MOLL FLANDERS

AN AUTHORITATIVE TEXT
BACKGROUNDS AND SOURCES
CRITICISM

➤➤➤ A NORTON CRITICAL EDITION ⫷⫷

DANIEL DEFOE

MOLL FLANDERS

AN AUTHORITATIVE TEXT
BACKGROUNDS AND SOURCES
CRITICISM

➤➤➤⫷⫷

Edited by

EDWARD KELLY

STATE UNIVERSITY OF NEW YORK
COLLEGE AT ONEONTA

W · W · NORTON & COMPANY

New York · London

W. W. Norton & Company, Inc., 500 Fifth Avenue, New York, N.Y. 10110
W. W. Norton & Company Ltd., 37 Great Russell Street, London WC1B 3NU

Library of Congress Cataloging in Publication Data
Defoe, Daniel, 1661?–1731.
  Moll Flanders.

  (A Norton critical edition)
  Original ed. published in 1722 under title: The
fortunes and misfortunes of the famous Moll Flanders.
  Bibliography: p.
  I. Kelly, Edward, 1930–   ed. II. Title.
PZ3.D362Mo7 [PR3404]   823'.5   72–13807
ISBN 0-393-04291-X
ISBN 0-393-09412-X {pbk}
PRINTED IN THE UNITED STATES OF AMERICA

5 6 7 8 9 0

Contents

Foreword

For more than 250 years Moll Flanders has endured extremes of praise and blame heaped on her by generations of authors, critics, and scholars. And just as she survived birth in Newgate Prison and the risks of shifting for herself in a society hostile to her goal of becoming a "gentlewoman," so her narrative has triumphed over calculated abridgement, piracy, and adaptation to achieve a fairly respectable status among the classics of English literature. The text of *Moll Flanders* printed here is that of the unabridged first edition, the only one known surely to have Defoe's authority; the first part of this Norton Critical Edition also includes historical and contextual annotation, a commentary on the text and publishing history of the work, and a list of all substantive editorial departures from the first edition.

Whether or not Defoe's main source for Moll originated in the real-life experiences of a female criminal he knew personally, Moll's history appeared at a time when criminal biography enjoyed unusual popularity. Pamphlets, ballads, and broadsides describing the crimes, confessions, and dying words of thieves and murderers were common reading in the first half of the eighteenth century. Some of this traditional sub-literature—which may have contributed to Defoe's concept of his heroine and to the events of her history—is included in the second section, entitled "Backgrounds and Sources." This section also offers selections from Defoe's periodicals which foreshadow events in Moll's career. Moreover, *Moll Flanders* became the basis of a number of abridgements, piracies, and adaptations throughout the eighteenth century, culminating in a variety of lesser versions and chapbooks. This second section contains parts of the first adaptation of *Moll Flanders*, which, in striving for authenticity, includes her "real name," her last will and testament, and a disrespectful elegy "composed by the Wits of Trinity College, Dublin." Concluding "Backgrounds and Sources," as if fulfilling George A. Aitken's long-standing conjecture that "Defoe's story was probably taken from the life of some real criminal [whose] . . . name will some day be traced," is a modern scholarly attempt to identify Moll.

The third section offers brief eighteenth- and nineteenth-century opinions of Defoe; it also includes early evaluations of his methods and alleged intentions in writing, and it cites positive and negative remarks on *Moll Flanders* by eminent men of letters. This short survey of criticism, although not designed to be an historical over-view, represents a wide range of estimates which, in a few instances, foreshadow the current critical attitudes presented in part four, "Twentieth-Century Criticism of *Moll Flanders.*" In order that the critical appraisals illustrated in section three not mislead one into believing that *Moll Flanders* enjoyed the same kind of popularity in the nineteenth century that it did in the eighteenth, I should point out that the novel was often dismissed by nineteenth-century critics and biographers of Defoe as unimportant, "secondary," or immoral. However, since current attitudes toward an author and his works are frequently influenced by voices from the past, I hope the pot pourri of opinions assembled will prove of interest to students in college literature courses.

At the turn of the twentieth century, critical appreciation of *Moll Flanders* increased sharply, due in part to a general reaction against Victorian standards and to the new interest in realism and natural-ism. Not only did literary historians tracing the development of English fiction find the history of Defoe's heroine significant in the growth of the novel, but highly regarded novelists also praised the work. James Joyce, Virginia Woolf, and E. M. Forster, for ex-ample, lauded Defoe's ability to create one of the most sublime characters in English literature; and a host of modern scholars, although not always in agreement with this opinion, have examined *Moll* within the theory and practice of standard forms of criticism. Since 1950, *Moll Flanders* has undergone critical discussion in por-tions of more than twenty scholarly books and in some thirty sepa-rate articles. (Our generation has also celebrated Moll in verse, recording, and a film, wherein she becomes a victim of Hollywood, rather than society.) From this abundance of twentieth-century commentary I have tried to choose essays and excerpts which illus-trate a wide range of important critical statements. Although the criticism in section four is not especially meant to exhibit conflict-ing interpretations, a number of the writers included do concern themselves with Defoe's conscious irony and artistic intent, a topic that has lately been of interest to many critics of *Moll Flanders*, and therefore one which should be represented in some depth. Hope-fully balancing these assessments of Defoe's intentions, however, are other essays that analyze form, character, method, and philosophical statement in the novel. I am grateful to these critics for allowing me to include their work. A chronology of Defoe's life, a map of Moll's London, and an up-to-date bibliography complete the edi-tion.

For initial encouragement and advice in undertaking this edition I thank George H. Ford and James William Johnson of the Univer-sity of Rochester. For patient and helpful responses to a variety of difficult major queries I am grateful to the following distinguished Defoe scholars: John Robert Moore, Emeritus Distinguished Professor, Indiana University; the late George Harris Healey, Cornell University; and Angus Ross, the University of Sussex. I have also been fortunate in receiving useful information from Peter A. Tasch, Temple University; William A. Gibson, Idaho State University; William T. Hagestad, Wisconsin State University (River Falls); and Ben R. Schneider, Jr., Lawrence University. Further, I owe especial thanks to David A. Randall, Lilly Librarian, Indiana University, for generously allowing me to borrow the rare Brotherton second edition. Also, I have found helpful the textual insights of Donald D. Eddy, Olin Library, Cornell University. And I am grateful for the enduring support of the library staff of State University of New York College, Oneonta. And I thank my colleagues Steven H. Rubin and Paul G. Italia for careful and patient proofreading. Finally, I acknowledge the important debt of gratitude I owe my wife, Barbara, whose unflinching assistance benefited all parts of this edition. None of the good people cited in this paragraph should be associated with any shortcomings of this edition.

The Text of
Moll Flanders

THE
FORTUNES
AND
MISFORTUNES
Of the FAMOUS
Moll Flanders, &c.

Who was Born in NEWGATE, and during a
Life of continu'd Variety for Threescore Years,
besides her Childhood, was Twelve Year a
Whore, five times a *Wife* (whereof once to her
own Brother) Twelve Year a *Thief*, Eight Year a
Transported *Felon* in *Virginia*, at last grew *Rich*,
liv'd *Honest*, and died a *Penitent*.

Written from her own MEMORANDUMS.

LONDON: Printed for, and Sold by W.
CHETWOOD, at *Cato's-Head*, in *Russel-
street, Covent-Garden*; and T. EDLING, at
the *Prince's-Arms*, over-against *Exerter-Change*
in the *Strand*. MDDCXXI.

The Preface

The World is so taken up of late with Novels and Romances, that it will be hard for a private History[1] to be taken for Genuine, where the Names and other Circumstances of the Person are concealed, and on this Account we must be content to leave the Reader to pass his own Opinion upon the ensuing Sheets, and take it just as he pleases.

The Author is here suppos'd to be writing her own History, and in the very beginning of her Account, she gives the Reasons why she thinks fit to conceal her true Name, after which there is no Occasion to say any more about that.

It is true, that the original of this Story is put into new Words, and the Stile of the famous Lady we here speak of is a little alter'd, particularly she is made to tell her own Tale in modester Words than she told it at first; the Copy which came first to Hand, having been written in Language more like one still in *Newgate*,[2] than one grown Penitent and Humble, as she afterwards pretends[3] to be.

The Pen employ'd in finishing her Story, and making it what you now see it to be, has had no little difficulty to put it into a Dress fit to be seen, and to make it speak Language fit to be read: When a Woman debauch'd from her Youth, nay, even being the Off-spring of Debauchery and Vice, comes to give an Account of all her vicious Practises, and even to descend to the particular Occasions and Circumstances by which she first became wicked, and of all the progression of Crime which she run through in threescore Year, an Author must be hard put to it to wrap it up so clean, as not to give room, especially for vicious Readers to turn it to his Disadvantage.

All possible Care however has been taken to give no lewd Ideas, no immodest Turns in the new dressing up this Story, no not to the worst parts of her Expressions; to this Purpose some of the vicious part of her Life, which cou'd not be modestly told, is quite left out, and several other Parts are very much shortn'd; what is left 'tis hop'd will not offend the chastest Reader or the modestest Hearer; and as the best use is made even of the worst Story, the Moral 'tis hop'd will keep the Reader serious even where the Story might incline him to be otherwise: To give the History of a wicked Life repented of, necessarily requires that the wicked Part should be made as wicked as the real History of it will bear, to illustrate and give a

1. A "history" in the eighteenth century purported to represent literal occurrences in the lives of persons who had actually lived; therefore, a history would be accorded more serious consideration by the reading public than would "novels and romances" depicting fictitious events and characters.
2. Famous London prison of the seventeenth and eighteenth century.
3. Proposes, aspires, not necessarily falsely.

Beauty to the Penitent part, which is certainly the best and brightest, if related with equal Spirit and Life.

It is suggested there cannot be the same Life, the same Brightness and Beauty, in relating the penitent Part, as is in the criminal Part: If there is any Truth in that Suggestion, I must be allow'd to say, 'tis because there is not the same taste and relish in the Reading, and indeed it is too true that the difference lyes not in the real worth of the Subject so much as in the Gust[4] and Palate of the Reader.

But as this Work is chiefly recommended to those who know how to Read it, and how to make the good Uses of it, which the Story all along recommends to them, so it is to be hop'd that such Readers will be much more pleas'd with the Moral than the Fable, with the Application than with the Relation, and with the End of the Writer than with the Life of the Person written of.

There is in this Story abundance of delightful Incidents, and all of them usefully apply'd. There is an agreeable turn Artfully given them in the relating, that naturally Instructs the Reader either one way or other. The first part of her lewd Life with the young Gentleman at *Colchester* has so many happy Turns given it to expose the Crime, and warn all whose Circumstances are adapted to it, of the ruinous End of such things, and the foolish Thoughtless and abhorr'd Conduct of both the Parties, that it abundantly attones for all the lively Discription she gives of her Folly and Wickedness.

The Repentance of her Lover at the *Bath*, and how brought by the just alarm of his fit of Sickness to abandon her; the just Caution given there against even the lawful Intimacies of the dearest Friends, and how unable they are to preserve the most solemn Resolutions of Virtue without divine Assistance; these are Parts, which to a just Discernment will appear to have more real Beauty in them than all the amorous Chain of Story which introduces it.

In a Word, as the whole Relation is carefully garbl'd[5] of all the Levity and Looseness that was in it: So it is all applied, and with the utmost care, to virtuous and religious Uses. None can, without being guilty of manifest Injustice, cast any Reproach upon it, or upon our Design in publishing it.

The Advocates for the Stage have in all Ages made this the great Argument to persuade People that their Plays are useful, and that they ought to be allow'd in the most civiliz'd, and in the most religious Government; Namely, That they are applyed to virtuous Purposes, and that by the most lively Representations, they fail not to recommend Virtue and generous Principles, and to discourage and expose all sorts of Vice and Corruption of Manners; and were it true that they did so, and that they constantly adhered to that

4. Taste.   5. **Sifted; the good is extracted from the bad.**

Rule, as the Test of their acting on the *Theatre*, much might be said in their Favour.

Throughout the infinite variety of this Book, this Fundamental is most strictly adhered to; there is not a wicked Action in any Part of it, but is first or last rendered Unhappy and Unfortunate: There is not a superlative Villain brought upon the Stage, but either he is brought to an unhappy End, or brought to be a Penitent: There is not an ill thing mention'd, but it is condemn'd, even in the Relation, nor a virtuous just Thing, but it carries its Praise along with it: What can more exactly answer the Rule laid down, to recommend, even those Representations of things which have so many other just Objections lying against them? Namely, of Example, of bad Company, obscene Language, and the like.

Upon this Foundation this Book is recommended to the Reader, as a Work from every part of which something may be learned, and some just and religious Inference is drawn, by which the Reader will have something of Instruction, if he pleases to make use of it.

All the Exploits of this Lady of Fame, in her Depredations upon Mankind stand as so many warnings to honest People to beware of them, intimating to them by what Methods innocent People are drawn in, plunder'd and robb'd, and by Consequence how to avoid them. Her robbing a little innocent Child, dress'd fine by the vanity of the Mother, to go to the Dancing-School, is a good Memento to such People hereafter; as is likewise her picking the Gold-Watch from the young Ladies side in the *Park*.

Her getting a parcel from a hair-brained Wench at the Coaches in St. *John-street*; her Booty made at the Fire, and again at *Harwich*; all give us excellent Warnings in such Cases to be more present to ourselves in sudden Surprizes of every Sort.

Her application to a sober Life, and industrious Management at last in *Virginia*, with her Transported Spouse, is a Story fruitful of Instruction to all the unfortunate Creatures who are oblig'd to seek their Re-establishment abroad; whether by the Misery of Transportation, or other Disaster; letting them know, that Diligence and Application have their due Encouragement, even in the remotest Parts of the World, and that no Case can be so low, so despicable, or so empty of Prospect, but that an unwearied Industry will go a great way to deliver us from it, will in time raise the meanest[6] Creature to appear again in the World,[7] and give him a new Cast[8] for his Life.

These are a few of the serious Inferences which we are led by the

---

6. Most debased, poorest in condition.
7. To raise himself, repair his fortunes and spirits.
8. Chance, opportunity. Samuel Johnson's *Dictionary of the English Language*

(1755) lists more than four dozen meanings of "cast." Defoe employs the word in a variety of its usages throughout *Moll Flanders*.

Hand to in this Book, and these are fully sufficient to Justifie any Man in recommending it to the World, and much more to Justifie the Publication of it.

There are two of the most beautiful Parts still behind,[9] which this Story gives some idea of, and lets us into the Parts of them, but they are either of them too long to be brought into the same Volume; and indeed are, *as I may call them*, whole Volumes of themselves, (*viz.*) I. The Life of her Governess, as she calls her, who had run thro', it seems in a few Years all the eminent degrees of a Gentlewoman, a Whore, and a Bawd; a Midwife, and a Midwife-keeper, as *they are call'd*, a Pawn-broker, a Child-taker,[1] a Receiver of Thieves, and of Thieves purchase, that is to say, of stolen Goods; and in a Word, her self a Thief, a Breeder up of Thieves, and the like, and yet at last a Penitent.

The second is the Life of her Transported Husband, a Highwayman; who it seems liv'd a twelve Years Life of successful Villany upon the Road, and even at last came off so well, as to be a Vountier Transport, not a Convict; and in whose Life there is an incredible Variety.

But as I have said, these are things too long to bring in here, so neither can I make a Promise of their coming out by themselves.[2]

We cannot say indeed, that this History is carried on quite to the End of the Life of this famous *Moll Flanders*, as she calls her self, for no Body can write their own Life to the full End of it, unless they can write it after they are dead; but her Husband's Life being written by a third Hand, gives a full Account of them both, how long they liv'd together in that Country, and how they came both to *England* again, after about eight Year, in which time they were grown very Rich, and where she liv'd it seems, to be very old; but was not so extraordinary a Penitent as she was at first; it seems only that indeed she always spoke with abhorence of her former Life, and of every Part of it.

In her last Scene at *Maryland* and *Virginia*, many pleasant things happen'd, which makes that part of her Life very agreeable, but they are not told with the same Elegancy as those accounted for by herself; so it is still to the more Advantage that we break off here.

9. Remaining to be told.
1. One who places illegitimate infants in foster homes.
2. Defoe is hinting at possible sequels to *Moll Flanders*. After the success of *Robinson Crusoe* (1719), he brought out *The Farther Adventures of Robinson Crusoe* later the same year. In 1730 *Fortune's*

Fickle Distribution appeared in Dublin, containing an abridged life of Moll, and purporting to give an account of the governess mentioned, along with the adventures of Moll's highwayman husband; however, this work has not been attributed to Defoe.

The History and Misfortunes
of the Famous Moll Flanders, &c.

My True Name is so well known in the Records, or Registers at *Newgate*, and in the *Old-Baily*,[1] and there are some things of such Consequence still depending there, relating to my particular Conduct, that it is not to be expected I should set my Name, or the Account of my Family to this Work; perhaps, after my Death it may be better known; at present it would not be proper, no, not tho' a general Pardon should be issued, even without Exceptions and reserve of Persons or Crimes.

It is enough to tell you, that as some of my worst Comrades, who are out of the Way of doing me Harm, having gone out of the World by the Steps and the String,[2] as I often expected to go, knew me by the Name of *Moll Flanders*; so you may give me leave to speak of myself under that Name till I dare own who I have been, as well as who I am.

I have been told, that in one of our Neighbour Nations, whether it be in *France*, or where else, I know not, they have an Order from the King, that when any Criminal is condemn'd, either to Die, or to the Gallies, or to be Transported,[3] if they leave any Children, as such are generally unprovided for, by the Poverty or Forfeiture of their Parents, so they are immediately taken into the Care of the Government, and put into an Hospital call'd the *House* of *Orphans*, where they are Bred up, Cloath'd, Fed, Taught, and when fit to go out, are plac'd out to Trades, or to Services, so as to be well able to provide for themselves by an honest industrious Behaviour.

Had this been the Custom in our Country, I had not been left a poor desolate Girl without Friends, without Cloaths, without Help or Helper in the World, as was my Fate; and by which, I was not only expos'd to very great Distresses, even before I was capable either of Understanding my Case, or how to Amend it, nor brought into a Course of Life, which was not only scandalous in itself, but which in its ordinary Course, tended to the swift Destruction both of Soul and Body.

1. Criminal court, adjoining Newgate Prison.
2. The "steps" to the gallows and the hangman's "string," or rope.
3. To be banished as a felon, usually to the tobacco and cotton plantations in America, where the convicted served a period of time in servitude. Transportation was an alternative to capital punishment, the sentence for a wide range of crimes in eighteenth-century England.

But the Case was otherwise here; my Mother was convicted of Felony for a certain petty Theft, scarce worth naming, (*viz.*) Having an opportunity of borrowing three Pieces of fine *Holland*,[4] of a certain Draper in *Cheapside*: The Circumstances are too long to repeat, and I have heard them related so many Ways, that I can scarce be certain which is the right Account.

However it was, this they all agree in, that my Mother pleaded her Belly,[5] and being found quick with Child, she was respited for about seven Months, in which time having brought me into the World, and being about again, she was call'd Down, as they term it, to her former Judgment, but obtain'd the Favour of being Transported to the Plantations, and left me about Half a Year old; and in bad Hands you may be sure.

This is too near the first Hours of my Life for me to relate any thing of myself, but by hear say; 'tis enough to mention, that as I was born in such an unhappy Place, I had no Parish[6] to have Recourse to for my Nourishment in my Infancy, nor can I give the least Account how I was kept alive, other, than that as I have been told, some Relation of my Mothers took me away for a while as a Nurse, but at whose Expence or by whose Direction I know nothing at all of it.

The first account that I can Recollect, or could ever learn of myself, was, that I had wandred among a Crew of those People they call *Gypsies*, or *Egyptians*; but I believe it was but a very little while that I had been among them, for I had not had my Skin discolour'd, or blacken'd,[7] as they do very young to all the Children they carry about with them, nor can I tell how I came among them, or how I got from them.

It was at *Colchester* in *Essex*, that those People left me; and I have a Notion in my Head, that I left them there, (that is, that I hid myself and wou'd not go any farther with them) but I am not able to be particular in that Account; only this I remember, that being taken up by some of the Parish Officers of *Colchester*, I gave an Account that I came into the Town with the *Gypsies*, but that I would not go any farther with them, and that so they had left me, but whither they were gone that I knew not, nor could they expect it of me; for tho' they sent round the Country to enquire after them, it seems they could not be found.

I was now in a Way to be provided for; for tho' I was not a

---

4. Expensive linen cloth.
5. Requested that her sentence be postponed because she was pregnant. The sentencing of a pregnant female criminal was deferred until after the birth of her child.
6. A district of a county, often corresponding to an ecclesiastical parish, but for purposes of civil government. The parish was responsible for the well-being of unfortunates within its confines. Born in Newgate Prison, Moll is not entitled to parish support.
7. The dark-skinned Gypsies were believed to dye the skin of kidnapped English children so that their light color would not disclose the crime.

Parish Charge upon this or that part of the Town by Law, yet as my Case came to be known, and that I was too young to do any Work, being not above three Years old, Compassion mov'd the Magistrates of the Town to order some Care to be taken of me, and I became one of their own, as much as if I had been born in the Place.

In the Provision they made for me, it was my good hap to be put to Nurse, as they call it, to a Woman who was indeed Poor, but had been in better Circumstances, and who got a little Livelihood by taking such as I was suppos'd to be, and keeping them with all Necessaries, till they were at a certain Age, in which it might be suppos'd they might go to Service, or get their own Bread.

This Woman had also a little School, which she kept to teach Children to Read and to Work; and having, as I have said, liv'd before that in good Fashion, she bred up the Children she took with a great deal of Art, as well as with a great deal of Care.

But that which was worth all the rest, she bred them up very Religiously, being herself a very sober pious Woman. (2.) Very Housewifly and Clean, and (3.) Very Mannerly, and with good Behaviour: So that in a Word, excepting a plain Diet, coarse Lodging, and mean Cloths, we were brought up as Mannerly and as Genteely as if we had been at the Dancing School.

I was continu'd here till I was eight years Old, when I was terrified with News that the Magistrates, as I think they call'd them, had order'd that I should go to Service; I was able to do but very little Service where ever I was to go, except it was to run of Errands, and be a Drudge to some Cook-Maid, and this they told me of often, which put me into a great Fright; for I had a thorough Aversion to going to Service, as they call'd it, that is to be a Servant, tho' I was so young; and I told my Nurse, as we call'd her, that I believ'd I could get my Living without going to Service if she pleas'd to let me; for she had Taught me to Work with my Needle, and Spin Worsted, which is the chief Trade of that City, and I told her that if she wou'd keep me, I wou'd Work for her, and I would Work very hard.

I talk'd to her almost every Day of Working hard; And in short, I did nothing but Work and Cry all Day, which griev'd the good kind Woman so much, that at last she began to be concern'd for me, for she lov'd me very well.

One Day after this, as she came into the Room where all we poor Children were at Work, she sat down just over against me, not in her usual Place as Mistress, but as if she set herself on purpose to observe me, and see me Work: I was doing something she had set me to, as I remember, it was Marking some Shirts, which she had taken to Make, and after a while she began to Talk to me: Thou foolish Child, says she, thou art always Crying; (for I was Crying then) Prithee, What dost Cry for? because they will take me away, *says I*, and put me to Service, and I can't Work House-Work; well Child, says she, but tho' you can't Work House-Work, as you call it, you will learn it in time, and they won't put you to hard Things at first; yes they will, says I, and if I can't do it, they will Beat me, and the Maids will Beat me to make me do great Work, and I am but a little Girl, and I can't do it; and then I cry'd again, till I could not speak any more to her.

This mov'd my good Motherly Nurse, so that she from that time resolv'd I should not go to Service yet, so she bid me not Cry, and she wou'd speak to Mr. *Mayor*, and I should not go to Service till I was bigger.

Well, this did not Satisfie me, for to think of going to Service was such a frightful Thing to me, that if she had assur'd me I should not have gone till I was 20 years old, it wou'd have been the same to me; I shou'd have cry'd, I believe all the time, with the very Apprehension of its being to be so at last.

When she saw that I was not pacify'd yet, she began to be angry with me; and what wou'd you have? *says she*, don't I tell you that you shall not go to Service till you are bigger? Ay, says I, but then I must go at last; why, what? said she, is the Girl mad? what, would you be a Gentlewoman? Yes *says I*, and cry'd heartily, till I roar'd out again.

This set the old Gentlewoman a Laughing at me, as you may be sure it would: Well, Madam, forsooth, says she, *Gibing at me*, you would be a Gentlewoman, and pray how will you come to be a Gentlewoman? what, will you do it by your Fingers Ends?

Yes, *says I again*, very innocently.

Why, what can you Earn, *says she*, what can you get at your Work?

Three-Pence, *said I*, when I Spin, and 4*d*. when I Work plain Work.[8]

Alas! poor Gentlewoman, *said she again*, Laughing, what will that do for thee?

It will keep me, *says I*, if you will let me live with you; and this I *said*, in such a poor petitioning Tone, that it made the poor Womans Heart yearn to me, as she told me afterwards.

But, *says she*, that will not keep you, and buy you Cloths too; and who must buy the little Gentlewoman Cloths, *says she*, and smil'd all the while at me.

I will Work Harder then, *says I*, and you shall have it all.

Poor Child! it won't keep you, *says she*, it will hardly keep you in Victuals.

8. Plain sewing without elaborate needle-work would bring Moll a penny a day more than she might earn from spinning thread, a livelihood not uncommon to children her age.

Then I will have no Victuals, *says I*, again very Innocently, let me but live with you.

Why, can you live without Victuals? *says she;* yes, *again says I*, very much like a Child, you may be sure, and still I cry'd heartily.

I had no Policy in all this, you may easily see it was all Nature, but it was joyn'd with so much Innocence, and so much Passion, That in short, it set the good Motherly Creature a weeping too, and she cry'd at last as fast as I did, and then took me, and led me out of the teaching Room; come *says she*, you shan't go to Service, you shall live with me, and this pacify'd me for the present.

Sometime after this, she going to wait on the *Mayor*, and talking of such things as belong'd to her Business, at last my Story came up, and my good Nurse told Mr. *Mayor* the whole Tale: He was so pleas'd with it, that he would call his Lady, and his two Daughters to hear it, and it made Mirth enough among them, you may be sure.

However, not a Week had pass'd over, but on a sudden comes Mrs. *Mayoress* and her two Daughters to the House to see my old Nurse, and to see her School and the Children: When they had look'd about them a little: Well, Mrs. ——— says the *Mayoress* to my Nurse, and pray which is the little Lass that intends to be a Gentlewoman? I heard her, and I was terrible frighted at first, tho' I did not know why neither; but Mrs. *Mayoress* comes up to me, Well Miss says she, And what are you at Work upon? The Word Miss[9] was a Language that had hardly been heard of in our School, and I wondred what sad Name it was she call'd me; However, I stood up, made a Curtsy, and she took my Work out of my Hand, look'd on it, and said it was very well; then she took up one of my Hands; nay, says she, the Child may come to be a Gentlewoman for ought any body knows; she has a Gentlewoman's Hand, says she; this pleas'd me mightily you may be sure, but Mrs. *Mayoress* did not stop there, but giving me my Work again, she put her Hand in her Pocket, gave me a Shilling, and bid me mind my Work, and learn to Work well, and I might be a Gentlewoman for ought she knew.

Now all this while, my good old Nurse, Mrs. *Mayoress*, and all the rest of them did not understand me at all, for they meant one Sort of thing, by the Word Gentlewoman,[1] and I meant quite another; for alas, all I understood by being a Gentlewoman, was to be able to Work for myself, and get enough to keep me without

9. "Miss," a term strange to Moll's ears, is used with mild irony, for it had two main meanings in the late seventeenth and eighteenth century. It could be used as a term of honor to a young girl of high quality who would become a lady; or it might be applied pejoratively to a whore, concubine, or strumpet. In neither case would it have appropriately been used by Moll's nurse.

1. In its first sense "gentlewoman" means a woman of good birth or breeding, a lady; Moll uses the term in its second sense: a woman who attends or waits on a lady. Later, she confuses "gentlewoman" and "madam," a kept woman or prostitute.

that terrible Bug-bear *going to Service*, whereas they meant to live Great, Rich, and High, and I know not what.

Well, after Mrs. *Mayoress* was gone, her two Daughters came in, and they call'd for the Gentlewoman too, and they talk'd a long while to me, and I answer'd them in my Innocent way; but always if they ask'd me whether I resolv'd to be a Gentlewoman, I answer'd YES: At last one of them ask'd me, what a Gentlewoman was? that puzzel'd me much; but however, I explain'd myself negatively, that it was one that did not go to Service, to do House-Work; they were pleas'd to be familiar with me, and lik'd my little Prattle to them, which it seems was agreeable enough to them, and they gave me Money too.

As for my Money I gave it all to my Mistress Nurse, as I call'd her, and told her she should have all I got for myself when I was a Gentlewoman, as well as now; by this and some other of my talk, my old Tutoress began to understand me, about what I meant by being a Gentlewoman; and that I understood by it no more than to be able to get my Bread by my own Work; and at last, she ask'd me whether it was not so.

I told her *yes*, and insisted on it, that to do so, was to be a Gentlewoman; for says I, there is such a one, naming a Woman that mended Lace, and wash'd the Ladies Lac'd-heads,[2] she, *says I,* is a Gentlewoman, and they call her Madam.

Poor Child, says my good old Nurse, you may soon be such a Gentlewoman as that, for she is a Person of ill Fame, and has had two or three Bastards.

I did not understand any thing of that; but I answer'd, I am sure they call her Madam, and she does not go to Service nor do House-Work, and therefore I insisted that she was a Gentlewoman, and I would be such a Gentlewoman as that.

The Ladies were told all this again, to be sure, and they made themselves Merry with it, and every now and then the young Ladies, Mr. *Mayor's* Daughters would come and see me, and ask where the little Gentlewoman was, which made me not a little Proud of myself.

This held a great while, and I was often visited by these young Ladies, and sometimes they brought others with them; so that I was known by it, almost all over the Town.

I was now about ten Years old, and began to look a little Womanish, for I was mighty Grave and Humble; very Mannerly, and as I had often heard the Ladies say I was Pretty, and would be a very handsome Woman, so you may be sure, that hearing them say so, made me not a little Proud; however, that Pride had no ill effect upon me yet, only as they often gave me Money, and I gave it my

2. **Head-dresses** trimmed with lace or ribbons.

old Nurse, she *honest Woman*, was so just to me, as to lay it all out again for me, and gave me Head-Dresses, and Linnen, and Gloves and Ribbons, and I went very Neat, and always Clean; for that I would do, and if I had Rags on, I would always be Clean, or else I would dabble them in Water myself; but *I say*, my good Nurse, when I had Money given me, very honestly laid it out for me, and would always tell the Ladies, this, or that, was bought with their Money; and this made them oftentimes give me more; Till at last, I was indeed call'd upon by the Magistrates as I understood it, to go out to Service; but then I was come to be so good a Workwoman myself, and the Ladies were so kind to me, that it was plain I could maintain myself, that is to say, I could Earn as much for my Nurse as she was able by it to keep me; so she told them, that if they would give her leave, she would keep the Gentlewoman as she call'd me, to be her Assistant, and teach the Children, which I was very well able to do; for I was very nimble at my Work, and had a good Hand with my Needle, though I was yet very young.

But the kindness of the Ladies of the Town did not End here, for when they came to understand that I was no more maintain'd by the publick Allowance, as before, they gave me Money oftner than formerly; and as I grew up, they brought me Work to do for them; such as Linnen to Make, and Laces to Mend, and Heads to Dress up, and not only paid me for doing them, but even taught me how to do them; so that now I was a Gentlewoman indeed, as I understood that Word, and as I desir'd to be; for by that time, I was twelve Years old, I not only found myself Cloathes, and paid my Nurse for my keeping, but got Money in my Pocket too before-hand.

The Ladies also gave me Cloaths frequently of their own, or their Childrens, some Stockings, some Petticoats, some Gowns, some one thing, some another, and these my old Woman Managed for me like a meer Mother,[3] and kept them for me, oblig'd me to Mend them, and turn them and twist them to the best Advantage, for she was a rare House-Wife.

At last one of the Ladies took so much Fancy to me that she would have me Home to her House for a Month she said, to be among her Daughters.

Now tho' this was exceeding kind in her, yet as my old good Woman said to her, unless she resolv'd to keep me for good and all, she would do the little Gentlewoman more harm than good: Well, says the Lady, that's true and therefore I'll only take her Home for a Week then, that I may see how my Daughters and she agree together, and how I like her Temper, and then I'll tell you more;

3. Complete; as if she were, in fact, Moll's mother. This edition follows the first and second editions' spelling of "meer" (mere) throughout, which in Defoe's usage usually means total, absolute.

and in the mean time, if any Body comes to see her as they us'd to do, you may only tell them, you have sent her out to my House.

This was prudently manag'd enough, and I went to the Ladies House, but I was so pleas'd there with the young Ladies, and they so pleas'd with me, that I had enough to do to come away, and they were as unwilling to part with me.

However, I did come away, and liv'd almost a Year more with my honest old Woman, and began now to be very helpful to her; for I was almost fourteen Years old, was tall of my Age, and look'd a little Womanish; but I had such a Taste of Genteel living at the Ladies House, that I was not so easie in my old Quarters as I us'd to be, and I thought it was fine to be a Gentlewoman indeed, for I had quite other Notions of a Gentlewoman now than I had before; and as I thought, I say, that it was fine to be a Gentlewoman, so I lov'd to be among Gentlewomen, and therefore I long'd to be there again.

About the Time that I was fourteen Years and a quarter Old, my good old Nurse, Mother I ought rather to call her, fell Sick and Dyed; I was then in a sad Condition indeed, for as there is no great Bustle in putting an end to a Poor bodies Family when once they are carried to the Grave, so the poor good Woman being Buried, the Parish Children she kept were immediately remov'd by the Church-Wardens; the School was at an End, and the Children of it had no more to do but just stay at Home till they were sent some where else; and as for what she left, her Daughter, a married Woman with six or seven Children, came and swept it all away at once, and removing the Goods, they had no more to say to me, than to Jest with me, and tell me that the little Gentlewoman might set up for her self if she pleas'd.

I was frighted out of my Wits almost, and knew not what to do, for I was, as it were, turn'd out of Doors to the wide World, and that which was still worse, the old honest Woman had two and twenty Shillings of mine in her Hand, which was all the Estate the little Gentlewoman had in the World; and when I ask'd the Daughter for it, she huft[4] me and laught at me, and told me, she had nothing to do with it.

It was true the good poor Woman had told her Daughter of it, and that it lay in such a Place, that it was the Child's Money, and had call'd once or twice for me to give it me, but I was unhappily out of the way, some where or other; and when I came back she was past being in a Condition to speak of it: However, the Daughter was so Honest afterward as to give it me, tho' at first she us'd me Cruelly about it.

Now was I a poor Gentlewoman indeed, and I was just that very

4. Blustered at, fumed at.

Night to be turn'd into the wide World; for the Daughter remov'd all the Goods, and I had not so much as a Lodging to go to, or a bit of Bread to Eat: But it seems some of the Neighbours who had known my Circumstances, took so much Compassion of me, as to acquaint the Lady in whose Family I had been a Week, as I mention'd above; and immediately she sent her Maid to fetch me away, and two of her Daughters came with the Maid tho' unsent; so I went with them Bag and Baggage, and with a glad Heart you may be sure: The fright of my Condition had made such an Impression upon me, that I did not want now to be a Gentlewoman, but was very willing to be a Servant, and that any kind of Servant they thought fit to have me be.

But my new generous Mistress had better thoughts for me; I call her generous for she exceeded the good Woman I was with before in every Thing, as well as in the matter of Estate; I say in every Thing except Honesty; and for that, tho' this was a Lady most exactly Just, yet I must not forget to say on all Occasions, that the First tho' Poor, was as uprightly Honest as it was possible for any One to be.

I was no sooner carried away as I have said by this good Gentlewoman, but the first Lady, *that is to say*, the *Mayoress* that was, sent her two Daughters to take Care of me; and another Family which had taken Notice of me when I was the little Gentlewoman, and had given me Work to do, sent for me after her, so that I was mightily made of, as we say; nay, and they were not a little Angry, especially, Madam the *Mayoress*, that her Friend had taken me away from her as she call'd it; for as she said, I was Hers by Right, she having been the first that took any Notice of me; but they that had me wou'd not part with me; and as for me, tho' I shou'd have been very well Treated with any of the others, yet I could not be better than where I was.

Here I continu'd till I was between 17 and 18 Years old, and here I had all the Advantages for my Education that could be imagin'd; the Lady had Masters home to the House to teach her Daughters to Dance, and to speak *French*, and to Write, and others to teach them Musick; and as I was always with them, I learn'd as fast as they; and tho' the Masters were not appointed to teach me, yet I learn'd by Imitation and enquiry, all that they learn'd by Instruction and Direction. So that in short, I learn'd to Dance and speak *French* as well as any of them, and to Sing much better, for I had a better Voice than any of them; I could not so readily come at playing on the Harpsicord or Spinnet, because I had no Instrument of my own to Practice on, and could only come at theirs in the intervals, when they left it, which was uncertain; but yet I learn'd tollerably well too, and the young Ladies at length got two Instruments, that is to say, a Harpsicord, and a Spinnet too, and then they Taught me themselves; But as to Dancing they could hardly help my learning Country Dances, because they always wanted me to make up even Number; and on the other Hand, they were as heartily willing to learn me every thing that they had been Taught themselves, as I could be to take the Learning.

By this Means I had, as I have said above, all the Advantages of Education that I could have had, if I had been as much a Gentlewoman as they were with whom I liv'd, and in some things, I had the Advantage of my Ladies, tho' they were my Superiors; but they were all the Gifts of Nature, and which all their Fortunes could not furnish. First, I was apparently Handsomer than any of them. Secondly, I was better shap'd, and Thirdly, I Sung better, by which I mean, I had a better Voice; in all which you will I hope allow me to say, I do not speak my own Conceit of myself, but the Opinion of all that knew the Family.

I had with all these the common Vanity of my Sex (*viz.*) That being really taken for very Handsome, or if you please for a great Beauty, I very well knew it, and had as good an Opinion of myself as any body else could have of me; and particularly I lov'd to hear any body speak of it, which could not but happen to me sometimes, and was a great Satisfaction to me.

Thus far I have had a smooth Story to tell of myself, and in all this Part of my Life, I not only had the Reputation of living in a very good Family, and a Family Noted and Respected every where, for Virtue and Sobriety, and for every valluable Thing; but I had the Character too of a very sober, modest, and virtuous young Woman, and such I had always been; neither had I yet any occasion to think of any thing else, or to know what a Temptation to Wickedness meant.

But that which I was too vain of, was my Ruin, or rather my vanity was the Cause of it. The lady in the House where I was had two Sons, young Gentlemen of very promising Parts,[5] and of extraordinary Behaviour; and it was my Misfortune to be very well with them both, but they manag'd themselves with me in a quite different Manner.

The eldest, a gay Gentleman that knew the Town as well as the Country, and tho' he had Levity enough to do an ill natur'd thing, yet had too much Judgment of things to pay too dear for his Pleasures, he began with that unhappy Snare to all Women, (*viz.*) taking Notice upon all Occasions how pretty I was, as he call'd it; how agreeable, how well Carriaged, and the like; and this he contriv'd so subtilly, as if he had known as well, how to catch a

5. Qualities.

Woman in his Net as a Partridge when he went a Setting; for he wou'd contrive to be talking this to his Sisters when tho' I was not by, yet when he knew I was not so far off, but that I should be sure to hear him: His Sisters would return softly to him, Hush Brother, she will hear you, she is but in the next Room; then he would put it off, and Talk softlier, as if he had not known it, and begin to acknowledge he was Wrong; and then as if he had forgot himself, he would speak aloud again, and I that was so well pleas'd to hear it, was sure to Lissen for it upon all Occasions.

After he had thus baited his Hook, and found easily enough the Method how to lay it in my Way, he play'd an opener Game; and one Day going by his Sister's Chamber when I was there doing something about Dressing her, he comes in with an Air of gayty, O! Mrs. *Betty*,[6] said he to me, How do you do Mrs. *Betty*? don't your Cheeks burn, Mrs. *Betty*? I made a Curtsy and blush'd, but said nothing; What makes you talk so Brother, *says the Lady*; Why, says he, we have been talking of her below Stairs this half Hour; *Well says his Sister*, you can say no Harm of her, that I am sure; so 'tis no matter what you have been talking about; nay, *says he*, 'tis so far from talking Harm of her, that we have been talking a great deal of good, and a great many fine Things have been said of Mrs. *Betty*, I assure you; and particularly, that she is the Handsomest young Woman in *Colchester*; and, in short, they begin to Toast her Health in the Town.

I wonder at you Brother, *says the Sister*; *Betty* wants but one Thing, but she had as good want every Thing, for the Market is against our Sex just now; and if a young Woman have Beauty, Birth, Breeding, Wit, Sense, Manners, Modesty, and all these to an Extream; yet if she have not Money, she's no Body, she had as good want them all, for nothing but Money now recommends a Woman; the Men play the Game all into their own Hands.

Her younger Brother, who was by, cry'd *Hold Sister*, you run too fast, I am an Exception to your Rule; I assure you, if I find a Woman so Accomplish'd as you Talk of, *I say*, I assure you, I would not trouble myself about the Money.

O, says the Sister, but you will take Care not to Fancy one then, without the Money.

You don't know that neither, *says the Brother*.

---

6. "Betty" was a stock name applied to female servants. The name also could connote female promiscuity. In 1683 Charles Cotton wrote *Erotopolis: The Present State of Bettyland*, a pornotopia. Many risqué ballads praising the charms of maid-servants named Betty appeared in the late seventeenth and early eight-eenth centuries; and in the criminal jargon of the day, a "Betty" was used to break locks. Defoe also uses the name as a general appellation in other episodes of *Moll Flanders*.

The polite term "Mrs." i.e., the abbreviation for "Mistress," was equivalent to the modern "Miss."

But why Sister, (*says the elder Brother*) why do you exclaim so at the Men for aiming so much at the Fortune? you are none of them that want a Fortune, what ever else you want.

I understand you Brother, (*replies the Lady very smartly,*) you suppose I have the Money, and want the Beauty; but as Times go now, the first will do without the last, so I have the better of my Neighbours.

Well, *says the younger Brother,* but your Neighbours, as you call them may be even with you; for Beauty will steal a Husband sometimes in spite of Money; and when the Maid chances to be Handsomer than the Mistress, she oftentimes makes as good a Market, and rides in a Coach before her.

I thought it was time for me to withdraw and leave them, and I did so; but not so far but that I heard all their Discourse, in which I heard abundance of fine things said of myself, which serv'd to prompt my Vanity; but as I soon found, was not the way to encrease my Interest in the Family; for the Sister and the younger Brother fell grievously out about it; and as he said some very disobliging things to her, upon my Account, so I could easily see that she Resented them by her future Conduct to me; which indeed was very unjust to me, for I had never had the least thought of what she suspected, as to her younger Brother: Indeed the elder Brother in his distant remote Way, had said a great many things, as in Jest, which I had the folly to believe were in earnest, or to flatter myself, with the hopes of what I ought to have suppos'd he never intended, and perhaps never thought of.

It happen'd one Day that he came running up Stairs, towards the Room where his Sisters us'd to sit and Work, as he often us'd to do; and calling to them before he came in, as was his way too, I being there alone, step'd to the Door, and said, Sir, the Ladies are not here, they are Walk'd down the Garden; as I step'd forward, to say this towards the Door, he was just got to the Door, and clasping me in his Arms, as if it had been by Chance, O! Mrs. *Betty, says he,* are you here? that's better still; I want to speak with you, more than I do with them, and then having me in his Arms he Kiss'd me three or four times.

I struggl'd to get away, and yet did it but faintly neither, and he held me fast, and still Kiss'd me, till he was almost out of Breath, and then sitting down, says, *dear Betty* I am in Love with you.

His Words I must confess fir'd my Blood; all my Spirits flew about my Heart, and put me into Disorder enough, which he might easily have seen in my Face: He repeated it afterwards several times, that he was in Love with me, and my Heart spoke as plain as a Voice, that I lik'd it; nay, when ever he said, I am in Love with you, my Blushes plainly reply'd, *wou'd you were* Sir.

However nothing else pass'd at that time; it was but a Surprise, and when he was gone, I soon recover'd myself again. He had stay'd longer with me, but he happen'd to look out at the Window and see his Sisters coming up the Garden, so he took his leave, Kiss'd me again, told me he was very serious, and I should hear more of him very quickly, and away he went leaving me infinitely pleas'd tho' surpris'd; and had there not been one Misfortune in it, I had been in the Right, but the Mistake lay here, that Mrs. *Betty* was in Earnest, and the Gentleman was not.

From this time my Head run upon strange Things, and I may truly say, I was not myself; to have such a Gentleman talk to me of being in Love with me, and of my being such a charming Creature, as he told me I was, these were things I knew not how to bear; my vanity was elevated to the last Degree: It is true, I had my Head full of Pride, but knowing nothing of the Wickedness of the times, I had not one Thought of my own Safety or of my Virtue about me; and had my young Master offer'd it at first Sight, he might have taken any Liberty he thought fit with me; but he did not see his Advantage, which was my happiness for that time.

After this Attack, it was not long but he found an opportunity to catch me again, and almost in the same Posture, indeed it had more of Design in it on his Part, tho' not on my Part; *it was thus*; the young Ladies were all gone a Visiting with their Mother; his Brother was out of Town; and as for his Father, he had been at *London* for a Week before; he had so well watched me, that he knew where I was, tho' I did not so much as know that he was in the House; and he briskly comes up the Stairs, and seeing me at Work comes into the Room to me directly, and began just as he did before with taking me in his Arms, and Kissing me for almost a quarter of an Hour together.

It was his younger Sisters Chamber, that I was in, and as there was no Body in the House but the Maids below Stairs, he was it may be the ruder: In short, he began to be in Earnest with me indeed; perhaps he found me a little too easie, for God knows I made no Resistance to him while he only held me in his Arms and Kiss'd me; indeed I was too well pleas'd with it, to resist him much.

However as it were, tir'd with that kind of Work, we sat down, and there he talk'd with me a great while; *he said*, he was charm'd with me, and that he could not rest Night or Day till he had told me how he was in Love with me; and if I was able to Love him again, and would make him happy, I should be the saving of his Life; and many such fine things. I said little to him again, but easily discover'd[7] that I was a Fool, and that I did not in the least perceive what he meant.

7. Displayed to him.

Then he walk'd about the Room, and taking me by the Hand, I walk'd with him; and by and by, taking his Advantage, he threw me down upon the Bed, and Kiss'd me there most violently; but to give him his Due, offer'd no manner of Rudeness to me, only Kiss'd me a great while; after this he thought he had heard some Body come up Stairs, so he got off from the Bed, lifted me up, professing a great deal of Love for me, but told me it was all an honest Affection, and that he meant no ill to me; and with that he put five Guineas into my Hand, and went away down Stairs.

I was more confounded with the Money than I was before with the Love, and began to be so elevated, that I scarce knew the Ground I stood on: I am the more particular in this part, that if my Story comes to be read by any innocent young Body, they may learn from it to Guard themselves against the Mischiefs which attend an early Knowledge of their own Beauty; if a young Woman once thinks herself Handsome, she never doubts the Truth of any Man that tells her he is in Love with her; for if she believes herself Charming enough to Captivate him, 'tis natural to expect the Effects of it.

This young Gentleman had fir'd his Inclinations as much as he had my vanity, and as if he had found that he had an opportunity and was sorry he did not take hold of it, he comes up again in half an Hour, or thereabouts, and falls to Work with me again as before, only with a little less Introduction.

And First, when he enter'd the Room, he turn'd about, and shut the Door. Mrs. *Betty*, said he, I fancy'd before, some Body was coming up Stairs, but it was not so; however, *adds he*, if they find me in the Room with you, they shan't catch me a Kissing of you; I told him I did not know who should be coming up Stairs, for I believ'd there was no Body in the House but the Cook and the other Maid, and they never came up those Stairs; well my Dear, *says he*, 'tis good to be sure however; and so he sits down and we began to Talk; and now, tho' I was still all on fire with his first visit, and said little, he did, as it were, put Words in my Mouth, telling me how passionately he lov'd me, and that tho' he could not mention such a thing till he came to his Estate, yet he was resolv'd to make me happy then, and himself too; *that is to say, to Marry me*, and abundance of such fine things, which I poor Fool did not understand the drift of, but acted as if there was no such thing as any kind of Love but that which tended to Matrimony; and if he had spoke of that, I had no Room, as well as no Power to have said No; but we were not come that length yet.

We had not sat long, but he got up, and stoping my very Breath with Kisses, threw me upon the Bed again; but then being both well warm'd, he went farther with me than Decency permits me to mention, nor had it been in my power to have deny'd him at that Moment, had he offer'd much more than he did.

However, tho' he took these Freedoms with me, it did not go to that, which they call the last Favour, which, to do him Justice, he did not attempt; and he made that Self-denial of his a Plea for all his Freedoms with me upon other Occasions after this: When this was over, he stay'd but a little while, but he put almost a Handful of Gold in my Hand, and left me; making a thousand Protestations of his Passion for me, and of his loving me above all the Women in the World.

It will not be strange if I now began to think, but alas! it was but with very little solid Reflection: I had a most unbounded Stock of Vanity and Pride, and but a very little Stock of Virtue; I did indeed cast[8] sometimes with myself what my young Master aim'd at, but thought of nothing but the fine Words, and the Gold; whether he intended to Marry me, or not to Marry me, seem'd a Matter of no great Consequence to me; nor did my Thoughts so much as suggest to me the Necessity of making any Capitulation for myself, till he came to make a kind of formal Proposal to me, as you shall hear presently.

Thus I gave up myself to a readiness of being ruined without the least concern, and am a fair *Memento*[9] to all young Women, whose Vanity prevails over their Virtue: Nothing was ever so stupid on both Sides, had I acted as became me, and resisted as Virtue and Honour requir'd, this Gentleman had either Desisted his Attacks, finding no room to expect the Accomplishment of his Design, or had made fair, and honourable Proposals of Marriage; in which Case, whoever had blam'd him, no Body could have blam'd me. In short, if he had known me, and how easy the Trifle he aim'd at, was to be had, he would have troubled his Head no farther, but have given me four or five Guineas, and have lain with me the next time he had come at me; and if I had known his Thoughts, and how hard he thought I would be to be gain'd, I might have made my own Terms with him; and if I had not Capitulated for an immediate Marriage, I might for a Maintenance till Marriage, and might have had what I would; for he was already Rich to Excess, besides what he had in Expectation; but I seem'd wholly to have abandoned all such Thoughts as these, and was taken up Only with the Pride of my Beauty, and of being belov'd by such a Gentleman; as

8. Deliberated, pondered.
9. Reminder. The term served to describe ruined women, and also as a warning of man's final end. Defoe may have in mind lines from the poetry of John Wilmot, Earl of Rochester (1647–1680), dissolute courtier and brilliant poet in the court of Charles II. "A Letter . . . from Artemisia," a poem of Lord Rochester's which Moll cites later (p. 58), tells the story of Corinna, who is misused by her rake lover:

Now scorn'd of all, forsaken and opprest,
She's a *Memento Mori* to the rest.

for the Gold, I spent whole Hours in looking upon it; I told[1] the Guineas over and over a thousand times a Day: Never poor vain Creature was so wrapt up with every part of the Story, as I was, not Considering what was before me, and how near my Ruin was at the Door; indeed I think, I rather wish'd for that Ruin, than studyed to avoid it.

In the mean time however, I was cunning enough, not to give the least room to any in the Family to suspect me, or to imagine that I had the least Correspondence[2] with this young Gentleman; I scarce ever look'd towards him in publick, or Answer'd if he spoke to me, if any Body was near us; but for all that, we had every now and then a little Encounter, where we had room for a Word or two, and now and then a Kiss; but no fair opportunity for the Mischief intended; and especially considering that he made more Circumlocution than if he had known my Thoughts he had occasion for, and the Work appearing Difficult to him, he really made it so.

But as the Devil is an unwearied Tempter, so he never fails to find opportunity for that Wickedness he invites to: It was one Evening that I was in the Garden with his two younger Sisters and himself, and all very innocently Merry, when he found Means to convey a Note into my Hand, by which he Directed me to understand that he would to Morrow desire me publickly to go of an Errand for him into the Town, and that I should see him somewhere by the Way.

Accordingly after Dinner, he very gravely says to me, his Sisters being all by, Mrs. *Betty*, I must ask a Favour of you: What's that? *says his second Sister*; nay, Sister *says he*, very gravely, if you can't spare Mrs. *Betty* to Day, any other time will do; *yes they said*, they could spare her well enough, and the Sister beg'd Pardon for asking; which she did but of meer Course, without any Meaning; Well, but Brother? says the eldest Sister, you must tell Mrs. *Betty* what it is; if it be any private Business that we must not hear, you may call her out; there she is; Why Sister, says the Gentleman, very gravely, What do you mean? *I* only desire her to go into the *High-street*, (and then he pulls out a Turn-Over)[3] to such a Shop, and then he tells them a long Story of two fine Neckcloths he had bid Money for, and he wanted to have me go and make an Errand to buy a Neck to the Turn-Over that he showed, to see if they would take my Money[4] for the Neckcloths; to bid a Shilling more, and Haggle with them; and then he made more Errands, and so continued to have such petty Business to do, that *I* should be sure to stay a good while.

When he had given me my Errands, he told them a long Story of

1. Counted.
2. Relationship, familiarity.
3. Turned-down collar.

4. Accept from Moll the price refused him.

a Visit he was going to make to a Family they all knew, and where was to be such and such Gentlemen, and how Merry they were to be; and very formally asks his Sisters to go with him, and they as formally excus'd themselves, because of Company that they had Notice was to come and Visit them that Afternoon, which by the Way he had contriv'd on purpose.

He had scarce done speaking to them, and giving me my Errand, but his Man came up to tell him that Sir W—— H——s[5] Coach stop'd at the Door; so he runs down, and comes up again immediately, alas! *says he*, aloud, there's all my Mirth spoil'd at once; Sir W—— has sent his Coach for me, and desires to speak with me upon some earnest Business: It seems this Sir W—— was a Gentleman, who liv'd about three Miles out of Town, to whom he had spoken on purpose the Day before, to lend him his Charriot for a particular occasion, and had appointed it to call for him, as it did about three a-Clock.

Immediately he calls for his best Wig, Hat and Sword, and ordering his Man to go to the other Place to make his Excuse, that was to say, he made an Excuse to send his Man away, he prepares to go into the Coach: As he was going, he stop'd a while, and speaks mighty earnestly to me about his Business, and finds an Opportunity to say very softly to me, *come away my Dear as soon as ever you can.* I said nothing, but made a Curtsy, as if I had done so to what he said in publick; in about a Quarter of an Hour I went out too; I had no Dress, other than before, except that I had a Hood, a Mask,[6] a Fan and a pair of Gloves in my Pocket; so that there was not the least Suspicion in the House: He waited for me in the Coach in a back *Lane*, which he knew I must pass by; and had directed the Coachman whither to go, which was to a certain Place, call'd *Mile-End*, where lived a Confident of his, where we went in, and where was all the Convenience in the World to be as Wicked as we pleas'd.

When we were together, he began to Talk very Gravely to me, and to tell me, he did not bring me there to betray me; that his Passion for me would not suffer him to Abuse me; that he resolv'd to Marry me as soon as he came to his Estate; that in the mean time, if I would grant his Request, he would Maintain me very Honourably; and made me a thousand Prostestations of his Sincerity and of his Affection to me; and That he would never abandon me, and as I may say, made a thousand more Preambles than he need to have done.

5. To lend authenticity to supposedly true narratives, Defoe often hints at names and places in this manner, as though he were concealing a distinguished, real person.

6. Face masks were fashionable for protecting the complexion from wind and sun, and they were also convenient for concealment.

However as he press'd me to speak, I told him, I had no Reason to question the Sincerity of his Love to me, after so many Protestations, But —— and there I stopp'd, as if I left him to Guess the rest; BUT WHAT my Dear? *says he*, I guess what you mean; what if you should be with Child, is not that it? Why then, *says he*, I'll take Care of you and Provide for you, and the Child too, and that you may see I am not in Jest, *says he*, here's an Earnest for you; and with that he pulls out a silk Purse, with an Hundred Guineas in it, and gave it me; and I'll give you such another, *says he*, every Year till I Marry you.

My Colour came and went, at the Sight of the Purse, and with the fire of his Proposal together; so that I could not say a Word, and he easily perceiv'd it; so putting the Purse into my Bosom, I made no more Resistance to him, but let him do just what he pleas'd; and as often as he pleas'd; and thus I finish'd my own Destruction at once, for from this Day, being forsaken of my Virtue, and my Modesty, I had nothing of Value left to recommend me, either to God's Blessing, or Man's Assistance.

But things did not End here; I went back to the Town, did the Business he publickly directed me to, and was at Home before any Body thought me long; as for my Gentleman, he staid out as he told me he would, till late at Night, and there was not the least Suspicion in the Family, either on his Account or on mine.

We had after this, frequent Opportunities to repeat our Crime; chiefly by his contrivance; especially at home, when his Mother and the young Ladies went Abroad a Visiting, which he watch'd so narrowly as never to miss; knowing always before-hand when they went out, and then fail'd not to catch me all alone, and securely enough; so that we took our fill of our wicked Pleasure for near half a Year; and yet, which was the most to my Satisfaction, I was not with Child.

But before this half Year was expir'd, his younger Brother, of whom I have made some mention in the beginning of the Story, falls to work with me; and he finding me alone in the Garden one Evening, begins a Story of the same Kind to me, made good honest Professions of being in Love with me, and in short, proposes fairly and Honourably to Marry me, and that before he made any other Offer to me at all.

I was now confounded and driven to such an Extremity as the like was never known; at least not to me; I resisted the Proposal with Obstinancy; and now I began to Arm myself with Arguments: I laid before him the inequallity of the Match; the Treatment I should meet with in the Family; the Ingratitude it wou'd be to his good Father and Mother, who had taken me into their House upon such generous Principles, and when I was in such a low Condition;

and in short, I said every thing to dissuade him from his Design that I could imagine, except telling him the Truth, which wou'd indeed have put an end to it all, but that I durst not think of mentioning.

But here happen'd a Circumstance that I did not expect indeed, which put me to my Shifts;[7] for this young Gentleman as he was plain and Honest, so he pretended to nothing with me, but what was so too; and knowing his own Innocence, he was not so careful to make his having a Kindness for Mrs. *Betty* a Secret in the House, as his Brother was; and tho' he did not let them know that he had talk'd to me about it, yet he said enough to let his Sisters perceive he Lov'd me, and his Mother saw it too, which tho' they took no Notice of it to me, yet they did to him, and immediately I found their Carriage to me alter'd, more than ever before.

I saw the Cloud, tho' I did not foresee the Storm; it was easie, *I say*, to see that their Carriage to me was alter'd, and that it grew worse and worse every Day, till at last I got Information among the Servants, that I shou'd, in a very little while, be desir'd to remove.

I was not alarm'd at the News, having a full Satisfaction that I should be otherwise provided for; and especially, considering that I had Reason every Day to expect I should be with Child, and that then I should be oblig'd to remove without any Pretences for it.

After some time, the younger Gentleman took an Opportunity to tell me that the Kindness he had for me, had got vent[8] in the Family; he did not Charge me with it, *he said*, for he knew well enough which way it came out; he told me his plain way of Talking had been the Occasion of it, for that he did not make his respect for me so much a Secret as he might have done, and the Reason was that he was at a Point; that if I would consent to have him, he would tell them all openly that he lov'd me, and that he intended to Marry me: That it was true his Father and Mother might Resent it, and be unkind, but that he was now in a Way to live, being bred to[9] the Law, and he did not fear Maintaining me, agreeable to what I should expect; and that in short, as he believed I would not be asham'd of him, so he was resolv'd not to be asham'd of me, and that he scorn'd to be afraid to own me now, who he resolv'd to own after I was his Wife, and therefore I had nothing to do but to give him my Hand, and he would Answer for all the rest.

I was now in a dreadful Condition indeed, and now I repented heartily my easiness with the eldest Brother, not from any Reflection of Conscience, but from a View of the Happiness I might have enjoy'd, and had now made impossible; for tho' I had no great Scruples of Conscience *as I have said* to struggle with, yet I could not

7. Stratagems.
8. Had become known, was aired.
9. Being educated to become a lawyer.

think of being a Whore to one Brother, and a Wife to the other; but then it came into my Thoughts, that the first Brother had promis'd to make me his Wife when he came to his Estate; but I presently remember'd what I had often thought of, that he had never spoken a Word of having me for a Wife after he had Conquer'd me for a Mistress; and indeed till now, tho' I said I thought of it often, yet it gave me no Disturbance at all, for as he did not seem in the least to lessen his Affection to me, so neither did he lessen his Bounty, tho' he had the Discretion himself to desire me not to lay out a Penny of what he gave me in Cloaths, or to make the least show Extraordinary, because it would necessarily give Jealousie in the Family, since every Body knew I could come at such things no manner of ordinary Way, but by some private Friendship, which they would presently have suspected.

But I was now in a great strait, and really knew not what to do; the main Difficulty was this: the younger Brother not only laid close Siege to me, but suffered it to be seen; he would come into his Sisters Room, and his Mothers Room, and sit down, and Talk a Thousand kind things of me, and to me, even before their Faces, and when they were all there: This grew so Publick, that the whole House talk'd of it, and his Mother reprov'd him for it, and their Carriage to me appear'd quite Altered: In short, his Mother had let fall some Speeches, as if she intended to put me out of the Family; that is, in *English*, to turn me out of Doors. Now I was sure this could not be a Secret to his Brother, only that he might not think, as indeed no Body else yet did, that the youngest Brother had made any Proposal to me about it; But as I easily cou'd see that it would go farther, so I saw likewise there was an absolute Necessity to speak of it to him, or that he would speak of it to me, and which to do first I knew not; that is, whether I should break it to him, or let it alone till he should break it to me.

Upon serious Consideration, for indeed now I began to Consider things very seriously, and never till now: I say, upon serious Consideration, I resolv'd to tell him of it first, and it was not long before I had an Opportunity, for the very next Day his Brother went to *London* upon some Business, and the Family being out a Visiting, just as it had happen'd before, and as indeed was often the Case, he came according to his Custom to spend an Hour or Two with Mrs. *Betty*.

When he came and had sat down a while, he easily perceiv'd there was an alteration in my Countenance, that I was not so free and pleasant with him as I us'd to be, and particularly, that I had been a Crying; he was not long before he took notice of it, and ask'd me in very kind Terms what was the Matter, and if any thing Troubl'd me: I wou'd have put it off if I could, but it was not to be Conceal'd; so after suffering many Importunities to draw that out of

me, which I long'd as much as possible to Disclose; I told him that
it was true, something did Trouble me, and something of such a
Nature that I could not Conceal from him, and yet, that I could
not tell how to tell him of it neither; that it was a thing that not
only Surpriz'd me, but greatly perplex'd me, and that I knew not
what Course to take, unless he would Direct me: He told me with
great Tenderness, that let it be what it wou'd, I should not let it
Trouble me, for he would Protect me from all the World.

I then begun at a Distance, and told him I was afraid the Ladies
had got some secret Information of our Correspondence; for that it
was easie to see that their Conduct was very much chang'd towards
me for a great while, and that now it was come to that pass, that
they frequently found Fault with me, and sometimes fell quite out
with me, tho' I never gave them the least Occasion: That whereas I
us'd always to lye with the Eldest Sister, I was lately put to lye by
my self, or with one of the Maids; and that I had over-heard them
several times talking very Unkindly about me; but that which confirm'd it all, was, that one of the Servants had told me, that she had
heard I was to be Turn'd out, and that it was not safe for the
Family that I should be any longer in the House.

He smil'd when he heard all this, and I ask'd him how he could
make so light of it, when he must needs know that if there was any
Discovery, I was Undone for ever? and that even it would hurt him,
tho' not Ruin him, as it would me: I upbraided him, that he was
like all the rest of the Sex, that when they had the Character and
Honour of a Woman at their Mercy, often times made it their Jest,
and at least look'd upon it as a Trifle, and counted the Ruin of
those, they had had their Will of, as a thing of no value.

He saw me Warm and Serious, and he chang'd his Stile immediately; *he told me*, he was sorry I should have such a thought of him;
that he had never given me the least Occasion for it, but had been
as tender of my Reputation as he could be of his own; that he was
sure our Correspondence had been manag'd with so much Address,
that not one Creature in the Family had so much as a Suspicion of
it; that if he smil'd when I told him my Thoughts, it was at the
Assurance he lately receiv'd, that our understanding one another,
was not so much as known or guess'd at; and that when he had told
me, how much Reason he had to be Easie, I should Smile as he
did, for he was very certain, it would give me a full Satisfaction.

This is a Mystery I cannot understand, *says I*, or how it should
be to my Satisfaction that I am to be turn'd out of Doors; for if our
Correspondence is not discover'd, I know not what else I have done
to change the Countenances of the whole Family to me, or to have
them Treat me as they do now, who formerly used me with so
much Tenderness, as if I had been one of their own Children.

Why look you Child, *says he*, that they are Uneasie about you,

that is true; but that they have the least Suspicion of the Case as it
is, and as it respects you and I, is so far from being True, that they
suspect my Brother *Robin*;[1] and in short, they are fully persuaded
he makes Love to you: Nay, the Fool has put it into their Heads
too himself, for he is continually Bantring them about it, and
making a Jest of himself; I confess, I think he is wrong to do so,
because he can not but see it vexes them, and makes them Unkind
to you; but 'tis a Satisfaction to me, because of the Assurance it
gives me that they do not suspect me in the least, and I hope this
will be to your Satisfaction too.

So it is, *says I*, one way, but this does not reach my Case at all,
nor is this the chief Thing that Troubles me, tho' I have been concern'd about that too: What is it then, *says he*? With which, I fell
into Tears, and could say nothing to him at all: He strove to pacifie
me all he could, but began at last to be very pressing upon me to
tell what it was; at last *I answer'd*, that I thought I ought to tell
him too, and that he had some right to know it, besides, that I
wanted his Direction in the Case, for I was in such Perplexity, that
I knew not what Course to take, and then I related the whole Affair
to him: *I told him* how imprudently his Brother had manag'd himself, in making himself so Publick; for that if he had kept it a
Secret, as such a Thing ought to have been, I could but have
Denied him Positively, without giving any Reason for it, and he
would in Time have ceas'd his Sollicitations; but that he had the
Vanity, first, to depend upon it that I would not Deny him, and
then had taken the Freedom to tell his Resolution of having me, to
the whole House.

I *told him* how far I had resisted him, and *told him* how Sincere
and Honourable his Offers were, but *says I*, my Case will be doubly
hard; for as they carry it Ill to me now, because he desires to have
me, they'll carry it worse when they shall find I have Deny'd him;
and they will presently say, there's something else in it, and then
out it comes, that I am Marry'd already to somebody else, or else
that I would never refuse a Match so much above me as this was.

This Discourse surpriz'd him indeed very much: He *told me*, that
it was a critical Point indeed for me to Manage, and he did not see
which way I should get out of it; but he would consider of it, and
let me know next time we met, what Resolution he was come to
about it; and in the mean time, desir'd I would not give my Consent to his Brother, nor yet give him a flat Denial, but that I would
hold him in Suspence a while.

I seem'd to start at his saying I should not give him any Consent;
I *told him*, he knew very well I had no Consent to give; that he had

---

1. Just as "Betty" is a generic name for maidservants, so "Robin" (short for "Robert") is a common tag-name for country bumpkins or dull-witted, boorish characters.

Engag'd himself to Marry me, and that my Consent was at the same time Engag'd to him; that he had all along told me I was his Wife, and I look'd upon my self as effectually so, as if the Ceremony has pass'd; and that it was from his own Mouth that I did so, he having all along persuaded me to call myself his Wife.

Well, my Dear *says he*, don't be Concern'd at that now, if I am not your Husband, I'll be as good as a Husband to you, and do not let those things Trouble you now, but let me look a little farther into this Affair, and I shall be able to say more next time we meet.

He pacify'd me as well as he could with this, but I found he was very Thoughtful, and that tho' he was very kind to me, and kiss'd me a thousand Times, and more I believe, and gave me Money too, yet he offer'd no more all the while we were together, which was above two Hours, and which I much wonder'd at, indeed at that Time, considering how it us'd to be, and what Opportunity we had.

His Brother did not come from *London* for five or six Days, and it was two Days more, before he got an Opportunity to talk with him; but then getting him by himself, he began to talk very Close to him about it; and the same Evening got an Opportunity, (for we had a long Conference together) to repeat all their Discourse to me, which as near as I can remember, was to the purpose following. He *told him* he heard strange News of him since he went, (*viz.*) that he made Love to Mrs. *Betty*: Well, *says his* Brother, a little Angrily, and so *I do*, And what then? What has any body to do with that? Nay, *says his* Brother, don't be Angry *Robin*, I don't pretend to have any thing to do with it; nor do I pretend to be Angry with you about it: But I find they do concern themselves about it, and that they have used the poor Girl Ill about it, which I should take as done to my self; Who do you mean by THEY? *says* Robin, I mean my Mother, and the Girls, *says the* elder Brother.

But hark ye, *says his* Brother, are you in Earnest? do you really Love the Girl? you may be free with me you know. Why then *says* Robin, I will be free with you; I do Love her above all the Women in the World, and I will have Her; let *them say*, and do what they will, I believe the Girl will not Deny me.

It stuck me to the Heart when he *told me* this, for tho' it was most rational to think I would not Deny him, yet I knew in my own Conscience I must Deny him, and I saw my Ruin in my being oblig'd to do so; but I knew it was my business to Talk otherwise then, so I interrupted him in his Story thus.

Ay! *said I*, does he think I can not Deny him? but he shall find I can Deny him, for all that.

Well my dear *says he*, but let me give you the whole Story as it went on between us, and then say what you will.

Then he went on and *told me*, that he reply'd thus: But Brother, you know She has nothing, and you may have several Ladies with good Fortunes: 'Tis no matter for that, *said* Robin, I Love the Girl; and I will never please my Pocket in Marrying, and not please my Fancy; and so my Dear *adds he*, there is no Opposing him.

Yes, yes, *says I*, you shall see I can Oppose him; I have learnt to say NO now, tho' I had not learnt it before; if the best Lord in the Land offer'd me Marriage now, I could very chearfully say NO to him.

Well, but my Dear *says he*, What can you say to him? You know, as you said when we talk'd of it before, he will ask you many Questions about it, and all the House will wonder what the meaning of it should be.

Why *says I* smiling, I can stop all their Mouths at one Clap, by telling him and them too, that I am Married already to his elder Brother.

He smil'd a little too at the Word, but I could see it Startled him, and he could not hide the disorder it put him into; however, he return'd, Why tho' that may be true in some Sense, yet I suppose you are but in Jest when you talk of giving such an Answer as that, it may not be Convenient on many Accounts.

No, no, *says I* pleasantly, I am not so fond of letting that Secret come out without your Consent.

But what then can you say to him, or to them, *says he*, when they find you positive against a Match, which would be apparently so much to your Advantage?

Why, *says I*, should I be at a loss? First of all, I am not oblig'd to give them any Reason at all, on the other hand, I may tell them I am Married already, and stop there, and that will be a full Stop too to him, for he can have no Reason to ask one Question after it.

Ay, *says he*, but the whole House will tease you about that, even to Father and Mother, and if you deny them positively, they will be Disoblig'd at you, and Suspicious besides.

Why, *says I*, What can I do? What would you have me do? I was in strait enough before, and as I *told you*, I was in Perplexity before, and acquainted you with the Circumstances, that I might have your Advice.

My dear, *says he*, I have been considering very much upon it, you may be sure, and tho' it is a piece of Advice that has a great many Mortifications in it to me, and may at first seem Strange to you, yet all Things consider'd, I see no better way for you, than to let him go on; and if you find him hearty and in Earnest, Marry him.

I gave him a look full of Horror at those Words, and turning Pale as Death, was at the very point of sinking down out of the Chair I sat in: When giving a start, my Dear, *says he* aloud, What's the matter with you? Where are you a going? and a great many such things; and with jogging and calling to me, fetch'd me a little to my self, tho' it was a good while before I fully recover'd my Senses, and was not able to speak for several Minutes more.

When I was fully recover'd he began again; My dear *says he*, What made you so Surpriz'd at what I said? I would have you consider Seriously of it; you may see plainly how the Family stand in this Case, and they would be stark Mad if it was my Case, as it is my Brothers, and for ought I see, it would be my Ruin and yours too.

Ay! *says I*, still speaking angrily; are all your Protestations and Vows to be shaken by the dislike of the Family? Did I not always object that to you, and you made a light thing of it, as what you were above, and would not Value; and is it come to this now? *Said I*, is this your Faith and Honour, your Love, and the Solidity of your Promises?

He continued perfectly Calm, notwithstanding all my Reproaches, and I was not sparing of them at all; but *he reply'd* at last, My Dear, I have not broken one Promise with you yet; I did tell you I would Marry you when I was come to my Estate; but you see My Father is a hail healthy Man, and may live these thirty Years still, and not be Older than several are round us in the Town; and you never propos'd my Marrying you sooner, because you know it might be my Ruin; and as to all the rest, I have not fail'd you in any thing; you have wanted for nothing.

I could not deny a Word of this, and had nothing to say to it in general; but why then, *says I*, can you perswade me to such a horrid stop,[2] as leaving you, since you have not left me? Will you allow no Affection, no Love on my Side, where there has been so much on your Side? Have I made you no Returns? Have I given no Testimony of my Sincerity, and of my Passion? are the Sacrifices I have made of Honour and Modesty to you, no Proof of my being ty'd to you in Bonds too strong to be broken?

But here my Dear, *says he*, you may come into a safe Station, and appear with Honour and with splendor at once, and the Remembrance of what we have done may be wrapt up in an eternal Silence, as if it had never happen'd; you shall always have my Respect, and my sincere Affection, only then it shall be Honest, and perfectly Just to my Brother; you shall be my Dear Sister, as now you are my Dear ———— and there he stop'd.

Your Dear whore, *says I*, you would have said, if you had gone on, and you might as well have said it; but I understand you: However, I desire you to remember the long Discourses you have had with me, and the many Hours pains you have taken to perswade me to believe myself an honest Woman; that I was your Wife inten-

2. Impasse, impediment.

tionally, tho' not in the Eye of the World, and that it was as effectual a Marriage that had pass'd between us as if we had been publickly Wedded by the Parson of the Parish; you know and cannot
but remember, that these have been your own Words to me.

I found this was a little too close upon him, but I made it up in
what follows; he stood stock still for a while and said nothing, and I
went on thus: you cannot, *says I*, without the highest injustice
believe that I yielded upon all these Perswasions without a Love not
to be questioned, not to be shaken again by any thing that could
happen afterward: If you have such dishonourable Thoughts of me,
I must ask you what Foundation in any of my Behaviour have I given
for such a Suggestion.

If then I have yielded to the Importunities of my Affection, and
if I have been perswaded to believe that I am really, and in the
Essence of the Thing your Wife, shall I now give the Lye to all
those Arguments, and call myself your Whore, or Mistress, which is
the same thing? And will you Transfer me to your Brother? Can
you Transfer my Affection? Can you bid me cease loving you, and
bid me love him? is it in my Power think you to make such a
Change at Demand? No Sir, *said I*, depend upon it 'tis impossible,
and whatever the Change of your Side may be, I will ever be True;
and I had much rather, since it is come that unhappy Length, be
your Whore than your Brothers Wife.

He appear'd pleas'd, and touch'd with the impression of this last
Discourse, and told me that he stood where he did before; that he
had not been Unfaithful to me in any one Promise he had ever
made yet, but that there were so many terrible things presented
themselves to his View in the Affair before me, and that on my
Account in particular, that he had thought of the other as a
Remedy so effectual, as nothing could come up to it: That he
thought this would not be an entire parting us, but we might love
as Friends all our Days, and perhaps with more Satisfaction, than
we should in the Station we were now in, as things might happen:
That he durst say, I could not apprehend any thing from him, as to
betraying a Secret, which could not but be the Destruction of us
both, if it came out: That he had but one Question to ask of me,
that could lye in the way of it, and if that Question was answer'd in
the Negative, he could not but think still it was the only Step I
could take.

I guess'd at his Question presently, namely, Whether I was sure I
was not with Child? As to that, *I told him*, he need not be concern'd about it, for I was not with Child; why then my Dear, *says
he*, we have no time to Talk farther now; consider of it, and think
closely about it, I cannot but be of the Opinion still, that it will be
the best Course you can take; and with this, he took his Leave, and

the more hastily too, his Mother and Sisters Ringing at the Gate, just at the Moment that he had risen up to go.

He left me in the utmost Confusion of Thought; and he easily perceiv'd it the next Day, and all the rest of the Week, for it was but *Tuesday* Evening when we talked; but he had no Opportunity to come at me all that Week, till the *Sunday* after, when I being indispos'd did not go to Church, and he making some Excuse for the like, stay'd at Home.

And now he had me an Hour and a Half again by myself, and we fell into the same Arguments all over again, or at least so near the same, as it would be to no purpose to repeat them; at last, *I ask'd him* warmly what Opinion he must have of my Modesty, that he could suppose, I should so much as Entertain a thought of lying with two Brothers? And assur'd him it could never be: *I added* if he was to tell me that he would never see me more, than which nothing but Death could be more Terrible, yet I could never entertain a thought so Dishonourable to my self, and so Base to him; and therefore, I entreated him if he had one Grain of Respect or Affection left for me, that he would speak no more of it to me, or that he would pull his Sword out and Kill me. He appear'd surpriz'd at my Obstinancy as he call'd it, *told me* I was unkind to my self, and unkind to him in it; that it was a Crisis unlook'd for upon us both, and impossible for either of us to foresee; but that he did not see any other way to save us both from Ruin, and therefore he thought it the more Unkind; but that if he must say no more of it to me, he added with an unusual Coldness, that he did not know any thing else we had to talk of; and so he rose up to take his leave; I rose up too, as if with the same Indifference, but when he came to give me as it were a parting Kiss, I burst out into such a Passion of Crying, that tho' I would have spoke, I could not, and only pressing his Hand, seem'd to give him the Adieu, but cry'd vehemently.

He was sensibly mov'd with this; so he sat down again, and said a great many kind things to me to abate the excess of my Passion; but still urg'd the necessity of what he had proposed; all the while insisting, that if I did refuse, he would notwithstanding provide for me; but letting me plainly see that he would decline me in the main Point; nay, even as a Mistress; making it a point of Honour not to lye with the Woman, that for ought he knew, might come to be his Brothers Wife.

The bare loss of him as a Gallant[3] was not so much my Affliction, as the loss of his Person, whom indeed I Lov'd to Distraction; and the loss of all the Expectations I had, and which I always had built my Hopes upon, of having him one Day for my Husband: These things oppress'd my Mind so much, that in short, I fell very

3. Lover.

ill; the agonies of my Mind, in a word, threw me into a high Feaver, and long it was that none in the Family expected my Life.

I was reduc'd very low indeed, and was often Delirious and light Headed; but nothing lay so near me, as the fear that when I was light Headed, I should say something or other to his Prejudice; I was distress'd in my Mind also to see him, and so he was to see me, for he really Lov'd me most passionately; but it could not be; there was not the least Room to desire it, on one side, or other, or so much as to make it Decent.

It was near five Weeks that I kept my Bed, and tho' the violence of my Feaver abated in three Weeks, yet it several times Return'd; and the Physicians said two or three times, they could do no more for me, but that they must leave Nature and the Distemper to fight it Out, only strengthening the first with Cordials to maintain the Struggle: After the end of five Weeks I grew better, but was so Weak, so Alter'd, so Melancholly, and recover'd so Slowly, that the Physicians apprehended I should go into a Consumption; and which vex'd me most, they gave it as their Opinion, that my Mind was Oppress'd, that something Troubl'd me, and in short, that I was In Love; upon this, the whole House was set upon me to Examine me, and to press me to tell whether I was in Love or not, and with who? but as I well might, I deny'd my being in Love at all.

They had on this Occasion a Squable one Day about me at Table, that had like to have put the whole Family in an Uproar, and for sometime did so; they happen'd to be all at Table, but the Father; as for me I was Ill, and in my Chamber: At the beginning of the Talk, which was just as they had finish'd their Dinner, the old Gentlewoman who had sent me somewhat to Eat, call'd her Maid to go up, and ask me if I would have any more; but the Maid brought down Word I had not Eaten half what she had sent me already.

Alas, *says the* old Lady, that poor Girl; I am afraid she will never be well.

Well! *says the* elder Brother, How should Mrs. *Betty* be well, *they say* she is in Love?

I believe nothing of it *says the* old Gentlewoman.

I don't know *says the* eldest Sister, what to say to it, they have made such a rout[4] about her being so Handsome, and so Charming, and I know not what, and that in her hearing too, that has turn'd the Creatures Head I believe, and who knows what possessions[5] may follow such Doings? for my Part I don't know what to make of it.

4. Fuss.   5. States of mind.

Why Sister, you must acknowledge she is very Handsome, *says the* elder Brother.

Ay, and a great deal Handsomer than you Sister, *says* Robin, and that's your Mortification.

Well, well, that is not the Question, *says his* Sister, the Girl is well[6] enough, and she knows it well enough; she need not be told of it to make her Vain.

We are not a talking of her being Vain, *says the* elder Brother, but of her being in Love; it may be she is in Love with herself, it seems my Sisters think so.

I would she was in Love with me, *says* Robin, I'd quickly put her out of her Pain.

What d' ye mean by that Son, *says the* old Lady, How can you talk so?

Why Madam, *says* Robin again, very honestly, Do you think I'd let the poor Girl Die for Love, and of one that is near at hand to be had too?

Fye Brother, *says the* second Sister, how can you talk so? would you take a Creature that has not a Groat[7] in the World?

Prithee Child *says* Robin, Beauty's a Portion,[8] and good Humour with it, is a double Portion; I wish thou hadst half her Stock of both for thy Portion: So there was her Mouth stopp'd.

I find, *says the* eldest Sister, if *Betty* is not in Love, my Brother is; I wonder he has not broke his Mind to *Betty*, I warrant she won't say NO.

They that yield when they're ask'd *says* Robin, are one step before them that were never ask'd to yield, Sister, and two Steps before them that yield before they are ask'd: And that's an Answer[9] to you Sister.

This fir'd the Sister, and she flew into a Passion, and said, things were come to that pass, that it was time the Wench, *meaning me,* was out of the Family; and but that she was not fit to be turn'd out, she hop'd her Father and Mother would consider of it as soon as she could be remov'd.

Robin reply'd, That was business for the Master and Mistress of the Family, who were not to be taught by One that had so little Judgment as his eldest Sister.

It run up a great deal farther; the Sister Scolded, *Robin* Rally'd and Banter'd, but poor *Betty* lost Ground by it extreamly in the Family: I heard of it, and I cry'd heartily, and the old Lady came up to me, some body having told her that I was so much concern'd

---

6. Attractive.
7. An obsolete English coin worth four-pence; therefore, "not a penny to her name."
8. A portion equal to money, a dowry.
9. Robin's "answer" is clarified by Moll, p. 36.

about it: I complain'd to her, that it was very hard the Doctors should pass such a Censure[1] upon me, for which they had no Ground; and that it was still harder, considering the Circumstances I was under in the Family; that I hop'd I had done nothing to lessen her Esteem for me, or given any Occasion for the Bickering between her Sons and Daughters; and I had more need to think of a Coffin than of being in Love, and beg'd she would not let me suffer in her Opinion for any body's Mistakes, but my own.

She was sensible of the Justice of what I said, but *told me*, since there had been such a Clamour among them, and that her younger Son Talk'd after such a rattling[2] way as he did, she desir'd I would be so Faithful to her as to Answer her but one Question sincerely; I told her I would with all my heart, and with the utmost plainess and Sincerity: Why then the Question was, Whether there was any thing between her Son *Robert* and me? I told her with all the Protestations of Sincerity that I was able to make, and as I might well do, that there was not, nor ever had been; I *told her* that Mr. *Robert* had rattled and jested, as she knew it was his way, and that I took it always as I suppos'd he meant it, to be a wild airy way of Discourse that had no Signification in it: And again assured her that there was not the least tittle of what she understood by it between us; and that those who had Suggested it had done me a great deal of Wrong, and Mr. *Robert* no Service at all.

The old Lady was fully satisfy'd, and kiss'd me, spoke chearfully to me, and bid me take care of my Health and want for nothing, and so took her leave: But when she came down, she found the Brother and all his Sisters together by the Ears;[3] they were Angry even to Passion, at his upbraiding them with their being Homely, and having never had any Sweet hearts, never having been ask'd the Question, and their being so forward as almost to ask first: He rallied them upon the Subject of Mrs. *Betty*; how Pretty, how good Humour'd, how she Sung better than they did, and Danc'd better, and how much Handsomer she was; and in doing this, he omitted no Ill-natur'd Thing that could vex them, and indeed, push'd too hard upon them: The old Lady came down in the height of it, and to put a stop to it, told them all the Discourse she had had with me, and how I answer'd, that there was nothing between Mr. *Robert* and I.

She's wrong there, *says* Robin, for if there was not a great deal between us, we should be closer together than we are: I told her I Lov'd her hugely, *says he*, but I could never make the Jade believe I was in Earnest; I do not know how you should *says his* Mother, no body in their Senses could believe you were in Earnest, to Talk so to a poor Girl, whose Circumstances you know so well.

1. Unfair diagnosis.   3. Arguing loudly.
2. Obstreperous.

But prithee Son *adds she*, since you tell me that you could not make her believe you were in Earnest, what must we believe about it? for you ramble so in your Discourse, that no body knows whether you are in Earnest or in Jest: But as I find the Girl by your own Confession has answer'd truely, I wish you would do so too, and tell me seriously, so that I may depend upon it; Is there any thing in it or no? Are you in Earnest or no? Are you Distracted indeed, or are you not? 'Tis a weighty Question, and I wish you would make us easie about it.

By my Faith Madam, *says* Robin, 'tis in vain to mince the Matter, or tell any more Lyes about it; I am in Earnest, as much as a Man is that's going to be Hang'd. If Mrs. *Betty* would say she Lov'd me, and that she would Marry me, I'd have her to morrow Morning fasting, and say, *To have, and to hold,* instead of eating my Breakfast.

Well, *says the Mother,* then there's one Son lost; and she said it in a very mournful Tone, as one greatly concern'd at it.

I hope not Madam, *says* Robin, no Man is lost, when a good Wife has found him.

Why but Child, *says the* old Lady, she is a Beggar.

Why then Madam, she has the more need of Charity *says* Robin; I'll take her off of the hands of the Parish, and she and I'll Beg together.

Its bad Jesting with such things, *says the Mother.*

I don't Jest Madam, *says* Robin: We'll come and beg your Pardon Madam; and your Blessing Madam, and my Fathers.

This is all out of the way Son, *says the Mother,* if you are in Earnest you are Undone.

I am afraid not *says he,* for I am really afraid she won't have me, after all my Sisters huffing and blustring; I believe I shall never be able to persuade her to it.

That's a fine Tale indeed, she is not so far out of her Senses neither; Mrs. *Betty* is no Fool, *says the youngest Sister,* Do you think she has learnt to say NO, any more than other People?

No Mrs. *Mirth-Wit*[4] says Robin, Mrs. *Betty's* no Fool; but Mrs. *Betty* may be Engag'd some other way, And what then?

Nay, *says the eldest Sister,* we can say nothing to that, Who must it be to then? She is never out of the Doors, it must be between you.

I have nothing to say to that *says* Robin, I have been Examin'd enough; there's my Brother, if it must be *between us,* go to Work with him.

This stung *the elder Brother* to the Quick, and he concluded that

4. Perhaps this reference is to Mistress Mirth, a gossiping, impromptu critic in Ben Jonson's comedy *The Staple of News* (1626). Another possible Jonsonian allusion occurs on p. 170.

Robin had discover'd something: However, he kept himself from appearing disturb'd; Prithee *says he*, don't go to sham your Stories off upon me, I tell you, I deal in no such Ware; I have nothing to say to Mrs. *Betty*, nor to any of the *Miss Betty's*[5] in the Parish; and with that he rose up and brush'd off.[6]

No, *says the eldest Sister*, I dare answer for my Brother, he knows the World better.

Thus the Discourse ended; but it left *the elder Brother* quite confounded: He concluded his Brother had made a full Discovery, and he began to doubt whether I had been concern'd in it or not; but with all his Management, he could not bring it about to get at me; at last, he was so perplex'd, that he was quite Desperate, and resolv'd he wou'd come into my Chamber and see me, whatever came of it: In order to this, he contriv'd it so, that one Day after Dinner, watching *his eldest Sister* till he could see her go up Stairs, he runs after her: *Hark ye Sister, says he*, Where is this sick Woman? may not a body see her? YES, *says the Sister*, I believe you may, but let me go first a little, and I'll tell you; so she run up to the Door and gave me notice; and presently call'd to him again: BROTHER, *says she*, you may come if you please; so in he came, just in the same kind of Rant: Well, *says he*, at the Door *as he came in*, Where is this sick Body that's in Love? How do ye do Mrs. *Betty*? I would have got up out of my Chair, but was so Weak I could not for a good while; and he saw it and his Sister too, and she said, *Come do not strive to stand up*, my Brother desires no Ceremony, especially, now you are so Weak. No, No, Mrs. *Betty*, pray sit still *says he*, and so sits himself down in a Chair over-against me, and appear'd as if he was mighty Merry.

He talk'd a deal of rambling Stuff to his Sister and to me; sometimes of one thing, sometimes of another, on purpose to Amuse[7] his Sister; and every now and then, would turn it upon the old Story, directing it to me: Poor Mrs. *Betty*, *says he*, it is a sad thing to be in Love, why it has reduced you sadly; at last I spoke a little; I am glad to see you so merry, Sir, *says I*, but I think the Doctor might have found some thing better to do than to make his Game at his Patients: If I had been Ill of no other Distemper, I know the Proverb too well to have let him come to me: What Proverb *says he*? O! I remember it now: What,

> *Where Love is the Case,*
> *The* Doctor's *an Ass.*[8]

5. "Miss Betty's" refers to the loose women of the parish.
6. Departed hastily.
7. Delude.
8. Defoe's plain English style accommodates numerous proverbs, apothegms, and maxims. This saying appears in both John Ray's *A Collection of English Proverbs*, 1678, and Francisco de Quevedo y Villegas' *Visions*, 1667. (See Helmut Heidenreich, *The Library of Daniel Defoe and Phillips Farewell*, Berlin, 1970, which lists editions of both works.)

Is not that it Mrs. *Betty*? I smil'd, and said nothing: Nay, *says he*, I think the effect has prov'd it to be Love, for it seems the Doctor has been able to do you but little Service; you mend very slowly they say, I doubt there's somewhat in it Mrs. *Betty*, I doubt[9] you are sick of the Incureables, and that is Love; I smil'd and said, No, *indeed Sir*, that's none of my Distemper.

We had a deal of such Discourse, and sometimes others that signify'd as little; by and by He ask'd me to Sing them a Song; at which I smil'd, and said, my singing Days were over: At last he ask'd me, if he should Play upon his Flute to me; his Sister said she believ'd it wou'd hurt me, and that my Head could not bear it; I bow'd and said, No, it would not hurt me: And pray Madam, *said I*, do not hinder it, I love the Musick of the Flute very much; then his Sister said, well do then Brother; with that he pull'd out the Key of his Closet; Dear Sister, *says he*, I am very Lazy, do step to my Closet and fetch my Flute, it lies in *such a Drawer*, naming a Place where he was sure it was not, that she might be a little while a looking for it.

As soon as she was gone, he related the whole Story to me, of the Discourse his Brother had about me, and of his pushing it at him, and his concern about it, which was the Reason of his contriving this Visit to me: I assur'd him, I had never open'd my Mouth either to his Brother, or to any Body else: I told him the dreadful Exigence I was in; that my Love to him, and his offering to have me forget that Affection and remove it to another, had thrown me down; and that I had a thousand Times wish'd I might Die rather than Recover, and to have the same Circumstances to struggle with as I had before; and that this backwardness to Life had been the great Reason of the slowness of my Recovering: I added that I foresaw, that as soon as I was well, I must quit the Family; and that as for Marrying his *Brother*, I abhor'd the thoughts of it, after what had been my Case with him, and that he might depend upon it, I would never see his Brother again upon that Subject: That if he would break all his Vows and Oaths, and Engagements with me, be that between his Conscience and his Honour, and himself: But he should never be able to say that I who he had persuaded to call my self his Wife, and who had given him the Liberty to use me as a Wife, was not as Faithful to him as a Wife ought to be, what ever he might be to me.

He was going to reply, and had said That he was sorry I could not be persuaded, and was a going to say more, but he heard his Sister a coming, and so did I; and yet I forc'd out these few Words as a reply, That I could never be persuaded to Love one Brother

9. In each case meaning "I *don't* doubt"; standard British usage of the word "doubt" may imply its opposite, and De-foe uses the word in this sense throughout the narrative.

and Marry another: He shook his Head and said, *Then I am Ruin'd*, meaning himself; and that Moment his Sister enter'd the Room and told him she could not find the Flute; Well, *says he* merrily, this Laziness won't do, so he gets up, and goes himself to go to look for it, but comes back without it too; not but that he could have found it, but because his Mind was a little Disturb'd, and he had no mind to Play; and besides, the Errand he sent his Sister of, was answer'd another way; for he only wanted an Opportunity to speak to me, which he gain'd, tho' not much to his Satisfaction.

I had however, a great deal of Satisfaction in having spoken my Mind to him with Freedom, and with such an honest Plainess, as I have related; and tho' it did not at all Work the way, I desir'd, *that is to say*, to oblige the Person to me the more, yet it took from him all possibility of quitting me but by a down right breach of Honour, and giving up all the Faith of a Gentleman to me, which he had so often engaged by, never to abandon me, but to make me his Wife as soon as he came to his Estate.

It was not many Weeks after this before I was about the House again, and began to grow well; but I continu'd Melancholly, silent, dull, and retir'd, which amaz'd the whole Family, except he that knew the Reason of it; yet it was a great while before he took any Notice of it, and I *as backward to speak as he*, carried[1] respectfully to him, but never offer'd to speak a Word to him, that was particular of any kind whatsoever; and this continu'd for sixteen or seventeen Weeks, so that as I expected every Day to be dismiss'd the Family, on Account of what Distaste they had taken another Way, in which I had no Guilt; so I expected to hear no more of this Gentleman, after all his solemn Vows, and Protestations, but to be ruin'd and abandon'd.

At last I broke the way myself in the Family for my Removing; for being talking seriously with the old Lady one Day, about my own Circumstances in the World, and how my Distemper had left a heaviness upon my Spirits, that I was not the same thing I was before: The old Lady said, I am afraid *Betty*, what I have said to you, about my Son has had some Influence upon you, and that you are Melancholly on his Account; Pray will you let me know how the Matter stands with you both? if it may not be improper, for as for *Robin*, he does nothing but Rally and Banter when I speak of it to him: Why truly Madam, *said I*, that Matter stands as I wish it did not, and I shall be very sincere with you in it, what ever befalls me for it; Mr. *Robert* has several times propos'd Marriage to me, which is what I had no Reason to expect, my poor Circumstances consider'd; but I have always resisted him, and that perhaps in Terms

1. Behaved.

more positive than became me, considering the Regard that I ought to have for every Branch of your Family: But *said I,* Madam, I could never so far forget my Obligations to you and all your House, to offer to Consent to a Thing, which I know must needs be Disobliging to you, and this I have made my Argument to him, and have possitively told him, that I would never entertain a Thought of that kind, unless I had your Consent, and his Fathers also, to whom I was bound by so many invincible Obligations.

And is this possible Mrs. *Betty*? says the old Lady, then you have been much Juster to us, than we have been to you; for we have all look'd upon you as a kind of a Snare to my Son; and I had a Proposal to make to you for your Removing, for fear of it; but I had not yet mention'd it to you, because I thought you were not thorough Well, and I was afraid of grieving you too much, lest it should throw you down again, for we have all a Respect for you still, tho' not so much, as to have it be the Ruin of my Son; but if it be as you say, we have all wrong'd you very much.

As to the Truth of what I say, Madam, *said I,* I refer you to your Son himself; if he will do me any Justice, he must tell you the Story just as I have told it.

Away goes the old Lady to her Daughters, and tells them the whole Story, just as I had told it her, and they were surpris'd at it, you may be sure, as I believ'd they would be; one *said,* she could never have thought it; another said, *Robin* was a Fool, a *Third* said, she would not believe a Word of it, and she would warrant that *Robin* would tell the Story another way; but the old Gentlewoman, who was resolv'd to go to the bottom of it, before I could have the least Opportunity of Acquainting her Son, with what had pass'd, resolv'd too that she would Talk with her Son immediately, and to that purpose sent for him, for he was gone but to a Lawyers House in the Town, upon some petty Business of his own, and upon her sending, he return'd immediately.

Upon his coming up to them, for they were all still together: sit down *Robin, says the old Lady,* I must have some talk with you; with all my Heart, Madam, *says Robin, looking very Merry;* I hope it is about a good Wife, for I am at a great loss in that Affair: How can that be, *says his Mother,* did not you say, you resolved to have Mrs. *Betty*? Ay Madam, says *Robin*; but there is one has *forbid the Banns:* Forbid the Banns! *says his Mother,* who can that be? Even Mrs. *Betty* herself, says *Robin.* How so, *says his Mother*; Have you ask'd her the Question then? *Yes, indeed Madam, says* Robin; I have attack'd her in Form,[2] five times since she was Sick, and am beaten off; the Jade is so stout, she won't Capitulate, nor yield upon any Terms, except such as I cannot effectually Grant: Explain your

2. Proposed to her properly.

self, *says the Mother*, for I am surpris'd; I do not understand you, I hope you are not in Earnest.

Why, Madam, *says he*, the Case is plain enough upon me, it explains itself; she wont have me, *she says*; is not that plain enough? I think 'tis plain, and pretty rough too; well but *says the Mother*, you talk of Conditions, that you cannot Grant, what, does she want a Settlement? her Jointure[3] ought to be according to her Portion; but what Fortune does she bring you? Nay, as to Fortune, *says* Robin, she is rich enough; I am satisfy'd in that Point; but *'tis* I that am not able to come up to her Terms, and she is positive she will not have me without.

Here the Sisters put in, Madam, *says the second Sister*, 'tis impossible to be serious with him; he will never give a direct Answer to any thing; you had better let him alone, and talk no more of it to him; you know how to dispose of her out of his way if you thought there was any thing in it; *Robin* was a little warm'd with his Sisters rudeness, but he was even with her; and yet with good Manners too: There are two sorts of People, Madam, *says he, turning to his Mother*, that there is no contending with, that is a wise Body and a Fool, 'tis a little hard I should engage with both of them together.

The younger Sister then put in, we must be Fools indeed, *says she*, in my Brother's Opinion, that he should think we can believe he has seriously ask'd Mrs. *Betty* to Marry him, and that she has refus'd him.

Answer, and *Answer not*, says Solomon,[4] *replyed her Brother*: When your Brother had said to your Mother that he had ask'd her no less than five Times, and that it was so, that she positively Denied him, methinks a younger Sister need not question the Truth of it when her Mother did not: My Mother, you see, did not understand it, *says the second Sister*: There's some difference *says* Robin, between desiring me to Explain it, and telling me she did not believe it.

Well but Son, *says the old Lady*, if you are dispos'd to let us into the Mystery of it, What were these hard Conditions? Yes Madam *says* Robin, I had done it before now, if the *Teazers* here had not worried me by way of Interruption: The Conditions are that I bring my Father and you to Consent to it, and without that, she protests she will never see me more upon that Head; and these Conditions *as I said*, I suppose I shall never be able to Grant; I hope my warm Sisters will be Answer'd now, and Blush a little; if not, I have no more to say till I hear farther.

---

3. A settlement made by a husband on his wife.
4. Proverbs 26:4, 5: "Answer not a fool according to his folly, lest thou also be like unto him." And, "Answer a fool according to his folly, lest he be wise in his conceit."

This Answer was surprizing to them all, tho' less to the Mother, because of what I had said to her; as to the Daughters they stood Mute a great while; but the Mother said with some Passion, WELL, I had heard this before, *but I cou'd not believe it*; but if it is so, then we have all done *BETTY* wrong, and she has behav'd better than I ever expected: Nay, *says the eldest Sister*, if it is so, she has acted Handsomely indeed: I confess *says the Mother*, it was none of her Fault, if he was Fool enough to take a Fancy to her; but to give such an Answer to him shews more Respect to your Father and me than I can tell how to Express; I shall value the Girl the better for it as long as I know her. But I shall not *says* Robin, unless you will give your Consent: I'll consider of that a while *says the Mother*; I assure you, if there were not some other Objections in the way, this Conduct of hers would go a great way to bring me to Consent: I wish it would go quite thro' with it, *says* Robin; if you had as much thought about making me Easie,[5] as you have about making me Rich, you would soon Consent to it.

Why *Robin, says the Mother again*, Are you really in Earnest? Would you so fain have her as you pretend? Really Madam *says* Robin, I think 'tis hard you should Question me upon that Head after all I have said: I won't say that I will have her, how can I resolve that point when you see I cannot have her without your Consent? besides I am not bound to Marry at all: But this I will say, I am in Earnest in, that I will never have any body else if I can help it; so you may Determine for me; *Betty* or no Body is the Word; and the Question which of the Two shall be in your Breast to decide Madam; provided only, that *my good humour'd Sisters here, may have no Vote in it.*

All this was dreadful to me, for the Mother began to yield, and *Robin* press'd her Home in it: On the other hand, she advised with the eldest Son, and he used all the Arguments in the World to persuade her to Consent; alledging his Brothers passionate Love for me, and my generous Regard to the Family in refusing my own Advantages upon such a nice point of Honour, and a thousand such Things: And as to the Father, he was a Man in a hurry of publick Affairs and getting Money, seldom at Home, thoughtful of the main Chance;[6] but left all those Things to his Wife.

You may easily believe, that when the Plot was thus, as *they thought* broke out,[7] and that every one thought they knew how Things were carried: It was not so Difficult or so Dangerous for the elder Brother, who no body suspected of any thing, to have a freer Access to me than before: Nay the Mother, *which was just as he wish'd*, Propos'd it to him to Talk with Mrs. *Betty*; for it may be

5. Putting his mind at ease.
6. Thinking about and seeking after financial gain.

7. When the family thought that they knew the whole scheme.

Son *said she,* you may see farther into the Thing than I; and see if you think she has been so Positive as *Robin* says she has been, or no. This was as well as he could wish, and he as it were yielding to Talk with me at his Mother's Request, She brought me to him into her own Chamber, told me her Son had some Business with me at her Request, and desir'd me to be very Sincere with him; and then she left us together, and he went and shut the Door after her.

He came back to me, and took me in his Arms and kiss'd me very Tenderly; but told me, he had a long Discourse to hold with me, and it was now come to that Crisis, that I should make my self Happy or Miserable, as long as I Liv'd: That the Thing was now gone so far, that if I could not comply with his Desire, we should be both Ruin'd: Then he told me the whole Story between *Robin,* as he call'd him, and his Mother and Sisters and himself; as it is above: And now dear Child, *says he,* consider what it will be to Marry a Gentleman of a good Family, in good Circumstances, and with the Consent of the whole House, and to enjoy all that the World can give you: And what on the other Hand, to be sunk into the dark Circumstances of a Woman that has lost her Reputation; and that tho' I shall be a private Friend to you while I live, yet as I shall be suspected always, so you will be afraid to see me, and I shall be afraid to own you.

He gave me no time to Reply, but went on with me thus: What has happen'd between us Child, so long as we both agree to do so, may be buried and forgotten: I shall always be your sincere Friend, without any Inclination to nearer Intimacy, when you become my Sister; and we shall have all the honest part of Conversation without any Reproaches between us of having done amiss: I beg of you to consider it, and do not stand in the way of your own Safety and Prosperity; and to satisfie you that I am Sincere, *added he,* I here offer you 500 *l.* in Money, to make you some Amends for the Freedoms I have taken with you, which we shall look upon as some of the Follies of our Lives, which 'tis hop'd we may Repent of.

He spoke this in so much more moving Terms than it is possible for me to Express, and with so much greater force of Argument than I can repeat, that I only recommend it to those who Read the Story, to suppose, that as he held me above an Hour and Half in that Discourse, so he answer'd all my Objections, and fortified his Discourse with all the Arguments, that humane[8] Wit and Art could Devise.

I cannot say however, that any thing he said, made Impression enough upon me, so as to give me any thought of the Matter, till he told me at last very plainly, that if I refus'd, he was sorry to add, that he could never go on with me in that Station as we stood

8. Human.

before; that tho' he Lov'd me as well as ever, and that I was as
agreeable to him, as ever; yet, Sense of Virtue had not so far forsaken him, as to suffer him to lye with a Woman, that his Brother
Courted to make his Wife; and if he took his leave of me, with a
denial in this Affair, whatever he might do for me in the Point of
support, grounded on his first Engagement of maintaining me, yet
he would not have me be surpriz'd, that he was oblig'd to tell me,
he could not allow himself to see me any more; and that indeed I
could not expect it of him.

I receiv'd this last part with some tokens of Surprize and Disorder, and had much ado, to avoid sinking down, for indeed I lov'd
him to an Extravagance not easie to imagine; but he perceiv'd my
Disorder; he entreated me to consider seriously of it, assur'd me
that it was the only way to Preserve our mutual Affection; that in
this Station we might love as Friends, with the utmost Passion, and
with a love of Relation untainted, free from our just Reproaches,
and free from other Peoples Suspicions; that he should ever
acknowledge his happiness owing to me; that he would be Debtor
to me as long as he liv'd, and would be paying that Debt as long as
he had Breath; Thus he wrought me up, in short, to a kind of Hesi-
tation in the Matter; having the Dangers on one Side represented in
lively Figures, and indeed heightn'd by my Imagination of being
turn'd out to the wide World, a meer cast off Whore, *for it was no
less*, and perhaps expos'd as such; with little to provide for myself;
with no Friend, no Acquaintance in the whole World, *out of that
Town*, and there I could not pretend to Stay; all this terrify'd me to
the last Degree, and he took care upon all Occasions to lay it home
to me, in the worst Colours that it could be possible to be drawn
in; on the other Hand, he fail'd not to set forth the easy prosperous
Life which I was going to live.

He answer'd all that I could object from Affection, and from
former Engagements, with telling me the Necessity that was before
us of taking other Measures now; and as to his Promises of Marriage, the nature of things *he said*, had put an End to that, by the
probability of my being his Brothers Wife, before the time to
which his Promises all referr'd.

Thus in a Word, I may say, he Reason'd me out of my Reason;
he conquer'd all my Arguments, and I began to see a Danger that I
was in, which I had not consider'd of before, and that was of being
drop'd by both of them, and left alone in the World to shift for
myself.

This, and his perswasion, at length Prevail'd with me to Consent,
tho' with so much Reluctance, that it was easie to see I should go
to Church, like a Bear to the Stake;[9] I had some little Apprehen-

9. I.e., reluctantly. Moll's comparison is drawn from the sport of bear-baiting, popular in early-eighteenth-century Eng-land.

sions about me too, lest my new Spouse, who by the way, I had not
the least Affection for, should be skilful enough to Challenge me on
another Account, upon our first coming to Bed together; but
whether he did it with Design or not, I know not, but his elder
Brother took care to make him very much Fuddled before he went
to Bed, so that I had the Satisfaction of a drunken Bedfellow the
first Night: How he did it I know not, but I concluded that he certainly contriv'd it that his Brother might be able to make no Judgment of the difference between a Maid and a married Woman; nor
did he ever Entertain any Notions of it, or disturb his Thoughts
about it.

I should go back a little here, to where I left off; the elder
Brother having thus manag'd me, his next business was to Manage
his Mother, and he never left till he had brought her to acquiesce,
and be passive in the thing; Even without acquainting the Father,
other than by Post Letters: So that she consented to our Marrying
privately, and leaving her to manage the Father afterwards.

Then he Cajol'd with his Brother, and perswaded him what Service he had done him, and how he had brought his Mother to Consent, which tho' *True*, was not indeed done to serve him, but to
serve himself; but thus diligently did he cheat him, and had the
Thanks of a faithful Friend for shifting off his Whore into his
Brothers Arms for a Wife. So certainly does Interest banish all
manner of Affection, and so naturally do Men give up Honour and
Justice, Humanity, and even Christianity, to secure themselves.

I must now come back to Brother *Robin*, as we always call'd him,
who having got his Mother's Consent *as above*, came big[1] with the
News to me, and told me the whole Story of it, with a Sincerity so
visible, that I must confess it griev'd me that I must be the Instrument to abuse so honest a Gentleman; but there was no Remedy;
he would have me, and I was not oblig'd to tell him, that I was his
Brother's Whore, tho' I had no other way to put him off; so I came
gradually into it, to his Satisfaction, and behold, we were Married.

Modesty forbids me to reveal the Secrets of the Marriage Bed,
but nothing could have happen'd more suitable to my Circumstances than that, *as above*, my Husband was so Fuddled when he
came to Bed, that he could not remember in the Morning, whether
he had had any Conversation[2] with me or no, and I was oblig'd to
tell him *he had*, tho' in reallity *he had not*, that I might be sure he
could make no enquiry about any thing else.

It concerns the Story in hand very little to enter into the farther
particulars of the Family, or of myself, for the five Years that I liv'd
with this Husband; only to observe that I had two Children by him,
and that at the end of five Year he Died: He had been really a very

1. Pregnant, bursting. 2. Sexual intercourse.

good Husband to me, and we liv'd very agreeably together; But as he had not receiv'd much from them, and had in the little time he liv'd acquir'd no great Matters, so my Circumstances were not great; nor was I much mended[3] by the Match: Indeed I had pre-serv'd the elder Brother's Bonds to me, to pay me 500 *l.* which he offer'd me for my Consent to Marry his Brother; and this, with what I had saved of the Money he formerly gave me, and about as much more by my Husband, left me a Widow with about 1200 *l.* in my Pocket.

My two Children were indeed taken happily off of my Hands by my Husband's Father and Mother, and that by the way was all they got by Mrs. *Betty.*

I confess I was not suitably affected with the loss of my Hus-band; nor indeed can I say that I ever Lov'd him as I ought to have done, or as was proportionable to the good Usage I had from him, for he was a tender, kind, good humour'd Man as any Woman could desire; but his Brother being so always in my sight, *at least*, while we were in the Country, was a continual Snare to me; and I never was in Bed with my Husband, but I wish'd my self in the Arms of his Brother; and tho' his Brother never offer'd me the least Kindness that way, after our Marriage, but carried it just as a Brother ought to do; yet, it was impossible for me to do so to him: In short, I committed Adultery and Incest with him every Day in my Desires, which without doubt, was as effectually Criminal in the Nature of the Guilt, as if I had actually done it.

Before my Husband Died, his elder Brother was Married, and we being then remov'd to *London,* were written to by the old Lady to come and be at the Wedding; my Husband went, but I pretended Indisposition, and that I could not possibly Travel, so I staid behind; for in short, I could not bear the sight of his being given to another Woman, tho' I knew I was never to have him my self.

I was now *as above,* left loose to the World, and being still Young and Handsome, as every body said of me, *and I assure you I thought my self so,* and with a tollerable Fortune in my Pocket, I put no small value upon my self: I was Courted by several very con-siderable Tradesmen, and particularly, very warmly by one, a *Lin-nen-Draper,* at whose House after my Husband's Death I took a Lodging, his Sister being my Acquaintance; here I had all the Lib-erty and all the Opportunity to be Gay, and appear in Company that I could desire; my Landlord's Sister being one of the Maddest, Gayest things alive, and not so much Mistress of her Virtue, as I thought at first she had been: She brought me into a World of wild Company, and even brought home several Persons, *such as she lik'd well enough to Gratifie,* to see her pretty Widow, *so she was pleas'd*

3. Financially improved.

48 · *Moll Flanders*

to call me, and that Name I got in a little time in Publick; now as Fame and Fools make an Assembly, I was here wonderfully Caress'd;[4] had abundance of Admirers, and such as call'd them-selves *Lovers*; but I found not one fair Proposal among them all; as for their common Design, that I understood too well to be drawn into any more Snares of that Kind: The Case was alter'd with me, I had Money in my Pocket, and had nothing to say to them: I had been trick'd once by *that Cheat call'd* LOVE, but the Game was over; I was resolv'd now to be Married or Nothing, and to be well Married or not at all.

I lov'd the Company indeed of Men of Mirth and Wit, Men of Gallantry and Figure, and was often entertain'd with such, as I was also with others; but I found by just Observation, that the brightest Men came upon the dullest Errand, *that is to say*, the Dullest as to what I aim'd at; on the other Hand, those who came with the best Proposals were the Dullest and most disagreeable Part of the World: I was not averse to a Tradesman, but then I would have a Tradesman forsooth, that was something of a Gentleman too; that when my Husband had a mind to carry me to the Court, or to the Play, he might become a Sword,[5] and look as like a Gentleman, as another Man; and not be one that had the mark of his Apron-strings upon his Coat, or the mark of his Hat upon his Perriwig;[6] that should look as if he was set on to his Sword, when his Sword was put on to him, and that carried his Trade in his Countenance.

Well, at last I found this amphibious Creature, this *Land-water-thing* call'd, *a Gentleman-Tradesman*; and as a just Plague upon my Folly, I was catch'd in the very Snare, which *as I might say*, I laid for my self; *I say laid for my self*, for I was not Trepan'd[7] I confess, but I betray'd my self.

This was a *Draper* too, for tho' my Comrade would have brought me to a Bargain with her Brother, yet when it came to the Point, it was it seems for a Mistress, not a Wife, and I kept true to this Notion, that a Woman should never be kept for a Mistress, that had Money to keep her self.

Thus my Pride, not my Principle, my Money, not my Virtue, kept me Honest; tho' as it prov'd, I found I had much better have been Sold by my *She Comrade* to her Brother, than have Sold my self as I did to a Tradesman that was Rake,[8] Gentleman, Shop keeper, and Beggar all together.

But I was hurried on[9] (by my Fancy to a Gentleman) to Ruin my self in the grossest Manner that ever Woman did; for my new

4. Flattered, sought after.
5. Wear a sword gracefully, look well with.
6. Wig. Moll doesn't want her trades-man's daily occupation to betray him when he dresses for occasions.
7. Tricked. ("Trepan" was a common term in the criminal cant of the day.)
8. A man of loose habits, idle and im-moral.
9. Moll blindly obeyed the dictates of her fancy rather than her reason.

Husband coming to a lump of Money at once, fell into such a pro-
fusion of Expence, that all I had, and all he had before, if he had
any thing worth mentioning, would not have held it out above one
Year.

He was very fond of me for about a quarter of a Year, and what I
got by that, was, that I had the pleasure of seeing a great deal of
my Money spent upon my self, and as I may say, had some of the
spending it too: Come, my dear, *says he to me one Day,* Shall we
go and take a turn into the Country for about a Week? Ay, my
Dear, *says I,* Whither would you go? I care not whither *says he,* but
I have a mind to look like Quality for a Week; we'll go to Oxford
says he: How *says I,* shall we go, I am no Horse Woman, and 'tis
too far for a Coach; too far *says he,* no Place is too far for a Coach
and Six: If I carry you out, you shall Travel like a Dutchess; hum
says I, my Dear 'tis a Frolick, but if you have a mind to it I don't
care. Well the time was appointed, we had a rich Coach, very good
Horses, a Coachman, Postilion, and two Footmen in very good Liveries; a Gentleman on Horseback, and a Page with a Feather in his
Hat upon another Horse; The Servants all call'd him my Lord, and
the Inn-Keepers you may be sure did the like, and I was *her
Honour,* the Countess; and thus we Travel'd to Oxford, and a very
pleasant Journey we had; for, give him his due, not a Beggar alive
knew better how to be a Lord than my Husband: We saw all the
Rareties at Oxford, talk'd with two or three Fellows of Colleges,
about putting out a young Nephew, that was left to his Lordship's
Care, to the University, and of their being his Tutors; we diverted
our selves with bantering several other poor Scholars, with hopes of
being at least his Lordship's Chaplains and putting on a Scarf;[1] and
thus having liv'd like Quality indeed, as to Expence, we went away
for *Northampton,* and in a word, in about twelve Days ramble came
Home again, to the Tune of about 93 *l.* Expence.

Vanity is the perfection of a Fop;[2] my Husband had this Excellence, that he valued nothing of Expence, and as his History you
may be sure, has very little weight[3] in it; 'tis enough to tell you,
that in about two Years and a Quarter he Broke, and was not so
happy to get over into the *Mint,*[4] but got into a *Spunging-House,*[5]
being Arrested in an Action too heavy for him to give Bail to, so he
sent for me to come to him.

It was no surprize to me, for I had foreseen *sometime* that all

1. An official silk neck scarf worn by a
nobleman's chaplain.
2. Dr. Johnson defined a "fop" as "a
man of small understanding and much
ostentation" (*Dictionary,* 1755).
3. Little of substance.
4. The Mint, in Southwark, was legal
sanctuary for insolvent debtors. Mint
Street and several adjoining streets and
alleys became the haunt of criminals
generally, and its privileges were abol-
ished in 1723.
5. A place of preliminary confinement
for debtors who had hopes of paying or
having someone else pay their debts.
Spunging Houses were under the sur-
veillance of a bailiff or sheriff's officer.

was going to Wreck, and had been taking care to reserve something if I could, *tho' it was not much* for myself: But when he sent for me, he behav'd much better than I expected, and told me plainly, he had played the Fool and suffer'd himself to be Surpriz'd which he might have prevented; that now he foresaw he could not stand it, and therefore he would have me go Home, and in the Night take away every thing I had in the House of any Value and secure it; and after that, he told me that if I could get away 100 *l.* or 200 *l.* in Goods out of the Shop, I should do it, only *says he*, let me know nothing of it, neither what you take, or whither you carry it; for as for me *says he*, I am resolv'd to get out of this House and be gone; and if you never hear of me more, my Dear, *says he*, I wish you well; I am only sorry for the Injury I have done you: He said some very handsome Things to me indeed at Parting; for I *told you* he was a *Gentleman*, and that was all the benefit I had of his being so; that he used me very handsomely, and with good Manners upon all Occasions, even to the last, only spent all I had, and left me to Rob the Creditors for something to Subsist on.

However, I did as he bade me, *that you may be sure*, and having thus taken my leave of him, I never saw him more; for he found means to break out of the Bailiff's House that Night or the next, and got over into *France*;[6] and for the rest, the Creditors scrambl'd for it as well as they could: How I knew not, for I could come at no Knowledge of any thing more than this, that he came Home about three a Clock in the Morning, caus'd the rest of his Goods to be remov'd into the *Mint*, and the Shop to be shut up; and having rais'd what Money he could get together, he got over as I said to *France*, from whence I had one or two Letters from him, and no more.

I did not see him when he came Home, for he having given me such Instructions as above, and I having made the best of my Time, I had no more Business back again at the House, not knowing but I might have been stop'd there by the Creditors; for a *Commission of Bankrupt*, being soon after Issued, they might have stop'd me by Orders from the *Commissioners*: But my Husband having so dextrously got out of the Bailiff's House by letting himself down in a most desperate Manner from almost the top of the House, to the top of another Building, and leaping from thence which was almost two Stories, and which was enough indeed to have broken his Neck: He came home and got away his Goods, before the Creditors could come to Seize, *that is to say*, before they could get out the Commission,[7] and be ready to send their Officers to take Possession.

My Husband was so civil to me, *for still I say, he was much of a*

6. A common practice of persecuted debtors. In *Review*, V, no. 149 (March 10, 1709), Defoe estimates that more than 5,000 insolvent debtors had left England for France.
7. Legal authority of confiscation.

Gentleman, that in the first Letter he wrote me from *France*, he let me know where he had Pawn'd 20 Pieces of fine *Holland* for 30 *l*. which were really worth above 90 *l*. and enclos'd me the Token, and an order for the taking them up, paying the Money, which I did, and made in time above 100 *l*. of them, having Leisure to cut them and sell them, some and some,[8] to private Families, as opportunity offer'd.

However with all this, and all that I had secur'd before, I found upon casting things up, my Case was very much alter'd, and my Fortune much lessen'd, for including the Hollands, and a parcel of fine Muslins, which I carry'd off before, and some Plate, and other things; I found I could hardly muster up 500 *l*. and my Condition was very odd, for tho' I had no Child, (*I had had one by my Gentleman* Draper, *but it was buried,*) yet I was a Widow bewitched, I had a Husband, and no Husband, and I could not pretend to Marry again, tho' I knew well enough my Husband would never see *England* any more, if he liv'd fifty Years: *Thus I say,* I was limitted from Marriage, what Offer soever might be made me: and I had not one Friend to advise with, in the Condition I was in, at least not one I durst Trust the Secret of my Circumstances to, for if the Commissioners were to have been inform'd where I was, I should have been fetch'd up and examin'd upon Oath, and all I had sav'd be taken away from me.

Upon these Apprehensions the first thing I did, was to go quite out of my Knowledge,[9] and go by another Name: This I did effectually, for I went into the *Mint* too, took Lodgings in a very private Place, drest me up in the Habit of a Widow, and call'd myself Mrs. *Flanders.*

Here, however I conceal'd myself, and tho' my new Acquaintances knew nothing of me, yet I soon got a great deal of Company about me; and whether it be that Women are scarce among the Sorts of People that generally are to be found there, or that some Consolation in the Miseries of the Place are more Requisite than on other Occasions, I soon found an agreeable Woman was exceedingly valuable among the Sons of Affliction[1] there; and that those that wanted Money to pay Half a Crown in the Pound to their Creditors, and that run in Debt at the Sign of the *Bull*[2] for their Dinners, would yet find Money for a Supper, if they lik'd the Woman.

However, I kept myself Safe yet, tho' I began like my Lord *Rochester's* Mistress,[3] that lov'd his Company, but would not admit him

8. "Now some and then some"; that is, when and where she could.
9. Go where she was unknown and the region was new to her.
1. See Proverbs 31:5–9.
2. The identifying sign of a tavern in the confines of the Mint.
3. Moll is recalling lines from Lord

Rochester's "Song" (Phillis, be gentler . . .), which concludes,
  Then if to make your ruin more,
  You'll peevishly be coy,
  Dye with the scandal of a *whore*,
  And never know the joy.
See also pp. 21, 58.

farther, to have the Scandal of a Whore, without the Joy; and upon
this score tir'd with the Place and indeed with the Company too, I
began to think of Removing.

It was indeed a Subject of strange Reflection to me to see Men
who were overwhelm'd in perplex'd Circumstances, who were
reduc'd some Degrees below being Ruin'd; whose Families were
Objects of their own Terror and other Peoples Charity; yet while a
Penny lasted, nay, even beyond it, endeavouring to drown their
Sorrow in their Wickedness; heaping up more Guilt upon themselves, labouring to forget former things, which now it was the
proper time to remember, making more Work for Repentance, and
Sinning on, as a Remedy for Sin past.

But it is none of my Talent to preach; these Men were too
wicked, even for me; there was something horrid and absurd in
their way of Sinning, for it was all a Force even upon themselves;
they did not only act against Conscience, but against Nature; they
put a Rape upon their Temper to drown the Reflections, which
their Circumstances continually gave them; and nothing was more
easie than to see how Sighs would interrupt their Songs, and pale-
ness, and anguish sit upon their Brows, in spite of the forc'd Smiles
they put on; nay, sometimes it would break out at their very
Mouths when they had parted with their Money for a lewd Treat,
or a wicked Embrace; I have heard them, turning about, fetch a
deep Sigh, and cry *what a Dog am I!* Well *Betty*, my Dear, I'll
drink thy Health tho', *meaning the Honest Wife*, that perhaps had
not a Half a Crown for herself, and three or four Children: The
next Morning they are at their Penitentials again, and perhaps the
poor weeping Wife comes over to him, either brings him some
Account of what his Creditors are doing, and how she and the Children are turn'd out of Doors, or some other dreadful News; and this
adds to his self Reproaches; but when he has Thought and Por'd on
it till he is almost Mad, having no Principles to Support him,
nothing within him or above him, to Comfort him; but finding it
all Darkness on every Side, he flyes to the same Relief again, (*viz.*)
to Drink it away, Debauch it away, and falling into Company of
Men in just the same Condition with himself, he repeats the
Crime, and thus he goes every Day one Step onward of his way to
Destruction.

I was not wicked enough for such Fellows as these *yet*; on the
contrary, I began to consider here *very seriously* what I had to do,
how things stood with me, and what Course I ought to take: I
knew I had no Friends, no not one Friend or Relation in the
World; and that little I had left apparently wasted, which when it
was gone, I saw nothing but Misery and Starving was before me:
Upon these Considerations, I say, and fill'd with Horror at the

Place I was in, and the dreadful Objects, which I had always before me, *I resolv'd to be gone.*

I had made an Acquaintance with a very sober good sort of a Woman, who was a Widow too like me, but in better Circumstances; her Husband had been a Captain of a Merchant Ship, and having had the Misfortune to be Cast away coming Home on a Voyage from the *West-Indies*, which would have been very profitable, if he had come safe, was so reduc'd by the Loss, that tho' he had saved his Life then, it broke his Heart, and kill'd him afterwards; and his Widow being persued by the Creditors was forc'd to take Shelter in the *Mint:* She soon made things up with the help of Friends, and was at Liberty again; and finding that I rather was there to be conceal'd, than by any particular Prosecutions, and finding also that I agreed with her, *or rather she with me* in a just Abhorrence of the Place and of the Company, she invited me to go Home with her, till I could put myself in some posture of settling in the World to my Mind; withal telling me that it was ten to one, but some good good Captain of a Ship might take a Fancy to me, and Court me, in that part of the Town where she liv'd.

I accepted her Offer, and was with her Half a Year, and should have been longer, but in that interval what she propos'd to me happen'd to herself, and she marry'd very much to her Advantage; but whose Fortune soever was upon the Encrease, mine seem'd to be upon the Wane, and I found nothing present, except two or three Boatswains, or such Fellows, but as for the Commanders they were generally of two Sorts. 1. Such as having good Business, *that is to say*, a good Ship, resolv'd not to Marry but with Advantage, that is, with a good Fortune. 2. Such as being out of Employ, wanted a Wife to help them to a Ship, I mean. (1). A Wife, who having some Money could enable them to hold, as they call it, a good part of a Ship themselves, so to encourage Owners to come in; Or. (2.) A Wife who if she had not Money, had Friends who were concern'd in Shipping, and so could help to put the young Man into a good Ship, which to them is as good as a Portion, and neither of these was my Case; so I look'd like one that was to *lye on Hand.*

This Knowledge I soon learnt by Experience, (*viz.*) That the State of things was altered as to Matrimony, and that I was not to expect at *London*, what I had found in the Country; that Marriages were here the Consequences of politick Schemes for forming Interests, and carrying on Business, and that Love had no Share, or but very little in the Matter.

That as my Sister in Law at *Colchester* had said, Beauty, Wit, Manners, Sence, good Humour, good Behaviour, Education, Virtue, Piety, or any other Qualification, whether of Body or Mind, had no power to recommend: That Money only made a Woman agreeable:

That Men chose Mistresses indeed by the gust of their Affection, and it was requisite to a Whore to be Handsome, well shap'd, have a good Mien, and a graceful Behaviour; but that for a Wife, no Deformity would shock the Fancy, no ill Qualities, the Judgement; the Money was the thing; the Portion was neither crooked or Monstrous, but the Money was always agreeable, whatever the Wife was.

On the other Hand, as the Market run very Unhappily on the Mens side, I found the Women had lost the Privilege of saying No, that it was a Favour now for a Woman to have THE QUESTION ask'd, and if any young Lady had so much Arrogance as to Counterfeit a Negative, she never had the Opportunity given her of denying twice; much less of Recovering that false Step, and accepting what she had but seem'd to decline: The Men had such Choice every where, that the Case of the Women was very unhappy; for they seem'd to Ply at every Door, and if the Man was by great Chance refus'd at one House, he was sure to be receiv'd at the next.

Besides this, I observ'd that the Men made no scruple to set themselves out, and to go a Fortune Hunting, *as they call it*, when they had really no Fortune themselves to Demand it, or Merit to deserve it; and That they carry'd it so high,[4] that a Woman was scarce allow'd to enquire after the Character or Estate of the Person that pretended to her. This I had an Example of in a young Lady at the next House to me, and with whom I had Contracted an intimacy; she was Courted by a young Captain, and though she had near 2000 *l.* to her Fortune, she did but enquire of some of his Neighbours about his Character, his Morals, or Substance; and he took Occasion at the next Visit to let her know, truly, that he took it very ill, and that he should not give her the Trouble of his Visits any more: I heard of it, and as I had begun my Acquaintance with her, I went to see her upon it: She enter'd into a close Conversation with me about it, and unbosom'd herself very freely; I perceiv'd presently that tho' she thought herself very ill us'd, yet she had no power to resent it, and was exceedingly Piqu'd that she had lost him, and particularly that another of less Fortune had gain'd him.

I fortify'd her Mind against such a Meanness, *as I call'd it*; I told her, that as low as I was in the World, I would have despis'd a Man that should think I ought to take him upon his own Recommendation only, without having the liberty to inform myself of his Fortune, and of his Character; also I *told her,* that as she had a good Fortune, she had no need to stoop to the Dissaster of the times; that it was enough that the Men could insult us that had but little Money to recommend us, but if she suffer'd such an Affront to pass

4. Acted so arrogantly.

upon her without Resenting it, she would be render'd low-priz'd upon all Occasions, and would be the Contempt of all the Women in that part of the Town; that a Woman can never want an Opportunity to be Reveng'd of a Man that has us'd her ill, and that there were ways enough to humble such a Fellow as that, or else certainly Women were the most unhappy Creatures in the World.

I found she was very well pleas'd with the Discourse, and she told me seriously that she would be very glad to make him sensible of her just Resentment, and either to bring him on again, or have the Satisfaction of her Revenge being as publick as possible.

I told her, that if she would take my Advice, I would tell her how she should obtain her Wishes in both those things; and that I would engage I would bring the Man to her Door again, and make him beg to be let in: *She smil'd at that*, and soon let me see that if he came to her Door, her Resentment was not so great as to give her leave to let him stand long there.

However, she lissened very willingly to my offer of Advice; so *I told her* that the first thing she ought to do, was a piece of Justice to herself; namely, that whereas she had been told by several People, that he had reported among the Ladies that he had left her, and pretended to give the Advantage of the Negative to himself; she should take care to have it well spread among the Women, which she could not fail of an Opportunity to do in a Neighbourhood, so addicted to Family News, as that she liv'd in was, that she had enquired into his Circumstances, and found he was not the Man as to Estate he pretended to be: Let them be told Madam, *said I*, that you had been well inform'd that he was not the Man that you expected, and that you thought it was not safe to meddle with him, that you heard he was of an ill Temper, and that he boasted how he had us'd the Women ill upon many Occasions, and that particularly he was Debauch'd in his Morals, *&c.* The last of which indeed had some Truth in it; but at the same time, I did not find that she seem'd to like him much the worse for that part.

As I had put this into her Head, she came most readily into it; immediately she went to Work to find Instruments,[5] and she had very little difficulty in the Search, for telling her Story in general to a Couple of Gossips in the Neighbourhood, it was the Chat of the Tea Table all over that part of the Town, and I met with it where ever I visited: Also, as it was known that I was Acquainted with the young Lady herself, my Opinion was ask'd very often, and I confirm'd it with all the necessary Aggravations, and set out his Character in the blackest Colours; but then as a piece of secret Intelligence, I added, as what the other Gossips knew nothing of (*viz.*) That I had heard he was in very bad Circumstances; that he was

---

5. Those who would listen and gossip; tools to be used in Moll's scheme.

under a Necessity of a Fortune to support his Interest with the Owners of the Ship he Commanded: That his own Part was not paid for, and if it was not paid quickly his Owners would put him out of the Ship, and his Chief Mate was likely to Command it, who offer'd to buy that Part which the Captain had promis'd to take.

I *added,* for I confess I was heartily piqu'd at the Rogue, *as I call'd him,* that I had heard a Rumour too, that he had a Wife alive at *Plymouth,* and another in the *West Indies,* a thing which they all knew was not very uncommon for such kind of Gentlemen.

This work'd as we both desir'd it, for presently the young Lady at next Door, *who had a Father and Mother that Govern'd both her and her Fortune,* was shut up, and her Father forbid him the House: Also in one Place more where he went, the Woman had the Courage, *however strange it was,* to say No, and he could try no where but he was Reproached with his Pride, and that he pretended not to give the Women leave to enquire into his Character, *and the like.*

Well, by this time he began to be sensible of his mistake, and having allarm'd[6] all the Women on that side the Water, he went over to *Ratcliff,* and got access to some of the Ladies there; but tho' the young Women there too, were according to the Fate of the Day, pretty willing to be ask'd, yet such was his ill luck, that his Character follow'd him over the Water, and his good Name was much the same there, as it was on our side; so that tho' he might have had Wives enough, yet it did not happen among the Women that had good Fortunes, which was what he wanted.

But this was not all; she very ingeniously manag'd another thing her self, for she got a young Gentleman, who was a Relation, and was indeed a marry'd Man, to come and visit her Two or Three times a Week in a very fine Chariot and good Liveries, and her Two Agents and I also, presently spread a Report all over, that this Gentleman came to Court her; that he was a Gentleman of a Thousand Pounds a Year, and that he was fallen in Love with her, and that she was going to her Aunt's in the City, because it was inconvenient for the Gentleman to come to her with his Coach in *Redriff,*[7] the Streets being so narrow and difficult.

This took immediately; the Captain was laugh'd at in all Companies, and was ready to hang himself; he tryed all the ways possible to come at her again, and wrote the most passionate Letters to her in the World, excusing his former Rashness, and in short, by great Application, obtained leave to wait on her again, *as he said,* to clear his Reputation.

---

6. Through the effect of the rumors.
7. Redriff (a slang name for "Rotherhithe") is on the south bank of the Thames. The colloquial pronunciation of "Rotherhithe" is "rod' rith" or "red' rif"; hence, "Redriff"; an area largely inhabited by seamen.

At this meeting she had her full Revenge of him; for *she told him* she wondred what he took her to be, that she should admit any Man to a Treaty of so much Consequence as that of Marriage, without enquiring very well into his Circumstances; that if he thought she was to be huff'd into Wedlock, and that she was in the same Circumstances which her Neighbours might be in, (*viz.*) to take up with the first good Christian that came, he was mistaken; that in a word his Character was really bad, or he was very ill beholding to his Neighbours; and that unless he could clear up some Points, in which she had justly been Prejudiced, she had no more to say to him, but to do herself Justice, and give him the Satisfaction of knowing that she was not afraid to say NO, either to him, or any Man else.

With that she told him what she had heard, *or rather rais'd*[8] *herself by my means, of his Character*; his not having paid for the Part he pretended to Own of the Ship he Commanded; of the Resolution of his Owners to put him out of the Command, and to put his Mate in his stead; and of the Scandal rais'd on his Morals; his having been reproach'd with such and such Women; and his having a Wife at *Plymouth* and in the *West-Indies, and the like*; and she ask'd him, whether he could deny that she had good Reason, if these things were not clear'd up, to refuse him, and in the mean time to insist upon having Satisfaction in Points so significant as they were.

He was so confounded at her Discourse that he could not answer a word, and she almost began to believe that all was true, by his disorder, tho' at the same time she knew that she had been the raiser of all those Reports herself.

After some time he recover'd himself a little, and from that time became the most humble, the most modest, and the most importunate Man alive in his Courtship.

She carried her jest on a great way, she ask'd him, if he thought she was so at her last shift,[9] that she could or ought to bear such Treatment, and if he did not see that she did not want[1] those who thought it worth their while to come farther to her than he did, meaning the Gentleman who she had brought to visit her by way of sham.

She brought him by these tricks to submit to all possible measures to satisfie her, as well of his Circumstances, as of his Behaviour. He brought her undeniable Evidence of his having paid for his part of the Ship; he brought her Certificates from his Owners, that the Report of their intending to remove him from the Command of the Ship and put his chief Mate in, was false and groundless; in short, he was quite the reverse of what he was before.

8. Spread by the rumors she and Moll had made up to damage his character.
9. Resort.
1. Lack.

Thus I convinc'd her, that if the Men made their Advantage of our Sex in the Affair of Marriage, upon the supposition of there being such Choice to be had, and of the Women being so easie, it was only owing to this, that the Women wanted Courage to maintain their Ground, and to play their Part; and that according to my Lord *Rochester*,

> A Woman's *ne'er so ruin'd but she can*
> *Revenge herself on her undoer*, Man.[2]

After these things, this young Lady played her part so well, that tho' she resolved to have him, and that indeed having him was the main bent of her design, yet she made his obtaining her be TO HIM the most difficult thing in the World; and this she did, not by a haughty Reserv'd Carriage, but by a just Policy, turning the Tables upon him, and playing back upon him his own Game; for as he pretended by a kind of lofty Carriage, to place himself above the occasion of a Character,[3] and to make enquiring into his Character a kind of an affront to him, she broke with him upon that Subject; and at the same time that she made him submit to all possible enquiry after his Affairs, she apparently shut the Door against his looking into her own.

It was enough to him to obtain her for a Wife, as to what she had, she told him plainly that as he knew her Circumstances, it was but just she should know his; and tho' at the same time he had only known her Circumstances by common Fame, yet he had made so many Protestations of his Passion for her, that he could ask no more but her Hand to his grand Request, *and the like ramble*[4] *according to the Custom of Lovers*: In short, he left himself no room to ask any more questions about her Estate, and she took the advantage of it like a prudent Woman, for she plac'd part of her Fortune so in Trustees, without letting him know any thing of it, that it was quite out of his reach, and made him be very well content with the rest.

It is true she was pretty well besides, that is to say, she had about 1400 *l.* in Money, which she gave him, and the other, after some time, she brought to light, as a perquisite to her self; which he was to accept as a mighty Favour, seeing though it was not to be his, it might ease him in the Article of her particular Expences; and I must add, that by this Conduct the Gentleman himself became not only the more humble in his Applications to her to obtain her, but also was much the more an obliging Husband to her when he had her: I cannot but remind the Ladies here how much they place

2. In "A Letter fancy'd from *Artemisia* in the Town, to *Chloe* in the Country." The lines in the poem actually read:
   A Woman's *ne're so ruin'd but she can Be still reveng'd, on her undoer* Man.

See also p. 21.
3. Any inquiry concerning his personal qualities.
4. Empty discourse.

themselves below the common Station of a Wife, which if I may be allow'd not to be Partial is low enough already; *I say* they place themselves below their common Station, and prepare their own Mortifications, by their submitting so to be insulted by the Men before-hand, which I confess I see no Necessity of.

This Relation may serve therefore to let the Ladies see that the Advantage is not so much on the other Side as the Men think it is; and tho' it may be true that the Men have but too much Choice among us, and that some Women may be found who will dishonour themselves, be Cheap, and Easy to come at, and will scarce wait to be ask'd; yet if they will have Women, *as I may say*, worth having, they may find them as uncomeatable[5] as ever; and that those that are otherwise, are a Sort of People that have such Defficiencies, *when had*, as rather recommend the Ladies that are Difficult than encourage the Men to go on with their easie Courtship, and expect Wives equally valluable that will come at first call.

Nothing is more certain than that the Ladies always gain of the Men by keeping their Ground, and letting their pretended Lovers see they can Resent being slighted, and that they are not affraid of saying No. They, I observe insult us mightily with telling us of the Number of Women; that the Wars and the Sea, and Trade, and other Incidents have carried the Men so much away, that there is no Proportion between the Numbers of the Sexes, and therefore the Women have the Disadvantage; but I am far from Granting that the Number of the Women is so great, or the Number of the Men so small; but if they will have me tell the Truth, the Disadvantage of the Women is a terrible Scandal upon the Men, and it lyes here, and here only; *Namely*, that the Age is so Wicked, and the Sex so Debauch'd, that in short the Number of such Men, as an honest Woman ought to meddle with, is small indeed, and it is but here and there that a Man is to be found who is fit for a Woman to venture upon.

But the Consequence even of that too amounts to no more than this; that Women ought to be the more Nice;[6] For how do we know the just Character of the Man that makes the offer? To say that the Woman should be the more easie on this Occasion, is to say we should be the forwarder to venture, because of the greatness of the Danger, which in my way of Reasoning is very absurd.

On the contrary, the Women have ten Thousand times the more Reason to be wary and backward, by how much the hazard of being betray'd is the greater; and would the Ladies consider this, and act the wary Part, they would discover every Cheat that offer'd; for, *in*

---

5. Unapproachable.
6. Discriminating, scrupulous. "Nice" carried a different primary meaning in the Restoration and eighteenth century from the one that it generally does now; it usually suggested delicacy, exactness, difficulty, or fine discrimination.

short, the Lives of very few Men now a-Days will bear a Character; and if the Ladies do but make a little Enquiry, they will soon be able to distinguish the Men and deliver[7] themselves: As for Women that do not think their own Safety worth their Thought, that impatient of their present State, resolve *as they call it* to take the first good Christian that comes, that run into Matrimony, as a Horse rushes into the Battle, I can say nothing to them, but this, that they are a Sort of Ladies that are to be pray'd for among the rest of distemper'd People, and to me they look like People that venture their whole Estates in a Lottery where there is a Hundred Thousand Blanks to one Prize.

No Man of common Sense will value a Woman the less for not giving up herself at the first Attack, or for not accepting his Proposal without enquiring into his Person or Character; on the contrary, he must think her the weakest of all Creatures in the World, as the Rate of Men now goes; In short, he must have a very contemptible Opinion of her Capacities, nay, even of her Understanding, that having but one Cast[8] for her Life, shall cast that Life away at once, and make Matrimony like Death, be *a Leap in the Dark*.[9]

I would fain have the Conduct of my Sex a little Regulated in this particular, which is the Thing, in which of all the parts of Life, I think at this Time we suffer most in: 'Tis nothing but lack of Courage, the fear of not being Marry'd at all, and of that frightful State of Life, call'd *an old Maid*; of which I have a Story to tell by itself: This I say, is the Woman's Snare; but would the Ladies once but get above that Fear and manage rightly, they would more certainly avoid it by standing their Ground, in a Case so absolutely Necessary to their Felicity, than by exposing themselves as they do; and if they did not Marry so soon as they may do otherwise, they would make themselves amends by Marrying safer; she is always Married too soon who gets a bad Husband, and she is never Married too late who gets a good one: In a word, there is no Woman, *Deformity, or lost Reputation excepted*, but if she manages well, may be Marry'd safely one time or other; but if she precipitates herself, it is ten Thousand to one but she is undone.

But I come now to my own Case, in which there was at this time no little Nicety. The Circumstances I was in, made the offer of a

7. Save, free.
8. Here "cast" means chance, as in a cast or throw of the dice. "Cast" also means to be condemned to death at trial. In another important sense throughout the novel, "cast" means to contrive, to weigh one's chances, and in this usage the word reinforces the idea of "fortunes" in Defoe's title. See also note 8, p. 5.

9. The expression "a leap in the dark" suggests a variety of meanings. Primarily it describes any undertaking that involves a risk, in this instance marriage. The phrase also applied to illicit copulation (leap); and in the criminal jargon of the day, "a leap at Tyburn" meant hanging; i.e., a leap into the darkness of the next world.

good Husband the most necessary Thing in the World to me; but I found soon that to be made Cheap and Easy was not the way: It soon began to be found that the Widow had no Fortune, and to say this, was to say all that was Ill of me, for I began to be dropt in all the Discourses of Matrimony: Being well Bred, Handsome, Witty, Modest and agreeable; all which I had allowed to my Character, whether justly or no, is not to the Purpose; I say, all these would not do without the Dross,[1] which was now become more valuable than Virtue itself. In short, *the Widow*, they said, *had no Money*.

I resolv'd therefore, as to the State of my present Circumstances; that it was absolutely Necessary to change my Station, and make a new Appearance in some other Place where I was not known, and even to pass by another Name if I found Occasion.

I communicated my Thoughts to my intimate Friend the Captain's Lady, who I had so faithfully serv'd in her Case with the Captain; and who was as ready to serve me in the same kind as I could desire: I made no scruple to lay my Circumstances open to her; my Stock was but low, for I had made but about 540 *l.* at the Close of my last Affair, and I had wasted some of that; However, I had about 460 *l.* left, a great many very rich Cloaths, a gold Watch, and some Jewels, tho' of no extraordinary value, and about 30 or 40 *l.* left in Linnen not dispos'd of.

My Dear and faithful Friend, the Captain's Wife was so sensible of the Service I had done her in the Affair above, that she was not only a steddy Friend to me, but knowing my Circumstances, she frequently made me Presents as Money came into her Hands; such as fully amounted to a Maintenance, so that I spent none of my own; and at last she made this unhappy Proposal to me (*viz.*) that as we had observ'd, *as above*, how the Men made no scruple to set themselves out as Persons meriting a Woman of Fortune, when they had really no Fortune of their own; it was but just to deal with them in their own way, and if it was possible, to Deceive the Deceiver.[2]

The Captain's Lady, in short, put this Project into my Head, and told me if I would be rul'd by her I should certainly get a Husband of Fortune, without leaving him any room to Reproach me with want of my own; I told her as I had Reason to do, That I would give up myself wholly to her Directions, and that I would have neither Tongue to speak, or Feet to step in that Affair, but as she should direct me, depending that she would Extricate one out of

1. Money, that which in the light of all Moll's favorable qualities might seem excessive.
2. "To deceive the deceiver is no deceit" (*Fallere fallentum non est fraus*), a popular Latin proverb (e.g., Ovid, *Artis* *Amatoriae*, Book 1, line 645; Heidenreich cites various editions of Ovid in Defoe's library) included in most books of English proverbs. Moll applies its sentiments in this incident, and again when she dupes Jemmy's mistress, pp. 113 ff.

every Difficulty that she brought me into, which she said she would Answer for.

The first step she put me upon was to call her Cousin, and go to a Relations House of hers in the Country, where she directed me, and where she brought her Husband to visit me; and calling me Cousin, she work'd Matters so about, that her Husband and she together Invited me most passionately to come to Town and be with them, for they now liv'd in a quite different Place from where they were before. In the next Place she tells her Husband, that I had at least 1500 *l*. Fortune, and that after some of my Relations I was like to have a great deal more.

It was enough to tell her Husband this, there needed nothing on my Side; I was but to sit still and wait the Event, for it presently went all over the Neighbourhood that the young Widow at Captain ———s was a Fortune, that she had at least 1500 *l*. and perhaps a great deal more, and *that the Captain said so*; and if the Captain was ask'd at any time about me, he made no scruple to affirm it, tho' he knew not one Word of the Matter, other than that his Wife had told him so; and in this he thought no Harm, for he really believ'd it to be so, because he had it from his Wife; so slender a Foundation will those Fellows build upon, if they do but think there is a Fortune in the Game: With the Reputation of this Fortune, I presently found myself bless'd with admirers enough, and that I had my Choice of Men, as scarce as they said they were, *which by the way confirms what I was saying before*: This being my Case, I who had a subtile Game to play, had nothing now to do but to single out from them all, the properest Man that might be for my Purpose; *that is to say*, the Man who was most likely to depend upon the *hear say* of a Fortune, and not enquire too far into the particulars; and unless I did this, *I did nothing*, for my Case would not bear much Enquiry.

I Pick'd out my Man without much difficulty, by the judgment I made of his way of Courting me; I had let him run on with his Protestations and Oaths that he lov'd me above all the World; that if I would make him happy, that was enough; all which I knew was upon Supposition, nay, it was upon a full Satisfaction,[3] that I was very Rich, tho' I never told him a Word of it myself.

This was my Man, but I was to try him to the bottom, and indeed in that consisted my Safety; for if he baulk'd, I knew I was undone, as surely as he was undone if he took me; and if I did not make some scruple about his Fortune, it was the way to lead him to raise some about mine; and first therefore, I pretended on all occasions to doubt his Sincerity, and told him, perhaps he only courted me for my Fortune; he stop'd my Mouth in that part, with the

3. Belief, conviction.

Thunder of his Protestations, *as above*, but still I pretended to doubt.

One Morning he pulls off his Diamond Ring, and writes upon the Glass[4] of the Sash in my Chamber this Line,

You I Love, and you alone.

I read it, and ask'd him to lend me his Ring, with which I wrote under it thus,

And so in Love says every one.

He takes his Ring again, and writes another Line thus,

Virtue alone is an Estate.

I borrow'd it again, and I wrote under it,

But Money's Virtue; Gold is Fate.

He colour'd as red as Fire to see me turn so quick upon him, and in a kind of a Rage told me he would Conquer me, and writes again *thus*,

I scorn your Gold, and yet I Love.

I ventur'd all upon the last cast of Poetry, as you'll see, for I wrote boldly under his last,

I'm Poor: Let's see how kind you'll prove.

This was a sad Truth to me, whether he believ'd me or no I cou'd not tell; I supposed then that he did not. However he flew to me, took me in his Arms, and kissing me very eagerly, and with the greatest Passion imaginable he held me fast till he call'd for a Pen and Ink, and then *told me* he could not wait the tedious writing on the Glass, but pulling out a piece of Paper, he began and wrote again,

Be mine, with all your Poverty.

I took his Pen and follow'd him immediately thus,

Yet secretly you hope I lie.

He told me that was unkind, because it was not just, and that I put him upon contradicting me, which did not consist with good Manners, any more than with his Affection; and therefore since I had insensibly drawn him into this poetical scribble, he beg'd I would not oblige him to break it off, so he writes again,

Let Love alone be our Debate.

I wrote again,

She Loves enough, that does not hate.

This he took for a favour, and so laid down the Cudgels,[5] that is to say the Pen; I say he took it for a favour, and a mighty one it was, if he had known all: However he took it as I meant it, that is, to let him think I was inclin'd to go on with him, as indeed I had all the Reason in the World to do, for he was the best humoured merry

---

4. Writing on windows, especially of inns, was a custom in the eighteenth century. Some writers carried diamond-pointed pencils for the purpose, or used stones in rings or jewelry to inscribe epigrams, verses, names, and sayings on windows. Jonathan Swift is supposed to have written a series of verses upon the windows of inns in 1726.

5. Quit the controversy.

sort of a Fellow that I ever met with; and I often reflected on my self, how doubly criminal it was to deceive such a Man; but that Necessity, which press'd me to a Settlement suitable to my Condition, was my Authority for it; and certainly his Affection to me, and the Goodness of his Temper, however they might argue against using him ill, yet they strongly argued to me that he would better take the Disappointment than some fiery tempered Wretch, who might have nothing to recommend him but those Passions which would serve only to make a Woman miserable all her Days.

Besides, tho' I had jested with him, as he suppos'd it, so often about my Poverty, yet, when he found it to be true, he had foreclosed all manner of objection, seeing whether he was in jest or in earnest, he had declar'd he took me without any regard to my Portion, and whether I was in jest or in earnest, I had declar'd my self to be very Poor, so that *in a word*, I had him fast both ways; and tho' he might say afterwards he was cheated, yet he could never say that I had cheated him.

He persued me close after this, and as I saw there was no need to fear losing him, I play'd the indifferent part with him longer than Prudence might otherwise have dictated to me: But I considered how much this caution and indifference would give me the advantage over him, when I should come to be under the Necessity of owning my own Circumstances to him; and I manag'd it the more warily, because I found he inferr'd from thence, as indeed he ought to do, that I either had the more Money, or the more Judgment, and would not venture at all.

I took the freedom one Day, after we had talk'd pretty close to the Subject, to tell him, that it was true I had receiv'd the Compliment of a Lover from him; namely, that he would take me without enquiring into my Fortune, and I would make him a suitable return in this, (*viz.*) that I would make as little enquiry into his as consisted with Reason, but I hoped he would allow me to ask a few Questions, which he should answer or not as he thought fit; and that I would not be offended if he did not answer me at all; one of these Questions related to our manner of living, and the place where, because I had heard he had a great Plantation in *Virginia*, and that he had talk'd of going to live there, and I told him I did not care to be Transported.

He began from this Discourse to let me voluntarily into all his Affairs, and to tell me in a frank open way all his Circumstances, by which I found he was very well to pass in the World; but that great part of his Estate consisted of three Plantations, which he had in *Virginia*, which brought him in a very good Income, generally speaking, to the tune of 300 *l.* a Year; but that if he was to live upon them, would bring him in four times as much; very well, thought I, you shall carry me thither as soon as you please, tho' I won't tell you so before-hand.

I jested with him extremely about the Figure he would make in *Virginia*; but I found he would do any thing I desired, tho' he did not seem glad to have me undervalue his Plantations, so I turn'd my Tale; I told him I had good reason not to desire to go there to live, because if his Plantations were worth so much there, I had not a Fortune suitable to a Gentleman of 1200 *l.* a Year, as he said his Estate would be.

He reply'd generously, he did not ask what my Fortune was, he had told me from the beginning he would not, and he would be as good as his word; But whatever it was, he assur'd me he would never desire me to go to *Virginia* with him, or go thither himself without me, unless I was perfectly willing, and made it my Choice.

All this, you may be sure, was as I wish'd, and indeed nothing could have happen'd more perfectly agreeable; I carried it on as far as this with a sort of indifferency that he often wondred at, more than at first, But which was the only support of his Courtship; and I mention it the rather to intimate again to the Ladies, that nothing but want of Courage for such an Indifferency, makes our Sex so cheap, and prepares them to be ill us'd as they are; would they venture the loss of a pretending Fop now and then, who carries it high upon the point of his own Merit, they would certainly be slighted less and courted more; had I discovered really and truly what my great Fortune was, and that in all I had not full 500 *l.* when he expected 1500 *l.* yet I had hook'd him so fast, and play'd him so long, that I was satisfied he would have had me in my worst Circumstances; and indeed it was less a surprize to him when he learnt the Truth than it would have been, because having not the least blame to lay on me, who had carried it with an air of indifference to the last, he could not say one word, except that indeed he thought it had been more, but that if it had been less he did not repent his bargain; only that he should not be able to maintain me so well as he intended.

In short, we were married, and very happily married on my side I assure you, *as to the Man*; for he was the best humour'd Man that ever Woman had, but his Circumstances were not so good as I imagined, as on the other hand he had not bettered himself by marrying so much as he expected.

When we were married I was shrewdly put to it to bring him that little Stock I had, and to let him see it was no more; but there was a necessity for it, so I took my opportunity one Day when we were alone, to enter into a short Dialogue with him about it; MY DEAR, *said I*, we have been married a Fortnight, is it not time to let you know whether you have got a Wife with something, or with

nothing? Your own time for that, my Dear, *says he*, I am satisfied
that I have got the Wife I love, I have not troubled you much, *says
he*, with my enquiry after it.

That's true, *said I*, but I have a great difficulty upon me about it,
which I scarce know how to manage.

What's that, my Dear, *says he*?

Why, *says I*, 'tis a little hard upon me, and 'tis harder upon you;
I am told that Captain ———— (meaning my Friend's Husband)
has told you I had a great deal more Money than I ever pretended
to have, and I am sure I never employ'd him to do so.

Well, *says he*, Captain ———— may have told me so, but what
then, if you have not so much that may lye at his Door, but you
never told me what you had, so I have no reason to blame you if
you have nothing at all.

That is so just, *said I*, and so generous, that it makes my having
but a little a double Affliction to me.

The less you have, *my Dear*, *says he*, the worse for us both; but I
hope your Affliction you speak of is not caus'd for fear I should be
unkind to you, for want of a Portion, No No, if you have nothing
tell me plainly, and at once; I may perhaps tell the Captain he has
cheated me, but I can never say you have cheated me, for did you
not give it under your Hand that you were Poor, and so I ought to
expect you to be.

Well, said I, *my Dear*, I am glad I have not been concern'd in
deceiving you before Marriage, if I deceive you since, 'tis ne'er the
worse; *that I am Poor* is too true, but not so Poor as to have
nothing neither; so I pull'd out some Bank Bills, and gave him
about a Hundred and Sixty Pounds; there's something, my Dear,
says I, and not quite all neither.

I had brought him so near to expecting nothing, by what I had
said before, that the Money, tho' the Sum was small in it self, was
doubly welcome to him; he own'd it was more than he look'd for,
and that he did not question by my Discourse to him, but that my
fine Cloths, Gold Watch, and a Diamond Ring or two had been all
my Fortune.

I let him please himself with that 160 *l.* two or three Days, and
then having been abroad that Day, and as if I had been to fetch it,
I brought him a Hundred Pounds more home in Gold, and told
him there was a little more Portion for him; and in short in about a
Week more I brought him 180 *l.* more, and about 60 *l.* in Linnen,
which I made him believe I had been oblig'd to take with the 100 *l.*
which I gave him in Gold, as a Composition for a Dept[6] of 600 *l.*
being little more than Five Shilling in the Pound, and overvalued
too.

---

6. As a partial payment for money owed her.

And now, My Dear, *says I to him*, I am very sorry to tell you, that there is all, and that I have given you my whole Fortune; I added, that if the Person who had my 600 *l.* had not abus'd me, I had been worth a Thousand Pound to him, but that as it was, I had been faithful to him, and reserv'd nothing to my self, but if it had been more he should have had it.

He was so oblig'd by the Manner, and so pleas'd with the Sum, for he had been in a terrible fright lest it had been nothing at all, that he accepted it very thankfully: And thus I got over the Fraud of *passing for a Fortune without Money*, and cheating a Man into Marrying me on pretence of a Fortune; which, *by the way*, I take to be one of the most dangerous Steps a Woman can take, and in which she runs the most hazard of being ill us'd afterwards.[7]

My Husband, *to give him his due*, was a Man of infinite good Nature, but he was no Fool; and finding his Income not suited to the manner of Living which he had intended, if I had brought him what he expected, and being under a Disappointment in his return[8] of his Plantations in *Virginia*, he discover'd many times his inclination of going over to *Virginia* to live upon his own; and often would be magnifying the way of living there, how cheap, how plentiful, how pleasant, *and the like*.

I began presently to understand his meaning, and I took him up very plainly one Morning, and told him that I did so; that I found his Estate turn'd to no account at this distance, compar'd to what it would do if he liv'd upon the spot, and that I found he had a mind to go and live there; and I added, that I was sensible he had been disappointed in a Wife, and that finding his Expectations not answer'd that way, I could do no less to make him amends than tell him that I was very willing to go over to *Virginia* with him and live there.

He said a thousand kind things to me upon the subject of my making such a Proposal to him: He told me, that however he was disappointed in his Expectations of a Fortune, he was not disappointed in a Wife, and that I was all to him that a Wife could be, and he was more than satisfied in the whole when the particulars were put together; but that this offer was so kind, that it was more than he could express.

To bring the story short, we agreed to go; *he told me*, that he had a very good House there, that it was well Furnish'd, that his Mother was alive and liv'd in it, and one Sister, which was all the Relations he had; that as soon as he came there, his Mother would remove to another House which was her own for life, and his after her Decease; so that I should have all the House to my self; and I found all this to be exactly as he had said.

7. As early as 1705 Defoe described just such a case in *Review*, I, no. 96 (Satur- day, February 3, 1705).
8. Profit from.

To make this part of the story short, we put on board the Ship *which we went in*, a large quantity of good Furniture for our House, with stores of Linnen and other Necessaries, and a good Cargoe for Sale, and away we went.

To give an account of the manner of our Voyage, which was long and full of Dangers, is out of my way; I kept no Journal, neither did my Husband; all that I can say is, that after a terrible passage, frighted twice with dreadful Storms, and once with what was still more terrible, I mean a Pyrate, who came on board and took away almost all our Provisions; and which would have been beyond all to me, they had once taken my Husband to go along with them but by entreaties were prevail'd with to leave him: I say, after all these terrible things, we arriv'd in *York River* in *Virginia*, and coming to our Plantation, we were receiv'd with all the Demonstrations of Tenderness and Affection (by my Husband's Mother) that were possible to be express'd.

We liv'd here all together, my Mother-in-law, *at my entreaty* continuing in the House, for she was too kind a Mother to be parted with; my Husband likewise continued the same as at first, and I thought my self the happiest Creature alive; when an odd and surprizing Event put an end to all that Felicity in a moment, and rendred my Condition the most uncomfortable, if not the most miserable, in the World.

My Mother was a mighty chearful good humour'd old Woman, I may call her old Woman, for her Son was above Thirty; I say she was very pleasant, good Company, and us'd to entertain *me, in particular*, with abundance of Stories to divert me, as well of the Country we were in, as of the People.

Among the rest, she often told me how the greatest part of the Inhabitants of the Colony came thither in very indifferent Circumstances from *England*; that, generally speaking, they were of two sorts, either (1.) such as were brought over by Masters of Ships to be sold as Servants, *such as we call them*, my Dear, *says she*, but they are more properly call'd *Slaves*.[9] Or, (2.) Such as are Transported from *Newgate* and other Prisons, after having been found guilty of Felony and other Crimes punishable with Death.

When they come here, *says she*, we make no difference; the Planters buy them, and they work together in the Field till their time is out; when 'tis expir'd, *said she*, they have Encouragement given them to Plant for themselves; for they have a certain number of Acres of Land allotted them by the Country, and they go to work to Clear and Cure[1] the Land, and then to Plant it with Tobacco and Corn[2] for their own use; and as the Tradesmen and

9. To call indentured servants—that is, those who would be free after completing a specified time in servitude—"slaves" is somewhat inexact. A third class of servitude was, of course, that of the black slave.
1. Prepare for planting.
2. Grain.

Merchants will trust them with Tools, and Cloaths, and other Necessaries, upon the Credit of their Crop before it is grown, so they
again Plant every Year a little more than the Year before, and so
buy whatever they want with the Crop that is before them.

Hence Child, *says she,* many a *Newgate* Bird becomes a great
Man, and we have, *continued she,* several Justices of the Peace,
Officers of the Train Bands,[3] and Magistrates of the Towns they live
in, that have been burnt in the Hand.[4]

She was going on with that part of the Story, when her own part
in it interrupted her, and with a great deal of good-humour'd Confidence she told me she was one of the second sort of Inhabitants
herself; that she came away openly, having ventur'd too far in a particular Case, so that she was become a Criminal; and here's the
Mark of it, CHILD, *says she,* and pulling off her Glove, look ye here,
says she, turning up the Palm of her Hand, and shewed me a very
fine white Arm and Hand, but branded in the inside of the Hand,
as in such cases it must be.

This Story was very moving to me, but my Mother (smiling)
said, you need not think such a thing strange, *Daughter,* for as I
told you, some of the best Men in this Country are burnt in the
Hand, and they are not asham'd to own it; there's Major ———
says she, he was an Eminent Pickpocket; there's Justice *Ba*——*r*
was a Shoplifter, and both of them were burnt in the Hand, and I
could name you several, such as they are.

We had frequent Discourses of this kind, and abundance of
instances she gave me of the like; after some time, as she was telling
some Stories of one that was Transported but a few Weeks ago, I
began in an intimate kind of way to ask her to tell me something of
her own Story, which she did with the utmost plainness and Sincerity; how she had fallen into very ill Company in *London* in her
young Days, occasion'd by her Mother sending her frequently to
carry Victuals and other Relief to a Kinswoman of hers who was
Prisoner in *Newgate,* and who lay in a miserable starving Condition, was afterwards Condemned to be Hang'd but having got Respite by pleading her Belly, dyed afterwards in the Prison.

Here my Mother-in-Law ran out in a long account of the wicked
practices in that dreadful Place, and how it ruin'd more young
People than all the Town besides; and Child, *says my Mother,* perhaps you may know little of it, or it may be have heard nothing
about it, but depend upon it, *says she,* we all know here, that there
are more Thieves and Rogues made by that one Prison of *Newgate,*
than by all the Clubs and Societies of Villains in the Nation; 'tis
that cursed Place, *says my Mother,* that half Peoples this Colony.

3. Trained bands or militias organized
from the citizenry for defense and keeping law and order.

4. Branded; persons convicted of felony
might be burned on the hand, indicating
that they had been convicted.

Here she went on with her own Story so long, and in so particular a manner, that I began to be very uneasy; but coming to one
Particular that requir'd telling her Name, I thought I should have
sunk down in the place; she perceived I was out of order, and asked
me if I was not well, and what ail'd me? I told her I was so affected
with the melancholy Story she had told, and the terrible things she
had gone thro', that it had overcome me; and I beg'd of her to talk
no more of it: *Why*, my Dear, *says she, very kindly*, what need
these things trouble you? These Passages were long before your
time, and they give me no trouble at all now; nay I look back on
them with a particular Satisfaction, as they have been a means to
bring me to this place. Then she went on to tell me how she very
luckily fell into a good Family, where behaving herself well, and her
Mistress dying, her Master married her, by whom she had my Husband and his Sister, and that by her Diligence and good Management after her Husband's Death, she had improv'd the Plantations
to such a degree as they then were, so that most of the Estate was
of her getting, not her Husband's, for she had been a Widow
upwards of sixteen Year.

I heard this part of the Story with very little attention, because I
wanted much to retire and give vent to my Passions, which I did
soon after; and let any one judge what must be the Anguish of my
Mind, when I came to reflect that this was certainly no more or less
than my own Mother, and I had now had two Children, and was
big with another by my own Brother, and lay with him still every
Night.

I was now the most unhappy of all Women in the World: O had
the Story never been told me, all had been well; it had been no
Crime to have lain with my Husband, since as to his being my
Relation, I had known nothing of it.

I had now such a load on my Mind that it kept me perpetually
waking; to reveal it, *which would have been some ease to me*, I
cou'd not find wou'd be to any purpose, and yet to conceal it wou'd
be next to impossible; nay, I did not doubt but I should talk of it in
my sleep, and tell my Husband of it whether I would or no:[5] If I
discover'd it, the least thing I could expect was to lose my Husband,
for he was too nice and too honest a Man to have continued my
Husband after he had known I had been his Sister, so that I was
perplex'd to the last degree.

I leave it any Man to judge what Difficulties presented to my
view, I was away from my native Country at a distance prodigious,
and the return to me unpassable; I liv'd very well, but in a Circumstance unsufferable in it self; if I had discover'd my self to my

---

5. Moll is interested in this kind of involuntary disclosure throughout; see pp. 34, 255.

Mother, it might be difficult to convince her of the Particulars, and I had no way to prove them: *On the other hand,* if she had question'd or doubted me, I had been undone, for the bare Suggestion would have immediately separated me from my Husband, without gaining[6] my Mother or him, who would have been neither a Husband or a Brother; so that between the surprise on one hand, and the uncertainty on the other, I had been sure to be undone.

In the mean time, as I was but too sure of the Fact, I liv'd therefore in open avowed Incest and Whoredom, and all under the appearance of an honest Wife; and tho' I was not much touched with the Crime of it, yet the Action had something in it shocking to Nature, and made my Husband, *as he thought himself* even nauseous to me.

However, upon the most sedate Consideration, I resolv'd, that it was absolutely necessary to conceal it all, and not make the least Discovery of it either to Mother or Husband; and thus I liv'd with the greatest Pressure imaginable for three Year more, but had no more Children.

During this time my Mother used to be frequently telling me old Stories of her former Adventures, which however were no ways pleasant to me; for by it, tho' she did not tell it me in plain terms, yet I could easily understand, joyn'd with what I had heard my self, of my first Tutors, that in her younger Days she had been both Whore and Thief; but I verily believe she had lived to repent sincerely of both, and that she was then a very Pious sober and religious Woman.

Well, let her Life have been what it would then, it was certain that my Life was very uneasie to me; for I liv'd, as I have said, but in the worst sort of Whoredom, and as I cou'd expect no Good of it, so really no good Issue came of it, and all my seeming Prosperity wore off and ended in Misery and Destruction; it was some time indeed before it came to this, for, but I know not by what ill Fate guided, every thing went wrong with us afterwards, and that which was worse, my Husband grew strangely alter'd, froward,[7] jealous, and unkind, and I was as impatient of bearing his Carriage, as the Carriage was unreasonable and unjust: These things proceeded so far, that we came at last to be in such ill Terms with one another, that I claim'd a promise of him which he entered willingly into with me, when I consented to come from *England* with him (*viz.*) that if I found the Country not to agree with me, or that I did not like to live there, I should come away to *England* again when I pleas'd, giving him a Year's warning to settle his Affairs.

I say *I now claim'd this promise of him,* and I must confess I did

6. Gain to, advantage to.   7. Perverse.

it not in the most obliging Terms that could be in the World neither; but I insisted that he treated me ill, that I was remote from
my Friends, and could do my self no Justice, and that he was Jealous without cause, my Conversation[8] having been unblameable,
and he having no pretence for it, and that to remove to *England*,
would take away all Occasion from him.

I insisted so peremptorily upon it, that he could not avoid
coming to a point, either to keep his word with me or to break it;
and this notwithstanding he used all the skill he was master of, and
employ'd his Mother and other Agents to prevail with me to alter
my Resolutions; indeed the bottom of the thing lay at my Heart,
and that made all his Endeavours fruitless, for my Heart was alienated from him, *as a Husband*; I loathed the Thoughts of Bedding
with him, and used a thousand Pretences of Illness and Humour[9]
to prevent his touching me, fearing nothing more than to be with
Child again by him, which to be sure would have prevented, or at
least delay'd my going over to *England*.

However, at last I put him so out of Humour, that he took up a
rash and fatal Resolution. In short I should not go to *England*; and
tho' he had promis'd me, yet it was an unreasonable thing for me to
desire it, that it would be ruinous to his Affairs, would Unhinge his
whole Family, and be next to an Undoing him in the World; That
therefore I ought not to desire it of him, and that no Wife in the
World that valu'd her Family and her Husbands prosperity would
insist upon such a thing.

This plung'd[1] me again, for when I considered the thing calmly,
and took my Husband as he really was, a diligent careful Man in
the main Work of laying up an Estate for his Children, and that he
knew nothing of the dreadful Circumstances that he was in, I could
not but confess to myself that my Proposal was very unreasonable,
and what no Wife that had the good of her Family at Heart wou'd
have desir'd.

But my Discontents were of another Nature; I look'd upon him
no longer as a Husband, but as a near Relation, the Son of my own
Mother, and I resolv'd some how or other to be clear of him, but
which way I did not know, nor did it seem possible.

It is said *by the ill-natured World*, of our Sex, that if we are set
on a thing, it is impossible to turn us from our Resolutions: *In
short*, I never ceas'd poreing upon the Means to bring to pass my
Voyage, and came that length with my Husband at last, as to propose going without him. This provok'd him to the last degree, and
he call'd me not only an unkind Wife, but an unnatural Mother,
and ask'd me how I could entertain such a Thought without horror

8. Relations with the opposite sex, conduct.

9. Temperament, mood.

1. Plunged her spirits, depressed her.

as that of leaving my two Children (for one was dead) without a
Mother, and to be brought up by Strangers, and never to see them
more? *It was true*, had things been right, I should not have done it,
but now, *it was* my real desire never to see them, or him either, any
more; and as to the Charge of unnatural I could easily answer it to
myself, while I knew that the whole Relation was Unnatural in the
highest degree in the World.

However, it was plain there was no bringing my Husband to any
thing; he would neither go with me, or let me go without him, and
it was quite out of my Power to stir without his Consent, as any
one that knows the Constitution of the Country I was in, knows
very well.

We had many Family quarrels about it, and they began (in time)
to grow up to a dangerous Height, for as I was quite Estrang'd from
my Husband (*as he was call'd*) in Affection, so I took no heed to
my Words, but sometimes gave him Language that was provoking:
And, *in short*, strove all I could to bring him to a parting with me,
which was what above all things in the World I desir'd most.

He took my Carriage very ill, and indeed he might well do so, for
at last I refus'd to Bed with him, and carrying on the Breach upon
all occasions to extremity he told me once he thought I was Mad,
and if I did not alter my Conduct, he would put me under Cure;
that is to say, into a Madhouse: I told him he should find I was far
enough from Mad, and that it was not in his power, or any other
Villains to Murther[2] me; I confess at the same time I was heartily
frighted at his Thoughts of putting me into a *Mad-House*, which
would at once have destroy'd all the possibility of breaking the
Truth out, whatever the occasion might be; for that then, no one
would have given Credit to a word of it.

This therefore brought me to a Resolution, *whatever came of it*
to lay open my whole Case; but which way to do it, or to whom,
was an inextricable Difficulty, and took me up many Months to
Resolve; *in the mean time*, another Quarrel with my Husband happen'd, which came up to such a mad Extream as almost push'd me
on to tell it him all to his Face; but tho' I kept it in so as not to
come to the particulars, I spoke so much as put him into the
utmost Confusion, and in the End brought out the whole Story.

He began with a calm Expostulation upon my being so resolute
to go to *England*; I defended it, and one hard Word bringing on
another as is usual in all Family strife, *he told me* I did not Treat
him as if he was my Husband, or talk of my Children as if I was a
Mother; and *in short*, that I did not deserve to be us'd as a Wife:
That he had us'd all the fair Means possible with me; that he had

2. Destroy. Obsolete spelling of *murder*.

Argu'd with all the kindness and calmness that a Husband or a Christian ought to do, and that I made him such a vile return, that I Treated him rather like a Dog than a Man, and rather like the most contemptible Stranger than a Husband: That he was very loth to use Violence with me, but that *in short*, he saw a Necessity of it now, and that for the future he should be oblig'd to take such Measures as should reduce me to my Duty.

My blood was now fir'd to the utmost, *tho' I knew what he had said was very true*, and nothing could appear more provok'd; I told him for his fair means and his foul they were equally contemn'd[3] by me; that for my going to *England*, I was resolv'd on it, come what would; and that as to treating him not like a Husband, and not showing my self a Mother to my Children, there might be something more in it than he understood at present; but, for his farther consideration, I thought fit to tell him thus much, that he neither was my lawful Husband, nor they lawful Children, and that I had reason to regard neither of them more than I did.

I confess I was mov'd to pity him when I spoke it, for he turn'd pale as Death, and stood mute as one Thunder struck, and once or twice I thought he would have fainted; *in short*, it put him in a Fit something like an Apoplex; he trembl'd, a Sweat or Dew ran off his Face, and yet he was cold as a Clod, so that I was forced to run and fetch something for him to keep Life in him; when he recover'd of that, he grew sick and vomited, and in a little after was put to Bed, and in the next Morning was, as he had been indeed all Night, in a violent Fever.

However it went off again, and he recovered tho' but slowly, and when he came to be a little better, he told me, I had given him a mortal Wound with my Tongue, and he had only one thing to ask before he desir'd an Explanation; I interrupted him, and told him I was sorry I had gone so far, since I saw what disorder it put him into, but I desir'd him not to talk to me of Explanations, for that would but make things worse.

This heighten'd his impatience, and indeed perplex'd him beyond all bearing; for now he began to suspect that there was some Mystery yet unfolded, but could not make the least guess at the real Particulars of it; all that run in his Brain was, that I had another Husband alive, which I could not say in fact might not be true; but I assur'd him however, there was not the least of that in it; and indeed as to my other Husband he was effectually dead in Law to me, and had told me I should look on him as such, so I had not the least uneasiness on that score.

But now I found the thing too far gone to conceal it much longer, and my Husband himself gave me an opportunity to ease

3. Despised.

my self of the Secret much to my Satisfaction; he had laboured
with me three or four Weeks, *but to no purpose,* only to tell him,
whether I had spoken those words only as the effect of my Passion
to put him in a Passion? Or whether there was anything of Truth
in the bottom of them? But I continued inflexible, and would
explain nothing, unless he would first consent to my going to *England,* which he would never do, *he said,* while he liv'd; on the other
hand I said it was in my power to make him willing when I pleas'd,
NAY to make him entreat me to go; and this increased his Curiosity, and made him importunate to the highest degree, *but it was all
to no purpose.*

At length he tells all this Story to his Mother, and sets her upon
me to get the main Secret out of me, and she us'd her utmost Skill
with me indeed; but I put her to a full stop at once, *by telling her*
that the Reason and Mystery of the whole matter lay in herself; and
that it was my Respect to her that had made me conceal it, and
that in short I could go no farther, and therefore conjur'd her not
to insist upon it.

She was struck dumb at this Suggestion, and could not tell what
to say or to think; but laying aside the supposition as a Policy of
mine, continued her importunity on account of her Son, and if possible to make up the breach between us two; as to that, *I told her,*
that it was indeed a good design in her, but that it was impossible
to be done; and that if I should reveal to her the Truth of what she
desir'd, she would grant it to be impossible, and cease to desire it:
At last I seem'd to be prevail'd on by her importunity, and told her
I dar'd trust her with a Secret of the greatest Importance, and she
would soon see that this was so, and that I would consent to lodge
it in her Breast, if she would engage solemnly not to acquaint her
Son with it without my consent.

She was long in promising this part, but rather than not come at
the main Secret she agreed to that too, and after a great many other
Preliminaries, I began and told her the whole Story: First I told her
how much she was concern'd in all the unhappy breach which had
happen'd between her Son and me, by telling me her own Story
and her *London* Name; and that the surprize she see I was in was
upon that Occasion: Then I told her my own Story and my Name,
and assur'd her by such other Tokens as she could not deny that I
was no other, nor more or less than her own Child, *her Daughter*
born of her Body in *Newgate;* the same that had sav'd her from the
Gallows by being in her Belly, and the same that she left in such
and such Hands when she was Transported.

It is impossible to express the Astonishment she was in; she was
not inclin'd to believe the Story, or to remember the Particulars, for
she immediately foresaw the Confusions that must follow in the

Family upon it; but every thing concurr'd so exactly with the Stories she had told me of her self, and which if she had not told me, she would perhaps have been content to have denied, that she had stop'd her own Mouth, and she had nothing to do but to take me about the Neck and kiss me, and cry most vehemently over me, without speaking one word for a long time together; at last she broke out, *Unhappy Child! says she*, what miserable chance could bring thee hither? And in the Arms of my own Son too! *Dreadful Girl!* says she, *why we are all undone!* Married to thy own Brother! Three Children, and two alive, all of the same Flesh and Blood! My Son and my Daughter lying together as Husband and Wife! All Confusion and Destraction for ever! *miserable Family!* what will become of us? what is to be said? what is to be done? and thus she run on for a great while, nor had I any power to speak, or if I had, did I know what to say, for every word wounded me to the Soul: With this kind of Amasement on our Thoughts we parted for the first time, tho' my Mother was more surpriz'd than I was, because it was more News to her than to me: However, she promis'd again to me at parting, that she would say nothing of it to her Son till we had talk'd of it again.

It was not long, you may be sure, before we had a second Conference upon the same Subject; when, as if she had been willing to forget the Story she had told me of herself, or to suppose that I had forgot some of the Particulars, she began to tell them with Alterations and Omissions; but I refresh'd her Memory, and set her to rights in many things which I supposed she had forgot, and then came in so opportunely with the whole History, that it was impossible for her to go from it; and then she fell into her Rhapsodies[4] again, and Exclamations at the Severity of her Misfortunes: When these things were a little over with her we fell into a close Debate about what should be first done before we gave an account of the matter to my Husband, but to what purpose could be all our Consultations? we could neither of us see our way thro' it, nor see how it could be safe to open such a Scene to him; it was impossible to make any judgment, or give any guess at what Temper he would receive it in, or what Measures he would take upon it; and if he should have so little Government of himself as to make it publick, we easily foresaw that it would be the ruin of the whole Family, and expose my Mother and me to the last degree; and if at last he should take the Advantage the Law would give him, he might put me away with disdain, and leave me to Sue for the little Portion that I had, and perhaps waste it all in the Suit, and then be a Beggar; the Children would be ruin'd too, having no legal Claim to any of his Effects; and thus I should see him perhaps in the Arms

4. Excited, unconnected expressions of extravagant emotion.

of another Wife in a few Months, and be my self the most miserable Creature alive.

My Mother was as sensible of this as I; and upon the whole, we knew not what to do; after some time, we came to more sober Resolutions, but then it was with this Misfortune too, that my Mother's Opinion and mine were quite different from one another, and indeed inconsistent with one another; for my Mother's Opinion was that I should bury the whole thing entirely, and continue to live with him as my Husband, till some other Event should make the discovery of it more convenient; and that in the mean time she would endeavour to reconcile us together again, and restore our mutual Comfort and Family Peace; that we might lie as we us'd to do together, and so let the whole matter remain a secret as close as Death; for Child, *says she*, we are both undone if it comes out.

To encourage me to this, she promis'd to make me easy in my Circumstances as far as she was able, and to leave me what she could at her Death, secur'd for me separately from my Husband; so that if it should come out afterwards, I should not be left destitute, but be able to stand on my own Feet and procure Justice from him.

This Proposal did not agree at all with my Judgment of the thing, tho' it was very fair and kind in my Mother, but my Thoughts run quite another way.

As to keeping the thing in our own Breasts, and letting it all remain as it was, I told her it was impossible; and I ask'd her how she cou'd think I cou'd bear the thoughts of lying with my own Brother? In the next place I told her that her being alive was the only support of the Discovery, and that while she own'd me for her Child, and saw reason to be satisfyed that I was so, no body else would doubt it; but that if she should die before the Discovery, I should be taken for an impudent Creature that had forg'd such a thing to go away from my Husband, or should be counted Craz'd and Distracted: Then I told her how he had threaten'd already to put me into a Mad-house, and what concern I had been in about it, and how that was the thing that drove me to the necessity of discovering it to her as I had done.

From all which I told her, that I had on the most serious Reflections I was able to make in the Case, come to this Resolution, which I hop'd she would like, as a medium between both, (*viz.*) that she should use her endeavours with her Son to give me leave to go for *England*, as I had desired, and to furnish me with a sufficient Sum of Money, either in Goods along with me, or in Bills for my Support there, all along suggesting, that he might one time or other think it proper to come over to me.

That when I was gone she should then in cold Blood, and after first obliging him in the solemnest manner possible to Secresie, discover the Case to him; doing it gradually, and as her own Discretion should guide her, so that he might not be surpriz'd with it, and fly out into any Passions and Excesses on my account, or on hers; and that she should concern herself to prevent his slighting the Children, or Marrying again, unless he had a certain account of my being Dead.

This was my Scheme, and my Reasons were good; I was really alienated from him in the Consequence of these things; indeed I mortally hated him as a Husband, and it was impossible to remove that riveted Aversion I had to him; *at the same time* it being an unlawful incestuous living added to that Aversion; and tho' I had no great concern about it in point of Conscience, yet every thing added to make Cohabiting with him the most nauseous thing to me in the World; and I think verily it was come to such a height, that I could almost as willingly have embrac'd a Dog, as have let him offer any thing of that kind to me, for which Reason I could not bear the thoughts of coming between the Sheets with him; I cannot say that I was right in point of Policy in carrying it such a length, while at the same time I did not resolve to discover the thing to him; but I am giving an account of what was, not of what ought or ought not to be.

In this directly opposite Opinion to one another my Mother and I continued a long time, and it was impossible to reconcile our Judgments; many Disputes we had about it, but we could never either of us yield our own, or bring over the other.

I insisted on my Aversion to lying with my own Brother, and she insisted upon its being impossible to bring him to consent to my going from him to *England*; and in this uncertainty we continued, not differing so as to quarrel, or any thing like it, but so as not to be able to resolve what we should do to make up that terrible breach that was before us.

At last I resolv'd on a desperate course, and *told my Mother* my Resolution, (*viz.*) that in short, I would tell him of it my self; my Mother was frighted to the last degree at the very thoughts of it; but *I bid her be easie*, told her I would do it gradually and softly, and with all the Art and good Humour I was Mistress of, and time it also as well as I could, taking him in good Humour too: *I told her* I did not question but if I cou'd be Hypocrite enough to feign more Affection to him than I really had, I should succeed in all my Design, and we might part by Consent, and with a good Agreement, for I might love him well enough for a Brother, tho' I could not for a Husband.

All this while he lay at[5] my Mother to find out, if possible, what was the meaning of that dreadful Expression of mine, as he call'd

5. Persisted in questioning.

it, which I mention'd before; namely, *That I was not his lawful Wife, nor my Children his legal Children:* My Mother put him off, told him she could bring me to no Explanations, but found there was something that disturb'd me very much, and she hop'd she should get it out of me in time, and in the mean time recommended to him earnestly to use me more tenderly, and win me with his usual good Carriage; *told him* of his terrifying and affrighting me with his Threats of sending me to a Mad-house, and the like, and advis'd him not to make a Woman Desperate on any account whatever.

He promis'd her to soften his Behaviour, and bid her assure me that he lov'd me as well as ever, and that he had no such design as that of sending me to a Mad-house, whatever he might say in his Passion; also he desir'd my Mother to use the same Perswasions to me too, that our Affections might be renew'd, and we might live together in a good understanding as we us'd to do.

I found the Effects of this Treaty presently; my Husband's Conduct was immediately alter'd, and he was quite another Man to me; nothing could be kinder and more obliging than he was to me upon all Occasions; and I could do no less than make some return to it, *which I did as well as I cou'd*; but it was but in an awkward manner at best, for nothing was more frightful to me than his Caresses, and the Apprehensions of being with Child again by him was ready to throw me into Fits; and this made me see that there was an absolute necessity of breaking the Case to him without any more delay, which however I did with all the caution and reserve imaginable.

He had continued his alter'd Carriage to me near a Month, and we began to live a new kind of Life with one another; and could I have satisfied my self to have gone on with it, I believe it might have continued as long as we had continued alive together. One Evening as we were sitting and talking very friendly together under a little Awning, which serv'd as an Arbour at the entrance from our House into the Garden, he was in a very pleasant agreeable Humour, and said abundance of kind things to me, relating to the Pleasure of our present good Agreement, and the Disorders of our past breach, and what a Satisfaction it was to him that we had room to hope we should never have any more of it.

I fetch'd a deep Sigh, and told him there was no Body in the World could be more delighted than I was in the good Agreement we had always kept up, or more afflicted with the Breach of it, and should be so still; but I was sorry to tell him that there was an unhappy Circumstance in our Case, which lay too close to my Heart, and which I knew not how to break to him, that rendred my part of it very miserable, and took from me all the Comfort of the rest.

He importun'd me to tell him what it was; I told him I could not tell how to do it; that while it was conceal'd from him, I alone was unhappy; but if he knew it also, we should be both so, and that therefore to keep him in the dark about it was the kindest thing that I could do, and it was on that account alone that I kept a secret from him, the very keeping of which I thought would first or last be my Destruction.

It is impossible to express his Surprize at this Relation, and the double importunity which he used with me to discover it to him: He told me I could not be call'd kind to him, nay, I could not be faithful to him if I conceal'd it from him; I told him I thought so too, and yet I could not do it. He went back to what I had said before to him, and told me he hoped it did not relate to what I had said in my Passion, and that he had resolv'd to forget all that, as the Effect of a rash provok'd Spirit; I told him I wish'd I could forget it all too, but that it was not to be done, the Impression was too deep, and I cou'd not do it; it was impossible.

He then told me he was resolved not to differ with me in any thing, and that therefore he would importune me no more about it, resolving to acquiesce in whatever I did or said; only begg'd I would then agree, that whatever it was, it should no more interrupt our quiet and our mutual kindness.

This was the most provoking thing he could have said to me, for I really wanted his farther importunities, that I might be prevail'd with to bring out that which indeed it was like Death to me to conceal; so I answer'd him plainly, that I could not say I was glad not to be importuned, tho' I could not tell how to comply; but come, *my Dear, said I*, what Conditions will you make with me upon the opening this Affair to you?

Any Conditions in the World, *said he*, that you can in reason desire of me; well, *said I*, come, give it me under your Hand,[6] that if you do not find I am in any fault, or that I am willingly concern'd in the Causes of the Misfortune that is to follow, you will not blame me, use me the worse, do me any Injury, or make me be the Sufferer for that which is not my fault.

That, *says he*, is the most reasonable demand in the World; not to blame you for that which is not your fault; give me a Pen and Ink, *says he*, so I ran in and fetch'd a Pen, Ink, and Paper, and he wrote the Condition down in the very words I had proposed it, and sign'd it with his Name; well, says he, *what is next*, my Dear?

Why, *says I*, the next is, that you will not blame me for not discovering the Secret of it to you before I knew it.

Very just again, *says he*, with all my Heart; so he wrote down that also and sign'd it.

6. Put your agreement in writing.

Well, *my Dear*, says I, then I have but one Condition more to
make with you, and that is, that as there is no body concern'd in it
but you and I, you shall not discover it to any Person in the World,
except your own Mother; and that in all the Measures you shall
take upon the discovery, as I am equally concern'd in it with you,
tho' as innocent as your self, you shall do nothing in a Passion,
nothing to my Prejudice, or to your Mother's Prejudice, without my
knowledge and consent.

This a little amaz'd him, and he wrote down the words distinctly,
but read them over and over before he Sign'd them, hesitating at
them several times, and repeating them; *my Mother's* Prejudice!
and your Prejudice! what mysterious thing can this be? however, at
last he Sign'd it.

Well, *says I*, my Dear, I'll ask you no more under your Hand,
but as you are to bear the most unexpected and surprizing thing
that perhaps ever befel any Family in the World, I beg you to
promise me you will receive it with Composure and a Presence of
Mind suitable to a Man of Sense.

I'll do my utmost, *says he*, upon Condition you will keep me no
longer in suspence, for you Terrify me with all these Preliminaries.

Well, then, *says I*, it is this; as I told you before in a Heat, that I
was not your lawful Wife, and that our Children were not legal
Children, so I must let you know now in calmness and in kindness,
but with Affliction enough that *I am* your own Sister, *and you* my
own Brother, and that we are both the Children of our Mother now
alive, and in the House, who is convinc'd of the Truth of it, in a
manner not to be denied or contradicted.

I saw him turn pale, and look wild, and I said, now remember
your Promise, and receive it with Presence of mind; for who cou'd
have said more to prepare you for it, than I have done? However I
call'd a Servant, and got him a little Glass of Rum, which is the
usual Dram[7] of the Country, for he was just fainting away.

When he was a little recover'd, *I said to him*, this Story you may
be sure requires a long Explanation, and therefore have patience
and compose your Mind to hear it out, and I'll make it as short as I
can; and with this, I told him what I thought was needful of the
Fact, and particularly how my Mother came to discover it to me, as
above; and now my Dear, *says I*, you will see Reason for my Capitu-
lations, and that I neither have been the Cause of this Matter, nor
could be so, and that I could know nothing of it before now.

I am fully satisfy'd of that, *says he*, but 'tis a dreadful Surprize to
me; however, I know a Remedy for it all, and a Remedy that shall
put an End to all your Difficulties, without your going to *England*;
That would be strange, *said I*, as all the rest; No, No, *says he*, I'll

7. Drink.

make it easie, there's no Body in the way of it all, but myself: He look'd a little disorder'd, when he said this, but I did not apprehend any thing from it at that time, believing as it us'd to be said, that they who do those things never talk of them; or that they who talk of such things never do them.

But things were not come their height[8] with him, and I observ'd he became Pensive and Melancholly; and in a Word, as I thought a little Distemper'd in his Head; I endeavour'd to talk him into Temper, and to Reason him into a kind of Scheme for our Government in the Affair, and sometimes he would be well, and talk with some Courage about it; but the Weight of it lay too heavy upon his Thoughts, and in short, it went so far that he made two attempts upon himself, and in one of them had actually strangled himself, and had not his Mother come into the Room in the very Moment, he had died; but with the help of a *Negro* Servant, she cut him down and recover'd him.

Things were now come to a lamentable height in the Family: My pity for him now began to revive that Affection which at first I really had for him, and I endeavour'd sincerely by all the kind Carriage I could to make up the Breach; but in short, it had gotten too great a Head, it prey'd upon his Spirits, and it threw him into a long ling'ring Consumption, tho' it happen'd not to be Mortal. In this Distress I did not know what to do, as his Life was apparently declining, and I might perhaps have Marry'd again there, very much to my Advantage, it had been certainly my Business to have staid in the Country, but my Mind was restless too, and uneasie; I hanker'd after coming to *England*, and nothing would satisfie me without it.

In short, by an unwearied importunity my Husband who was apparently decaying, as I observ'd, was at last prevail'd with; and so *my own Fate pushing me on*, the way was made clear for me, and *my Mother concurring*, I obtain'd a very good Cargo for my coming to *England*.

When I parted with my Brother, for such I am now to call him, we agreed that after I arriv'd he should pretend to have an Account that I was Dead in *England*, and so might Marry again when he would; he promis'd, and engag'd me to Correspond with me as a Sister, and to Assist and Support me as long as I liv'd; and that if he dy'd before me, he would leave sufficient to his Mother to take Care of me still, in the Name of a Sister, and he was in some respect Careful of me, when he heard of me; but it was so oddly

8. Some modern editions print, "But things were not come *to* their height. . . ." Or, "But things were *now* come to their height. . . ." The first and second editions leave the clause as it stands above, which makes the same idiomatic good sense as the current expression, "But things were not come full circle" (*Editor's italics*).

manag'd that I felt the Disappointments very sensibly afterwards, as you shall hear in its time.

I came away for *England* in the Month of *August*, after I had been Eight Years in that Country, and now a new Scene of Misfortunes attended me, which perhaps few Women have gone thro' the like of.

We had an indifferent good Voyage till we came just upon the Coast of *England*, and where we arriv'd in two and thirty Days, but were then Ruffled with two or three Storms, one of which drove us away to the Coast of *Ireland*, and we put in at *Kinsale*: We remain'd there about thirteen Days, got some Refreshment on Shore, and put to Sea again, tho' we met with very bad Weather again in which the Ship sprung her Main-mast, *as they call'd it, for I knew not what they meant*: But we got at last into *Milford Haven* in *Wales*, where tho' it was remote from our Port, yet having my Foot safe upon the firm Ground of my Native Country the Isle of *Britain*, I resolv'd to venture it no more upon the Waters, which had been so terrible to me; so getting my Cloths and Money on Shore with my Bills of Loading and other Papers, I resolv'd to come for *London*, and leave the Ship to get to her Port as she could; the Port whither she was bound, was to *Bristol*, where my Brothers chief Correspondent[9] liv'd.

I got to *London* in about three Weeks, where I heard a little while after that the Ship was arriv'd in *Bristol*; but at the same time had the Misfortune to know that by the violent Weather she had been in, and the breaking of her Mainmast; she had great damage on board, and that a great part of her Cargo was spoil'd.

I had now a new Scene of Life upon my Hands, and a dreadful Appearance it had; I was come away with a kind of final Farewel; what I brought with me was indeed considerable, had it come safe, and by the help of it I might have married again tollerably well; but as it was, I was reduc'd to between two or three Hundred Pounds in the whole, and this without any hope of Recruit:[1] I was entirely without Friends, nay, even so much as without Acquaintance, for I found it was absolutely necessary not to revive former Acquaintances; and as for my subtle Friend that set me up formerly for a Fortune she was Dead, and her Husband also; as I was inform'd upon sending a Person unknown to enquire.

The looking after my Cargo of Goods soon after oblig'd me to take a Journey to *Bristol*, and during my attendance upon that Affair, I took the Diversion of going to the *Bath*,[2] for as I was still

9. The official executor of the brother's business in England.
1. New source.
2. Well-known spa in southwest England, famous for its hot springs, Roman antiquities, and variety of vacationers.

far from being old, so my Humour, which was always Gay, continu'd so to an Extream; and being now, *as it were*, a Woman of Fortune, tho' I was a Woman without a Fortune, I expected something or other might happen in my way, that might mend my Circumstances as had been my Case before.

The *Bath* is a Place of Gallantry enough; Expensive, and full of Snares; I went thither indeed in the view of taking any thing that might offer, but I must do myself that Justice, as to protest I knew nothing amiss; I meant nothing but in an honest way; nor had I any Thoughts about me at first that look'd the way, which afterwards I suffered them to be guided.

Here I stay'd the whole latter Season,[3] *as it is call'd there*, and Contracted some unhappy Acquaintance, which rather prompted the Follies, I fell afterwards into, than fortify'd me against them: I liv'd pleasantly enough, kept good Company, *that is to say*, gay fine Company; but had the Discouragement to find this way of Living sunk me exceedingly, and that as I had no settl'd Income, so spending upon the main Stock was but a certain kind of *bleeding to Death*; and this gave me many sad Reflections in the Intervals of my other Thoughts: However I shook them off, and still flatter'd myself that something or other might offer for my Advantage.

But I was in the wrong Place for it; I was not now at *Redriff*, where If I had set myself tollerably up, some honest Sea Captain or other might have talk'd with me upon the honourable terms of Matrimony; but I was at the *Bath* where Men find a Mistress sometimes, but very rarely look for a Wife; and Consequently all the particular Acquaintances a Woman can Expect to make there must have some Tendency that way.

I had spent the first Season[4] well enough, for tho' I had Contracted some Acquaintance with a Gentleman who came to the *Bath* for his Diversion, yet I had enter'd into no *felonious Treaty*, as it might be call'd: I had resisted some Casual offers of Gallantry, and had manag'd that way well enough; I was not wicked enough to come into the Crime for the meer Vice of it, and I had no extraordinary Offers made me that tempted me with the main thing which I wanted.

However I went this length the first Season, (*viz.*) I contracted an Acquaintance with a Woman in whose House I Lodg'd, who tho' she did not keep an ill House,[5] *as we call it*, yet had none of the best Principles in herself: I had on all Occasions behav'd myself so well as not to get the least Slur upon my Reputation on any

3. The late vacation period, after spring and summer tourism waned. Moll arrived in the fall after leaving America in August.
4. Moll's first season at Bath.

5. Bawdy house. The reputations of many who frequented Bath were questionable. British writers have long treated Bath as a place of artificial entertainment and corrupting influences.

Account whatever, and all the Men that I had Convers'd with, were of so good Reputation that I had not given the least Reflection by Conversing with them; nor did any of them seem to think there was room for a wicked Correspondence, if they had any of them offered it; yet there was one Gentleman, *as above*, who always singl'd me out for the Diversion of my Company, as he call'd it, which *as he was pleas'd to say* was very agreeable to him, but at that time there was no more in it.

I had many melancholly Hours at the *Bath* after all the Company was gone, for tho' I went to *Bristol* sometimes for the disposing my Effects and for Recruits of Money, yet I chose to come back to *Bath* for my Residence, because being on good Terms with the Woman in whose House I lodg'd in the Summer, I found that during the Winter I liv'd rather cheaper there than I could do any where else; here, *I say*, I pass'd the Winter as heavily as I had pass'd the Autumn chearfully; But having contracted a nearer intimacy with the said Woman, in whose House I Lodg'd, I could not avoid communicating to her something of what lay hardest upon my Mind, and particularly the narrowness of my Circumstances, and the loss of my Fortune by the Damage of my Goods by Sea: I told her also that I had a Mother and a Brother in *Virginia* in good Circumstances, and as I had really written back to my Mother in particular to represent my Condition, and the great Loss I had receiv'd, which indeed came to almost 500 *l.* so I did not fail to let my new Friend know that I expected a Supply from thence, and so indeed I did; and as the Ships went from *Bristol* to *York* River in *Virginia*, and back again generally in less time than from *London*, and that my Brother Corresponded chiefly at *Bristol*, I thought it was much better for me to wait here for my Returns than to go to *London*, where also I had not the least Acquaintance.

My new Friend appear'd sensibly affected with my Condition, and indeed was so very kind, as to reduce the Rate of my living with her to so low a Price during the Winter, that she convinced me she got nothing by me; and as for Lodging during the Winter, I paid nothing at all.

When the Spring Season came on, she continu'd to be as kind to me as she could, and I lodg'd with her for a time, till it was found necessary to do otherwise; she had some Persons of Character that frequently lodg'd in her House, and in particular the Gentleman who, as I said, singl'd me out for his Companion the Winter before; and he came down again with another Gentleman in his Company and two Servants, and lodg'd in the same House: I suspected that my Landlady had invited him thither, letting him know that I was still with her, but she deny'd it, and protested to me that she did not, and he said the same.

In a Word, this Gentleman came down and continu'd to single me out for his peculiar Confidence as well as Conversation; he was a compleat Gentleman, *that must be confess'd*, and his Company was very agreeable to me, as mine, *if I might believe him*, was to him; he made no Professions to me but of an extraordinary Respect, and he had such an Opinion of my Virtue, that *as he often professs'd*, he believ'd if he should offer any thing else, I should reject him with Contempt; he soon understood from me that I was a Widow; that I had arriv'd at *Bristol* from *Virginia* by the last ships; and that I waited at *Bath* till the next *Virginia Fleet* should arrive, by which I expected considerable Effects; I understood by him, and by others of him, that he had a Wife, but that the Lady was distemper'd in her Head, and was under the Conduct of her own Relations, which he consented to, to avoid any Reflections that might, *as was not unusual in such Cases*, be cast on him for mismanaging her Cure; and in the mean time he came to the *Bath* to divert his Thoughts from the Disturbance of such a melancholy Circumstance as that was.

My Landlady, who of her own accord encourag'd the Correspondence on all Occasions, gave me an advantageous Character of him, as of a Man of Honour and of Virtue, as well as of a great Estate; and indeed I had a great deal of Reason to say so of him too; for tho' we lodg'd both on a Floor, and he had frequently come into my Chamber, even when I was in Bed; and I also into his when he was in Bed,[6] yet he never offered any thing to me farther than a kiss, or so much as solicited me to any thing till long after, as you shall hear.

I frequently took notice to my Landlady of his exceeding Modesty, and she again used to tell me, she believ'd it was so from the beginning; however she used to tell me that she thought I ought to expect some Gratification from him for my Company, for indeed he did, as it were, engross me,[7] and I was seldom from him; *I told her* I had not given him the least occasion to think I wanted it, or that I would accept of it from him; *she told me* she would take that part upon her, and she did so, and manag'd it so dextrously, that the first time we were together alone, after she had talk'd with him, he began to enquire a little into my Circumstances, as how I had subsisted my self since I came on shore? and whether I did not want Money? I stood off very boldly, I told him that tho' my Cargo of Tobacco was damag'd, yet that it was not quite lost; that the Merchant I had been consign'd to, had so honestly manag'd for me that I had not wanted, and that I hop'd, with frugal Management, I should make it hold out till more would come, which I expected by

---

6. Morning visits of this kind were acceptable in polite company among good friends; however, Moll is stressing the innocence of the relationship.
7. Occupy most of my time.

the next Fleet; that in the mean time I had retrench'd my Expences, and whereas I kept a Maid last Season, now I liv'd without;
and whereas I had a Chamber and a Dining-room then on the first
Floor, *as he knew*, I now had but one Room two pair of Stairs,[8]
and the like; but I live *said I*, as well satisfy'd now as I did then;
adding, that his Company had been a means to make me live much
more chearfully than otherwise I should have done, for which I was
much oblig'd to him; and so I put off all room for any offer for the
present: However, it was not long before he attack'd me again, and
told me he found that I was backward to trust him with the Secret
of my Circumstances, *which he was sorry for*; assuring me that he
enquir'd into it with no design to satisfie his own Curiosity, but
meerly to assist me, if there was any occasion; but since I would not
own my self to stand in need of any assistance, he had but one
thing more to desire of me, and that was that I would promise him
that when I was any way streighten'd, or like to be so, I would
frankly tell him of it, and that I would make use of him with the
same freedom that he made the offer, *adding*, that I should always
find I had a true Friend, tho' perhaps I was afraid to trust him.

I omitted nothing *that was fit to be said by one infinitely oblig'd*,
to let him know, that I had a due Sense of his Kindness; and
indeed from that time, I did not appear so much reserv'd to him as
I had done before, tho' still within the Bounds of the strictest
Virtue on both sides; but how free soever our Conversation was, I
cou'd not arrive to that sort of Freedom which he desir'd, (*viz.*) to
tell him I wanted Money, tho' I was secretly very glad of his offer.

Some Weeks pass'd after this, and still I never ask'd him for
Money; when my Landlady, a cunning Creature, who had often
press'd me to it, but found that I cou'd not do it, makes a Story of
her own inventing, and comes in bluntly to me when we were
together, O Widow, *says she*, I have bad News to tell you this
Morning; What is that, said I, are the *Virginia* Ships taken by the
French? for that was my fear. No, no, *says she*, but the Man you
sent to *Bristol* Yesterday for Money is come back, and says he has
brought none.

Now I could by no means like her Project; I thought it look'd too
much like prompting him, which indeed he did not want, and I saw
clearly that I should lose nothing by being backward to ask, so I
took her up short; I can't imagine why he should say so to you, *said
I*, for I assure you he brought me all the Money I sent him for, and
here it is *said I*, (pulling out my Purse with about 12 Guineas in it)
and added, I intend you shall have most of it by and by.

He seem'd distasted a little at her talking as she did at first, as
well as I, taking it as I fancied he would as something forward of

8. A third-floor room.

her; but when he saw me give such an Answer, he came immediately to himself again: The next Morning we talk'd of it again, when I found he was fully satisfy'd, and smiling said, he hop'd I would not want Money and not tell him of it, and that I had promis'd him otherwise: I told him I had been very much dissatisfy'd at my Landladies talking so publickly the Day before of what she had nothing to do with; but I suppos'd she wanted what I ow'd her, which was about Eight Guineas, which I had resolv'd to give her, and had accordingly given it her the same Night she talk'd so foolishly.

He was in a mighty good Humour, when he heard me say, *I had paid her*, and it went off into some other Discourse at that time; but the next Morning he having heard me up about my Room before him, he call'd to me, *and I answering*, he ask'd me to come into his Chamber; he was in bed when I came in, and he made me come and sit down on his Bed side, *for he said* he had something to say to me, which was of some Moment: After some very kind Expressions he ask'd me if I would be very honest to him, and give a sincere Answer to one thing he would desire of me? after some little Cavil with him at the word *Sincere*, and asking him if I had ever given him any Answers which were not Sincere, I promis'd him I would; why then his Request was, *he said*, to let him see my Purse; I immediately put my Hand into my Pocket, *and Laughing at him*, pull'd it out, and there was in it three Guineas and a Half; *then he ask'd me*, if there was all the Money I had? I told him no, *Laughing again*, not by a great deal.

Well then, *he said*, he would have me promise to go and fetch him all the Money I had, every Farthing: *I told him I would*, and I went into my Chamber and fetch'd him a little private Drawer, where I had about six Guineas more, and some Silver, and threw it all down upon the Bed, and told him there was all my Wealth, honestly to a Shilling: He look'd a little at it, but did not tell it, and Huddled it all into the Drawer again, and reaching his Pocket, pull'd out a Key, and then bade me open a little Walnut-tree box, he had upon the Table, and bring him such a Drawer, which I did, in which Drawer there was a great deal of Money in Gold, I believe near 200 Guineas, but I knew not how much: He took the Drawer, and taking my Hand, made me put it in and take a whole handful; I was backward at that, but he held my Hand hard in his Hand, and put it into the Drawer, and made me take out as many Guineas almost as I could well take up at once.

When I had done so, he made me put them into my Lap, and took my little Drawer, and pour'd out all my own Money among his, and bade me get me gone, and carry it all Home into my own Chamber.

I relate this Story the more particularly because of the good Humour there was in it, and to show the temper with which we Convers'd: It was not long after this but he began every Day to find fault with my Cloths, with my Laces, and Head-dresses, and in a Word, press'd me to buy better, which by the way I was willing enough to do, tho' I did not seem to be so; for I lov'd nothing in the World better than fine Clothes; I told him I must Housewife the Money he had lent me, or else I should not be able to pay him again. He then told me in a few Words, that as he had a sincere Respect for me, and knew my Circumstances, he had not Lent me that Money, but given it me, and that he thought I had merited it from him by giving him my Company so intirely as I had done: After this, he made me take a Maid, and keep House, and his Friend that came with him to *Bath*, being gone, he oblig'd me to Dyet[9] him, which I did very willingly, believing *as it appear'd*, that I should lose nothing by it, nor did the Woman of the House fail to find her Account in it too.

We had liv'd thus near three Months, when the Company beginning to wear away at the *Bath*, he talk'd of going away, and fain he would have me to go to *London* with him: I was not very easie in that Proposal, not knowing what Posture I was to live in there, or how he might use me: But while this was in Debate he fell very Sick; he had gone out to a place in *Somersetshire* called *Shepton*, where he had some Business, and was there taken very ill, and so ill that he could not Travel; so he sent his Man back to *Bath* to beg me that I would hire a Coach and come over to him. Before he went, he had left all his Money and other things of Value with me, and what to do with them I did not know, but I secur'd them as well as I could, and Lock'd up the Lodgings and went to him, where I found him very ill indeed; however, I perswaded him to be carry'd in a Litter[1] to the *Bath*, where there was more help and better advice to be had.

He consented, and I brought him to the *Bath*, which was about fifteen Miles, *as I remember*: here he continued very ill of a Fever, and kept his Bed five Weeks, all which time I nurs'd him and tended him my self, as much and as carefully as if I had been his Wife; indeed if I had been his Wife I could not have done more; I sat up with him so much and so often, that at last indeed he would not let me sit up any longer, and then I got a Pallet[2] Bed into his Room, and lay in it just at his Bed's Feet.

I was indeed sensibly affected with his Condition, and with the Apprehension of losing such a Friend as he was, and was like to be to me, and I us'd to sit and Cry by him many Hours together:

9. Board.
1. A horse-drawn vehicle containing a
couch shut in by curtains.
2. A couch.

However at last he grew Better, and gave hopes that he would recover, as indeed he did, tho' very slowly.

Were it otherwise than what I am going to say, I should not be backward to disclose it, as it is apparent I have done in other Cases in this Account; but I affirm, that thro' all this Conversation, abating the freedom of coming into the Chamber when I or he was in Bed, and abating the necessary Offices of attending him Night and Day when he was Sick, there had not pass'd the least immodest Word or Action between us. O! that it had been so to the last.

After some time he gathered Strength and grew well apace, and I would have remov'd my Pallet Bed, but he would not let me till he was able to venture himself without any Body to sit up with him, and then I remov'd to my own Chamber.

He took many Occasions to express his Sense of my Tenderness and Concern for him; and when he grew quite well, he made me a Present of Fifty Guineas for my Care, and, as he call'd it, for hazarding my Life to save his.

And now he made deep Protestations of a sincere inviolable Affection for me, but all along attested it to be with the utmost reserve for my Virtue and his own: I told him I was fully satisfyed of it; he carried it that length that he protested to me, that if he was naked in Bed with me, he would as sacredly preserve my Virtue, as he would defend it if I was assaulted by a Ravisher; I believ'd him, and told him I did so; but this did not satisfie him; he would, *he said,* wait for some opportunity to give me an undoubted Testimony of it.

It was a great while after this that I had Occasion, on my own Business, to go to *Bristol,* upon which he hir'd me a Coach, and would go with me, and did so; and now indeed our intimacy increas'd: From *Bristol* he carry'd me to *Gloucester,* which was meerly a Journey of Pleasure to take the Air; and here it was our hap to have no Lodging in the Inn but in one large Chamber with two Beds in it: The Master of the House going up with us to show his Rooms, and coming into that Room, said very frankly to him, Sir, *It is none of my business to enquire whether the Lady be your Spouse or no,* but if not, *you may lie as honestly in these two Beds as if you were in two Chambers,* and with that he pulls a great Curtain which drew quite cross the Room, and effectually divided the Beds; well, *says my Friend,* very readily, these Beds will do, and as for the rest, we are too near a kin to lye together, tho' we may Lodge near one another; and this put an honest Face on the thing too. When we came to go to Bed he decently went out of the Room till I was in Bed, and then went to Bed in the Bed on his own side of the Room, but lay there talking to me a great while.

At last repeating his usual saying, that he could lye naked in the Bed with me and not offer me the least Injury, he starts out of his Bed, and now, *my Dear, says he,* you shall see how just I will be to you, and that I can keep my word, and away he comes to my Bed.

I resisted a little, but I must confess I should not have resisted him much if he had not made those Promises at all; so after a little struggle, *as I said,* I lay still and let him come to Bed; when he was there he took me in his Arms, and so I lay all Night with him, but he had no more to do with me, or offer'd any thing to me other than embracing me, as I say, in his Arms, no not the whole Night, but rose up and dress'd him in the Morning, and left me as innocent for him as I was the Day I was born.

This was a surprizing thing to me, and perhaps may be so to others who know how the Laws of Nature work; for he was a strong vigorous brisk Person; nor did he act thus on a principle of Religion at all, *but of meer Affection;* insisting on it, that tho' I was to him the most agreeable Woman in the World, yet because he lov'd me he cou'd not injure me.

I own it was a noble Principle, but as it was what I never understood before, so it was to me perfectly amazing. We Travel'd the rest of the Journey as we did before, and came back to the *Bath,* where, as he had opportunity to come to me when he would, he often repeated the Moderation, and I frequently lay with him, and he with me, and altho' all the familiarities between Man and Wife were common to us, yet he never once offered to go any farther, and he valued himself much upon it; I do not say that I was so wholly pleas'd with it as he thought I was: For I own I was much wickeder than he, *as you shall hear presently.*

We liv'd thus near two Year, only with this exception, that he went three times to *London* in that time, and once he continued there four Months; but, to do him Justice, he always supply'd me with Money to subsist me very handsomly.

Had we continued thus, I confess we had had much to boast of; but as wise Men say, it is ill venturing too near the brink of a Command,[3] so we found it; and here again I must do him the Justice to own that the first Breach was not on his part: It was one Night that we were in Bed together warm and merry, and having drank, I think, a little more Wine that Night, both of us, than usual, tho' not in the least to disorder either of us, when after some other follies which I cannot name, and being clasp'd close in his Arms, *I told him, (I repeat it with shame and horror of Soul)* that I cou'd find in my Heart to discharge him of his Engagement[4] for one Night and no more.

3. Commandment. (See G. A. Starr, below, p. 431).   4. Promise.

He took me at my word immediately, and after that, there was no resisting him; neither indeed had I any mind to resist him any more, let what would come of it.

Thus the Government of our Virtue was broken, and I exchang'd the Place of Friend for that unmusical harsh-sounding Title of WHORE. In the Morning we were both at our Penitentials; I cried very heartily, he express'd himself very sorry; but that was all either of us could do at that time; and the way being thus clear'd, and the bars of Virtue and Conscience thus removed, we had the less difficulty afterwards to struggle with.

It was but a dull kind of Conversation that we had together for all the rest of that Week, I look'd on him with Blushes, and every now and then started that melancholy Objection, *what if I should be with Child now? What will become of me then?* He encourag'd me by telling me, that as long as I was true to him he would be so to me; and since it was gone such a length, (which indeed he never intended) yet if I was with Child, he would take care of that, and of me too: This harden'd us both; I assur'd him if I was with Child, I would die for want of a Midwife rather than Name him as the Father of it; and he assur'd me I should never want if I should be with Child: These mutual assurances harden'd us in the thing; and after this we repeated the crime as often as we pleas'd, till at length, as I had fear'd so it came to pass, and I was indeed with Child.

After I was sure it was so, and I had satisfied him of it too, we began to think of taking measures for the managing it, and I propos'd trusting the Secret to my Landlady, and asking her Advice, which he agreed to: My Landlady, a Woman (as I found) us'd to such things, made light of it; she said she knew it would come to that at last, and made us very merry about it: As I said above, we found her an Experienc'd old Lady at such Work; she undertook every thing, engag'd to procure a Midwife and a Nurse, to satisfie all Enquiries, and bring us off with Reputation, and she did so very dexterously indeed.

When I grew near my time, she desir'd my Gentleman to go away to *London*, or make as if he did so; when he was gone, she acquainted the Parish Officers that there was a Lady ready to lye in[5] at her House, but that she knew her Husband very well, and gave them, as she pretended, an account of his Name, which she called Sir *Walter Cleave*; telling them, he was a very worthy Gentleman, and that she would answer for all Enquiries, and the like: This satisfied the Parish Officers presently and I lay INN with as

---

5. Defoe also spells the term "Lye Inn" and "Lie Inn," which means to be confined while awaiting childbirth. Since the parish was responsible for indigents, its officers wanted to ascertain that Moll and baby had financial support.

much Credit as I could have done if I had really been my Lady
Cleave;[6] and was assisted in my Travail by three or four of the best
Citizens Wives of *Bath*, who liv'd in the Neighbourhood, which
however made me a little the more expensive to him; I often
expressed my concern to him about it, but he bid me not be concern'd at it.

As he had furnish'd me very sufficiently with Money for the
extraordinary Expences of my Lying Inn, I had every thing very
handsome about me; but did not affect to be Gay or Extravagant
neither; besides, knowing my own Circumstances, and knowing the
World as I had done, and that such kind of things do not often last
long, I took care to lay up as much Money as I could for a wet Day,
as I call'd it; making him believe it was all spent upon the extraordinary appearance of things in my Lying Inn.

By this means, and including what he had given me as above, I
had at the end of my Lying Inn about 200 Guineas by me, including
also what was left of my own.

I was brought to Bed of a fine Boy indeed, and a charming
Child it was; and when he heard of it he wrote me a very kind
obliging Letter about it, and then told me, he thought it would
look better for me to come away for *London* as soon as I was up
and well, that he had provided Appartments for me at *Hammersmith* as if I came thither only from *London*, and that after a little
while I should go back to the *Bath*, and he would go with me.

I lik'd this offer very well, and accordingly hir'd a Coach on purpose, and taking my Child and a Wet-Nurse to Tend and Suckle it,
and a Maid Servant with me, away I went for *London*.

He met me at *Reading* in his own Chariot, and taking me into
that, left the Servant and the Child in the hir'd Coach, and so he
brought me to my new Lodgings at *Hammersmith*; with which I
had abundance of Reason to be very well pleas'd, for they were very
handsome Rooms, and I was very well accommodated.

And now I was indeed in the height of what I might call my
Prosperity, and I wanted nothing but to be a Wife, which however
could not be in this Case, there was no room for it; and therefore
on all Occasions I study'd to save what I could, as I have said above,
against a time of scarcity; knowing well enough that such things as
these do not always continue, that Men that keep Mistresses often
change them, grow weary of them, or Jealous of them, or something
or other happens to make them withdraw their Bounty; and some-

6. Seemingly a pun on the word "cleave," which in the slang of the century meant a wanton woman, a slut. Moreover, Moll's excellent treatment may be an ironic reference to the chaste and virtuous wife in Mme. de Lafayette's novel of sentiment *La Princesse de Clèves* (1678). The Restoration dramatist Nat Lee wrote an English play entitled *The Princess of Cleve* (1689), debasing the popular French romance.

times the Ladies that are thus well us'd, are not careful by a prudent Conduct to preserve the Esteem of their Persons, or the nice Article of their Fidelity, and then they are justly cast off with Contempt.

But I was secur'd in this Point, for as I had no Inclination to change, so I had no manner of Acquaintance in the whole House, and so no Temptation to look any farther; I kept no Company but in the Family where I Lodg'd, and with a Clergyman's Lady at next Door; so that when he was absent I visited no Body, nor did he ever find me out of my Chamber or Parlor whenever he came down; if I went any where to take the Air it was always with him.

The living in this manner with him, and his with me, was certainly the most undesigned thing in the World; he often protested to me, that when he became first acquainted with me, and even to the very Night when we first broke in upon our Rules, he never had the least Design of lying with me; that he always had a sincere Affection for me, but not the least real inclination to do what he had done; I assur'd him I never suspected him, that if I had, I should not so easily have yielded to the freedoms which brought it on, but that it was all a surprize, and was owing to the Accident of our having yielded too far to our mutual Inclinations that Night; and indeed I have often observ'd since, and leave it as a caution to the Readers of this Story, that we ought to be cautious of gratifying our Inclinations in loose and lewd Freedoms, lest we find our Resolutions of Virtue fail us in the juncture when their Assistance should be most necessary.

It is true, *and I have confess'd it before*, that from the first hour I began to converse with him, I resolv'd to let him lye with me if he offer'd it; but it was because I wanted his help and assistance, and I knew no other way of securing him than that: But when we were that Night together, and, as I have said, had gone such a length, I found my Weakness, the Inclination was not to be resisted, but I was oblig'd to yield up all even before he ask'd it.

However he was so just to me that he never upbraided me with that; nor did he ever express the least dislike of my Conduct on any other Occasion, but always protested he was as much delighted with my Company as he was the first Hour we came together, I mean came together as Bedfellows.

It is true that he had no Wife, that is to say, she was as no Wife to him, and so I was in no Danger that way, but the just Reflections of Conscience oftentimes snatch a Man, especially a Man of Sense, from the Arms of a Mistress, as it did him at last, tho' on another Occasion.

On the other hand, tho' I was not without secret Reproaches of my own Conscience for the Life I led, and that even in the greatest height of the Satisfaction I ever took, yet I had the terrible prospect of Poverty and Starving which lay on me as a frightful Spectre, so that there was no looking behind me: But as Poverty brought me into it, so fear of Poverty kept me in it, and I frequently resolv'd to leave it quite off, if I could but come to lay up Money enough to maintain me: But these were Thoughts of no weight, and whenever he came to me they vanish'd; for his Company was so delightful, that there was no being melancholly when he was there; the Reflections were all the Subject of those Hours when I was alone.

I liv'd six Year in this happy but unhappy Condition, in which time I brought him three Children, but only the first of them liv'd; and tho' I remov'd twice in those six Years, yet I came back the sixth Year to my first Lodgings at *Hammersmith*: Here it was that I was one Morning surpriz'd with a kind but melancholy Letter from my Gentleman; intimating, that he was very ill, and was afraid he should have another fit of Sickness, but that his Wife's Relations being in the House with him, it would not be practicable to have me with him, which however he express'd his great Dissatisfaction in, and that he wish'd I cou'd be allowed to Tend and Nurse him as I did before.

I was very much concern'd at this Account, and was very impatient to know how it was with him; I waited a Fortnight or thereabouts, and heard nothing, which surpriz'd me, and I began to be very uneasy indeed; I think I may say, that for the next Fortnight I was near to distracted: It was my particular difficulty, that I did not know directly where he was; for I understood at first he was in the Lodgings of his Wife's Mother; but having remov'd my self to *London*, I soon found by the help of the Direction I had for writing my Letters to him, how to enquire after him; and there I found that he was at a House in *Bloomsbury*, whither he had, a little before he fell Sick, remov'd his whole Family; and that his Wife and Wife's Mother were in the same House, tho' the Wife was not suffered to know that she was in the same House with her Husband.

Here, I also soon understood that he was at the last Extremity, which made me almost at the last Extremity too, to have a true account: One Night I had the Curiosity to disguise my self like a Servant Maid in a Round Cap and Straw Hat, and went to the Door, as[7] sent by a Lady of his Neighbourhood, where he liv'd before, and giving Master and Mistresses Service, I said I was sent to know how Mr. ——— did, and how he had rested that Night; in delivering this Message I got the opportunity I desir'd, for speaking with one of the Maids, I held a long Gossips Tale with her, and had all the Particulars of his Illness, which I found was a Pleurisie

7. As if.

attended with a Cough and a Fever; she told me also who was in the House, and how his Wife was, who, by her Relation,[8] they were in some hopes might Recover her Understanding; but as to the Gentleman himself, *in short* she told me the Doctors said there was very little hopes of him, that in the Morning they thought he had been dying, and that he was but little better then, for they did not expect that he could live over the next Night.

This was heavy News for me, and I began now to see an end of my Prosperity, and to see also that it was very well I had play'd the good Housewife, and secur'd or saved something while he was alive, for that now I had no view of *my own living* before me.

It lay very heavy upon my Mind too, that I had a Son, a fine lovely Boy, above five Years old, and no Provision made for it, at least that I knew of; with these Considerations, and a sad Heart, I went home that Evening, and began to cast with my self how I should live, and in what manner to bestow[9] my self, for the residue of my Life.

You may be sure I could not rest without enquiring again very quickly what was become of him; and not venturing to go my self, I sent several sham Messengers, till after a Fortnights waiting longer, I found that there was hopes of his Life, tho' he was still very ill; then I abated my sending any more to the House, and in some time after I learnt in the Neighbourhood that he was about House, and then that he was Abroad[1] again.

I made no doubt then but that I shou'd soon hear of him, and began to comfort my self with my Circumstances being, as I thought, recovered; I waited a Week, and two Weeks, and with much surprize and amazement I waited near two Months and heard nothing, but that being recover'd he was gone into the Country for the Air, and for the better Recovery after his Distemper; after this it was yet two Months more, and then I understood he was come to his City-House again, but still I heard nothing from him.

I had written several Letters for[2] him, and Directed them as usual, and found two or three of them had been call'd for, *but not the rest*: I wrote again in a more pressing manner than ever, and in one of them let him know, that I must be forc'd to wait on him myself, Representing my Circumstances, the Rent of Lodgings to pay, and the Provision for the Child wanting, and my own deplorable Condition, destitute of Subsistence after his most solemn Engagement to take Care of, and Provide for me; I took a Copy of this Letter, and finding it lay at the House near a Month and was not call'd for, I found means to have the Copy of it put into his own Hands at a Coffee-House, where I had by Enquiry found he us'd to go.

8. As the maid told it.
9. Employ, apply myself.

1. Able to go outdoors.
2. To (for to be sent to).

This Letter forc'd an Answer from him, by which, tho' I found I was to be abandon'd, yet I found he had sent a Letter to me sometime before, desiring me to go down *to the Bath again*; its Contents I shall come to presently.

It is True that Sick Beds are the times when such Correspondences as this are look'd on with different Countenance, and seen with other Eyes than we saw them with, or than they appear'd with before: My Lover had been at the Gates of Death, and at the very brink of Eternity; and it seems had been struck with a due remorse, and with sad Reflections upon his past Life of Gallantry and Levity; and among the rest, this criminal Correspondence with me, which was neither more or less than a long continu'd Life of Adultery had represented it self, as it really was, not as it had been formerly thought by him to be, and he look'd upon it now with a just, and a religious Abhorrence.

I cannot but observe also, and leave it for the Direction of my Sex in such Cases of Pleasure, that when ever sincere Repentance succeeds such a Crime as this, there never fails to attend a Hatred of the Object; and the more the Affection might seem to be before, the Hatred will be the more in Proportion: It will always be so, indeed it can be no otherwise; for there cannot be a true and sincere Abhorrence of the Offence, and the Love to the Cause of it remain, there will with an Abhorrence of the Sin be found a detestation of the fellow Sinner; you can expect no other.

I found it so here, tho' good Manners and Justice in this Gentleman kept him from carrying it on to any extream; but the short History of his Part in this Affair, was thus; he perceiv'd by my last Letter, and by all the rest, which he went for after, that I was not gone to the *Bath*, that his first Letter had not come to my Hand, upon which he writes me this following,

Madam,

I am surpriz'd that my Letter Dated the 8th of last Month did not come to your Hand; I give you my Word it was deliver'd at your Lodgings, and to the Hands of your Maid.

I need not acquaint you with what has been my condition for sometime past; and how having been at the Edge of the Grave, I am by the unexpected and undeserv'd Mercy of Heaven restor'd again: In the Condition I have been in, it cannot be strange to you that our unhappy Correspondence has not been the least of the Burthens which lay upon my Conscience; I need say no more, those things that must be repented of, must be also reform'd.

I wish you would think of going back to the Bath; *I enclose you here a Bill for 50 l. for clearing your self at your Lodgings, and carrying you down, and hope it will be no surprize to you to add, that on this account only, and not for any Offence given me on your side, I can* SEE YOU NO MORE; *I will take due care of the Child; leave him where he is, or take him with you, as you please; I wish you the like Reflections,[3] and that they may be to your Advantage. I am, &c.*

I was struck with this Letter as with a thousand Wounds, such as I cannot describe; the Reproaches of my own Conscience were such as I cannot express, for I was not blind to my own Crime: and I reflected that I might with less Offence have continued with my Brother, and liv'd with him as a Wife, since there was no Crime in our Marriage on that score, neither of us knowing it.

But I never once reflected that I was all this while a marry'd Woman, a Wife to Mr. ———— the Linnen Draper, who tho' he had left me by the Necessity of his Circumstances, had no power to Discharge me from the Marriage Contract which was between us, or to give me a legal liberty to marry again; so that I had been no less than a Whore and an Adultress all this while: I then reproach'd my self with the Liberties I had taken, and how I had been a Snare to this Gentleman, and that indeed I was principal in the Crime; that now he was mercifully snatch'd out of the Gulph[4] by a convincing Work upon his Mind, but that I was left as if I was forsaken of God's Grace, and abandon'd by Heaven to a continuing in my wickedness.

Under these Reflections I continu'd very pensive and sad for near a Month, and did not go down to the *Bath*, having no inclination to be with the Woman who I was with before; lest, as I thought, she should prompt me to some wicked course of Life again, as she had done; and besides, I was very loth she should know I was cast off as above.

And now I was greatly perplex'd about my little Boy; it was Death to me to part with the Child, and yet when I consider'd the Danger of being one time or other left with him to keep without a Maintenance to support him, I then resolv'd to leave him where he was; but then I concluded also to be near him my self too, that I might have the satisfaction of seeing him, without the Care of providing for him.

I sent my Gentleman a short Letter therefore, that I had obey'd his Orders in all things, but that of going back to the *Bath*, which I cou'd not think of for many Reasons; that however parting from him was a Wound to me that I could never recover, yet that I was fully satisfied his Reflections were just, and would be very far from desiring to obstruct his Reformation or Repentance.

Then I represented my own Circumstances to him in the most moving Terms that I was able: I told him that those unhappy Distresses which first mov'd him to a generous and an honest Friendship for me, would, I hope, move him to a little concern for me

3. Similar thoughts of repentance.   4. Gulf, abyss; depths of degradation.

now; tho' the Criminal part of our Correspondence, which I believed neither of us intended to fall into at that time, was broken off; that I desir'd to Repent as sincerely as he had done, but entreated him to put me in some Condition that I might not be expos'd to the Temptations which the Devil never fails to excite us to from the frightful prospect of Poverty and Distress; and if he had the least Apprehensions of my being troublesome to him, I beg'd he would put me in a Posture to go back to my Mother in *Virginia*, from whence he knew I came, and that would put an end to all his Fears on that account; I concluded, that if he would send me 50 *l*. more to facilitate my going away, I would send him back a general Release, and would promise never to disturb him more with any Importunities; unless it was to hear of the well-doing of the Child, who if I found my Mother living, and my Circumstances able, I would send for to come over to me, and take him also effectually off of his Hands.

This was indeed all a Cheat thus far, *viz.* that I had no intention to go to *Virginia*, as the Account of my former Affairs there may convince any Body of; but the business was to get this last Fifty Pounds of him, if possible, knowing well enough it would be the last Penny I was ever to expect.

However, the Argument I us'd, namely, of giving him a general Release, and never troubling him any more, prevail'd effectually with him, and he sent me a Bill for the Money by a Person who brought with him a general Release for me to sign, and which I frankly sign'd, and receiv'd the Money; and thus, tho' full sore against my will, a final End was put to this Affair.

And here I cannot but reflect upon the unhappy Consequence of too great Freedoms between Persons stated[5] as we were, upon the pretence of innocent intentions, Love of Friendship, *and the like*; for the Flesh has generally so great a share in those Friendships, that it is great odds but inclination prevails at last over the most solemn Resolutions; and that Vice breaks in at the breaches of Decency, which really innocent Friendship ought to preserve with the greatest strictness; but I leave the Readers of these things to their own just Reflections, which they will be more able to make effectual than I, who so soon forgot my self, and am therefore but a very indifferent Monitor.[6]

I was now a single Person again, *as I may call my self*, I was loos'd from all the Obligations either of Wedlock or Mistressship in the World; except my Husband the Linnen Draper, who I having not now heard from in almost Fifteen Year, no Body could blame

---

5. Situated.   'Indifferent Monitor,' " p. 414, below.
6. See Maximilian E. Novak's "Defoe's

me for thinking my self entirely freed from; seeing also he had at his going away told me, that if I did not hear frequently from him, I should conclude he was dead, and I might freely marry again to whom I pleas'd.

I now began to cast up my Accounts; I had by many Letters, and much Importunity, and with the Intercession of my Mother too, had a second return of some Goods from my Brother, *as I now call him*, in *Virginia*, to make up the Damage of the Cargo I brought away with me, and this too was upon the Condition of my sealing a general Release to him, and to send it him by his Correspondent at *Bristol*, which though I thought hard, but yet I was oblig'd to promise to do: However, I manag'd so well in this case, that I got my Goods away before the Release was sign'd, and then I always found something or other to say to evade the thing, and to put off the signing it at all; till *at length* I pretended I must write to my Brother, and have his Answer, before I could do it.

Including this Recruit, and before I got the last 50 *l*. I found my strength to amount, put all together, to about 400 *l*. so that with that I had above 450 *l*. I had sav'd above 100 *l*. more, but I met with a Disaster with that, which was this; that a Goldsmith in whose Hands I had trusted it, broke, so I lost 70 *l*. of my Money, the Man's Composition not making above 30 *l*. out of his 100 *l*.[7] I had a little Plate, but not much, and was well enough stock'd with Cloaths and Linnen.

With this Stock I had the World to begin again; but you are to consider that I was not now the same Woman as when I liv'd at *Redriff*; for first of all I was near 20 Years older, and did not look the better for my Age, nor for my Rambles to *Virginia* and back again; and tho' I omitted nothing that might set me out to Advantage, except Painting,[8] for that I never stoop'd to, and had Pride enough to think I did not want it, yet there would always be some difference seen between Five and Twenty, and Two and Forty.

I cast about innumerable ways for my future State of Life and began to consider very seriously what I should do, *but nothing offer'd*; I took care to make the World take me for something more than I was, and had it given out that I was a Fortune, and that my Estate was in my own Hands, the last of which was very true, the first of it was as above: I had no Acquaintance, which was one of my worst Misfortunes, and the Consequence of that was, I had no adviser, at least who cou'd advise and assist together; and above all, I had no Body to whom I could in confidence commit the Secret of my Circumstances to, and could depend upon for their Secresie and Fidelity; and I found by experience, that to be Friendless is the

---

7. In this incident the goldsmith "broke" — went bankrupt— and was able to re- pay only £30 on the £100.

8. Using cosmetics, "painting" her face.

worst Condition, next to being in want, that a Woman can be reduc'd to: *I say a Woman*, because 'tis evident Men can be their own Advisers, and their own Directors, and know how to work themselves out of Difficulties and into Business better than Women; but if a Woman has no Friend to Communicate her Affairs to, and to advise and assist her, 'tis ten to one but she is undone; nay, and the more Money she has, the more Danger she is in of being wrong'd and deceiv'd; and this was my Case in the Affair of the Hundred Pound which I left in the Hand of the Goldsmith, *as above*, whose Credit, it seems, was upon the Ebb before, but I that had no knowledge of things, and no Body to consult with, knew nothing of it, and so lost my Money.

In the next place, when a Woman is thus left desolate and void of Council,[9] she is just like a Bag of Money, or a Jewel dropt on the Highway, which is a Prey to the next Comer; if a Man of Virtue and upright Principles happens to find it, he will have it cried,[1] and the Owner may come to hear of it again; but how many times shall such a thing fall into Hands that will make no scruple of seizing it for their own, to once that it shall come into good Hands.

This was evidently my Case, for I was now a loose unguided Creature, and had no Help, no Assistance, no Guide for my Conduct: I knew what I aim'd at, and what I wanted, but knew nothing how to pursue the End by direct means; I wanted to be plac'd in a settled State of Living, and had I happen'd to meet with a sober good Husband, I should have been as faithful and true a Wife to him as Virtue it self could have form'd: If I had been otherwise, the Vice came in always at the Door of Necessity, not at the Door of Inclination; and I understood too well, by the want of it, what the value of a settl'd Life was, to do any thing to forfeit the felicity of it; nay, I should have made the better Wife for all the Difficulties I had pass'd thro', by a great deal; nor did I in any of the Time that I had been a Wife, give my Husbands the least uneasiness on account of my Behaviour.

But all this was nothing; I found no encouraging Prospect; I waited, I liv'd regularly, and with as much frugality as became my Circumstances, but nothing offer'd; nothing presented, and the main Stock wasted apace; what to do I knew not, the Terror of approaching Poverty lay hard upon my Spirits: I had some Money, but where to place it I knew not, nor would the Interest of it maintain me, at least not in *London*.

At length a new Scene open'd: There was in the House where I Lodg'd, a North Country Woman that went for a Gentlewoman, and nothing was more frequent in her Discourse than her account

9. Counsel.
1. Have his find publicly announced (cried about town—or advertised) so the owner might claim it.

of the cheapness of Provisions, and the easie way of living in her County; how plentiful and how cheap every thing was, what good Company they kept, and the like; till at last I told her she almost tempted me to go and live in her County; for I that was a Widow, tho' I had sufficient to live on, yet had no way of encreasing it; and that *London* was an expensive and extravagant Place; that I found I could not live here under a Hundred Pound a Year, unless I kept no Company, no Servant, made no Appearance, and buried my self in Privacy, as if I was oblig'd to it by Necessity.

I should have observ'd, that she was always made to believe, as every Body else was, that I was a great Fortune, or at least that I had Three or Four Thousand Pounds, if not more, and all in my own Hands; and she was mighty sweet upon me when she thought me inclin'd in the least to go into her Country; she said she had a Sister liv'd near *Liverpool*, that her Brother was a considerable Gentleman there, and had a great Estate also in *Ireland*; that she would go down there in about two Months, and if I would give her my Company thither, I should be as welcome as her self for a Month or more as I pleas'd, till I should see how I lik'd the Country; and if I thought fit to live there, she would undertake they would take care, tho' they did not entertain Lodgers themselves, they would recommend me to some agreeable Family, where I shou'd be plac'd to my content.

If this Woman had known my real Circumstances, she would never have laid so many Snares, and taken so many weary steps to catch a poor desolate Creature that was good for little when it was caught; and indeed I, whose case was almost desperate, and thought I cou'd not be much worse, was not very anxious about what might befall me, provided they did me no personal Injury; so I suffered my self, tho' not without a great deal of Invitation and great Professions of sincere Friendship and real Kindness, *I say* I suffer'd my self to be prevail'd upon to go with her, and accordingly I pack'd up my Baggage, and put my self in a Posture for a Journey, tho' I did not absolutely know whither I was to go.

And now I found my self in great Distress; what little I had in the World was all in Money, except as before, a little Plate, some Linnen, and my Cloaths; as for Household stuff I had little or none, for I had liv'd always in Lodgings; but I had not one Friend in the World with whom to trust that little I had, or to direct me how to dispose of it, and this perplex'd me Night and Day; I thought of the Bank, and of the other Companies in *London*, but I had no Friend to commit the Management of it to, and to keep and carry about with me Bank Bills, Talleys, Orders, and such things, I look'd upon it as unsafe; that if they were lost my Money was lost, and then I was undone; and on the other hand I might be robb'd, and perhaps murder'd in a strange place for them; this perplex'd me strangely, and what to do I knew not.

It came in my Thoughts one Morning that I would go to the *Bank* my self, where I had often been to receive the Interest of some Bills I had, which had Interest payable on them, and where I had found the Clark,[2] to whom I applyed my self, very Honest and Just to me, and particularly so fair one time, that when I had miss-told my Money, and taken less than my due, and was coming away, he set me to rights and gave me the rest, which he might have put into his own Pocket.

I went to him, and represented my Case very plainly, *and ask'd if he would trouble himself to be my Adviser, who was a poor friendless Widow, and knew not what to do:* He told me, if I desir'd his Opinion of any thing within the reach of his Business, he would do his Endeavour that I should not be wrong'd, but that he would also help me to a good sober Person who was a grave Man of his Acquaintance, who was a Clark in such business too, tho' not in their House, whose Judgment was good, and whose Honesty I might depend upon, *for,* added he, *I will answer for him, and for every step he takes; if he wrongs you,* Madam, *of one Farthing, it shall lye at my door, I will make it good;* and he delights to assist People in such Cases, he does it as an act of Charity.

I was a little at a stand at this Discourse, but after some pause I told him, I had rather have depended upon him because I had found him honest, but if that cou'd not be, I would take his Recommendation sooner than any ones else; *I dare say,* Madam, says he, *that you will be as well satisfied with my Friend as with me, and he is thoroughly able to assist you, which I am not*; it seems he had his Hands full of the Business of the Bank, and had engag'd to meddle with no other Business than that of his Office, which I heard afterwards, but did not understand then: He added, that his Friend should take nothing of me for his Advice or Assistance, and this indeed encourag'd me very much.

He appointed the same Evening after the Bank was shut and Business over, for me to meet him and his Friend; and indeed as soon as I saw his Friend, and he began but to talk of the Affair, I was fully satisfied that I had a very honest Man to deal with; his Countenance spoke it, and his Character, as I heard afterwards, was every where so good, that I had no room for any more doubts upon me.

After the first meeting, in which I only said what I had said before, we parted, and he appointed me to come the next Day to him, *telling me* I might in the mean time satisfie my self of him by

2. Clerk.

enquiry, which however I knew not how well to do, having no
Acquaintance my self.

Accordingly I met him the next Day, when I entered more freely
with him into my Case, *I told him my* Circumstances at large, that
I was a Widow come over from *America,* perfectly desolate and
friendless; that I had a little Money, and but a little, and was
almost distracted for fear of losing it, having no Friend in the
World to trust with the management of it; that I was going into
the North of *England* to live cheap, that my stock might not waste;
that I would willingly Lodge my Money in the Bank, but that I
durst not carry the Bills about me, and the like, as above; and how
to Correspond about it, or with who, I knew not.

He told me I might lodge the Money in the Bank as an Account,
and its being entred in the Books would entitle me to the Money at
any time, and if I was in the North might draw Bills on the Cash-
ire and receive it when I would; but that then it would be esteem'd
as running Cash, and the Bank would give no Interest for it; that I
might buy Stock with it, and so it would lye in store for me, but
that then if I wanted to dispose of it, I must come up to Town on
purpose to Transfer it, and even it would be with some difficulty I
should receive the half yearly Dividend, unless I was here in Person,
or had some Friend I could trust with having the Stock in his
Name to do it for me, and that would have the same difficulty in it
as before; and with that he look'd hard at me and *smil'd a little*; at
last, *says he*, why do you not get a head Steward,[3] Madam, that
may take you and your Money together into keeping, and then you
would have the trouble taken off of your Hands? Ay, Sir, and the
Money too it may be, *said I*, for truly *I find the hazard that way is
as much as 'tis t'other way*; but I remember, *I said*, secretly to my
self, I wish you would ask me the Question fairly, I would consider
very seriously on it before I said NO.

He went on a good way with me, and I thought once or twice he
was in earnest, but to my real Affliction, I found at last he had a
Wife; but when he own'd he had a Wife he shook his Head, and
said with some concern, that indeed he had *a Wife,* and *no Wife:* I
began to think he had been in the Condition of my late Lover, and
that his Wife had been Distemper'd or Lunatick, or some such
thing: However, we had not much more Discourse at that time, but
he told me he was in too much hurry of business then, but that if I
would come home to his House after their Business was over, he
would by that time consider what might be done for me, to put my
Affairs in a Posture of Security: I told him I would come, and
desir'd to know where he liv'd: He gave me a Direction in Writing,
and when he gave it me he read it to me, and said, there 'tis,

3. A manager (specifically, a husband).

Madam, if you dare trust your self with me: Yes, Sir, *said I*, I believe I may venture to trust you with my self, for you have a Wife you say, and I don't want a Husband; besides, I dare trust you with my Money, which is all I have in the World, and if that were gone, I may trust my self any where.

He said some things in Jest that were very handsome and mannerly, and would have pleas'd me very well if they had been in earnest; *but that pass'd over*, I took the Directions, and appointed to attend him at his House at seven a Clock the same Evening.

When I came he made several Proposals for my placing my Money in the Bank, in order to my having Interest for it; but still some difficulty or other came in the way, which he objected as not safe; and I found such a sincere disinterested Honesty in him, that I began to muse with my self, that I had certainly found the honest Man I wanted; and that I could never put my self into better Hands; so I told him with a great deal of frankness that I had never met with Man or Woman yet that I could trust, or in whom I cou'd think my self safe, but that I saw he was so disinterestedly concern'd for my safety that *I said* I would freely trust him with the management of that little I had, if he would accept to be Steward for a poor Widow that could give him no Salary.

He smil'd, and standing up with great Respect saluted me; he told me he could not but take it very kindly that I had so good an Opinion of him; that he would not deceive me, that he would do any thing in his Power to serve me and expect no Sallary; but that he cou'd not by any means accept of a Trust, that it might bring him to be suspected of Self-interest, and that if I should die he might have Disputes with my Executors, which he should be very loth to encumber himself with.

I told him if those were all his Objections I would soon remove them, and convince him that there was not the least room for any difficulty; for that *first* as for suspecting him, if ever I should do it now was the time to suspect him, and not put the Trust into his Hands, and whenever I did suspect him, he could but throw it up then and refuse to go any farther; *Then* as to Executors, I assur'd him I had no Heirs, nor any Relations in *England*, and I would have neither Heirs or Executors but himself, unless I should alter my Condition before I died, and then his Trust and Trouble should cease together, which however I had no prospect of yet; but I told him if I died as I was, it should be all his own, and he would deserve it by being so faithful to me as I was satisfied he would be.

He chang'd his Countenance at this Discourse, and ask'd me how I came to have so much good will for him? and looking very much pleas'd, said, he might very lawfully wish he was a single Man for my sake; I smil'd and told him, that as he was not, my offer could have no design upon him in it, and to wish as he did was not to be allow'd, 'twas Criminal to his Wife.

He told me I was wrong; for, *says he*, Madam, as I said before, I have a Wife and no Wife, and 'twould be no Sin to me to wish her hang'd, if that were all; I know nothing of your Circumstances that way, Sir, *said I*; but it cannot be innocent to wish your Wife dead; I tell you, *says he again*, she is a Wife and no Wife; you don't know what I am, or what she is.

That's true, *said I*, Sir, I do not know what you are, but I believe you to be an honest Man, and that's the cause of all my Confidence in you.

Well, well, *says he*, and so I am, *I hope*, too; but I am something else too, Madam; for, *says he*, to be plain with you, I am a *Cuckold*, and she is a *Whore*; he spoke it in a kind of Jest, but it was with such an awkward smile, that I perceiv'd it was what stuck very close to him, and he look'd dismally when he said it.

That alters the case indeed, Sir, *said I*, as to that part you were speaking of; but a *Cuckold* you know may be an honest Man, it does not alter that Case at all; besides I think, *said I*, since your Wife is so dishonest to you, you are too honest to her to own her for your Wife; but that, *said I*, is what I have nothing to do with.

Nay, *says he*, I do think to clear my Hands of her, for to be plain with you, Madam, *added he*, I am no contented Cuckold neither: *On the other hand*, I assure you it provokes me to the highest degree, but I can't help my self, she that will be *a Whore*, will be a *Whore*.

I wav'd[4] the Discourse, and began to talk of my Business, but I found he could not have done with it, so I let him alone, and he went on to tell me all the Circumstances of his Case, too long to relate here; particularly, that having been out of *England* some time before he came to the Post he was in, she had had two Children in the mean time by an Officer of the Army; and that when he came to *England*, and, upon her Submission,[5] took her again, and maintain'd her very well, yet she run away from him with a Linnen-Draper's Apprentice, robb'd him of what she could come at, and continued to live from him still; so that, Madam, *says he*, she is a Whore not by Necessity, which is the common Bait of your Sex, but by Inclination, and for the sake of the Vice.

Well, I pitied him and wish'd him well rid of her, and still would have talk'd of my Business, but it would not do; at last he looks steadily at me, *look you*, Madam, *says he*, you came to ask Advice of me, and I will serve you as faithfully as if you were my own Sister; but I must turn the Tables, since you oblige me to do it, and

4. Waived (abandoned).
5. Agreeing to be corrected, her sup- posed humiliation.

are so friendly to me, and I think I must ask advice of you; *tell me
what must a poor abus'd Fellow do with* a Whore? *what can I do
to do my self Justice upon her?*

Alas, *Sir, says I,* 'tis a Case too nice for me to advise in, but it
seems she has run away from you, so you are rid of her fairly; what
can you desire more? Ay, she is gone indeed, *said he,* but I am not
clear of her for all that.

That's true, *says I,* she may indeed run you into Debt, but the
Law has furnish'd you with Methods to prevent that also, you may
Cry her down,[6] *as they call it.*

No, no, *says he,* that is not the Case neither, I have taken care of
all that; 'tis not that part that I speak of, but I would be rid of her
so that I might marry again.

Well, Sir, *says I,* then you must Divorce her; if you can prove
what you say, you may certainly get that done, and then, I suppose,
you are free.

That's very tedious and expensive, *says he.*

Why, *says I,* if you can get any Woman you like to take your
word, I suppose your Wife would not dispute the Liberty with you
that she takes herself.

Ay, *says he,* but 'twou'd be hard to bring an honest Woman to
do that; and for the other sort, *says he,* I have had enough of her to
meddle with any more Whores.

It occurr'd to me presently, I would have taken your word with
all my Heart, if you had but ask'd me the Question; but that was to
my self; *to him I reply'd,* why you shut the Door against any honest
Woman accepting you, for you condemn all that should venture
upon you at once, and conclude, that really a Woman that takes
you now, can't be honest.

Why, *says he,* I wish you would satisfie me that an honest
Woman would take me, I'd venture it; and then turns short upon
me, *will you take me,* Madam?

That's not a fair Question, *says I,* after what you have said; however, lest you should think I wait only for a Recantation of it, I
shall answer you plainly NO *not I;* my Business is of another kind
with you, and I did not expect you would have turn'd my serious
Application to you in my own distracted Case, into a Comedy.

Why, Madam, *says he,* my Case is as distracted as yours can be,
and I stand in as much need of Advice as you do, for I think if I
have not Relief some where, I shall be mad my self, and I know not
what course to take, I protest to you.

Why, Sir, *says I,* 'tis easie to give Advice in your Case, much
easier than it is in mine; speak then, *says he,* I beg of you, for now
you encourage me.

6. Publicly abrogate all responsibility for her debts.

Why, *says I*, if your Case is so plain as you say it is, you may be legally Divorc'd, and then you may find honest Women enough to ask the Question of fairly, the Sex is not so scarce that you can want a Wife.

Well then, *said he*, I am in earnest; I'll take your Advice, but shall I ask you one Question seriously before hand?

Any Question, *said I*, but that you did before.

No, that Answer will not do, *said he*, for, in short, that is the Question I shall ask.

You may ask what Questions you please, but you have my Answer to that already, *said I*; besides Sir, *said I*, can you think so Ill of me as that I would give any Answer to such a Question beforehand? Can any Woman alive believe you in earnest, or think you design any thing but to banter her?

Well, well, *says he*, I do not banter you, I am in earnest; consider of it.

But, Sir, *says I, a little gravely*, I came to you about my own Business; I beg of you let me know, what you will advise me to do?

I will be prepar'd, *says he*, against you come again.

Nay, *says I*, you have forbid my coming any more.

Why so, *said he*, and look'd a little surpriz'd?

Because, *said I*, you can't expect I should visit you on the account you talk of.

Well, *says he*, you shall promise me to come again however, and I will not say any more of it till I have gotten the Divorce, but I desire you will prepare to be better condition'd when that's done, for you shall be the Woman, or I will not be Divorc'd at all: Why I owe it to your unlooked for kindness, if it were to nothing else, but I have other Reasons too.

He could not have said any thing in the World that pleas'd me better; however, I knew that the way to secure him was to stand off while the thing was so remote, as it appear'd to be, and that it was time enough to accept of it when he was able to perform it; so I said very respectfully to him, it was time enough to consider of these things, when he was in a Condition to talk of them; in the mean time I told him, I was going a great way from him, and he would find Objects enough to please him better: We broke off here for the present, and he made me promise him to come again the next Day, for his Resolutions upon my own Business, which after some pressing I did; tho' had he seen farther into me, I wanted no pressing on that Account.

I came the next Evening accordingly, and brought my Maid with me, *to let him see* that I kept a Maid, but I sent her away, as soon as I was gone in: He would have had me let the Maid have staid, but I would not, but order'd her aloud to come for me again about Nine a-Clock, but he forbid that, and told me he would see me safe Home, which by the way I was not very well pleas'd with, supposing he might do that to know where I liv'd, and enquire into my Character and Circumstances: However, I ventur'd that, for all that the People there or thereabout knew of me, was to my Advantage; and all the Character he had of me, after he had enquir'd, was *that I was a Woman of Fortune*, and that I was a very modest sober Body; which whether true or not in the Main, yet you may see how necessary it is, for all Women who expect any thing in the World to preserve the Character of their Virtue, even when perhaps they may have sacrific'd the Thing itself.

I found, *and was not a little pleas'd with it*, that he had provided a Supper for me: I found also he liv'd very handsomely, and had a House very handsomely furnish'd, all which I was rejoyc'd at indeed, for I look'd upon it as all my own.

We had now a second Conference upon the Subject matter of the last Conference: He laid his business very Home indeed; he protested his Affection to me, and indeed I had no room to doubt it; he declar'd that it began from the first Moment I talk'd with him, and long before I had mention'd leaving my Effects with him; 'tis no matter when it begun, *thought I*, if it will but hold, 'twill be well enough: *He then told me*, how much the offer I had made of trusting him with my Effects, and leaving them to him, had engag'd him; so I intended it should, *thought I*, but then I thought you had been a single Man too: After we had Supp'd, I observ'd he press'd me very hard to drink two or three Glasses of Wine, which however I declin'd, but Drank one Glass or two: He then told he had a Proposal to make to me, which I should promise him I would not take ill, if I should not grant it: I told him I hop'd he would make no dishonourable Proposal to me, especially in his own House, and that if it was such, I desir'd he would not propose it, that I might not be oblig'd to offer any Resentment to him that did not become the respect I profess'd for him, and the Trust I had plac'd in him, in coming to his House; and beg'd of him he would give me leave to go away, and accordingly began to put on my Gloves and prepare to be gone, tho' at the same time I no more intended it than he intended to let me.

Well, he importun'd me not to talk of going; he assur'd me he had no dishonourable thing in his Thoughts about me, and was very far from offering any thing to me that was dishonourable and if I thought so, he would chuse to say no more of it.

That part I did not relish at all; I told him I was ready to hear any thing that he had to say, depending that he would say nothing unworthy of himself, or unfit for me to hear; upon this, he told me his Proposal was this, That I would Marry him, tho' he had not yet

obtain'd the Divorce from the Whore his Wife; and to satisfie me
that he meant honourably, he would promise not to desire me to
live with him, or go to Bed to him till the Divorce was obtain'd:
My Heart said yes to this offer at first Word, but it was necessary to
Play the Hypocrite a little more with him; so I seem'd to decline
the Motion with some warmth, and besides a little Condemning
the thing as unfair, told him that such a Proposal could be of no
Signification, but to entangle us both in great Difficulties; for if he
should not at last obtain the Divorce, yet we could not dissolve the
Marriage, neither could we proceed in it; so that if he was disappointed in the Divorce, I left him to consider what a Condition we
should both be in.

In short, I carried on the Argument against this so far, that I
convinc'd him, it was not a Proposal that had any Sense in it:
WELL then he went from it to another, and that was, that I would
Sign and Seal a Contract with him, Conditioning to Marry him as
soon as the Divorce was obtain'd, and to be void if he could not
obtain it.

I told him such a thing was more Rational than the other; but
as this was the first time that ever I could imagine him weak
enough to be in earnest in this Affair, I did not use to say YES at
first asking, I would consider of it.

I play'd with this Lover as an Angler does with a Trout: I found
I had him fast on the Hook, so I jested with his new Proposal and
put him off: I told him he knew little of me, and bade him enquire
about me; I let him also go Home with me to my Lodging, tho' I
would not ask him to go in, for I told him it was not Decent.

In short, I ventur'd to avoid Signing a Contract of Marriage, and
the Reason why I did it, was because the Lady that had invited me
so earnestly to go with her into *Lancashire* insisted so possitively
upon it, and promised me such great Fortunes, and such fine things
there, that I was tempted to go and try; perhaps, *said I*, I may
mend myself very much, and then I made no scruple in my
Thoughts of quitting my honest Citizen, who I was not so much in
Love with, as not to leave him for a Richer.

In a Word I avoided a Contract; but told him I would go into
the *North*, that he should know where to write to me by the Consequence of the Business I had entrusted with him, that I would give
him a sufficient Pledge of My Respect for him; for I would leave
almost all I had in the World in his Hands; and I would thus far
give him my Word, that as soon as he had sued out a Divorce from
his first Wife, if he would send me an Account of it, I would come
up to *London*, and that then we would talk seriously of the Matter.

It was a base Design I went with, *that I must confess*, tho' I
was invited thither with a Design much worse than mine was,

as the Sequel will discover; well I went with my Friend, *as I call'd her*, into *Lancashire*; all the way we went she Caressed me with the utmost appearance of a sincere undissembled Affection; treated me except my Coach hire all the way; and her Brother brought a Gentleman's Coach to *Warrington* to receive us, and we were carried from thence to *Liverpool* with as much Ceremony as I could desire: We were also entertain'd at a Merchant's House in *Liverpool* three or four Days very handsomely: I forbear to tell his Name, because of what follow'd; then she told me she would carry me to an Uncles House of hers, where we should be nobly entertain'd; she did so, her Uncle as she call'd him, sent a Coach and four Horses for us, and we were carried near forty Miles, I know not whither.

We came however to a Gentleman's Seat, where was a numerous Family, a large Park, extraordinry Company indeed, and where she was call'd Cousin; I told her if she had resolv'd to bring me into such Company as this, she should have let me have prepar'd my self, and have furnish'd my self with better Cloths; the Ladies took notice of that, and told me very genteely, they did not value People in their Country so much by their Cloths, as they did in *London*; that their Cousin had fully inform'd them of my Quality, and that I did not want Cloths to set me off; in short, they entertain'd me not like what I was, but like what they thought I had been, Namely, a Widow Lady of a great Fortune.

The first Discovery I made here was that the Family were all *Roman Catholicks*,[7] and the Cousin too, who I call'd my Friend; however, *I must say*, that nothing in the World could behave better to me; and I had all the Civility shown me that I could have had if I had been of their Opinion: The Truth is, I had not so much Principle of any kind, as to be Nice in Point of Religion; and I presently learn'd to speak favourably of the *Romish Church*; particularly I told them I saw little, but the prejudice of Education in all the Differences that were among Christians about Religion, and if it had so happen'd that my Father had been a *Roman Catholick*, I doubted not but I should have been as well pleas'd with their Religion as my own.

This oblig'd them in the highest Degree, and as I was besieg'd Day and Night with good Company and pleasant Discourse, so I had two or three old Ladies that lay at me upon the Subject of Religion too; I was so Complaisant that tho' I would not compleatly engage, yet I made no scruple to be present at their Mass, and to conform to all their Gestures as they shew'd me the Pattern, but I would not come too cheap;[8] so that I only in the main

---

7. A large Catholic populace lived in the northwestern county of Lancashire, which was a chief center of Jacobite sympathy during the rebellion of 1715.
8. Seem to be converted too easily.

encourag'd them to expect that I would turn *Roman Catholick,*
if I was instructed in the *Catholick Doctrine* as they call'd it, and
so the matter rested.

I stay'd here about six Weeks; and then my Conducter led me
back to a Country Village about six Miles from *Liverpool,* where
her Brother, (as she call'd him) came to Visit me in his own Chariot, and in a very good Figure, with two Footmen in a good Livery;
and the next thing was to make Love to me: As it had happen'd to
me, one would think I could not have been cheated, and indeed I
thought so myself, having a safe Card at home, which I resolv'd not
to quit, unless, I could mend myself very much: However in all
appearance this Brother was a Match worth my lissening to, and
the least his Estate was valued at was a 1000 *l.* a Year, but the
Sister said it was worth 1500 *l.* a Year, and lay most of it in *Ireland.*

I that was a great Fortune, and pass'd for such, was above being
ask'd how much my Estate was; and my false Friend taking it upon
a foolish hearsay had rais'd it from 500 *l.* to 5000 *l.* and by the time
she came into the Country she call'd it 15000 *l.* The *Irishman,* for
such I understood him to be, was stark Mad at this Bait: In short,
he Courted me, made me Presents, and run in Debt like a mad
Man for the Expences of his Equipage, and of his Courtship: He
had, to give him his due, the Appearance of an extraordinary fine
Gentleman; he was Tall, well Shap'd, and had an extraordinary
Address; talk'd as naturally of his Park and his Stables, of his
Horses, his Game-Keepers, his Woods, his Tenants, and his Servants, as if we had been in the Mansion-House, and I had seen them
all about me.

He never so much as ask'd me about my Fortune or Estate, but
assur'd me that when we came to *Dublin* he would Joynture[9] me in
600 *l.* a Year good Land; and that he would enter into a Deed of
Settlement or Contract here, for the performance of it.

This was such Language indeed as I had not been us'd to, and I
was here beaten out of all my Measures;[1] I had a she Devil in my
Bosom, every Hour telling me how great her Brother liv'd: One
time she would come for my Orders, how I would have my Coaches
painted, and how lin'd; and another time what Cloths my Page
should wear: In short, my Eyes were dazl'd, I had now lost my
Power of saying No, and to cut the Story short, I consented to be
married, but to be the more private we were carried farther into the
Country, and married by a Romish Clergyman,[2] which I was assur'd
would marry us as effectually as a Church of *England* Parson.

I cannot say, but I had some Reflections in this Affair, upon the

9. He would hold the acreage in both
their names, which was usually done only
among husband and wife; therefore, he
is, in effect, proposing to marry Moll.

1. Standards of judgment.
2. Roman Catholic priest, who could in
fact perform legal marriages.

dishonourable forsaking my faithful Citizen, who lov'd me sincerely, and who was endeavouring to quit himself of a scandalous Whore, by whom he had been indeed barbarously us'd, and promis'd himself infinite Happiness in his new choice; which choice was now giving up her self to another in a manner almost as scandalous as hers could be.

But the glittering show of a great Estate, and of fine Things, which the deceived Creature that was now my Deceiver represented every Hour to my Imagination, hurried me away, and gave me no time to think of *London*, or of any thing there, much less of the Obligation I had to a Person of infinitely more real Merit than what was now before me.

But the thing was done, I was now in the Arms of my new Spouse, who appear'd still the same as before; great even to Magnificence, and nothing less than a Thousand Pound a Year could support the ordinary Equipage he appear'd in.

After we had been marry'd about a Month, he began to talk of my going to *West-chester* in order to embark for *Ireland*. However, he did not hurry me, for we staid near three Weeks longer, and then he sent to *Chester* for a Coach to meet us at the *Black Rock*, as they call it, over-against *Liverpool*: Thither we went in a fine Boat they call a Pinnace with Six Oars, his Servants, and Horses, and Baggage going in the Ferry Boat. He made his excuse to me, that he had no Acquaintance at *Chester*, but he would go before and get some handsome Apartment for me at a private House; I ask'd him how long we should stay at *Chester*? he said not at all any longer than one Night or two, but he would immediately hire a Coach to go to *Holyhead*; then I told him he should by no means give himself the trouble to get private Lodgings for one Night or two, for that *Chester* being a great Place, I made no doubt but there would be very good Inns and Accommodation enough; so we lodg'd at an Inn in the West Street, not far from the Cathedral, I forget what Sign it was at.

Here my Spouse talking of my going to *Ireland*, ask'd me if I had no Affairs to settle at *London* before we went off; I told him no not of any great Consequence, but what might be done as well by Letter from *Dublin*: Madam, says he very respectfully, I suppose the greatest part of your Estate, which my Sister tells me is most of it in Money in the Bank of *England*, lies secure enough, but in case it requir'd Transferring, or any way altering its Property, it might be necessary to go up to *London* and settle those things before we went over.

I seemed to look strange at it, and told him I knew not what he meant; that I had no Effects in the Bank of *England* that I knew of; and I hoped he could not say that I had ever told him I had:

No, he said, I had not told him so, but his Sister had said the greatest part of my Estate lay there; and *I only mention'd it my Dear*,
said he, *that if there was any occasion to settle it, or order any
thing about it, we might not be oblig'd to the hazard and trouble of
another Voyage back again*, for he added, that he did not care to
venture me too much upon the Sea.

I was surpriz'd at this talk, and began to consider very seriously,
what the meaning of it must be? and it presently occurr'd to me
that my Friend, who call'd him Brother, had represented me in
Colours which were not my due; and I thought, since it was come
to that pitch, that I would know the bottom of it before I went out
of *England*, and before I should put my self into I knew not whose
Hands, in a strange Country.

Upon this I call'd his Sister into my Chamber the next Morning,
and letting her know the Discourse her Brother and I had been
upon the Evening before, I conjur'd her to tell me, what she had
said to him, and upon what Foot[3] it was that she had made this
Marriage? She own'd that she had told him that I was a great Fortune, and said, that she was told so at *London: Told so*, says I
warmly, *did I ever tell you so*? No, she said, it was true I did not
tell her so, but I had said several times that what I had was in my
own disposal: I did so, *return'd I very quickly and hastily*, but I
never told you I had any thing call'd a Fortune; no not that I had
one Hundred Pounds, or the value of an Hundred Pounds in the
World; and how did it consist with my being a Fortune, *said I*, that
I should come here into the North of *England* with you, only upon
the account of living cheap? At these words which I spoke warm
and high, my Husband, and her Brother, as she call'd him, came
into the Room, and I desir'd him to come and sit down, for I had
something of moment to say before them both, which it was absolutely necessary he should hear.

He look'd a little disturb'd at the assurance with which I seem'd
to speak it, and came and sat down by me, having first shut the
Door; upon which I began, for I was very much provok'd, and turning my self to him, I am afraid, says I, *my Dear*, for I spoke with
kindness on his side, that you have a very great abuse put upon you,
and an Injury done you never to be repair'd in your marrying me,
which however as I have had no hand in it, I desire I may be fairly
acquitted of it, and that the blame may lie where it ought to lie,
and no where else, for I wash my Hands of every part of it.

What Injury can be done me, *my Dear*, says he, in marrying you?
I hope it is to my Honour and Advantage every way; I will soon
explain it to you, says I, and I fear you will have no reason to think

3. Arrangement.

your self well us'd, but I will convince you, *my Dear, says I again*, that I have had no hand in it, and there I stop'd a while.

He look'd now scar'd and wild, and began, I believ'd, to suspect what follow'd; however, looking towards me, and saying only *go on*, he sat silent, as if to hear what I had more to say; so I went on; I ask'd you last Night, said I, speaking to him, if ever I made any boast to you of my Estate, or ever told you I had any Estate in the Bank of *England*, or any where else, and you own'd I had not, as is most true; and I desire you will tell me here, before your Sister, if ever I gave you any Reason from me to think so, or that ever we had any Discourse about it; and he own'd again I had not, *but said*, I had appeared always as a Woman of Fortune, and he depended on it that I was so, and hoped he was not deceived. I am not enquiring yet whether you have been deceived or not, *said I*, I fear you have, *and I too*; but I am clearing my self from the unjust Charge of being concern'd in deceiving you.

I have been now asking your Sister if ever I told her of any Fortune or Estate I had, or gave her any Particulars of it; and she owns I never did: And pray, Madam, *said I, turning my self to her*, be so just to me, before your Brother, to charge me, if you can, if ever I pretended to you that I had an Estate; and why, if I had, should I come down into this Country with you on purpose to spare *that little I had*, and live cheap? She could not deny one word, but said she had been told in *London* that I had a very great Fortune, and that it lay in the Bank of *England*.

And now, *Dear Sir*, said I, *turning my self to my new Spouse again*, be so just to me as to tell me who has abus'd both you and me so much as to make you believe I was a Fortune, and prompt you to court me to this Marriage? He cou'd not speak a word, but pointed to her; and after some more pause, flew out in the most furious Passion that ever I saw a Man in my Life; cursing her, and calling her all the Whores and hard Names he could think of; and that she had ruin'd him, declaring that she had told him I had Fifteen Thousand Pounds, and that she was to have Five Hundred Pounds of him for procuring this Match for him: He then added, directing his Speech to me, that she was none of his Sister, but had been his Whore for two Years before, that she had had One Hundred Pound of him in part of this Bargain, and that he was utterly undone if things were as I said; and in his raving *he swore* he would let her Heart's Blood out immediately, which frighted her and me too; *she cried*, said she had been told so in the House where I Lodg'd; but this aggravated him more than before, that she should put so far upon him, and run things such a length upon no other Authority than *a hear-say*; and then turning to me again, said very honestly, he was afraid we were both undone; for to be plain, *my Dear*, I have no Estate, *says he*, what little I had, this Devil has made me run out in waiting on you, and putting me into this Equipage; she took the opportunity of his being earnest in talking with me, and got out of the Room, and I never saw her more.

I was confounded now as much as he, and knew not what to say: I thought many ways that I had the worst of it, but his saying he was undone, and that he had no Estate neither, put me into a meer distraction; why, *says I to him*, this has been a hellish Juggle, for we are married here upon the foot of a double Fraud; you are undone by the Disappointment it seems, and if I had had a Fortune I had been cheated too, for you say you have nothing.

You would indeed have been cheated, my Dear, *says he*, but you would not have been undone, for Fifteen Thousand Pound would have maintain'd us both very handsomly in this Country; and I assure you, *added he*, I had resolv'd to have dedicated every Groat of it to you; I would not have wrong'd you of a Shilling, and the rest I would have made up in my Affection to you, and Tenderness of you as long as I liv'd.

This was very honest indeed, and I really believe he spoke as he intended, and that he was a Man that was as well qualified to make me happy, as to his Temper and Behaviour, as any Man ever was; but his having no Estate, and being run into Debt on this ridiculous account in the Country, made all the Prospect dismal and dreadful, and I knew not what to say, or what to think of my self.

I told him it was very unhappy that so much Love, and so much Good-nature, as I discovered in him, should be thus precipitated into Misery; that I saw nothing before us but Ruin, for as to me, it was my unhappiness that what little I had was not able to relieve us a Week, and with that I pull'd out a Bank Bill of 20 *l.* and eleven Guineas, which I told him I had saved out of my little Income; and that by the account that Creature had given me of the way of living in that Country, I expected it would maintain me three or four Year; that if it was taken from me I was left destitute, and he knew what the Condition of a Woman among strangers must be, if she had no Money in her Pocket; however, I told him if he would take it, there it was.

He told me with a great concern, and I thought I saw Tears stand in his Eyes, that he would not touch it, that he abhorr'd the thoughts of stripping me, and making me miserable; that on the contrary, he had Fifty Guineas left, which was all he had in the World, and he pull'd it out and threw it down on the Table, bidding me take it, tho' he were to starve for want of it.

I return'd, with the same concern for him, that I could not bear to hear him talk so; that on the contrary, if he could propose any probable method of living, I would do any thing that became me on my part, and that I would live as close and as narrow as he cou'd desire.

He beg'd of me to talk no more at that rate, for it would make him Distracted; he said he was bred a Gentleman, tho' he was reduced to a low Fortune; and that there was but one way left which he cou'd think of, and that would not do, unless I cou'd answer him one Question, which however he said he would not press me to; I told him I would answer it honestly; whether it would be to his Satisfaction or no, that I could not tell.

Why then, my Dear, tell me plainly, *says he* will the little you have keep us together in any Figure, or in any Station or Place, or will it not?

It was my happiness hitherto that I had not discovered myself or my Circumstances at all; no not so much as my Name; and seeing there was nothing to be expected from him, however good Humoured and however honest he seem'd to be, but to live on what I knew would soon be wasted, I resolv'd to conceal everything but the *Bank Bill*, and the Eleven Guineas which I had own'd; and I would have been very glad to have lost that, and have been set down where he took me up; I had indeed another *Bank Bill* about me of 30 *l*. which was the whole of what I brought with me as well to Subsist on in the Country, as not knowing what might offer; because this Creature, the *go-between* that had thus betray'd us both, had made me believe strange things of my Marrying to my Advantage in the Country, and I was not willing to be without Money whatever might happen. This Bill I concealed, and that made me the freer of the rest, in Consideration of his Circumstances, for I really pittied him heartily.

But to return to his Question, I told him I never willingly Deceiv'd him, and I never would: I was very sorry to tell him that the little I had would not Subsist us; that it was not sufficient to Subsist me alone in the *South* Country; and that this was the Reason that made me put my self into the Hands of that Woman, who call'd him Brother, she having assur'd me that I might Board very handsomely at a Town call'd *Manchester*, where I had not yet been, for about six Pound a Year, and my whole Income not being above 15 *l*. a Year, I thought I might live easie upon it, and wait for better things.

He shook his Head, and remain'd Silent, and a very melancholly Evening we had; however we Supped together, and lay together that Night, and when we had almost Supp'd he look'd a little better and more chearful, and call'd for a Bottle of Wine; *come my Dear, says he*, tho' the Case is bad, it is to no purpose to be dejected, come be as easie as you can, I will endeavour, to find out some way or other to live; if you can but Subsist your self, that is better than nothing, I must try the World again; a Man ought to think like a Man: To be Discourag'd, is to yield to the Misfortune; with this he fill'd a Glass, and Drank to me, holding my Hand, and pressing it hard in his Hand all the while the Wine went down, and Protesting afterward his main concern was for me.

It was really a truly gallant Spirit he was of, and it was the more Grievous to me: 'Tis something of Relief even to be undone by a Man of Honour, rather than by a Scoundrel; but here the greatest Disappointment was on his side, for he had really spent a great deal of Money, deluded by this Madam the Procuress; and it was very remarkable on what poor Terms she proceeded; first the baseness of the Creature herself is to be observ'd, who for the getting One Hundred Pound herself, could be content to let him spend Three or Four more, tho' perhaps it was all he had in the World, and more than all; when she had not the least Ground, more than a little Tea-Table Chat, to say that I had any Estate, or was a Fortune, *or the like*: It is true the Design of deluding a Woman of a Fortune, if I had been so, was base enough; the putting the Face of great Things upon poor Circumstances was a Fraud, and bad enough; but the Case a little differ'd too, and that in his Favour, for he was not a Rake that made a Trade to delude Women, and as some have done get six or seven Fortunes after one another, and then rifle and run away from them; but he was really a Gentleman, unfortunate and low, but had liv'd well; and tho' if I had had a Fortune I should have been enrag'd at the Slut for betraying me; yet really for the Man, a Fortune would not have been ill bestow'd on him, for he was a lovely Person indeed; of generous Principles, good Sense, and of abundance of good Humour.

We had a great deal of close Conversation that Night, for we neither of us Slept much; he was as Penitent for having put all those Cheats upon me as if it had been Felony, and that he was going to Execution; he offer'd me again every Shilling of the Money he had about him, and said, he would go into the Army and seek the World for more.

I ask'd him, why he would be so unkind to carry me into *Ireland*, when I might suppose he cou'd not have Subsisted me there? He took me in his Arms, my Dear, *said he*, depend upon it, I never design'd to go to *Ireland* at all, much less to have carried you thither, but came hither to be out of the Observation of the People who had heard what I pretended to, and withal, that No Body might ask me for Money before I was furnish'd to supply them.

But where then, *said I*, were we to have gone next?

Why my Dear, *said he*, I'll confess the whole Scheme to you as I had laid it; I purpos'd here to ask you something about your Estate, as you see I did, and when you, as I expected you would had enter'd into some Account with me of the particular, I would have made an excuse to you, to have put off our Voyage to *Ireland* for some time, and to have gone first towards *London*.

Then my Dear, *said he*, I resolv'd to have confess'd all the Circumstances of my own Affairs to you, and let you know I had indeed made use of these Artifices to obtain your Consent to marry me, but had now nothing to do but to ask you Pardon, and to tell you abundantly, *as I have said above*,⁴ I would endeavour to make you forget what was past, by the felicity of the Days to come.

Truly, *said I to him*, I find you would soon have conquer'd me; and it is my Affliction now, that I am not in a Condition to let you see how easily I should have been reconcil'd to you; and have pass'd by all the Tricks you had put upon me, in Recompence of so much good Humour; but my Dear, *said I*, what can we do now? We are both undone, and what better are we for our being reconcil'd together, seeing we have nothing to live on.

We propos'd a great many things, but nothing could offer, where there was nothing to begin with: He beg'd me at last to talk no more of it, for *he said*, I would break his Heart; so we talk'd of other things a little, till at last he took a Husbands leave of me, and so we went to Sleep.

He rise⁵ before me in the Morning, and indeed having lain Awake almost all Night, I was very sleepy, and lay till near Eleven a-Clock, in this time he took his Horses and three Servants, and all his Linnen and Baggage, and away he went, leaving a short, but moving Letter for me on the Table, as follows:

My Dear,

I am a Dog; I have abus'd you; but I have been drawn in to do it by a base Creature, contrary to my Principle and the general Practice of my Life: Forgive me, my Dear! I ask you Pardon with the greatest Sincerity; I am the most miserable of Men, in having deluded you: I have been so happy to Possess you, and am now so wretch'd as to be forc'd to fly from you: Forgive me, my Dear; once more I say forgive me! I am not able to see you Ruin'd by me, and myself unable to Support you: Our Marriage is nothing, I shall never be able to see you again: I here discharge you from it; if you can Marry to your Advantage do not decline it on my Account; I here swear to you on my Faith, and on the Word of a Man of Honour, I will never disturb your Repose if I should know of it, which however is not likely: On the other Hand, if you should

4. The editor of the second edition deleted "as I have said above," correctly realizing that only Moll can use these words since she is narrator. Moll and other characters use the expression, "as I have said" throughout the narrative, and although the oversight of adding "above" is probably attributable to Defoe, a composing stick error is possible. 5. "Rise" would be acceptable eighteenth-century past tense and should be pronounced to rhyme with "his."

not Marry, and if good Fortune should befall me, it shall be all yours where ever you are.

I have put some of the Stock of Money I have left into your Pocket; take Places for your self and your Maid in the Stage-Coach, and go for London; *I hope it will bear your Charges thither, without breaking into your own: Again I sincerely ask your Pardon, and will do so, as often as I shall ever think of you.*

Adieu my Dear for Ever,

I am yours most Affectionatly,

J. E.

Nothing that ever befel me in my Life sunk so deep into my Heart as this Farewel: I reproach'd him a Thousand times in my Thoughts for leaving me, for I would have gone with him thro' the World, if I had beg'd my Bread. I felt in my Pocket, and there I found ten Guineas, his Gold Watch, and two little Rings, one a small Diamond Ring worth only about six Pound, and the other a plain Gold Ring.

I sat me down and look'd upon these Things two Hours together, and scarce spoke a Word, till my Maid interrupted me by telling me my Dinner was ready: I eat[6] but little, and after Dinner I fell into a vehement Fit of crying, every now and then, calling him by his Name, which was *James*, O *Jemy!* said I, *come back, come back*, I'll give you all I have; I'll beg, I'll starve with you, and thus I run Raving about the Room several times, and then sat down between whiles, and then walking about again, call'd upon him to *come back*, and then cry'd again; and thus I pass'd the Afternoon; till about seven a-Clock when it was near Dusk in the Evening, being *August*, when to my unspeakable Surprize he comes back into the Inn, but without a Servant, and comes directly up into my Chamber.

I was in the greatest Confusion imaginable, and so was he too: I could not imagine what should be the Occasion of it, and began to be at odds with myself whether to be glad or sorry; but my Affection byass'd all the rest, and it was impossible to conceal my Joy, which was too great for Smiles, for it burst out into Tears. He was no sooner entered the Room, but he run to me and took me in his Arms, holding me fast and almost stopping my Breath with his Kisses, but spoke not a Word; at length I began: my Dear, *said I*, how could you go away from me? To which he gave no Answer, for it was impossible for him to speak.

When our Extasies were a little over, he told me he was gone about 15 Mile, but it was not in his Power to go any farther, without coming back to see me again, and to take his Leave of me once more.

6. "Eat," in this instance, is another past tense commonly used in the eighteenth century; pronounced to rhyme with "get."

I told him how I had pass'd my time, and how loud I had call'd him to *come back* again; he told me he heard me very plain upon *Delamere Forest*, at a Place about 12 Miles off: *I smil'd; Nay says he*, do not think I am in Jest, for if ever I heard your Voice in my Life, I heard you call me aloud, and sometimes I thought I saw you running after me; why said I, what did I say? for I had not nam'd the Words to him; you call'd aloud, says he, and said, O *Jemy! O Jemy! come back, come back.*

I Laught at him; *my Dear says he*, do not Laugh, for depend upon it, I heard your Voice as plain as you hear mine now; if you please, I'll go before a Magistrate and make Oath of it; I then began to be amaz'd and surpriz'd, and indeed frighted, and told him what I had really done, and how I had call'd after him, as above.[7]

When we had amus'd ourselves a while about this, I said to him, well, you shall go away from me no more; I'll go all over the World with you rather: *He told me*, it would be a very difficult thing for him to leave me, but since it must be, he hoped I would make it as easie to me as I could; but as for him, it would be his Destruction, that he foresaw.

However he told me that he Consider'd he had left me to Travel to *London* alone, which was too long a Journey; and that as he might as well go that way, as any way else, he was resolv'd to see me safe thither, or near it; and if he did go away then without taking his leave, I should not take it ill of him, and this he made me promise.

He told me how he had dismiss'd his three Servants, sold their Horses, and sent the Fellows away to seek their Fortunes, and all in a little time, at a Town on the Road, I know not where; and *says he*, it cost me some Tears all alone by myself, to think how much happier they were than their Master, for they could go to the next Gentleman's House to see for a Service, whereas, *said he*, I knew not whither to go, or what to do with myself.

I told him, I was so compleatly miserable in parting with him, that I could not be worse; and that now he was come again, I would not go from him, if he would take me with him, let him go whither he would, or do what he would; and in the mean time I agreed that we would go together to *London*; but I could not be brought to Consent he should go away at last and not take his leave of me, as he propos'd to do; but told him Jesting, that if he did, I would call him back again as loud as I did before; Then I pull'd out his Watch and gave it him back, and his two Rings, and his Ten Guineas; but he would not take them, which made me very much suspect that he resolv'd to go off upon the Road, and leave me.

7. For a discussion of Defoe's interest in the supernatural see Rodney M. Baine, *Daniel Defoe and the Supernatural* (Athens, Ga., 1969).

The truth is, the Circumstances he was in, the passionate Expressions of his Letter, the kind Gentlemanly Treatment I had from him in all the Affair, with the Concern he show'd for me in it, his manner of Parting with that large Share which he gave me of his little Stock left, all these had joyn'd to make such Impressions on me, that I really lov'd him most tenderly, and could not bear the Thoughts of parting with him.

Two Days after this we quitted *Chester*, I in the Stage Coach, and he on Horseback; I dismiss'd my Maid at *Chester*; he was very much against my being without a Maid, but she being a Servant hired in the Country, and I resolving to keep no Servant at *London*, I told him it would have been barbarous to have taken the poor Wench, and have turn'd her away as soon as I came to Town; and it would also have been a needless Charge on the Road, so I satisfy'd him, and he was easie enough on that Score.

He came with me as far as *Dunstable*, within 30 Miles of *London*, and then he told me Fate and his own Misfortunes oblig'd him to leave me, and that it was not Convenient for him to go to *London* for Reasons which it was of no value to me to know, and I saw him preparing to go. The Stage Coach we were in did not usually stop at *Dunstable*, but I desiring it but for a Quarter of an Hour, they were content to stand at an Inn-Door a while, and we went into the House.

Being in the Inn, I told him I had but one Favour more to ask of him, and that was, that since he could not go any farther, he would give me leave to stay a Week or two in the Town with him, that we might in that time think of something to prevent such a ruinous thing to us both, as a final Separation would be; and that I had something of Moment to offer to him, that I had never said yet, and which perhaps he might find Practicable to our mutual Advantage.

This was too reasonable a Proposal to be denied, so he call'd the Landlady of the House *and told her* his Wife was taken ill, and so ill that she cou'd not think of going any farther in the Stage Coach, which had tyr'd her almost to Death, and ask'd if she cou'd not get us a Lodging for two or three Days in a private House, where I might rest me a little, for the Journey had been too much for me. The Landlady, a good sort of Woman, well bred, and very obliging, came immediately to see me; *told me* she had two or three very good Rooms in a part of the House quite out of the noise, and if I saw them, she did not doubt but I would like them, and I should have one of her Maids, that should do nothing else but be appointed to wait on me; this was so very kind, that I could not but accept of it and thank her; so I went to look on the Rooms, and lik'd them very well, and indeed they were extraordinarily Furnish'd, and very pleasant Lodgings; so we paid the Stage Coach, took out our Baggage, and resolv'd to stay here a while.

Here I *told him* I would live with him now till all my Money was spent, but would not let him spend a Shilling of his own: We had some kind squabble about that, but I *told him* it was the last time I was like to enjoy his Company, and I desir'd he would let me be Master in that thing only, and he should govern in every thing else, so he acquiesc'd.

Here one Evening taking a Walk into the Fields, I *told him* I would now make the Proposal to him I had told him of; accordingly I related to him how I had liv'd in *Virginia*, that I had a Mother, I believ'd, was alive there still, tho' my Husband was dead some Years; I *told him*, that had not my Effects miscarry'd, which by the way I magnify'd pretty much, I might have been Fortune good enough to him to have kept us from being parted in this manner: Then I entered into the manner of Peoples going over to those Countries to settle, how they had a quantity of Land given them by the Constitution of the Place; and if not, that it might be purchased at so easie a Rate that it was not worth naming.

I then gave him a full and distinct account of the nature of Planting, how with carrying over but two or three Hundred Pounds value in *English* Goods, with some Servants and Tools, a Man of Application would presently lay a Foundation for a Family, and in a very few Years be certain to raise an Estate.

I let him into the nature of the Product of the Earth, how the Ground was Cur'd and Prepared, and what the usual encrease of it was; and demonstrated to him, that in a very few Years, with such a beginning, we should be as certain of being Rich, as we were now certain of being Poor.

He was surpriz'd at my Discourse; for we made it the whole Subject of our Conversation for near a Week together, in which time I laid it down in black and white, *as we say*, that it was morally impossible, with a supposition of any reasonable good Conduct,[8] but that we must thrive there and do very well.

Then I told him what measures I would take to raise such a Sum as 300 *l.* or thereabouts; and I argued with him how good a Method it would be to put an end to our Misfortunes and restore our Circumstances in the World, to what we had both expected, and I added, that after seven Years, if we liv'd, we might be in a Posture to leave our Plantation in good Hands, and come over again and receive the Income of it, and live here and enjoy it; and I gave him Examples of some that had done so, and liv'd now in very good Circumstances in *London*.

8. Management.

In short, I press'd him so to it, that he almost agreed to it, but still something or other broke it off again; till at last he turn'd the Tables, and he began to talk almost to the same purpose of *Ireland*.

He told me that a Man that could confine himself to a Country Life, and that cou'd but find Stock to enter upon any Land, should have Farms there for 50 *l.* a Year, as good as were here let for 200 *l.* a Year; that the Produce was such, and so Rich the Land, that if much was not laid up, we were sure to live as handsomely upon it as a Gentleman of 3000 *l.* a Year could do in *England;* and that he had laid a Scheme to leave me in *London,* and go over and try; and if he found he could lay a handsome Foundation of living suitable to the Respect he had for me, as he doubted not he should do, he would come over and fetch me.

I was dreadfully afraid that upon such a Proposal he would have taken me at my Word, (*viz.*) to sell my little Income, as I call'd it, and turn it into Money, and let him carry it over into *Ireland* and try his Experiment with it; but he was too just to desire it, or to have accepted it if I had offered it; and he anticipated me in that, for he added, that he would go and try his Fortune that way, and if he found he cou'd do any thing at it to live, then, by adding mine to it when I went over, we should live like our selves; but that he would not hazard a Shilling of mine till he had made the Experiment with a little, and he assur'd me that if he found nothing to be done in *Ireland,* he would then come to me and join in my Project for *Virginia.*

He was so earnest upon his Project being to be try'd first, that I cou'd not withstand him; how ever, he promis'd to let me hear from him in a very little time after his arriving there, to let me know whether his prospect answer'd his Design, that if there was not a probability of Success, I might take the Occasion to prepare for our other Voyage, and then, he assur'd me, he would go with me to *America* with all his Heart.

I could bring him to nothing farther than this: However, those Consultations entertain'd us near a Month, during which I enjoy'd his Company, which indeed was the most entertaining that ever I met with in my life before. In this time he let me into the whole Story of his own Life, which was indeed surprizing, and full of an infinite Variety sufficient to fill up a much brighter History for its Adventures and Incidents, that any I ever saw in Print: But I shall have occasion to say more of him hereafter.

We parted at last, tho' with the utmost reluctance on my side, and indeed he took his leave very unwillingly too, but Necessity oblig'd him, for his Reasons were very good why he would not come to *London,* as I understood more fully some time afterwards.

I gave him a Direction how to write to me, tho' still I reserv'd the grand Secret, and never broke my Resolution, which was not to let him ever know my true Name, who I was, or where to be found; he likewise let me know how to write a Letter to him, so that he said he wou'd be sure to receive it.

I came to *London* the next Day after we parted, but did not go directly to my old Lodgings; but for another nameless Reason took a private Lodging in St. *John's-street*, or as it is vulgarly call'd St. *Jones's* near *Clarkenwell*; and here being perfectly alone, I had leisure to sit down and reflect seriously upon the last seven Months Ramble I had made, for I had been abroad no less; the pleasant Hours I had with my last Husband I look'd back on with an infinite deal of Pleasure; but that Pleasure was very much lessen'd, when I found some time after that I was really with Child.

This was a perplexing thing because of the Difficulty which was before me, where I should get leave to Lye Inn; it being one of the nicest things in the World at that time of Day, for a Woman that was a Stranger, and had no Friends, to be entertain'd in that Circumstance without Security,[9] which by the way I had not, neither could I procure any.

I had taken care all this while to preserve a Correspondence with my honest Friend at the Bank, or rather he took care to Correspond with me, for he wrote to me once a Week; and tho' I had not spent my Money so fast as to want any from him, yet I often wrote also to let him know I was alive; I had left Directions in *Lancashire*, so that I had these Letters, which he sent, convey'd to me; and during my Recess at St. *Jones's* I receiv'd a very obliging Letter from him, assuring me that his Process for a Divorce from his Wife went on with Success, tho' he met with some Difficulties in it that he did not expect.

I was not displeas'd with the News that his Process was more tedious than he expected; for tho' I was in no condition to have had him yet, not being so foolish to marry him when I knew my self to be with Child by another Man, as some I know have ventur'd to do; yet I was not willing to lose him, and in a word, resolv'd to have him if he continu'd in the same mind, as soon as I was up again; for I saw apparently I should hear no more from my other Husband; and as he had all along press'd me to Marry, and had assur'd me he would not be at all disgusted at it, or ever offer to claim me again, so I made no scruple to resolve to do it if I could, and if my other Friend stood to his Bargain; and I had a great deal of Reason to be assur'd that he would stand to it, by the Letters he wrote to me, which were the kindest and most obliging that could be.

9. Proof of financial support, which would be sought by the parish officers.   See also pp. 8, 92, 127.

I now grew Big, and the People where I Lodg'd perceiv'd it, and began to take notice of it to me, and as far as Civility would allow, intimated that I must think of removing; this put me to extreme perplexity, and I grew very melancholy, for indeed I knew not what Course to take; I had Money, but no Friends, and was like now to have a Child upon my Hands to keep, which was a difficulty I had never had upon me yet, as the Particulars of my Story hitherto makes appear.

In the course of this Affair I fell very ill, and my Melancholy really encreas'd my Distemper; my illness prov'd at length to be only an Ague, but my Apprehensions were really that I should Miscarry; I should not say Apprehensions, for indeed I would have been glad to miscarry, but I cou'd never be brought to entertain so much as a thought of endeavouring to Miscarry, or of taking any thing to make me Miscarry; I abhorr'd, I say so much as the thought of it.

However, speaking of it in the House, the Gentlewoman who kept the House propos'd to me to send for a Midwife; I scrupled it at first, but after some time consented to it, but told her I had no particular Acquaintance with any Midwife, and so left it to her.

It seems the Mistress of the House was not so great a Stranger to such Cases as mine was, as I thought at first she had been, as will appear presently, and she sent for a Midwife of the right sort, that is to say, the right sort for me.

The Woman appear'd to be an experienc'd Woman in her Business, I mean as a Midwife, but she had another Calling too, in which she was as expert as most Women, if not more: My Landlady had told her I was very Melancholy, and that she believ'd that had done me harm; and once, *before me*, said to her, Mrs. B—— *meaning the Midwife*, I believe this Lady's Trouble is of a kind that is pretty much in your way, and therefore if you can do any thing for her, pray do, for she is a very civil Gentlewoman, and so she went out of the Room.

I really did not understand her, but my Mother Midnight[1] began very seriously to explain what she meant, as soon as she was gone: Madam, *says she*, you seem not to understand what your Landlady means, and when you do understand it, you need not let her know at all that you do so.

She means that you are under some Circumstances that may render your Lying-Inn difficult to you, and that you are not willing to be expos'd; I need say no more, but to tell you, that if you think fit to communicate so much of your Case to me, *if it be so*, as is necessary; for I do not desire to pry into those things; I perhaps

---

1. Slang term for a midwife who engaged in practices outside the law. Also slang for a bawd or procuress.

may be in a Condition to assist you, and to make you perfectly easie, and remove all your dull Thoughts upon that Subject.

Every word this Creature said was a Cordial to me, and put new Life and new Spirit into my very Heart; my Blood began to circulate immediately, and I was quite another Body; I eat my Victuals again, and grew better presently after it: She said a great deal more to the same purpose, and then having press'd me to be free with her, and promis'd in the solemnest manner to be secret, she stop'd a little, as if waiting to see what Impression it made on me, and what I would say.

I was too sensible of the want I was in of such a Woman, not to accept her offer; *I told her* my Case was partly as she guess'd, and partly not, for I was really married, and had a Husband, tho' he was in such Circumstances, and so remote at that time, as that he cou'd not appear publickly.

She took me short, *and told me*, that was none of her Business, all the Ladies that came under her Care were married Women to her; every Woman, *says she*, that is with Child has a Father for it, and whether that Father was a Husband or no Husband, was no Business of hers; her Business was to assist me in my present Circumstances, whether I had a Husband or no; for, *Madam, says she*, to have a Husband that cannot appear, is to have no Husband in the sense of the Case, and therefore whether you are a Wife or a Mistress is all one to me.

I found presently, that whether I was a Whore or a Wife, I was to pass for a Whore here, so I let that go; *I told her* it was true as she said, but that however, if I must tell her my Case, I must tell it her as it was: So I related it to her as short as I could, and I concluded it to her thus: *I trouble you with all this*, Madam, said I, *not that, as you said before, it is much to the purpose* in your Affair, but this is to the purpose, *namely, that I am not in any pain about being seen, or being publick or conceal'd, for 'tis perfectly indifferent to me; but my difficulty is, that I have no Acquaintance in this part of the Nation.*

I understand you, Madam, *says she*, you have no Security to bring to prevent the Parish Impertinences usual in such Cases; and perhaps, *says she*, do not know very well how to dispose of the Child when it comes; the last, *says I*, is not so much my concern as the first: Well, Madam, *answers the Midwife*, dare you put your self into my Hands, I live in such a place, tho' I do not enquire after you, you may enquire after me; my Name is *B——* I live in such a Street, naming the Street, at the Sign of the *Cradle*; my Profession is a Midwife, and I have many Ladies that come to my House to Lye-Inn; I have given Security to the Parish in General Terms to secure them from any Charge from whatsoever shall come into the World under my Roof; I have but one Question to ask in the whole Affair, Madam, *says she*, and if that be answer'd, you shall be entirely easie for all the rest.

I presently understood what she meant, and told her, Madam, *I believe I understand you*; I thank God, *tho' I want Friends in this Part of the World, I do not want Money, so far as may be Necessary, tho' I do not abound in that neither*: This I added, because I would not make her expect great things; well Madam, *says she*, that is the thing indeed, without which nothing can be done in these Cases; and yet, *says she*, you shall see that I will not impose upon you, or offer any thing that is unkind to you, and if you desire it, you shall know every thing before hand, that you may suit your self to the Occasion, and be either costly or sparing as you see fit.

I told her, she seem'd to be so perfectly sensible of my Condition, that I had nothing to ask of her but this, that as I had told her that I had Money sufficient, but not a great Quantity, she would order it so, that I might be at as little superfluous Charge as possible.

She replyed, that she would bring in an Account of the Expences of it, in two or three Shapes, and like a *Bill of Fare*, I should chuse as I pleas'd, and I desir'd her to do so.

The next Day she brought it, and the Copy of her three Bills was as follows:

	l.	s.	d.
1. For Three Months Lodging in her House, including my Dyet at 10s. a Week	06	00	0
2. For a Nurse for the Month, and Use of Child-bed Linnen	01	10	0
3. For a Minister to Christen the Child, and to the Godfathers and Clark	01	10	0
4. For a Supper at the Christening if I had five Friends at it	01	00	0
For her Fees as a Midwife, and the taking off the Trouble of the Parish	03	03	0
To her Maid-Servant attending	00	10	0
	13	13	0

This was the first Bill, the second was in the same Terms.

1. For Three Months Lodging and Diet, &c. at 20s. *per* Week	13	00	0
2. For a Nurse for the Month, and the Use of Linnen and Lace	02	10	0
3. For the Minister to Christen the Child, &c. as above	02	00	0

4. For a Supper, and for Sweetmeats	03	03	0
For her Fees, as above	05	05	0
For a Servant-Maid	01	00	0
	26	18	0

This was the second rate Bill, the third, *she said*, was for a degree Higher, and when the Father, or Friends appeared.

	l.	*s.*	*d.*
1. For Three Months Lodging and Diet, having two Rooms and a Garret for a Servant }	30	00	0
2. For a Nurse for the Month, and the finest Suit of Child-bed Linnen }	04	04	0
3. For the Minister to Christen the Child, &c.	02	10	0
4. For a Supper, the Gentlemen to send in the Wine }	06	00	0
For my Fees, &c.	10	10	0
The Maid, besides their own Maid only	00	10	0
	53	14	0

I look'd upon all the three Bills, and smil'd, *and told her* I did not see but that she was very reasonable in her Demands, all things Consider'd, and for that I did not doubt but her Accommodations were good.

She told me I should be Judge of that when I saw them: *I told her*, I was sorry to tell her that I fear'd I must be her lowest rated Customer; and *perhaps Madam*, said I, *you will make me the less Welcome upon that Account*. No not at all, *said she*, for where I have One of the third Sort, I have Two of the Second, and Four to One of the First, and I get as much by them in Proportion, as by any; but if you doubt my Care of you, I will allow any Friend you have to overlook, and see if you are well waited on, or no.

Then she explain'd the particulars of her Bill; in the first place, Madam, *said she*, I would have you Observe, that here is three Months Keeping; you are but 10s. a Week; I undertake to say you will not complain of my Table: I suppose, *says she*, you do not live Cheaper where you are now; no indeed, *said I*, nor so Cheap, for I give six Shillings *per* Week for my Chamber, and find my own Diet as well as I can, which costs me a great deal more.

Then Madam, *says she*, If the Child should not live, or should be dead Born, as you know sometime happens, then there is the Minister's Article saved; and if you have no Friends to come to you, you may save the Expence of a Supper; so that take those Articles out Madam, *says she*, your Lying-In will not cost you above 5l. 3s. in all, more than your ordinary Charge of Living.

This was the most reasonable thing that I ever heard of; so I smil'd, and told her I would come and be her Customer; but *I told her also*, that as I had two Months, and more to go, I might perhaps be oblig'd to stay longer with her than three Months, and desir'd to know if she would not be oblig'd to remove me before it was proper; no, *she said*, her House was large, and besides, she never put any Body to remove that had lain Inn till they were willing to go; and if she had more Ladies offer'd, she was not so ill belov'd among her Neighbours but she could provide Accommodation for Twenty, if there was occasion.

I found she was an eminent Lady in her way, and *in short*, I agreed to put myself into her Hands, and promis'd her: She then talk'd of other things, look'd about into my Accommodations, where was found fault with my wanting Attendance, and Conveniences, and that I should not be us'd so at her House: *I told her*, I was shy of speaking, for the Woman of the House look'd stranger, or at least I thought so since I had been Ill, because I was with Child; and I was afraid she would put some Affront or other upon me, supposing that I had been able to give but a slight Account of myself.

O Dear, *said she*, her Ladyship is no stranger to these things; she has try'd to entertain Ladies in your Condition several times, but could not secure the Parish;[2] and besides, she is not such a nice Lady as you take her to be; however, since you are agoing you shall not meddle with her, but I'll see you are a little better look'd after while you are here, than I think you are, and it shall not cost you the more neither.

I did not understand her at all; however I thank'd her, and so we parted; the next Morning she sent me a Chicken roasted and hot, and a pint Bottle of Sherry, and order'd the Maid to tell me that she was to wait on me every Day as long as I stay'd there.

This was surprisingly good and kind, and I accepted it very willingly: At Night she sent to me again, to know if I wanted any thing, and how I did, and to order the Maid to come to her in the morning for my Dinner; the Maid had order to make me some Chocolat in the Morning before she came away, and did so, and at Noon she brought me the Sweetbread of a Breast of Veal whole, and a Dish of Soup for my Dinner, and after this manner she Nurs'd me up at a distance, so that I was mightily well pleas'd, and quickly well, for indeed my Dejections before were the principal Part of my Illness.

I expected as usually is the Case among such People, that the Servant she sent me would have been some impudent brazen Wench of *Drury-Lane*[3] Breeding and I was very uneasie at having

2. Influence or bribe the parish officers.
3. A London district north of the Strand, noted for its theater and its brothels; the term "Drury-Lane Ague" was another name for venereal disease, and a "Drury-Lane Virgin" was a prostitute.

her with me upon that Account, so I would not let her lie in that House, the first Night by any means, but had my Eyes about me as narrowly as if she had been a publick Thief.

My Gentlewoman guess'd presently what was the matter, and sent her back with a short Note, that I might depend upon the honesty of her Maid; that she would be answerable for her upon all Accounts; and that she took no Servants into her House, without very good Security for their Fidelity: I was then perfectly easie, and indeed the Maids behaviour spoke for its self, for a modester, quieter, soberer Girl never came into any bodies Family, and I found her so afterwards.

As soon as I was well enough to go Abroad, I went with the Maid to see the House, and to see the Apartment I was to have; and every thing was so handsome and so clean and well, that in short, I had nothing to say, but was wonderfully pleas'd and satisfy'd with what I had met with, which considering the melancholy Circumstances I was in, was far beyond what I look'd for.

It might be expected that I should give some Account of the Nature of the wicked Practice of this Woman, in whose Hands I was now fallen; but it would be but too much Encouragement to the Vice, to let the World see what easie Measures were here taken to rid the Women's unwelcome Burthen of a Child clandestinely gotten:[4] This grave Matron had several sorts of Practise, and this was one particular, that if a Child was born, tho' not in her House, for she had the occasion to be call'd to many private Labours, she had People at Hand, who for a Peice of Money would take the Child off their Hands, and off from the Hands of the Parish too; and those Children, as she said were honestly provided for, and taken care of: What should become of them all, Considering so many, as by her Account she was concern'd with, I cannot conceive.

I had many times Discourses upon the Subject with her; but she was full of this Argument, that she sav'd the Life of many an innocent Lamb, as she call'd them, which would otherwise perhaps have been Murder'd; and of many a Woman, who made Desperate by the Misfortune, would otherwise be tempted to Destroy their Children, and bring themselves to the Gallows: I granted her that this was true, and a very commendable thing, provided the poor Children fell into good Hands afterwards, and were not abus'd, starv'd, and neglected by the Nurses that bred them up; she answer'd, that she always took care of that, and had no Nurses in her Business, but what were very good honest People, and such as might be depended upon.

I cou'd say nothing to the contrary, and so was oblig'd to say, Madam I do not question you do your part honestly, but what those People do afterwards is the main Question, and she stop'd my Mouth again with saying, that she took the utmost Care about it.

4. Illicitly begotten, born out of wedlock.

The only thing I found in all her Conversation on these Subjects that gave me any distaste, was, that one time in Discoursing about my being so far gone with Child, and the time I expected to come, she said something that look'd as if she could help me off with my Burthen sooner, if I was willing; or in *English*, that she could give me something to make me Miscarry, if I had a desire to put an end to my Troubles that way; but I soon let her see that I abhorr'd the Thoughts of it, and to do her Justice, she put it off so cleverly, that I cou'd not say she really intended it, or whether she only mentioned the practise as a horrible thing; for she couch'd her words so well, and took my meaning so quickly, that she gave her Negative before I could explain my self.

To bring this part into as narrow a Compass as possible, I quitted my Lodging at St. *Jones*'s and went to my new Governess, for so they call'd her in the House, and there I was indeed treated with so much Courtesy, so carefully look'd to, so handsomely provided, and every thing so well, that I was surpris'd at it, and cou'd not at first see what Advantage my Governess made of it; but I found afterwards that she profess'd to make no Profit of the Lodgers Diet, nor indeed cou'd she get much by it, but that her Profit lay in the other Articles of her Management, and she made enough that way, I assure you; for 'tis scarce credible what Practice she had, as well Abroad as at Home, and yet all upon the private Account, or in plain *English*, the whoring Account.

While I was in her House, which was near Four Months, she had no less than Twelve Ladies of Pleasure brought to Bed within Doors, and I think she had Two and Thirty, or thereabouts, under her Conduct without Doors, whereof one, as nice as she was with me, was Lodg'd with my old Landlady at St. *Jones*'s.

This was a strange Testimony of the growing Vice of the Age, and such a one, that as bad as I had been my self, it shock'd my very Senses, I began to nauceate the place I was in, and above all, the wicked Practice; and yet I must say that I never saw, or do I believe there was to be seen, the least indecency in the House the whole time I was there.

Not a Man was ever seen to come up Stairs, except to visit the Lying-Inn Ladies within their Month, nor then without the old Lady with them, who made it a piece of the Honour of her Management, that no Man should touch a Woman, no not his own Wife, within the Month; nor would she permit any Man to lye in the House upon any pretence whatever, no not tho' she was sure it was with his own Wife, and her general saying for it was, that she car'd not how many Children was born in her house, but she would have none got there if she could help it.

It might perhaps be carried farther than was needful, but it was an Error of the right Hand[5] if it was an Error, for by this she kept up the Reputation, such as it was, of her Business, and obtain'd this Character, that tho' she did take Care of the Women when they were Debauch'd, yet she was not Instrumental to their being Debauch'd at all; and yet it was a wicked Trade she drove too.

While I was here, and before I was brought to Bed, I receiv'd a Letter from my Trustee at the Bank full of kind obliging things, and earnestly pressing me to return to *London:* It was near a Fortnight old when it came to me, because it had been first sent into *Lancashire*, and then return'd to me; he concludes with telling me that he had obtain'd a Decree,[6] I think he call'd it, against his Wife, and that he would be ready to make good his Engagement to me, if I would accept of him, adding a great many Protestations of Kindness and Affection, such as he would have been far from offering if he had known the Circumstances I had been in, and which as it was I had been very far from deserving.

I returned an Answer to this Letter, and dated it at *Leverpool*, but sent it by a Messenger, alledging that it came in Cover to a Friend in Town; I gave him Joy of his Deliverance, but rais'd some Scruples at the Lawfulness of his Marrying again, and told him I suppos'd he would consider very seriously upon that Point before he resolv'd on it, the Consequence being too great for a Man of his Judgment to venture rashly upon a thing of that Nature; so concluded, wishing him very well in whatever he resolv'd, without letting him into any thing of my own Mind, or giving any Answer to his Proposal of my coming to *London* to him, but mention'd at a distance my intention to return the latter end of the Year, this being dated in *April*.

I was brought to Bed about the middle of *May*, and had another brave[7] Boy, and my self in as good Condition as usual on such Occasions: My Governess did her part as a Midwife with the greatest Art and Dexterity imaginable, and far beyond all that ever I had had any Experience of before.

Her Care of me in my Travail, and after in my Lying-Inn, was such, that if she had been my own Mother it cou'd not have been better; let none be encourag'd in their loose Practises from this Dexterous Lady's Management; for she is gone to her place, and I dare say has left nothing behind her that can or will come up to it.

I think I had been brought to Bed about twenty two Days when I receiv'd another Letter from my Friend at the Bank, with the surprizing News that he had obtain'd a final Sentence of Divorce against his Wife, and had serv'd her with it on such a Day, and that he had such an Answer to give to all my Scruples about his

---

5. In the right direction.
6. An authoritative but not final decision
in his divorce proceedings.
7. Grand, excellent.

Marrying again, as I could not expect, and as he had no Desire of; for that his wife, who had been under some Remorse before for her usage of him, as soon as she had the account that he had gain'd his Point, had very unhappily destroy'd her self that same Evening.

He express'd himself very handsomly as to his being concern'd at her Disaster, but clear'd himself of having any hand in it, and that he had only done himself Justice in a Case in which he was notoriously Injur'd and Abus'd: However, he said that he was extremely afflicted at it, and had no view of any Satisfaction left in this World, but only in the hope that I wou'd come and relieve him by my Company; and then he press'd me violently indeed to give him some hopes that I would at least come up to Town and let him see me, when he would farther enter into Discourse about it.

I was exceedingly surpriz'd at the News, and began now seriously to reflect on my present Circumstances, and the inexpressible Misfortune it was to me to have a Child upon my Hands, and what to do in it I knew not; at last I open'd my Case at a distance to my Governess; I appear'd melancholy and uneasie for several Days, and she lay at me continually to know what troubl'd me; I could not for my life tell her that I had an offer of Marriage, after I had so often told her that I had a Husband, so that I really knew not what to say to her; I own'd I had something which very much troubl'd me, but at the same time told her I cou'd not speak of it to any one alive.

She continued importuning me several Days, but it was impossible, *I told her*, for me to commit the Secret to any Body; this, instead of being an Answer to her, encreas'd her Importunities; she urg'd her having been trusted with the greatest Secrets of this Nature, that it was her business to Conceal every thing, and that to Discover things of that Nature would be her Ruin; she ask'd me if ever I had found her Tatling of other People's Affairs, and how could I suspect her? *she told me to* unfold my self to her was telling it to no Body; that she was silent as Death; that it must be a very strange Case indeed, that she could not help me out of; but to conceal it, was to deprive myself of all possible Help, or means of Help, and to deprive her of the Opportunity of Serving me. *In short*, she had such a bewitching Eloquence, and so great a power of Perswasion, that there was no concealing any thing from her.

So I resolv'd to unbosome myself to her; I told her the History of my *Lancashire* Marriage, and how both of us had been Disappointed; how we came together, and how we parted: How he absolutely Discharg'd me, as far as lay in him, and gave me free Liberty to Marry again, protesting that if he knew it he would never Claim me, or Disturb, or Expose me; that I thought I was free, but was dreadfully afraid to venture, for the fear of Consequences that might follow in case of a Discovery.

Then I told her what a good Offer I had; show'd her my Friends two last Letters, inviting me to come to *London*, and let her see with what Affection and Earnestness they were written, but blotted out the Name, and also the Story about the Dissaster of his Wife, only that she was dead.

She fell a Laughing at my scruples about marrying, and told me the other was no Marriage, but a cheat on both Sides; and that as we were parted by mutual Consent, the nature of the Contract was destroy'd, and the Obligation was mutually discharg'd:[8] She had Arguments for this at the tip of her Tongue; and *in short*, reason'd me out of my Reason; not but that it was too by the help of my own Inclination.

But then came the great and main Difficulty, and that was the Child; this she told me in so many Words must be remov'd, and that so, as that it should never be possible for any one to discover it: I knew there was no Marrying without entirely concealing that I had had a Child, for he would soon have discover'd by the Age of it, that it was born, nay and gotten too, since my Parly[9] with him, and that would have destroy'd all the Affair.

But it touch'd my Heart so forcibly to think of Parting entirely with the Child, and for ought I knew, of having it murther'd, or starv'd by Neglect and Ill-usuage (which was much the same) that I could not think of it without Horror; I wish all those Women who consent to the disposing their Children out of the way, *as it is call'd* for Decency sake, would consider that 'tis only a contriv'd Method for Murther; that is to say, a killing their Children with safety.

It is manifest to all that understand any thing of Children, that we are born into the World helpless and uncapable either to supply our own Wants, or so much as make them known; and that without help we must Perish; and this help requires not only an assisting Hand, whether of the Mother or some Body else; but there are two Things necessary in that assisting Hand, that is, Care and Skill, without both which, half the Children that are born would die, nay, tho' they were not to be deny'd Food; and one half more of those that remain'd would be Cripples or Fools, lose their Limbs, and perhaps their Sense: I Question not, but that these are partly the Reasons why Affection was plac'd by Nature in the Hearts of Mothers to their Children; without which they would never be able to give themselves up, as 'tis necessary they should, to the Care and waking Pains needful to the Support of their Children.

Since this Care is needful to the Life of Children, to neglect

8. The casuistical reasoning of the governess would not necessarily apply to the morality or legality of Moll's marriage. See G. A. Starr's "Defoe and Casuistry: *Moll Flanders*" in Twentieth-Century Criticism, pp. 421, below.
9. Parley.

them is to Murther them; again to give them up to be Manag'd by those People, who have none of that needful Affection, plac'd by Nature in them, is to Neglect them in the highest Degree; nay, in some it goes farther, and is a Neglect in order to their being Lost; so that 'tis even an intentional Murther, whether the Child lives or dies.

All those things represented themselves to my View, and that in the blackest and most frightful Form; and as I was very free with my Governness, who I had now learn'd to call Mother, I represented to her all the dark Thoughts which I had upon me about it, and told her what distress I was in: She seem'd graver by much at this Part than at the other; but as she was harden'd in these things beyond all possibility of being touch'd with the Religious part, and the Scruples about the Murther, so she was equally impenetrable in that Part which related to Affection; She ask'd me if she had not been Careful and Tender of me in my Lying-Inn, as if I had been her own Child? I told her I own'd she had. Well my Dear, *says she*, and when you are gone, what are you to me? and what would it be to me if you were to be Hang'd? Do you think there are not Women, who as it is their Trade, and they get their Bread by it, value themselves upon their being as careful of Children as their own Mothers can be, and understand it rather better? Yes, yes, Child, *says she*, fear it not, How were we Nurs'd ourselves? Are you sure, you was Nurs'd up by your own Mother? and yet you look fat, and fair Child, says the old Beldam,[1] and with that she stroak'd me over the Face; never be concern'd Child, *says she*, going on in her drolling way; I have no Murtherers about me; I employ the best, and the honestest Nurses that can be had, and have as few Children miscarry under their Hands as there would if they were all Nurs'd by Mothers; we want neither Care nor Skill.

She touch'd me to the Quick, when she ask'd if I was sure that I was Nurs'd by my own Mother; on the contrary I was sure I was not; and I trembled, and look'd pale at the very Expression; sure said I, to myself, this Creature cannot be a Witch, or have any Conversation with a Spirit that can inform her what was done with me before I was able to know it myself; and I look'd at her as if I had been frighted; but reflecting that it cou'd not be possible for her to know any thing about me, that Disorder went off, and I began to be easie, but it was not presently.

She perceiv'd the Disorder I was in, but did not know the meaning of it; so she run on in her wild Talk upon the weakness of my supposing that Children were murther'd, because they were not all Nurs'd by the Mother; and to perswade me that the Children she

1. Old woman; in the sixteenth century the term signified "nurse"; later, however, it took on the connotation of "hag" or "witch."

dispos'd of were as well us'd as if the Mothers had the Nursing of them themselves.

It may be true Mother, *says I*, for ought I know, but my Doubts are very strongly grounded, indeed; come then, *says she*, lets hear some of them: Why first, *says I*, you give a Piece of Money to these People to take the Child off the Parents Hands, and to take Care of it as long as it lives; now we know Mother, *said I*, that those are poor People, and their Gain consists in being quit of the Charge as soon as they can; how can I doubt but that, as it is best for them to have the Child die, they are not over Solicitous about its Life?

This is all Vapours² and Fancy, *says the old Woman*, I tell you their Credit depends upon the Child's Life, and they are as careful as any Mother of you all.

O Mother, *says I*, if I was but sure my little Baby would be carefully look'd to, and have Justice done it, I should be happy indeed; but it is impossible I can be satisfy'd in that Point unless I saw it, and to see it would be Ruin and Destruction to me, as now my Case stands, so what to do I know not.

A Fine Story! *says the Governess*, you would see the Child, and you would not see the Child; you would be Conceal'd and Discover'd both together; these are things impossible my Dear, so you must e'n do as other conscientious Mothers have done before you, and be contented with things as they must be, tho' they are not as you wish them to be.

I understood what she meant by conscientious Mothers; she would have said conscientious Whores, but she was not willing to disoblige me, for really in this Case I was not a Whore, because legally Married, the force of my former Marriage excepted.

However let me be what I would, I was not come up to that pitch of Hardness common to the Profession; I mean to be unnatural, and regardless of the Safety of my Child, and I preserv'd this honest Affection so long, that I was upon the Point of giving up my Friend at the *Bank*, who lay so hard at me to come to him and Marry him, that *in short*, there was hardly any room to deny him.

At last my old Governess came to me, with her usual Assurance. Come my Dear, *says she*, I have found out a way how you shall be at a certainty, that your Child shall be used well, and yet the People that take Care of it shall never know you, or who the Mother of the Child is.

O Mother, *says I*, If you can do so, you will engage me to you for ever: Well, *says she*, are you willing to be at some small Annual Expence, more than what we usually give to the People we Contract with? Ay, *says I*, with all my Heart, provided I may be con-

2. Melancholy, spiritual depression; a term often used in the eighteenth cen- tury; thought to be caused by exhalations from principal organs of the body.

ceal'd; as to that, says *the Governess*, you shall be Secure, for the
Nurse shall never so much as dare to Enquire about you, and you
shall once or twice a Year go with me and see your Child, and see
how 'tis used, and be satisfy'd that it is in good Hands, no Body
knowing who you are.

Why, *said I*, do you think Mother, that when I come to see my
Child, I shall be able to conceal my being the Mother of it, do you
think that possible?

Well, well, *says my Governess*, if you discover it, the Nurse shall
be never the wiser; for she shall be forbid to ask any Questions
about you, or to take any Notice; if she offers it she shall lose the
Money which you are to be suppos'd to give her, and the Child be
taken from her too.

I was very well pleas'd with this; so the next Week a Country
Woman was brought from *Hertford*, or thereabouts, who was to
take the Child off our Hands entirely, for 10 *l*. in Money; but if I
would allow 5 *l*. a Year more to her, she would be obliged to bring
the Child to my Governesses House as often as we desired, or we
should come down and look at it, and see how well she us'd it.

The Woman was a very wholesome look'd likely Woman, a Cot-
tager's Wife, but she had very good Cloaths and Linnen, and every
thing well about her; and with a heavy Heart and many a Tear I let
her have my Child: I had been down at *Hertford* and look'd at her
and at her Dwelling, which I lik'd well enough; and I promis'd her
great Things if she would be kind to the Child, so she knew at first
word that I was the Child's Mother; but she seem'd to be so much
out of the way, and to have no room to enquire after me, that I
thought I was safe enough, so in short I consented to let her have
the Child, and I gave her Ten Pound, that is to say I gave it to my
Governess, who gave it the poor Woman before my Face, she agreeing never to return the Child back to me, or to claim any thing
more for its keeping or bringing up; only that I promised, if she
took a great deal of Care of it, I would give her something more as
often as I came to see it; so that I was not bound to pay the Five
Pound, only that I promised my Governess I would do it: And thus
my great Care was over, after a manner, which tho' it did not at all
satisfie my Mind, yet was the most convenient for me, as my Affairs
then stood, of any that cou'd be thought of at that time.

I then began to write to my Friend at the Bank in a more kindly
Style, and particularly about the beginning of *July* I sent him a
Letter, that I purpos'd to be in Town sometime in *August*; he
return'd me an Answer in the most Passionate Terms imaginable,
and desir'd me to let him have timely Notice, and he would come
and meet me two Days Journey: This puzzl'd me scurvily,[3] and I

3. Sorely, vilely.

did not know what Answer to make to it; once I was resolv'd to take the Stage Coach to *West-Chester* on purpose only to have the satisfaction of coming back, that he might see me really come in the same Coach; for I had a jealous[4] thought, though I had no Ground for it at all, lest he should think I was not really in the Country, and it was no ill-grounded Thought, as you shall hear presently.

I endeavour'd to Reason my self out of it, but it was in vain, the Impression lay so strong on my Mind, that it was not to be resisted; at last it came as an Addition to my new Design of going in the Country, that it would be an excellent Blind to my old governess, and would cover entirely all my other Affairs, for she did not know in the least whether my new Lover liv'd in *London* or in *Lancashire*; and when I told her my Resolution, she was fully perswaded it was in *Lancashire*.

Having taken my Measures for this Journey, I let her know it, and sent the Maid that tended me from the beginning, to take a Place for me in the Coach; she would have had me let the Maid have waited on me down to the last Stage, and come up again in the Waggon, but I convinc'd her it wou'd not be convenient; when I went away she told me, she would enter into no Measures for Correspondence, for she saw evidently that my Affection to my Child would cause me to write to her, and to visit her too when I came to Town again; I assur'd her it would, and so took my leave, well satisfied to have been freed from such a House, however good my Accommodations there had been, as I have related above.

I took the Place in the Coach not to its full Extent, but to a place call'd *Stone* in *Cheshire*,[5] I think it is, where I not only had no manner of Business, but not so much as the least Acquaintance with any Person in the Town or near it: But I knew that with Money in the Pocket one is at home any where, so I Lodg'd there two or three Days, till watching my opportunity, I found room in another Stage Coach, and took Passage back again for *London*, sending a Letter to my Gentleman, that I should be such a certain Day at *Stony-Stratford*, where the Coachman told me he was to Lodge.

It happen'd to be a Chance Coach that I had taken up, which having been hired on purpose to carry some Gentlemen to *West-Chester* who were going for *Ireland*, was now returning, and did not tye it self up to exact Times or Places as the Stages did; so that having been oblig'd to lye still a *Sunday*, he had time to get himself ready to come out, which otherwise he cou'd not have done.

---

4. Apprehensive.
5. C. A. Johnson points out that Stone is not in Cheshire but in Staffordshire, about 140 miles from London. Defoe's *Tour through the Whole Island of Great Britain* (1724–26) contains a map that properly shows Stone's location. See *Notes and Queries*, CCVII (1962), 455.

However, his warning was so short, that he could not reach to
Stony-Stratford time enough to be with me at Night, but he met
me at a Place call'd *Brickill* the next Morning, as we were just
coming into the Town.

I confess I was very glad to see him, for I had thought my self a
little disappointed over Night, seeing I had gone so far to contrive
my coming on purpose: He pleas'd me doubly too by the Figure he
came in, for he brought a very handsome (Gentleman's) Coach and
four Horses with a Servant to attend him.

He took me out of the Stage Coach immediately, which stop'd at
an Inn in *Brickill*, and putting in to the same Inn he set up his own
Coach, and bespoke[6] his Dinner; I ask'd him what he meant by
that, for I was for going forward with the Journey; he said no, I had
need of a little Rest upon the Road, and that was a very good sort
of a House, tho' it was but a little Town; so we would go no farther
that Night, whatever came of it.

I did not press him much, for since he had come so far to meet
me, and put himself to so much Expence, it was but reasonable I
should oblige him a little too, so I was easy as to that Point.

After Dinner we walk'd to see the Town, to see the Church, and
to view the Fields, and the Country as is usual for Strangers to do,
and our Landlord was our Guide in going to see the Church; I
observ'd my Gentleman enquir'd pretty much about the Parson,
and I took the hint immediately that he certainly would propose to
be married; and tho' it was a sudden thought, it follow'd presently,
that in short I would not refuse him; for to be plain with my Circumstances, I was in no condition now to say NO; I had no reason
now to run any more such hazards.

But while these Thoughts run round in my Head, which was the
work but of a few Moments, I observ'd my Landlord took him aside
and whisper'd to him, tho' not very softly neither, for so much I
over-heard, *Sir, if you shall have occasion*—the rest I cou'd not hear,
but it seems it was to this purpose, *Sir, if you shall have occasion
for a Minister, I have a Friend a little way off that will serve you,
and be as private as you please*; my Gentleman answer'd loud enough
for me to hear, *very well, I believe I shall.*

I was no sooner come back to the Inn, but he fell upon me with
irresistable Words, that since he had had the good Fortune to meet
me, and every thing concurr'd, it wou'd be hastening his Felicity if
I would put an end to the matter just there; what do you mean,
says I, colouring a little, what in an Inn, and upon the Road! Bless
us all, *said I,* as if I had been surpriz'd; how can you talk so! O I
can talk so very well, *says he,* I came a purpose to talk so, and I'll
show you that I did, and with that he pulls out a great Bundle of

6. Stated his need for; ordered.

Papers; you fright me, *said* I, what are all these; don't be frighted, my Dear, *said he*, and kiss'd me; *this was the first time that he had been so free to call me my Dear*; then he repeated it, don't be frighted, you shall see what it is all; then he laid them all abroad;[7] there was first the Deed or Sentence of Divorce from his Wife, and the full Evidence of her playing the Whore; then there was the Certificates of the Minister and Church-wardens of the Parish where she liv'd, proving that she was buried, and intimating the manner of her Death; the Copy of the Coroner's Warrant for a Jury to sit upon her, and the Verdict of the Jury, who brought it in *Non Compos Mentis*;[8] all this was indeed to the purpose, and to give me Satisfaction, tho', by the way, I was not so scrupulous, had he known all, but that I might have taken him without it: However, I look'd them all over as well as I cou'd, and told him, that this was all very clear indeed, but that he need not have given himself the Trouble to have brought them out with him, for it was time enough: Well *he said*, it might be time enough for me, but no time but the present time was time enough for him.

There were other Papers roll'd up, and I ask'd him, what they were? Why, Ay, *says he*, that's the Question I wanted to have you ask me; so he unrolls them, and takes out a little Chagreen[9] Case, and gives me out of it a very fine Diamond Ring; I could not refuse it, if I had a mind to do so, for he put it upon my Finger; so I made him a Curtsy, and accepted it; then he takes out another Ring, and this, *says he*, is for another Occasion, so he puts that in his Pocket. Well, but let me see it tho', *says I*, and smil'd, I guess what it is, I think you are Mad: I should have been Mad if I had done less, *says he*, and still he did not show it me, and I had a great mind to see it; so I says, well but let me see it; hold, *says he*, first look here, then he took up the Roll again, and read it, and behold! it was a License for us to be married: Why, *says I*, are you Distracted? why you were fully satisfy'd that I would comply and yield at first Word, or resolv'd to take no denial; the last is certainly the Case, *said he*; but you may be mistaken, *said I*; no, no, *says he*, how can you think so? I must not be denied, I can't be denied, and with that he fell to Kissing me so violently, I could not get rid of him.

There was a Bed in the Room, and we were walking to and again,[1] eager in the Discourse, at last he takes me by surprize in his Arms, and threw me on the Bed and himself with me, and holding me fast in his Arms, but without the least offer of any Undecency, Courted me to Consent with such repeated Entreaties and Arguments; protesting his Affection and vowing he would not let me go, till I had promised him, that at last I said, why you resolve not to

7. Spread them out.
8. That the wife was mentally unbalanced; i.e., insane in the eyes of the law.
9. Rough leather; usually spelled "shagreen."
1. Back and forth.

be deny'd indeed, I think: No, no, *says he*, I must not be denyed, I won't be deny'd, I can't be deny'd: Well, well, *said* I, and giving him a slight Kiss, then you shan't be deny'd, *said I*, let me get up.

He was so Transported with my Consent, and the kind manner of it, that I began to think Once, he took it for a Marriage, and would not stay for the Form, but I wrong'd him, for he gave over Kissing me, took me by the Hand, pull'd me up again, and then giving me two or three Kisses again, thank'd me for my kind yielding to him; and was so overcome with the Satisfaction and Joy of it, that I saw Tears stand in his Eyes.

I turn'd from him, for it fill'd my Eyes with Tears too; and I ask'd him leave to retire a little to my Chamber: If ever I had a Grain of true Repentance for a vicious and abominable Life for 24 Years past, it was then. O! what a felicity is it to Mankind, *said I*, to myself, that they cannot see into the Hearts of one another! How happy had it been for me, if I had been Wife to a Man of so much honesty, and so much Affection from the Beginning?

Then it occurr'd to me what an abominable Creature am I! and how is this innocent Gentleman going to be abus'd by me! How little does he think, that having Divorc'd a Whore, he is throwing himself into the Arms of another! that he is going to Marry one that has lain with two Brothers, and has had three Children by her own Brother! one that was born in *Newgate*, whose Mother was a Whore, and is now a transported Thief; one that has lain with thirteen Men,[2] and has had a Child since he saw me! poor Gentleman! *said I*, What is he going to do? After this reproaching my self was over, it followed thus: Well, if I must be his Wife, if it please God to give me Grace, I'll be a true Wife to him, and love him suitably to the strange Excess of his Passion for me; I will make him amends, if possible, by what he shall see, for the Cheats and Abuses I put upon him, which he does not see.

He was impatient for my coming out of my Chamber, but finding me long, he went down Stairs and talk'd with my Landlord about the Parson.

My Landlord, an Officious tho' well-meaning Fellow, had sent away for the Neighbouring Clergy Man; and when my Gentleman began to speak of it to him, and talk of sending for him, Sir, says he to him, my Friend is in the House; so without any more words he brought them together: When he came to the Minister, he ask'd him if he would venture to marry a couple of Strangers that were both willing? The Parson said that Mr. ——— had said something to him of it; that he hop'd it was no Clandestine Business; that he seem'd to be a grave Gentleman, and he suppos'd Madam was not a Girl, so that the consent of Friends should be wanted; to put you

---

2. As the Preface indicates (p. 3), Moll has not told all of her experiences.

out of doubt of that, says my Gentleman, read this Paper, and out he pulls the License; I am satisfied, says the Minister, where is the Lady? you shall see her presently, says my Gentleman.

When he had said thus, he comes up Stairs, and I was by that time come out of my Room; so he tells me the Minister was below, and that he had talk'd with him, and that upon showing him the License, he was free to marry us with all his Heart, but he asks to see you; so he ask'd if I would let him come up.

'Tis time enough, *said I*, in the Morning, is it not? Why, *said he*, my Dear, he seem'd to scruple whether it was not some young Girl stolen from her Parents, and I assur'd him we were both of Age to command our own Consent; and that made him ask to see you; well, *said I*, do as you please; so up they brings the Parson, and a merry good sort of Gentleman he was; he had been told, it seems, that we had met there by accident, that I came in the *Chester* Coach, and my Gentleman in his own Coach to meet me; that we were to have met last Night at *Stony-Stratford*, but that he could not reach so far: Well, Sir, *says the Parson*, every ill turn has some good in it; the Disappointment, Sir, *says he to my Gentleman*, was yours, and the good Turn is mine, for if you had met at *Stony-Stratford* I had not had the Honour to Marry you: LANDLORD *have you a Common-Prayer Book?*[3]

I started as if I had been frighted; Lord, *says I*, what do you mean? what to marry in an Inn, and at Night too: Madam, *says the Minister*, if you will have it be in the Church you shall; but I assure you your Marriage will be as firm here as in the Church; we are not tyed by the Canons to Marry no where but in the Church; and if you will have it in the Church it will be as publick as a Country Fair; and as for the time of Day it does not at all weigh in this Case; our Princes are married in their Chambers, and at Eight or Ten a Clock at Night.

I was a great while before I could be perswaded, and pretended not to be willing at all to be married but in the Church; but it was all Grimace;[4] so I seem'd at last to be prevail'd on, and my Landlord, and his Wife, and Daughter were call'd up: My Landlord was Father and Clark and all together, and we were married, and very Merry we were; tho' I confess the self-reproaches which I had upon me before lay close to me, and extorted every now and then a deep sigh from me, which my Bridegroom took notice of, and endeavour'd to encourage me, thinking, poor Man, that I had some little hesitations at the Step I had taken so hastily.

We enjoy'd our selves that Evening compleatly, and yet all was kept so private in the Inn, that not a Servant in the House knew of

3. *The Book of Common Prayer* contains the liturgy of the Church of England, including the sacraments of Baptism, Confirmation, and Matrimony.
4. Sham, hypocrisy.

it, for my Landlady and her Daughter waited on me, and would not let any of the Maids come up Stairs, except while we were at Supper: My Landlady's Daughter I call'd my Bride-maid, and sending for a Shop-keeper the next Morning, I gave the young Woman a good Suit of Knots,[5] as good as the Town would afford, and finding it was a Lace-making Town, I gave her Mother a piece of Bone-lace[6] for a Head.

One Reason that my Landlord was so close[7] was, that he was unwilling the Minister of the Parish should hear of it; but for all that somebody heard of it, so as that we had the Bells set a Ringing the next Morning early, and the Musick,[8] such as the Town would afford, under our Window; but my Landlord brazen'd it out, that we were marry'd before we came thither, only that being his former Guests, we would have our Wedding Supper at his House.

We cou'd not find in our Hearts to stir the next Day; for in short having been disturb'd by the Bells in the Morning, and having perhaps not slept over much Before, we were so sleepy afterwards that we lay in Bed till almost Twelve a Clock.

I beg'd my Landlady that we might not have any more Musick in the Town, nor Ringing of Bells, and she manag'd it so well that we were very quiet: But an odd Passage interrupted all my Mirth for a good while; the great Room of the House look'd into the Street, and my new Spouse being below Stairs, I had walk'd to the end of the Room, and it being a pleasant warm Day, I had opened the Window, and was standing at it for some Air, when I saw three Gentlemen come by on Horseback and go into an Inn just against[9] us.

It was not to be conceal'd, nor was it so doubtful as to leave me any room to question it, but the second of the three was my *Lancashire* Husband: I was frighted to Death, I never was in such a Consternation in my Life, I thought I should have sunk into the Ground, my Blood run Chill in my Veins, and I trembl'd as if I had been in a cold Fit of an Ague: I say there was no room to question the Truth of it, I knew his Cloaths, I knew his Horse, and I knew his Face.

The first sensible Reflection I made was, that my Husband was not by to see my Disorder, and that I was very glad of: The Gentlemen had not been long in the House but they came to the Window of their Room, as is usual; but my Window was shut you may be sure: However, I cou'd not keep from peeping at them, and there I

5. A set of ribbons to decorate apparel.
6. Lace made by knitting upon a pattern with bobbins of bone, used to trim head-dresses.
7. Close-mouthed, secretive. The parish minister would want the banns announced formally and would require the wedding to be performed in church in daylight.
8. The shivaree (from the French *charivari*), a loud, mock serenade for a newly married couple, was a longstanding custom for which the "musicians" generally expected a gratuity.
9. Opposite.

saw him again, heard him call out to one of the Servants of the House for something he wanted, and receiv'd all the terrfying Confirmations of its being the same Person that were possible to be had.

My next concern was to know, if possible, what was his Business there; but that was impossible; sometimes my Imagination form'd an Idea of one frightful thing, sometimes of another; sometimes I thought he had discover'd me, and was come to upbraid me with Ingratitude and Breach of Honour; and every Moment I fancied he was coming up the Stairs to Insult me; and innumerable fancies came into my Head of what was never in his Head, nor ever could be, unless the Devil had reveal'd it to him.

I remain'd in this fright near two Hours, and scarce ever kept my Eye from the Window or Door of the Inn where they were: At last hearing a great clutter in the Passage of their Inn, I run to the Window, and, to my great Satisfaction, see them all three go out again and Travel on Westward; had they gone toward *London*, I should have been still in a fright, lest I should meet him on the Road again, and that he should know me; but he went the contrary way, and so I was eas'd of that Disorder.

We resolv'd to be going the next Day, but about six a Clock at Night we were alarm'd with a great uproar in the Street, and People riding as if they had been out of their Wits, and what was it but a Hue and Cry[1] after three Highway Men, that had rob'd two Coaches, and some other Travellers near *Dunstable* Hill, and notice had, it seems, been given, that they had been seen at *Brickill* at such a House, meaning the House where those Gentlemen had been.

The House was immediately beset and search'd, but there were witnesses enough that the Gentlemen had been gone above three Hours; the Crowd having gathered about, we had the News presently; and I was heartily concern'd now another way: I presently told the People of the House, that I durst to say those were not the Persons, for that I knew one of the Gentlemen to be a very honest Person, and of a good Estate in *Lancashire*.

The Constable who came with the Hue and Cry was immediately inform'd of this, and came over to me to be satisfy'd from my own Mouth, and I assur'd him that I saw the three Gentlemen as I was at the Window; that I saw them afterwards at the Windows of the Room they din'd in; that I saw them afterwards take Horse, and I could assure him I knew one of them to be such a Man, that he was a Gentleman of a very good Estate, and an undoubted Character in *Lancashire*, from whence I was just now upon my Journey.

1. A great public clamor; specifically, the pursuit of a felon by a constable and a posse of shouting citizens, with all who heard being obliged to join the chase.

The assurance with which I deliver'd this gave the Mob Gentry a Check,[2] and gave the Constable such Satisfaction, that he immediately sounded a Retreat, told his People these were not the Men, but that he had an account they were very honest Gentlemen; and so they went all back again; what the Truth of the matter was I knew not, but certain it was that the Coaches were rob'd at *Dunstable* Hill, and 560 *l.* in Money taken, besides some of the Lace Merchants that always Travel that way had been visited too; as to the three Gentlemen, that remains to be explain'd hereafter.

Well, this Allarm stop'd us another Day, tho' my Spouse was for Travelling, and told me that it was always safest Travelling after a Robbery, for that the Thieves were sure to be gone far enough off when they had allarm'd the Country; but I was afraid and uneasy, and indeed principally lest my old Acquaintance should be upon the Road still, and should chance to see me.

I never liv'd four pleasanter Days together in my life; I was a meer Bride all this while, and my new Spouse strove to make me entirely easie in every thing; O could this State of Life have continued! how had all my past Troubles been forgot, and my future Sorrows been avoided! but I had a past life of a most wretched kind to account for, some of it in this World as well as in another.

We came away the fifth Day; and my Landlord, because he saw me uneasie, mounted himself, his Son, and three honest Country Fellows with good Fire-Arms, and, without telling us of it, follow'd the Coach, and would see us safe into *Dunstable*; we could do no less than treat them very handsomely at *Dunstable*, which Cost my Spouse about Ten or Twelve Shillings, and something he gave the Men for their Time too, but my Landlord would take nothing for himself.

This was the most happy Contrivance for me that could have fallen out, for had I come to *London* unmarried, I must either have come to him for the first Night's Entertainment, or have discovered to him that I had not one Acquaintance in the whole City of *London* that could receive a poor Bride for the first Night's Lodging with her Spouse: But now being an old married Woman, I made no scruple of going directly home with him, and there I took Possession at once of a House well Furnish'd, and a Husband in very good Circumstances, so that I had a prospect of a very happy Life, if I knew how to manage it; and I had leisure to consider of the real Value of the Life I was likely to live; how different it was to be from the loose ungovern'd part I had acted before, and how much happier a Life of Virtue and Sobriety is, than that which we call a Life of Pleasure.

O had this particular Scene of Life lasted, or had I learnt from

2. Disappointed the lower classes comprising the Hue and Cry.

that time I enjoy'd it, to have tasted the true sweetness of it, and had I not fallen into the Poverty which is the sure Bane of Virtue, how happy had I been, not only here, but perhaps for ever? for while I liv'd thus, I was really a Penitent for all my Life pass'd, I look'd back on it with Abhorrence, and might truly be said to hate my self for it; I often reflected how my Lover at the *Bath*, strook by the Hand of God, repented and abandon'd me, and refus'd to see me any more, tho' he lov'd me to an extreme; but I, prompted by that worst of Devils, Poverty, return'd to the vile Practice, and made the Advantage of what they call a handsome Face, be the Relief to my Necessities, and Beauty be a Pimp to Vice.

Now I seem'd landed in a safe Harbour, after the Stormy Voyage of Life past was at an end; and I began to be thankful for my Deliverance; I sat many an Hour by my self, and wept over the Remembrance of past Follies, and the dreadful Extravagances of a wicked Life, and sometimes I flatter'd my self that I had sincerely repented.

But there are Temptations which it is not in the Power of Human Nature to resist, and few know what would be their Case, if driven to the same Exigences: As Covetousness is the Root of all Evil, so Poverty is, I believe, the worst of all Snares: But I wave that Discourse till I come to the Experiment.[3]

I liv'd with this Husband in the utmost Tranquility; he was a Quiet, Sensible, Sober Man, Virtuous, Modest, Sincere, and in his Business Diligent and Just: His Business was in a narrow Compass, and his Income sufficient to a plentiful way of Living in the ordinary way; I do not say to keep an Equipage,[4] and make a Figure as the World calls it, nor did I expect it, or desire it; for as I abhorr'd the Levity and Extravagance of my former Life, so I chose now to live retir'd, frugal, and within our selves; I kept no Company, made no Visits; minded my Family, and oblig'd my Husband; and this kind of Life became a Pleasure to me.

We liv'd in an uninterrupted course of Ease and Content for Five Years, when a sudden Blow from an almost invisible Hand, blasted all my Happiness, and turn'd me out into the World in a Condition the reverse of all that had been before it.

My Husband having trusted one of his Fellow Clarks with a Sum of Money too much for our Fortunes to bear the Loss of, the Clark fail'd, and the Loss fell very heavy on my Husband, yet it was not so great neither, but that if he had had Spirit and Courage to have look'd his Misfortunes in the Face, his Credit was so good, that as I told him, he would easily recover it; for to sink under Trouble is to

3. Trial itself, the experience; i.e., Moll intends illustrating how necessity leads her into temptation.

4. Accoutrements of wealth, such as a carriage, horses, and attendants.

double the Weight, and he that will Die in it shall Die in it.[5]

It was in vain to speak comfortably to him, the Wound had sunk too deep, it was a Stab that touch'd the Vitals; he grew Melancholy and Disconsolate, and from thence Lethargick, and died; I foresaw the Blow, and was extremely oppress'd in my Mind, for I saw evidently that if he died I was undone.

I had had two Children by him and no more, for to tell the Truth, it began to be time for me to leave bearing Children, for I was now Eight and Forty, and I suppose if he had liv'd I should have had no more.

I was now left in a dismal and disconsolate Case indeed, and in several things worse than ever: First it was past the flourishing time with me when I might expect to be courted for a Mistress; that agreeable part had declin'd some time, and the Ruins only appear'd of what had been; and that which was worse than all was this, that I was the most dejected, disconsolate Creature alive; I that had encourag'd my Husband, and endeavour'd to support his Spirits under his Trouble, could not support my own; I wanted that Spirit in Trouble which I told him was so necessary to him for bearing the burthen.

But my Case was indeed Deplorable, for I was left perfectly Friendless and Helpless, and the Loss my Husband had sustain'd had reduc'd his Circumstances so low, that tho' indeed I was not in Debt, yet I could easily foresee that what was left would not support me long; that while it wasted daily for Subsistence, I had no way to encrease it one Shilling, so that it would be soon all spent, and then I saw nothing before me but the utmost Distress, and this represented it self so lively to my Thoughts, that it seem'd as if it was come, before it was really very near; also my very Apprehensions doubl'd the Misery, for I fancied every Sixpence that I paid but for a Loaf of Bread, was the last that I had in the World, and that Tomorrow I was to fast, and be starv'd to Death.

In this Distress I had no Assistant, no Friend to comfort or advise me, I sat and cried and tormented my self Night and Day; wringing my Hands, and sometimes raving like a distracted Woman; and indeed I have often wonder'd it had not affected my Reason, for I had the Vapours to such a degree, that my Understanding was sometimes quite lost in Fancies and Imaginations.

I liv'd Two Years in this dismal Condition wasting that little I had, weeping continually over my dismal Circumstances, and as it were only bleeding to Death, without the least hope or prospect of help from God or Man; and now I had cried so long, and so often, that Tears were, as I might say, exhausted, and I began to be Desperate, for I grew Poor apace.

5. He who has not the will to resist despair shall succumb to it.

For a little Relief I had put off my House and took Lodgings, and as I was reducing my Living so I sold off most of my Goods, which put a little Money in my Pocket, and I liv'd near a Year upon that, spending very sparingly, and eeking things out to the utmost; but still when I look'd before me, my very Heart would sink within me at the inevitable approach of Misery and Want: O let none read this part without seriously reflecting on the Circumstances of a desolate State, and how they would grapple with meer want of Friends and want of Bread; it will certainly make them think not of sparing what they have only, but of looking up to Heaven for support, and of the wise Man's Prayer, *Give me not Poverty lest I Steal.*[6]

Let 'em remember that a time of Distress is a time of dreadful Temptation, and all the Strength to resist is taken away; Poverty presses, the Soul is made Desperate by Distress, and what can be done? It was one Evening, when being brought, as I may say, to the last Gasp, I think I may truly say I was Distracted and Raving, when prompted by I know not what Spirit, and as it were, doing I did not know what, or why, I dress'd me, for I had still pretty good Cloaths, and went out: I am very sure I had no manner of Design in my Head when I went out, I neither knew or considered where to go, or on what Business; but as the Devil carried me out and laid his Bait for me, so he brought me to be sure to the place, for I knew not whither I was going or what I did.

Wandring thus about I knew not whither, I pass'd by an Apothecary's Shop in *Leadenhall-street,*[7] where I saw lye on a Stool just before the Counter a little Bundle wrapt in a white Cloth; beyond it, stood a Maid Servant with her Back to it, looking up towards the top of the Shop, where the Apothecary's Apprentice, as I suppose, was standing up on the Counter, with his Back also to the Door, and a Candle in his Hand, looking and reaching up to the upper Shelf for something he wanted, so that both were engag'd mighty earnestly, and no Body else in the Shop.

This was the Bait; and the Devil who I said laid the Snare, as readily prompted me, as if he had spoke, for I remember, and shall never forget it, 'twas like a Voice spoken to me over my Shoulder, take the Bundle; be quick; do it this Moment; it was no sooner said but I step'd into the Shop, and with my Back to the Wench, as if I had stood up for a Cart that was going by,[8] put my Hand behind me and took the Bundle, and went off with it, the Maid or the Fellow not perceiving me, or any one else.

6. A constant theme in Defoe's writings. See especially *Review*, VII, no. 75 (Saturday, September 15, 1711), which is devoted to the "wise man's prayer." The source may be Proverbs 30:9.
7. A market site east of the Royal Ex-change.
8. I.e., as if she had flattened herself against the entrance to avoid being splashed by a passing cart in a narrow street.

It is impossible to express the Horror of my Soul all the while I did it: When I went away I had no Heart to run, or scarce to mend my pace; I cross'd the Street indeed, and went down the first turning I came to, and I think it was a Street that went thro' into *Fen-church-street*, from thence I cross'd and turn'd thro' so many ways and turnings that I could never tell which way it was, nor where I went, for I felt not the Ground, I stept on, and the farther I was out of Danger, the faster I went, till tyr'd and out of Breath, I was forc'd to sit down on a little Bench at a Door, and then I began to recover, and found I was got into *Thames-street* near *Billinsgate*:[9] I rested me a little and went on, my Blood was all in a Fire, my Heart beat as if I was in a sudden Fright: In short, I was under such a Surprize that I still knew not whither I was a going, or what to do.

After I had tyr'd my self thus with walking a long way about, and so eagerly, I began to consider and make home to my Lodging, where I came about Nine a Clock at Night.

What the Bundle was made up for, or on what Occasion laid where I found it, I knew not, but when I came to open it I found there was a Suit of Child-bed Linnen in it, very good and almost new, the Lace very fine; there was a Silver Porringer[1] of a Pint, a small Silver Mug and Six Spoons, some other Linnen, a good Smock, and Three Silk Handkerchiefs, and in the Mug wrap'd up in a Paper Eighteen Shillings and Six-pence in Money.

All the while I was opening these things I was under such dreadful Impressions of Fear, and in such Terror of Mind, tho' I was per-fectly safe, that I cannot express the manner of it; I sat me down and cried most vehemently; Lord, *said I*, what am I now? a Thief! why I shall be taken next time and be carry'd to *Newgate* and be Try'd for my Life! and with that I cry'd again a long time, and I am sure, as poor as I was, if I had durst for fear, I would certainly have carried the things back again, but that went off after a while: Well, I went to Bed for that Night, but slept little, the Horror of the Fact was upon my Mind, and I knew not what I said or did all Night, and all the next Day: Then I was impatient to hear some News of the Loss; and would fain know how it was, whether they were a Poor Bodies Goods, or a Rich; perhaps, *said I*, it may be some poor Widow like me, that had pack'd up these Goods to go and sell them for a little Bread for herself and a poor Child, and are now starving and breaking their Hearts, for want of that little they would have fetch'd, and this Thought tormented me worse than all the rest, for three or four Days time.

But my own Distresses silenc'd all these Reflections, and the

9. The area of the robbery and Moll's escape route may be located on the Map of Moll Flanders' London, pp. 438–439.
1. Child's bowl.

prospect of my own Starving, which grew every Day more frightful to me, harden'd my Heart by degrees; it was then particularly heavy upon my Mind, that I had been reform'd, and had, as I hop'd, repented of all my pass'd wickednesses; that I had liv'd a sober, grave, retir'd Life for several Years, but now I should be driven by the dreadful Necessity of my Circumstances to the Gates of Destruction, Soul and Body; and two or three times I fell upon my Knees, praying to God, as well as I could, for Deliverance; but I cannot but say my Prayers had no hope in them; I knew not what to do, it was all Fear without, and Dark within; and I reflected on my pass'd Life as not sincerely repented of, that Heaven was now beginning to punish me on this side the Grave, and would make me as miserable as I had been wicked.

Had I gone on here I had perhaps been a true Penitent; but I had an evil Counsellor within, and he was continually prompting me to relieve my self by the worst means; so one Evening he tempted me again by the same wicked Impulse that had said, *take that Bundle*, to go out again and seek for what might happen.

I went out now by Day-light, and wandred about I knew not whither, and in search of I knew not what, when the Devil put a Snare in my way of a dreadful Nature indeed, and such a one as I have never had before or since; going thro' *Aldersgate-street* there was a pretty little Child had been at a Dancing-School, and was going home, all alone, and my Prompter, like a true Devil, set me upon this innocent Creature; I talk'd to it, and it prattl'd to me again, and I took it by the Hand and led it a long till I came to a pav'd Alley that goes into *Batholomew Close*, and I led it in there; the Child said that was not its way home; I said, yes, my Dear it is, I'll show you the way home; the Child had a little Necklace on of Gold Beads, and I had my Eye upon that, and in the dark of the Alley I stoop'd, pretending to mend the Child's Clog that was loose, and took off her Necklace and the Child never felt it, and so led the Child on again: Here, I say, the Devil put me upon killing the Child in the dark Alley, that it might not Cry; but the very thought frighted me so that I was ready to drop down, but I turn'd the Child about and bade it go back again, for that was not its way home; the Child said so she would, and I went thro' into *Bartholo-mew Close*, and then turn'd round to another Passage that goes into *Long-lane*, so away into *Charterhouse-Yard* and out into *St. John's-street*, then crossing into *Smithfield*, went down *Chick-lane* and into *Field-lane* to *Holbourn-bridge*, when mixing with the Crowd of People usually passing there, it was not possible to have been found out; and thus I enterpriz'd my second Sally into the World.[2]

2. I.e., world of crime.

The thoughts of this Booty put out all the thoughts of the first, and the Reflections I had made wore quickly off; Poverty, as I have said, harden'd my Heart, and my own Necessities made me regardless of any thing: The last Affair left no great Concern upon me, for as I did the poor Child no harm, I only said to my self, I had given the Parents a just Reproof for their Negligence in leaving the poor little Lamb to come home by it self, and it would teach them to take more Care of it another time.

blame it on the victim to avoid feeling guilty

This String of Beads was worth about Twelve or Fourteen Pounds; I suppose it might have been formerly the Mother's, for it was too big for the Child's wear, but that, perhaps, the Vanity of the Mother to have her Child look Fine at the Dancing School, had made her let the Child wear it; and no doubt the Child had a Maid sent to take care of it, but she, like a careless Jade, was taken up perhaps with some Fellow that had met her by the way, and so the poor Baby wandred till it fell into my Hands.

However, I did the Child no harm; I did not so much as fright it, for I had a great many tender Thoughts about me yet, and did nothing but what, as I may say, meer Necessity drove me to.

I had a great many Adventures after this, but I was young in the Business, and did not know how to manage, otherwise than as the Devil put things into my Head; and indeed he was seldom backward to me: One Adventure I had which was very lucky to me; I was going thro' *Lombard-street* in the dusk of the Evening, just by the end of *Three King Court*, when on a sudden comes a Fellow running by me as swift as Lightning, and throws a Bundle that was in his Hand just behind me, as I stood up against the corner of the House at the turning into the Alley; just as he threw it in he said, God bless you Mistress let it lie there a little, and away he runs swift as the Wind: After him comes two more, and immediately a young Fellow without his Hat, crying stop Thief, and after him two or three more, they pursued the two last Fellows so close, that they were forced to drop what they had got, and one of them was taken into the bargain, the other got off free.

I stood stock still all this while till they came back, dragging the poor Fellow they had taken, and lugging the things they had found, extremely well satisfied that they had recovered the Booty and taken the Thief; and thus they pass'd by me, for I look'd only like one who stood up while the Crowd was gone.

Once or twice I ask'd what was the matter, but the People neglected answering me, and I was not very importunate; but after the Crowd was wholly pass'd, I took my opportunity to turn about and take up what was behind me and walk away: This indeed I did with less Disturbance than I had done formerly, for these things I did not steal, but they were stolen to my Hand: I got safe to my

Lodgings with this Cargo, which was a Peice of fine black Lustring Silk,[3] and a Peice of Velvet; the latter was but part of a Peice of about 11 Yards; the former was a whole Peice of near 50 Yards; it seems it was a *Mercer's* Shop that they had rifled, I say rifled, because the Goods were so considerable that they had Lost; for the Goods that they Recover'd were pretty many, and I believe came to about six or seven several[4] Peices of Silk: How they came to get so many I could not tell; but as I had only robb'd the Thief I made no scruple at taking these Goods, and being very glad of them too.

I had pretty good Luck thus far, and I made several Adventures more, tho' with but small Purchase;[5] yet with good Success, but I went in daily dread that some mischief would befal me, and that I should certainly come to be hang'd at last: The impression this made on me was too strong to be slighted, and it kept me from making attempts that for ought I know might have been very safely perform'd; but one thing I cannot omit, which was a Bait to me many a Day. I walk'd frequently out into the Villages round the Town to see if nothing would fall in my Way there; and going by a House near *Stepney*, I saw on the Window-board two Rings, one a small Diamond Ring, and the other a plain Gold Ring, to be sure laid there by some thoughtless Lady, that had more Money than Forecast,[6] perhaps only till she wash'd her Hands.

I walk'd several times by the Window to observe if I could see whether there was any Body in the Room or no, and I could see no Body, but still I was not sure; it came presently into my Thoughts to rap at the Glass, as if I wanted to speak with some Body, and if any Body was there they would be sure to come to the Window, and then I would tell them to remove those Rings, for that I had seen two suspicious Fellows take notice of them: This was a ready Thought, I rapt once or twice and no Body came, when seeing the Coast clear, I thrust hard against the Square of Glass, and broke it with very little Noise, and took out the two Rings, and walk'd away with them very safe; the Diamond Ring was worth about 3*l.* and the other about 9*s.*

I was now at a loss for a Market for my Goods, and especially for my two Peices of Silk, I was very loth to dispose of them for a Trifle; as the poor unhappy Theives in general do, who after they have ventured their Lives for perhaps a thing of Value, are fain to sell it for a Song when they have done; but I was resolv'd I would not do thus whatever shift I made, unless I was driven to the last Extremity; however I did not well know what Course to take: At last I resolv'd to go to my old Governess, and acquaint myself with her again: I had punctually supply'd the 5*l.* a Year to her for my

---

3. Light silk with a glossy surface.
4. Different.

5. Gain, booty.
6. Foresight.

little Boy as long as I was able; but at last was oblig'd to put a stop to it: However I had written a Letter to her, wherein I had told her that my Circumstances were reduc'd very low; that I had lost my Husband, and that I was not able to do it any longer, and so beg'd that the poor Child might not suffer too much for its Mother's Misfortunes.

I now made her a Visit, and I found that she drove something of the old Trade still, but that she was not in such flourishing Circumstances as before; for she had been Sued by a certain Gentleman who had had his Daughter stolen from him, and who it seems she had helped to convey away; and it was very narrowly that she escap'd the Gallows; the Expence also had ravag'd her, and she was become very poor; her House was but meanly Furnished, and she was not in such repute for her Practice as before; however she stood upon her Legs, as they say, and as she was a stirring bustling Woman, and had some Stock left, she was turn'd *Pawn Broker, and liv'd pretty well.*

She receiv'd me very civilly, and with her usual obliging manner told me she would not have the less respect for me, for my being reduc'd; that she had taken Care my Boy was very well look'd after, tho' I could not pay for him, and that the Woman that had him was easie,[7] so that I needed not to Trouble myself about him, till I might be better able to do it effectually.

I told her I had not much Money left, but that I had some things that were Monies worth, if she could tell me how I might turn them into Money; she ask'd me what it was I had, I pull'd out the string of gold Beads, and told her it was one of my Husbands Presents to me; then I show'd her the two Parcels of Silk which I told her I had from *Ireland*, and brought up to Town with me; and the little Diamond Ring; as to the small Parcel of Plate and Spoons, I had found means to dispose of them myself before; and as for the Childbed Linnen I had, she offer'd me to take it herself, believing it to have been my own; she told me that she was turn'd *Pawn-Broker*, and that she would sell those things for me as pawn'd to her; and so she sent presently for proper Agents that bought them, being in her Hands, without any scruple, and gave good Prizes[8] too.

I now began to think this necessary Woman might help me a little in my low Condition to some Business, for I would gladly have turn'd my Hand to any honest Employment if I could have got it; but here she was defficient; honest Business did not come within her reach; if I had been younger, perhaps she might have helped me to a Spark,[9] but my Thoughts were off of that kind of

7. Not pressed financially.
8. Prices.

9. Beau, suitor.

Livelihood, as being quite out of the way after 50, which was my Case, and so I told her.

She invited me at last to come, and be at her House till I could find something to do, and it should cost me very little, and this I gladly accepted of, and now living a little easier, I enter'd into some Measures to have my little Son by my last Husband taken off;[1] and this she made easie too, reserving a Payment only of 5*l.* a Year, if I could pay it. This was such a help to me, that for a good while I left off the wicked Trade that I had so newly taken up; and gladly I would have got my Bread by the help of my Needle if I cou'd have got Work, but that was very hard to do for one that had no manner of Acquaintance in the World.

However at last I got some Quilting-Work for Ladies Beds, Petti-coats, and the like; and this I lik'd very well and work'd very hard, and with this I began to live; but the diligent Devil who resolv'd I should continue in his Service, continually prompted me to go out and take a Walk, that is to say, to see if any thing would offer in the old Way.

One Evening I blindly obeyed his Summons, and fetch'd a long Circuit thro' the Streets, but met with no purchase and came Home very weary, and empty; but not content with that, I went out the next Evening too, when going by an Alehouse I saw the Door of a little room open, next the very Street, and on the Table a silver Tankard, things much in use in publick Houses at that time; it seems some Company had been drinking there, and the careless Boys had forgot to take it away.

I went into the Box frankly,[2] and setting the silver Tankard on the Corner of the Bench, I sat down before it, and knock'd with my Foot, a Boy came presently, and I bade him fetch me a pint of warm Ale, for it was cold Weather; the Boy run, and I heard him go down the Cellar to draw the Ale; while the Boy was gone, another Boy come into the Room, and cried, *d' ye call?* I spoke with a melancholly Air, and said, no Child, the Boy is gone for a Pint of Ale for me.

While I sat here, I heard the Woman in the Bar say are they all gone in the Five? which was the Box I sat in, and the Boy said *yes*; who fetch'd the Tankard away? *says the Woman*; I did, *says another Boy*, that's it, pointing it seems to another Tankard, which he had fetch'd from another Box by Mistake; or else it must be, that the Rogue forgot that he had not brought it in, which certainly he had not.

I heard all this, much to my satisfaction, for I found plainly that the Tankard was not mist, and yet they concluded it was fetch'd away; so I drank my Ale, call'd to Pay, and as I went away, *I said,*

---

1. Taken off her hands.   2. Entered the booth openly.

take care of your Plate Child, meaning a silver pint Mug, which he
brought me Drink in; the Boy said, *yes Madam, very welcome*, and
away I came.

I came Home to my Governess, and now I thought it was a time
to try her, that if I might be put to the Necessity of being expos'd,
she might offer me some assistance; when I had been at Home
some time, and had an opportunity of Talking to her, I told her I
had a Secret of the greatest Consequence in the World to commit
to her if she had respect enough for me to keep it a Secret: She told
me she had kept one of my Secrets faithfully; why should I doubt
her keeping another? I told her the strangest thing in the World
had befallen me, and that it had made a Thief of me, even without
any design; and so told her the whole Story of the Tankard: And
have you brought it away with you my Dear? *says she*, to be sure I
have, *says I*, and shew'd it her. But what shall I do now, *says I*,
must not I carry it again?

Carry it again! *says she*, Ay, if you are minded to be sent to
Newgate for stealing it; why, *says I*, they can't be so base to stop
me, when I carry it to them again? You don't know those Sort of
People Child, *says she*, they'll not only carry you to *Newgate*, but
hang you too without any regard to the honesty of returning it; or
bring in an Account of all the other Tankards they have lost for you
to pay for: What must I do then? *says I*; Nay, *says she*, as you have
played the cunning part and stole it, you must e'n keep it, there's
no going back now; besides Child, *says she*, Don't you want it more
than they do? I wish you cou'd light of such a Bargain once a
Week.

This gave me a new Notion of my *Governess*, and that since she
was turn'd *Pawn Broker*, she had a Sort of People about her, that
were none of the honest ones that I had met with there before.

I had not been long there, but I discover'd it more plainly than
before, for every now and then I saw Hilts of Swords, Spoons,
Forks, Tankards, and all such kind of Ware brought in, not to be
Pawn'd, but to be sold down right; and she bought every thing that
came without asking any Questions, but had very good Bargains as I
found by her Discourse.

I found also that in the following this Trade, she always melted
down the Plate she bought, that it might not be challeng'd; and she
came to me and told me one Morning that she was going to Melt,
and if I would, she would put my Tankard in, that it might not be
seen by any Body; I told her with all my Heart; so she weigh'd it,
and allow'd me the full value in Silver again; but I found she did
not do the same to the rest of her Customers.

Sometime after this, as I was at Work, and very melancholly, she
begins to ask me what the Matter was? as she was us'd to do; I told

her my Heart was heavy, I had little Work, and nothing to live on, and knew not what Course to take; she Laugh'd and told me I must go out again and try my Fortune; it might be that I might meet with another Peice of Plate. O, Mother! *says I*, that is a Trade I have no skill in, and if I should be taken I am undone at once; *says she*, I cou'd help you to a School-Mistress,[3] that shall make you as dexterous as her self: I trembled at that Proposal for hitherto I had had no Confederates, nor any Acquaintance among that Tribe; but she conquer'd all my Modesty, and all my Fears; and in a little time, by the help of this Confederate I grew as impudent a Thief, and as dexterous as ever *Moll Cut-Purse*[4] was, tho' if Fame does not belie her, not half so Handsome.

The Comrade she helped me to dealt in three sorts of Craft, (*viz.*) Shop-lifting, stealing of Shop-Books and Pocket-Books, and taking off Gold Watches from the Ladies Sides, and this last she did so dexteriously that no Woman ever arriv'd to the Perfection of that Art, so as to do it like her: I lik'd the first and the last of these things very well, and I attended her some time in the Practise, just as a Deputy attends a Midwife without any Pay.

At length she put me to Practise; she had shewn me her Art, and I had several times unhook'd a Watch from her own side with great dexterity; at last she show'd me a Prize, and this was a young Lady big with Child who had a charming Watch; the thing was to be done as she came out of Church; she goes on one side of the Lady, and pretends, just as she came to the Steps, to fall, and fell against the Lady with so much violence as put her into a great fright, and both cry'd out terribly; in the very moment that she jostl'd the Lady, I had hold of the Watch, and holding it the right way, the start she gave drew the Hook out and she never felt it; I made off immediately, and left my Schoolmistress to come out of her pretended Fright gradually, and the Lady too; and presently the Watch was miss'd; ay, says my Comrade, then it was those Rogues that thrust me down, I warrant ye; I wonder the Gentlewoman did not miss her Watch before, then we might have taken them.

She humour'd[5] the thing so well that no Body suspected her, and I was got home a full Hour before her: This was my first Adventure in Company; the Watch was indeed a very fine one, and had a great many Trinkets about it, and my Governess allow'd us 2*ol.* for

3. Tutoress in crime.
4. Alias of Mary Frith (c. 1584–1659), famous thief of the seventeenth century. Her life appears in Captain Alexander Smith's *Complete History of the Lives and Robberies of the Most Notorious Highwaymen, Footpads, Shoplifts and Cheats of Both Sexes* (London, 1714). Middleton and Dekker celebrated her character in *The Roaring Girle, or Moll Cut-Purse* (1611), and she also exhibited her "merry prankes" in Field's *Amends for Ladies* (c. 1618). Several incidents in her life parallel happenings in *Moll Flanders*, especially where both Molls practice crime while disguised as men. The term "cut-purse" derives from thieves' practice of cutting purses loose from belts worn about the waist.
5. Managed so delicately.

it, of which I had half, and thus I was enter'd a compleat Thief, Harden'd to a Pitch above all the Reflections of Conscience or Modesty, and to a Degree which I must acknowledge I never thought possible in me.

Thus the Devil who began, by the help of an irresistable Poverty, to push me into this Wickedness, brought me on to a height beyond the common Rate, even when my Necessities were not so great, or the prospect of my Misery so terrifying; for I had now got into a little Vein of Work, and as I was not at a loss to handle my Needle, it was very probable, as Acquaintance came in, I might have got my Bread honestly enough.

I must say, that if such a prospect of Work had presented it self at first, when I began to feel the approach of my miserable Circumstances, I say, had such a prospect of getting my Bread by working presented it self then, I had never fallen into this wicked Trade, or into such a wicked Gang as I was now embark'd with; but practise had hardened me, and I grew audacious to the last degree; and the more so, because I had carried it on so long, and had never been taken; for in a word, my new Partner in Wickedness *and I* went on together so long, without being ever detected, that we not only grew Bold, but we grew Rich, and we had at one time One and Twenty Gold Watches in our Hands.

I remember that one Day being a little more serious than ordinary, and finding I had so good a Stock before-hand as I had, for I had near 200 *l*. in Money for my Share, it came strongly into my Mind, no doubt from some kind Spirit, if such there be, that as at first Poverty excited me, and my Distresses drove me to these dreadful Shifts; so seeing those Distresses were now relieved, and I could also get something towards a Maintenance by working, and had so good a Bank to support me, why should I not now leave off, as they say, while I was well; that I could not expect to go always free; and if I was once surpris'd, and miscarry'd, I was undone.

This was doubtless the happy Minute, when if I had hearken'd to the blessed hint from whatsoever hand it came, I had still a cast for an easie Life; but my Fate was otherwise determin'd; the busie Devil that so industriously drew me in, had too fast hold of me to let me go back; but as Poverty brought me into the Mire, so Avarice kept me in, till there was no going back; as to the Arguments which my Reason dictated for perswading me to lay down, Avarice stept in and said, go on, go on; you have had very good luck, go on till you have gotten Four or Five Hundred Pound, and then you shall leave off, and then you may live easie without working at all.

Thus I that was once in the Devil's Clutches, was held fast there as with a Charm, and had no Power to go without the Circle, till I was ingulph'd in Labyrinths of Trouble too great to get out at all.

However, these Thoughts left some Impression upon me, and made me act with some more caution than before, and more than my Directors us'd for themselves. My Comerade, as I call'd her, but rather she should have been called my Teacher, with another of her Scholars,[6] was the first in the Misfortune, for happening to be upon the hunt for Purchase, they made an attempt upon a Linnen-Draper in *Cheapside,* but were snap'd by a Hawks-ey'd Journey-man,[7] and seiz'd with two pieces of Cambrick, which were taken also upon them.

This was enough to Lodge them both in *Newgate,* where they had the Misfortune to have some of their former Sins brought to remembrance; two other Indictments being brought against them, and the Facts being prov'd upon them, they were both condemned to Die; they both pleaded their Bellies, and were both voted Quick with Child;[8] tho' my Tutress was no more with Child than I was.

I went frequently to see them, and Condole with them, expecting that it would be my turn next; but the place gave me so much Horror, reflecting that it was the place of my unhappy Birth, and of my Mother's Misfortunes, that I could not bear it, so I was forc'd to leave off going to see them.

And O! cou'd I have but taken warning by their Disasters, I had been happy still, for I was yet free, and had nothing brought against me; but it could not be, my Measure was not yet fill'd up.

My Comerade having the Brand of an old Offender, was Executed; the young Offender was spar'd, having obtain'd a Reprieve; but lay starving a long while in Prison, till at last she got her Name into what they call a Circuit Pardon,[9] and so came off.

This terrible Example of my Comerade frighted me heartily, and for a good while I made no Excursions; but one Night, in the Neighbourhood of my Governesses House, they cryed Fire; my Governess look'd out, for we were all up, and cryed immediately that such a Gentlewoman's House was all of a light Fire a top, and so indeed it was: Here she gives me a jog, now, Child, says she, there is a rare opportunity, the Fire being so near that you may go to it before the Street is block'd up with the Crowd;[1] she presently gave me my Cue, go, Child, *says she,* to the House, and run in and tell the Lady, or any Body you see, that you come to help them, and that you came from such a Gentlewoman (that is one of her Acquaintance farther up the Street); she gave me the like Cue to

6. The idea of criminals as scholars who would matriculate at "Newgate College" was popular early in the eighteenth century. See "Hell upon Earth" . . . in Backgrounds and Sources, p. 289, below.
7. Caught ("snap'd") by a sharp-eyed journeyman, a worker whose rank was between those of apprentice and master.
8. Adjudged to be pregnant.
9. Apparently a remission of punishment by having her name included in a general pardon.
1. A forerunner of this fire episode appears in Defoe's *Review.* See Backgrounds and Sources, p. 296, below.

the next House, naming another Name that was also an Acquaintance of the Gentlewoman of the House.

Away I went, and coming to the House I found them all in Confusion, you may be sure; I run in, and finding one of the Maids,
Lord! Sweetheart, *said I*, how came this dismal Accident? Where is
your Mistress? And how does she do? Is she safe? And where are
the Children? I come from Madam —————— to help you; away runs
the Maid; Madam, Madam, *says she*, screaming as loud as she cou'd
yell, *here is a Gentlewoman come from Madam —————— to help us.*
The poor Woman half out of her Wits, with a Bundle under her
Arm, and two little Children, comes towards me, *Lord, Madam,
says I*, let me carry the poor Children to Madam ——————, she
desires you to send them; she'll take care of the poor Lambs, and
immediately I takes one of them out of her Hand, and she lifts the
tother[2] up into my Arms; *ay, do, for God sake*, says she, *carry them
to her*; *O thank her for her kindness*: Have you *any thing else to
secure*, Madam? says I, *she will take care of it*: O dear! ay, says she,
*God bless her, and thank her, take this bundle of Plate and carry it
to her too*; *O she is a good Woman*; *O Lord, we are utterly ruin'd,
utterly undone*; and away she runs from me out of her Wits, and
the Maids after her, and away comes I with the two Children and
the Bundle.

I was no sooner got into the Street, but I saw another Woman
come to me, O! *says she*, Mistress, in a piteous Tone, you will let
fall the Child; come, this is a sad time, let me help you, and immediately lays hold of my Bundle to carry it for me; no, *says I*, if you
will help me, take the Child by the Hand, and lead it for me but to
the upper end of the Street, I'll go with you and satisfie you for
your pains.

She cou'd not avoid going, after what I said, but the Creature, in
short, was one of the Same Business with me, and wanted nothing
but the Bundle; however, she went with me to the Door, for she
cou'd not help it; when we were come there I whisper'd her, *go
Child*, said I, *I understand your Trade*, you may meet with Purchase enough.

She understood me and walk'd off; I thundered at the Door with
the Children, and as the People were rais'd before by the noise of
the Fire, I was soon let in, and I said, *is Madam awake, pray tell
her* Mrs. —————— *desires the favour of her to take the two Children
in*; poor Lady, *she will be undone, their House is all of a Flame*;
they took the Children in very civily, pitied the Family in Distress,
and away came I with my Bundle; one of the Maids ask'd me if I
was not to leave the Bundle too? I said no, Sweetheart, 'tis to go to
another place, it does not belong to them.

2. The other; written variously "tother" or "t'other."

I was a great way out of the hurry now, and so I went on, clear of any Body's enquiry, and brought the bundle of Plate, which was very considerable, strait home, and gave it to my old Governess; she told me she would not look into it, but bade me go out again to look for more.

She gave me the like Cue to the Gentlewoman of the next House to that which was on Fire, and I did my endeavour to go, but by this time the allarm of Fire was so great, and so many Engines play-ing,[3] and the Street so throng'd with People, that I cou'd not get near the House, whatever I cou'd do; so I came back again to my Governesses, and taking the Bundle up into my Chamber, I began to examine it: It is with Horror that I tell what a Treasure I found there; 'tis enough to say, that besides most of the Family Plate, which was considerable, I found a Gold Chain, an old fashion'd thing, the Locket of which was broken, so that I suppose it had not been us'd some Years, but the Gold was not the worse for that; also a little Box of burying Rings,[4] the Lady's Wedding-Ring, and some broken bits of old Lockets of Gold, a Gold Watch, and a Purse with about 24 *l.* value in old pieces of Gold Coin, and several other things of Value.

This was the greatest and the worst Prize that ever I was con-cern'd in, for indeed, tho' as I have said above, I was harden'd now beyond the Power of all Reflection in other Cases, yet it really touch'd me to the very Soul, when I look'd into this Treasure, to think of the poor disconsolate Gentlewoman who had lost so much by the Fire besides; and who would think to be sure that she had sav'd her Plate and best things; how she wou'd be surpriz'd and afflicted when she should find that she had been deceiv'd, and should find that the Person that took her Children and her Goods, had not come, as was pretended, from the Gentlewoman in the next Street, but that the Children had been put upon her without her own knowledge.

I say I confess the inhumanity of this Action mov'd me very much, and made me relent exceedingly, and Tears stood in my Eyes upon that Subject: But with all my Sense of its being cruel and Inhuman, I cou'd never find in my Heart to make any Restitution: The Reflection wore off, and I began quickly to forget the Circum-stances that attended the taking them.

Nor was this all, for tho' by this jobb I was become considerably Richer than before, yet the Resolution I had formerly taken of leav-ing off this horrid Trade, when I had gotten a little more, did not

3. Playing streams of water on the fire. The engines were basically equipped with manual pumps and grappling hooks. See John Gay, *Trivia*, III, 353–386, for a de-scription of engines at a London fire.
4. Mourners were often given commem-orative rings at eighteenth-century fun-erals. For example, see Read's adaptation of *Moll Flanders*, which includes the last will and testament of Elizabeth At-kins, in Backgrounds and Sources, p. 306, below.

return; but I must still get farther, and more; and the Avarice join'd so with the Success, that I had no more thoughts of coming to a timely Alteration of Life; tho' without it I cou'd expect no Safety, no Tranquility in the Possession of what I had so wickedly gain'd; but a little more, and a little more, was the Case still.

At length yielding to the Importunities of my Crime, I cast off all Remorse and Repentance; and all the Reflections on that Head, turn'd to no more than this, that I might perhaps come to have one Booty more that might compleat my Desires; but tho' I certainly had that one Booty, yet every hit look'd towards another, and was so encouraging to me to go on with the Trade, that I had no Gust to the Thought of laying it down.

In this Condition, harden'd by Success, and resolving to go on, I fell into the Snare in which I was appointed to meet with my last Reward for this kind of Life: But even this was not yet, for I met with several successful Adventures more in this way of being undone.

I remain'd still with my Governess, who was for a while really concern'd for the Misfortune of my Comerade that had been hang'd, and who it seems knew enough of my Governess to have sent her the same way, and which made her very uneasy; indeed she was in a very great fright.

It is true that when she was gone, and had not open'd her Mouth to tell what she knew, my Governess was easy as to that Point, and perhaps glad she was hang'd; for it was in her power to have obtain'd a Pardon at the Expence of her Friends; But on the other Hand, the loss of her, and the Sense of her Kindness in not making her Market[5] of what she knew, mov'd my Governess to Mourn very sincerely for her: I comforted her as well as I cou'd, and she in return harden'd me to Merit more compleatly the same Fate.

However as I have said it made me the more wary, and particularly I was very shie of Shoplifting, especially among the *Mercers*, and *Drapers* who are a Set of Fellows that have their Eyes very much about them: I made a Venture or two among the Lace Folks, and the Milliners, and particularly at one Shop, where I got Notice of two young Women who were newly set up, and had not been bred to the Trade: There, I think I carried off a Peice of Bonelace, worth six or seven pound, and a Paper of Thread; but this was but once, it was a Trick that would not serve again.

It was always reckon'd a safe Job when we heard of a new Shop, especially when the People were such as were not bred to Shops; such may depend upon it, that they will be visited once or twice at their beginning, and they must be very Sharp indeed if they can prevent it.

I made another Adventure or two, but they were but Trifles too,

5. Saving herself by informing on others.

tho' sufficient to live on; after this nothing considerable offering for a good while, I began to think that I must give over the Trade in Earnest; but my Governess, who was not willing to lose me, and expected great Things of me, brought me one Day into Company with a young Woman and a Fellow that went for her Husband, tho' as it appear'd afterwards she was not his Wife, but they were Partners it seems in the Trade they carried on, and Partners in something else too. *In short*, they robb'd together, lay together, were taken together, and at last were hang'd together.

I came into a kind of League with these two, by the help of my Governess, and they carried me out into three or four Adventures, where I rather saw them commit some Coarse and unhandy Robberies, in which nothing but a great Stock of impudence on their Side, and gross Negligence on the Peoples Side who were robb'd, could have made them Successful; so I resolv'd from that time forward to be very Cautious how I Adventur'd upon any thing with them; and indeed when two or three unlucky Projects were propos'd by them, I declin'd the offer, and perswaded them against it: One time they particularly propos'd Robbing a Watchmaker of 3 Gold Watches, which they had Ey'd in the Day time, and found the Place where he laid them; one of them had so many Keys of all kinds, that he made no Question to open the Place where the Watchmaker had laid them; and so we made a kind of an Appointment; but when I came to look narrowly into the Thing, I found they propos'd breaking open the House; and this as a thing out of my Way, I would not Embark in; so they went without me: They did get into the House by main Force, and broke up the lock'd Place where the Watches were, but found but one of the Gold Watches, and a Silver one, which they took, and got out of the House again very clear, but the Family being alarm'd cried out, Thieves, and the Man was pursued and taken, the young Woman had got off too, but unhappily was stop'd at a Distance, and the Watches found upon her; and thus I had a second Escape, for they were convicted, and both hang'd, being old Offenders, tho' but young People; as *I said before*, that they robbed together, and lay together, so now they hang'd together, and there ended my new Partnership.

I began now to be very wary, having so narrowly escap'd a Scouring,[6] and having such an Example before me; but I had a new Tempter, who prompted me every Day, I mean my Governess; and now a Prize presented, which as it came by her Management, so she expected a good Share of the Booty; there was a good Quantity of Flanders-Lace Lodg'd in a private House, where she had gotten Intelligence of it; and Flanders-Lace, being then Prohibited,[7] it was a good Booty to any Custom-House Officer that could come at it: I

---

6. Severe punishment.
7. There was a ban on importing Flanders lace "made in the dominion of the French King," so Moll is reporting contraband to the customs officer.

had a full Account from my Governess, as well of the Quantity as of the very Place where it was conceal'd, and I went to a Custom-House Officer, and told him I had such a Discovery to make to him, of such a Quantity of Lace, if he would assure me that I should have my due Share of the Reward: This was so just an offer, that nothing could be fairer; so he agreed, and taking a Constable and me with him, we beset the House; as I told him I could go directly to the Place, He left it to me, and the Hole being very dark, I squeez'd myself into it with a Candle in my Hand, and so reach'd the Peices out to him, taking care as I gave him some, so to secure as much about myself as I could conveniently Dispose of: There was near 300 *l.* worth of Lace in the whole, and I secur'd about 50 *l.* worth of it to myself: The People of the House were not owners of the Lace, but a Merchant who had entrusted them with it; so that they were not so surpriz'd as I thought they would be.

I left the Officer overjoy'd with his Prize, and fully satisfy'd with what he had got, and appointed to meet him at a House of his own directing, where I came after I had dispos'd of the Cargo I had about me, of which he had not the least Suspicion; when I came to him, he began to Capitulate[8] with me, believing I did not understand the right I had to a Share in the Prize, and would fain have put me off with Twenty Pound, but I let him know that I was not so ignorant as he suppos'd I was; and yet I was glad too, that he offer'd to bring me to a certainty;[9] I ask'd 100 *l.* and he rise up to 30 *l.* I fell to 80 *l.* and he rise again to 40 *l.* in a Word, he offer'd 50 *l.* and I consented, only demanding a Peice of Lace, which I thought came to about 8 or 9 Pound, as if it had been for my own Wear, and he agreed to it, so I got 50 *l.* in Money paid me that same Night, and made an End of the Bargain; nor did he ever know who I was, or where to enquire for me; so that if it had been discover'd, that part of the Goods were embezzel'd; he could have made no Challenge upon me for it.

I very punctually divided this Spoil with my Governess, and I pass'd with her from this time for a very dexterous Manager in the nicest Cases; I found that this last was the best, and easiest sort of Work that was in my way, and I made it my business to enquire out prohibited Goods; and after buying some usually betray'd them, but none of these Discoveries amounted to any thing Considerable, not like that I related just now; but I was willing to act safe, and was still Cautious of running the great Risques which I found others did, and in which they Miscarried every Day.

The next thing of Moment was an attempt at a Gentlewoman's gold Watch, it happen'd in a Crowd, at a Meeting-House, where I was in very great Danger of being taken; I had full hold of her

8. Bargain.   9. Agreed price.

Watch, but giving a great Jostle, as if some body had thrust me against her, and in the Juncture giving the Watch a fair pull, I found it would not come, so I let it go that Moment, and cried out as if I had been kill'd, that some body had Trod upon my Foot, and that there was certainly *Pick-pockets* there; for some body or other had given a pull at my Watch; for you are to observe, that on these Adventures we always went very well Dress'd, and I had very good Cloaths on, and a Gold Watch by my Side, as like a Lady as other Folks.

I had no sooner said so, but the tother Gentlewoman cried out *a Pick-pocket* too, for some body, *she said*, had try'd to pull her Watch away.

When I touch'd her Watch, I was close to her, but when I cry'd out, I stop'd as it were short, and the Crowd bearing her forward a little, she made a Noise too, but it was at some Distance from me, so that she did not in the least suspect me; but when she cried out *a Pickpocket*, some body cried Ay, and here has been another, this Gentlewoman has been attempted too.

At that very instant, a little farther in the Crowd, and very Luckily too, they cried out *a Pick-pocket* again, and really seiz'd a young Fellow in the very Fact. This, tho' unhappy for the Wretch was very opportunely for my Case, tho' I had carried it off handsomely enough before, but now it was out of Doubt, and all the loose part of the Crowd run that way, and the poor Boy was deliver'd up to the Rage of the Street,[1] which is a Cruelty I need not describe, and which however they are always glad of, rather than to be sent to *Newgate*, where they lie often a long time, till they are almost perish'd, and sometimes they are hang'd, and the best they can look for, if they are Convicted, is to be Transported.

This was a narrow Escape to me, and I was so frighted, that I ventur'd no more at Gold Watches a great while; there was indeed a great many concurring Circumstances in this Adventure, which assisted to my Escape; but the chief was, that the Woman whose Watch I had pull'd at was a Fool; that is to say, she was Ignorant of the nature of the Attempt, which one would have thought she should not have been, seeing she was wise enough to fasten her Watch, so, that it could not be slipt up; but she was in such a Fright, that she had no thought about her proper for the Discovery; for she, when she felt the pull scream'd out, and push'd herself forward, and put all the People about her into disorder, but said not a Word of her Watch, or of a *Pick-pocket*, for at least two Minutes

1. The brutality of London street crowds could result in the severe injury or death of a criminal, such as Moll describes, caught in the act of public thievery. A similar incident described in more detail, occurs later, p. 192. Gay describes the fate of a young pickpocket at the hands of a London crowd, *Trivia*, III, lines 63–76.

time, which was time enough for me, and to spare; for as I had cried out behind her, *as I have said,* and bore myself back in the Crowd as she bore forward, there were several People, at least seven or eight, the Throng being still moving on, that were got between me and her in that time, and then I crying out *a Pick-pocket,* rather sooner than she, or at least as soon, she might as well be the Person suspected as I, and the People were confus'd in their Enquiry; whereas, had she with a Presence of Mind needful on such an Occasion, as soon as she felt the pull, not skream'd out as she did, but turn'd immediately round, and seiz'd the next Body that was behind her, she had infallibly taken me.

This is a Direction not of the kindest Sort to the Fraternity; but 'tis certainly a Key to the Clue of a *Pick-pockets* Motions, and whoever can follow it, will as certainly catch the Thief as he will be sure to miss if he does not.

I had another Adventure, which puts this Matter out of doubt, and which may be an Instruction for Posterity in the Case of *a Pick-pocket;* my good old Governess to give a short touch at her History, tho' she had left off the Trade, was as I may say, born *a Pick-pocket,* and as I understood afterward had run thro' all the several Degrees of that Art, and yet had never been taken but once, when she was so grossly detected, that she was convicted and orderd to be Transported; but being a Woman of a rare Tongue, and withal having Money in her Pocket; she found Means, the Ship putting into *Ireland* for Provisions, to get on Shore there, where she liv'd and practis'd her old Trade for some Years; when falling into another sort of bad Company, she turn'd Midwife and Procuress, and play'd a Hundred Pranks there, which she gave me a little History of in Confidence between us as we grew more intimate; and it was to this wicked Creature that I ow'd all the Art and Dexterity I arriv'd to, in which there were few that ever went beyond me, or that practis'd so long without any Misfortune.

It was after those Adventures in *Ireland,* and when she was pretty well known in that Country, that she left *Dublin,* and came over to *England,* where the time of her Transportation being not expir'd, she left her former Trade, for fear of falling into bad Hands again, for then she was sure to have gone to Wreck: Here she set up the same Trade she had followed in *Ireland,* in which she soon by her admirable Management, and a good Tongue, arriv'd to the Height, which I have already describ'd, and indeed began to be Rich tho' her Trade fell off again afterwards; as I have hinted before.

I mention thus much of the History of this Woman here, the better to account for the concern she had in the wicked Life I was now leading; into all the particulars of which she led me as it were by the Hand, and gave me such Directions, and I so well follow'd them, that I grew the greatest Artist of my time, and work'd myself out of every Danger with such Dexterity, that when several more of my Comrades run themselves into *Newgate* prescntly, and by that time they had been Half a Year at the Trade, I had now Practis'd upwards of five Year, and the People at *Newgate*, did not so much as know me; they had heard much of me indeed, and often expected me there, but I always got off, tho' many times in the extreamest Danger.

One of the greatest Dangers I was now in, was that I was too well known among the Trade, and some of them whose hatred was owing rather to Envy than any Injury I had done them began to be Angry that I should always Escape when they were always catch'd and hurried to *Newgate*. These were they that gave me the Name of *Moll Flanders*: For it was no more of Affinity with my real Name, or with any of the Names I had ever gone by, than black is of Kin to white, except that once, as before I call'd my self Mrs. *Flanders*, when I sheltered myself in the *Mint*; but that these Rogues never knew, nor could I ever learn how they came to give me the Name, or what the Occasion of it was.[2]

I was soon inform'd that some of these who were gotten fast into *Newgate*, had vowed to Impeach[3] me; and as I knew that two or three of them were but too able to do it, I was under a great concern about it, and kept within Doors for a good while; but my Governess who I always made Partner in my Success, and who now played a sure[4] Game with me, for that she had a Share of the Gain, and no Share in the hazard, *I say*, my Governess was something impatient of my leading such a useless unprofitable Life, as she call'd it; and she laid a new Contrivance for my going Abroad, and this was to Dress me up in Mens Cloths,[5] and so put me into a new kind of Practise.

I was Tall and Personable, but a little too smooth Fac'd for a Man; however as I seldom went Abroad but in the Night, it did well enough; but it was a long time before I could behave in my new Cloths: I mean, as to my Craft; it was impossible to be so Nimble, so Ready, so Dexterous at these things, in a Dress so contrary to Nature; and as I did every thing Clumsily, so I had neither the success, or the easiness of Escape that I had before, and I resolv'd to leave it off; but that Resolution was confirm'd soon after by the following Accident.

As my Governess had disguis'd me like a Man, so she joyn'd me with a Man, a young Fellow that was Nimble enough at his Business, and for about three Weeks we did very well together. Our

2. For possible identification of the real "Moll Flanders" see Gerald Howson's "Who Was Moll Flanders?" in Backgrounds and Sources, p. 312, below.

3. Testify against, "peach" on.
4. Safe, secure.
5. This type of disguise had been used by Moll Cut-Purse (see note 4, p. 157).

principal Trade was watching Shop-Keepers Compters,[6] and Slipping off any kind of Goods we could see carelesly laid any where, and we made several very good Bargains as we call'd them at this Work: And as we kept always together, so we grew very intimate, yet he never knew that I was not a Man; nay, tho' I several times went home with him to his Lodgings, according as our business directed, and four or five times lay with him all Night: But our Design lay another way, and it was absolutely necessary to me to conceal my Sex from him, as appear'd afterwards: The Circumstances of our Living, coming in late, and having such and such Business to do as requir'd that no Body should be trusted with coming into our Lodgings, were such as made it impossible to me to refuse lying with him, unless I would have own'd my Sex, and as it was I effectually conceal'd my self.

But his ill, and my good Fortune, soon put an end to this Life, which I must own I was sick of too, on several other Accounts: We had made several Prizes in this new way of Business, but the last would have been extraordinary; there was a Shop in a certain Street which had a Warehouse behind it that look'd into another Street, the House making the corner of the turning.

Through the Window of the Warehouse we saw lying on the Counter or Show-board which was just before it, Five pieces of Silks, besides other Stuffs; and tho' it was almost dark, yet the People being busie in the fore shop with Customers, had not had time to shut up those Windows, or else had forgot it.

This the young Fellow was so overjoy'd with, that he could not restrain himself; it lay all within his reach he said, and he swore violently to me that he would have it, if he broke down the House for it; I disswaded him a little, but saw there was no remedy, so he run rashly upon it, slipt out a Square out of the Sash Window dexterously enough, and without noise, and got out four pieces of the Silks, and came with them towards me; but was immediately pursued with a terrible Clutter and Noise; we were standing together indeed, but I had not taken any of the Goods out of his Hand, when I said to him hastily, you are undone, fly for God sake; he run like Lightning, and I too, but the pursuit was hotter after him because he had the Goods, than after me; he dropt two of the Pieces which stop'd them a little, but the Crowd encreas'd and pursued us both; they took him soon after with the other two pieces upon him, and then the rest followed me; I run for it and got into my Governesses House, whither some quick-eyed People follow'd me so warmly as to fix[7] me there; they did not immediately knock at the Door, by which I got time to throw off my Disguise, and

6. Counters.
7. The crowd pursued closely enough to be certain that Moll had entered there.

dress me in my own Cloths; besides, when they came there, my Governess, who had her Tale ready, kept her Door shut, and call'd out to them and told there was no Man came in there; the People affirm'd there did a Man come in there, and swore they would break open the Door.

My Governess, not at all surpriz'd, spoke calmly to them, told them they should very freely come and search her House, if they would bring a Constable, and let in none but such as the Constable would admit, for it was unreasonable to let in a whole Crowd; this they could not refuse, tho' they were a Crowd; so a Constable was fetch'd immediately, and she very freely open'd the Door; and the Constable kept the Door, and the Men he appointed search'd the House, my Governess going with them from Room to Room; when she came to my Room she call'd to me, and said aloud; Cousin, pray open the Door, here's some Gentlemen that must come and look into your Room.

I had a little Girl with me, which was my Governesses Grand-child, as she call'd her; and I bade her open the Door, and there sat I at work with a great litter of things about me, as if I had been at Work all Day, being my self quite undress'd, with only Night-cloaths on my Head, and a loose Morning Gown wrapt about me: My Governess made a kind of excuse for their disturbing me, telling me partly the occasion of it, and that she had no Remedy but to open the Doors to them, and let them satisfie themselves, for all she could say to them would not satisfie them: I sat still, and bid them search the Room if they pleas'd, for if there was any Body in the House, I was sure they was not in my Room; and as for the rest of the House I had nothing to say to that, I did not understand what they look'd for.

Every thing look'd so innocent and so honest about me, that they treated me civiller than I expected, but it was not till they had search'd the Room to a nicety, even under the Bed, in the Bed, and every where else, where it was possible any thing cou'd be hid; when they had done this, and cou'd find nothing, they ask'd my Pardon for troubling me, and went down.

When they had thus searched the House from Bottom to Top, and then from Top to Bottom, and cou'd find nothing, they appeas'd the Mob pretty well; but they carried my Governess before the Justice: Two Men swore that they see the Man who they pur-sued go into her House: My Governess rattled and made a great noise that her House should be insulted, and that she should be used thus for nothing; that if a Man did come in, he might go out again presently for ought she knew, for she was ready to make Oath that no Man had been within her Doors all that Day as she knew of, and that was very true indeed; that it might be indeed that as she was above Stairs, any Fellow in a Fright might find the Door open, and run in for shelter when he was pursued, but that she knew nothing of it; and if it had been so, he certainly went out again, perhaps at the other Door, for she had another Door into an Alley, and so had made his escape and cheated them all.

This was indeed probable enough, and the Justice satisfied himself with giving her an Oath, that she had not receiv'd or admitted any Man into her House to conceal him, or protect or hide him from Justice: This Oath she might justly take, and did so, and so she was dismiss'd.

It is easie to judge what a fright I was in upon this occasion, and it was impossible for my Governess ever to bring me to Dress in that Disguise again; for, as I told her, I should certainly betray my self.

My poor Partner in this Mischief was now in a bad Case, for he was carried away before my Lord Mayor, and by his Worship committed to *Newgate*, and the People that took him were so willing, as well as able, to Prosecute him, that they offer'd themselves to enter into Recognisances[8] to appear at the Sessions, and persue the Charge against him.

However, he got his Indictment deferr'd, upon promise to discover his Accomplices, and particularly, the Man that was concern'd with him in this Robbery, and he fail'd not to do his endeavour, for he gave in my Name who he call'd *Gabriel Spencer*,[9] which was the Name I went by to him, and here appear'd the Wisdom of my concealing my Name and Sex from him, which if he had ever known, I had been undone.

He did all he cou'd to discover this *Gabriel Spencer*; he describ'd me, he discover'd the place where he said I Lodg'd, and in a word, all the Particulars that he cou'd of my Dwelling; but having conceal'd the main Circumstances of my Sex from him, I had a vast Advantage, and he never cou'd hear of me; he brought two or three Families into Trouble by his endeavouring to find me out, but they knew nothing of me, any more than that he had a Fellow with him that they had seen, but knew nothing of; and as for my Governess, tho' she was the means of his coming to me, yet it was done at second hand, and he knew nothing of her.

This turn'd to his Disadvantage, for having promis'd Discoveries, but not being able to make it good, it was look'd upon as a trifling with the Justice of the City, and he was the more fiercely persued by the Shopkeepers who took him.

8. Posted bonds assuring that they would testify in court against him at his trial.
9. Ben Jonson killed an actor named Gabriel Spencer in a duel in 1598; Jonson claimed benefit of clergy and merely suf- fered the Tyburn brand on his thumb as punishment. Defoe's use of the name may be coincidence. See also note 4, p. 37.

I was however terribly uneasie all this while, and that I might be quite out of the way, I went away from my Governesses for a while; but not knowing whither to wander, I took a Maid Servant with me, and took the Stage Coach to *Dunstable* to my old Landlord and Landlady, where I had liv'd so handsomly with my *Lancashire* Husband: Here I told her a formal Story, that I expected my Husband every Day from *Ireland,* and that I had sent a Letter to him that I would meet him at *Dunstable* at her House, and that he would certainly Land, if the Wind was fair, in a few Days, so that I was come to spend a few Days with them till he should come, for he would either come Post,[1] or in the *West-Chester* Coach, I knew not which, but which soever it was, he would be sure to come to that House to meet me.

My Landlady was mighty glad to see me, and My Landlord made such a stir with me, that if I had been a Princess I cou'd not have been better used, and here I might have been welcome a Month or two if I had thought fit.

But my Business was of another Nature; I was very uneasie (tho' so well Disguis'd that it was scarce possible to Detect me) lest this Fellow should some how or other find me out; and tho' he cou'd not charge me with this Robbery, having perswaded him not to venture, and having also done nothing in it my self but run away, yet he might have charg'd me with other things, and have bought his own Life at the Expence of mine.

This fill'd me with horrible Apprehensions: I had no Recourse, no Friend, no Confident but my old Governess, and I knew no Remedy but to put my Life in her Hands, and so I did, for I let her know where to send to me, and had several Letters from her while I stayed here, some of them almost scar'd me out of my Wits; but at last she sent me the joyful News that he was hang'd, which was the best News to me that I had heard a great while.

I had stay'd here five Weeks, and liv'd very comfortably indeed, (the secret Anxiety of my Mind excepted) but when I receiv'd this Letter I look'd pleasantly again, and told my Landlady that I had receiv'd a Letter from my Spouse in *Ireland,* that I had the good News of his being very well, but had the bad News that his business would not permit him to come away so soon as he expected, and so I was like to go back again without him.

My Landlady complemented me upon the good News however, that I had heard he was well, for I have observ'd, Madam, *says she,* you han't been so pleasant as you us'd to be; you have been over Head and Ears in Care for him, I dare say, *says the good Woman;* 'tis easie to be seen there's an alteration in you for the better, *says she:* Well, I am sorry the Esquire can't come yet, *says my Land-*

1. On horseback.

lord, I should have been heartily glad to have seen him, but I hope, when you have certain News of his coming, you'll take a step hither again, Madam; *says he*, you shall be very welcome whenever you please to come.

With all these fine Complements we parted, and I came merry enough to *London*, and found my Governess as well pleas'd as I was; and now she told me she would never recommend any Partner to me again, for she always found, *she said*, that I had the best luck when I ventur'd by my self; and so indeed I had, for I was seldom in any Danger when I was by my self, or if I was, I got out of it with more Dexterity than when I was entangled with the dull Measures of other People, who had perhaps less forecast, and were more rash and impatient than I; for tho' I had as much Courage to venture as any of them, yet I used more caution before I undertook a thing, and had more Presence of Mind when I was to bring my self off.

I have often wondered even at my own hardiness another way, that when all my Companions were surpriz'd, and fell so suddenly into the Hand of Justice, and that I so narrowly escap'd, yet I could not all that while enter into one serious Resolution to leave off this Trade; and especially Considering that I was now very far from being poor, that the Temptation of Necessity, which is generally the Introduction of all such Wickedness was now remov'd; for I had near 500 *l.* by me in ready Money, on which I might have liv'd very well, if I had thought fit to have retir'd; but *I say*, I had not so much as the least inclination to leave off; no not so much as I had before when I had but 200 *l.* before-hand, and when I had no such frightful Examples before my Eyes as these were; From hence 'tis Evident to me, that when once we are harden'd in Crime, no Fear can affect us, no Example give us any warning.

I had indeed one Comrade whose Fate went very near[2] me for a good while, tho' I wore it off too in time; that Case was indeed very unhappy; I had made a Prize of a Piece of very good Damask in a *Mercers* Shop, and went clear off[3] myself; but had convey'd the Peice to this Companion of mine, when we went out of the Shop, and she went one way, and I went another: We had not been long out of the Shop, but the *Mercer* mist his Peice of Stuff, and sent his Messengers, one, one way, and one another, and they presently seiz'd her that had the Peice, with the Damask upon her; as for me, I had very Luckily step'd into a House where there was a Lace Chamber, up one Pair of Stairs, and had the Satisfaction, or the Terror indeed of looking out of the Window upon the Noise they made, and seeing the poor Creature drag'd away in Triumph to the Justice, who immediately committed her to *Newgate*.

2. Touched me closely. Moll almost shared in her fate and was saddened by her capture.

3. Had escaped undetected.

I was careful to attempt nothing in the Lace-Chamber, but tumbl'd their Goods pretty much to spend time; then bought a few Yards of Edging, and paid for it, and came away very sad Hearted indeed for the poor Woman who was in Tribulation for what I only had stolen.

Here again my old Caution stood me in good stead; Namely, that tho' I often robb'd with these People, yet I never let them know who I was, or where I Lodg'd; nor could they ever find out my Lodging, tho' they often endeavour'd to Watch me to it. They all knew me by the Name of *Moll Flanders*, tho' even some of them rather believ'd I was she, than knew me to be so; my Name was publick among them indeed; but how to find me out they knew not, nor so much as how to guess at my Quarters, whether they were at the East-End of the Town, or the West; and this wariness was my safety upon all these Occasions.

I kept close a great while upon the Occasion of this Womans disaster; I knew that if I should do any thing that should Miscarry, and should be carried to Prison she would be there, and ready to Witness against me, and perhaps save her Life at my Expence; I consider'd that I began to be very well known by Name at the *Old Baily*, tho' they did not know my Face; and that if I should fall into their Hands, I should be treated as an old Offender; and for this Reason, I was resolv'd to see what this poor Creatures Fate should be before I stirr'd Abroad, tho' several times in her Distress I convey'd Money to her for her Relief.

At length she came to her Tryal, she pleaded she did not steal the Things; but that one Mrs. *Flanders*, as she heard her call'd, (for she did not know her) gave the Bundle to her after they came out of the Shop, and bade her carry it Home to her Lodging. They ask'd her where this Mrs. *Flanders* was? but she could not produce her, neither could she give the least Account of me; and the *Mercers* Men swearing positively that she was in the Shop when the Goods were stolen; that they immediately miss'd them, and pursu'd her, and found them upon her; Thereupon the Jury brought her in Guilty; but the Court considering that she really was not the Person that stole the Goods, an inferiour Assistant, and that it was very possible she could not find out this Mrs. *Flanders*, *meaning me*, tho' it would save her Life, which indeed was true, I say considering all this, they allow'd her to be Transported, which was the utmost Favour she could obtain, only that the Court told her, that if she could in the mean time produce the said Mrs. *Flanders*, they would intercede for her Pardon; that is to say, if she could find me out, and hang me, she should not be Transported: This I took care to make impossible to her, and so she was Shipp'd off in pursuance of her Sentence a little while after.

I must repeat it again, that the Fate of this poor Woman

troubl'd me exceedingly, and I began to be very pensive, knowing that I was really the Instrument of her disaster; but the Preservation of my own Life, which was so evidently in Danger, took off all my tenderness; and seeing she was not put to Death, I was very easie at her Transportation, because she was then out of the way of doing me any Mischief whatever should happen.

The Disaster of this Woman was some Months before that of the last recited Story, and was indeed partly the Occasion of my Governess proposing to Dress me up in Mens Cloths, that I might go about unobserv'd, as indeed I did; but I was soon tir'd of that Disguise, as *I have said*, for indeed it expos'd me to too many Difficulties.

I was now easie as to all Fear of Witnesses against me, for all those, that had either been concern'd with me, or that knew me by the Name of *Moll Flanders*, were either hang'd or Transported; and if I should have had the Misfortune to be taken, I might call myself any thing else, as well as *Moll Flanders*, and no old Sins could be plac'd to my Account; so I began to run a Tick[4] again, with the more freedom, and several successful Adventures I made, tho' not such as I had made before.

We had at that time another Fire happen'd not a great way off from the Place where my Governess liv'd, and I made an attempt there, as before, but as I was not soon enough before the Crowd of People came in, and could not get to the House I aim'd at, instead of a Prize, I got a mischief, which had almost put a Period to my Life, and all my wicked doings together; for the Fire being very furious, and the People in a great Fright in removing their Goods, and throwing them out of Window; a Wench from out of a Window threw a Featherbed just upon me; it is true, the Bed being soft it broke no Bones; but as the weight was great, and made greater by the Fall, it beat me down, and laid me dead for a while; nor did the People concern themselves much to deliver me from it, or to recover me at all; but I lay like one Dead and neglected a good while, till some body going to remove the Bed out of the way, helped me up; it was indeed a wonder the People in the House had not thrown other Goods out after it, and which might have fallen upon it, and then I had been inevitably kill'd; but I was reserved for further Afflictions.

This Accident however spoil'd my Market for that time, and I came Home to my Governess very much hurt, and Bruised, and Frighted to the last degree, and it was a good while before she could set me upon my Feet again.

---

4. A tally or tab on which debts are scored. Moll is beginning a new ledger of crime.

It was now a Merry time of the Year, and *Bartholomew* Fair[5] was begun; I had never made any Walks that Way, nor was the common Part of the Fair of much Advantage to me; but I took a turn this Year into the Cloisters,[6] and among the rest, I fell into one of the Raffling Shops:[7] It was a thing of no great Consequence to me, nor did I expect to make much of it; but there came a Gentleman extreamly well Dress'd, and very Rich, and as 'tis frequent to talk to every Body in those Shops he singl'd me out, and was very particular with me; first he told me he would put in for me to Raffle, and did so; and some small matter coming to his Lot, he presented it to me, I think it was a Feather Muff: Then he continu'd to keep talking to me with a more than common Appearance of Respect; but still very civil and much like a Gentleman.

He held me in talk so long till at last he drew me out of the Raffling Place to the Shop-Door, and then to take a walk in the Cloister, still talking of a Thousand things Cursorily without any thing to the purpose; at last he told me that without Complement he was charm'd with my Company, and ask'd me if I durst trust myself in a Coach with him; he told me he was a Man of Honour, and would not offer any thing to me unbecoming him as such: I seem'd to decline it a while, but suffer'd myself to be importun'd a little, and then yielded.

I was at a loss in my Thoughts to conclude at first what this Gentleman design'd; but I found afterward he had had some drink in his Head; and that he was not very unwilling to have some more: He carried me in the Coach to the *Spring-Garden*,[8] at *Knight's-Bridge*, where we walk'd in the Gardens, and he Treated me very handsomely; but I found he drank very freely, he press'd me also to drink, but I declin'd it.

Hitherto he kept his Word with me, and offer'd me nothing amiss; we came away in the Coach again, and he brought me into the Streets and by this time it was near Ten a-Clock at Night, and he stop'd the Coach at a House, where it seems he was acquainted, and where they made no scruple to show us up Stairs into a Room with a Bed in it; at first I seem'd to be unwilling to go up, but after a few Words, I yielded to that too, being indeed willing to see the End of it, and in Hopes to make something of it at last; as for the Bed, &c. I was not much concern'd about that Part.

Here he began to be a little freer with me than he had promis'd;

5. Famous fair held annually during the last week in August in West Smithfield. Other fairs were held throughout the year in Smithfield, an area which gained a reputation for oddities and raucous merriment.

6. A circle of shops, an arcade.

7. A shop offering games of chance, especially dice.

8. On the western outskirts of London; a place of questionable reputation in the late seventeenth and early eighteenth centuries.

and I by little and little yielded to every thing, so that in a Word, he did what he pleas'd with me; I need say no more; all this while he drank freely too, and about One in the Morning we went into the Coach again; the Air, and the shaking of the Coach made the Drink he had get more up in his Head than it was before, and he grew uneasy in the Coach, and was for acting over again, what he had been doing before; but as I thought my Game now secure, I resisted him, and brought him to be a little still, which had not lasted five Minutes, but he fell fast asleep.

I took this opportunity to search him to a Nicety; I took a gold Watch, with a silk Purse of Gold, his fine full bottom Perrewig, and silver fring'd Gloves, his Sword, and fine Snuff-box, and gently opening the Coach-door, stood ready to jump out while the Coach was going on; but the Coach stopping in the narrow Street beyond *Temple-Bar* to let another Coach pass, I got softly out, fasten'd the Door again, and gave my Gentleman and the Coach the slip both together, and never heard more of them.[9]

This was an Adventure indeed unlook'd for, and perfectly unde-sign'd by me; tho' I was not so past the Merry part of Life, as to forget how to behave, when a Fop so blinded by his Appetite should not know an old Woman from a young: I did not indeed look so old as I was by ten or twelve Year; yet I was not a young Wench of Seventeen, and it was easie enough to be distinguish'd: There is nothing so absurd, so surfeiting, so ridiculous as a Man heated by Wine in his Head, and a wicked Gust in his Inclination together; he is in the possession of two Devils at once, and can no more govern himself by his Reason than a Mill can Grind without Water; His Vice tramples upon all that was in him that had any good in it, if any such thing there was; nay, his very Sense is blinded by its own Rage, and he acts Absurdities even in his View;[1] such is Drinking more, when he is Drunk already; picking up a common Woman, without regard to what she is, or who she is; whether Sound or rotten, Clean or Unclean;[2] whether Ugly or Handsome, whether Old or Young, and so blinded, as not really to distinguish; such a Man is worse than Lunatick; prompted by his vicious corrupted Head he no more knows what he is doing than this Wretch of mine knew when I pick'd his Pocket of his Watch and his Purse of Gold.

These are the Men of whom *Solomon* says, *they go like an Ox to the slaughter, till a Dart strikes through their Liver;*[3] an admirable

9. Evidently meaning, "she got away clean; gave them the slip," for this epi-sode is developed at length. The second edition deletes "and never heard more of them."

1. Moll commented similarly on such men in her stay at the Mint, p. 52.

2. "Rotten . . . unclean," whether or not she carries venereal disease.

3. Moll alludes to the harlot in Pro-verbs 7:22–23, and traces the progress of syphilis. The liver was thought to be the seat of passion.

Description, *by the way*, of the foul Disease, which is a poisonous deadly Contagion mingling with the Blood, whose Center or Fountain is in the Liver; from whence, by the swift Circulation of the whole Mass, that dreadful nauceous Plague strikes immediately thro' his Liver, and his Spirits are infected, his Vitals stab'd thro' as with a Dart.

It is true this poor unguarded Wretch was in no Danger from me, tho' I was greatly apprehensive at first of what Danger I might be in from him; but he was really to be pityed in one respect, that he seem'd to be a good sort of a Man in himself; a Gentleman that had no harm in his Design; a Man of Sense, and of a fine Behaviour; a comely handsome Person, a sober solid Countenance, a charming beautiful Face, and everything that cou'd be agreeable; only had unhappily had some Drink the Night before, had not been in Bed, as he told me when we were together, was hot, and his Blood fir'd with Wine, and in that Condition his Reason *as it were* asleep, had given him up.

As for me, my Business was his Money, and what I could make of him, and after that if I could have found out any way to have done it, I would have sent him safe home to his House and to his Family, for 'twas ten to one but he had an honest virtuous Wife and innocent Children, that were anxious for his Safety, and would have been glad to have gotten him Home, and have taken care of him till he was restor'd to himself; and then with what Shame and Regret would he look back upon himself? how would he reproach himself with associating himself with a Whore? pick'd up in the worst of all Holes, the Cloister, among the Dirt and Filth of all the Town? how would he be trembling for fear he had got the Pox,[4] for fear a Dart had struck through his Liver, and hate himself every time he look'd back upon the Madness and Brutality of his Debauch? how would he, if he had any Principles of Honour, as I verily believe he had, I say how would he abhor the Thought of giving any ill Distemper, if he had it, as for ought he knew he might, to his Modest and Virtuous Wife, and thereby sowing the Contagion in the Life-blood of his Posterity?

Would such Gentlemen but consider the contemptible Thoughts which the very Women they are concern'd with, in such Cases as these, have of them, it wou'd be a surfeit to them: As I said above, they value not the Pleasure, they are rais'd by no Inclination to the Man, the passive Jade thinks of no Pleasure but the Money; and when he is as it were drunk in the Extasies of his wicked Pleasure, her Hands are in his Pockets searching for what she can find there, and of which he can no more be sensible in the Moment of his Folly, than he can fore-think of it when he goes about it.

4. Syphilis.

I knew a Woman that was so dexterous with a Fellow, who indeed deserv'd no better usage, that while he was busie with her another way, convey'd his Purse with twenty Guineas in it out of his Fob Pocket, where he had put it for fear of her, and put another Purse with guilded Counters[5] in it into the room of it: After he had done, he says to her, now han't you pick'd my Pocket? she jested with him, and told him she suppos'd he had not much to lose; he put his Hand to his Fob, and with his Fingers felt that his Purse was there, which fully satisfy'd him, and so she brought off his Money; and this was a Trade with her, she kept a sham Gold Watch, that is a Watch of Silver Guilt, and a purse of Counters in her Pocket to be ready on all such Occasions; and I doubt not practis'd it with Success.

I came home with this last Booty to my Governess, and really when I told her the Story it so affected her that she was hardly able to forbear Tears, to think how such a Gentleman run a daily Risque of being undone, every time a Glass of Wine got into his Head.

But as to the Purchase I got, and how entirely I stript him, she told me it pleas'd her wonderfully; nay, Child, *says she*, the usage may, for ought I know, do more to reform him, than all the Sermons that ever he will hear in his Life, and if the remainder of the Story be true, so it did.

I found the next Day she was wonderful inquisitive about this Gentleman; the description I had given her of him, his Dress, his Person, his Face, every thing concur'd to make her think of a Gentleman whose Character she knew, and Family too; she mus'd a while, and I going still on with the Particulars, she starts up, *says she*, I'll lay a Hundred Pound I know the Gentleman.

I am sorry you do, *says I*, for I would not have him expos'd on any account in the World; he has had Injury enough already by me, and I would not be instrumental to do him any more: No, no *says she*, I will do him no Injury, I assure you, but you may let me satisfie my Curiosity a little, for if it is he, I warrant you I find it out: I was a little startled at that, and told her with an apparent concern in my Face, that by the same Rule he might find me out, and then I was undone: *she return'd warmly*, why, do you think I will betray you, Child? No, no, *says she*, not for all he is worth in the World; I have kept your Counsel in worse things than these, sure you may trust me in this: So I said no more at that time.

She laid her Scheme another way, and without acquainting me of it, but she was resolv'd to find it out, if possible; so she goes to a certain Friend of hers who was acquainted in the Family, that she guess'd at, and told her Friend she had some extraordinary business

5. Imitation coins.

with such a Gentleman (who by the way was no less than a Baronet, and of a very good Family) and that she knew not how to come at him without somebody to introduce her: Her Friend promis'd her very readily to do it, and accordingly goes to the House to see if the Gentleman was in Town.

The next Day she comes to my Governess and tells her that Sir ———— was at Home, but that he had met with a Disaster and was very ill, and there was no speaking with him; what Disaster, *says my Governess hastily*, as if she was surpriz'd at it? Why, *says her Friend*, he had been at *Hampstead*[6] to Visit a Gentleman of his Acquaintance, and as he came back again he was set upon and Robb'd, and having got a little Drink too, as they suppose, the Rogues abus'd him, and he is very ill: Robb'd, *says my Governess*, and what did they take from him? why, *says her Friend*, they took his Gold Watch, and his Gold Snuff-box, his fine Perriwig, and what Money he had in his Pocket, which was considerable to be sure, for Sir ———— never goes without a Purse of Guineas about him.

Pshaw! says my old Governess jeering, I warrant you he has got drunk now and got a Whore, and she has pick'd his Pocket, and so he comes home to his Wife and tells her he has been Robb'd; that's an old sham, a thousand such tricks are put upon the poor Women every Day.

Fye, says her Friend, I find you don't know Sir ————, why he is as Civil a Gentleman, there is not a finer Man, nor a soberer grave modester Person in the whole City; he abhors such things, there's no Body that knows him will think such a thing of him: Well, well, *says my Governess*, that's none of my Business, if it was, I warrant I should find there was something of that kind in it; your Modest Men in common Opinion are sometimes no better than other People, only they keep a better Character, or if you please, are the better Hypocrites.

No, no, *says her Friend*, I can assure you Sir ———— is no Hypocrite; he is really an honest sober Gentleman, and he has certainly been Robb'd: Nay, *says my Governess*, it may be he has, it is no Business of mine I tell you; I only want to speak with him, my Business is of another Nature; but, *says her Friend*, let your Business be of what nature it will, you cannot see him yet, for he is not fit to be seen, for he is very ill, and bruis'd very much: Ay, *says my Governess*, nay then he has fallen into bad Hands to be sure; and then she ask'd gravely, pray where is he bruised? Why in his Head, *says her Friend*, and one of his Hands, and his Face, for they us'd him barbarously. Poor Gentleman, *says my Governess*, I must wait

6. Northwest of London and some miles from both Smithfield and Knightsbridge, Hampstead Heath was an area frequented by highwaymen.

then till he recovers, and adds, I hope it will not be long, for I want very much to speak with him.

Away she comes to me and tells me this Story; I have found out your fine Gentleman, and a fine Gentleman he was, *says she*, but Mercy on him, he is in a sad pickle now; I wonder what the D——l you have done to him; why you have almost kill'd him: I look'd at her with disorder enough; I kill'd him! *says I*, you must mistake the Person, I am sure I did nothing to him, he was very well when I left him, *said I*, only drunk and fast asleep; I know nothing of that, *says she*, but he is in a sad pickle now, and so she told me all that her Friend had said to her: Well then, *says I*, he fell into bad Hands after I left him, for I am sure I left him safe enough.

About ten Days after, or a little more, my Governess goes again to her Friend, to introduce her to this Gentleman; she had enquir'd other ways in the mean time, and found that he was about again, if not abroad again, so she got leave to speak with him.

She was a Woman of an admirable Address, and wanted no Body to introduce her; she told her Tale much better than I shall be able to tell it for her, for she was a Mistress of her Tongue, as I have said already: She told him that she came, tho' a Stranger, with a single design of doing him a Service, and he should find she had no other End in it; that as she came purely on so Friendly an account, she beg'd a promise from him, that if he did not accept what she should officiously[7] propose, he would not take it ill, that she meddl'd with what was not her Business; she assur'd him that as what she had to say was a Secret that belong'd to him only, so whether he accepted her offer or not, it should remain a Secret to all the World, unless he expos'd it himself; nor should his refusing her Service in it, make her so little show her Respect, as to do him the least Injury, so that he should be entirely at liberty to act as he thought fit.

He look'd very shy at first, and said he knew nothing that related to him that requir'd much secresie; that he had never done any Man any wrong, and car'd not what any Body might say of him; that it was no part of his Character to be unjust to any Body, nor could he imagine in what any Man cou'd render him any Service; but that if it was so disinterested a Service as she said, he could not take it ill from any one that they should endeavour to serve him; and so, as it were, left her at liberty either to tell him, or not to tell him, as she thought fit.

She found him so perfectly indifferent, that she was almost afraid to enter into the point with him; but however, after some other Circumlocutions, she told him that by a strange and unaccountable Accident she came to have a particular knowledge of the late

7. With kind intentions.

unhappy Adventure he had fallen into; and that in such a manner, that there was no Body in the World but herself and him that were acquainted with it, no not the very Person that was with him.

He look'd a little angrily at first; what Adventure? *said he*; why, Sir, *said she*, of your being Robb'd coming from *Knightsbr——*, *Hampstead*, Sir, I should say, *says she*; be not surpris'd, Sir, *says she*, that I am able to tell you every step you took that Day from the *Cloyster* in *Smithfield*, to the *Spring-Garden* at *Knightsbridge*, and thence to the ——— in the *Strand*, and how you were left asleep in the Coach afterwards; I say let not this surprize you, for Sir I do not come to make a Booty of you, I ask nothing of you, and I assure you the Woman that was with you knows nothing who you are, and never shall; and yet perhaps I may serve you farther still, for I did not come barely to let you know that I was inform'd of these things, as if I wanted a Bribe to conceal them; assure your self, Sir, *said she*, that whatever you think fit to do or say to me, it shall be all a secret as it is, as much as if I were in my Grave.

He was astonish'd at her Discourse, and said gravely to her, Madam, you are a Stranger to me, but it is very unfortunate that you should be let into the Secret of the worst action of my Life, and a thing that I am so justly asham'd of, that the only satisfaction of it to me was that I thought it was known only to God and my own Conscience: Pray, Sir, *says she*, do not reckon the Discovery of it to me, to be any part of your Misfortune; it was a thing, I believe, you were surprised into, and perhaps the Woman us'd some Art to prompt you to it; however, you will never find any just Cause, *said she*, to repent that I came to hear of it; nor can your own Mouth be more silent in it than I have been, and ever shall be.

Well, *says he*, but let me do some Justice to the Woman too, whoever she is, I do assure you she prompted me to nothing, she rather declin'd me; it was my own Folly and Madness that brought me into it all, ay and brought her into it too; I must give her her due so far; as to what she took from me, I cou'd expect no less from her in the condition I was in, and to this Hour I know not whether she Robb'd me or the Coachman; if she did it I forgive her, and I think all Gentlemen that do so,[8] should be us'd in the same manner; but I am more concern'd for some other things than I am for all that she took from me.

My Governess now began to come into the whole matter, and he open'd himself freely to her; first, she said to him, in answer to what he had said about me, I am glad Sir you are so just to the Person that you were with; I assure you she is a Gentlewoman, and no Woman of the Town; and however you prevail'd with her so far as you did, I am sure 'tis not her Practise; you run a great venture[9]

---

8. As I did. 9. Risk (of venereal disease).

indeed, Sir, but if that be any part of your Care, I am perswaded
you may be perfectly easie, for I dare assure you no Man has
touch'd her, before you, since her Husband, and he has been dead
now almost eight Year.

It appear'd that this was his Grievance, and that he was in a very
great fright about it; however, when my Governess said this to him
he appeared very well pleased; and said, well, Madam, to be plain
with you, if I was satisfy'd of that, I should not so much value what
I lost; for as to that, the Temptation was great, and perhaps she was
poor and wanted it: If she had not been poor Sir ———, *says my
Governess,* I assure you she would never have yielded to you; and as
her Poverty first prevailed with her to let you do as you did, so the
same Poverty prevail'd with her to pay her self at last, when she saw
you was in such a Condition, that if she had not done it, perhaps
the next Coach-man or Chair-man[1] might have done it.

Well, *says he,* much good may it do her; I say again, all the Gentlemen that do so, ought to be us'd in the same manner, and then
they would be cautious of themselves; I have no more concern
about it, but on the score which you hinted at before, Madam:
Here he entered into some freedoms with her on the Subject of
what pass'd between us, which are not so proper for a Woman to
write, and the great Terror that was upon his Mind with relation to
his Wife, for fear he should have receiv'd any Injury from me, and
should communicate it farther; and ask'd her at last if she cou'd not
procure him an opportunity to speak with me; my Governess gave
him farther assurances of my being a Woman clear from any such
thing, and that he was as entirely safe in that respect, as he was
with his own Lady; but as for seeing me, she said it might be of
dangerous consequence; but however, that she would talk with me,
and let him know my Answer; using at the same time some Arguments to perswade him not to desire it, and that it cou'd be of no
Service to him, seeing she hop'd he had no desire to renew a Correspondence with me, and that on my account it was a kind of putting my Life in his Hands.

He told her, he had a great desire to see me, that he would give
her any assurances that were in his Power, not to take any Advantages of me, and that in the first place he would give me a general
release from all Demands of any kind; she insisted how it might
tend to a farther divulging the Secret, and might in the end be inju-
rious to him, entreating him not to press for it, so at length he desisted.

They had some Discourse upon the Subject of the things he had
lost, and he seem'd to be very desirous of his Gold Watch, and told

1. Chairmen carried passengers in closed sedan chairs suspended on poles, usually
for a shilling a mile.

her if she cou'd procure that for him, he would willingly give as much for it as it was worth, she told him she would endeavour to procure it for him and leave the valuing it to himself.

Accordingly the next Day she carried the Watch, and he gave her 30 Guineas for it, which was more than I should have been able to make of it, tho' it seems it cost much more; he spoke something of his Perriwig, which it seems cost him threescore Guineas, and his Snuff-box, and in a few Days more, she carried them too; which oblig'd him very much, and he gave her Thirty more, the next Day I sent him his fine Sword, and Cane *Gratis*, and demanded nothing of him, but I had no mind to see him, unless it had been so, that he might be satisfy'd I knew who he was, which he was not willing to.

Then he entered into a long Talk with her of the manner how she came to know all this matter; she form'd a long Tale of that part; how she had it from one that I had told the whole Story to, and that was to help me dispose of the Goods, and this Confident brought the Things to her, she being by Profession a *Pawn-Broker*; and she hearing of his Worship's dissaster, guess'd at the thing in general; that having gotten the Things into her Hands, she had resolv'd to come and try as she had done: She then gave him repeated Assurances that it should never go out of her Mouth, and tho' she knew the Woman very well, yet she had not let her know, *meaning me*, any thing of it; *that is to say*, who the Person was, which by the way was false; but however it was not to his Damage, for I never open'd my Mouth of it to any Body.

I had a great many Thoughts in my Head about my seeing him again, and was often sorry that I had refus'd it; I was perswaded that if I had seen him, and let him know that I knew him, I should have made some Advantage of him, and perhaps have had some Maintenance from him; and tho' it was a Life wicked enough, yet it was not so full of Danger as this I was engag'd in. However those Thoughts wore off, and I declin'd seeing him again, for that time; but my Governess saw him often, and he was very kind to her, giving her something almost every time he saw her; one time in particular she found him very Merry, and as she thought he had some Wine in his Head, and he press'd her again very earnestly to let him see that Woman, that *as he said*, had Bewitch'd him so that Night; my Governess, who was from the beginning for my seeing him, told him, he was so desirous of it, that she could almost yield to it, if she cou'd prevail upon me; adding that if he would please to come to her House in the Evening she would endeavour it, upon his repeated Assurances of forgetting what was pass'd.

Accordingly she came to me and told me all the Discourse; *in short*, she soon byass'd me to consent, in a Case which I had some regret in my mind for declining before: so I prepar'd to see him: I dress'd me to all the Advantage possible I assure you, and for the first time us'd a little Art; I say for the first time, for I had never yielded to the baseness of Paint before, having always had vanity enough to believe I had no need of it.

At the Hour appointed he came; and as she observ'd before, so it was plain still, that he had been drinking, tho' very far from what we call being in drink: He appear'd exceeding pleas'd to see me, and enter'd into a long Discourse with me, upon the old Affair; I beg'd his pardon very often, for my share of it; protested I had not any such design when first I met him; that I had not gone out with him, but that I took him for a very civil Gentleman; and that he made me so many promises of offering no uncivility to me.

He alledg'd[2] the Wine he drank, and that he scarce knew what he did, and that if it had not been so, I should never have let him take the freedom with me that he had done: He protested to me that he never touch'd any Woman but me since he was married to his Wife, and it was a surprise upon him; Complimented me upon being so particularly agreeable to him, and the like, and talk'd so much of that kind, till I found he had talk'd himself almost into a temper to do the same thing over again: But I took him up short, I protested I had never suffer'd any Man to touch me since my Husband died, which was near eight Year; he said he believed it to be so truly; and added that Madam, had intimated as much to him, and that it was his Opinion of that part which made him desire to see me again; and that since he had once broke in upon his Virtue with me, and found no ill Consequences, he cou'd be safe in venturing there again; and so in short it went on to what I expected, and to what will not bear relating.

My old Governess had foreseen it, as well as I, and therefore led him into a Room which had not a Bed in it, and yet had a Chamber within it, which had a Bed, whither we withdrew for the rest of the Night, and in short, after some time being together, he went to Bed, and lay there all Night; I withdrew, but came again undress'd in the Morning before it was Day, and lay with him the rest of the time.

Thus you see having committed a Crime once, is a sad Handle to the committing of it again; whereas all the Regret, and Reflections wear off when the Temptation renews it self; had I not yielded to see him again, the Corrupt desire in him had worn off, and 'tis very probable he had never fallen into it, with any Body else, as I really believe he had not done before.

When he went away, I told him I hop'd he was satisfy'd he had

2. Blamed.

not been robb'd again; he told me he was satisfy'd in that Point, and cou'd trust me again; and putting his Hand in his Pocket gave me five Guineas, which was the first Money I had gain'd that way for many Years.

I had several Visits of the like kind from him, but he never came into a settled way of Maintenance, which was what I would have been best pleas'd with: Once indeed he ask'd me how I did to live, I answer'd him pretty quick, that I assur'd him I had never taken that Course that I took with him; but that indeed I work'd at my Needle, and could just Maintain myself, that sometimes it was as much as I was able to do, and I shifted hard enough.

He seem'd to reflect upon himself that he should be the first Person to lead me into that, which he assur'd me he never intended to do himself; and it touch'd him a little, *he said*, that he should be the Cause of his own Sin, and mine too: He would often make just Reflections also upon the Crime itself, and upon the particular Circumstances of it, with respect to himself; how Wine introduc'd the Inclinations, how the Devil led him to the Place, and found out an Object to tempt him, and he made the Moral always himself.

When these thoughts were upon him he would go away, and perhaps not come again in a Months time or longer; but then as the serious part wore off, the lewd Part would wear in, and then he came prepar'd for the wick'd Part; thus we liv'd for some time; tho' he did not KEEP,[3] as they call it, yet he never fail'd doing things that were Handsome, and sufficient to Maintain me without working, and which was better, without following my old Trade.

But this Affair had its End too; for after about a Year, I found that he did not come so often as usual, and at last he left it off altogether without any dislike,[4] or bidding adieu; and so there was an End of that short Scene of Life, which added no great Store to me, only to make more Work for Repentance.

However during this interval, I confin'd my self pretty much at Home; at least being thus provided, I made no Adventures, no not for a Quarter of a Year after he left me; but then finding the Fund fail, and being loth to spend upon the main Stock, I began to think of my old Trade, and to look Abroad into the Street again; and my first Step was lucky enough.

I had dress'd myself up in a very mean Habit, for as I had several Shapes[5] to appear in I was now in an ordinary Stuff-Grown, a blue Apron and a Straw-Hat; and I plac'd myself at the Door of the three Cups-Inn in St. *John Street*: There were several Carriers[6] us'd

---

3. Did not formally maintain Moll as a kept mistress.
4. Without any apparent absence of affection; without a quarrel.
5. Disguises.
6. Coach lines.

the Inn, and the Stage Coaches for *Barnet*, for *Toteridge*, and other
Towns that way, stood always in the Street in the Evening, when
they prepar'd to set out, so that I was ready for any thing that
offer'd for either one or other: The meaning was this, People come
frequently with Bundles and small Parcels to those Inns, and call
for such Carriers, or Coaches as they want, to carry them into the
Country; and there generally attends Women, Porters Wives, or
Daughters, ready to take in such things for their respective People
that employ them.

It happen'd very odly that I was standing at the Inn-Gate, and a
Woman that had stood there before, and which was the Porter's
Wife belonging to the *Barnet* Stage Coach, having observ'd me,
ask'd if I waited for any of the Coaches; I told her yes, I waited for
my Mistress, that was coming to go to *Barnet*; she ask'd me who
was my Mistress, and I told her any Madam's Name that came next
me;[7] but as it seem'd I happen'd upon a Name, a Family of which
Name liv'd at *Hadly* just beyond *Barnet*.

I said no more to her, or she to me a good while, but by and by,
some body calling her at a Door a little way off, she desir'd me that
if any body call'd for the *Barnet* Coach, I would step and call her at
the House, which it seems was an Ale-house; I said yes very readily,
and away she went.

She was no sooner gone, but comes a Wench and a Child, puffing
and sweating, and asks for the *Barnet* Coach; I answer'd presently,
here. Do you belong to the *Barnet* Coach? *says she*. Yes, Sweetheart, *said I*, what do ye want? I want Room for two Passengers
says she; Where are they Sweetheart? *said I*. Here's this Girl, pray
let her go into the Coach, *says she*, and I'll go and fetch my Mistress; make haste then Sweetheart, *says I*, for we may be full else;
the Maid had a great Bundle under Arm; so she put the Child into
the Coach, and *I said*, you had best put your Bundle into the
Coach too; No, *says she*, I am afraid some body should slip it away
from the Child; give it me then, *said I*, and I'll take care of it; do
then, *says she*, and be sure you take care of it; I'll answer for it, *said
I*, if it were for Twenty Pound value. There take it then, *says she*,
and away she goes.

As soon as I had got the Bundle, and the Maid was out of Sight,
I goes on towards the Ale-house, where the Porter's Wife was, so
that if I had met her, I had then only been going to give her the
Bundle, and to call her to her Business, as if I was going away, and
cou'd stay no longer; but as I did not meet her I walk'd away, and
turning into *Charter-house-Lane*, made off thro' *Charter-house-
Yard*, into *Long-Lane*, then cross'd into *Bartholomew-Close*, so into

7. The first name that came into her head.

Little Britain, and thro' the *Blue-Coat-Hospital*[8] into *Newgate-Street.*

To prevent my being known, I pull'd off my blue Apron, and wrapt the Bundle in it, which before was made up in a Piece of painted Callico, and very Remarkable;[9] I also wrapt up my Straw-Hat in it, and so put the Bundle upon my Head; and it was very well, that I did thus, for coming thro' the *Blue-Coat Hospital,* who should I meet but the Wench, that had given me the Bundle to hold; it seems she was going with her Mistress, who she had been gone to fetch to the *Barnet* Coaches.

I saw she was in haste, and I had no Business to stop her: so away she went, and I brought my Bundle safe Home to my Governess; there was no Money, nor Plate, or Jewels in the Bundle, but a very good Suit of *Indian* Damask, a Gown and Petticoat, a lac'd Head and Ruffles of very good Flanders-Lace, and some Linnen, and other things, such as I knew very well the value of.

This was not indeed my own Invention, but was given me by one that had practis'd it with Success, and my Governess lik'd it extreamly; and indeed I try'd it again several times, tho' never twice near the same Place; for the next time I try'd it in *White-Chappel* just by the Corner of *Petty-Coat-Lane,* where the Coaches stand that go out to *Stratford* and *Bow,* and that Side of the Country, and another time at the *Flying-Horse,* without[1] *Bishops-gate,* where the *Chester* Coaches then lay, and I had always the good Luck to come off with some Booty.

Another time I plac'd myself at a Warehouse by the Waterside, where the Coasting Vessels[2] from the *North* come, such as from *New-Castle* upon *Tyne, Sunderland,* and other Places; here, the Warehouse being shut, comes a young Fellow with a Letter; and he wanted a Box, and a Hamper[3] that was come from *New-Castle* upon *Tyne,* I ask'd him if he had the Marks[4] of it, so he shows me the Letter, by Virtue of which he was to ask for it, and which gave an Account of the Contents, the Box being full of Linnen, and the Hamper full of Glass-Ware; I read the Letter, and took care to see the Name, and the Marks, the Name of the Person that sent the Goods, the Name of the Person that they were sent to, then I bade the Messenger come in the Morning, for that the Warehouse Keeper, would not be there any more that Night.

---

8. "Hospital" in this case means a charitable institution for the education of the young. Blue Coat School was another name for the famous Christ's Hospital on Newgate Street, until it moved to Horsham in 1902. "Blue Coat" was derived from the traditional blue dress of the scholars. Samuel Taylor Coleridge and Charles Lamb were educated there.

9. Easily recognizable because of its bright pattern.
1. Outside.
2. Ships that traded along the coastal ports of England.
3. A large, covered wicker basket used as a packing case.
4. Identification indicating ownership, such as a bill of lading.

Away went I, and getting Materials in a publick House, I wrote a Letter from Mr. *John Richardson* of *New-Castle* to his Dear Cousin *Jemey Cole*, in *London*, with an Account that he had sent by such a Vessel, (for I remember'd all the Particulars to a tittle,) so many pieces of Huckaback Linnen,[5] so many Ells[6] of *Dutch* Holland and the like, in a Box, and a Hamper of Flint Glasses from Mr. *Henzill's* Glass-house,[7] and that the Box was mark'd I C. No I. and the Hamper was directed by a Label on the Cording.

About an Hour after, I came to the Warehouse, found the Warehouse-keeper, and had the Goods deliver'd me without any scruple; the value of the Linnen being about 22 Pound.

I could fill up this whole Discourse with the variety of such Adventures which daily Invention directed to, and which I manag'd with the utmost Dexterity, and always with Success.

At length, as when does the Pitcher come safe home that goes so very often to the Well, I fell into some small Broils,[8] which tho' they cou'd not affect me fatally, yet made me known, which was the worst thing next to being found Guilty, that cou'd befall me.

I had taken up the Disguise of a Widow's Dress; it was without any real design in view, but only waiting for any thing that might offer, as I often did: It happen'd that while I was going along the Street in *Covent Garden*, there was a great Cry of stop Thief, stop Thief; some Artists had it seems put a trick upon a Shop-keeper, and being pursued, some of them fled one way, and some another; and one of them was, they said, dress'd up in Widow's Weeds, upon which the Mob gathered about me, and some said I was the Person, others said no; immediately came the Mercer's Journeyman, and he swore aloud I was the Person, and so seiz'd on me; however, when I was brought back by the Mob to the Mercer's Shop, the Master of the House said freely that I was not the Woman that was in his Shop, and would have let me go immediately; but another Fellow said gravely, pray stay till Mr. ———, *meaning the Journeyman*, comes back for he knows her; so they kept me by force near half an Hour; they had call'd a Constable, and he stood in the Shop as my Jayler; and in talking with the Constable I enquir'd where he liv'd, and what Trade[9] he was; the Man

5. Rough linen used for toweling.
6. The English ell was 45 inches, the Flemish 27 inches.
7. Defoe visited Newcastle upon Tyne while in the service of Robert Harley, Earl of Oxford, and in lending authenticity to this episode he recalled John Henzell's glass-house on Tyneside. The Henzell-Tizacke glass-works was established in 1679. Dr. Constance Fraser, Joint Secretary, Society of Antiquaries of Newcastle upon Tyne, advises, however, that flint glass (clear, lustrous glass made with ground flint) was not processed in Newcastle until 1684 by Edward Dagnia, who operated the only flint glasshouse in the town.
8. Hassles, difficulties.
9. Constabulary duties were a secondary occupation to which fairly substantial middle-class London citizens were required by parish officials to contribute their time. The unsalaried position often attracted individuals who sought whatever graft the occupation might offer.

not apprehending in the least what happened afterwards, readily told me his Name, and Trade, and where he liv'd; and told me as a Jest, that I might be sure to hear of his Name when I came to the *Old Bayley*.

Some of the Servants likewise us'd me saucily, and had much ado to keep their Hands off of me, the Master indeed was civiler to me than they; but he would not yet let me go, tho' he owned he could not say I was in his Shop before.

I began to be a little surly with him, and told him I hop'd he would not take it ill, if I made my self amends upon him in a more legal way another time; and desir'd I might send for Friends to see me have right done me: No, *he said*, he could give no such liberty, I might ask it when I came before the Justice of Peace, and seeing I threaten'd him, he would take care of me in the mean time, and would lodge me safe in *Newgate*: I told him it was his time now, but it would be mine by and by, and govern'd my Passion as well as I was able; however, I spoke to the Constable to call me a Porter, which he did, and then I call'd for Pen, Ink, and Paper, but they would let me have none; I ask'd the Porter his Name, and where he liv'd, and the poor Man told it me very willingly; I bade him observe and remember how I was treated there; that he saw I was detain'd there by Force; I told him I should want his Evidence in another place, and it should not be the worse for him to speak; the Porter said he would serve me with all his Heart; but, Madam, *says he*, let me hear them refuse to let you go, then I may be able to speak the plainer.

With that I spoke aloud to the Master of the Shop, and said, Sir, you know in your own Conscience that I am not the Person you look for, and that I was not in your Shop before, therefore I demand that you detain me here no longer, or tell me the reason of your stopping me; the Fellow grew surlier upon this than before, and said he would do neither till he thought fit; very well, said I to the Constable and to the Porter, you will be pleas'd to remember this, Gentlemen, another time; the Porter said, *yes, Madam*, and the Constable began not to like it, and would have perswaded the Mercer to dismiss him, and let me go, since, as he said, he own'd I was not the Person; Good Sir, *says the Mercer to him Tauntingly*, are you a Justice of Peace, or a Constable? I charg'd you with her, pray do you do your Duty: The Constable told him a little mov'd, but very handsomely, *I know my Duty, and what I am, Sir, I doubt you hardly know what you are doing*; they had some other hard words, and in the mean time the Journey-men, impudent and unmanly to the last degree, used me barbarously, and one of them, the same that first seized upon me, pretended he would search me, and began to lay Hands on me: I spit in his Face, call'd out to the

Constable, and bade him take notice of my usage; and pray, Mr. Constable, *said I*, ask that Villain's Name, pointing to the Man; the Constable reprov'd him decently, told him that he did not know what he did, for he knew that his Master acknowledg'd I was not the Person that was in his Shop; and, says the Constable, I am afraid your Master is bringing himself and me too into Trouble, if this Gentlewoman comes to prove who she is, and where she was, and it appears that she is not the Woman you pretend to; *Dam her, says the Fellow again*, with an impudent harden'd Face, she is the Lady, you may depend upon it, I'll swear she is the same Body that was in the Shop, and that I gave the pieces of Satin that is lost into her own hand, you shall hear more of it when Mr. *William* and *Anthony, those were other Journeymen*, come back, they will know her again as well as I.

Just as the insolent Rogue was talking thus to the Constable, comes back Mr. *William* and Mr. *Anthony*, as he call'd them, and a great Rabble with them, bringing along with them the true Widow that I was pretended to be; and they came sweating and blowing into the Shop, and with a great deal of Triumph dragging the poor Creature in a most butcherly manner up towards their Master, who was in the back Shop, and cryed out aloud, here's the Widow, Sir, we have catch'd her at last; what do ye mean by that? *says the Master*, why we have her already, there she sits, *says he*, and Mr. ———— *says he*, can swear this is she: The other Man who they call'd Mr. *Anthony* replyed, Mr. ———— may say what he will, and swear what he will, but this is the Woman, and there's the Remnant of Sattin she stole, I took it out of her Cloaths with my own Hand.

I sat still now, and began to take a better Heart, but smil'd and said nothing; the Master look'd Pale; the Constable turn'd about and look'd at me; *let 'em alone Mr. Constable*, said I, *let 'em go on*; the Case was plain and could not be denied, so the Constable was charg'd with the right Thief, and the Mercer told me very civilly he was sorry for the mistake, and hoped I would not take it ill; that they had so many things of this nature put upon them every Day, that they cou'd not be blam'd for being very sharp in doing themselves Justice; Not take it ill, Sir! *said I*, how can I take it well? if you had dismiss'd me when your insolent Fellow seiz'd on me in the Street, and brought me to you; and when you your self acknowledg'd I was not the Person, I would have put it by, and not taken it ill, because of the many ill things I believe you have put upon you daily; but your Treatment of me since has been unsufferable, and especially that of your Servant, I must and will have Reparation for that.

Then he began to parly with me, said he would make me any rea-

sonable Satisfaction, and would fain have had me told him what it
was I expected; I told him I should not be my own Judge, the Law
should decide it for me, and as I was to be carried before a Magistrate, I should let him hear there what I had to say; he told me
there was no occasion to go before the Justice now, I was at liberty
to go where I pleased, and so calling to the Constable told him, he
might let me go, for I was discharg'd; the Constable said calmly to
him, Sir, you ask'd me just now, if I knew whether I was a Constable or a Justice, and bade me do my Duty, and charg'd me with
this Gentlewoman as a Prisoner; now, Sir, I find you do not understand what is my Duty, for you would make me a Justice indeed; but
I must tell you it is not in my Power: I may keep a Prisoner when I
am charg'd with him, but 'tis the Law and the Magistrate alone
that can discharge that Prisoner; therefore 'tis a mistake, Sir, I must
carry her before a Justice now, whether you think well of it or not:
The Mercer was very high with the Constable at first; but the Constable happening to be not a hir'd Officer,[1] but a good Substantial
kind of Man, I think he was a Corn-chandler, and a Man of good
Sense, stood to his Business, would not discharge me without going
to a Justice of the Peace; and I insisted upon it too: When the
Mercer see that, well, *says he to the Constable*, you may carry her
where you please, I have nothing to say to her; but Sir, *says the
Constable*, you will go with us, I hope, for 'tis you that charg'd me
with her; no not I, *says the Mercer*, I tell you I have nothing to say
to her: But pray Sir do, *says the Constable*, I desire it of you for your
own sake, for the Justice can do nothing without you: Prithee,
Fellow, *says the Mercer*, go about your Business, I tell you I have
nothing to say to the Gentlewoman, I charge you in the King's
Name to dismiss her: Sir, *says the Constable*, I find you don't know
what it is to be a Constable, I beg of you don't oblige me to be rude
to you; I think I need not, you are rude enough already, *says the
Mercer*: No, Sir, *says the Constable*, I am not rude, you have broken
the Peace in bringing an honest Woman out of the Street, when she
was about her lawful Occasion, confining her in your Shop, and ill
using her here by your Servants; and now can you say I am rude to
you? I think I am civil to you in not commanding or charging you
in the King's Name to go with me, and charging every Man I see,
that passes your Door, to aid and assist me in carrying you by Force,
this you cannot but know I have power to do, and yet I forbear it,
and once more entreat you to go with me: Well, he would not for
all this, and gave the Constable ill Language: However, the Con-

1. Since the solid citizens of London usually sought to be exempted from constabulary duties, those assuming the position generally had a reputation for
being surly, ignorant, grasping, and
readily bribed. This citizen evidently
seeks none of the especial financial gain
often available in the duty. See Gay's
description of a constable's yielding to
a bribe in *Trivia*, III, lines 307–320.

stable kept his Temper, and would not be provoked; and then I put
in and said, come, Mr. Constable, let him alone, I shall find ways
enough to fetch him before a Magistrate, I don't fear that; but
there's the Fellow, *says I*, he was the Man that seized on me, as I
was innocently going along the Street, and you are a Witness of
his Violence with me since; give me leave to charge you with him,
and carry him before the Justice; yes, Madam, *says the Constable*;
and turning to the Fellow, come young Gentleman, *says he to the
Journey-man*, you must go along with us, I hope you are not above
the Constable's Power, tho' your Master is.

The Fellow look'd like a condemn'd Thief, and hung back, then
look'd at his Master, as if he cou'd help him; and he, like a Fool,
encourag'd the Fellow to be rude, and he truly resisted the Constable, and push'd him back with a good Force when he went to lay
hold on him, at which the Constable knock'd him down, and call'd
out for help; and immediately the Shop was fill'd with People, and
the Constable seiz'd the Master and Man, and all his Servants.

The first ill Consequence of this Fray was, that the Woman they
had taken, who was really the Thief, made off, and got clear away
in the Crowd; and two others that they had stop'd also, whether
they were really Guilty or not, that I can say nothing to.

By this time some of his Neighbours having come in, and, upon
inquiry, seeing how things went, had endeavour'd to bring the hot-
brain'd Mercer to his Senses; and he began to be convinc'd that he
was in the wrong; and so at length we went all very quietly before
the Justice, with a Mob of about 500 People at our Heels; and all
the way I went I could hear the People ask what was the matter?
and others reply and say, a Mercer had stop'd a Gentlewoman
instead of a Thief, and had afterwards taken the Thief, and now
the Gentlewoman had taken the Mercer, and was carrying him
before the Justice; this pleas'd the People strangely,[2] and made the
Crowd encrease, and they cry'd out as they went, which is the
Rogue? which is the Mercer? and especially the Women; then
when they saw him they cryed out, *that's he, that's he*; and every
now and then came a good dab of Dirt at him; and thus we
march'd a good while, till the Mercer thought fit to desire the Constable to call a Coach to protect himself from the Rabble; so we
Rode the rest of the way, the Constable and I, and the Mercer and
his Man.

When we came to the Justice, which was an ancient Gentleman
in *Bloomsbury*, the Constable giving first a summary account of the
Matter the Justice bade me speak, and tell what I had to say; and
first he asked my Name, which I was very loath to give, but there
was no remedy, so I told him my Name was *Mary Flanders*, that I

2. Wonderfully.

was a Widow, my Husband being a Sea Captain, dyed on a Voyage to *Virginia*; and some other Circumstances I told, which he cou'd never contradict, and that I lodg'd at present in Town with such a Person, naming my Governess; but that I was preparing to go over to *America*, where my Husband's Effects lay, and that I was going that Day to buy some Cloaths to put my self into second Mourning,[3] but had not yet been in any Shop, when that Fellow, pointing to the Mercer's Journeyman came rushing upon me with such fury, as very much frighted me, and carried me back to his Masters Shop; where tho' his Master acknowledg'd I was not the Person; yet he would not dismiss me, but charg'd a constable with me.

Then I proceeded to tell how the Journeyman treated me; how they would not suffer me to send for any of my Friends; how afterwards they found the real Thief, and took the very Goods they had Lost upon her, and all the particulars as before.

Then the Constable related his Case; his Dialogue with the Mercer about Discharging me, and at last his Servants refusing to go with him, when I had Charg'd him with him, and his Master encouraging him to do so; and at last his striking the Constable, and the like, all as I have told it already.

The Justice then heard, the *Mercer* and his Man; the *Mercer* indeed made a long Harangue of the great loss they have daily by Lifters and Thieves; that it was easy for them to Mistake, and that when he found it, he would have dismiss'd me, &c. as above; as to the Journeyman he had very little say, but that he pretended other of the Servants told him, that I was really the Person.

Upon the whole, the Justice first of all told me very courteously I was Discharg'd; that he was very sorry that the *Mercers* Man should in his eager pursuit have so little Discretion, as to take up an innocent Person for a guilty Person; that if he had not been so unjust as to detain me afterward, he believ'd I would have forgiven the first Affront; that however it was not in his Power to award me any Reparation for any thing, other than by openly reproving them, which he should do; but he suppos'd I would apply to such Methods as the Law directed; in the mean time he would bind him over.

But as to the Breach of the Peace committed by the Journeyman, he told me he should give me some satisfaction for that, for he should commit him to *Newgate* for Assaulting the Constable, and for Assaulting of me also.

Accordingly he sent the Fellow to *Newgate* for that Assault, and his Master gave Bail, and so we came away; but I had the satisfaction of seeing the Mob wait upon them both as they came out,

3. A style of dress allowed by the etiquette of the age to be worn when strict mourning clothes (severe, unrelieved black) were put aside.

Holooing, and throwing Stones and Dirt at the Coaches they rode in, and so I came Home to my Governess.

After this hustle,[4] coming home and telling my Governess the Story, she falls a Laughing at me; Why are you merry, *says I?* the Story has not so much Laughing room in it as you imagine; I am sure I have had a great deal of Hurry and Fright too, with a Pack of uɜly Rogues. *Laugh*, says my Governess, I laugh Child to see what a lucky Creature you are; why this Jobb will be the best Bargain to you, that ever you made in your Life, if you manage it well: I warrant you, says she, you shall make the *Mercer* pay you 500 *l.* for Damages, besides what you shall get of the Journeyman.

I had other Thoughts of the Matter than she had; and especially, because I had given in my name to the Justice of Peace; and I knew that my Name was so well known among the People at *Hick's Hall*,[5] the *Old Baily*, and such Places, that if this Cause came to be tryed openly, and my Name came to be enquir'd into, no Court would give much Damages, for the Reputation of a Person of such a Character; however, I was oblig'd to begin a Prosecution in Form, and accordingly my Governess found me out a very creditable sort of a Man to manage it, being an Attorney of very good Business, and of good Reputation, and she was certainly in the right of this; for had she employ'd a petty Fogging hedge Soliciter,[6] or a Man not known, and not in good Reputation, I should have brought it to but little.

I met this Attorney, and gave him all the particulars at large, as they are recited above; and he assur'd me, it was a Case, *as he said*, that would very well support itself, and that he did not Question, but that a Jury would give very considerable Damages on such an Occasion; so taking his full Instructions, he began the Prosecution, and the *Mercer* being Arrested, gave Bail; a few Days after his giving Bail, he Comes with his Attorney to my Attorney, to let him know that he desir'd to Accommodate[7] the matter; that it was all carried on in the Heat of an unhappy Passion; that his Client, *meaning me*, had a sharp provoking Tongue, that I us'd them ill, gibing at them, and jeering them, even while they believed me to be the very Person, and that I had provok'd them, and the like.

My Attorney manag'd as well on my Side; made them believe I was a Widow of Fortune, that I was able to do myself Justice, and had great Friends to stand by me too, who had all made me promise to Sue to the utmost, and that if it cost me a Thousand Pound, I would be sure to have satisfaction, for that the Affronts I had receiv'd were unsufferable.

4. Rough handling.
5. Sessions Court of Middlesex County.
6. A shyster; a lawyer who deals with insignificant cases and who resorts to trickery.
7. I.e., to settle out of court.

However they brought my Attorney to this, that he promis'd he would not blow the Coals,[8] that if I enclin'd to an Accommodation, he would not hinder me, and that he would rather perswade me to Peace than to War; for which they told him he should be no loser, all which he told me very honestly, and told me that if they offer'd him any Bribe, I should certainly know it; but upon the whole he told me very honestly that if I would take his Opinion, he would Advise me to make it up with them; for that as they were in a great Fright, and were desirous above all things to make it up, and knew that let it be what it would, they would be alotted to bear all the Costs of the Suit; he believ'd they would give me freely more than any Jury or Court of Justice would give upon a Trial: I ask'd him what he thought they would be brought to; he told me he could not tell, as to that; but he would tell me more when I saw him again.

Some time after this, they came again to know if he had talk'd with me: He told them he had, that he found me not so Averse to an Accommodation as some of my Friends were, who resented the Disgrace offer'd me, and set me on; that they blow'd the Coals in secret, prompting me to Revenge, or to do myself Justice, as they call'd it; so that he could not tell what to say to it; he told them he would do his endeavour to persuade me, but he ought to be able to tell me what Proposal they made: They pretended they could not make any Proposal, because it might be made use of against them; and he told them, that by the same Rule he could not make any offers, for that might be pleaded in Abatement of what Damages a Jury might be inclin'd to give: However after some Discourse and mutual Promises that no Advantage should be taken on either Side, by what was transacted then, or at any other of those Meetings, they came to a kind of a Treaty; but so remote, and so wide from one another, that nothing could be expected from it; for my Attorney demanded 500 *l*. and Charges, and they offer'd 50 *l*. without Charges; so they broke off, and the *Mercer* propos'd to have a Meeting with me myself; and my Attorney agreed to that very readily.

My Attorney gave me Notice to come to this Meeting in good Cloaths, and with some State,[9] that the *Mercer* might see I was something more than I seem'd to be that time they had me: Accordingly I came in a new Suit of second Mourning, according to what I had said at the Justices; I set myself out[1] too, as well as a Widows dress in second Mourning would admit; my Governess, also furnish'd me with a good Pearl Neck-lace, that shut in behind

8. Fan the flames of Moll's supposed indignation, should she be willing to settle without trial.
9. Show of wealth.
1. Wore accessories.

with a Locket of Diamonds, which she had in Pawn; and I had a very good gold Watch by my Side; so that in a Word, I made a very good Figure, and as I stay'd,[2] till I was sure they were come, I came in a Coach to the Door with my Maid with me.

When I came into the Room, the *Mercer* was surpriz'd; he stood up and made his Bow, which I took a little Notice of, and but a little, and went and Sat down where my own Attorney had pointed to me to sit, for it was his House; after a little while, the *Mercer* said, he did not know me again, and began to make some Compliments his way,[3] I told him, I believ'd he did not know me at first, and that if he had, I believ'd he would not have treated me as he did.

He told me he was very sorry for what had happen'd, and that it was to testifie the willingness he had to make all possible Reparation, that he had appointed this Meeting; that he hop'd I would not carry things to extremity, which might be not only too great a Loss to him, but might be the ruin of his Business and Shop, in which Case I might have the satisfaction of repaying an Injury with an Injury ten times greater; but that I would then get nothing, whereas he was willing to do me any Justice that was in his Power, without putting himself or me to the Trouble or Charge of a Suit at Law.

I told him I was glad to hear him talk so much more like a Man of Sense than he did before; that it was true, acknowledgement in most Cases of Affronts was counted Reparation sufficient; but this had gone too far to be made up so; that I was not Revengeful, nor did I seek his Ruin, or any Mans else, but that all my Friends were unanimous not to let me so far neglect my Character as to adjust a thing of this kind without a sufficient Reparation of Honour: That to be taken up for a Thief was such an Indignity as could not be put up, that my Character was above being treated so by any that knew me; but because in my Condition of a Widow, I had been for sometime Careless of myself, and Negligent of myself, I might be taken for such a Creature, but that for the particular usage I had from him afterward; and then I repeated all as before, it was so provoking I had scarce Patience to repeat it.

Well he acknowledg'd all, and was mighty humble indeed; he made Proposals very handsome; he came up to a Hundred Pounds, and to pay all the Law Charges, and added that he would make a Present of a very good Suit of Cloths; I came down to three Hundred Pounds, and I demanded that I should publish an Advertisement of the particulars in the common News Papers.

This was a Clause he never could comply with, however at last he came up by good Management of my Attorney to 150 *l.* and a Suit

2. Waited.   3. In his way.

of black silk Cloaths, and there I agreed and as it were at my Attornies request complied with it; he paying my Attornies Bill and Charges, and gave us a good Supper into the Bargain.

When I came to receive the Money, I brought my Governess with me, dress'd like an old Dutchess, and a Gentleman very well dress'd, who we pretended Courted me, but I call'd him Cousin, and the Lawyer was only to hint privately to him, that this Gentleman Courted the Widow.

He treated us handsomely indeed, and paid the Money chearfully enough; so that it cost him 200 *l.* in all, or rather more: At our last Meeting when all was agreed, the Case of the Journeyman came up, and the *Mercer* beg'd very hard for him, told me he was a Man that had kept a Shop of his own, and been in good Business, had a Wife and several Children, and was very poor, that he had nothing to make satisfaction with, but he should come to beg my pardon on his Knees, if I desir'd it as openly as I pleas'd: I had no Spleen at the sawcy Rogue, nor were his Submissions any thing to me, since there was nothing to be got by him; so I thought it was as good to throw that in generously as not, so I told him I did not desire the Ruin of any Man, and therefore at his Request I would forgive the Wretch, it was below me to seek any Revenge.

When we were at Supper he brought the poor Fellow in to make acknowledgement, which he would have done with as much mean Humility, as his Offence was with insulting Haughtiness and Pride, in which he was an Instance of a compleat baseness of Spirit, imperious, cruel, and relentless when Uppermost, and in Prosperity; abject and low Spirited when Down in Affliction: However I abated his Cringes, told him I forgave him, and desir'd he might withdraw, as if I did not care for the sight of him, tho' I had forgiven him.

I was now in good Circumstances indeed, if I could have known my time for leaving off, and my Governess often said I was the richest of the Trade in *England,* and so I believe I was; for I had 700 *l.* by me in Money, besides Cloaths, Rings, some Plate, and two gold Watches, and all of them stol'n, for I had innumerable Jobbs besides these I have mention'd; O! had I even now had the Grace of Repentance, I had still leisure to have look'd back upon my Follies, and have made some Reparation; but the satisfaction I was to make for the publick Mischiefs I had done, was yet left behind; and I could not forbear going Abroad again, *as I call'd it now,* any more than I could when my Extremity really drove me out for Bread.

It was not long after the Affair with the *Mercer* was made up, that I went out in an Equipage[4] quite different from any I had ever appear'd in before; I dress'd myself like a Beggar Woman, in the coarsest and most despicable Rags I could get, and I walk'd about

4. Outfit, attire.

peering, and peeping into every Door and Window I came near; and indeed I was in such a Plight[5] now, that I knew as ill how to behave in as ever I did in any; I naturally abhorr'd Dirt and Rags; I had been bred up Tite[6] and Cleanly, and could be no other, whatever Condition I was in; so that this was the most uneasie Disguise to me that ever I put on. I said presently to myself that this would not do, for this was a Dress that every body was shy, and afraid of; and I thought every body look'd at me, as if they were afraid I should come near them, lest I should take something from them, or afraid to come near me, lest they should get something from me: I wandered about all the Evening the first time I went out, and made nothing of it, but came home again wet, draggl'd and tired; However I went out again, the next Night, and then I met with a little Adventure, which had like to have cost me dear; as I was standing near a Tavern Door, there comes a Gentleman on Horse back, and lights at the Door, and wanting to go into the Tavern, he calls one of the Drawers[7] to hold his Horse; he stay'd pretty long in the Tavern, and the Drawer heard his Master call, and thought he would be angry with him; when seeing me stand by him, he call'd to me, here Woman, *says he*, hold this Horse a while, till I go in, if the Gentleman comes, he'll give you something; *yes says* I, and takes the Horse and walks off with him very soberly, and carry'd him to my Governess.

This had been a Booty to those that had understood it; but never was poor Thief more at a loss to know what to do with any thing that was stolen; for when I came home, my Governess was quite confounded, and what to do with the Creature, we neither of us knew; to send him to a Stable was doing nothing, for it was certain that publick Notice would be given in the *Gazette*,[8] and the Horse describ'd, so that we durst not go to fetch it again.

All the remedy we had for this unlucky Adventure was to go and set up the Horse at an Inn, and sent a Note by a Porter to the Tavern, that the Gentleman's Horse that was lost such a time, was left at such an Inn, and that he might be had there; that the poor Woman that held him, having led him about the Street, not being able to lead him back again, had left him there; we might have waited till the owner had publish'd, and offer'd a Reward, but we did not care to venture the receiving the Reward.

So this was a Robbery and no Robbery, for little was lost by it, and nothing was got by it, and I was quite Sick of going out in a Beggar's dress, it did not answer at all, and besides I thought it was Ominous and Threatning.

5. Condition (due to her uncomfortable disguise).
6. Brought up to be tidy.
7. Waiter or bartender, one who draws liquors.

8. *The London Gazette*, an official newspaper printed semi-weekly in London containing information pertaining to all branches of public interest.

While I was in this Disguise, I fell in with a parcel of Folks of a worse kind than any I ever sorted[9] with, and I saw a little into their ways too, these were Coiners[1] of Money, and they made some very good offers to me, as to profit; but the part they would have had me have embark'd in, was the most dangerous Part; I mean that of the very working the Dye,[2] as they call it, which had I been taken, had been certain Death, and that at a Stake, *I say*, to be burnt to Death at a Stake; so that tho' I was to Appearance, but a Beggar; and they promis'd Mountains of Gold and Silver to me to engage; yet it would not do; it is True if I had been really a Beggar, or had been desperate as when I began, I might perhaps have clos'd with it; for what care they to Die, that can't tell how to Live? But at present this was not my Condition, at least I was for no such terrible Risques as those; besides the very Thoughts of being burnt at a Stake, struck terror into my very Soul, chill'd my Blood, and gave me the Vapours to such a degree as I could not think of it without trembling.

This put an End to my Disguise too, for as I did not like the Proposal, so I did not tell them so, but seem'd to relish it, and promis'd to meet again; but I durst see them no more, for if I had seen them, and complied, tho' I had declin'd it with the greatest assurances of Secresy in the World, they would have gone near to have murther'd me to make sure Work, and make themselves easy, *as they call it*; what kind of easiness that is, they may best Judge that understand how easy Men are that can Murther People to prevent Danger.

This and Horse stealing were things quite out of my way, and I might easily resolve I would have no more to say to them; my business seem'd to lye another way, and tho' it had hazard enough in it too, yet it was more suitable to me, and what had more of Art in it, more room to Escape, and more Chances for a coming off, if a Surprize should happen.

I had several Proposals made also to me about that time, to come into a Gang of House-Breakers; but that was a thing I had no mind to venture at neither, any more than I had at the Coining Trade; I offer'd to go along with two Men, and a Woman, that made it their Business to get into Houses by Stratagem, and with them I was willing enough to venture; but there was three of them already, and they did not care to part,[3] nor I to have too many in a Gang,

9. Consorted.
1. Counterfeiters. The offense was considered to be treasonable and was punishable by burning at the stake.
2. Engraved stamp (die) for pressing a design into the metal coin. The apparent puns and verbal associations in Moll's description of the episode with the coun-

terfeiters indicates grim humor. Not only is the money itself a "stake" in risking such an enterprise, but Moll also savors the word play on "die" as she dwells on the consequences of the scheme.
3. To separate into couples; "to part" could also mean "to share the loot further."

so I did not close with them, but declin'd them, and they paid dear for their next Attempt.

But at length I met with a Woman that had ofen told me what Adventures she had made, and with Success at the Water-side, and I clos'd with her, and we drove on our Business pretty well: One Day we came among some *Dutch* People at St. *Catherines*,[4] where we went on pretence to buy Goods that were privately got on Shore: I was two or three times in a House, where we saw a good Quantity of prohibited Goods, and my Companion once brought away three Peices of *Dutch* black Silk that turn'd to good Account, and I had my Share of it; but in all the Journeys I made by myself, I could not get an Opportunity to do any thing, so I laid it aside, for I had been so often, that they began to suspect something, and were so shy, that I saw nothing was to be done.

This baulk'd[5] me a little, and I resolv'd to push at something or other, for I was not us'd to come back so often without Purchase; so the next Day I dress'd myself up fine, and took a Walk to the other End of the Town; I pass'd thro' the *Exchange*[6] in the *Strand*, but had no Notion of finding any thing to do there, when on a sudden I saw a great Clutter in the Place, and all the People, Shop-keepers as well as others, standing up, and staring, and what should it be? but some great Dutchess come into the *Exchange*; and they said the Queen was coming; I set myself close up to a Shop-side with my back to the Compter, as if to let the Crowd pass by, when keeping my Eye upon a parcel of Lace, which the Shop-keeper was showing to some Ladies that stood by me; the Shop-keeper and her Maid were so taken up with looking to see who was a coming, and what Shop they would go to, that I found means to slip a Paper of Lace into my Pocket, and come clear off with it, so the Lady Mille-ner paid dear enough for her gaping after the Queen.

I went off from the Shop, as if driven along by the Throng, and mingling myself with the Crowd, went out at the other Door of the *Exchange*, and so got away before they miss'd their Lace; and because I would not be follow'd, I call'd a Coach and shut myself up in it; I had scarse shut the Coach Doors up, but I saw the Mille-ners Maid, and five or six more come running out into the Street, and crying out as if they were frighted; they did not cry stop Thief, because no body ran away, but I cou'd hear the Word robb'd, and Lace, two or three times, and saw the Wench wringing her Hands, and run staring, to and again, like one scar'd; the Coachman that had taken me up was getting up into the Box, but was not quite up, so that the Horses had not begun to move, so

---

4. Waterfront area on the Thames adjacent to the Tower of London.
5. Frustrated, disappointed.
6. The New Exchange, a bazaar on the south side of the Strand.

that I was terrible uneasy; and I took the Packet of Lace and laid it ready to have dropt it out at the Flap of the Coach, which opens before, just behind the Coachman;[7] but to my great satisfaction in less than a Minute, the Coach began to move, that is to say, as soon as the Coachman had got up and spoken to his Horses; so he drove away without any interruption, and I brought off my Pur-chase, which was worth near twenty Pound.

The next Day I dress'd me up again, but in quite different Cloths, and walk'd the same way again; but nothing offer'd till I came into *St. James's Park*,[8] where I saw abundance of fine Ladies in the *Park*, walking in the *Mall*, and among the rest, there was a little Miss, a young Lady of about 12 or 13 Years old, and she had a Sister, as I suppose it was, with her, that might be about Nine Year old: I observ'd the biggest had a fine gold Watch on, and a good Necklace of Pearl, and they had a Footman in Livery with them; but as it is not usual for the Footmen to go[9] behind the Ladies in the *Mall*; so I observ'd the Footman stop'd at their going into the *Mall*, and the biggest of the Sisters spoke to him, which I perceiv'd was to bid him be just there when they came back.

When I heard her dismiss the Footman, I step'd up to him, and ask'd him, what little Lady that was? and held a little Chat with him, about what a pretty Child it was with her, and how Genteel and well Carriag'd the Lady, the eldest would be, how Womanish, and how Grave; and the Fool of a Fellow told me presently who she was, that she was Sir *Thomas* ———'s eldest Daughter of *Essex*, and that she was a great Fortune, that her Mother was not come to Town yet; but she was with Sir *William* ———'s Lady of *Suffolk*, at her Lodgings in *Suffolk-Street*, and a great deal more; that they had a Maid and a Woman to wait on them, besides, Sir *Thomas's* Coach, the Coachman and himself, and that young Lady was Governess to the whole Family as well here, as at Home too; and in short, told me abundance of things enough for my business.

I was very well dress'd, and had my gold Watch, as well as she; so I left the Footman, and I puts myself in a Rank with[1] this young Lady, having stay'd till she had taken one double Turn in the *Mall*, and was going forward again, by and by, I saluted her by her Name, with the Title of Lady *Betty*: I ask'd her when she heard from her Father? when my Lady her Mother would be in Town and how she did?

I talk'd so familiarly to her of her whole Family that she cou'd not suspect but that I knew them all intimately: I ask'd her why

she would come Abroad without Mrs. *Chime* with her (that was
the Name of her Woman)[2] to take care of Mrs. *Judith* that was her
Sister. Then I enter'd into a long Chat with her about her Sister,
what a fine little Lady she was, and ask'd her if she had learn'd
French, and a Thousand such little things to entertain her, when
on a sudden we see the Guards come, and the Crowd run to see the
King go by to the Parliament-House.

The Ladies run all to the Side of the *Mall*, and I help'd my Lady
to stand upon the edge of the Boards on the side of the *Mall*, that
she might be high enough to see; and took the little one and lifted
her quite up; during which, I took care to convey the gold Watch
so clean away from the Lady *Betty*, that she never felt it, nor miss'd
it, till all the Crowd was gone, and she was gotten into the middle
of the *Mall* among the other Ladies.

I took my leave of her in the very Crowd, and said to her, as if in
haste, dear Lady *Betty* take care of your little Sister, and so the
Crowd did, as it were Thrust me away from her, and that I was
oblig'd unwillingly to take my leave.

The hurry in such Cases is immediately over, and the Place clear
as soon as the King is gone by; but as there is always a great running and clutter just as the King passes; so having drop'd the two
little Ladies, and done my Business with them, without any Miscar-
riage, I kept hurrying on among the Crowd, as if I run to see the
King, and so I got before the Crowd and kept so, till I came to the
End of the *Mall*, when the King going on toward the Horse-
Guards;[3] I went forward to the Passage, which went then thro'
against the lower End of the *Hay-Market*, and there I bestow'd a
coach upon myself, and made off; and I confess I have not yet been
so good as my word (*viz.*) to go and visit my Lady *Betty*.

I was once of the mind to venture staying with Lady *Betty* till
she mist the Watch, and so have made a great Out-cry about it
with her, and have got her into her Coach, and put my self in the
Coach with her, and have gone Home with her; for she appear'd so
fond of me, and so perfectly deceiv'd by my so readily talking to her
of all her Relations and Family, that I thought it was very easy to
push the thing farther, and to have got at least the Neck-lace of
Pearl; but when I consider'd that tho' the Child would not perhaps
have suspected me, other People might, and that if I was search'd I
should be discover'd; I thought it was best to go off with what I
had got, and be satisfy'd.

I came accidentally afterwards to hear, that when the young Lady
miss'd her Watch, she made a great Out-cry in the *Park*, and sent

---

2. Not a common British surname. Defoe seems to be playfully using the word
"chime" to reflect its meaning in the
criminal jargon of the day: to flatter a
victim while at the same time taking advantage of him.
3. Horse Guards Parade Grounds.

her Footman up and down, to see if he could find me out, she having describ'd me so perfectly that he knew presently that it was the same Person that had stood and talked so long with him, and ask'd him so many Questions about them; but I was gone far enough out of their reach before she could come at her Footman to tell him the Story.

I made another Adventure after this, of a Nature different from all I had been concern'd in yet, and this was at a Gaming-House near *Covent-Garden.*

I saw several People go in and out; and I stood in the Passage a good while with another Woman with me, and seeing a Gentleman go up that seem'd to be of more than ordinary Fashion, I said to him, Sir, pray don't they give Women leave to go up? *yes Madam, says he,* and to play too if they please; I mean so Sir, *said I*; and with that, he said he would introduce me if I had a mind; so I followed him to the Door, and he looking in: there, Madam, *says he,* are the Gamesters, if you have a mind to venture; I look'd in and said to my Comrade, aloud, here's nothing but Men, I won't venture among them; at which one of the Gentlemen cry'd out, you need not be afraid Madam, here's none but fair Gamesters, you are very welcome to come and Set[4] what you please; so I went a little nearer and look'd on, and some of them brought me a Chair, and I sat down and see the Box and Dice go round a pace;[5] then I said to my Comrade, the Gentlemen play too high for us, come let us go.

The People were all very civil, and one Gentleman in particular encourag'd me, and said, come Madam, if you please to Venture, if you dare Trust me I'll answer for it; you shall have nothing put upon you here; no Sir, *said I*, smiling, I hope the Gentlemen wou'd not Cheat a Woman; but still I declin'd venturing, tho' I pull'd out a Purse with Money in it, that they might see I did not want Money.

After I had sat a while, one Gentleman said to me Jeering, come Madam, I see you are afraid to venture for yourself; I always had good luck with the Ladies, you shall Set for me, if you won't Set for yourself; I told him, Sir I should be very loth to lose your Money, tho' I added, I am pretty lucky too; but the Gentlemen play so high, that I dare not indeed venture my own.

Well, well, *says he,* there's ten Guineas Madam, Set them for me; so I took his Money and set, himself looking on; I run out Nine of the Guineas by One and Two at a Time, and then the Box coming to the next Man to me, my Gentleman gave me Ten Guineas more, and made me Set Five of them at once, and the Gentleman who had the Box threw out,[6] so there was Five Guineas of his

Money again; he was encourag'd at this, and made me take the Box, which was a bold Venture: However, I held the Box so long that I had gain'd him his whole Money, and had a good handful of Guineas in my Lap; and which was the better Luck, when I threw out, I threw but at One or Two of those that had Set me, and so went off easie.

When I was come this length, I offer'd the Gentleman all the Gold, for it was his own; and so would have had him play for himself, pretending I did not understand the Game well enough: He laugh'd, and said if I had but good Luck, it was no matter whether I understood the Game or no; but I should not leave off: However he took out the 15 Guineas that he had put in at first, and bade me play with the rest: I would have told[7] them to see how much I had got, but he said no, no, don't tell them, I believe you are very honest, and 'tis bad Luck to tell them, so I play'd on.

I understood the Game well enough, tho' I pretended I did not, and play'd cautiously; it was to keep a good Stock in my Lap, out of which I every now and then convey'd some into my Pocket, but in such a manner, and at such convenient times, as I was sure he cou'd not see it.

I play'd a great while, and had a very good Luck for him, but the last time I held the Box, they Set me high, and I threw boldly at all; I held the Box till I gain'd near Fourscore Guineas, but lost above half of it back at the last throw; so I got up, for I was afraid I should lose it all back again, and said to him, pray come Sir now and take it and play for your self, I think I have done pretty well for you; he would have had me play'd on, but it grew late, and I desir'd to be excus'd. When I gave it up to him, I told him I hop'd he would give me leave to tell it now, that I might see what I had gain'd, and how lucky I had been for him; when I told them, there was Threescore, and Three Guineas. Ay, *says I*, if it had not been for that unlucky Throw I had got you a Hundred Guineas; so I gave him all the Money, but he would not take it till I had put my Hand into it, and taken some for myself, and bid me please myself; I refus'd it, and was positive I would not take it myself, if he had a mind to any thing of that kind it should be all his own doings.

The rest of the Gentlemen seeing us striving, cry'd give it her all; but I absolutely refus'd that; then one of them said, D——n ye *Jack*, half it with her, don't you know you should be always upon even Terms with the Ladies; so in short, he divided it with me, and I brought away 30 Guineas, besides about 43, which I had stole privately, which I was sorry for afterwards, because he was so generous.

Thus I brought Home 73 Guineas, and let my old Governess see what good Luck I had at Play: However, it was her Advice that I

---

7. Counted.

should not venture again, and I took her Council, for I never went there any more; for I knew as well as she, if the Itch of Play came in, I might soon lose that, and all the rest of what I had got.

Fortune had smil'd upon me to that degree, and had Thriven so much, and my Governess too, for she always had a Share with me, that really the old Gentlewoman began to talk of leaving off while we were well, and being satisfy'd with what we had got; but, I know not what Fate guided me, I was as backward to it now as she was when I propos'd it to her before, and so in an ill Hour we gave over the Thoughts of it for the Present, and in a Word, I grew more hardn'd and audacious than ever, and the Success I had, made my Name as famous as any Thief of my sort ever had been at *Newgate*, and in the *Old-Bayly*.

I had sometimes taken the liberty to Play the same Game over again, which is not according to Practice, which however succeeded not amiss; but generally I took up new Figures, and contriv'd to appear in new Shapes every time I went abroad.

It was now a rumbling[8] time of the Year, and the Gentlemen being most of them gone out of Town, *Tunbridge*, and *Epsom*,[9] and such Places were full of People, but the City was Thin, and I thought our Trade felt it a little, as well as others; so that at the latter End of the Year I joyn'd myself with a Gang, who usually go every Year to *Sturbridge* Fair, and from thence to *Bury* Fair,[1] in *Suffolk*: We promis'd our selves great things here, but when I came to see how things were, I was weary of it presently; for except meer Picking of Pockets, there was little worth meddling with; neither if a Booty had been made, was it so easy carrying it off, nor was there such a variety of occasion for Business in our way, as in *London*; all that I made of the whole Journey, was a gold Watch at *Bury* Fair, and a small parcel of Linnen at *Cambridge*, which gave me an occasion to take leave of the Place: It was an old Bite,[2] and I thought might do with a Country Shop keeper, tho' in *London* it would not.

I bought[3] at a Linnen Draper's shop, not in the Fair, but in the Town of *Cambridge*, as much fine Holland and other things as came to about seven Pound; when I had done, I bade them be sent to such an Inn, where I had purposely taken up my being[4] the same Morning, as if I was to Lodge there that Night.

I order'd the Draper to send them Home to me, about such an Hour to the Inn where I lay, and I would pay him his Money; at

8. A time for travel; possibly from "rumbling": to move or travel with a continuous low, rolling sound, as in coaches, or to be conveyed in rumbling vehicles. The second edition prints "rambling," suggesting a possible misprint in the first.
9. Both fashionable spas.
1. Famous fairs held in autumn outside London.
2. Trick, dodge.
3. Ordered to be delivered.
4. Residence; Moll registered as if she intended to stay one night.

the time appointed the Draper sends the Goods, when the Innkeeper's Maid brought the Messenger to the Door, who was a young Fellow, an Apprentice, almost a Man, she tells him her Mistress was a sleep, but if he would leave the things, and call in about an Hour, I should be awake, and he might have the Money; he left the Parcel very readily, and goes his way, and in about half an Hour my Maid and I walk'd off, and that very Evening I hired a Horse, and a Man to ride before me, and went to *Newmarket*, and from thence got my Passage in a Coach that was not quite full to St. *Edmund's Bury*; Where as I told you I could make but little of my Trade, only at a little Country *Opera*-House, made a shift to carry off a gold Watch from a Ladies side, who was not only intollerably Merry, but as I thought a little Fuddled,[5] which made my Work much easier.

I made off with this little Booty to *Ipswich*, and from thence to *Harwich*;[6] where I went into an Inn, as if I had newly arriv'd from *Holland*, not doubting but I should make some Purchase among the Foreigners that came on shore there; but I found them generally empty of things of value, except what was in their Portmanteaus,[7] and *Dutch* Hampers, which were generally guarded by Footmen; however, I fairly[8] got one of their Portmanteaus one Evening out of the Chamber where the Gentleman lay, the Footman being fast a sleep on the Bed, and I suppose very Drunk.

The room in which I lodg'd lay next to the *Dutchman's*, and having dragg'd the heavy thing with much a-do out of the Chamber into mine, I went out into the Street to see if I could find any possibility of carrying it off; I walk'd about a great while but could see no probability either of getting out the thing, or of conveying away the Goods that was in it if I had open'd it, the Town being so small, and I a perfect Stranger in it; so I returning with a resolution to carry it back again, and leave it where I found it: Just in that very Moment I heard a Man make a Noise to some People to make haste, for the Boat was going to put off, and the Tide would be spent; I call'd to the Fellow, What Boat is it Friend, *says I*, that you belong to? the *Ipswich* Wherry, Madam, *says he*: When do you go off, *says I*? this Moment Madam, *says he*, do you want to go thither? yes, *said I*, if you can stay till I fetch my things: Where are your things Madam, *says he*? At such an Inn, *said I*: Well I'll go with you Madam, *says he*, very civilly, and bring them for you; come away then, *says I*, and takes him with me.

The People of the Inn were in great hurry, the Packet-Boat[9] from *Holland*, being just come in, and two Coaches just come also

5. Drunk.
6. A main port for travel between England and Holland.
7. Portmanteau: a case or valise; however, Moll later describes it as a trunk.
8. Cleanly.
9. A scheduled boat between two ports carrying mail and passengers.

with Passengers from *London*, for another Packet-Boat that was going off for *Holland*, which Coaches were to go back next Day with the Passengers that were just Landed: In this hurry it was not much minded,[1] that I came to the Bar,[2] and paid my Reckoning, telling my Landlady I had gotten my Passage by Sea in a Wherry.

These Wherries are large Vessels, with good Accommodation for carrying Passengers from *Harwich* to *London*; and tho' they are call'd Wherries, which is a word us'd in the *Thames* for a small Boat, Row'd with one or two Men; yet these are Vessels able to carry twenty Passengers, and ten or fifteen Ton of Goods, and fitted to bear the Sea; all this I had found out by enquiring the Night before into the several ways of going to *London*.

My Landlady was very Courteous, took my Money for my Reckoning, but was call'd away, all the House being in a hurry; so I left her, took the Fellow up to my Chamber, gave him the Trunk, or Portmanteau, for it was like a Trunk, and wrapt it about with an old Apron, and he went directly to his Boat about it; as for the drunken *Dutch* Footman he was still a sleep, and his Master with other Foreign Gentlemen at Supper, and very Merry below; so I went clean off with it to *Ipswich*, and going in the Night, the People of the House knew nothing, but that I was gone to *London*, by the *Harwich* Wherry as I had told my Landlady.

I was plagu'd at *Ipswich* with the Custom-House Officers, who stopt my Trunk, *as I call'd it*, and would open, and search it; I was willing I told them, they should search it, but my Husband had the Key, and he was not yet come from *Harwich*; this I said, that if upon searching it, they should find all the things be such as properly belong'd to a Man rather than a Woman, it should not seem strange to them; however, they being possitive to open the Trunk, I consented to have it be broken open, that is to say, to have the Lock taken off, which was not difficult.

They found nothing for their turn, for the Trunk had been search'd before, but they discover'd several things very much to my satisfaction, as particularly a parcel of Money in *French* Pistoles,[3] and some *Dutch* Ducatoons, or *Rix* Dollars,[4] and the rest was chiefly two Perriwigs, wearing Linnen, and Razors, Wash-balls,[5] Perfumes and other useful things, Necessaries for a Gentleman; which all pass'd for my Husband's, and so I was quit of them.

It was now very early in the Morning, and not Light, and I knew not well what Course to take; for I made no doubt but I should be

---

1. No one noticed.
2. Counter.
3. Gold coins, worth from 16 to 18 shillings each.
4. The ducatoon was a silver coin which varied in value from 5 to 6 shillings sterling. The Rix-dollar, also silver, varied from 4s. 6d. to 2s. 3d.
5. Balls of soap, usually scented with orris root and tinted various colors. More fancy than efficient as soap, they were often carried to keep clothes smelling fresh and sweet.

pursued in the Morning, and perhaps be taken with the things about me; so I resolv'd upon taking new Measures; I went publickly to an Inn in the Town with my Trunk, *as I call'd it*, and having taken the Substance out, I did not think the Lumber[6] of it worth my concern; however, I gave it the Landlady of the House with a Charge to take great Care of it, and lay it up safe till I should come again, and away I walk'd into the Street.

When I was got into the Town a great way from the Inn, I met with an antient Woman who had just open'd her Door, and I fell into Chat with her, and ask'd her a great many wild Questions of things all remote to my Purpose and Design, but in my Discourse I found by her how the Town was situated, that I was in a Street which went out towards *Hadly*, but that such a Street went towards the Water-side, such a Street went into the Heart of the Town, and at last such a Street went towards *Colchester*, and so the *London* Road lay there.

I had soon my Ends[7] of this old Woman; for I only wanted to know which was *London* Road, and away I walk'd as fast as I could; not that I intended to go on Foot, either to *London* or to *Colchester*, but I wanted to get quietly away from *Ipswich*.

I walk'd about two or three Mile, and then I met a plain Countryman,[8] who was busy about some Husbandry work I did not know what; and I ask'd him a great many Questions first, not much to the purpose, but at last told him I was going for *London*, and the Coach was full, and I cou'd not get a Passage, and ask'd him if he cou'd not tell me where to hire a Horse that would carry double, and an honest Man to ride before me to *Colchester*, so that I might get a Place there in the Coaches; the honest Clown, look'd earnestly at me, and said nothing for above half a Minute; when scratching his Pole,[9] a Horse say you, and to *Colchester* to carry double; why yes Mistress, alack-a-day, you may have Horses enough for Money; well Friend, *says I*, that I take for granted, I don't expect it without Money: Why but Mistress, *says he*, how much are you willing to give; nay, says I again, Friend, I don't know what your Rates are in the Country here, for I am a Stranger; but if you can get one for me, get it as Cheap as you can, and I'll give you somewhat for your Pains.

Why that's honestly said too, says the Countryman; *not so honest neither*, said I, to myself, *if thou knewest all*; why Mistress, *says he*, I have a Horse that will carry Double, and I don't much care if I go my self with you; *and the like*:[1] Will you, *says I*? well I

6. The body of it; the trunk itself.
7. Used the woman to purpose.
8. Farmer, rustic.
9. Poll (the top of his head).
1. The second edition emends to read "an you like"; however, "and the like" is a standard expression of Defoe's meaning "and so forth." The original manuscript may have contained Defoe's shorthand "ye" ("the"), which was rendered "you" in the second edition.

believe you are an honest Man, if you will, I shall be glad of it, I'll pay you in Reason; why look ye Mistress, *says he,* I won't be out of Reason with you then, if I carry you to *Colechester,* it will be worth five Shillings for myself and my Horse, for I shall hardly come back to Night.

In short, I hir'd the honest Man and his Horse; but when we came to a Town upon the Road, I do not remember the Name of it, but it stands upon a River, I pretended myself very ill, and I could go no farther that Night, but if he would stay there with me, because I was a Stranger I would pay him for himself and his Horse with all my Heart.

This I did because I knew the *Dutch* Gentlemen and their Servants would be upon the Road that Day, either in the Stage Coaches, or riding Post, and I did not know but the drunken Fellow, or somebody else that might have seen me at *Harwich,* might see me again, and so I thought that in one Days stop they would be all gone by.

We lay all that Night there, and the next Morning it was not very early when I set out, so that it was near Ten a-Clock by that time I got to *Colechester:* It was no little Pleasure that I saw the Town, where I had so many pleasant Days, and I made many Enquires after the good old Friends I had once had there, but could make little out, they were all dead or remov'd: The young Ladies had been all married or gone to *London*; the old Gentleman, and the old Lady that had been my early Benefactress all dead; and which troubled me most the young Gentleman my first Lover, and afterwards my Brother-in-Law was dead; but two Sons Men grown, were left of him, but they too were Transplanted to *London.*

I dismiss'd my old Man here, and stay'd incognito for three or four Days in *Colechester,* and then took a Passage in a Waggon, because I would not venture being seen in the *Harwich* Coaches; but I needed not have used so much Caution, for there was no Body in *Harwich* but the Woman of the House could have known me; nor was it rational to think that she, considering the hurry she was in, and that she never saw me but once, and that by Candle light, should have ever discover'd me.

I was now return'd to *London,* and tho' by the Accident of the last Adventure, I got something considerable, yet I was not fond of any more Country rambles, nor should I have ventur'd Abroad again if I had carried the Trade on to the End of my Days; I gave my Governess a History of my Travels, she lik'd the *Harwich* Journey well enough, and in Discoursing of these things between our selves she observ'd, that a Theif being a Creature that Watches the Advantages of other Peoples mistakes, 'tis impossible but that to one that is vigilant and industrious many Opportunities must happen, and therefore she thought that one so exquisitely keen in the Trade as I was, would scarce fail of something extraordinary where ever I went.

On the other hand, every Branch of my Story, if duly consider'd, may be useful to honest People, and afford a due Caution to People of some sort or other to Guard against the like Surprizes, and to have their Eyes about them when they have to do with Strangers of any kind, for 'tis very seldom that some Snare or other is not in their way. The Moral indeed of all my History is left to be gather'd by the Senses and Judgment of the Reader; I am not Qualified to preach to them, let the Experience of one Creature compleatly Wicked, and compleatly Miserable be a Storehouse of useful warning to those that read.

I am drawing now towards a new Variety of the Scenes of Life: Upon my return, being hardened by a long Race of Crime, and Success unparalell'd, at least in the reach of my own Knowledge, I had, as I have said, no thoughts of laying down a Trade, which if I was to judge by the Example of others, must however End at last in Misery and Sorrow.

It was on the *Christmas-day* following in the Evening, that to finish a long Train of Wickedness, I went Abroad to see what might offer in my way; when going by a Working Silver-Smiths in *Foster-lane*, I saw a tempting Bait indeed, and not to be resisted by one of my Occupation; for the Shop had no Body in it, as I could see, and a great deal of loose Plate lay in the Window, and at the Seat of the Man, who usually as I suppose Work'd at one side of the Shop.

I went boldly in and was just going to lay my Hand upon a peice of Plate, and might have done it, and carried it clear off, for any care that the Men who belong'd to the Shop had taken of it; but an officious Fellow in a House, not a Shop, on the other side of the Way, seeing me go in, and observing that there was no Body in the Shop, comes running over the Street, and into the Shop, and without asking me what I was, or who, seizes upon me, and cries out for the People of the House.

I had not as I said above, touch'd any thing in the Shop, and seeing a glimpse of some Body running over to the Shop, I had so much presence of Mind, as to knock very hard with my Foot on the Floor of the House, and was just calling out too, when the Fellow laid Hands on me.

However as I had always most Courage when I was in most danger, so when the Fellow laid Hands on me, I stood very high upon it that I came in to buy half a Dozen of silver Spoons, and to my good Fortune, it was a Silversmith's that sold Plate, as well as work'd Plate, for other Shops: The Fellow laugh'd at that Part, and put such a value upon the Service that he had done his Neighbour, that he would have it be that I came not to buy, but to steal; and raising a great Crowd, I said to the Master of the Shop, who by this time was fetch'd Home from some Neighbouring Place, that it was in vain to make Noise, and enter into Talk there of the Case; the Fellow had insisted, that I came to steal, and he must prove it, and I desir'd we might go before a Magistrate without any more Words; for I began to see I should be too hard for the Man that had seiz'd me.

The Master and Mistress of the Shop were really not so violent as the Man from tother side of the Way, and the Man said, Mistress you might come into the Shop with a good Design for ought I know, but it seem'd a dangerous thing for you to come into such a Shop as mine is, when you see no Body there, and I cannot do Justice to my Neighbour, who was so kind to me, as not to acknowledge he had reason on his Side; tho' upon the whole I do not find you attempt'd to take any thing, and I really know not what to do in it: I press'd him to go before a Magistrate with me, and if any thing cou'd be prov'd on me that was like a design of Robbery, I should willingly submit, but if not I expected reparation.

Just while we were in this Debate, and a Crowd of People gather'd about the Door, came by Sir *T. B.* an Alderman of the City, and Justice of the Peace, and the Goldsmith[2] hearing of it goes out, and entreated his Worship to come in and decide the Case.

Give the Goldsmith his due, he told his Story with a great deal of Justice and Moderation, and the Fellow that had come over, and seiz'd upon me, told his with as much Heat and foollish Passion, which did me good still, rather than Harm: It came then to my turn to speak, and I told his Worship that I was a Stranger in *London*, being newly come out of the *North*, that I Lodg'd in such a Place, that I was passing this Street, and went into the Goldsmiths Shop to buy half a Dozen of Spoons; by great good Luck I had an old silver Spoon in my Pocket, which I pull'd out, and told him I had carried that Spoon to match it with half a Dozen of new ones, that it might match some I had in the Country.

That seeing no Body in the Shop, I knock'd with my Foot very hard to make the People hear, and had also call'd aloud with my Voice: Tis true, there was loose Plate in the Shop, but that no Body cou'd say I had touch'd any of it, or gone near it; that a Fellow came running into the Shop out of the Street, and laid Hands on me in a furious manner, in the very Moments while I was calling, for the People of the House; that if he had really had a mind to have done his Neighbour any Service, he should have stood

2. Moll shifts from silversmith to goldsmith in this episode; however, a working silversmith made and sold both silver and gold plate, which may help explain the shift.

at a distance, and silently watch'd to see whether I had touch'd any thing, or no, and then have clap'd in upon me,[3] and taken me in the Fact: That is very true, *says* Mr. *Alderman,* and turning to the Fellow that stopt me, he ask'd him if it was true that I knock'd with my Foot, he said yes I had knock'd, but that might be because of his coming; Nay, says *the Alderman,* taking him short, now you contradict yourself, for just now you said, she was in the Shop with her back to you, and did not see you till you came upon her; now it was true, that my back was partly to the Street, but yet as my Business was of a kind that requir'd me to have my Eyes every way, so I really had a glance of him running over, as I said before, tho' he did not perceive it.

After a full Hearing, the Alderman gave it as his Opinion, that his Neighbour was under a mistake, and that I was Innocent, and the Goldsmith acquiesc'd in it too, and his Wife, and so I was dismiss'd; but as I was going to depart, Mr. *Alderman* said, but *hold Madam,* if you were designing to buy Spoons I hope you will not let my Friend here lose his Customer by the Mistake: I readily answer'd, no Sir, I'll buy the Spoons still if he can Match my odd Spoon, which I brought for a Pattern; and the Goldsmith shew'd me some of the very same Fashion; so he weigh'd the Spoons, and they came to five and thirty Shillings, so I pulls out my Purse to pay him, in which I had near 20 Guineas, for I never went without such a Sum about me, what ever might happen, and I found it of use at other times as well as now.

When Mr. *Alderman* saw my Money, *he said,* well Madam, now I am satisfy'd you were wrong'd, and it was for this Reason that I mov'd you should buy the Spoons, and staid till you had bought them, for if you had not had Money to pay for them, I should have suspected that you did not come into the Shop with an intent to buy, for indeed the sort of People who come upon those Designs that you have been Charg'd with, are seldom troubl'd with much Gold in their Pockets, as I see you are.

I smil'd, and told his Worship, that then I ow'd something of his Favour to my Money, but I hop'd he saw reason also in the Justice he had done me before; he said, yes he had, but this had confirm'd his Opinion, and he was fully satisfy'd now of my having been injur'd; so I came off with flying Colours, tho' from an Affair, in which I was at the very brink of Destruction.

It was but three Days after this, that not at all made Cautious by my former Danger as I us'd to be, and still pursuing the Art which I had so long been employ'd in, I ventur'd into a House where I saw the Doors open, and furnish'd myself as I thought verily without being perceiv'd, with two Peices of flower'd Silks, such as they

3. Appeared suddenly.

call Brocaded Silk, very rich; it was not a Mercers Shop, nor a
Warehouse of a Mercer, but look'd like a private Dwelling-House,
and was it seems Inhabited by a Man that sold Goods for the
Weavers to the Mercers, like a Broker or Factor.

That I may make short of this black Part of this Story, I was
attack'd by two Wenches that came open Mouth'd at me just as I
was going out at the Door, and one of them pull'd me back into the
Room, while the other shut the Door upon me; I would have given
them good Words, but there was no room for it; two fiery Dragons
cou'd not have been more furious than they were; they tore my
Cloths, bully'd and roar'd as if they would have murther'd me; the
Mistress of the House came next, and then the Master, and all out-
rageous, for a while especially.

I gave the Master very good Words, told him the Door was open,
and things were a Temptation to me, that I was poor, and distress'd, and Poverty was what many could not resist, and beg'd him
with Tears to have pity on me; the Mistress of the House was
mov'd with Compassion, and enclin'd to have let me go, and had
almost perswaded her Husband to it also, but the sawcy Wenches
were run even before they were sent, and had fetch'd a Constable,
and then the Master said, he could not go back, I must go before a
Justice, and answer'd his Wife that he might come into Trouble
himself if he should let me go.

The sight of the Constable indeed struck me with terror, and I
thought I should have sunk into the Ground; I fell into faintings,
and indeed the People themselves thought I would have died, when
the Woman argued again for me, and entreated her Husband,
seeing they had lost nothing to let me go: I offer'd him to pay for
the two Peices whatever the value was, tho' I had not got them,
and argued that as he had his Goods, and had really lost nothing, it
would be cruel to pursue me to Death, and have my Blood for the
bare Attempt of taking them; I put the Constable in mind that I
had broke no Doors, nor carried any thing away; and when I came
to the Justice, and pleaded there that I had neither broken any
thing to get in, nor carried any thing out, the Justice was enclin'd
to have releas'd me; but the first sawcy Jade that stop'd me, affirm-
ing that I was going out with the Goods, but that she stop'd me
and pull'd me back as I was upon the Threshold, the Justice upon
that point committed me, and I was carried to _Newgate_; that horrid
Place! my very Blood chills at the mention of its Name; the Place,
where so many of my Comrades had been lock'd up, and from
whence they went to the fatal Tree;[4] the Place where my Mother
suffered so deeply, where I was brought into the World, and from
whence I expected no Redemption, but by an infamous Death: To

4. Tyburn Tree (the gallows).

conclude, the Place that had so long expected me, and which with so much Art and Success I had so long avoided.

I was now fix'd indeed; 'tis impossible to describe the terror of my mind, when I was first brought in, and when I look'd round upon all the horrors of that dismal Place: I look'd on myself as lost, and that I had nothing to think of, but of going out of the World, and that with the utmost Infamy; the hellish Noise, the Roaring, Swearing and Clamour, the Stench and Nastiness, and all the dreadful croud of Afflicting things that I saw there; joyn'd together to make the Place seem an Emblem of Hell itself,[5] and a kind of an Entrance into it.

Now I reproach'd myself with the many hints I had had, *as I have mentioned above*, from my own Reason, from the Sense of my good Circumstances, and of the many Dangers I had escap'd to leave off while I was well, and how I had withstood them all, and hardened my Thoughts against all Fear; it seem'd to me that I was hurried on by an inevitable and unseen Fate to this Day of Misery, and that now I was to Expiate all my Offences at the Gallows, that I was now to give satisfaction to Justice with my Blood, and that I was come to the last Hour of my Life, and of my Wickedness together: These things pour'd themselves in upon my Thoughts in a confus'd manner, and left me overwhelm'd with Melancholly and Despair.

Then I repented heartily of all my Life past, but that Repentance yielded me no Satisfaction, no Peace, no not in the least, because, *as I said to myself*, it was repenting after the Power of farther Sinning was taken away: I seem'd not to Mourn that I had committed such Crimes, and for the Fact, as it was an Offence against God and my Neighbour; but I mourn'd that I was to be punish'd for it; I was a Penitent as I thought, not that I had sinn'd, but that I was to suffer, and this took away all the Comfort, and even the hope of my Repentance in my own Thoughts.

I got no sleep for several Nights or Days after I came into that wretch'd Place, and glad I wou'd have been for some time to have died there, tho' I did not consider dying as it ought to be consider'd neither; indeed nothing could be fill'd with more horror to my Imagination than the very Place, nothing was more odious to me than the Company that was there: O! if I had but been sent to any Place in the World, and not to *Newgate*, I should have thought myself happy.

In the next Place, how did the harden'd Wretches that were there before me Triumph over me? what! Mrs. *Flanders* come to

Handwritten margin note: "I told you so."

5. See "Hell upon Earth," in Backgrounds and Sources, for a corroborating description of Newgate Prison which De- foe may have used along with his own experiences in being a prisoner there.

Newgate at last? what Mrs. *Mary*, Mrs. *Molly*, and after that plain *Moll Flanders*? They thought the Devil had help'd me they said, that I had reign'd so long, they expected me there many Years ago, and was I come at last? then they flouted me with my Dejections, welcom'd me to the Place, wish'd me Joy, bid me have a good Heart, not to be cast down, things might not be so bad as I fear'd, and the like; then call'd for Brandy, and drank to me; but put it all up to my Score,[6] for they told me I was but just come to the College, *as they call'd it*, and sure I had Money in my Pocket, tho' they had none.

I ask'd one of this Crew how long she had been there? she said four Months; I ask'd her, how the Place look'd to her when she first came into it? just as it did now to me, *says she*, dreadful and frightful, that she thought she was in Hell, and I believe so still, *adds she, but it is natural to me now, I don't disturb myself about it:* I suppose says I, you are in no danger of what is to follow: Nay, *says she*, for you are mistaken there I assure you, for I am under Sentence,[7] only I pleaded my Belly, but I am no more with Child than the Judge that try'd me, and I expect to be call'd down next Sessions; *this* CALLING DOWN, is calling down *to their former Judgement, when a Woman has been respited for her Belly, but proves not to be with Child, or if she has been with Child, and has been brought to Bed.* Well says I, and are you thus easy? ay, *says she*, I can't help myself, what signifyes being sad? If I am hang'd there's an End of me, *says she*, and away she turns Dancing, and Sings as she goes the following Peice of *Newgate* Wit,

> *If I swing by the String,*
> *I shall hear the[8] Bell ring.*
> And then there's an End of poor *Jenny*.

I mention this, because it would be worth the Observation of any Prisoner, who shall hereafter fall into the same Misfortune and come to that dreadful Place of *Newgate*; how Time, Necessity, and Conversing with the Wretches that are there Familiarizes the Place to them; how at last they become reconcil'd to that which at first was the greatest Dread upon their Spirits in the World, and are as impudently Chearful and Merry in their Misery, as they were when out of it.

I can not say, as some do, this Devil is not so black, as he is painted; for indeed no Colours can represent the Place to the Life, nor any Soul conceive aright of it, but those who have been Suffer-

---

6. Charged the drinks to Moll. Newgate jailers held a license to sell beer, wine, and spirits to prisoners, according to their ability to pay.
7. Sentence of death.

8. The Bell at St. *Sepulcher's* which Tolls upon Execution Day [*Defoe's note*]. The bell of St. Sepulchre's Church, across from Newgate, tolled from 6:00 A.M. to 10:00 A.M. on execution mornings.

ers there: But how Hell should bcome by degrees so natural, and not only tollerable, but even agreeable, is a thing Unintelligible, but by those who have Experienc'd it, as I have.

The same Night that I was sent to *Newgate*, I sent the News of it to my old Governess, who was surpriz'd at it you may be sure, and spent the Night almost as ill out of *Newgate*, as I did in it.

The next Morning, she came to see me, she did what she cou'd to Comfort me, but she saw that was to no purpose; however, as she said, to sink under the Weight, was but to encrease the Weight, she immediately applied her self to all the proper Methods to prevent the Effects of it, which we fear'd; and first she found out the two fiery Jades that had surpriz'd me; she tamper'd with them, persuad'd them, offer'd them Money, and in a Word, try'd all imaginable ways to prevent a Prosecution; she offer'd one of the Wenches 100 *l.* to go away from her Mistress, and not to appear against me; but she was so resolute, that tho' she was but a Servant-Maid, at 3 *l.* a Year Wages or thereabouts, she refus'd it, and would have refus'd it, as my Governess said she believ'd, if she had offer'd her 500 *l.* Then she attack'd the tother Maid, she was not so hard Hearted in appearance as the other; and sometimes seem'd inclin'd to be merciful; but the first Wench kept her up, and chang'd her Mind, and would not so much as let my Governess talk with her, but threatn'd to have her up for Tampering with the Evidence.

Then she apply'd to the Master, that is to say, the Man whose Goods had been stol'n, and particularly to his Wife, who as I told you was enclin'd at first to have some Compassion for me; she found the Woman the same still, but the Man alledg'd he was bound by the Justice that committed me, to Prosecute, and that he should forfeit his Recognizance.[9]

My Governess offer'd to find Friends that should get his Recognizances off of the File, as they call it, and that he should not suffer;[1] but it was not possible to Convince him, that could be done, or that he could be safe any way in the World, but by appearing against me; so I was to have three Witnesses of Fact against me, the Master and his two Maids; that is to say, I was as certain to be cast[2] for my Life, as I was certain that I was alive, and I had nothing to do, but to think of dying, and prepare for it: I had but a sad foundation to build upon, as I said before, for all my Repentance appear'd to me to be only the Effect of my fear of Death, not a sincere regret for the wicked Life that I had liv'd, and which had brought this Misery upon me, or for the offending my Creator, who was now suddenly to be my Judge.

9. The bond which he posted assuring that he would continue the prosecution and appear to testify.
1. The governess would have the record removed from the docket without his being involved or losing money.
2. Condemned to death by hanging.

I liv'd many Days here under the utmost horror of Soul; I had Death as it were in view, and thought of nothing Night and Day, but of Gibbets and Halters, evil Spirits and Devils; it is not to be express'd by Words how I was harrass'd, between the dreadful Apprehensions of Death and the Terror of my Conscience reproaching me with my past horrible Life.

The Ordinary[3] of *Newgate* came to me, and talk'd a little in his way, but all his Divinity run upon Confessing my Crime, as he call'd it, (tho' he knew not what I was in for) making a full Discovery, and the like, without which he told me God would never forgive me; and he said so little to the purpose, that I had no manner of Consolation from him; and then to observe the poor Creature preaching Confession and Repentance to me in the Morning, and find him drunk with Brandy and Spirits by Noon; this had something in it so shocking, that I began to Nauseate the Man more than his Work, and his Work too by degrees for the sake of[4] the Man; so that I desir'd him to trouble me no more.

I know not how it was, but by the indefatigable Application of my diligent Governess I had no Bill preferr'd against me the first Sessions, I mean to the Grand Jury, at *Guild-Hall*;[5] so I had another Month, or five Weeks before me, and without doubt this ought to have been accepted by me, as so much time given me for Reflection upon what was past, and preparation for what was to come, or in a Word, I ought to have esteem'd it, as a space given me for Repentance, and have employ'd it as such, but it was not in me, I was sorry (*as before*) for being in *Newgate*, but had very few Signs of Repentance about me.

On the contrary, like the Waters in the Caveties, and Hollows of Mountains, which petrifies and turns into Stone whatever they are suffer'd to drop upon, so the continual Conversing with such a Crew of Hell-Hounds as I was, which had the same common Operation upon me as upon other People, I degenerated into Stone; I turn'd first Stupid and Senseless, then Brutish and thoughtless, and at last raving Mad as any of them were; and in short, I became as naturally pleas'd and easie with the Place, as if indeed I had been Born there.[6]

It is scarce possible to imagine that our Natures should be capable of so much Degeneracy, as to make that pleasant and agreeable

3. The chaplain, whose duty it was to prepare condemned prisoners for death. Like all those in important positions at Newgate, he had opportunity to misuse power. One of the most famous Ordinaries of Newgate was Paul Lorrain (d. 1719), who compiled texts of the last words of penitent criminals sentenced to death at Newgate. He is mentioned in *Tatler* 63 and *Spectator* 338.
4. Because of.

5. The council hall of the city of London.
6. Moll, of course, was born in Newgate, and has just repeated the fact, p. 213. Her comment should probably be interpreted as a statement that reinforces the sense of her current degenerate condition. In other words, although somewhat circuitously, she sees her birth in the dreaded prison and her return to it as causative of her abject mental state.

that in it self is the most compleat Misery. Here was a Circum-stance, that I think it is scarce possible to mention a worse; I was as exquisitely[7] miserable as speaking of common Cases, it was possible for any one to be that had Life and Health, and Money to help them as I had.

I had a weight of Guilt upon me enough to sink any Creature who had the least power of Reflection left, and had any Sense upon them of the Happiness of this Life, or the Misery of another; then I had at first remorse indeed, but no Repentance; I had now neither Remorse or Repentance: I had a Crime charg'd on me, the Punish-ment of which was Death by our Law; the Proof so evident, that there was no room for me so much as to plead not Guilty; I had the Name of old Offender, so that I had nothing to expect but Death in a few Weeks time, neither had I myself any thoughts of Escap-ing, and yet a certain strange Lethargy of Soul possess'd me; I had no Trouble, no Apprehensions, no Sorrow about me, the first Sur-prize was gone; I was, I may well say I know not how, my Senses, my Reason, nay, my Conscience were all a-sleep; my Course of Life for forty Years had been a horrid Complication of Wickedness, Whore-dom, Adultery, Incest, Lying, Theft, and in a Word, every thing but Murther and Treason had been my Practice from the Age of Eighteen, or thereabouts to Threescore; and now I was ingulph'd in the misery of Punishment, and had an infamous Death just at the Door, and yet I had no Sense of my Condition, no Thought of Heaven or Hell at least, that went any farther than a bare flying Touch, like the Stitch or Pain that gives a Hint and goes off; I nei-ther had a Heart to ask God's Mercy, or indeed to think of it, and in this I think I have given a brief Description of the compleatest Misery on Earth.

All my terrifying Thoughts were past, the Horrors of the Place, were become Familiar, and I felt no more uneasinesses at the Noise and Clamours of the Prison, than they did who made that Noise; in a Word, I was become a meer *Newgate-Bird*, as Wicked and as Outragious as any of them; nay, I scarce retain'd the Habit and Custom of good Breeding and Manners, which all along till now run thro' my Conversation; so thoro' a Degeneracy had pos-sess'd me, that I was no more the same thing that I had been, than if I had never been otherwise than what I was now.

In the middle of this harden'd Part of my Life, I had another sudden Surprize, which call'd me back a little to that thing call'd Sorrow, which indeed I began to be past the Sense of before: They told me one Night, that there was brought into the Prison late the Night before three Highway-Men, who had committed a Robbery

7. Consummately bad; perfectly, in an ill sense.

somewhere on the Road to *Windsor, Hounslow-Heath,* I think it
was, and were pursu'd to *Uxbridge* by the Country,[8] and were taken
there after a gallant Resistance, in which I know not how many of
the Country People were wounded, and some kill'd.

It is not to be wonder'd that we Prisoners were all desirous
enough to see these brave topping Gentleman[9] that were talk'd up
to be such, as their Fellows had not been known, and especially
because it was said they would in the Morning be remov'd into the
Press-Yard,[1] having given Money to the Head-Master of the Prison,
to be allow'd the liberty of that better Part of the Prison: So we
that were Women plac'd ourselves in the way that we would be
sure to see them; but nothing cou'd express the Amazement and
Surprize I was in, when the very first Man that came out I knew to
be my *Lancashire* Husband, the same with whom I liv'd so well at
Dunstable, and the same who I afterwards saw at *Brickill,* when I
was married to my last Husband, as has been related.

I was struck Dumb at the Sight, and knew neither what to say, or
what to do; he did not know me, and that was all the present Relief
I had; I quitted my Company, and retir'd as much as that dreadful
Place suffers any Body to retire, and I cry'd vehemently for a great
while; dreadful Creature, that I am, *said I,* How many poor People
have I made Miserable? How many desperate Wretches have I sent
to the Devil; This Gentleman's Misfortunes I plac'd all to my own
Account: He had told me at *Chester,* he was ruin'd by that Match,
and that his Fortunes were made Desperate on my Account; for
that thinking I had been a Fortune he was run into Debt more
than he was able to pay, and that he knew not what Course to take;
that he would go into the Army, and carry a Musquet, or buy a
Horse and take a Tour,[2] as he call'd it; and tho' I never told him
that I was a Fortune, and so did not actually Deceive him myself,
yet I did encourage the having it thought that I was so, and by that
means I was the occasion originally of his Mischief.

The Surprize of this thing only, struck deeper into my Thoughts,
and gave me stronger Reflections than all that had befallen me
before; I griev'd Day and Night for him, and the more, for that
they told me, he was the Captain of the Gang, and that he had

8. Country folk citizens of the area.
9. Brave beyond comparison; seventeenth-and eighteenth-century highwaymen were heroes to the public at large.
1. A less crowded area of Newgate which provided greater physical freedom than the inner confines. The term "Press" refers to the heavy weights placed upon the chests of prisoners ("peine forte et dure") who refused to plead guilty or not guilty to charges. By refusing to plead, the prisoner preserved any property he may have owned, which would have been confiscated had he pleaded and been found guilty of felony.
2. In the criminal jargon of the day, "to take a tour" meant "to become a highwayman"; the word is sometimes spelled "toure," "towre," or "tower": "to tower over and watch closely, as a bird watches its prey and then swoops down."

220 · *Moll Flanders*

committed so many Robberies, that *Hind*, or *Whitney*, or the *Golden Farmer* were Fools to him;[3] that he would surely be hang'd if there were no more Men left in the Country he was born in; and that there would be abundance of People come in against him.

I was overwhelm'd with grief for him; my own Case gave me no disturbance compar'd to this, and I loaded my self with Reproaches on his Account; I bewail'd his Misfortunes, and the ruin he was now come to, at such a Rate, that I relish'd nothing now, as I did before, and the first Reflections I made upon the horrid detestable Life I had liv'd, began to return upon me, and as these things return'd my abhorrence of the Place I was in, and of the way of living in it, return'd also; in a word, I was perfectly chang'd, and become another Body.

While I was under these influences of sorrow for him, came Notice to me that the next Sessions approaching, there would be a Bill preferr'd to the Grand Jury against me, and that I should be certainly try'd for my Life at the *Old-Baily*: My Temper was touch'd before, the harden'd wretch'd boldness of Spirit, which I had acquir'd abated, and conscious in the Prison, Guilt[4] began to flow in upon my Mind: In short, I began to think, and to think is one real Advance from Hell to Heaven; all that Hellish harden'd state and temper of Soul, which I have said so much of before, is but a deprivation of Thought; he that is restor'd to his Power of thinking, is restor'd to himself.

As soon as I began, I say to Think, the first thing that occurr'd to

3. The adventures of these well-known highwaymen were insignificant when compared to his. The three were famous robbers whose lives were celebrated in the criminal literature and chapbooks of the day. James Hind was hanged in 1652. His head was set on Bridge-Gate, over the Severn River, and other portions of his drawn and quartered body on the gates of the city of London. James Whitney, also known as the "Jacobite Robber," was hanged in 1694. William Davis, alias the "Golden Farmer," supposedly because he paid his debts in gold and pretended to be a farmer in order to conceal his criminal activities, was executed in 1689. An inn was named after his alias.

4. Perhaps to be interpreted as "in-the-prison guilt," as opposed to sincere repentance for her crimes; or changed through accidental transposition in composing from the manuscript, which may have read, "the hardened wretch'd boldness of Spirit, which I had acquir'd in the prison abated, and the Conscious guilt began to flow. . . ." At any rate, Moll is not yet sincerely sorry for her acts, just for her punishment. The second edition deletes "in the prison." In a letter (1717?) to Samuel Keimer, a publisher, Defoe defined true repentance, the kind

Moll says she experiences later:

"Shall I recommend a sincere Prayer put up to Heaven, tho' in Verse, by one I knew under deep and dreadful Afflictions? I'll write you but a few of them;

Lord, whatsoever Troubles wrack my Breast,
Till Sin removes too, let me take no Rest,
How dark soe'er my Case, or sharp my Pain,
O let no Sorrows cease, and Sin remain!
For *Jesus Sake*, remove not my Distress
Till thy Almighty Grace shall repossess
The vacant Throne, from whence my Crimes depart,
And makes a willing Captive of my Heart.

These are serious Lines, tho' Poetical. Its a Prayer, I doubt few can make: But the Moral is excellent; if Afflictions cease, and Cause of Afflictions remain, the Joy of your Deliverance will be short. . . " (*The Letters of Daniel Defoe*, ed. George Harris Healey [Oxford, 1955], p. 448.) Professor Healey attributes the lines to Defoe.

me broke out thus; Lord! what will become of me, I shall certainly die! I shall be cast to be sure, and there is nothing beyond that but Death! I have no Friends, what shall I do? I shall be certainly cast; Lord, have Mercy upon me, what will become of me? This was a sad Thought, you will say, to be the first after so long time that had started into my Soul of that kind, and yet even this was nothing but fright at what was to come; there was not a Word of sincere Repentance in it all: However, I was indeed dreadfully dejected, and disconsolate to the last degree; and as I had no Friend in the World to communicate my distress'd Thoughts to, it lay so heavy upon me, that it threw me into Fits, and Swoonings several times a-Day: I sent for my old Governess, and she, *give her her due*, acted the Part of a true Friend, she left me no Stone unturn'd to prevent the Grand Jury finding the Bill,[5] she went to one or two of the Jury Men, talk'd with them, and endeavour'd to possess them with favourable Dispositions,[6] on Account that nothing was taken away, and no House broken, &c. but all would not do, they were over-ruled by the rest, the two Wenches swore home to the Fact, and the Jury found the Bill against me for Robbery and Housebreaking, that is for Felony and Burglary.

I sunk down when they brought me News of it, and after I came to myself again, I thought I should have died with the weight of it: My Governess acted a true Mother to me, she pittied me, she cryed with me, and for me; but she cou'd not help me; and to add to the Terror of it, 'twas the Discourse all over the House, that I should die for it; I cou'd hear them talk it among themselves very often; and see them shake their Heads, and say they were sorry for it, and the like, as is usual in the Place; but still no Body came to tell me their Thoughts, till at last one of the Keepers came to me privately, and said with a Sigh, well Mrs. *Flanders*, you will be tried a *Friday*, (this was but a *Wednesday*,) what do you intend to do? I turn'd as white as a Clout,[7] and said, God knows what I shall do, for my part I know not what to do; why, *says he*, I won't flatter[8] you, I would have you prepare for Death, for I doubt you will be Cast, and as they say, you are an old Offender, I doubt you will find but little Mercy; They say, *added he*, your Case is very plain, and that the Witnesses swear so home against you, there will be no standing it.

This was a stab into the very Vitals of one under such a Burthen as I was oppress'd with before, and I cou'd not speak to him a Word good or bad, for a great while, but at last I burst out into Tears, and said to him, Lord! Mr. ——— What must I do? Do, *says he*, send for the Ordinary, send for a Minister, and talk with

---

5. Finding a true bill; a bill of indictment found by a Grand Jury to be supported by evidence sufficient to justify trying a case.

6. Opinions that would indicate the evidence was insufficient to try Moll.

7. Cloth; i.e., "as white as a sheet."

8. Raise your hopes.

him, for indeed Mrs. *Flanders*, unless you have very good Friends, you are no Woman for this World.

This was plain dealing indeed, but it was very harsh to me, at least I thought it so: He left me in the greatest Confusion imaginable, and all that Night I lay awake; and now I began to say my Prayers, which I had scarce done before since my last Husband's Death, or from a little while after; and truly I may well call it, saying my Prayers; for I was in such a Confusion, and had such horrour upon my Mind, that tho' I cry'd, and repeated several times the Ordinary Expression of, *Lord have Mercy upon me*; I never brought my self to any Sense of my being a miserable Sinner, as indeed I was, and of Confessing my Sins to God, and begging Pardon for the sake of Jesus Christ; I was overwhelm'd with the Sense of my Condition, being try'd for my Life, and being sure to be Condemn'd, and then I was as sure to be Executed, and on this Account, I cry'd out all Night, Lord! what will become of me? Lord! what shall I do? Lord! I shall be hang'd, Lord have mercy upon me, and the like.

My poor afflicted Governess was now as much concern'd as I, and a great deal more truly Penitent; tho' she had no prospect of being brought to Tryal and Sentence, not but that she deserv'd it as much as I, and so she said herself; but she had not done any thing herself for many Years, other than receiving what I, and others stole, and encouraging us to steal it: But she cry'd and took on like a distracted Body, wringing her Hands, and crying out that she was undone, that she believ'd there was a Curse from Heaven upon her, that she should be damn'd, that she had been the Destruction of all her Friends, that she had brought such a one, and such a one, and such one to the Gallows; and there she reckon'd up ten or eleven People, some of which I have given an Account of that came to untimely Ends, and that now she was the occasion of my Ruin, for she had persuaded me to go on, when I would have left off: I interrupted her there; no Mother, no, *said I*, don't speak of that, for you would have had me left off when I got the Mercer's Money again, and when I came home from *Harwich*, and I would not hearken to you, therefore you have not been to blame, it is I only have ruin'd myself. I have brought myself to this Misery, and thus we spent many Hours together.

Well there was no Remedy, the Prosecution went on, and on the *Thursday* I was carried down to the Sessions-House, where I was arraign'd, as they call'd it, and the next Day I was appointed to be Try'd. At the Arraignment I pleaded not Guilty, and well I might, for I was indicted for Felony and Burglary; that is for feloniously stealing two Pieces of Brocaded Silk, value 46 *l.* the Goods of

Anthony Johnson, and for breaking open his Doors; whereas I knew very well they could not pretend to prove I had broken up the Doors, or so much as lifted up a Latch.

On the *Friday* I was brought to my Tryal, I had exhausted my Spirits with Crying for two or three Days before, that[9] I slept better the *Thursday* Night than I expected, and had more Courage for my Tryal, than indeed I thought possible for me to have.

When the Tryal began, and the Indictment was read, I would have spoke, but they told me the Witnesses must be heard first, and then I should have time to be heard. The Witnesses were the two Wenches, a Couple of hard Mouth'd[1] Jades indeed, for tho' the thing was Truth in the main, yet they aggravated it to the utmost extremity, and swore I had the Goods wholly in my possession, that I had hid them among my Cloaths, that I was going off with them, that I had one Foot over the Threshold when they discovered themselves, and then I put tother over, so that I was quite out of the House in the Street with the Goods before they took hold of me, and then they seiz'd me, and brought me back again, and they took the Goods upon me: The Fact in general was all true, but I believe, and insisted upon it, that they stop'd me before I had set my Foot clear of the Threshold of the House; but that did not argue much, for certain it was, that I had taken the Goods, and that I was bringing them away, if I had not been taken.

But I pleaded that I had stole nothing, they had lost nothing, that the Door was open, and I went in seeing the Goods lye there, and with Design to buy, if seeing no Body in the House, I had taken any of them up in my Hand, it cou'd not be concluded that I intended to steal them, for that I never carried them farther than the Door to look on them with the better Light.

The Court would not allow that by any means, and make a kind of a Jest of my intending to buy the Goods, that being no Shop for the Selling of any thing, and as to carrying them to the Door to look at them, the Maids made their impudent Mocks upon that, and spent their Wit upon it very much; told the Court I had look'd at them sufficiently, and approv'd them very well, for I had pack'd them up under my Cloaths, and was a going with them.

In short, I was found Guilty of Felony, but acquited of the Burglary, which was but small Comfort to me, the first bringing me to a Sentence of Death, and the last would have done no more: The next Day, I was carried down to receive the dreadful Sentence, and

9. So that, as a result.
1. Unreasonable, insensitive. As Defoe refers to the two witnesses as jades, which in the first sense means worthless, unmanageable horses, so he reinforces the metaphor with the exact description "hard-mouthed," literally meaning "insensitive," as such "jades" might indeed be not sensible to the bit or rein. The adjective could also mean "willful" or "coarse in speech."

when they came to ask me what I had to say, why Sentence should
not pass, I stood mute a while, but some Body that stood behind
me, prompted me aloud to speak to the Judges, for that they cou'd
represent things favourably for me: This encourag'd me to speak,
and I told them I had nothing to say to stop the Sentence; but that
I had much to say, to bespeak the Mercy of the Court, that I hop'd
they would allow something in such a Case, for the Circumstances
of it, that I had broken no Doors, had carried nothing off, that no
Body had lost any thing; that the Person whose Goods they were
was pleas'd to say, he desir'd Mercy might be shown, which indeed
he very honestly did, that at the worst it was the first Offence, and
that I had never been before any Court of Justice before: And in a
Word, I spoke with more Courage than I thought I cou'd have
done, and in such a moving Tone, and tho' with Tears, yet not so
many Tears as to obstruct my Speech, that I cou'd see it mov'd
others to Tears that heard me.

The Judges sat Grave and Mute, gave me an easy Hearing, and
time to say all that I would, but saying neither Yes or No to it,
Pronounc'd the Sentence of Death upon me, a Sentence that was to
me like Death itself, which after it was read confounded me; I had
no more Spirit left in me, I had no Tongue to speak, or Eyes to
look up either to God or Man.

My poor Governess was utterly Disconsolate, and she that was
my Comforter before, wanted Comfort now herself, and sometimes
Mourning, sometimes Raging, was as much out of herself (as to all
outward Appearance) as any mad Woman in *Bedlam*:[2] Nor was
she only Disconsolate as to me, but she was struck with Horror at
the Sense of her own wicked Life, and began to look back upon it
with a Taste quite different from mine; for she was Penitent to the
highest Degree for her Sins, as well as Sorrowful for the Misfortune: She sent for a Minister too, a serious pious good Man, and
apply'd herself with such earnestness by his assistance to the Work
of a sincere Repentance, that I believe, and so did the Minister too,
that she was a true Penitent, and which is still more, she was not
only so for the Occasion, and at that Juncture, but she continu'd so,
as I was inform'd to the Day of her Death.

It is rather to be thought of than express'd what was now my
Condition; I had nothing before me but present Death; and as I
had no Friends to assist me, or to stir for me, I expected nothing
but to find my Name in the Dead Warrant,[3] which was to come
down for the Execution the *Friday* afterward, of five more and
myself.

In the mean time my poor distress'd Governess sent me a Minis-

2. A corrupted form of "Bethlehem";
Bethlehem Hospital, an institution for the
insane.

3. Listing names of those to be hanged.

ter, who at her request first, and at my own afterwards came to visit me: He exhorted me seriously to repent of all my Sins, and to dally no longer with my Soul; not flattering myself with hopes of Life, which he said, he was inform'd there was no room to expect, but unfeignedly to look up to God with my whole Soul, and to cry for Pardon in the Name of Jesus Christ. He back'd his Discourses with proper Quotations of Scripture, encouraging the greatest Sinner to Repent, and turn from their Evil way, and when he had done, he kneel'd down and pray'd with me.

It was now that for the first time I felt any real signs of Repentance; I now began to look back upon my past Life with abhorrence, and having a kind of view into the other Side of time, the things of Life, as I believe they do with every Body at such a time, began to look with a different Aspect, and quite another Shape, than they did before; the greatest and best things, the views of felicity, the joy, the griefs of Life were quite other things; and I had nothing in my Thoughts but what was so infinitely Superior to what I had known in Life, that it appear'd to me to be the greatest stupidity in Nature to lay any weight upon any thing tho' the most valuable in this World.

The word Eternity represented itself with all its incomprehensible Additions, and I had such extended Notions of it, that I know not how to express them: Among the rest, how vile, how gross, how absurd did every pleasant thing look? I mean, that we had counted pleasant before; especially when I reflected that these sordid Trifles were the things for which we forfeited eternal Felicity.

With these Reflections came in, of meer Course, severe Reproaches of my own Mind for my wretched Behaviour in my past Life; that I had forfeited all hope of any Happiness in the Eternity that I was just going to enter into, and on the contrary was entitul'd to all that was miserable, or had been conceiv'd of Misery; and all this with the frightful Addition of its being also Eternal.

I am not capable of reading Lectures of Instruction to any Body, but I relate this in the very manner in which things then appear'd to me, as far as I am able; but infinitely short of the lively impressions which they made on my Soul at that time; indeed those Impressions are not to be explain'd by words, or if they are, I am not Mistress of Words enough to express them; It must be the Work of every sober Reader to make just Reflections on them, as their own Circumstances may direct; and without Question, this is what every one at sometime or other may feel something of; I mean a clearer Sight into things to come, than they had here, and a dark view of their own Concern in them.

But I go back to my own Case; the Minister press'd me to tell him, as far as I thought convenient, in what State I found myself as to the Sight I had of things beyond Life; he told me he did not come as Ordinary of the Place, whose business it is to extort Confessions from Prisoners, for private Ends, or for the farther detecting of other Offenders; that his business was to move me to such freedom of Discourse as might serve to disburthen my own Mind, and furnish him to administer Comfort to me as far as was in his Power; and assur'd me, that whatever I said to him should remain with him, and be as much a Secret as if it was known only to God and myself; and that he desir'd to know nothing of me, but as above, to qualifie him to apply proper Advice and Assistance to me, and to pray to God for me.

This honest friendly way of treating me unlock'd all the Sluices of my Passions: He broke into my very Soul by it; and I unravell'd all the Wickedness of my Life to him: In a word, I gave him an Abridgement of this whole History; I gave him the Picture of my Conduct for 50 Years in Miniature.

I hid nothing from him, and he in return exhorted me to a sincere Repentance, explain'd to me what he meant by Repentance, and then drew out such a Scheme of infinite Mercy, proclaim'd from Heaven to Sinners of the greatest Magnitude, that he left me nothing to say, that look'd like despair or doubting of being accepted, and in this Condition he left me the first Night.

He visited me again the next Morning, and went on with his Method of explaining the Terms of Divine Mercy, which according to him consisted of nothing more, or more Difficult than that of being sincerely desirous of it, and willing to accept it; only a sincere Regret for, and hatred of those things I had done, which render'd me so just an Object of divine Vengeance: I am not able to repeat the excellent Discourses of this extraordinary Man; 'tis all that I am able to do to say, that he reviv'd my Heart, and brought me into such a Condition, that I never knew any thing of in my Life before: I was cover'd with Shame and Tears for things past, and yet had at the same time a secret surprizing Joy at the Prospect of being a true Penitent, and obtaining the Comfort of a Penitent, I mean the hope of being forgiven; and so swift did Thoughts circulate, and so high did the impressions they had made upon me run, that I thought I cou'd freely have gone out that Minute to Execution, without any uneasiness at all, casting my Soul entirely into the Arms of infinite Mercy as a Penitent.[4]

The good Gentleman was so mov'd also in my behalf, with a view of the influence, which he saw these things had on me, that he blessed God he had come to visit me, and resolv'd not to leave me till the last Moment, that is not to leave visiting me.

It was no less than 12 Days after our receiving Sentence, before

4. G. A. Starr discusses Moll's repentance in the light of traditional spiritual awakenings in literature (*Defoe and Spiritual Autobiography*, Princeton, 1965, pp. 126–162).

any were order'd for Execution, and then upon a *Wednesday* the Dead Warrant, *as they call it*, came down, and I found my Name was among them; a terrible blow this was to my new Resolutions; indeed my Heart sunk within me, and I swoon'd away twice, one after another, but spoke not a word: The good Minister was sorely Afflicted for me, and did what he could to comfort me with the same Arguments, and the same moving Eloquence that he did before, and left me not that Evening so long as the Prison-keepers would suffer him to stay in the Prison, unless he wou'd be lock'd up with me all Night, which he was not willing to be.

I wonder'd much that I did not see him all the next Day, *it being but the Day before the time appointed for Execution*; and I was greatly discouraged, and dejected in my Mind, and indeed almost sunk for want of that Comfort, which he had so often, and with such Success yeilded me on his former Visits; I waited with great impatience, and under the greatest oppressions of Spirits imaginable; till about four a-Clock he came to my Apartment,[5] for I had obtain'd the Favour by the help of Money, nothing being to be done in that Place without it, not to be kept in the Condemn'd Hole,[6] as they call it, among the rest of the Prisoners, who were to die, but to have a little dirty Chamber to my self.

My heart leap'd within me for Joy, when I heard his Voice at the Door even before I saw him; but let any one Judge what kind of Motion I found in my Soul, when after having made a short excuse for his not coming, he shew'd me that his time had been employ'd on my Account; that he had obtain'd a favourable Report from the Recorder[7] to the Secretary of State in my particular Case, and in short that he had brought me a Reprieve.

He us'd all the Caution that he was able in letting me know a thing which it would have been a double Cruelty to have conceal'd; and yet it was too much for me; for as Grief had overset me before, so did Joy overset now, and I fell into a much more dangerous Swooning than I did at first, and it was not without a great Difficulty that I was recover'd at all.

The good Man having made a very Christian Exhortation to me, not to let the Joy of my Reprieve put the Remembrance of my past Sorrow out of my Mind, and having told me that he must leave me to go and enter the Reprieve in the Books, and show it to the Sheriffs, stood up just before his going away, and in a very earnest manner pray'd to God for me that my Repentance might be made Unfeign'd and Sincere; and that my coming back as it were into

5. Private cell, which was available to prisoners able to pay for the privilege.
6. That portion of Newgate confining prisoners sentenced to death.
7. A magistrate or layman with wide legal knowledge, who was appointed Recorder by the Court of Aldermen in London. His opinions were held in the highest esteem.

Life again, might not be a returning to the Follies of Life which I
had made such solemn Resolutions to forsake, and to repent of
them; I joyn'd heartily in the Petition, and must needs say I had
deeper Impressions upon my Mind all that Night, of the Mercy of
God in sparing my Life; and a greater Detestation of my past Sins,
from a Sense of the goodness which I had tasted in this Case, than
I had in all my Sorrow before.

This may be thought inconsistent in it self, and wide from the
Business of this Book; Particularly, I reflect that many of those who
may be pleas'd and diverted with the Relation of the wild and
wicked part of my Story, may not relish this, which is really the best
part of my Life, the most Advantageous to myself, and the most
instructive to others; such however will I hope allow me the liberty
to make my Story compleat: It would be a severe Satyr on such,[8] to
say they do not relish the Repentance as much as they do the
Crime; and that they had rather the History were a compleat Tragedy, as it was very likely to have been.

But I go on with my Relation; the next Morning there was a sad
Scene indeed in the Prison; the first thing I was saluted with in the
Morning was the Tolling of the great Bell at St. *Sepulchres*, as they
call it, which usher'd in the Day: As soon as it began to Toll, a
dismal groaning and crying was heard from the Condemn'd Hole,
where there lay six poor Souls, who were to be Executed that Day,
some for one Crime, some for another, and two of them for
Murther.

This was follow'd by a confus'd Clamour in the House among
the several sorts of Prisoners, expressing their awkward Sorrows for
the poor Creatures that were to die, but in a manner extreamly differing one from another; some cried for them; some huzza'd,[9] and
wish'd them a good Journey; some damn'd and curst those that had
brought them to it, that is meaning the Evidence, or Prosecutors;
many pittying them; and some few, but very few praying for them.

There was hardly room for so much Composure of Mind, as was
requir'd for me to bless the merciful Providence that had as it were
snatch'd me out of the Jaws of this Destruction: I remained as it
were Dumb and Silent, overcome with the Sense of it, and not able
to express what I had in my Heart; for the Passions on such Occasions as these, are certainly so agitated as not to be able presently to
regulate their own Motions.

All the while the poor condemn'd Creatures were preparing to
their Death, and the Ordinary *as they call him*, was busy with
them, disposing them to submit to their Sentence: I say all this
while I was seiz'd with a fit of trembling, as much as I cou'd have

8. Satire on such readers of Moll's life   9. Hurrahed, cheered loudly.
who enjoy only the seamy side.

been if I had been in the same Condition, as to be sure the Day
before I expected to be; I was so violently agitated by this Surprising Fit, that I shook as if it had been in the cold Fit of an Ague; so
that I could not speak or look but like one Distracted: As soon as
they were all put into the Carts and gone, which however I had not
Courage enough to see, *I say*, as soon as they were gone, I fell into
a fit of crying involuntarily, and without Design, but as a meer Distemper, and yet so violent, and it held me so long, that I knew not
what Course to take, nor could I stop, or put a Checque to it, no
not with all the Strength and Courage I had.

This fit of crying held me near two Hours and as I believe held
me till they were all out of the World, and then a most humble
Penitent serious kind of Joy succeeded; a real transport it was, or
Passion of Joy, and Thankfulness, but still unable to give vent to it
by Words, and in this I continued most part of the Day.

In the Evening the Good Minister visited me again, and then fell
to his usual good Discourses; he Congratulated my having a space
yet allow'd me for Repentance, whereas the state of those six poor
Creatures was determin'd, and they were now pass'd the offers of
Salvation; he earnestly press'd me to retain the same Sentiments of
the things of Life, that I had when I had a view of Eternity; and at
the End of all, told me I should not conclude that all was over, that
a Reprieve was not a Pardon, that he could not yet answer for the
Effects of it; however, I had this Mercy, that I had more time given
me, and that it was my business to improve that time.

This Discourse, tho' very seasonable, left a kind of sadness on my
Heart, as if I might expect the Affair would have a tragical Issue
still, which however he had no certainty of, and I did not indeed at
that time question him about it, he having said that he would do
his utmost to bring it to a good End, and that he hoped he might,
but he would not have me secure;[1] and the Consequence prov'd
that he had Reason for what he said.

It was about a Fortnight after this, that I had some just Apprehensions that I should be included in the next dead Warrant at the
ensuing Sessions; and it was not without great difficulty, and at last
an humble Petition for Transportation, that I avoided it, so ill was I
beholding to Fame, and so prevailing was the fatal Report of being
an old Offender, tho' in that they did not do me strict Justice, for I
was not in the Sense of the Law an old Offender, whatever I was in
the Eye of the Judge; for I had never been before them in a judicial
way before, so the Judges could not Charge me with being an old
Offender, but the Recorder was pleas'd to represent my Case as he
thought fit.

I had now a certainty of Life indeed, but with the hard Condi-

1. Feel secure in the idea that a pardon must surely follow a reprieve.

tions of being order'd for Transportation, which indeed was a hard Condition in it self, but not when comparatively considered; and therefore I shall make no Comments upon the Sentence, nor upon the Choice I was put to; we shall all choose any thing rather than Death, especially when 'tis attended with an uncomfortable prospect beyond it, which was my Case.

The good Minister whose interest, tho' *a Stranger to me*, had obtain'd me the Reprieve, mourn'd sincerely for this part; he was in hopes, *he said*, that I should have ended my Days under the Influence of good Instruction, that I might not have forgot my former Distresses, and that I should not have been turned loose again among such a wretched a Crew as they generally are, who are thus sent Abroad where, *as he said*, I must have more than ordinary secret Assistance from the Grace of God, if I did not turn as wicked again as ever.

I have not for a good while mentioned my Governess, who had during most, if not all of this part been dangerously Sick, and being in as near a view of Death by her Disease, as I was by my Sentence, was a very great Penitent; I say, I have not mention'd her, nor indeed did I see her in all this time, but being now recovering, and just able to come Abroad, she came to see me.

I told her my Condition, and what a different flux and reflux of Fears and Hopes I had been agitated with; I told her what I had escap'd, and upon what Terms; and she was present, when the Minister express'd his fears of my relapsing into wickedness upon my falling into the wretch'd Companies that are generally Transported: Indeed I had a melancholly Reflection upon it in my own Mind, for I knew what a dreadful Gang was always sent away together, and I said to my Governess that the good Minister's fears were not without Cause: Well, well, *says she*, but I hope you will not be tempted with such a horrid Example as that; and as soon as the Minister was gone, she told me, she would not have me discourag'd, for perhaps ways and means might be found out to dispose of me in a particular way, by my self, of which she would talk farther to me afterward.

I look'd earnestly at her, and I thought she look'd more chearful than she usually had done, and I entertain'd immediately a Thousand Notions of being deliver'd, but could not for my Life imagine the Methods, or think of one that was in the least feasible; but I was too much concerned in it, to let her go from me without explaining herself, which tho' she was very loth to do, yet my importunity prevail'd, and while I was still pressing, she answer'd me in few Words, thus, Why, *you have Money, have you not?* did you ever know one in your Life that was Transported and had a Hundred Pound in his Pocket, I'll warrant you Child, *says she*.

I understood her presently, but told her I would leave all that to her, but I saw no room to hope for any thing but a strict Execution of the order, and as it was a severity that was esteem'd a Mercy, there was no doubt but it would be strictly observ'd; she said no more, but this, *we will try what can be done*, and so we parted for that Night.

I lay in the Prison near fifteen Weeks after this order for Transportation was sign'd; what the Reason of it was, I know not, but at the end of this time I was put on Board of a Ship in the *Thames*, and with me a Gang of Thirteen, as harden'd vile Creatures as ever *Newgate* produc'd in my time; and it would really well take up a History longer than mine to describe the degrees of Impudence, and audacious Villany that those Thirteen were arriv'd to; and the manner of their behaviour in the Voyage; of which I have a very diverting Account by me, which the Captain of the Ship, who carried them over gave me the Minutes of, and which he caus'd his Mate to write down at large.

It may perhaps be thought Trifling to enter here into a Relation of all the little incidents which attended me in this interval of my Circumstances; I mean between the final order for my Transportation and the time of my going on board the Ship, and I am too near the End of my Story, to allow room for it, but something relating to me, *and my Lancashire Husband*, I must not omit.

He had, *as I have observ'd already* been carried from the Master's side[2] of the ordinary Prison, into the Press-Yard, with three of his Comrades, for they found another to add to them after some time; here for what Reason I knew not, they were kept in Custody without being brought to Tryal almost three Months; it seems they found means to Bribe or buy off some of those who were expected to come in against them, and they wanted Evidence some time to Convict them: After some puzzle on this Account at first, they made a shift to get proof enough against two of them, to carry them off;[3] but the other two, of which my *Lancashire* Husband was one, lay still in Suspence: They had I think one positive Evidence against each of them; but the Law strictly obliging them to have two Witnesses, they cou'd make nothing of it; yet it seems they were resolv'd not to part with the Men neither, not doubting but a farther Evidence would at last come in; and in order to this, I think Publication was made, that such Prisoners being taken, any one that had been robb'd by them might come to the Prison and see them.

I took this opportunity to satisfy my Curiosity, pretending that I had been robb'd in the *Dunstable* Coach, and that I would go to

2. One of the main sections into which Newgate was divided. See "Hell upon Earth," Backgrounds and Sources, p. 289, below.
3. Convict and hang.

see the two Highway-Men; but when I came into the Press-Yard, I so disguis'd myself, and muffled my Face up so, that he cou'd see little of me, and consequently knew nothing of who I was; and when I came back, I said publickly that I knew them very well.

Immediately it was Rumour'd all over the Prison that *Moll Flanders* would turn Evidence against one of the Highway Men, and that I was to come off by it from the Sentence of Transportation.

They heard of it, and immediately my Husband desir'd to see this Mrs. *Flanders* that knew him so well, and was to be an Evidence against him, and accordingly, I had leave given to go to him. I dress'd myself up as well as the best Cloths that I suffer'd myself ever to appear in there would allow me, and went to the Press-Yard, but had for some time a Hood over my Face; he said little to me at first, but ask'd me if I knew him; I told him, yes, very well; but as I conceal'd my Face, so I Counterfeited my Voice, that he had not the least guess at who I was: He ask'd me where I had seen him; I told him between *Dunstable* and *Brickhill*, but turning to the Keeper that stood by, I ask'd if I might not be admitted to talk with him alone, he said, yes, yes, as much as I pleas'd, and so very civilly withdrew.

As soon as he was gone, and I had shut the Door, I threw off my Hood, and bursting out into Tears, *my Dear*, says I, *do you not know me?* He turn'd pale and stood Speechless, like one Thunder struck, and not able to conquer the Surprize, said no more but this, *let me sit down*; and sitting down by a Table, he laid his Elbow upon the Table, and leaning his Head on his Hand, fix'd his Eyes on the Ground as one stupid: I cry'd so vehemently, on the other Hand, that it was a good while e'er I could speak any more; but after I had given some vent to my Passion by Tears, I repeated the same Words: MY DEAR, *do you not know me?* at which he answer'd YES, and said no more a good while.

After some time continuing in the Surprize, *as above*, he cast up his Eyes towards me and said, *How could you be so cruel?* I did not readily understand what he meant; and I answer'd, How can you call me Cruel? What have I been Cruel to you in? *To come to me*, says he, *in such a Place as this, is it not to insult me? I have not robb'd you, at least not on the Highway?*

I perceiv'd by this that he knew nothing of the miserable Circumstances I was in, and thought that having got some Intelligence of his being there, I had come to upbraid him with his leaving me; but I had too much to say to him to be affronted, and told him in few Words that I was far from coming to Insult him, but at best I came to Condole mutually; that he would be easily satisfy'd that I had no such View, when I should tell him that *my Condition was worse than his, and that many ways*: He look'd a little concern'd at the general Expression of my Condition being worse than his; but with a kind of a smile, look'd a little wildly, and said, How can that be? when you see me Fetter'd, and in *Newgate*, and two of my Companions Executed already; can you say your Condition is worse than Mine?

Come my Dear, *says I*, we have a long piece of Work to do, if I should be to relate, or you to hear my unfortunate History; but if you are dispos'd to hear it, you will soon conclude with me that my Condition is worse than yours: How is that possible, *says he again*, when I expect to be cast for my Life the very next Sessions? Yes *says I*, 'tis very possible when I shall tell you that I have been cast for my Life three Sessions ago, and am under Sentence of Death, is not my Case worse than yours?

Then indeed he stood silent again, like one struck Dumb, and after a little while he starts up; unhappy Couple! *says he*, How can this be possible? I took him by the Hand; come MY DEAR, *said I*, sit down, and let us compare our Sorrows: I am a Prisoner in this very House, and in a much worse Circumstance than you, and you will be satisfy'd I do not come to Insult you, when I tell you the particulars; and with this we sat down together, and I told him so much of my Story as I thought was convenient, bringing it at last to my being reduc'd to great Poverty, and representing myself as fallen into some Company that led me to relieve my Distresses by a way that I had been utterly unacquainted with, and that they making an attempt at a Tradesman's House I was seiz'd upon, for having been but just at the Door, the Maid-Servant pulling me in; that I neither had broke any Lock, or taken any thing away, and that notwithstanding that I was brought in Guilty, and Sentenc'd to Die; but that the Judges having been made sensible of the Hardship of my Circumstances, had obtain'd leave to remit the Sentence upon my consenting to be transported.

I told him I far'd the worse for being taken in the Prison for one *Moll Flanders*, who was a famous successful Thief, that all of them had heard of, but none of them had ever seen, but that *as he knew well* was none of my Name; but I plac'd all to the account of my ill Fortune, and that under this Name I was dealt with as an old Offender, tho' this was the first thing they had ever known of me. I gave him a long particular of things that had befallen me, since I saw him; but I told him if[4] I had seen him since he might think I had, and then gave him an Account how I had seen him at *Brickhill*; how furiously he was pursued, and how by giving an Account that I knew him, and that he was a very honest Gentleman, one Mr. —— the *Hue and Cry* was stopp'd, and the High Constable went back again.

4. **Whether or not.**

He listen'd most attentively to all my Story, and smil'd at most of the particulars, being all of them petty Matters, and infinitely below what he had been at the Head of; but when I came to the Story of little *Brickill*, he was surpriz'd; *and was it you my Dear*, says he, *that gave the Check to the Mob that was at our Heels there at Brickill*: Yes *said I*, it was I indeed, and then I told him the particulars which I had observ'd of him there. *Why then*, said he, *it was you that sav'd my Life at that time*, and I am glad I owe my Life to you, for I will pay the Debt to you now, and I'll deliver you from the present Condition you are in, or I will die in the attempt.

I told him by no means; it was a Risque too great, not worth his running the hazard of, and for a Life not worth his saving; 'twas no matter for that he said, it was a Life worth all the World to him; a Life that had given him a new Life; for *says he*, I was never in real Danger of being taken, but that time; till the last Minute when I was taken: Indeed *he told* me his Danger then lay in his believing he had not been pursued that way; for they had gone off from *Hockly* quite another way, and had come over the enclos'd Country into *Brickill*, not by the Road and were sure they had not been seen by any Body.

Here he gave a long History of his Life, which indeed would make a very strange History, and be infinitely diverting. He told me he took to the Road about twelve Year before he marry'd me; that the Woman which call'd him Brother, was not really his Sister, or any Kin to him; but one that belong'd to their Gang, and who keeping Correspondence with them, liv'd always in Town, having good store of Acquaintance, that she gave them a perfect Intelligence of Persons going out of Town, and that they had made several good Booties by her Correspondence; that she thought she had fix'd a Fortune for him, when she brought me to him, but happen'd to be Disappointed, which he really could not blame her for: That, if it had been his good Luck, that I had had the Estate, which she was inform'd I had, he had resolv'd to leave off the Road, and live a retired sober Life, but never to appear in publick till some general Pardon had been pass'd, or till he could, for Money have got his Name into some particular Pardon, that so he might have been perfectly easy, but that as it had proved otherwise he was oblig'd to put off his Equipage, and take up the old Trade again.

He gave me a long Account of some of his Adventures, and particularly one, when he robb'd the *West Chester* Coaches, near *Lichfield*, when he got a very great Booty; and after that, how he robb'd five Grasiers,[5] in the *West*, going to *Burford* Fair in

5. Raisers of sheep or cattle.

Wiltshire[6] to buy Sheep; he told me he got so much Money on those two Occasions, that if he had known where to have found me, he would certainly have embrac'd my Proposal of going with me to *Virginia,* or to have settled in a Plantation on some other Parts of the *English* Colonies in *America.*

He told me.he wrote two or three Letters to me, directed according to my Order, but heard nothing from me: This I indeed knew to be true, but the Letters coming to my Hand in the time of my latter Husband, I could do nothing in it, and therefore chose to give no answer, that so he might rather believe they had miscarried.

Being thus Disappointed, *he said,* he carried on the old Trade ever since, tho' when he had gotten so much Money, *he said,* he did not run such desperate Risques as he did before; then he gave me some Account of several hard and desperate Encounters which he had with Gentlemen on the Road, who parted too hardly[7] with their Money; and shew'd me some Wounds he had receiv'd, and he had one or two very terrible Wounds indeed, as particularly one by a Pistol Bullet which broke his Arm; and another with a Sword, which ran him quite thro' the Body, but that missing his Vitals he was cur'd again; one of his Comrades having kept with him so faithfully, and so Friendly, as that he assisted him in riding near 80 Miles before his Arm was Set, and then got a Surgeon in a considerable City, remote from that Place where it was done, pretending they were Gentlemen Traveling towards *Carlisle,* and that they had been attack'd on the Road by Highway-Men, and that one of them had shot him into the Arm, and broke the Bone.

This *he said,* his Friend manag'd so well, that they were not suspected at all, but lay still till he was perfectly cur'd: He gave me so many distinct Accounts of his Adventures, that it is with great reluctance, that I decline the relating them; but I consider that this is my own Story, not his.

I then enquir'd into the Circumstances of his present Case at that time, and what it was he expected when he came to be try'd; he told me that they had no Evidence against him, or but very little; for that of three Robberies, which they were all Charg'd with, it was his good Fortune, that he was but in one of them, and that there was but one Witness to be had for that Fact, which was not sufficient; but that it was expected some others would come in against him; that he thought indeed, when he first see me, that I had been one that came of that Errand; but that if no Body came in against him, he hop'd he should be clear'd; that he had had some

6. C. A. Johnson points out that Burford is in Oxfordshire, not Wilshire. Again the maps in Defoe's *Tour through the Whole Island of Great Britain* (1724–1726) clearly show the location of Burford. See note 5, p. 139.
7. I.e., put up a fight.

intimation, that if he would submit to Transport himself, he might be admitted to it without a Tryal, but that he could not think of it with any Temper,[8] and thought he could much easier submit to be Hang'd.[9]

I blam'd him for that, and told him I blam'd him on two Accounts; first because if he was Transported, there might be an Hundred ways for him that was a Gentleman, and a bold enterprizing Man to find his way back again, and perhaps some Ways and Means to come back before he went.[1] He smil'd at that Part, and said he should like the last the best of the two, for he had a kind of Horror upon his Mind at his being sent over to the Plantations as *Romans* sent condemn'd Slaves to Work in the Mines; that he thought the Passage into another State,[2] let it be what it would, much more tolerable at the Gallows, and that this was the general Notion of all the Gentlemen who were driven by the Exigence of their Fortunes to take the Road; that at the Place of Execution there was at least an End of all the Miseries of the present State, and as for what was to follow, a Man was in his Opinion, as likely to Repent sincerely in the last Fortnight of his Life under the Pressures and Agonies of a Jayl, and the condemn'd Hole, as he would ever be in the Woods and Wildernesses of *America*; that Servitude and hard Labour were things Gentlemen could never stoop to, that it was but the way to force them to be their own Executioners afterwards, which was much worse; and that therefore he could not have any Patience when he did but think of being Transported.

I used the utmost of my endeavour to perswade him, and joyn'd that known Womans Rhetorick to it, I mean that of Tears: I told him the Infamy of a publick Execution was certainly a greater pressure upon the Spirits of a Gentleman, than any of the Mortifications that he could meet with Abroad could be; that he had at least in the other a Chance for his Life, whereas here he had none at all; that it was the easiest thing in the World for him to manage the Captain of the Ship, who were generally speaking, Men of good Humour and some Gallantry; and a small matter of Conduct, especially if there was any Money to be had, would make way for him to buy himself off, when he came to *Virginia*.

He look'd wishfully at me, and I thought I guess'd at what he meant, *that is to say*, that he had no Money, but I was mistaken, his meaning was another way; *you hinted just now*, my Dear said he, that there might be a way of coming back before I went, by

8. Tolerance, composure, patience.
9. In *Mercurius Politicus* (December, 1716), Defoe cited the case of one Samuel Kempton, who chose not to be transported to the colonies, stating "that he was bred a Gentleman, and could not labor." M. G. McClung offers this possible source for Moll's Lancashire husband (*Notes and Queries*, vol. 18, no. 9, 329–330).
1. Avoid going at all.
2. Death and whatever might follow.

which I understood you, that it might *be possible to buy it off here*; *I had rather give* 200 *l. to prevent going, than* 100 *l. to be set at Liberty when I came there.* That is my Dear, said I, *because you do not know the Place so well as I do*: that may be, said he, *and yet I believe as well as you know it, you would do the same unless it is because,* as you told me, *you have a Mother there.*

I told him, as to my Mother, it was next to impossible, but that she must be dead many Years before; and as for any other Relations that I might have there, I knew them not now: That since the Misfortunes I had been under, had reduc'd me to the Condition I had been in for some Years, I had not kept up any Correspondence with them, and that he would easily believe, I should find but a cold Reception from them, if I should be put to make my first visit in the Condition of a Transported Felon; that therefore if I went thither, I resolv'd not to see them; But that I had many Views in going there, if it should be my Fate, which took off all the uneasy Part of it; and if he found himself oblig'd to go also, I should easily Instruct him how to manage himself, so as never to go a Servant at all, especially since I found he was not destitute of Money, which was the only Friend in such a Condition.

He smil'd, and said, he did not tell me he had Money; I took him up short, and told him I hop'd he did not understand by my speaking, that I should expect any supply from him if he had Money; that on the other Hand, tho' I had not a great deal, yet I did not want, and while I had any I would rather add to him than weaken him in that Article, seeing what ever he had, I knew in the Case of Transportation he would have Occasion of it all.

He express'd himself in a most tender manner upon that Head: he told me what Money he had was not a great deal, but that he would never hide any of it from me if I wanted it; and that he assur'd me he did not speak with any such Apprehensions; that he was only intent upon what I had hinted to him before he went; that here he knew what to do with himself, but there he should be the most ignorant helpless Wretch alive.

I told him he frighted and terrify'd himself with that which had no Terror in it; that if he had Money, as I was glad to hear he had, he might not only avoid the Servitude suppos'd to be the Consequence of Transportation; but begin the World upon a new Foundation, and that such a one as he cou'd not fail of Success in, with but the common Application usual in such Cases; that he could not but call to Mind, that it was what I had recommended to him many Years before, and had propos'd it for our mutual Subsistence, and restoring our Fortunes in the World; and I would tell him now, that to convince him both of the certainty of it, and of my being fully acquainted with the Method, and also fully satisfy'd in the probability of Success, he should first see me deliver myself from the Necessity of going over at all, and then that I would go with him freely, and of my own Choice, and perhaps carry enough with me to satisfy him that I did not offer it for want of being able to live without Assistance from him; but that I thought our mutual Misfortunes had been such, as were sufficient to Reconcile us both to quitting this part of the World, and living where no Body could upbraid us with what was past, or we be in any dread of a Prison, and without the Agonies of a condemn'd Hole to drive us to it, where we should look back on all our past Disasters with infinite Satisfaction, when we should consider that our Enemies should entirely forget us, and that we should live as new People in a new World, no Body having any thing to say to us, or we to them.

I press'd this Home to him with so many Arguments, and answer'd all his own passionate Objections so effectually, that he embrac'd me, and told me I treated him with such a Sincerity, and Affection as overcame him; that he would take my Advice, and would strive to submit to his Fate, in hope of having the comfort of my Assistance, and of so faithful a Counsellor and such a Companion in his Misery; but still he put me in mind of what I had mention'd before, Namely, that there might be some way to get off before he went, and that it might be possible to avoid going at all, which he said would be much better. I told him he should see, and be fully satisfy'd that I would do my utmost in that Part too, and if it did not succeed, yet that I would make good the rest.

We parted after this long Conference with such Testimonies of Kindness and Affection as I thought were Equal if not Superior to that at our parting at *Dunstable*; and now I saw more plainly than before, the Reason why he declin'd coming at that time any farther with me toward *London* than *Dunstable*; and why when we parted there, he told me it was not convenient for him to come part of the way to *London* to bring me going, as he would otherwise have done: I have observ'd that the Account of his Life, would have made a much more pleasing History, than this of mine; and indeed nothing in it, was more strange than this Part, (*viz.*) that he had carried on that desperate Trade full five and Twenty Year, and had never been taken, the Success he had met with, had been so very uncommon, and such, that sometimes he had liv'd handsomely and retir'd, in one Place for a Year or two at a time, keeping himself and a Man-Servant to wait on him, and has often sat in the Coffee-Houses, and heard the very People who he had robb'd give Accounts of their being robb'd, and of the Places and Circumstances, so that he cou'd easily remember that it was the same.

In this manner it seems he liv'd near *Leverpool* at the time, he unluckily married me for a Fortune: Had I been the Fortune he expected, I verily believe, as he said, that he would have taken up and liv'd honestly all his Days.

He had with the rest of his Misfortunes the good luck not to be actually upon the spot when the Robbery was done which he was committed for; and so none of the Persons robb'd cou'd swear to him, or had any thing to Charge upon him; but it seems as he was taken, with the Gang, one hard-mouth'd Countryman swore home to him; and they were like to have others come in according to the Publication they had made, so that they expected more Evidence against him, and for that Reason he was kept in hold.[3]

However, the offer which was made to him of admitting him to Transportation was made, as I understood upon the intercession of some great Person who press'd him hard to accept of it before a Tryal; and indeed as he knew there were several that might come in against him, I thought his Friend was in the Right, and I lay at him Night and Day to delay it no longer.

At last, with much difficulty he gave his consent, and as he was not therefore admitted to Transportation in Court, and on his Petition as I was, so he found himself under a difficulty to avoid embarking himself as I had said he might have done; his great Friend, who was his Intercessor for the Favour of that Grant, having given Security for him that he should Transport himself, and not return within the Term.[4]

This hardship broke all my Measures,[5] for the steps I took afterwards for my own deliverance, were hereby render'd wholly ineffectual, unless I would abandon him, and leave him to go to *America* by himself; than which he protested he would much rather venture,[6] altho' he were certain to go directly to the Gallows.

I must now return to my own Case; the time of my being Transported according to my Sentence was near at Hand; my Governess who continu'd my fast Friend, had try'd to obtain a Pardon, but it could not be done unless with an Expence too heavy for my Purse, considering that to be left naked and empty, unless I had resolv'd to return to my old Trade again, had been worse than my Transportation, because there I knew I could live, here I could not. The good Minister stood very hard on another Account to prevent my being Transported also; but he was answer'd, that indeed my Life had been given me at his first Solicitations, and therefore he ought to ask no more; he was sensibly griev'd at my going, because, *as he said*, he fear'd I should lose the good impressions, which a prospect

---

3. Held in custody.
4. Since he volunteered for transportation, his friend's bond would be forfeited should he return before the term, so he cannot follow Moll's first plan "to come back before he went," which would be during the current court term. The British legal year is divided into four terms. A usual term of transportation was seven years.
5. Plans to foil transportation.
6. Take his chances at trial.

of Death had at first made on me, and which were since encreas'd by his Instructions, and the pious Gentleman was exceedingly concern'd about me on that Account.

On the other Hand, I really was not so sollicitous about it as I was before, but I industriously conceal'd my Reasons for it from the Minister, and to the last he did not know, but that I went with the utmost reluctance and affliction.

It was in the Month of *February* that I was with seven other Convicts, *as they call'd us*, deliver'd to a Merchant that Traded to *Virginia*, on board a Ship, riding, as they call'd it, in *Deptford* Reach: The Officer of the Prison deliver'd us on board, and the Master of the Vessel gave a Discharge for us.

We were for that Night clapt under Hatches,[7] and kept so close, that I thought I should have been suffocated for want of Air, and the next Morning the Ship weigh'd,[8] and fell[9] down the River to a Place they call *Bugby's Hole*, which was done, as they told us by the agreement of the Merchant, that all opportunity of Escape should be taken from us: However when the Ship came thither, and cast Anchor, we were allow'd more Liberty, and particularly were permitted to come upon the Deck, but not upon the Quarter-Deck, that being kept particularly for the Captain, and for Passengers.

When by the Noise of the Men over my Head, and the Motion of the Ship, I perceiv'd that they were under Sail, I was at first greatly surpriz'd, fearing we should go away directly, and that our Friends would not be admitted to see us any more; but I was easy soon after when I found they had come to an Anchor again, and soon after that we had Notice given by some of the Men where we were, that the next Morning we should have the Liberty to come upon Deck, and to have our Friends come and see us if we had any.

All that Night I lay upon the hard Boards of the Deck, as the other Prisoners did, but we had afterwards the Liberty of little Cabins for such of us as had any Bedding to lay in them; and room to stow any Box or Trunk for Cloths, and Linnen, if we had it, (which might well be put in) for some of them had neither Shirt or Shift, or a Rag of Linnen or Woollen, but what was on their Backs, or a Farthing of Money to help themselves; and yet I did not find but they far'd well enough in the Ship, especially the Women, who got Money of the Seamen for washing their Cloths sufficient to purchase any common things that they wanted.

When the next Morning we had the liberty to come upon the Deck, I ask'd one of the Officers of the Ship, whether I might not have the liberty to send a Letter on Shore to let my Friends know where the Ship lay, and to get some necessary things sent to me.

7. Confined below deck.
8. Weighed anchor.

9. Sailed downriver.

This was it seems the Boatswain, a very civil courteous sort of Man, who told me I should have that, or any other liberty that I desir'd, that he could allow me with Safety; I told him I desir'd no other; and he answer'd that the Ships Boat would go up to *London* the next Tide, and he would order my Letter to be carried.

Accordingly when the Boat went off, the Boatswain came to me, and told me the Boat was going off, and that he went in it himself, and ask'd me if my Letter was ready, he would take care of it; I had prepared myself you may be sure, Pen, Ink and Paper beforehand, and I had gotten a Letter ready directed to my Governess, and enclos'd another for my fellow Prisoner, which however I did not let her know was my Husband, not to the last; in that to my Governess, I let her know where the Ship lay, and press'd her earnestly to send me what things I knew she had got ready for me, for my Voyage.

When I gave the Boatswain the Letter, I gave him a Shilling with it, which I told him was for the Charge of a Messenger or Porter, which I entreated him to send with the Letter, as soon as he came on Shore, that if possible I might have an Answer brought back by the same Hand, that I might know what was become of my things; for SIR, *says I*, if the Ship should go away before I have them on Board I am undone.

I took care when I gave him the Shilling to let him see that I had a little better Furniture[1] about me, than the ordinary Prisoners, for he saw that I had a Purse, and in it a pretty deal of Money, and I found that the very sight of it, immediately furnish'd me with very different Treatment from what I should otherwise have met with in the Ship; for tho' he was very Courteous indeed before, in a kind of natural Compassion to me, as a Woman in distress; yet he was more than ordinarily so, afterwards, and procur'd me to be better treated in the Ship, than, *I say*, I might otherwise have been; as shall appear in its Place.

He very honestly had my Letter deliver'd to my Governess own Hands, and brought me back an Answer from her in writing; and when he gave me the Answer, gave me the Shilling again; *there*, says he, there's your Shilling again too, for I deliver'd the Letter my self; I could not tell what to say, I was so surpris'd at the thing; but after some Pause, *I said*, Sir you are too kind, it had been but Reasonable that you had paid yourself Coach hire then.

No, no, *says he*, I am over paid: What is the Gentlewoman, your Sister?

No, SIR, *says I*, she is no Relation to me, but she is a dear Friend, and all the Friends I have in the World: well, *says he*, there are few

---

1. Furnishings; personal possessions.

such Friends in the World: why she cryes after you like a Child, *Ay, says I again,* she would give a Hundred Pound, I believe, to deliver me from this dreadful Condition I am in.

Would she so? *says he,* for half the Money I believe, I cou'd put you in a way how to deliver yourself, but this he spoke softly that no Body cou'd hear.

Alas! Sɪʀ, *said I,* but then that must be such a Deliverance as if I should be taken again, would cost me my Life; Nay, *said he,* if you were once out of the Ship you must look to yourself afterwards, that I can say nothing to; so we drop'd the Discourse for that time.

In the mean time my Governess faithful to the last Moment, convey'd my Letter to the Prison to my Husband, and got an Answer to it, and the next Day came down herself to the Ship, bringing me in the first Place a *Sea-Bed* as they call it, and all its Furniture,[2] such as was convenient, but not to let the People think it was extraordinary; she brought with her a *Sea-Chest,* that is a Chest such as are made for Seamen with all the Conveniences in it, and fill'd with every thing almost that I could want; and in one of the corners of the Chest, where there was a Private Drawer was my Bank of Money, *that is to say,* so much of it as I had resolv'd to carry with me; for I order'd a part of my Stock to be left behind me, to be sent afterwards in such Goods as I should want when I came to settle; for Money in that Country is not of much use where all things are bought for Tobacco, much more is it a great loss to carry it from Hence.[3]

But my Case was particular; it was by no Means proper to me to go thither without Money or Goods, and for a poor Convict that was to be sold as soon as I came on Shore, to carry with me a Cargo of Goods would be to have Notice taken of it, and perhaps to have them seiz'd by the Publick; so I took part of my Stock with me thus, and left the other part with my Governess.

My Governess brought me a great many other things, but it was not proper for me to look too well provided in the Ship, at least, till I knew what kind of a Captain we should have. When she came into the Ship, I thought she would have died indeed; her Heart sunk at the sight of me, and at the thoughts of parting with me in that Condition, and she cry'd so intolerably, I cou'd not for a long time have any talk with her.

I took that time to read my fellow Prisoners Letter, which however greatly perplex'd me; he told me he was determin'd to go, but found it would be impossible for him to be Discharg'd time enough for going in the same Ship, and which was more than all, he began

2. Furnishings; bedclothes, linen.
3. From here (England). The money's purchasing power would be greatly de- creased in America, where tobacco was a main standard for trade.

to question whether they would give him leave to go in what Ship he pleas'd, tho' he did voluntarily Transport himself; but that they would see him put on Board such a Ship as they should direct, and that he would be charg'd upon the Captain as other convict Prisoners were; so that he began to be in dispair of seeing me till he came to *Virginia*, which made him almost desperate; seeing that on the other Hand, if I should not be there, if any Accident of the Sea, or of Mortality should take me away, he should be the most undone Creature there in the World.

This was very perplexing, and I knew not what Course to take; I told my Governess the Story of the Boatswain, and she was mighty eager with me to treat with him; but I had no mind to it, till I heard whether my Husband, or fellow Prisoner, *so she call'd him,* cou'd be at liberty to go with me or no; at last I was forc'd to let her into the whole matter, except only, that of his being my Husband; I told her I had made a positive Bargain or Agreement with him to go, if he could get the liberty of going in the same Ship, and that I found he had Money.

Then I read a long Lecture to her of what I propos'd to do when we came there, how we could Plant, Settle, and in short, grow Rich without any more Adventures, and as a great Secret, I told her that we were to Marry as soon as he came on Board.

She soon agreed chearfully to my going, when she heard this, and she made it her business from that time to get him out of the Prison in time, so that he might go in the same Ship with me, which at last was brought to pass tho' with great difficulty, and not without all the Forms of a Transported Prisoner *Convict,* which he really was not yet, for he had not been try'd, and which was a great Mortification to him. As our Fate was not determin'd, and we were both on Board, actually bound to *Virginia,* in the despicable Quality of Transported Convicts destin'd to be sold for Slaves, I for five Year, and he under Bonds and Security not to return to *England* any more, as long as he liv'd;[4] he was very much dejected and cast down; the Mortification of being brought on Board as he was, like a Prisoner, piqu'd him very much, since it was first told him he should Transport himself, and so that he might go as a Gentleman at liberty; it is true he was not order'd to be sold when he came there, as we were, and for that Reason he was oblig'd to pay for his Passage to the Captain, which we were not; as to the rest, he was as much at a loss as a Child what to do with himself, or with what he had, but by Directions.

Our first business was to compare our Stock: He was very honest to me, and told me his Stock was pretty good when he came into

4. This penalty is more severe than that contemplated for him earlier. See note 4, p. 239; see also Notes to the Text, p. 285.

the Prison, but the living there as he did in a Figure like a Gentle-man, *and which was ten times as much*, the making of Friends, and soliciting his Case, had been very Expensive; and in a Word, all his Stock that he had left was an Hundred and Eight Pounds, which he had about him all in Gold.

I gave him an Account of my Stock as faithfully, that is to say of what I had taken to carry with me, for I was resolv'd what ever should happen, to keep what I had left with my Governess, in Reserve; that in case I should die, what I had with me was enough to give him, and that which was left in my Governess Hands would be her own, which she had well deserv'd of me indeed.

My Stock which I had with me was two Hundred forty six Pounds, some odd Shillings; so that we had three Hundred and fifty four Pound between us, but a worse gotten Estate was scarce ever put together to begin the World with.

Our greatest Misfortune as to our Stock was that it was all in Money, which every one knows is an unprofitable Cargoe to be car-ryed to the Plantations; I believe his was really all he had left in the World, as he told me it was; but I who had between seven and eight Hundred Pounds in Bank when this Disaster befel me, and who had one of the faithfulest Friends in the World to manage it for me, considering she was a Woman of no manner of Religious Principles, had still Three Hundred Pounds left in her Hand, which I reserv'd, as above; besides some very valuable things, as particu-larly two gold Watches, some small Peices of Plate, and some Rings; all stolen Goods; the Plate, Rings and Watches were put up in my Chest with the Money, and with this Fortune, and in the Sixty first Year of my Age, I launch'd out into a new World, as I may call it, in the Condition (as to what appear'd) only of a poor nak'd Convict, order'd to be Transported in respite from the Gal-lows; my Cloaths were poor and mean, but not ragged or dirty, and none knew in the whole Ship that I had any thing of value about me.

However, as I had a great many very good Cloaths, and Linnen in abundance, which I had order'd to be pack'd up in two great Boxes, I had them Shipp'd on Board, not as my Goods, but as con-sign'd to my real Name in *Virginia*; and had the Bills of Loading sign'd by a Captain in my Pocket; and in these Boxes was my Plate and Watches, and every thing of value except my Money, which I kept by itself in a private Drawer in my Chest, which cou'd not be found, or open'd if found, without splitting the Chest to pieces.

In this Condition I lay for three Weeks in the Ship, not knowing whether I should have my Husband with me or no; and therefore not resolving how, or in what manner to receive the honest Boat-swain's proposal, which indeed he thought a little strange at first.

At the End of this time, behold my Husband came on Board; he look'd with a dejected angry Countenance, his great Heart was swell'd with Rage and Disdain; to be drag'd along with[5] three Keepers of *Newgate*, and put on Board like a Convict, when he had not so much as been brought to a Tryal; he made loud complaints of it by his Friends, for it seems he had some interest;[6] but his Friends got some Checque in their Application, and were told he had had *Favour enough*, and that they had receiv'd such an Account of him since the last Grant of his Transportation, that he ought to think himself very well treated that he was not prosecuted a new. This answer quieted him at once, for he knew too much what might have happen'd, and what he had room to expect; and now he saw the goodness of the Advice to him, which prevail'd with him to accept of the offer of a voluntary Transportation, and after his chagrin at these Hell Hounds, *as he call'd them*, was a little over, he look'd a little compos'd, began to be chearful, and as I was telling him how glad I was to have him once more out of their Hands, took me in his Arms, and acknowledg'd with great Tenderness, that I had given him the best Advice possible, *My Dear*, says he, *Thou hast twice sav'd my Life; from hence forward it shall be all employ'd for you, and I'll always take your Advice.*[7]

The Ship began now to fill, several Passengers came on Board who were embark'd on no Criminal account, and these had Accommodations assign'd them in the great Cabin, and other Parts of the Ship, whereas we *as Convicts* were thrust down below, I know not where; but when my Husband came on Board, I spoke to the Boatswain, who had so early given me Hints of his Friendship in carrying my Letter; I told him he had befriended me in many things, and I had not made any suitable Return to him, and with that I put a Guinea into his Hands; I told him that my Husband was now come on Board, that tho' we were both under the present Misfortunes, yet we had been Persons of a differing Character from the wretched Crew that we came with, and desir'd to know of him, whether the Captain might not be mov'd, to admit us to some Conveniences in the Ship, for which we would make him what Satisfaction he pleas'd, and that we would gratifie him for his Pains in procuring this for us. He took the Guinea as I cou'd see with great Satisfaction, and assur'd me of his Assistance.

Then he told us, he did not doubt but that the Captain, who was one of the best humour'd Gentlemen in the World, would be easily brought to Accommodate us, as well as we cou'd desire, and to

---

5. By.
6. Some influential persons who were interested in him.
7. In the second edition this paragraph and the preceding one are inserted earlier, following the paragraph on p. 243 ending ". . . or with what he had, but by directions." See A Comment on the Text, p. 273, below.

make me easie, told me he would go up the next Tide on purpose
to speak to the Captain about it. The next Morning happening to
sleep a little longer than ordinary, when I got up, and began to look
Abroad, I saw the Boatswain among the Men in his ordinary Business; I was a little melancholly at seeing him there, and going for-
wards to speak to him, he saw me, and came towards me, but not
giving him time to speak first, I said smiling, *I doubt, Sir, you have
forgot us*, for I see you are very busy; he return'd presently,[8] come
along with me, and you shall see, so he took me into the great
Cabbin, and there sat a good sort of a Gentlemanly Man for a
Seaman writing, and with a great many Papers before him.

Here says the Boatswain to him that was a writing, is the Gentlewoman that the Captain spoke to you of, and turning to me, he
said, I have been so far from forgetting your Business, that I have
been up at the Captain's House, and have represented faithfully to
the Captain what you said, relating to your being furnished with
better Conveniences for your self, and your Husband; and the Captain has sent this Gentleman, who is Mate of the Ship down with
me, on purpose to show you every thing, and to Accommodate you
fully to your Content, and bid me assure you that you shall not be
treated like what you were at first expected to be, but with the same
respect as other Passengers are treated.

The Mate then spoke to me, and not giving me time to thank
the Boatswain for his kindness confirm'd what the Boatswain had
said, and added that it was the Captain's delight to show himself
Kind and Charitable, especially, to those that were under any Misfortunes, and with that he shew'd me several Cabbins built up,
some in the Great Cabbin, and some partition'd off, out of the
Steerage,[9] but opening into the great Cabbin on purpose for the
Accommodation of Passengers, and gave me leave to choose where I
would; however I chose a Cabbin, which open'd into the Steerage,
in which was very good Conveniences to set our Chest, and Boxes,
and a Table to eat on.

The Mate then told me that the Boatswain had given so good a
Character of me, and of my Husband, as to our civil Behaviour,
that he had orders to tell me, we should eat with him, if we
thought fit, during the whole Voyage on the common Terms of
Passengers; that we might lay in some fresh Provisions, if we
pleas'd; or if not, he should lay in his usual Store, and we should
have Share with him: This was very reviving News to me, after so
many Hardships, and Afflictions as I had gone thro' of late; I
thank'd him, and told him, the Captain should make his own
Terms with us, and ask'd him leave to go and tell my Husband of it

8. Answered immediately.
9. That part of the vessel situated forward of the main cabin, but adjoining it
as Moll describes; not steerage in the
modern sense, i.e., space on lower decks
allotted to passengers paying lowest fares.

who was not very well, and was not yet out of his Cabbin: Accordingly I went, and my Husband whose Spirits were still so much sunk with the Indignity (as he understood it) offered him, that he was scarce yet himself, was so reviv'd with the Account I gave him of the Reception we were like to have in the Ship, that he was quite another Man, and new vigour and Courage appear'd in his very Countenance; so true is it, that the greatest of Spirits, when overwhelm'd by their Afflictions, are subject to the greatest Dejections, and are the most apt to Despair and give themselves up.

After some little Pause to recover himself, my Husband come up with me, and gave the Mate thanks for the kindness, which he express'd to us, and sent suitable acknowledgement by him to the Captain, offering to pay him by Advance, what ever he demanded for our Passage, and for the Conveniences he had help'd us to; the Mate told him that the Captain would be on Board in the Afternoon, and that he would leave all that till he came; accordingly, in the Afternoon the Captain came, and we found him the same courteous obliging Man, that the Boatswain had represented him to be; and he was so well pleas'd with my Husband's Conversation, that in short, he would not let us keep the Cabbin we had chosen, but gave us one, that as I said before, open'd into the great Cabbin.

Nor were his Conditions exorbitant, or the Man craving and eager to make a Prey of us, but for fifteen Guineas we had our whole Passage and Provisions, and Cabbin, eat at the Captain's Table, and were very handsomely Entertain'd.

The Captain lay himself in the other part of the Great Cabbin, having let his round House,[1] *as they call it,* to a rich Planter, who went over with his Wife and three Children, who eat by themselves; he had some other ordinary Passengers, who Quarter'd in the Steerage, and as for our old Fraternity, they were kept under the Hatches while the Ship lay there, and came very little on the Deck.

I could not refrain acquainting my Governess with what had happen'd, it was but just that she, who was so really concern'd for me, should have part in my good Fortune; besides I wanted her Assistance to supply me with several Necessaries, which before I was shy of letting any Body see me have, that it might not be publick; but now I had a Cabbin and room to set things in, I order'd abundance of good things for our Comfort in the Voyage, as Brandy, Sugar, Lemons, &c. to make Punch, and Treat our Benefactor, the Captain; and abundance of things for eating and drinking in the Voyage; also a larger Bed, and Bedding proportion'd to it; so that in a Word, we resolv'd to want for nothing in the Voyage.

All this while I had provided nothing for our Assistance when we

---

1. The roundhouse is a cabin on the aft part of the quarter-deck (the rear portion of a vessel's upper deck), usually reserved for officers. The captain rents these desirable quarters to a rich planter.

should come to the Place and begin to call ourselves Planters; and I was far from being ignorant of what was needful on that Occasion; particularly all sorts of Tools for the Planters-Work, and for building; and all kinds of Furniture for our Dwelling, which if to be bought in the Country, must necessarily cost double the Price.

So I discours'd that Point with my Governess, and she went and waited upon the Captain, and told him, that she hop'd ways might be found out, for her two unfortunate Cousins, *as she call'd us*, to obtain our Freedom when we came into the Country, and so enter'd into a Discourse with him about the Means and Terms also, of which I shall say more in its Place; and after thus sounding the Captain, she let him know, tho' we were unhappy in the Circumstance that occasion'd our going, yet that we were not unfurnish'd to set our selves to Work in the Country; and were resolv'd to settle, and live there as Planters, if we might be put in a way how to do it: The Captain readily offer'd his Assistance, told her the Method of entering upon such Business, and how easy, nay, how certain it was for industrious People to recover their Fortunes in such a manner: Madam, *says he*, 'tis no Reproach to any Man in that Country to have been sent over in worse Circumstances than I perceive your Cousins are in, provided they do but apply with diligence and good Judgment to the Business of that Place when they come there.

She then enquir'd of him what things it was Necessary we should carry over with us, and he like a very honest as well as knowing Man, told her thus: Madam, your Cousins in the first Place must procure some Body to buy them as Servants, in Conformity to the Conditions of their Transportation, and then in the Name of that Person, they may go about what they will; they may either Purchase some Plantations already begun, or they may purchase Land of the Government of the Country, and begin where they please, and both will be done reasonably; she bespoke his Favour in the first Article, which he promis'd to her to take upon himself, and indeed faithfull perform'd it; and as to the rest, he promis'd to recommend us to such as should give us the best Advice, and not to impose upon us, which was as much as could be desir'd.

She then ask'd him if it would not be Necessary to furnish us with a Stock of Tools and Materials for the Business of Planting, and he said, yes, by all means, and then she begg'd his Assistance in it; she told him she would furnish us with every thing that was Convenient whatever it cost her; he accordingly gave her a long particular of things Necessary for a Planter, which by his Account came to about fourscore, or an Hundred Pounds; and in short, she went about as dexterously to buy them, as if she had been an old *Virginia* Merchant; only that she bought by my Direction above twice as much of every thing as he had given her a List of.

These she put on Board in her own Name, took his Bills of Loading for them, and Endorst those Bills of Loading to my Husband, Ensuring the Cargo afterwards in her own Name, by our order; so that we were provided for all Events, and for all Disasters.

I should have told you that my Husband gave her all his whole Stock of 108 *l.* which as I have said, he had about him in Gold, to lay out thus, and I gave her a good Sum besides; so that I did not break into the Stock, which I had left in her Hands at all, but after we had sorted out our whole Cargo, we had yet near 200 *l.* in Money, which was more than enough for our purpose.

In this Condition, very chearful, and indeed joyful at being so happily Accommodated as we were, we set Sail from *Bugby's-Hole* to *Gravesend*, where the Ship lay about ten Days more, and where the Captain came on Board for good and all. Here the Captain offer'd us a civility, which indeed we had no Reason to expect. Namely, to let us go on Shore, and refresh ourselves, upon giving our Words in a solemn manner, that we would not go from him, and that we would return peaceably on Board again: This was such an Evidence of his Confidence in us, that it overcome my Husband, who in a meer Principle of Gratitude, told him as he could not be in any Capacity to make a suitable return for such a Favour, so he could not think of accepting of it, nor could he be easy that the Captain should run such a Risque: After some mutual Civilities, I gave my Husband a Purse, in which was 80 Guineas, and he puts it into the Captain's hand: There Captain, *says he*, there's part of a Pledge for our Fidelity, if we deal dishonestly with you on any Account, 'tis your own, and on this we went on Shore.

Indeed the Captain had assurance enough of our Resolutions to go, for that having made such Provision to Settle there, it did not seem Rational that we would chuse to remain here at the Expence and Peril of Life, for such it must have been, if we had been taken again. In a Word, we went all on Shore with the Captain, and Supp'd together in *Gravesend*; where we were very Merry, staid all Night, lay at the House where we Supp'd, and came all very honestly on Board again with him in the Morning. Here we bought ten dozen Bottles of good Beer, some Wine, some Fowls, and such things as we thought might be acceptable on Board.

My Governess was with us all this while, and went with us Round into the *Downs*,[2] as did also the Captain's Wife with whom she went back; I was never so sorrowful at parting with my own Mother as I was at parting with her, and I never saw her more: We had a fair Easterly Wind sprung up the third Day after we came to the *Downs*, and we sail'd from thence the 10th of *April*; nor did we touch any more at any Place, till being driven on the Coast of *Ire-*

---

2. A sheltered place of anchorage in the English Channel off the southeast coast of Kent.

land by a very hard Gale of Wind, the Ship came to an Anchor in a little *Bay*, near the Mouth of a River, whose Name I remember not, but they said the River came down from *Limerick*, and that it was the largest River in *Ireland*.[3]

Here being detain'd by bad Weather for some time, the Captain who continu'd the same kind good humour'd Man as at first, took us two on Shore with him again: He did it now in kindness to my Husband indeed, who bore the Sea very ill, and was very Sick, especially when it blew so hard: Here we bought in again, store of fresh Provisions, especially Beef, Pork, Mutton and Fowls, and the Captain stay'd to Pickle up five or six Barrels of Beef to lengthen out the Ships Store. We were here not above five Days, when the Weather turning mild, and a fair Wind; we set Sail again and in two and Forty Days came safe to the Coast of *Virginia*.

When we drew near to the Shore, the Captain call'd me to him, and told me that he found by my Discourse, I had some Relations in the Place, and that I had been there before, and so he suppos'd I understood the Custom, in their disposing the convict Prisoners when they arriv'd; I told him I did not, and that as to what Relations I had in the Place, he might be sure I would make my self known to none of them while I was in the Circumstances of a Prisoner, and that as to the rest, we left ourselves entirely to him to Assist us, as he was pleas'd to promise us he wou'd do. He told me I must get some Body in the Place to come and buy us as Servants, and who must answer for us[4] to the Governor of the Country, if he demanded us; I told him we should do as he should direct; so he brought a Planter to treat with him, as it were for the Purchase of these two Servants, my Husband and me, and there we were formally sold to him, and went a Shore with him: The Captain went with us, and carried us to a certain House whether it was to be call'd a Tavern or not, I know not, but we had a Bowl of Punch there made of Rum, &c. and were very Merry. After some time the Planter gave us a Certificate of Discharge, and an Acknowledgement of having serv'd him faithfully, and we were free from him the next Morning, to go whither we would.

For this Peice of Service the Captain demanded of us 6000

3. The River Shannon.
4. Although this paragraph contradicts Moll's statement that her husband was not to be sold (p. 243), it is consistent with the circumstances in his case which were changing for the worse, his being dragged aboard ship by three Newgate keepers, and his treatment on board as a prisoner. He goes to America as a privileged convict rather than a "Gentleman at liberty," as Moll suggested he might earlier. The editor of the second edition noticed the variance and changed the plurals to singulars throughout the paragraph, a procedure which creates additional problems by failing to account for Jemmy's treatment on being delivered to the vessel. Earlier Moll suggested that new evidence was coming in against him, and later she says that his influential friends had been checked in helping him, and that he could have been prosecuted anew. Apparently Defoe had in mind a turn of plot which he did not develop; hence, the confusion. For the alternate version see Notes to the Text, p. 285, below.

weight of Tobacco, which he said he was Accountable for to his Freighter, and which we immediately bought for him, and made him a present of 20 Guineas, besides, with which he was abundantly satisfy'd.

It is not proper to Enter here into the particulars of what Part of the Colony of *Virginia* we Settled in, for divers[5] Reasons; it may suffice to mention that we went into the great River of *Potomack,* the Ship being bound thither; and there we intended to have Settled at first, tho' afterwards we altered our Minds.

The first thing I did of Moment after having gotten all our Goods on Shore, and plac'd them in a Storehouse, or Warehouse, which with a Lodging we hir'd at the small Place or Village where we Landed; I say the first thing was to enquire after my Mother, and after my Brother, (that fatal Person who I married as a Husband, as I have related at large;) a little enquiry furnish'd me with Information that Mrs. ————, that is my Mother, was Dead; that my Brother (or Husband) was alive, which I confess I was not very glad to hear; but which was worse, I found he was remov'd from the Plantation where he liv'd formerly, and where I liv'd with him, and liv'd with one of his Sons in a Plantation just by the Place where we Landed, and where we had hir'd a Warehouse.

I was a little surpriz'd at first, but as I ventured to satisfy my self that he could not know me, I was not only perfectly easy, but had a great mind to see him, if it was possible to do so without his seeing me; in order to that I found out by enquiry the Plantation where he liv'd, and with a Woman of that Place who I got to help me, like what we call a *Chairwoman,*[6] I rambl'd about towards the Place, as if I had only a mind to see the Country, and look about me; at last I came so near that I saw the Dwelling-house: *I ask'd the Woman* whose Plantation that was, *she said,* it belong'd to such a Man, and looking out a little to our right Hands, there says she, is the Gentleman that owns the Plantation, and his Father with him: What are their Christian Names? said I, I know not, *said she,* what the old Gentlemans Name is, but his Sons Name is *Humphry,* and I believe, *says she,* the Fathers is so too; you may guess, if you can, what a confus'd mixture of Joy and Fright possest my Thoughts upon this Occasion, for I immediately knew that this was no Body else but my own Son, by that Father she shewed me, who was my own Brother: I had no Mask, but I ruffled my Hoods so about my Face, that I depended upon it that after above 20 Years absence, and withal not expecting any thing of me in that part of the World, he would not be able to know any thing of me; but I need not have us'd all that Caution, for the old Gentleman was grown

5. Diverse (archaic form); various.
6. Charwoman: a woman hired for day-   work to do odd jobs.

dim Sighted by some Distemper which had fallen upon his Eyes, and could but just see well enough to walk about, and not run against a Tree or into a Ditch. The Woman that was with me had told me that by a meer Accident, knowing nothing of what importance it was to me: As they drew near to us, *I said*, does he know you Mrs. *Owen?* so they call'd the Woman, yes, *said she*, if he hears me speak, he will know me; but he can't see well enough to know me, or any Body else; and so she told me the Story of his Sight, as I have related: This made me secure, and so I threw open my Hoods again, and let them pass by me: It was a wretched thing for a Mother thus to see her own Son, a handsome comely young Gentleman in flourishing Circumstances, and durst not make herself known to him; and durst not take any notice of him; let any Mother of Children that reads this consider it, and but think with what anguish of Mind I restrain'd myself; what yearnings of Soul I had in me to embrace him, and weep over him; and how I thought all my Entrails turn'd within me, that my very Bowels mov'd,[7] and I knew not what to do; as I now know not how to express those Agonies: When he went from me I stood gazing and trembling, and looking after him as long as I could see him; then sitting down on the Grass, just at a Place I had mark'd, I made as if I lay down to rest me, but turn'd from her, and lying on my Face wept, and kiss'd the Ground that he had set his Foot on.

I cou'd not conceal my Disorder so much from the Woman, but that she perceiv'd it, and thought I was not well, which I was oblig'd to pretend was true; upon which she press'd me to rise, the Ground being damp and dangerous, which I did accordingly, and walk'd away.

As I was going back again, and still Talking of this Gentleman and his Son, a new Occasion of melancholy offer'd itself *thus*: The Woman began, as if she would tell me a Story to divert me; there goes, *says she*, a very odd Tale among the Neighbours where this Gentleman formerly liv'd: What was that, *said I?* why, says she, that old Gentleman going to *England*, when he was a young Man, fell in Love with a young Lady there, one of the finest Women that ever was seen, and Married her, and brought her over hither to his Mother, who was then living. He liv'd here several Years with her, *continu'd she*, and had several Children by her, of which the young Gentleman that was with him now, was one, but after some time, the old Gentlewoman his Mother talking to her of something relating to herself when she was in *England*, and of her Circumstances in *England*, which were bad enough, the Daughter-in-Law, began to be very much surpriz'd, and uneasy; and in short, examining further

---

7. **Moll was deeply moved; the bowels were thought to be the center of tender emotions.**

into things it appear'd past all Contradiction, that she (the old Gentlewoman) was her own Mother, and that consequently that Son was his Wives own Brother, which struck the whole Family with Horror, and put them into such Confusion, that it had almost ruin'd them all; the young Woman would not live with him, the Son, her Brother and Husband, for a time went Distracted, and at last, the young Woman went away for *England*, and has never been heard of since.

It is easy to believe that I was strangely affected with this Story, but 'tis impossible to describe the Nature of my Disturbance: I seem'd astonish'd at the Story, and ask'd her a Thousand Questions about the particulars, which I found she was thoroughly acquainted with; at last I began to enquire into the Circumstances of the Family, how the old Gentlewoman, *I mean, my Mother* died, and how she left what she had; for my Mother had promis'd me very solemnly, that when she died, she would do something for me, and leave it so, as that, if I was Living, I should one way or other come at it, without its being in the Power of her Son, *my Brother and Husband* to prevent it: She told me she did not know exactly how it was order'd; but she had been told that *my* Mother had left a Sum of Money, and had tyed[8] her Plantation for the Payment of it, to be made good to the Daughter, if ever she could be heard of, either in *England*, or else where; and that the Trust was left with this Son, who was the Person that we saw with his Father.

This was News too good for me to make light of, and you may be sure fill'd my Heart with a Thousand Thoughts, what Course I should take, how, and when, and in what manner I should make myself known, or whether I should ever make myself known, or no.

Here was a Perplexity that I had not indeed skill to manage myself in, neither knew I what Course to take: It lay heavy upon my mind Night, and Day, I could neither Sleep or Converse, so that my Husband perceiv'd it, and wonder'd what ail'd me, strove to divert me, but it was all to no purpose; he press'd me to tell him what it was troubled me, but I put it off, till at last importuning me continually, I was forc'd to form a Story, which yet had a plain Truth to lay it upon too; I told him I was troubled because I found we must shift our Quarters and alter our Scheme of Settling, for that I found I should be known, if I stay'd in that part of the Country, for that my Mother being dead, several of my Relations were come into that Part where we then was, and that I must either discover myself to them, which in our present Circumstances was not proper on many Accounts, or remove; and which to do I knew not, and that this it was that made me so Melancholly, and so Thoughtful.

8. Tied, entailed, restricted the inheritance.

He joyn'd with me in this, that it was by no means proper for me to make myself known to any Body in the Circumstances in which we then were; and therefore he told me he would be willing to remove to any other part of the Country, or even to any other Country[9] if I thought fit; but now I had another Difficulty, which was, that if I remov'd to any other Colony, I put myself out of the way of ever making a due Search after those Effects which my Mother had left: Again, I could never so much as think of breaking the Secret of my former Marriage to my new Husband; It was not a Story, as I thought that would bear telling, nor could I tell what might be the Consequences of it; and it was impossible to search into the bottom of the thing without making it Publick all over the Country, as well who I was, as what I now was also.

In this perplexity I continu'd a great while, and this made my Spouse very uneasy; for he found me perplex'd, and yet thought I was not open with him, and did not let him into every part of my Grievance; and he would often say, he wondred what he had done, that I would not Trust him with what ever it was, especially if it was Grievous and Afflicting; the Truth is, he ought to have been trusted with every thing, for no Man in the World could deserve better of a Wife; but this was a thing I knew not how to open to him, and yet having no Body to disclose any part of it to, the Burthen was too heavy for my mind; for let them say what they please of our Sex not being able to keep a Secret, my Life is a plain Conviction to me of the contrary; but be it our Sex, or the Man's Sex, a Secret of Moment should always have a Confident, a bosom Friend, to whom we may Communicate the Joy of it, or the Grief of it, be it which it will, or it will be a double weight upon the Spirits, and perhaps become even insupportable in itself; and this I appeal to all human Testimony for the Truth of.

And this is the Cause why many times Men as well as Women, and Men of the greatest, and best Qualities other ways, yet have found themselves weak in this part, and have not been able to bear the weight of a secret Joy, or of a secret sorrow; but have been oblig'd to disclose it, even for the meer giving vent to themselves, and to unbend the Mind, opprest with the Load and Weights which attended it; nor was this any Token of Folly or Thoughtlessness at all, but a natural Consequence of the thing; and such People had they struggl'd longer with the Oppression, would certainly have told it in their Sleep, and disclos'd the Secret, let it have been of what fatal Nature soever, without regard to the Person to whom it might be expos'd: This Necessity of Nature, is a thing which Works sometimes with such vehemence in the Minds of

9. Colony.

those who are guilty of any atrocious Villany; such as secret Murther in particular, that they have been oblig'd to Discover it, tho' the Consequence would necessarily be their own Destruction: Now tho' it may be true that the divine Justice ought to have the Glory of all those Discoveries and Confessions, yet 'tis as certain that Providence which ordinarily Works by the Hands of Nature, makes use here of the same natural Causes to produce those extraordinary Effects.

I could give several remarkable Instances of this in my long Conversation with Crime and with Criminals; I knew one Fellow, that while I was a Prisoner in *Newgate*, was one of those they called then *Night-Flyers*,[1] I know not what other Word they may have understood it by since; but he was one, who by Connivance was admitted to go Abroad every Evening, when he play'd his Pranks, and furnish'd those honest People they call Thief-Catchers[2] with business to find out next Day, and restore *for a Reward*, what they had stolen the Evening before: This Fellow was as sure to tell in his sleep all that he had done, and every Step he had taken, what he had stole, and where, as sure as if he had engag'd to tell it waking, and that there was no Harm or Danger in it; and therefore he was oblig'd after he had been out to lock himself up, or be lock'd up by some of the Keepers that had him in Fee,[3] that no Body should hear him; but on the other Hand, if he had told all the Particulars, and given a full account of his Rambles and Success to any Comrade, any Brother Thief, or to his Employers, *as I may justly call them*, then all was well with him, and he slept as quietly as other People.

As the publishing this Account of my Life is for the sake of the just Moral of every part of it, and for Instruction, Caution, Warning and Improvement to every Reader, so this will not pass I hope for an unnecessary Digression concerning some People being oblig'd to disclose the greatest Secrets either of their own or other Peoples Affairs.

Under the certain Oppression of this weight upon my Mind, I

---

1. A cant term for criminals who were already imprisoned but who were allowed to sally out at night in order to steal whatever possible, the prison officials "going snacks" (sharing in the loot) with them.
2. Since London had no professional police force other than the constabulary until the early nineteenth century, "thief-takers" ("bounty hunters" would be an American equivalent) informed on and captured criminals in order to receive posted rewards. Occasionally such men would work hand-in-hand with the thief, returning stolen property to victims for a reward, much as Moll and her governess did with the goods of the drunken baronet. Moll's calling these men "honest" is ironic. Jonathan Wild (1682?–1725) was the most well-known and infamous of the "thief-catchers," and Defoe wrote his biography in 1725. Also, Henry Fielding satirized Wild's life in *Jonathan Wild the Great* (1743). See also Gerald Howson's *Thief-Taker General: The Rise and Fall of Jonathan Wild* (London, 1970).
3. Those in Newgate who had charge of him and who shared in the booty from his nightly escapades.

labour'd in the Case I have been Naming; and the only relief I found for it was to let my Husband into so much of it as I thought would convince him of the Necessity there was for us to think of Settling in some other Part of the World; and the next Consideration before us, was, which part of the *English* settlements we should go to; my Husband was a perfect Stranger to the Country, and had not yet so much as a Geographical knowledge of the Situation of the several Places; and I, that till I wrote this, did not know what the word Geographical signify'd, had only a general Knowledge from long Conversation with People that came from, or went to several Places; but this I knew, that *Maryland, Pensilvania,* East and West *Jersy, New York,* and *New England,* lay all North of *Virginia,* and that they were consequently all colder Climates, to which, for that very Reason, I had an Aversion; for that as I naturally lov'd warm Weather, so now I grew into Years, I had a stronger Inclination to shun a cold Climate; I therefore consider'd of going to *Carolina,* which is the most Southern Colony of the *English,* on the Continent of *America,* and hither I propos'd to go; and the rather, because I might with great ease come from thence at any time, when it might be proper to enquire after my Mothers effects, and to make myself known enough to demand them.

With this Resolution, I propos'd to my Husband our going away from where we was, and carrying all our Effects with us to *Carolina,* where we resolv'd to Settle, for my Husband readily agreed to the first Part (*viz.*) that it was not at all proper to stay where we was, since I had assur'd him we should be known there, and the rest I effectually conceal'd from him.

But now I found a new Difficulty upon me: The main Affair grew heavy upon my Mind still, and I could not think of going out of the Country without *some how or other* making enquiry into the grand Affair of what my Mother had done for me; nor cou'd I with any patience bear the thought of going away, and not make myself known to my old Husband, (*Brother*) or to my Child, his Son, only I would fain have had this done without my new Husband having any knowledge of it, or they having any knowledge of him, or that I had such a thing as a Husband.

I cast about innumerable ways in my Thoughts how this might be done: I would gladly have sent my Husband away to *Carolina,* with all our Goods, and have come after myself; but this was impracticable, he would never stir without me, being himself perfectly unacquainted with the Country, and with the Methods of settling there, or any where else: Then I thought we would both go first with part of our Goods, and that when we were Settled I should come back to *Virginia* and fetch the remainder; but even then I knew he would never part with me, and be left there to go on alone; the Case was plain; he was bred a Gentleman, and by Consequence was not only unacquainted,[4] but indolent, and when we did Settle, would much rather go out into the Woods with his Gun, which they call there Hunting,[5] and which is the ordinary Work of the *Indians,* and which they do as Servants; I say he would much rather do that, than attend the natural Business of his Plantation.

These were therefore difficulties unsurmountable, and such as I knew not what to do in; I had such strong impressions on my Mind about discovering myself to my *Brother,* formerly my *Husband,* that I could not withstand them; and the rather, because it run constantly in my Thoughts, that if I did not do it while he liv'd, I might in vain endeavour to convince my Son afterward that I was really the same Person, and that I was his Mother, and so might both lose the assistance and comfort of the Relation, and the benefit of whatever it was my Mother had left me; and yet on the other Hand, I cou'd never think it proper to discover myself to them in the Circumstances I was in; as well relating to the having a Husband with me, as to my being brought over by a legal Transportation as a Criminal; on both which Accounts it was absolutely necessary to me to remove from the Place where I was, and come again to him, as from another Place, and in another Figure.

Upon those Considerations, I went on with telling my Husband the absolute necessity there was of our not Settling in *Potomack* River, at least that we should be presently made publick there, whereas if we went to any other Place in the World, we should come in with as much Reputation as any Family that came to Plant: That as it was always agreeable to the Inhabitants to have Families come among them to Plant, who brought Substance with them, either to purchase Plantations, or begin New ones, so we should be sure of a kind agreeable Reception, and that without any possibility of a Discovery of our Circumstances.

I told him in general too, that as I had several Relations in the Place where we was, and that I durst not now let myself be known to them, because they would soon come into a knowledge of the Occasion and Reason of my coming over, which would be to expose myself to the last degree; so I had Reason to believe that my Mother who died here had left me something, and perhaps considerable, which it might be very well worth my while to enquire after; but that this too could not be done without exposing us publickly, unless we went from hence; and then, where ever we Settled, I might come as it were to visit and to see my Brother and Nephews, make myself known to them, claim and enquire after what was my

---

4. Inexperienced.   5. As opposed to "shooting" in England.

Due, be receiv'd with Respect, and at the same time have justice done me with chearfulness and good will; whereas if I did it
now, I could expect nothing but with trouble, such as exacting it by
force, receiving it with Curses and Reluctance, and with all kinds of
Affronts, which he would not perhaps bear to see; that in Case of
being oblig'd to legal Proofs of being really her Daughter, I might
be at loss, be oblig'd to have recourse to *England*, and it may be to
fail at last, and so lose it, whatever it might be: With these Arguments, and having thus acquainted my Husband with the whole
Secret so far as was needful to him, we resolv'd to go and seek a
Settlement in some other Colony, and at first Thoughts, *Carolina*
was the Place we pitch'd upon.

In order to this we began to make enquiry for Vessels going to
Carolina, and in a very little while got information, that on the
other side the *Bay, as they call it,* namely, in *Maryland* there was a
Ship, which came from *Carolina*, loaden with Rice, and other
Goods, and was going back again thither, and from thence to
Jamaica, with Provisions: On this News we hir'd a Sloop to take in
our Goods, and taking as it were a final farewel of *Potowmack*
River, we went with all our Cargo over to *Maryland*.

This was a long and unpleasant Voyage, and my Spouse said it
was worse to him than all the Voyage from *England*, because the
Weather was but indifferent, the Water rough, and the Vessel
small and inconvenient; in the next Place we were full a hundred
Miles up *Potowmack* River, in a part which they call *Westmor-
land* County, and as that River is by far the greatest in *Virginia*,
and I have heard say, it is the greatest River in the World that falls
into another River, and not directly into the Sea; so we had base
Weather in it, and were frequently in great Danger; for tho' they
call it but a River, 'tis frequently so broad, that when we were in
the middle, we could not see Land on either Side for many Leagues
together: Then we had the great River, or Bay of *Chesapeake* to
cross, which is where the River *Potowmack* falls into it, near thirty
Miles broad, and we entered more great vast Waters, whose Names
I know not, so that our Voyage was full two hundred Mile, in a
poor sorry Sloop with all our Treasure, and if any Accident had
happened to us, we might at last have been very miserable; supposing we had lost our Goods and saved our Lives only, and had then
been left naked and destitute, and in a wild strange Place, not
having one Friend or Acquaintance in all that part of the World?
The very thoughts of it gives me some horror, even since the
Danger is past.

Well, we came to the Place in five Days sailing, I think they call it *Phillips*'s *Point*,[6] and behold when we came thither, the Ship bound to *Carolina*, was loaded and gone away but three Days before. This was a Disappointment, but however, I that was to be discourag'd with nothing, told my Husband that since we could not get Passage to *Carolina*, and that the Country we was in was very fertile and good; we would if he lik'd of it, see if we could find out any thing for our Turn where we was, and that if he lik'd things we would Settle here.

We immediately went on Shore, but found no Conveniences just at that Place, either for our being on Shore, or preserving our Goods on Shore, but was directed by a very honest Quaker, who we found there to go to a Place, about sixty Miles East; that is to say, nearer the Mouth of the *Bay*, where he said he liv'd, and where we should be Accommodated, either to Plant, or to wait for any other Place to Plant in, that might be more Convenient, and he invited us with so much kindness and simple Honesty that we agreed to go, and the Quaker himself went with us.

Here we bought us two Servants, (*viz.*) an *English* Woman-Servant just come on Shore from a Ship of *Leverpool*, and a *Negro* Man-Servant; things absolutely necessary for all People that pretended to Settle in that Country: This honest Quaker was very helpful to us, and when we came to the Place that he propos'd to us, found us out a convenient Storehouse for our Goods, and Lodging for ourselves and our Servants; and about two Months, or thereabout afterwards, by his Direction we took up a large peice of Land from the Governor of that Country, in order to form our Plantation, and so we laid the thoughts of going to *Carolina* wholly aside, having been very well receiv'd here, and Accommodated with a convenient Lodging, till we could prepare things, and have Land enough cur'd, and Timber and Materials provid'd for building us a House, all which we manag'd by the Direction of the Quaker; so that in one Years time, we had near fifty Acres of Land clear'd, part of it enclos'd, and some of it Planted with Tobacco, tho' not much; besides, we had Garden ground, and Corn sufficient to help supply our Servants with Roots, and Herbs, and Bread.

And now I perswaded my Husband to let me go over the *Bay* again, and enquire after my Friends; he was the willinger to consent to it now, because he had business upon his Hands sufficient to employ him, besides his Gun to divert him, which they call Hunting there, and which he greatly delighted in; and indeed we us'd to look at one another, sometimes with a great deal of Pleasure,

6. George E. Gifford suggests that Moll landed at the present Clay Island, in the mouth of the Nanticoke River, Dorchester County ("Daniel Defoe and Maryland," *Maryland Historical Magazine*, LII, 307–315).

reflecting how much better that was, not than *Newgate* only, but than the most prosperous of our Circumstances in the wicked Trade that we had been both carrying on.

Our Affair was in a very good posture; we purchased of the Proprietors of the Colony, as much Land for 35 Pound, paid in ready Money, as would make a sufficient Plantation to employ between fifty and sixty Servants, and which being well improv'd, would be sufficient to us as long as we could either of us live; and as for Children I was past the prospect of any thing of that kind.

But our good Fortune did not End here; I went, *as I have said*, over the *Bay*, to the Place where my Brother, once a Husband liv'd; but I did not go to the same Village where I was before, but went up another great River, on the East side of the River *Potowmack*, call'd *Rapahannock* River, and by this means came on the back of his Plantation, which was large, and by the help of a Navigable Creek, or little River, that run into the *Rapahannock*, I came very near it.

I was now fully resolv'd to go up *Point-blank*, to my Brother (Husband) and to tell him who I was; but not knowing what Temper I might find him in, or how much out of Temper rather, I might make him by such a rash visit, I resolv'd to write a Letter to him first to let him know who I was, and that I was come not to give him any trouble upon the old Relation, which I hop'd was entirely forgot; but that I apply'd to him as a Sister to a Brother, desiring his Assistance in the Case of that Provision, which our Mother at her decease had left for my Support, and which I did not doubt but he would do me Justice in, especially considering that I was come thus far to look after it.

I said some very tender kind things in the Letter about his Son, which I told him he knew to be my own Child, and that as I was guilty of nothing in Marrying him any more than he was in Marrying me, neither of us having then known our being at all related to one another, so I hop'd he would allow me the most Passionate desire of once seeing my one, and only Child,[7] and of showing something of the Infirmities of a Mother in preserving a violent Affection for him, who had never been able to retain any thought of me one way or other.

I did believe that having receiv'd this Letter he would immediately give it to his Son to Read, I having understood his Eyes being so dim, that he cou'd not see to read it; but it fell out better than so, for as his Sight was dim, so he had allow'd his Son to open all Letters that came to his Hand for him, and the old Gentleman being from Home, or out of the way when my Messenger came, my Letter came directly to my Sons Hand, and he open'd and read it.

He call'd the Messenger in, after some little stay, and ask'd him

7. The remaining offspring of the children Moll bore her brother.

where the Person was who gave him the Letter, the Messenger told him the Place, which was about seven Miles off, so he bid him stay, and ordering a Horse to be got ready, and two Servants, away he came to me with the Messenger: Let any one judge the Consternation I was in when my Messenger came back, and told me the old Gentleman was not at Home, but his Son was come along with him, and was just coming up to me: I was perfectly confounded, for I knew not whether it was Peace or War, nor cou'd I tell how to behave: However, I had but a very few Moments to think, for my Son was at the Heels of the Messenger, and coming up into my Lodgings, ask'd the Fellow at the Door something, I suppose it was, *for I did not hear it so as to understand it,* which was the Gentlewoman that sent him, for the Messenger said, *there she is Sir,* at which he comes directly up to me, kisses me, took me in his Arms, and embrac'd me with so much Passion, that he could not speak, but I could feel his Breast heave and throb like a Child that Cries, but Sobs, and cannot cry it out.

I can neither express or describe the Joy that touch'd my very Soul when I found, *for it was easy to discover that Part,* that he came not as a Stranger, but as a Son to a Mother, and indeed as a Son, who had never before known what a Mother of his own was; in short, we cryed over one another a considerable while, when at last he broke out first, MY DEAR MOTHER, says he, *are you still alive! I never expected to have seen your Face*; as for me, I cou'd say nothing a great while.

After we had both recover'd ourselves a little, and were able to talk, he told me how things stood; as to what I had written to his Father, he told me he had not shewed my Letter to his Father, or told him any thing about it; that what his Grandmother left me, was in his Hands, and that he would do me Justice to my full Satisfaction; that as to his Father, he was old and infirm both in Body and Mind, that he was very Fretful, and Passionate, almost Blind, and capable of nothing; and he question'd whether he would know how to act in an Affair which was of so nice a Nature as this, and that therefore he had come himself, as well to satisfy himself in seeing me, which he could not restrain himself from, as also to put it into my Power, to make a Judgement after I had seen how things were, whether I would discover myself to his Father, or no.

This was really so prudently and wisely manag'd, that I found my Son was a Man of Sense, and needed no Direction from me; I told him, I did not wonder that his Father was, as he had describ'd him, for that his Head was a little touch'd before I went away; and principally his Disturbance was because I could not be perswaded to conceal our Relation and to live with him as my Husband, after I knew that he was my Brother: That as he knew better than I, what his Fathers present Condition was, I should readily joyn with him in such Measures as he would direct: That I was indifferent as to seeing his Father, since I had seen him first, and he cou'd not have told me better News, than to tell me that what his Grandmother had left me, was entrusted in his Hands, who I doubted not now he knew who I was, would *as he said,* do me Justice: I enquir'd then how long my Mother had been dead, and where she died, and told so many particulars of the Family, that I left him no room to doubt the Truth of my being really and truly his Mother.

My Son then enquir'd where I was, and how I had dispos'd myself; I told him I was on the *Maryland* side of the *Bay,* at the Plantation of a particular Friend, who came from *England* in the same Ship with me, that as for that side of the *Bay* where he was, I had no Habitation; he told me I should go Home with him, and live with him, if I pleas'd, as long as I liv'd: That as to his Father he knew no Body, and would never so much as guess at me; I consider'd of that a little, and told him, that tho' it was really no little concern to me to live at a distance from him; yet I could not say it would be the most comfortable thing in the World to me to live in the House with him, and to have that unhappy Object always before me, which had been such a blow to my Peace before; that tho' I should be glad to have his Company (my Son) or to be as near him as possible while I stay'd, yet I could not think of being in the House where I should be also under constant Restraint for fear of betraying myself in my Discourse, nor should I be able to refrain some Expressions in my Conversing with him as my Son, that might discover the whole Affair, which would by no means be Convenient.

He acknowledged that I was right in all this, but then DEAR MOTHER, says he, *you shall be as near me as you can*; so he took me with him on Horseback to a Plantation, next to his own, and where I was as well entertain'd as I cou'd have been in his own; having left me there he went away home, telling me we would talk of the main Business the next Day; and having first called me his Aunt, and given a Charge to the People, who it seems were his Tenants, to treat me with all possible Respect; about two Hours after he was gone, he sent me a Maid-Servant, and a *Negro* Boy to wait on me, and Provisions ready dress'd for my Supper; and thus I was as if I had been in a new World, and began secretly now to wish that I had not brought my *Lancashire* Husband from *England* at all.

However, that wish was not hearty neither, for I lov'd my *Lancashire* Husband entirely, as indeed I had ever done from the beginning; and he merited from me as much as it was possible for a Man to do, but that by the way.

The next Morning my Son came to visit me again almost as soon as I was up; after a little Discourse, he first of all pull'd out a Deer skin Bag, and gave it me, with five and fifty *Spanish* Pistoles[8] in it, and told me that was to supply my Expences from *England,* for tho' it was not his Business to enquire, yet he ought to think I did not bring a great deal of Money out with me; it not being usual to bring much Money into that Country: Then he pull'd out his Grandmother's Will, and read it over to me, whereby it appear'd, that she had left a small Plantation, *as he call'd it,* on *York* River, that is, where my Mother liv'd, to me, with the Stock of Servants and Cattle upon it, and given it in Trust to this Son of mine for my Use, when ever he should hear of my being alive, and to my Heirs, if I had any Children, and in default of Heirs, to whomsoever I should by Will dispose of it; but gave the Income of it, till I should be heard of, or found, to my said Son; and if I should not be living, then it was to him and his Heirs.

This Plantation, tho' remote from him, he said he did not let out;[9] but manag'd it by a head Clerk, Steward, as he did another that was his Fathers, that lay hard by it, and went over himself three or four times a Year to look after it; I ask'd him what he thought the Plantation might be worth; *he said,* if I would let it out, he would give me about sixty Pounds a Year for it; but if I would live on it, then it would be worth much more, and he believ'd would bring me in about 150 *l.* a Year; but seeing I was likely either to Settle on the other side the *Bay,* or might perhaps have a mind to go back to *England* again, if I would let him be my Steward he would manage it for me, as he had done for himself, and that he believ'd he should be able to send me as much Tobacco to *England* from it, as would yeild me about 100 *l.* a Year, sometimes more.

This was all strange News to me, and things I had not been us'd to; and really my Heart began to look up more seriously, than I think it ever did before, and to look with great Thankfulness to the Hand of Providence, which had done such wonders for me, who had been myself the greatest wonder of Wickedness, perhaps that had been suffered to live in the World; and I must again observe, that not on this Occasion only, but even on all other Occasions of Thankfulness, my past wicked and abominable Life never look'd so Monstruous to me, and I never so compleatly abhorr'd it, and reproach'd myself with it, as when I had a Sense upon me of Providence doing good to me, while I had been making those vile Returns on my part.

But I leave the Reader to improve these Thoughts, as no doubt they will see Cause, and I go on to the Fact; my Sons tender Carriage, and kind Offers fetch'd Tears from me, almost all the while he talk'd with me; indeed I could scarce Discourse with him, but in

8. Gold coins, worth approximately £48.   9. Rent, lease.

the intervals of my Passion; however, at length I began, and expressing myself with wonder at my being so happy to have the Trust of
what I had left put into the Hands of my own Child, I told him,
that as to the Inheritance of it, I had no Child but him in the
World,[1] and now was past having any, if I should Marry, and
therefore would desire him to get a Writing Drawn, which I was
ready to execute, by which I would after me give it wholly to him
and to his Heirs; and in the mean time smiling, I ask'd him, what
made him continue a Batchelor so long; his answer was kind, and
ready, that *Virginia* did not yield any great plenty of Wives, and
since I talk'd of going back to *England*, I should send him a Wife
from *London*.

This was the Substance of our first days Conversation, the pleas-
antest Day that ever past over my Head in my Life, and which gave
me the truest Satisfaction: He came every Day after this, and spent
great part of his time with me, and carried me about to several of
his Friends Houses, where I was entertain'd with great Respect; also
I Dined several times at his own House, when he took care always
to see his half dead Father so out of the way, that I never saw him,
or he me: I made him one Present, and it was all I had of value,
and that was one of the gold Watches, of which I mention'd above,
that I had two in my Chest, and this I happen'd to have with me,
and I gave it him at his third Visit: I told him, I had nothing of
any value to bestow but that, and I desir'd he would now and then
kiss it for my sake; I *did not indeed tell him* that I had stole it from
a Gentlewomans side, at a Meeting-House in *London*, that's by the
way.

He stood a little while Hesitating, as if doubtful whether to take
it or no; but I press'd it on him, and made him accept it, and it was
not much less worth than his Leather-pouch full of *Spanish* Gold;
no, tho' it were to be reckon'd, as if at *London*, whereas it was
worth twice as much there, where I gave it him;[2] at length he took
it, kiss'd it, told me the Watch should be a Debt upon him, that he
would be paying, as long as I liv'd.

A few Days after he brought the Writings of Gift,[3] and the
Scrivener[4] with them, and I sign'd them very freely, and deliver'd
them to him with a hundr'd Kisses; for sure nothing ever pass'd
between a Mother and a tender dutiful Child, with more Affection:
The next Day he brings me an Obligation under his Hand and Seal,
whereby he engag'd himself to Manage and Improve the Plantation
for my account, and with his utmost Skill, and to remit the Produce

1. Moll has not forgotten that she has had other children, and that some might be living; rather, she is specifically telling Humphrey that he will be her sole heir.
2. In London the watch would have been almost worth the 55 pistoles; in America, however, it was worth twice the amount.
3. Legal writs bestowing the titles to the property on Moll.
4. A professional clerk or copyist.

to my order where-ever I should be, and withal, to be oblig'd him-self to make up the Produce a hundred Pound a year to me: When he had done so, he told me, that as I came to demand it before the Crop was off,[5] I had a right to the Produce of the current Year, and so he paid me an hundred Pound in *Spanish* Peices of Eight, and desir'd me to give him a Receipt for it as in full for that Year, ending at *Christmas* following; this being about the latter End of *August*.

I stay'd here above five Weeks, and indeed had much a do to get away then. Nay, he would have come over the *Bay* with me, but I would by no means allow him to it; however, he would send me over in a Sloop of his own, which was built like a Yatch,[6] and serv'd him as well for Pleasure as Business: This I accepted of, and so after the utmost Expressions both of Duty and Affection, he let me come away, and I arriv'd safe in two Days at my Friends the Quakers.

I brought over with me for the use of our Plantation, three Horses with Harness, and Saddles; some Hogs, two Cows, and a thousand other things, the Gift of the kindest and tenderest Child that ever Woman had: I related to my Husband all the particulars of this Voyage, except that I called my Son my Cousin; and first I told him, that I had lost my Watch, which he seem'd to take as a Misfortune; but then I told him how kind my Cousin had been, that my Mother had left me such a Plantation, and that he had preserv'd it for me, in hopes some time or other he should hear from me; then I told him that I had left it to his Management, that he would render me a faithful Account of its Produce; and then I pull'd him out the hundred Pound in Silver, as the first Years pro-duce, and then pulling out the Deer skin Purse with the Pistoles, and here my Dear, *says I*, is the gold Watch. My Husband, *so is Heavens goodness sure to work the same Effects, in all sensible Minds, where Mercies touch the Heart*, lifted up both his Hands, and with an extasy of Joy, *What is God a doing* says he, *for such an ungrateful Dog as I am!* Then I let him know what I had brought over in the Sloop, besides all this; I mean the Horses, Hogs and Cows, and other Stores for our Plantation; all which added to his surprize, and fill'd his Heart with thankfulness; and from this time forward I believe he was as sincere a Penitent, and as thoroughly a reform'd Man, as ever God's goodness brought back from a Profli-gate, a Highway-man, and a Robber. I could fill a larger History than this, with the Evidences of this Truth, and but that I doubt that part of the Story will not be equally diverting as the wicked Part, I have had thoughts of making a Volume of it by itself.

5. Harvested that year.　　　6. Yacht.

As for myself, as this is to be my own Story, not my Husbands, I return to that Part which relates to myself; we went on with our Plantation, and manag'd it with the help and Diversion[7] of such Friends as we got there by our obliging Behaviour, and especially the honest Quaker, who prov'd a faithful generous and steady Friend to us; and we had very good Success; for having a flourishing Stock to begin with, as *I have said*; and this being now encreas'd, by the Addition of a Hundred and fifty Pound *Sterling* in Money, we enlarg'd our Number of Servants, built us a very good House, and cur'd every Year a great deal of Land. The second Year I wrote to my old Governess, giving her part[8] with us of the Joy of our Success, and order'd her how to lay out the Money I had left with her, which was 250 *l.* as above, and to send it to us in Goods, which she perform'd, with her usual Kindness and Fidelity, and all this arriv'd safe to us.

Here we had a supply of all sorts of Cloaths, as well for my Husband as for myself; and I took especial care to buy for him all those things that I knew he delighted to have; as two good long Wigs, two silver hilted Swords, three or four fine Fowling peices, a fine Saddle with Holsters and Pistoles[9] very handsome, with a Scarlet Cloak; and in a Word, every thing I could think of to oblige him; and to make him appear, as he really was, a very fine Gentleman: I order'd a good Quantity of such Houshold-Stuff, as we yet wanted, with Linnen of all sorts for us both; as for my self, I wanted very little of Cloths or Linnen, being very well furnished before: The rest of my Cargo consisted in Iron-Work of all sorts, Harness for Horses, Tools, Cloaths for Servants, and Woollen-Cloth, stuffs,[1] Serges, Stockings, Shoes, Hats and the like, such as Servants wear, and whole Peices[2] also, to make up for Servants, all by direction of the Quaker; and all this Cargo arriv'd safe, and in good Condition, with three Women Servants, lusty Wenches, which my old Governess had pick'd up for me, suitable enough to the Place, and to the Work we had for them to do; one of which happen'd to come double, having been got with Child by one of the Seamen in the Ship, as she own'd afterwards, before the Ship got so far as *Gravesend*; so she brought us a stout Boy, about 7 Months after her Landing.

My Husband you may suppose was a little surpriz'd at the arriving of all this Cargo from *England*, and talking with me after he saw the Account of the particular;[3] my Dear, *says he*, what is the meaning of all this? I fear you will run us too deep in Debt: When

---

7. That is, as they were diverted or turned from the courses of their own occupations to help Moll. The second edition prints "help and Direction."
8. Share; i.e., Moll informed the gover-

ness of their success.
9. Pistols.
1. Textile material.
2. Yard goods of various kinds of cloth.
3. Itemized bill.

shall we be able to make Return for it all? I smil'd, and told him that it was all paid for; and then I told him, that not knowing what might befal us in the Voyage, and considering what our Circumstances might expose us to; I had not taken my whole Stock with me, that I had reserv'd so much in my Friends Hands, which now we were come over safe, and was Settled in a way to live, I had sent for as he might see.

He was amaz'd, and stood a while telling upon his Fingers, but said nothing, at last he began thus: Hold, lets see, *says he, telling upon his Fingers still*; and first on his Thumb, there's 246 *l.* in Money at first, then two gold Watches, Diamond Rings, and Plate, *says he,* upon the fore Finger, then upon the next Finger, here's a Plantation on *York* River, a 100 *l.* a Year, then 150 in Money; then a Sloop load of Horses, Cows, Hogs and Stores, and so on to the Thumb again; and now, *says he,* a Cargo cost 250 *l.* in *England,* and worth here twice the Money; well, *says I,* What do you make of all that? make of it, *says he,* why who says I was deceiv'd, when I married a Wife in *Lancashire*? I think I have married a Fortune, and a very good Fortune too, *says he.*

In a Word, we were now in very considerable Circumstances, and every Year encreasing, for our new Plantation grew upon our Hands insensibly,[4] and in eight Year which we lived upon it, we brought it to such a pitch, that the Produce was, at least, 300 *l.* Sterling a Year; I mean, worth so much in *England.*

After I had been a Year at Home again, I went over the Bay to see my Son, and to receive another Year's Income of my Plantation; and I was surpriz'd to hear, just at my Landing there, that my old Husband was dead, and had not been bury'd above a Fortnight. This, I confess, was not disagreeable News, because now I could appear as I was in a marry'd Condition; so I told my Son before I came from him, that I believed I should marry a Gentleman who had a Plantation near mine; and tho' I was legally free to marry, as to any Obligation that was on me before, yet that I was shye of it, lest the Blot should some time or other be reviv'd, and it might make a Husband uneasy; my Son the same kind dutiful and obliging Creature as ever, treated me now at his own House, paid me my hundred Pound, and sent me Home again loaded with Presents.

Some time after this, I let my Son know I was marry'd, and invited him over to see us; and my Husband wrote a very obliging Letter to him also, inviting him to come and see him; and he came accordingly some Months after, and happen'd to be there just when my Cargo from *England* came in, which I let him believe belong'd all to my Husband's Estate, not to me.

4. Imperceptibly.

It must be observ'd, that when the old Wretch, my Brother (Husband) was dead, I then freely gave my Husband an Account of all that Affair, and of this Cousin, as I had call'd him befoie, being my own Son by that mistaken unhappy Match: He was perfectly easy in the Account, and told me he should have been as easy if the old Man, as we call'd him, had been alive; for, *said he*, it was no Fault of yours, nor of his; it was a Mistake impossible to be prevented; he only reproach'd him with desiring me to conceal it, and to live with him as a Wife, after I knew that he was my Brother, that, he said, was a vile part: Thus all these little Difficulties were made easy, and we liv'd together with the greatest Kindness and Comfort imaginable; we are now grown Old: I am come back to *England*, being almost seventy Years of Age, my Husband sixty eight, having perform'd much more than the limited Terms of my Transportation: And now notwithstanding all the Fatigues, and all the Miseries we have both gone thro', we are both in good Heart and Health; my Husband remain'd there sometime after me to settle our Affairs, and at first I had intended to go back to him, but at his desire I alter'd that Resolution, and he is come over to *England* also, where we resolve to spend the Remainder of our Years in sincere Penitence, for the wicked Lives we have lived.

Written in the Year 1683.

F I N I S.

Textual Appendix

A COMMENT ON THE TEXT

The first edition of *Moll Flanders* was published in January, 1722, by W. Chetwood and T. Edlin.[1] In July of that year two separate issues of "The Second Edition, Corrected" (an abridged version) appeared, one published by John Brotherton, the other by a group of six printers and booksellers, which included Chetwood, Edlin, and Brotherton, and also W. Mears, C. King, and J. Stagg. Except for the title page the Brotherton second is identical[2] with the one issued in association by the six publishers. Toward the end of the same year two issues of "The Third Edition, Corrected" were published, again one by Brotherton alone, and the other by the same six printers and sellers who had combined to bring out the corrected second edition. Over the years this "third" edition has been generally considered to have Defoe's authority, and most modern editions are based on it;[3] however, examination of the "third edition, corrected" proves it to be only a reissue of the "second edition, corrected" with a new title page. We have in fact, therefore, the first edition and four issues of the abridged second.[4]

Undoubtedly, the demand for *Moll Flanders* during the first six months of its publication was steady if not remarkable,[5] exhausting the supply of

1. William Lee lists January 27, 1722, as the date of publication in *Daniel Defoe: His Life and Recently Discovered Writings, 1716–1729* (London, 1869), III, xlvi; according to George Chalmers' eighteenth-century list of Defoe's works, Edlin registered the book at Stationers Hall, January 12, 1722; see *The Life of Daniel De Foe* (London, 1790), p. 79. The date on the title page of the first edition reads MDDCXXI [sic] for 1721 under the Julian calendar, in which the new year began in March. (England adopted the Gregorian calendar in 1752.)

2. I have compared Indiana University's second edition, corrected, published by Brotherton, with the Cornell University second edition, corrected, published by Chetwood, Edlin, Mears, Brotherton, King, and Stagg. Both editions are extremely rare in comparison to first and "third" editions, perhaps suggesting a somewhat limited or cautious print order.

3. Herbert Davis's World Classics edition (London, 1961) is the first notable exception to this practice. (Davis's edition follows Constable and Company's limited reprint [London, 1923, 775 copies] of the first edition.) Recently, two editions of *Moll Flanders* have appeared using the first edition as text: J. Paul

Hunter's Crowell Critical Library edition (New York, 1970) and G. A. Starr's Oxford English Novels edition (London, 1972).

4. Standard bibliographies of Defoe's works also list a reissue by W. Chetwood of the third edition in 1723; however, after checking with Henry C. Hutchins, the original compiler of the Defoe section of the *Cambridge Bibliography of English Literature*, and inquiring of holders of large collections of Defoe's works, it would appear that this edition is a ghost. Its existence seems to have been perpetuated by Lee, who, working from advertisements for the novel in eighteenth-century periodicals, may have recorded a Julian calendar date for the December, 1722, Chetwood et al. "third" or recorded it with the 1723 abridgment by T. Read, entitled *The Life and Actions of Moll Flanders.* The second edition, corrected, published by Chetwood et al., and the Brotherton "third" edition, corrected, are not recorded in most standard bibliographies.

5. The sales of *Moll* did not compare to those of a work like *Robinson Crusoe,* which went through six editions in four months. See K. I. D. Maslen, "Edition Quantities for *Robinson Crusoe,* 1719," *The Library,* XXIV (1969), 145–150.

printed first editions; and the type having been distributed, Thomas Edlin made shares of the work available to the five other publishers, who agreed to bring out jointly an abridged and corrected second edition. Since in 1722 the cost of paper alone amounted to as much as 60 percent of the total expense of printing a book, the savings on paper in a shorter edition could offset a good share of the charges for correction, composition, and press-work. Apparently, the group had foresight enough this time to let the type stand,[6] against the possibility of demand for a third edition, at which time another printing with a new title page could be offered for sale.

Moreover, after collating the first and second editions, I find it difficult to believe that Defoe made the second-edition "corrections"; rather, the alterations (almost four thousand word changes, mostly deletions) indicate that whoever revised the first edition was instructed mainly to shorten it and, of course, to correct obvious errors while in the process. That economy rather than aesthetic improvement was the central concern can be seen by examining the kind of editing done. The first edition contains an eleven-page preface and 424 pages of text, approximately twenty-eight octavo gatherings. The second edition has a six-page preface and 366 pages of text, almost four gatherings fewer. The printer saved space by using a smaller-point type in the preface, by compressing passages of dialogue into single paragraphs, and by occasionally eliminating whole lines—all suggesting that he acted as his own editor or that he worked hand-in-hand with whoever abridged the first edition.[7] The editor deleted prepositional phrases and dependent clauses (often changing and confusing meaning), substituted shorter words for polysyllables, eliminated adjectives, and generally simplified the sentence structure of the first edition.[8]

That the actual corrections of the second edition are helpful in many cases is unquestionable; however, most of the acceptable revisions occur in

6. My theory that the type was allowed to stand rather than that the "third" edition was composed of unsold second-edition sheets is based on examination of the British Museum's "third" edition, Indiana's and Cornell's second edition, and the Yale and Newberry "third" editions (for editions compared see "Notes to the Text," p. 277, below), which show the same peculiar traits of text, page-by-page, in all four issues of the second edition. For example, broken and upside-down letters correspond, the same words are garbled, the same pages misnumbered, and the like. However, in bringing out the Chetwood "third" edition at the end of 1722, portions of two pages had to be reset hurriedly, perhaps due to pied lines. As a result pp. 338 and 347 exhibit normal variations in spelling, as well as obvious composing-stick errors, such as "sore" for "shore" and "aext" for "next." Since corresponding pages of the gathering do not appear to have been reset, and because the cost of paper was a major consideration, ruling out the printing of an abundance of second-edition pages for future binding, I conjecture that the six publishers agreed to let the type stand, perhaps each being responsible for a number of

gatherings. It should be noted, however, that the Brotherton "third" does not contain corresponding errors on these two pages, which suggests that it was printed before the Chetwood.

7. I assume that the second-edition trimming was done by using both Defoe's written ms. and a printed copy of the first edition (which would become copy-text for the second), for on occasion the second is able to add sense to the first edition where a line had been dropped or a phrase or word omitted in composition. For example see "Notes to the Text," 15.13–14 and 175.35.

8. This process of shortening and simplication continues in the abridgements and adaptations of *Moll Flanders* which began in Defoe's lifetime, but which he apparently had no hand in, and continued after his death. For example, Read's abridgment, *The Life and Actions of Moll Flanders* runs 188 pages (12mo) and includes whole portions of Defoe's original work. *Fortune's Fickle Distribution* (London, 1730), containing the *Life and Death of Moll Flanders* (from Read) has 130 pages (12mo). Numerous chapbooks and other condensations also appeared, many based on Read's version.

spelling (not one of Defoe's strong points), grammar, and corrected accidentals. In having access to the original manuscript, the "corrector" would have had the singular advantage of being able to rectify misreadings that the compositor of the first edition may have made in setting type from Defoe's shorthand;[9] however, the amount and kinds of errors that emerge in the second edition make it extremely doubtful that Defoe himself had anything to do with the editing. The following random sample of revisions in the second edition illustrates a tendency to garble meaning, contradict essential facts, introduce nonsense, or rob the narrative of vivid and essential detail. Such "corrections" I assume to be the work of the printer-editor because the changes suggest a gross unfamiliarity with the work as a whole. In each instance the abridger seems to concentrate on trimming the material immediately before his eyes, without concern for past or future events in the narrative and certainly with little or no attention to aesthetic quality or linguistic intent. Words resulting in important shifts in meaning are printed in bold face.

FIRST EDITION A	SECOND EDITION, CORRECTED B

1

| he . . . told me he was very serious, and I should hear more of him very quickly, and away he went **leaving me** infinitely pleas'd. [p. 20] | he . . . told me he was very serious, and I should hear more of him very quickly, and away he went infinitely pleas'd. [p. 18] |

[Two words saved, meaning reversed.]

2

| When I was fully recover'd he began again; My dear says he, **What made you so Surpriz'd at what I said?** I would have you consider Seriously of it; [p. 40] | When I was fully recover'd he began again; My dear, *says he,* I would have you consider seriously of it? [p. 35] |

[The necessary question points up Moll's almost fainting at the brother's suggestion that she marry Robin.]

3

| Well! *says the* elder Brother, How should Mrs. *Betty* be well, *they say* she is in Love? I believe nothing of it, *says* the old **Gentlewoman**. [p. 46] | Well! *says the elder Brother,* How should Mrs. *Betty* be well, *they say she is in Love*? I believe nothing of it says the *old* **Gentleman**. [p. 46] |

[The father never appears in either edition; perhaps the letters "wo" were accidently omitted in composition, but at this point the editor is collapsing the dialogue of Robin, his brother, mother, and eldest sister into a single paragraph and may have been unfamiliar with the speakers.]

9. Defoe's system of shorthand is described by George Harris Healey in *The Letters of Daniel Defoe* (Oxford, 1955), pp. vii, viii. Defoe used such symbols as "y^e" = "the," "y^t" = "that," "y^m" = "them," "w^th" = "with," "w^ch" = "which," and the like. Also Karl D. Bülbring, editor of *The Compleat English Gentleman* (London, 1890), which Defoe began in 1729, comments on Defoe's ms., which contains faulty spellings and unusual contractions and abbreviations. Defoe's remarkable number of publications in 1722 (*Moll Flanders, A Journal of the Plague Year, Religious Courtship, Colonel Jack,* plus periodical writings) indicates that he was writing at top speed and, therefore, undoubtedly using the many shortened forms indicated.

272 · *Textual Appendix*

A   B

4

In short, I committed Adultery
and Incest with him every Day in my
Desires, which without doubt, was as
effectually Criminal **in the Nature of
the Guilt as if I had actually done it**.
[p. 66]

In short, I committed Adultery
and **Incence** with him every Day in
my Desires, which without doubt, was
as effectually Criminal. [p. 57]

[Although a line of type is saved, Moll's reflections on her guilt
give way to an incomplete idea.]

5

for I had foreseen **sometime** that all
was going to Wreck. [p. 70]

for I had foreseen **something before**
that all was going to Wreck. [p. 60]

[Seemingly, the reviser "corrects" Defoe's ms.; result: an added
word and a sensible passage garbled.]

6

The Men made no scruple to set
themselves out as Persons meriting a
Woman of Fortune, **when they had no
Fortune in their own way,** [p. 89]

The Men made no scruple to set
themselves out as Persons meriting a
Woman of Fortune of their own; [pp.
75–76]

[A typical omission, which in this case may be a compositorial
error since it occurs at the bottom of a page.]

7

There was in the House, where I
lodg'd, a North Country Woman **that
went for** [i.e., pretended to be] a Gentlewoman. [p. 155]

There was in the House, where I
lodg'd, a North Country Gentlewoman. [p. 131]

[The clue prepares readers for the woman's deception, and it is
necessary to support the context later.]

8

my Husband the Linnen Draper, who
I having not now heard from in almost
Fifteen **year**, no Body could blame me
for thinking my self entirely **freed**
from; [p. 152]

my Husband the Linnen Draper, who
I having not now heard from in almost
Fifteen **Years**, no Body could blame
me for thinking my self entirely from;
[p. 128]

[A typical grammatical improvement in idiom, i.e., "Years" for
"year," which is inconsistent with Moll's speech throughout, and
then the omission of the necessary word "freed."]

9

but my Governess who **I always made**
Partner in my Success, and who now
plaid a sure Game **with me**, for that
she had a Share of the Gain, and **no
Share of** the hazard [p. 263]

but my Governess who was Partner
in my Success, and who now plaid a
sure Game, for she had a Share in the
hazard [p. 224]

[The editor saves space but the result is nonsense.]

10

Some of the Servants likewise us'd
me saucily, and had much ado to keep
their Hands off **of** me, the Master indeed was civiler to me than they; but
he would not yet let me go, tho' he
owned **he could not say I was** in his
Shop before. [p. 297]

The Servants likewise us'd me
saucily, and had much ado to keep
their Hands off me, the Master indeed
was civiler to me than they; but he
would not let me go, tho' **he own'd I
was** in his Shop before. [p. 254]

[The edited words allow a reversal of an essential detail.]

A   B

11

A	B
Then I thought we would both go first **with part of our Goods**, and that when we were Settled I should come back to *Virginia*, **and fetch the remainder**; [p. 405]	Then I thought we would both go first, and that when we were settled I should come back to *Virginia*; [p. 348]

[Moll is trying to find an excuse to return to Virginia; therefore, details are necessary.]

Clearly, some of the above illustrations may be mere composing-stick errors, for example, numbers 3 and 6; however, had Defoe himself revised the work, he would have been able to avoid many similar mistakes as well as some more serious ones, such as the misplaced paragraphs (see "Notes to the Text," 243.42) and the confusion over Jemmy's being sold as a "slave" in Virginia when he had supposedly volunteered for transportation ("Notes to the Text," 250.23–35). The editor of the first edition notices the confusion in each case, yet in the first instance, his revision still leaves the sequence of events garbled; and in the latter, his "corrections" serve only to accentuate inconsistencies in earlier descriptions. The point is that had Defoe edited his own work, a few strokes of his pen could have satisfactorily eliminated the two most difficult textual problems of the first edition. Is it not futile to imagine that Defoe, or any author, would merely correct and regularize spelling (a formidable task for Defoe in the light of his orthographical habits), revise minor grammatical errors, and change faulty word order while at the same time misread his own manuscript and leave unresolved the major problems that supposedly had triggered the need for "correction," and then, in an attempt at deletion, actually add more errors than he was able to expunge? No, we must simply conclude that unless some evidence becomes available attesting to Defoe's hand in the corrected second edition, the first edition of *Moll Flanders* is the only text of the novel which has his authority.

The little evidence demonstrating Defoe's practices in revision suggests that he made his changes in manuscript, before the copy was set in type. The editor of Defoe's *Complete English Tradesman* (fourth edition, London, 1738)[1] observed of Defoe's writing habits,

> That to have a complete Work come out of his hands, it was necessary to give him so much *per* Sheet to write it in his own way; and half as much afterwards to lop off its excrescences, or abstract it: And then, especially if it were on a *Trading subject*, no author of his time could produce a more finished performance.

We also have Defoe's letter (September 10, 1729) to the printer John Watts, who had intentions of publishing the *Compleat English Gentleman*:

> Sir
>   I am to ask your Pardon for keeping the Enclosed so long, Mr. Baker having told me your Resolution of taking it in hand and Working it off, But I have been Exceeding ill.

1. It has been conjectured that the author of this preface was Samuel Richardson, but the evidence is doubtful. The publishing history of Defoe's *Tradesman* is far from clear, and revisions are known to have been made both after Defoe's death and in his lifetime; therefore, the comment may be an effort to establish the 1738 edition as authoritative. See John Robert Moore, *A Checklist of the Writings of Daniel Defoe* (Bloomington, Ind., 1966), pp. 198–199.

I have Revisd it again and Contracted it Very Much, and hope to bring it within the Bulk you Desire or as Near it as Possible.

But this and Some Needfull alterations will Oblige you to much Trouble in the first sheet, perhaps allmost as bad as Setting it over again, which Can not be avoided.

I will Endeavour to send the Rest of the Coppy So Well Corrected as to give you Very little Trouble.

I here Return the first sheet[2] and as much Coppy as Will make near 3 sheets more. You shall have all the remainder So as not to let you stand still atall.

> I am, Sir, Your Most Humble Servt
> De Foe

Moreover, if we consider to be sincere the remarks aimed by Defoe at T. Cox, who had abridged *Robinson Crusoe* without authorization, we may conclude that he had little sympathy for a process that tended to mutilate the artistic integrity of his work.[3] In his preface to *The Farther Adventures of Robinson Crusoe* (1719), he complained that this kind of trimming eliminated the "just Application of every incident [and] the religious and useful Inferences drawn from every part," and that such a loss

> . . . makes the abridging this Work, as scandalous, as it is knavish and ridiculous, seeing, while to shorten the Book, that they may seem to reduce the Value, they strip it of all those reflections, as well religious as moral, which are not only the greatest Beauties of the Work, but are calculated for the infinite Advantage of the Reader. By this they leave the Work naked of its brightest Ornaments; and if they would, at the same Time pretend, that the Author has supply'd the Story out of his invention, they take from it the Improvement, which alone recommends that Invention to wise and good Men.[4]

And he goes on to threaten legal action[5] in the name of the "proprieter" of the work W. Taylor. The attack, of course, smacks of self-righteous indignation in part, and also of a desire to authenticate as well as protect sales of his *Farther Adventures*; yet at the same time Defoe was putting his finger on the main faults of the process of abridgment, which, at the expense of the serious reflections and moral sentiments of a work, tended to retain only its most sensational aspects. In this instance, the publisher was wholly on the side of Defoe; however, in the case of the second edition of

2. Professor Healey notes "that a copy of this sheet, with corrections in a hand other than Defoe's, has been preserved with the manuscript of the book in the British Museum," *Letters*, p. 473.

3. That Defoe paid little attention to improving his writings aesthetically, once they were in print, has been observed by Ian Watt, who cites the "prefatory apology for the poetic imperfections" of *The True-Born Englishman* (1701), a work Defoe regarded with pride: ". . . I shall be cavilled at about my mean style, rough verse, and incorrect language, things I indeed might have taken more care in. But the book is printed; and though I see some faults, it is too late to mend them. And this is all I think needful to say. . . ." (*The Rise of the Novel* [London, 1957], p. 99). Defoe, of course, did revise this poem, (e.g., he

eliminated lines 624–649 to pacify John Tutchin, whose journal rivaled the *Review*), but Watt's point, made on artistic grounds, remains valid.

4. I quote from Lee, *Life*, I, 296.

5. As owner of the work, Taylor would be the one to initiate legal action, which would have been time-consuming, expensive, and uncertain of results. However, Defoe's argument touches on the very points lawyers would pursue in cases of unauthorized abridgments later in the century, i.e., "that the best parts, the moral reflections, had been edited from the abridgement and only the plot remained." I quote from William J. Howard, "Literature in the Law Courts, 1770–1800," *Editing Eighteenth Century Texts*, edited by D. I. B. Smith (University of Toronto Press, 1968), p. 87.

Moll Flanders and Read's later piratical abridgement, we do not know what position the proprietor (that is, the holder of the copyright), Thomas Edlin, and his associates may have taken.

In the absence of any clear and persuasive evidence that Defoe had a hand in revising the second edition, I have adopted the first edition as copy-text. My main objective in editing the text is to preserve the words of Defoe with no intention toward improvement where meaning is intelligible and unambiguous to the modern reader. However, to avoid confusion, I have regularized the spelling of the following words throughout: Defoe's "bad" becomes "bade," "hast"/"haste," "least"/"lest," "loose"/"lose," "off"/"of" ("of"/"off"), "plaid"/"played," "prethee"/"prithee," "then"/ "than" ("than"/"then"), "vertue"/"virtue," and "whether"/"whither"; and where necessary I have corrected a few other spellings which might present the reader with undue difficulties. In most cases, barring accidentals, I believe the peculiar and obsolete spellings to be Defoe's own; and in every instance of departure from the spelling of the first edition (except in compositorial errors such as upside-down letters, obvious redundancies, etc.), I record the readings of both the first and second edition in the "Notes to the Text."

Just as Defoe was an erratic speller, so was he inconsistent in his use of capital letters and punctuation.[6] Undoubtedly capitals, italics, and punctuation marks (which are copious and often misleading) were supplied by the compositor, according to the printing customs of the day; in these cases proper names and terms of emphasis are set in italics. Moreover, in the absence of quotation marks to indicate dialogue, italics also appear to particularize a speaker; for example, *told him, says his* Brother, *I answer'd,* and the like. To add special stress or weight to words or phrases, generally, the printer variously used larger-point italic and Roman type: learnt to say NO, and YES, *says the Sister.* While I have made no changes in capital letters or italics, I have, again for the sake of clarity and readability, frequently been obliged to delete or add commas and semicolons; yet the punctuation, overall, reflects eighteenth-century usage.

Although I adjudge the second edition, corrected, to be inferior to the first, I have in a few cases adopted its readings. From the evidence cited above and in the "Notes to the Text," it appears that the corrector of the second edition had access to Defoe's manuscript, and in doubtful passages in the printed first edition he would have had recourse to the actual words of the original. On this assumption, in addition to the examples cited in note 7, above, I have relied on the second edition in the following noteworthy emendations: "Notes to the Text," 91.1–2, 120.10, 170.20, 183.14–15, 221.13–14, and 256.17. However, whenever I defer to the second edition or am forced to assume editorial prerogative to preserve the sense of a word or phrase which in both editions is obviously confused (or deleted in the second), I say so in the "Notes to the Text," which contain the words of both the first and second editions in every case of editorial alteration.

6. Professor Healey's point (*Letters,* viii). Defoe's letters show his use of italics to be quite sparing and usually applied only for emphasis and to foreign words and phrases.

NOTES TO THE TEXT

The abbreviations used in the textual notes are to the following editions:

A =   First Edition: The/FORTUNES/and/MISFORTUNES of the Famous/*Moll Flanders*, &c./Who was Born in Newgate, and during a/Life of continu'd Variety for Threescore Years,/ besides her Childhood, was Twelve Year a/*Whore*, five times a *Wife*/(whereof once to her/own Brother) Twelve Year a *Thief*, Eight/Year a Transported *Felon* in *Virginia*, at last grew *Rich*,/ liv'd *Honest*, and died a *Penitent*,/*Written from her own* Memorandums/LONDON: Printed for, and Sold by W./ Chetwood, at *Cato's-Head*, in *Russel-street*, *Covent-Garden*: and T. Edling, at/the Prince's-Arms, over-against *Exerter-Change*/in the Strand. MDDCXXI [sic 1721]

B =   ⌈ Second Edition "Corrected": The/FORTUNES/and MISFOR-TUNES/Of the Famous/*Moll Flanders*, &c./Who Was Born in/NEWGATE,/And during a Life of continu'd Variety for/ Threescore Years, besides her Childhood,/was Twelve Years a *Whore*, five Times a *Wife*/ (whereof once to her own *Brother*) Twelve/Years a *Thief*, Eight Years a Transported/*Felon* in *Virginia*, at last grew *Rich*, liv'd *Honest*,/and died a Penitent,/ *Written from her own* Memorandums/*The Second Edition*, *Corrected*./LONDON:/Printed for John Brotherton, at/the *Bible* in *Cornhill*, against the *Royal*/*Exchange*. MDCCXXII. [1722]

Another "second edition corrected" was printed and sold jointly by T. Edlin, W. Chetwood, W. Mears, J. Brotherton, C. King, and J. Stag, along with the separate Brotherton.

Third Edition "Corrected": The/FORTUNES/and/MISFOR-TUNES/Of the Famous/*Moll Flanders*, &c./Who was Born in/NEWGATE/And during a Life of continu'd Variety for/ Threescore Years, besides her childhood, was/Twelve Year a *Whore*, five times a *Wife* (whereof/once to her own Brother) Twelve Year a *Thief*,/Eight Year a Transported *Felon* in *Virginia*, at last,/grew *Rich*, liv'd *Honest*, and died a *Penitent*./ *Written from her own Memorandums*./The Third Edition, Corrected./LONDON:/Printed for, and Sold by W. Chetwood, at *Cato's-Head* in *Russel-street*, *Covent-Garden*; and/ T. Edlin, at the *Prince's-Arms*, overagainst/*Exeter-Change* in the *Strand*; W. Mears, at the/*Lamb* without *Temple-Bar*; J. Brotherton, by/the *Royal-Exchange*; C. King, and J. Stags, in/ *Westminister-Hall*. MDCCXXII. [1722]

Brotherton also sold a "third edition corrected," as he had the second edition.

N.B. In preparing the Norton Critical edition of *Moll Flanders,* I have relied on the British Museum's first and third editions, listed above. For the use of the Brotherton corrected second edition, I am indebted to the Lilly Library, Indiana University.

With these editions I have compared copies of the corrected second edition printed and sold by Chetwood, Edlin, *et al.,* in possession of the Olin Library, Cornell University, and the Brotherton corrected third edition in the Beinecke Rare Book and Manuscript Library, Yale University. (I have also examined the Brotherton third of the Newberry Library.) For further purposes of comparison I have relied on the first editions of the Beinecke and New York Public Library (Berg Collection).

3.26	A.	vitious; B: *vicious*
3.27	A:	leud; B: *lew'd*
3.36	A:	wick'd; B: *wicked*
4.5	A:	relateing; B: *relating*
4.20	A:	leud; B: *lew'd*
4.31	A:	Vertue; B: *Virtue*
4.36	A:	vertuous; B: *vertuous*
4.42	A:	vertuous; B: *vertuous*
4.44	A:	Vertue; B: *Virtue*
5.6	A:	first and last; B: *first or last*
5.10	A:	vertuous; B: *vertuous*
7.12	A:	know; B: knew
8.36	A:	whether; B: whither
9.13	A:	had also had; B: had also
9.20	A, B:	course
9.27	A:	Druge; B: Drudge
9.40	A:	were; B: where
10.2	A:	prethee; B: Prithee
10.2	A:	doest; B: do'st
11.17	A:	suddain; B: sudden
12.10	A:	familiar me
12.16	A:	Tutress; B: Tuteress
12.17	A:	by it to no more
13.25	A:	for by that time; B: for before [*The word* "that" *may represent the compositor's misreading of Defoe's symbols in manuscript; i.e.,* y^e = "the," *and* y^t = "that," *in which case the line would read,* "for by the time."]
13.43	A:	then; B: than

14.10   A: Tast; B: taste

15.13–14   A: But my new generous Mistress, for she exceeded; B: But my new generous Mistress had better Thoughts for me, I call her generous, for she exceeded [*Evidently the compositor accidently dropped this line of roughly fifty spaces (one line) in the first edition.*]

15.30   A: other

16.26   A, B: Vertue
16.27   A, B: vertuous

17.1   A, B: Patridge
17.6   A: begun; B: begin
17.26   A: has good; B: as good

18.10   A, B: spight

19.16   A: Vertue; B: Virtue

20.11   A: scarse; B: scarce
20.39   A: off; B: of
20.45   A: then; B: than

21.5   A: self denyal; B: Self-denial
21.13   A: Vertue; B: Virtue
21.23   A: Vertue; B: Virtue
21.24   A: Vertue; B: Virtue
21.38   A: Onely; B: only

23.29   A: whether; B: whither

24.17   A: Vertue; B: Virtue

26.40   A, B: sate

30.30   A, B: teize

31.1   A, B: joging
31.8   A: for I ought I; B: for ought I

32.13   A: than; B: then

34.15   A: Strugle

35.20   A: Prethee; B: Prithee
35.20   A: Beauties; B: Beauty's
35.39   A: loss'd; B: lost

36.8   A: any bodies; B: an body's
36.29   A: Sweet-heart; B: Sweet hearts

37.1   A: prethee; B: Prithee

38.2   A: Prethee; B: Prithee

39.27   A: strugle; B: struggle

40.5   A: without too; B: without it too
40.13 A: that way; B: the way [*See p. 13, line 25, above.*]
40.15 A: quiting; B: quitting

41.9   A: than; B: *Then*
41.14 A: least; B: *least*
41.15 A: thro'; B: *throw*

42.22 A: than; B: then

45.2   A: Vertue; B: Virtue
45.11 A: a do; B: ado

46.1   A, B: least
46.9   A: off; B: of

47.40 A, B: Madest
47.41 A, B: Vertue

48.35 A, B: Vertue

49.10 A: Whether; B: Whither
49.10 A: whether; B: whither

50.4   A, B: plaid
50.10 A: whether; B: whither
50.19 A, B: bad

52.20 A, B: spight

53.30 A: good a
53.40 A: carring; B. carrying
53.43 A, B: Vertue
53.45 A: recomend; B: recommend

54.3   A, B: Mein
54.15 A: unhapy; B: unhappy
54.16 A: Plie; B: Ply

58.10 A, B: plaid

59.12 A: uncomatable; B: uncomeatable

60.6   A: runs; B: run
60.13 A: for accepting; B: for not accepting

62.31 A: bare; B: bear

63.11 A: V*ertue*; B: V*irtue*

65.8   A: 1200l. Year; B: 1200l. a Year

67.8   A, B: least

69.14 A: of

72.33 A: of an another; B: of another

73.25 A, B: Villians

76.42 A: wast; B: waste

78.36 A: off; B: of

79.33 A, B: Auning

83.1 A, B: mannag'd
83.21 A: whether; B: whither

84.22 A: not none at; B: not now at

88.34 A: bad then me open; B: bad me open
88.34 A: Walnuttree; B: Walnut-tree
88.44 A, B: bad

89.39 A: Pallate; B: Pallet

90.11 A: Palate; B: Pallet

91.1–2 A: lye in the naked Bed; B: lye naked in the Bed

93.2 A: Travel; B: Travail

94.23 A, B: least

95.26 A: Wive's; B: Wife's
95.29 A: whether; B: whither
95.31 A: Wive's; B: Wife's

97.9 A: strook; B: struck
97.15 A: Aborrence; B: Abhorrence
97.32 ff. In the first edition the letter is set in Roman type with open parenthesis preceding each line.

98.24 A, B: least

100.11 A: thought hard of, yet; B: thought hard, but yet

101.14 A, B: council
101.19 A: siezing; B: seizing

102.34 A: whether; B: whither

107.34 A, B: least

110.25 A, B: bad
110.41 A: su'd; B: sued

111.12 A: whether; B: whither

114.28 A: sigh'd; B: high

118.23 A: riffle; B: rifle

119.26 A: Bagage; B. Baggage

120.10 A: A.E.; B: J.E.

121.33   A: whether; B: whither
121.37   A: whether; B: whither
121.42   A: gave him back; B: gave it him back

126.31   A: prety; B: pretty

128.23   A: Follow; B: follows

133.22   A: being two great; B: being too great

134.31   A: Tatling to her of; B: Tatling of

135.36   A: loose; B: lose

137.40   A: Mother, *says she*; B: Mother, *say I*

139.2   A: W*est-chester*; B: W*est-Chester*
139.5   A: least; B: lest
139.38–39   A: W*est Chester*; B: W*est-Chester*

141.37–38   A, B: too and again

142.13   A: vitious
142.18   A: occour'd; B: occurr'd

144.14   A, B: Guess [*See below, p. 262, line 18, just as* "comfortabless," *for* "most comfortable," *would be a correct but obsolete usage—and the one Defoe probably wrote—so* "Guess" *for* "Guests," *would be similarly acceptable.*]

145.18   A, B: least
145.32   A: I and; B: and I

146.14   A, B: least

149.11   A, B: *least*
149.24   A: whether; B: whither
149.25   A: whether; B: whither

150.13   A: whether; B: whither

151.20   A: whether; B: whither
151.36   A, B: bad

152.36   A: luging; B: lugging

153.3   A, B: about a 11 Yards [*An obsolete but correct form which evidently expresses spelled-out usages, such as,* "a leven" *or* "enleven."]

155.13–14   A: Peticoats; B: Petticoats
155.29   A, B: bad
155.31   A: Sellar; B: Cellar

156.24   A, B: plaid

157.15   A: taking off Gold Watches; B: taking of Gold Watches
[*The first edition is clear; the second edition change seems to strive for parallelism with* "stealing of Shop-Books."

161.4   A, B: bad

162.29   A: sincerely her; B: sincerely for her
162.35   A, B: Mileners

163.12   A, B: Course

167.25   A, B: plaid

168.41   A: whether; B: whither

169.18   A, B: bad

170.20   A: against them; B: against him

171.3   A: whether; B: whither
171.19   A, B: least

172.18   A: suddainly; B: suddenly

173.29   A, B: bad

174.13   A: aganst; B: against
174.19   A: Adventurers; B: Adventures
174.31   A: for while; B: for a while

175.9   A: first told he me; B: first he told me
175.35   A: unwilling go up; B: unwilling to go up

178.8   A, B: loose

183.14   A: long Tale with; B: long Talk with
183.15   A: long Talk of; B: long Tale of

184.26   A: Vertue; B: Virtue
184.32   A: whether; B: whither

185.23   A: sometime; B: some Time

186.24–26   A: I answer'd presently *Here*, do you belong to the *Barnet* Coach, *says she*? yes Sweetheart; B: I answer'd presently, *here*. Do you belong to the *Barnet* Coach? says she. Yes, Sweetheart.

186.29   A: hast; B: haste

187.5   A: Remarkble; B: Remarkable
187.11   A: hast; B: haste
187.24   A, B: *Cheston*
187.32   A: Vertue; B: Virtue
187.36   A, B: bad

188.27–28   A: Journeman; B: Journey-man

189.20   A, B: bad

190.1 ·A, B: bad

191.9 A, B: bad

192.42 A, B: bad

193.18 A: when he had; B: when I had

194.1 A, B: rod
194.35 A, B: gibbing

195.5 A, B: looser

196.10 A: believe; B: believ'd
196.13 A: told me was; B: told me he was

197.26 A: impious, cruelter, and relentless; B: imperious, cruel, and relentless
197.44 A, B: coursest

198.9 A, B: least
198.10 A, B: least
198.17 A: prety; B: pretty
198.19 A: seeing me stand by him, when he call'd;
B: seeing me stand by him, he call'd
198.22 A: carri'd; B: carry'd

200.40 A, B: too, and again

202.16 A, B: hast
202.23 A: hurring; B: hurrying
202.27 A: off; B: of

203.36 A, B: loose
203.40 A: the of; B: of the
203.43 A: had at the box; B: had the box

204.12 A, B: bad

205.27 A: their; B: there
205.36 A, B: bad

206.19 A: Portmanteuas; B: Portmantuas
206.21 A: Portmanteuas; B: Portmantuas
206.33 A: hast; B: haste

207.16 A: Portmanteua; B: Portmantua
207.17 A: for as; B: as for

208.9 A: I and; B: and I
208.27 A: that so; B: so that

209.15 A: Follow; B: Fellow
209.16 A: ones Days; B: one days

210.8 A: Historys left; B: History is left

212.15 A: acquisc'd; B: acquiesc'd

213.9   A, B: firery
213.10 A: then

215.14 A:and lieve so; B: and I believe so
215.25 A: and End; B: an End

217.28–29 A: waters . . . putrifies; B: water . . . peterifies [*while the second edition attempts to correct the error in subject-verb agreement of the first edition, i.e.,* "water-petrifies," *it falls into the pronoun-antecedent error,* "water-they."]

218.26 A: Stich; B: Stitch
218.32 A: then; B: than
218.33 A: became meer a; B: became a meer
218.36 A: so thro' a; so thoro' a

219.1   A: to Road; B: Road to
219.5   A: we were Prisoners were; B: we Prisoners were
219.25 A: Desperate that on; B: desperate on
219.27 A: then; B: than

221.13–14 A: to prevent the Grand Jury finding out one or two of the Jury Men; B: to prevent the Grand Jury finding the Bill; she went to several of the Jury Men . .

223.28 A, B: then

226.11 A, B: Sluces

229.11 A: off; B: of
229.12 A: than; B: then

230.38 A: imagin; B: imagine
230.39 A: feizible; B: feizable

231.31 A: on for this Account; B: on this Account

233.3   A: Feter'd; B: Fetter'd
233.43 A, B: *Heu*

235.35 A, B: Roberries

237.35 A: terify'd

238.3   A: off; B: of

239.4   A: the was; B: they were

243.42 [*At this point the second edition inserts the last two paragraphs on pp. 244–245 beginning,* In this Condition . . . *and ending,* I'll always take your Advice.]

245.15 A: chagrine; B: chagrin

246.30 A: chose; B: choose

247.13 A: what ever the demanded; B: whatever he demanded
247.25 A: and where; B: and were

249.6   A: 180; B: 108

250.23–35   A: [See text]; B: . . . He told me I must get some Body
in the Place to come and buy me as a Servant, and who must
answer for me to the Governor of the Country, if he demanded
me; I told him we should do as he should direct; so he brought
a Planter to treat with him, as it were for the Purchase of me
for a Servant, my Husband not being order'd to be Sold, and
there I was formally sold to him, and went a Shore with him:
The Captain went with us, and carried us to a certain House
whether it was to be call'd a Tavern or not, I know not, but
we had a Bowl of Punch there made of Rum, &c. and were
very Merry. After some time the Planter gave us a Certificate
of Discharge, and an Acknowledgement of having serv'd him
faithfully, and I was free from him the next Morning, to go
whether I would. [*While the second edition strives for technical correctness, it does not take into consideration Jemmy's
worsening circumstances in Newgate, nor the manner in which
he is treated initially.*]

250.35   A, B: whether

251.25   A: a Plantation; B: the Plantation

253.1–2   A: she the old Gentlewoman; B: she (the old Gentlewoman)

256.17   A: only Southern; B: most Southern

262.18   A: comfortabless; B: most comfortable [*see p. 144, line 14,
above.*]

263.4   A: deal money; B: deal of money

265.21   A, B: my Son (my Cousin)
265.26   A: told that; B: told him that

266.27   A: Wollen-Cloth; B: Woolen-Cloth
266.29   A: and to whole Peices also make; B: and whole Peices also,
to make

268.16   A: both of in good heart; B: both in good heart
268.17   A: remain; B: remain'd

Backgrounds and Sources

Spelling, capitalization, and punctuation of eighteenth-century texts in this section have, on the whole, not been modernized; and the aim of annotation is to supplement, not repeat, footnotes to the text of *Moll Flanders*. Centered asterisks in a selection denote the omission of complete paragraph. All notes to eighteenth-century material are the editor's. Editorial commentary on Mr. Howson's essay is marked [*Editor*] in each case.

[JOHN HALL]

[Hell Upon Earth]†

* * *

Now you must know, that this ancient Gaol is divided into three Parts; to wit, the *Press-yard*, *Master-side*, and *Common-side*; as for the Manner of the *Press-yard* Building, tho' there are glaz'd Windows to the several Chambers thereof, yet are they well fortified inwardly by *Vulcan's* Craft, for fear any of the Students therein shou'd, when they get drunk and mad, tumble out at the Casements; for those Sinners who lie there, having well lin'd their Pockets by their several Vices and Irregularities committed in contempt of the *Law* are pretty often elevated with outlandish Liquors, taking more delight by half to spend their Time in Tipling, than spare an Hour in a Day to pray for their Deliverance from the Burden of Affliction.

The only Air they enjoy here is in a Yard, whose length is scarce so much as one may swing a cat in it; and as for the breadth 'tis but indifferent. * * * But to make amends for this close Confinement, they have another Conveniency above the rest of their Fellow Students secur'd in the other side of the Prison; for in case it shou'd Rain, they have a small Piazza to walk under, where they strut about in as great State as a Beadle before a Poor Harlot (who is not able to hire a Coach) to Bridewell or New-Prison.[1]

When the Wind sits North, blustering *Boreas* blows strongly through the Grate Entrance, where if any Swordsman comes to speak with a confin'd Friend, he must deform himself, by leaving his Tail[2] with one of the Keepers, who, holding in his Hand (as he leans over the Hatch, or sits on the Bench, under the *Dog-Tavern* Window) a Key, almost as big as that put up for a Weather-Cock on St. *Peter's* Church in *Cornhill*.

Now, as concerning the Humours of the *Master-side*, when a Scholar in Iniquity comes to *Newgate*, by Virtue of a *Mittimus*,[3] which word sounds as terrible in his Ears, as *God-damn-me* in the

---

† From *Hell upon Earth; or, the Most Pleasant and Delectable History of Whittington's Colledge, otherwise (vulgarly) Called Newgate* (London, 1703). This pamphlet has been attributed to John Hall (d. 1707), a famous housebreaker who was imprisoned in Newgate; his biography was written by Paul Lorrain (d. 1719), Ordinary of Newgate. Richard Whittington (d. 1423) was Lord Mayor of London; he left a legacy for the specific purpose of rebuilding Newgate Prison.
1. Bridewell and New Prison housed mainly prostitutes, vagrants, and disorderly persons.
2. His sword.
3. A warrant of commitment.

hearing of a good *Christian*, he is deliver'd up to the Paws of the
Wolves, lurking continually in the *Lodge* for a Prey; where, as soon
as a *Scribler* records him for a Villain, he's adorn'd with a pair of
Iron Boots, and from thence conducted (provided he has *Gilt*) over
the way to Hell; for really, no Place has a nearer Resemblance of
that Eternal Receptacle of Punishment than the *Master-side*, for
the *Cellar* (where poor relentless Sinners are guzling in the midst of
Debauchery and new invented *Oaths*, which rumble like Thunder
through their filthy Throats) is a lamentable Den of Horror and
Darkness; there being no Light. In this *Boozing Ken*[4] (where more
than *Cimmerian* Darkness dissipates its horrible Gloom) the Students, instead of holding Disputes in *Philosophy* or *Mathematicks*,
run altogether upon *Law*; For such as are committed for Housebreaking, swear stoutly they can't be cast for *Burglary*, because the
Fact was done in the Day-time; Such as are committed for stealing
a Horse-Cloath or Coachman's Cloak, swear they can't be cast for
Felony and *Robbery*, because the Coach was standing still, not
stop'd; And such as steal before a Man's Face, swear they value not
their Adversary, because they are out of the reach of the new Act
against *Private-Stealing*. Thus with an unparallel'd Impudence,
every brazen'd Face Rascal is harden'd in his Sin, because the *Law*
can't touch his Life.[5] But when Night has spun her Darkness to the
length of Nine a Clock, then are they hurry'd up before their Driv-
ers (like so many *Turkish* Slaves) to their Kennels; which are joyn'd
in the same manner as the Soldiers Lousie Beds, in the Barracks of
Portsmouth or *Plymouth* Garrison: And as in all Places of Disorder
and Confusion, all things go by Contraries, so here, instead of the
Men lying over the Women, the Women lie over the Men; in
whose several Apartments, both Male and Female are confin'd, till
they Distill a little Oyl of *Argentum*,[6] for the Favour of going into
the *Cellar*, to spend their ill got Coyn with speed; to make the old
Proverb good, *Lightly come, Lightly go*: Or rather, *What's got
over the Devils Back, is Spent under his Belly.*

* * *

But now passing by that part of the *Master-side*, into which Prisoners are brought upon real suspicion of Debt, I shall proceed to
the Humours of the *Common-side*: Those Scholars that come here,
have nothing to depend on but the Charity of the Foundation, in
which side very exact Rules are observ'd; for as soon as a Prisoner
comes into the Turnkey's Hands, three knocks are given at the Stair

4. Drinking place; alcoholic drinks were
allowed prisoners who could pay for
them.
5. Legal terminology which distinguished
a felony from a misdemeanor was often
ambiguous, and the life of the accused
could depend on interpretation of a
statute. Moll reasoned that her own conviction might be adjudged a lesser crime
and, therefore, not punishable by death.
6. Grease the keepers' palms with silver.

Foot, as a signal a *Collegian* is coming up, which Harmony makes those *Convicts* that stand for the *Garnish*,[7] as joyful as one knock, the signal of the Baker's coming every Morning, does those poor Prisoners, who for want of Friends, have nothing else to subsist on but Bread and Water: And no sooner are the Three stroaks given, but out jump Four Trunchion Officers (who only hate Religion because it condemns their Vices) from their Hovel, and with a sort of ill mannerly Reverence receive him at the Grate; then taking him into their Apartment, a couple of the good natur'd Sparks hold him, whilst the other two pick his Pockets, claiming Six pence a piece as a priviledge belonging to their Office; then they turn him out to the Convicts, who hover about him (like so many Crows about a piece of Carrion) for *Garnish*, which is Six Shillings and Eight pence, which they, from an old Custom, claim by Prescription, Time out of Mind, for entering into the *Society*, otherwise they strip the poor Wretch, if he has not wherewithal to pay it. * * * Then after the Gray-Pease-Woman comes through *Newgate* crying, hot Gray-Pease, hot, hot, which is between Seven and Eight at Night, he is conducted down Stairs, with an Illumination of Links[8] to his Lodging, and provided he has a Shilling for civility Money, may lie in the *Middle Ward*, which to give the Devils their due, is kept very neat and clean; Where he pays one Shilling and Four Pence more to his Comrades, and then is free of the *Colledge*, and *Metriculated*.

But the *Lower ward*, where the tight slovenly Dogs lying upon ragged Blanckets, one would take to be *Old-Nick's* Backyard, where all the damn'd go to ease their roasted Arses; and trampling on the Floor, the Lice crackling under Feet, make such a noise, as walking on Shells which are strew'd over Garden-Walks. To this nasty Place is adjoyning the *Stone-Hold*, where Convicts lie, till a Free Pardon grants 'em Liberty from Tribulation; but not making good use of Mercy, come tumbling headlong in again. This low Dungeon is a real House of meagre Looks, and ill Smells; for Lice, Drink, and Tobacco is all the Compound.

When the Prisoners are disposed to recreate themselves with walking, they go up into a spacious Room call'd the *High-Hall*; where when you see them taking a Turn together, it would puzzle one to know which is the Gentleman, which the *Mechanick*, and which the *Beggar*, for they are all suited in the same Form of a kind of nasty Poverty, which is a Spectacle of more Pity than Executions; only to be out at the Elbows is in Fashion here, and a great indecorum not to be threadbare. On the North-side, is a small Room call'd the *Buggering Hold*; but from whence it takes its Name I

7. An unauthorized fee demanded of new prisoners by old inmates.   8. Torchlights.

cannot well tell, unless it is a Fate attending this Place, that some confin'd there, may have been addicted to *Sodomy*; here the *Fines*[9] lie, and perhaps, as he behaves himself, an outlaw'd Person may creep in among them: But what Degree of Latitude this Chamber is situated in, I cannot positively demonstrate, unless it lies Ninety Degrees beyond the *Artick-Pole*; for instead of being dark here but half a Year, it is dark all the Year round. The Company, one with another there, is but a vying of Complaints, and the Causes they have, to rail on the ill success of Petitions, and in this they reckon there is a great deal of Good Fellowship: There they huddle up their Life as a thing of no use, and wear it out like an old Suit, the faster, the better, and he that deceives the Time at Cards, or Dice, thinks that he deceives it best, and best spends it. Just by them lie the *Tangerines*, in a large room call'd *Tangier*, which next to the *Lower-ward* is the nastiest place in the Gaol; the miserable Inhabitants hereof are *Debtors* who put what sorry Bedding they enjoy upon such an Ascent, where Solders lie when on Guard at the *Tilt-yard*:[1] These poor Wretches are commonly next their Creditors, most bitter against the *Lawyers*, as Men that have had a great Stroak in assisting them there; a *Bailiff* likewise, they mortally hate, because he makes them fear the *Queen's* Name, worse than the *Devil's*: But in this Apartment lie, besides real Debtors, such as are call'd your *Thieving Debtors*; who having for Theft satisfy'd the Queen, by being *burnt* in the Face, or *Whipt*, which is no satisfaction to the wrong'd Subject.

* * *

But the place which is most diverting to our *Collegians* (who sin to better their understanding) is in the *Cellar*, whose *Newgate* Fashion of having all Tables publick, all the Alehouses about Town now imitate, where we sit in the pleasant Prospect of a Range of *Butts* and *Barrels*; and the only grievance herein, is the paying for *Pipes* and *Candles*, which are placed in square Pyramidal Candlesticks made of Clay.

* * *

Now if there should be any great Tumult or Uproar among the Prisoners, whose deepest Endearment is a communication of Mischief, then a Bell, which hangs over the *High-Hall* Stairs (to call the Turnkey, when out of the way, by single ringing, to let People in and out) is rung double; and at the Alarm, several Officers belonging to the Gaol, come running up to quell the Mutiny, which being appeased, the Ringleaders thereof (who are such high spirited Fellows, that would sooner accept the Gallows than a mean Trade) are conducted to a low Dungeon, as dark as the inside of

9. Those subject to pecuniary penalty.
1. An enclosed yard at Whitehall Palace, once used for sporting combat and tour-naments; Hall uses the term in a pun-ning sense to indicate that the debtors almost had to sleep standing up.

the *Devils Arse in the Peak*, and hung all over with spider Texture, and there Shear'd, or put into *Bilboes*,[2] and *Handcuffed*; but in case the Place of Punishment should be first taken up by any Fractious Woman, that's given to Penknife, then are they punish'd in the *Press-Room*, where Men that stand mute at their Tryal, are Pres'd to Death, by having their Hands and Feet extended out to Four Iron Rings fix'd to the ground, and a great heavy Press of Wood made like a Hog-Trough, having a square Post at each end, reaching up to the Ceiling, let up and down full of Weights, by Ropes them upon, in which Torment he lies Three or Four Days, or less time, according as favour'd; having no Food or Drink, but Black Bread, or the Channel Water which runs under the Gaol, if his fainting Pains should make him crave to Eat or Drink.

But now I am arrived to the Women Felons Apartment, in the *Common-side*; where I view'd a Troop of *Hell-Cats*, lying Head and Tail together, in a dismal nasty, dark Room: Having no Place to divert themselves; but at the Grate, adjoyning to the Foot Passage under *Newgate*, where Passengers[3] may with admiration and pity hear them swear *extempory*, being so shamefully vers'd in that most odious Prophanation of Heaven, that Vollies of Oaths are discharg'd through their detestable Throats, whilst asleep. And if any of their riotous Acquaintance gives them *L'argent*, then they jump into their *Cellar*, to melt it; which is scarce so large as *Covent-Garden* Cage, and the Stock therein not much exceeding those pedling *Victuallers*, who fetch their Drink in Tubs, every brewing Day; as for the *Sutler*[4] there, I have no more to say of her, than that her Purity consists in the whiteness of her Linnen; and that the Licentiousness of the Women on this side is so detestable, that it is an unpardonable Crime to describe their Lewdness; which Sex, when bad, exceeds the prophaneness of Man.

* * *

But when the Time's approach'd, that a Gaol Delivery is made, then the Prisoners are betimes in the Morning conducted down to the *Sessions-House* in the *Old Baily*, making as they go along a jingling with their Fetters, like so many *Morrice-Dancers* in the *Christmas* Holy-Days; and such *Malefactors* as will not give Half a Crown to be in the *Bail-Dock*, where Criminals both Male and Female are secur'd, go into the Hold, where they resemble so many Sheep penn'd up in *Smithfield* on a Market Day: There the eldest Prisoners claim Twelve pence a piece of the youngest for *Hold Money*, with which Collection they make shift to get some of 'em Drunk before they go up to the *Bar*, to be arraign'd, or try'd; the same odious Custom is likewise observ'd by the Women in their *Hold*. And if it shou'd be a Prisoners good luck to be acquitted, he

2. Shackles.
3. Passers-by.
4. Barmaid, proprietress.

kneels on his Knees, and crys, *God bless the Queen, and all the honourable Court,* then joyfully returning to his Comrades, they make him spend his *quit⁵ Shilling,* for his happy Deliverance. But after they are all try'd, the Judge proceeds to pass Sentence on the several Offenders, then those cast for *single Felony* are brought up; but such as never broke their Friends for Learning, not venturing a *non legit,*⁶ throw themselves on the Mercy of the Court, and escape marking with an ignominious *T,* by entering themselves in Her Majesty's service; and such as can read and claim the *Benefit of the Clergy,* a favour only design'd at first for Scholars, but now through long Custom, claim'd by the illiterate, are forc'd (upon the account of clearing the Land of Villains) to save their Bacon by Listing too.⁷ But profligate Women (having not this Advantage) are Glim'd⁸ for that Villainy, for which, rather than leave it, they could freely die Martyrs. Next, Sentence of Death is past on Malefactors; but upon this Point, the Women have a great Advantage over the Men by pleading their Bellies, who are then search'd by a Jury of Matrons, impanell'd for that Purpose, but either for favour or profit some are brought often in quick with Child (when they are not gone an Hour) to the great abuse of the honourable Court, not but that they deserv'd for it, but as the saying is, *No grass grows on the Highway.* Those cast for *Petit-Larceny,* shove the Tumbler, *i.e.* are whipt at the Cart's Tail.

The *Court* being broke up, and by an *O yes,* appointed to begin again at another certain Time, the Prisoners not cast for their Lives return from whence they came, the *Thieftakers* ogling them as earnestly as they trudge along (to know their shameless Faces another time) as a Gypsie does ignorant Country Wenches Hands, to tell their Fortune: But those Condemn'd, go to the Condemn'd *Hold,* there being two, one for Males, another for Females: Who being relentless Wretches, unmindful of a future State, make their dark dismal Den the rendezvous of Spittle, where they Dialogue (as in Tobacco-shops) with their Noses, and their Communication is Smoak. * * *

Next *Sunday* following their fatal Doom, they go to Chapel to hear Mr. *Ordinary* preach the Condemnation Sermon; which is full of strangers, to see more the miserable Wretches sit round the con-

5. Acquittal.
6. A felon who could read was granted "Benefit of Clergy," which meant that he could not legally be punished by death for his crime. The prison Ordinary would hand the prisoner a book printed in black-letter (a late Gothic type) and ask him to read. The judge would then ask, "Legitne vel non?" (Does he read or not?). If the prisoner were successful, the Ordinary would answer, "Legit ut Clericus" (He reads as a clerk or scholar

reads). A "non legit" (He doesn't read) would condemn the man. Benefit of Clergy was originally designed to protect clergymen from prosecution in secular courts, but gradually took on the meaning of "benefit of scholarship" and was applied to laymen as well. The term, however, did not apply to literate female felons.
7. To save their skins, they enlisted in the Queen's (Anne's) service.
8. Branded, marked.

demn'd Table than to hear what is piously deliver'd from the Pulpet: The other Prisoners being separated from the Congregation by such wooden Grates * * * and the *Dead-Warrant* sign'd, and sent to the *Sheriffs*, and the Day appointed for their dying, a *Bell Man*, at dead of Night rings his Bell under *Newgate*, and then with a dismal Voice calls the condemn'd Persons to hear the following Speech.

> *All you that in the condemn'd Holds do lie,*
> *Prepare you, for to Morrow you shall die;*
> *Watch all and pray, the Hour's drawing near,*
> *That you before th' Almighty must appear:*
> *Examine well your selves, in time repent,*
> *That you may not t'eternal Flames be sent;*
> *And when St. Pulcher's Bell, to morrow, tolls,*
> *The Lord above have Mercy on your Souls.*

On the morning they die, they are brought from their dark Den (a lively Type of the Grave) to Chapel, where such as are disposed receive the blessed *Sacrament*; then brought into the *Stone-Hall* (where formerly Charity has been begg'd in old Shoes, hanging out at the Grates) their Irons are knock'd off, and the Yeoman of the Halter, there adorns them with a hempen Garment, which is to espouse them to a better World, according as their Contrition is sincere in this: Which solemn Ceremony performed, they are conducted down Stairs to the Cart, in which being seated and ty'd, a *Subaltern*,[9] with a white Wand, and Guard of *Serjeants* conveys them to the *World's end*; but in their final Voyage, they stop near the West-end of St. *Pulcher's* Church, where a Fellow leans over the Wall, tingling a small Bell, and makes a short *Harangue*, putting them in mind of their latter end; which ended, they proceed onwards again, the Bell tolling at St. *Andrew's* Church, as they ride backwards up the Hill, the same solemnity being likewise observed at Saint *Giles* Church; where by the *Pound* they may perhaps make another stop at the *Crown*,[1] to enliven their drooping Hearts with a Glass of *Canary*; then away they ride again, sometimes looking on the Mob, among whom they may chance to espy some of their ill Consorts following them to pick Pockets at *Tyburn*; other times casting up their Eyes (if endu'd with so much Grace) towards that Sacred Place, against which they have too often offended; next, with great earnestness throwing up their Hands (which are commonly deck'd with White gloves, book in one, and Nosegay or Orange[2] in t'other) in commiseration of the untimely end they've brought on themselves, and Disgrace to their Friends; then being arriv'd to the *Triple-Tree*,[3] consecrated by the Romish Church, for several of

9. Army officer.
1. A tavern on the route to the gallows.
2. To help overcome the stench of sweat and accumulated filth of the condemned in the wagon.
3. Tyburn, the gallows.

their *Martyrs* dying thereon, they declare their perplexed minds to Mr. *Ordinary*, and make a short speech to the People, whilst Mr. *Catch*[4] ogles their Habit, and gives instructions to his Man, who waits upon him with a Bag, in which he crams the Hats, Perukes, Neckcloths, and rest of the Cloaths of the executed Persons; but penitential Psalm being sung, and Night-cap pull'd over the Eyes, the Cart's drawn away, and with Dismal Screeches they bid the World adieu.

After swinging an Hour between Heaven and Earth, as unworthy of either, they are cut down, stript, and tumbled into a *Highway-grave* together, against *Hyde-Park* Gate, unless their Friends buy them for interment or *Chyrurgeons*[5] beg their Carcasses for Anatomizing Operations. This is all the Description I can give of this Place, whose Horror I hope may so much work on irregular Persons for the future, as to make them forsake wicked Courses; and it is my Wish that honest People will be more wary of giving Opportunities to graceless Wretches, who value not the Misery of this Mansion, where Villains Breathe their Discontents against *Magistracy* more securely, and have their Tongues at more liberty than abroad; and to conclude, this is a School which teaches much Wisdom, but too late, and with Danger; and it is better be a Fool than come here to learn it.

[DANIEL DEFOE]

[Luxuries Before Loved-Ones] †

It is a Remark of my own, but, perhaps, too well to be justified by the Experience of most who shall read this Paper, that tho' the Trade of the Nation, by the Confession of all Men of Sense, was *never* more decayed, Money *never* scarcer, the Number of Bankrupts *never* greater, the Cries of the Poor *never* louder, and the rate of Provisions, for some Years past, one with another, *never* higher; yet the Pride, the Luxury, the Expensive Way of Living, the costly Furniture and Ostentation, both in Equipage, Cloaths, Feeding and Wearing, were never greater in this Nation.

* * *

I remember an Accident, which gave me a Sketch of this very

4. Jack Ketch (d. 1686) executioner. The name Jack "Catch" became an allusion to official hangmen.
5. Unclaimed corpses were often used by surgeons for experimental purposes and in classes of anatomy.
† From the *Review*, a periodical which Defoe wrote and edited for over nine years (February, 1704–June, 1713). The *Review* sometimes touched on topics and incidents which Defoe later used to advantage in his novels. The paragraphs omitted from this issue of the *Review* (I [IX], 53 [January 31, 1713]) discuss extravagance, bankruptcy, and the condition of trade in England.

Thing, and which I could not avoid taking Notice of: Sometime since, being upon Business, *very late*, in the City, it was my Lot to come along the Street, just as a sudden and terrible Fire broke out in a Citizens House, *in none of the Wealthiest part of the Town neither*; I forbear the Place, for the sake of the Particulars.—I could contribute little to the helping the Good People in their Distress; nor was I very well qualified to Carry Water, or Work an Engin; besides the Street was presently full of People for that Work: But, I plac'd my self in a convenient Corner, near the Fire, to look on, and, indeed, the Consternation of the Poor People was not fruitless of Remarks.

And First, I was, I confess, surprized to hear the Shreeks and Lamentations of the Poor Ladies, as well in the Houses on either side, as opposite to the House that was on Fire; after the first Fright was express'd with a great deal of Noise, terrible Gestures and Distortions, I observ'd all hands at Work to Remove: The Chamber-Maids were hurried down Stairs, *Betty, Betty*, says a Lady, aloud you may be sure, *have you got the Plate?* Yes, Madam, says *Betty*: *Here take the Cabinet*, says Madam, *Run to my Mothers; there's all my Jewels, have a Care of them Betty*: Away runs *Betty*: This, I think, was about the Degree of a Fish-monger's Lady—At a House that was in great Danger, they were, like Sea-Men in a Storm to lighten the Ship, throwing their Goods out at Window; and, *Indeed, I think, they had as good have let them be burnt*: Here I saw, out of a *Shopkeeper's* House, Velvet Hangings, Embroidered Chairs, Damask Curtains, Plumes of Feathers; and, in short, Furniture equal to what formerly suffis'd the greatest of our Nobility; thrown into a Street flowing a Foot Deep with Water and Mud, trodden Under-Foot by the Crowd, and then carried off Piece-Meal as well as they could: It was not the Fright the People were in, of the Error of their destroying their Goods in that Hurry that was so much matter of Observation to me, as to see the Furniture that came out of such Houses, far better than any Removed at the late Fire, at the *French* Ambassadors.

In the House which I stood nearest to, which was opposite to the Fire, and which was in great Danger too, the Wind blowing the Flame, which was very Furious, directly into the Windows; The Woman, or Mistress, or Lady, call her as you will, had several small Children; her Maids, or Nurses, or whatever they were, made great Diligence to bring the Poor Children half naked and asleep, Down-Stairs in their Arms; and wrapping them up carefully, run out of the House with them; One of the Maids coming again, as if to fetch Another, meets her Mistress, whose Concern, it seems, lay another way with a Great Bundle, the Mistress screams out to her, *Mary, Mary, Take care of my Cloaths; Carry them away; I'll go fetch the Rest*: The Maid, more concern'd for the Children, than the Mother, *Cries out louder* than her Mistress, *Lord, Madam, Where's Master* Tommy? *The Child will be burnt in the Bed*: Throws down the Cloaths, and runs up Stairs: The Mistress, whose fine Cloaths lay nearer her Heart, than her Child, Cries out, *Oh! There's all my Cloaths*; Snatches up the Great Bundle, and runs out of the House half naked, with it, and leaves the Wench to go fetch her Child; who, Poor Lamb, was almost suffocated with the Smoke and Heat.

The Mother was back again in an Instant, with two or three Porters and some Friend's Servants which she had got to help her; and away they run up Stairs with her, and came down as quickly, laden with Baskets, and Bundles of Rich Goods; and about half an Hour after, when the Good Lady had discharged her Passions of those Things that lay nearest her Heart, and was come a little to her Memory, I saw her in Dreadful Fury, Raving and Skreaming, and tearing her Hair for her Child; Her Child, Oh, her Child! for the House had taken Fire on the Top, and there was no bearing to be in the Rooms; and she remembered the Wench had cryed out, that the Child was in its Bed; but never saw the Maid who had fetch'd the Poor Child down, at the Hazard of her own Life, and had carried it well away, and came not back for some time; at last, Word was brought her that the Child was safe.

This scene eased me of the Wonder I had been in, to see our Citizens, who go all Day with Blue Frocks, and Blue-Aprons, Dirty Hands, and foul Linnen, have their Chambers hung with Velvet, and their Wives with Jewels: How should it be otherwise, when the Ladies love their Cloaths and Furniture so much better than their Children, and no doubt, as much in proportion, better than their Husbands Prosperity?

*   *   *

ALEXANDER SMITH

[Moll Hawkins, a Shop-Lift] †

This unfortunate Creature permitting her inclination to introduce her very early into all sorts of Vanity and to give Sense the

† From Captain Alexander Smith, *The History of the Lives of the Most Noted Highway-Men, Foot-pads, House-Breakers, Shoplifts, and Cheats of both Sexes . . . for above fifty Years last past*, 2nd ed., I (London, 1714). By the year 1719, this popular work had appeared in five editions. "Alexander Smith" is probably a pseudonym.

Preheminence above Reason, her Wits were always put on the Rack of Invention to support her in Actions which ever tended to meer Debauchery; for the greatest Darkness that ever muffled up our Hemisphere in Obscurity, could not exceed the Blackness of her Soul, which had been dead and rotten in Trespasses and Sin, long before she made her *Exit* on the Triple-Tree. Adultery and Fornication were her common Recreations, as well as Shop-lifting, for which last Crime, altho' she had seen many of her Acquaintance Monthly made Examples, yet would she not forebear nor desist from such Irregular and Life-destroying Courses, till it had brought her to the like miserable Catastrophe. But before *Moll Hawkins* projected Shop-lifting, she went upon the *Question-Lay*, which is putting herself into a good handsome Dress, like some Exchange Girl,[1] then she takes an empty Band-box in her Hand, and passing for a Milliner's or Sempstress's 'Prentice, she goes early to a Person of Quality's House, and knocking at the Door, she asks the Servant if the Lady is stirring yet; for if she was, she had brought home, according to order, the Suit of Knots,[2] (or what else the Devil puts in her Head) which Her Ladyship had bespoke over Night; then the Servant going up Stairs to acquaint the Lady of this Message, she in the mean time robs the House, and goes away without an Answer. Thus she one Day serv'd the Lady *Arabella Holland*, living in *Soho-Square*, when the Maid going up Stairs to acquaint her Ladyship that a Gentlewoman waited below with some Gloves and Fans, *Moll Hawkins* then took the Opportunity of carrying away above fifty Pounds worth of Plate, which stood on a Side-Board in the Parlor, to be clean'd against[3] Dinner-time.

Moll Hawkins, otherwise call'd *Fudge*, from her living with a Fellow of that Name, who was a most notorious Pick-pocket, was Condemn'd on the 3d of *March*, 1702 for privately stealing Goods out of the Shop of Mrs. *Hobday* in *Pater-noster-row*. She having been repriev'd for nine Months, upon the account of her being then found to be quick with Child, tho' she was not, she was now call'd down to her former Judgment. When she came to the Place of Execution at *Tyburn*, on *Wednesday* the 22d of *December* 1703, She said she was about twenty-six Years of Age, born in the Parish of St. *Giles's* in the Fields; that she serv'd three Years Apprenticeship to a Button-Maker in *Maiden-Lane*, by *Covent-Garden*, and follow'd that Employment for some Years after; but withal gave way to those ill Practices which she now finds to be the Cause of her shameful Death.

1. Working girl from a shop in the Exchange.
2. Suit adorned with lace or ribbons tied in knots.
3. Before.

ALEXANDER SMITH

[Anne Holland, a Pick-Pocket] †

This was her right Name, tho' she went by the Names of
Andrews, Charlton, Edwards, Goddard, and *Jackson,* which is very
usual for Thieves to change them, because falling often-times into
the Hands of Justice, and as often convicted of some Crimes, yet
thereby it appears sometimes that when they are arraign'd at the
Bar again, that is the first Time that they have been taken, and the
first Crime whereof they have ever been accus'd; moreover, if they
should happen to be cast, People, by not knowing their right
Names, cannot say, the Son or Daughter of such a Man or Woman
is to be whip'd, burnt, or hang'd on such a Day of the Month, in
such a Year; from whence would proceed more Sorrow to them
that suffer'd, as well as Disgrace to their Parents. For this Reason,
many such Persons are indicted with an *alias* prefix'd to several
Names. * * * But as concerning *Anne Holland,* her usual Way of
Thieving, was the *Service-Lay,* which was hiring herself for a Servant in any good Family, and then, as Opportunity serv'd, robb'd
them: Thus, living once with a Master Taylor in *York-Buildings* in
the *Strand,* her Mistress was but just gone out to a Christening as
her Master came Home booted and spurr'd out of the Country, and
going up into his Chamber where she was making his Bed, he had a
great Mind to try his Manhood with his Maid, and accordingly
threw her on her Back; but she made a great Resistance, and would
not grant him his Desire without he pull'd off his Boots; whereupon
she first pluck'd one off, and whilst she was pulling off the other,
one knocking at the Door, she ran down Stairs taking a Silver Tankard off the Window which would hold two Quarts, saying, she
must draw some Beer, for she was very dry: However, she returning
not presently, poor *Stitch*[1] was swearing, and staring, and bawling
for his Maid *Nan,* to pull off his t'other Boot, which was half on
and half off, but being extraordinary tight, could neither get his Leg
farther in nor out: And there he might remain 'till Dooms-day for
Nan, for she was gone far enough off with the *Wedge,* that's to say,
Plate, which she had converted into another Shape and Fashion in a
short time.

And once *Nan,* having been at a Fair in the Country, and
coming up to London, she lay at *Uxbridge,* where being a good Pair
of *Holland* Sheets to the Bed, she was so industrious as to sit up

† From Captain Alexander Smith, *Lives,*
2nd ed., I (London, 1714).

1. Cant term for "lying with a woman,"
usually a verb.

most part of the Night, to make her a couple of good Smocks out of one of 'em; so in the Morning, putting the other Sheet double towards the Head of the Bed, she came down Stairs to Breakfast. In the Interim, the Mistress sent up her Maid to see if the Sheets were there, who turning the single Sheet a little down as it lay folded, she came and whisper'd in her Mistress's Ear, that the Sheets were both there; so *Nan* discharging her Reckoning, she brought more Shifts to Town than she carry'd out with her; and truly she had a pretty many, or else she could not have liv'd as she did for some Years.

This unfortunate Creature, at her first launching out into the Region of Vice, was a very personable young Woman, being clear-skinn'd, well shap'd, having a sharp piercing Eye, a proportionable Face, and exceeding small hand; which natural Gifts serv'd rather to make her miserable, than happy; for several lewd Fellows flocking about her, like so many Ravens about a Piece of Carrion, to enter her under *Cupid's* Banners, and obtaining their Ends, she soon commenc'd and took Degrees in all manner of Debauchery; for if once a Woman passes the Bounds of Modesty, she seldom stops, 'till she hath arriv'd to the very Height of Impudence.

* * *

Nan Holland being thus oblig'd to shift among the Wicked for a Livelihood, for though but young, yet could she cant tolerably well, wheedle most cunningly, lie confoundedly, swear desperately, pick a Pocket dexterously, dissemble undiscernably, drink and smoak ever-lastingly, whore insatiately, and brazen out all her Actions impudently. A little after this Disaster, she was marry'd to one *James Wilson*, an eminent Highway-Man, very expert in his Occupation.

* * *

ALEXANDER SMITH

[Mary Carleton, Cheat, Thief, and Jilt]†

The Meanness of her Quality did not suit with her Spirit, and although she intended for herself no less a Fortune than a Knight or some great Man to be her Husband, yet she fail'd in her Expectation, for she was marry'd to one *Stedman* a Shoe-maker, by whom she had two Children, which soon died. But her Husband's Condi-

---

† From Captain Alexander Smith, *Lives*, 2nd ed., II (London, 1714). Smith retells Francis Kirkman's popular criminal biography, *The Counterfeit Lady Unveiled* ... *Life* ... *Actions* ... *and Death of that Famous Cheat Mary Carleton, Known by the Name of the German Princess* (1673).

tion being so mean, that he was not able to maintain her at that
Height which she always aim'd at, she was discontented, and was
resolv'd to seek her Fortune; so eloping from her Husband, she
went and married one Mr. *Day* a Surgeon at *Dover;* then she was
indicted for having two Husbands, but so carry'd the Matter that
she was acquitted, and this embolden'd her to undertake a third
Marriage with one *John Carleton*, which was the first Occasion of
her being publickly taken Notice of in *London*, for her former Marriages being discover'd to her last Husband's father, he took her up
with a Warrant, by Virtue whereof she was committed to the
Gate-House at *Westminster;* from whence after six Weeks Imprisonment she was carry'd to *Newgate*, then taking her Tryal at the
Old-Baily, where the Evidence was not sufficient to convict her, she
was acquitted once more of Bigamy.

* * *

After she came out of *Newgate*, she being generally acquainted
with, resorted to the Players in Hopes of gaining by entertaining as
an Actress. She who had acted on the large Theatre of the World
in publick now came to act in a small Theatre; we cannot say in
private, for it was publick enough at all times, but much more when
she presented her Part thereon, for it was a Play of her own self she
acted in; it was stil'd by her glorious Name of *The* German *Princess*,[1] the Epilogue whereof was spoken by herself, and is as follows.

> *I've past one Tryal, but it is my Fear*
> *I shall receive a rigid Sentence here;*
> *You think me a bold Cheat, put Case 'twere so,*
> *Which of you are not? Now you'd swear I know.*
> *But do not, lest that you deserve to be*
> *Censur'd worse than you can censure me.*
> *The World's a Cheat, and we that move in it,*
> *In our Degrees, do exercise our Wit;*
> *And better 'tis to get a glorious Name,*
> *However got, than live by common Fame.*

* * *

She went to a Mercer's Shop in *Cheapside* with her pretended
Maid, where agreeing for as much Silk as came to 6 *l.*, she pull'd
out a Purse to pay him, but having nothing but Gold in it, which
she was loth to part with, she desir'd the Mercer to let his Servant
ride along with her in the Coach which was at the Door to her
House, and she would pay him in Silver. The Mercer, willing to
accommodate his Customer, order'd his Servant to attend her,
whereupon being all coach'd, as they were riding along, she order'd the Coachman to set her down at the *Royal Exchange* to

1. The title of Defoe's *Roxana* (*The Fortunate Mistress*, 1724) suggests that the heroine was once the German Count-ess de Wintelsheim.

buy her some Knots suitable to the Colour of her Silk. Being arriv'd there the *German Princess* and her Maid alighting, she said
to the Mercer's Man, *Friend, you may sit here in the Coach, while
I and my Maid go up, and buy a few odd Things, and we will
instantly return.* The young Man thought it good Manners to obey
her Ladyship, and therefore sat still, permitting her Woman to take
the Silk to match with Ribbons, as they said, so they tript it up
Stairs, leaving the young Novice to take a Nap in the Coach; but it
might have bin a long one, had he stay'd till their Return, for
he ne'er saw 'em again.

A little after transacting this Project, she went to a *French*
Weaver in *Spittle-fields,* where seeing several Sorts of Silk, she
agreed for as much as came to 40 *l.,* but examining her Pocket she
had nothing but Gold, and not enough of that neither; wherefore
she tells him, that he must either go or send with her, and take his
Money. Accordingly the Weaver himself went with her in a Coach,
and as they were riding along, her Impudence also asking him where
she might buy some Gold and Silver Lace, he directs her to a
Friend of his; thither the Coachman was ordered to drive, who did
so, and she seeing and liking the Commodity agreed for as much as
came to 20 *l.;* she tells that Man as he had done the Weaver, that
he must go, or send with her, and receive his Money: The Lace-
man seeing his Friend the Weaver there, not doubting any thing,
did not think it necessary to go himself, but sent his Man, supposing him to be sufficient, and so they enter'd the Coach, ordering
the Coach-man to drive to the Lady's Lodgings. Thither being
come, she conducts 'em up Stairs, calls her Waiting-Woman to
bring a Bottle of Wine, that is brought, and they drank; she fetches
a Bag of Money, suppos'd to be 50 or 60 *l.,* chinks it on the Table,
but being about to open it, calls to her Attendant to bring Pen,
Ink, and Paper, and says to the Weaver and Lace-Man, *I must
desire you both to write down the Quantity and Prices of your
Goods, that I may have no Mistake, for I buy half of it for a Niece
of mine, who is above in her Chamber.* They were content with this,
and began to write, her Bag of Money and Hand on it was still on
the Table, and then she calls to her Attendant, *Here,* said she to
her, *carry this Silk and Lace to my Niece, and see how she likes it.*
The Attendant takes it away; and one of the two had now made
out his Bill, and the other begins to do so, she takes it in her hand
as to peruse it, walks 3 or 4 Steps towards a Curtain and turns in
there. The other had by and by made his Bill, and they both
expected the Return of the Lady with the Money, but she intends
no such Matter, they had seen their last of her; to conclude, after
much Stay they call and knock, and that so loudly, that one from
below came up, asks what is the Matter; they enquire for the Lady,

are answer'd, they know nothing of her, but thought she had been still with them; they draw the Curtain, and search the Room, but find no Body, but to their great Grief, see a Door and back-Pair of Stairs, which they concluded she and her Woman had went. * * *

A little after this she stole at least half a score Silver Tankards in *Covent-Garden, Milford-lane, Lothbury, New-Market, West-smith-field,* and several other Places; and for one of these Adventures was she at last taken and indicted, found guilty, condemn'd, repriev'd, and transported to *Jamaica;* where she had not been above Two Years, before she came to *England* again, and by pretending to be a rich Heiress, she was marry'd to a rich Apothecary at *Westminster,* whom she rob'd of above 300 *l.* in Money, and then ran away. Next taking Lodgings at *Charing-Cross,* she there invited her Landlady, and a Watch-maker lodging in the same House, to go see a Play at the Duke's Theatre in *Dorset-Garden;* in the mean time her Maid breaking open a Chamber-Door where she lodg'd, and a Trunk, she took thereout above 200 *l.* ready Money in Gold and Silver, and about 30 rich Watches, so that the Prize was in all valu'd at about 600 *l.* which she carry'd to her Mistress the *German Princess,* who after the Play was over, inviting her Landlady, and the Watch-maker to the *Green Dragon Tavern* in *Fleet-street,* she there gave them the Slip.

* * *

[Daniel Defoe]

[A Letter from Moll of Rag-Fair]†

Saturday, July 16, 1720.

To the Author of the Original Weekly-Journal.

Sir,

I find many People send their Cases to *Public Writers* for their Advice, and I suppose receive Satisfaction by the Answers their Eminences give them back again; or that the making their Cases Publick is *in its self* something of Assistance to them in the several Circumstances they are in, otherwise they would never give themselves and the Authors of *Journals* so much Trouble; now my Case being Extraordinary, you will easily see I have at least as much

† John Robert Moore points out that Defoe was a "principal contributor at times, and at intervals he influenced or controlled the editorial policy" of *Applebee's Journal,* which was first called *The Original Weekly Journal.* Defoe's association with this publication began in June, 1720, and formally ended in May, 1726; see *A Checklist of the Writings of Daniel Defoe* (Bloomington: Indiana University Press, 1960), pp. 231, 234.

reason to make it Public as other People, and therefore I desire to be heard with Patience.

I am, Sir, an *Elder,* and well known Sister, of the *File,* but lest all the Readers should not understand the Cant of our Profession, you may take it in plain *English,* I was, in the former part of my Life, an eminent *Pick-Pocket,* and you may observe also that while I kept in the Employment I was bred up to, I did very well, and kept out of Harms way, for I was so Wary, so Dexterous, kept so retir'd to my self, and did my Work so well, that I was never detected, *no never,* was never pump'd, never taken, and I may add I began to lay up Money, and be before-hand in the World; not that I had any Thought of leaving off my Trade neither; no, nor ever should have done it, if I had been as rich as the best of my Trade in *Exchange Alley.*

But *Curse of ill Company,* I was unhappily drawn a-side out of my ordinary and lawful Calling into the dangerous Business of *Shop-lifting,* and being not half so clever and nimble at that as I was at my own Trade, I was nab'd by a plaguy Hawks-Ey'd Journey-Man *Mercer,* and so I got into the Hands of the Law. It went very hard with me upon this Occasion, and to make my Story short, I run thro' all the *several Ways of being Undone;* I mean the *Newgate* Ways, for I was Tryed, Condemn'd, pleaded my Belly, had a Verdict of the *Jades* they call Matrons in my Favour, and at length having obtain'd a suspicion of Hanging, I got to be Transported.

How I was sent over, or whether sent over or no, and of what use the little Money I had laid up *as above,* has been to me in all my Tribulation, is not to the present Purpose, and besides is too long a Story to tell in a Letter; it may suffice to the Case in hand to let you know, *and the World by your Means,* that I am at the present Writing hereof among the Number of the Inhabitants of *Old England;* whether I was Transported, what Adventures I met with abroad, *if I was abroad,* and how I came hither again, I say, are too long for a Letter;[1] *But here I am.*

Now as my being here is a new Tresspass, and may bring me back to the Gallows, from whence it may be *truly* said I came, I am not quite so easie as I was before, tho' I am prudently retir'd to my first Employ, and find I can do pretty well at it; but that which makes me more in Danger is the meeting Yesterday with One of my old Acquaintance; he salutes me publickly in the Street, with a long out-cry, *O brave Moll,* says he, *Why what do you do out of your Grave? Was not you Transported?* Hold your Tongue *Jack,* says I, for God's Sake, what have you a mind to ruin me?

---

1. Moll's insistence that her story is too long for a letter seems to hint at the forthcoming "history."

D——me, says he, *you Jade* give me a Twelver[2] than, *or I'll tell this minute;* I was forc'd to do it, and so the Rogue has a Milch Cow[3] of me, as long as I live.[4]

But this is not all, for it may happen, that I may miscarry in my Business too, and if once I come into the Hands of the unmerciful again, I am gone for ever; pray give your Advice, how such a dexterous Sinner, *as I am*, must go on, for this kind of Life does not do now, so cleverly as it us'd to do:

your Friend and Servant,
Moll.

T. READ

[Her Last Will and Testament] †

* * *

Thus I past my latter Days in a total Resignation of myself to the Will and Pleasure of my heavenly Father, till he was pleas'd to visit me with a *Dropsie* and *Asthma,* or Shortness of Breath, whereby finding Nature daily to decay more and more, and that I was not a Woman for this World long, I began to set my House hold in Order, and made my last Will and Testament as follows:

I *Elizabeth Atkins,*[1] of the City of *Galway,* in the County of *Galway,* (being at this Time in good and perfect Memory, thro' the Mercy of God, but weak and sickly in Body) do make this my last Will and Testament, in Manner following; that is to say, I give to my deceased Husband's Brother, *Charles Carrol,* all my real Estate, lying about Athlone, in the Counties of *Roscommon,* and *West-Meath,* and to his Heirs and Assigns for ever.

Item, I give to my Gardiner, *Henry Kelly,* the sum of 50 Pounds of current Money of *England.*

2. Twelve pence.
3. Newgate slang for "a favor"; he will be able to "milk" Moll in the future.
4. Gerald Howson contends that the rogue who was blackmailing this Moll (who Howson says is really Moll King, from whose life Defoe derived his story of Moll Flanders) was none other than the infamous Jonathan Wild. See *Thief-Taker General: The Rise and Fall of Jonathan Wild* (London: Hutchinson, 1970), p. 162. See also Howson's essay "Who Was Moll Flanders?" (p. 312–319, below).
† Moll is speaking in this excerpt from

T. Read's abridged edition, *The Life and Actions of Moll Flanders* (London, c. 1723). Unlike Defoe's conclusion, Read sees Moll through her death and burial (chapbooks generally followed Read's version, but sometimes buried her in Virginia).
1. Striving for realism, Read assigns this name to Moll. As a child, Moll is called "Betty," a common name for maidservants in the literature of the period. Some later abridgements and adaptations used "Laetitia Atkins" as Moll's name. "Atkins" has long been a common British family name.

Item, To *Jane Burke*, my Chamber-maid, I give the Sum of 40 Pounds.

Item, To *Catherine O-Neal*, my Cook-Maid, I give the Sum of 30 Pounds.

Item, To *Dorothy Macknamarra*, my House-maid, I give the Sum of 20 Pounds.

Item, To my deceas'd Husband's Brother, *William Carrol*, I give all the rest of my Goods, and Chattels, and personal Estate whatsoever; but out of the same to be decently interr'd, and all Funeral Charges to be paid, by the said *William Carrol*.

Lastly, I make and constitute my abovesaid Brother-in-law, *Charles Carrol*, Executor of this my last Will and Testament, written with my own Hand this 30th Day of *March*, in the Year of our Lord Christ, according to the *English* Computation, 1722.

Eliz. Atkins

Seal'd, publish'd, and declar'd
by *the said* Elizabeth Atkins,
for and as her last Will and
Testament, in the Presence of
Patrick Magey, James Mullens, and
John Hara.

T. READ

[Her Death and Elegy]†

In the time of her Sickness, which held for about nine Months, she was very penitent, and most zealously fervent in her Devotion, not in the least minding the Affairs of this World, but entirely prepar'd herself for a future State. She was constantly attended by some eminent Divines, but particularly one Mr. *Price*,[1] Master of the Free-School in Galway. In this godly Disposition for her latter End she continu'd till the 10th of *April* following the Date of her last will and Testament, when she departed this mortal Life, in the 75th Year of her Age, to the no small Grief and Sorrow of the Poor, to whom she had been very charitable whilst alive; for she

† From T. Read, *The Life and Actions of Moll Flanders* (London, 1723).
1. The Reverend John Price (d. 1729) "was elected by the Governors as master of Galway Grammar School in succession to Rev. Feilding [sic] Shaw, as from October 1700." Michael Quane, "Galway Grammar School," *Journal of the Galway Archaeological and Historical Society*, XXXI (1964–1965), 39–70, p. 51.

allow'd 25 old Men 40 Shillings a-piece yearly; to 20 old Women she allow'd 30 shillings a-piece yearly; and forty Pounds a Year for putting out poor Children to be Apprentices.

No sooner was the Death of Moll Flanders nois'd over the Kingdom of *Ireland*, but the prime Wits of Trinity College in *Dublin* compos'd on her the following Elegy:

> Alas! what News doth now our Ears invade?
> What Havock has grim Death among us made?
> With the impetuous Fury of the Dart,
> *Moll Flanders* he has wounded thro' the Heart:
> *Moll Flanders*, once the Wonder of the Age,
> Whilst she remain'd on this terrestrial Stage,
> Is gone to take a Nap for many Years,
> For which ye ought to shed as many Tears.
> We mean her chiefest Mourners ought to be
> The chief Proficients in all Villany,
> Such Persons who go on the sneaking Budge,[2]
> And will for Mops and Pails thro' *Dublin* trudge;
> House-breakers, Doxies who can file a Cly,[3]
> And those who out of Shops steal privately.
> But you that can't cry, yet would seem to weep,
> Your Handkerchiefs in Juice of Onions steep,
> Then rail upon the cruel Hand of Fate,
> Which would not grant *Moll's* Reign a longer Date.
> A longer Date, said we? Indeed too long
> She liv'd to do some honest People wrong;
> Such Wrong, that had she her deserved Due,
> She had been whipt, and glimm'd, and hanged too;
> But all the Paths of Vice so much she trac'd,
> That hanging her had any Tree disgrac'd.
> Howe'er take care below, among the Dead,
> For tho' the mortal Life of *Moll* is fled,
> She may perhaps as now ye cannot feel,
> Your Shrouds, and Coffins, else your Bodies steal,
> As Grave-diggers in *England* do, to be
> Mangled to pieces in Anatomy.
> But hold, deceased *Moll* we must not blame
> Too much, for tho' she glory'd in her Shame,
> Of being dextrous Thief, and arrant Whore,
> Yet we some Pity for her must implore,
> And give her deathless Memory some Praise,
> In that she ended well her latter Days,
> For of her num'rous Sins she did repent,
> And dy'd a very hearty Penitent.

2. Who steal without the help of an accomplice.   3. Pick a pocket.

T. READ

[Her Funeral and Epitaph]†

Death having now clos'd the last Scene of her Life, she lay in
State in a very splendid Manner, her House being hung from Top
to Bottom with black Baize, a black Velvet Pall covering her Coffin
to the Ground, which was rail'd round, the Room being all dark,
and illuminated with several wax Tapers put into silver Sconces.
Having thus lain three Days, her Corpse was carried to St. *Nicho-
las's* Church, being attended thither by all her Husband's Relations,
both Men and Women, in deep Mourning, besides above one
hundred and twenty other Persons, who had gold Rings given them,
with these Words engrav'd in them, *Memento mori. Elizabetha
Atkins obiit* 1722; that is, Remember to die. *Elizabeth Atkins* died
in 1722.

Four Women went before strewing sweet Herbs and Flowers all
the Way; after whom follow'd two Beadles, with their Staves
cover'd with Cypress; next them two Ministers and the Clerk; the
Pall was supported by the Wives of the Recorder of *Galway*, the two
Sheriffs, the Town-Clerk, and two other Gentlewomen, led all by
their Husbands. When the Corps was brought into the Church,
after the usual Prayers were said, the Rev. Dr. *Shaw* preach'd the
Funeral Sermon, which being over, she was decently interr'd in the
same Grave with her Husband; and shortly after a fine white
Marble Tombstone was put over her, with the following Epitaph
cut on it:

> Behold the cruel Hand of Death,
> Hath snatch'd away Elizabeth.
> Twelve Years she was an arrant Whore;
> Was sometimes rich, and sometimes poor;
> Which made her, when she'd no Relief,
> Be full as many Years a Thief.
> In this Career of Wickedness,
> Poor Betty always had Success;
> Till caught at last, was doom'd to die,
> But Rope b'ing not her Destiny,
> Eight Years she was transported, where
> She Wealth obtain'd by Pains and Care.
> Of Husbands five, one was her Brother,

† From T. Read, *The Life and Actions of Moll Flanders* (London, 1723).

Which was discover'd by her Mother,
Yet tho' she was both Thief and Whore,
She with this Mate wou'd live no more.
When People all in after Times,
Shall read the Story of her Crimes,
They'll stand amaz'd, but more admire
That one so bad should e'er desire
To live a godly, righteous Life,
And be a loving, faithful Wife.
Of all her Sins she did repent,
And really dy'd a Penitent.

JOHN ROBERT MOORE

[Sources and Innovations in Defoe's *Moll Flanders*]†

Before January 27, 1722, there was perhaps no considerable literary work in the world which was based on an intelligent and sympathetic understanding of the misfortunes of an unprotected woman in contemporary society. Certain Renaissance painters had caught something of this understanding and sympathy from the teachings of Jesus. But the common attitude of writers before Defoe was a scornful presentation of the criminal or the fallen, or a jesting presentation of sullied humanity as a subject for mirth.

To Defoe, always seeing human experience with the eyes of a social historian, vice and crime were subjects not for scorn or mirth but for sympathetic concern. All too often it was society itself which caused the original crime, even in the attempt to correct other wrongs. Moll Flanders, born in Newgate, is allowed to speak for the author who created her: "there are more thieves and rogues made by that one prison of Newgate, than by all the clubs and societies of villains in the nation."

As early as July, 1720, Defoe had written a letter from "Moll of Rag-Fair," an expert pickpocket, but—like her more famous namesake—caught in the act when she attempted to rob a shop. This earlier Moll had returned to England before the end of her sentence of transportation to the colonies, so that she was in constant fear of being discovered or hanged; and she was being blackmailed by an acquaintance who threatened to inform on her.

As late as December of 1730, in his last tract, published about four months before his death, Defoe mentioned another Moll in his

† From *Daniel Defoe: Citizen of the Modern World* (Chicago: The University of Chicago Press, 1958), pp. 242–244.

account of the "night-houses" which served as training schools and as houses of refuge for the young criminals of London: "there are other sinks of Wickedness which want cleansing, besides there is the Dominion of MOLL HARVEY; tho' she was rampant enough, and has not many equals, yet there are other Ladies of Fame, whose Stock of Assurance has carried them great Lengths, in Defiance of the Laws, and of the Magistrate; and till these are attack'd, and that with the same Vigor and Resolution, our Reformation will never merit the Title of UNIVERSAL."

A more immediate source for the criminal career of Moll Flanders is to be traced in a news story which Defoe wrote for Mist's *Weekly-Journal.* This was not published until nearly eight months after the novel appeared, but it told of a female criminal whose record must have been long familiar to Defoe: "Moll King, a most notorious Offender, famous for stealing Gold Watches from the Ladies' Sides in the Churches, for which she has been several times convicted, being lately return'd from Transportation, has been taken, and is committed to Newgate."[1]

The great innovation in Defoe's first social novel was not in his vivid portrayal of the expert pickpocket and the accomplished prostitute, remarkable as this is in its way. It was not even in his account of the new life that beckoned in a new land—although no other writer of the age gave so encouraging and yet so realistic an account of the advantages a transported felon might have if he thought of himself as a colonist who might acquire a stake in the land of his enforced adoption. So far this would be the Crusoe story in another guise, with transportation serving instead of shipwreck, and with a thinly settled colony replacing the desert island.

Defoe's originality appeared more clearly in his going back to the beautiful little girl long before she acquired the notorious name of Moll Flanders—the innocent but sensuous Betty, born in Newgate to a mother who escaped hanging only because of the expected birth of her child. The crime for which Betty's mother was convicted, and which shaped little Betty's future life, was the stealing of three pieces of holland from a mercer in Cheapside—"a petty theft, scarce worth naming." Perhaps it was as well for Betty that her mother was transported, so that the infant daughter lived for a little while among her mother's relatives. Perhaps it was well that, after being carried about by gypsies for a brief time, Betty hid herself at Colchester and refused to go away with them, so that she was taken up by the parish officers and put in charge of a poor woman who kept a little school.

1. *Moll Flanders* (Tegg ed.) pp. 88–89. Applebee's *Weekly Journal,* January 26, 1723 (Lee, III, 95–97). *Ibid.,* July 16, 1720 (Lee, II, 256–58). *An Effectual* *Scheme for the Immediate Preventing of Street Robberies* (1731, for 1730), p. 62. Mist's *Weekly-Journal,* September 22, 1722 (Lee, III, 52).

In her old age Moll regretted that she had not been treated like the destitute children of criminals in France, who "are immediately taken into the care of the government, and put into an hospital called the House of Orphans, where they are bred up, clothed, fed, taught, and when fit to go out, are placed to trades, or to services, so as to be well able to provide for themselves by an honest industrious behaviour. Had this been the custom in our country, I had not been left a poor desolate girl without friends."

* * *

GERALD HOWSON

Who Was Moll Flanders?†

No doubt *Moll Flanders* (first published on January 27, 1722) has its dull passages, but I would disagree that many can be found in that part of the book which tells of her life as a London thief. Here, a different voice seems to be speaking. She divulges to Defoe, rather flatly and cold-bloodedly at times, as many different thieving techniques as she can remember. The result is very much the sort of thing he would have taken down in shorthand (at which he was skilled according to his own statement) during a series of interviews with a typical Newgate woman. Who could she have been?

The guessing-game began in 1723 with the first of a series of pamphlets[1] claiming that the real "Moll Flanders" died in Galway in April, 1722, under the name of Elizabeth Atkins. These were no more than condensations of the novel, with a few real names added to give an impression of truth. The most well-known of the series, *Fortune's Fickle Distribution* (1730), even gives the name of Moll's "Governess" as "Jane Hackabout". But this was borrowed from a real Kate Hackabout, a "Termagant and a Terrour" of Bridges Street, Drury Lane, who was in the newspapers a great deal that year. Her footpad brother, Francis, was hanged in 1730 and she was transported in 1731. Hogarth, too, borrowed her name for his "Harlot's Progress".

The last two volumes of William Lee's book *Defoe, His Life and Undiscovered Writings* (1869) contained hundreds of items in the *Weekly Journal or Saturday's Post* and *Applebee's Original Weekly Journal* which Lee thought Defoe contributed to those papers (though he says nothing of the *Daily Journal*, a paper which carried

† From *The Times Literary Supplement*, no. 3438 (January 18, 1968), 63–64. Mr. Howson uses this material in Chapter XVI of his *Thief-Taker General: The Rise and Fall of Jonathan Wild* (London: Hutchinson, 1970). Reprinted by permission of the publisher.
1. Read's text, "adorn'd with cuts," is a 188-page abridgement, not a pamphlet [*Editor*].

items in the week that the other two often reprinted verbatim on Saturdays). Among them are three pieces related to *Moll Flanders*. The first (A.O.W.J., July 20, 1720) was an article in the form of a letter from one "Moll, of Rag Fair", which told how she had returned illegally from transportation (a capital felony) and was being blackmailed by a man who threatened to impeach her if she did not share her earnings with him. The second was a news report concerning a notorious London pickpocket called Moll King (*W.J.S.P.*, September, 22, 1722). This was eight months *after* the publication of *Moll Flanders*, but Lee wondered if there might be a clue here. The third was an inquiry about why convicts stubbornly returned from the safety of Maryland and Virginia to the dangers of London (A.O.W.J., January 23, 1723).

This was where Lee left the matter, and no one since has taken it much farther, though one Moll Harvey, mentioned in Defoe's last pamphlet on street-robbery, has been suggested as a possible "original" for Defoe's heroine. What follows was discovered, at first accidentally, during researches on Jonathan Wild, the thief taker, and so literary history was not, and is not, my prime concern. Nevertheless, I hope it may be of interest, and possibly use, to Defoe scholars as well as to other readers.

A *True & Genuine Account of . . . Jonathan Wild* (published by Applebee on June 8, 1725) is generally believed now to have been written by Defoe. Lee knew the pamphlet well, but overlooked the fact (as others have overlooked it since) that it contains a reconstructed conversation between Wild and a lady whose watch had been stolen in St. Anne's Church, Soho. The thief, "a dextrous Jade", was "M——ll K——ng", who at the time was apparently working for Wild. The episode is intended to show how Wild managed the "Quality" by playing on their sensibilities and the thieves by extortion and blackmail. There are, besides, other news items about Moll King.

(i) On Friday, Moll King, one of the most notorious Pickpockets of the Town, and eminently famous for assisting in stealing Watches at Ladies' Sides at Church, was again committed to her old Mansion House, Newgate. [*D.J.* June 17, 1721.]

(ii) Moll King, a most notorious Offender, famous for stealing Gold Watches from Ladies' Sides in the Churches, for which she has been several Times convicted, being lately returned from Transportation, has been taken and is committed to Newgate. [*D.J.* September 20, 1722. This is identical to the one printed two days later in the *W.J.S.P.*, and quoted by Lee, vol. 3, p. 52, referred to above.]

(iii) The Gentleman who is bound to prosecute Moll King, the famous Robber of the Ladies of their Gold Watches at

Churches, for returning from Transportation, received a Reprimand the last Sessions for omitting Prosecution for several Sessions past; and the Court ordered her Tryal the next Sessions. [*British Journal*, March 16, 1723; a paper apparently unconnected with Defoe.]

These are the only ones I have been able to find, but there may have been more. The most important is (i), for this is six months before the publication of *Moll Flanders*. However, the first two are in a paper known to have been connected with Defoe. There is a further connexion in the novel itself. When Moll Flanders started as a thief, her "governess" put her under the instruction of an old hand:

The Comrade she helped me to, dealt in three Sorts of Craft; viz. Shoplifting, stealing of Shop-books, and Pockett-books, and taking-off Gold Watches from Ladies' Sides; and this last, she did so dextrously, that no Woman ever arrived to the Perfection of that Art, like her.

The similarity between this and the newspaper reports is immediately striking, though this instructress, in the novel, was shortly hanged.

My first surprise came when I turned to the Old Bailey Sessions records and, after a long search, could find no sign that she had been in Newgate, or any other prison, at any time at all between 1721 and 1723. These Sessions Records are fearsome documents for the novice to be confronted with. Scrawled in scarcely legible, highly abbreviated dog-Latin on crumbling dirt-encrusted parchments, they are divided into numerous bewildering categories. The main part are called "Rolls", because the case documents (recognizances, indictments, &c.) are rolled inside the largest skins, usually prison registers. The Gaol Delivery Rolls for this period are all wrapped, or filed, inside the Newgate Calendars. These were written a day or two before each Sessions and were a list of new arrivals since the last Sessions, with additional lists of "Prisoners Upon Orders" who were awaiting punishment or trial at the following Sessions. They were not complete lists of Newgate prisoners.

The rolls recording crimes committed in the City of London are kept in the City of London Guildhall Records Office; those for crimes committed in Westminster or Middlesex are at the Middlesex Records Office in Queen Anne's Gate Buildings, near St. James's Park. Besides the GD Rolls are SP (Sessions of the Peace) Rolls for each prison (Gatehouse, New Prison, &c.), GD and SP Books, Calendars of Indictments, and Sessions Papers of various kinds, including the useful Transportation Bonds, of which something should be said here. The concession to transport prisoners at

£40 a head to Maryland or other colonies was granted to an agent (at this time, Jonathan Forward). An Order for a draft of prisoners was written in the GD Book. Then Mr. Forward signed a Bond undertaking to contract a ship and deliver the prisoners at their destination. A fairly high death rate was usual (between one in ten and one in four), and so when the ship arrived in America the Cap-, tain obtained a Landing Certificate from the local J.P. This gave a list of those who survived the journey and were sold off at £10 a head. The numbers of prisoners transported in a ship varied between about seventy and 130. Defoe made a slight mistake here. He tells how the bulk of prisoners were put on board and locked below after the more privileged prisoners had settled into their cabins. This was supposed to be at the end of the seventeenth century, but the wholesale transportation of convicts did not begin until 1718.[2] At any rate, the Captain took the certificate back to London so that he could claim his fee. I am not sure what happened to the moneys earned from the sale of the prisoners, but the certificates have been preserved in Guildhall. All these documents are invaluable in following the fortunes of various criminals and in discovering the pattern of the underworld at any given moment during these years. However, to trace the history of a thief like Moll King, who robbed all over London, involves a great deal of travelling to and fro to compare the different sets of records against one another.

The only mention of Moll King on the records was a cryptic "Maria King—f" on the July, 1721, page of the Middlesex Calender Book of Indictments. This meant she had been indicted for felony at the July Sessions of Gaol Delivery. Her indictment was not on the GD Roll (2370) and she was not on the Calendar. Yet she appeared twice in newspapers connected with Defoe and in Defoe's life of Wild. Her real existence was proved by her presence in the BJ (iii) and on two authentic documents relating to Wild himself. When he petitioned for the Freedom of the City of London (June 2, 1724), he added a list of people he had delivered to "justice" since 1720, and she is among those who had returned from transportation and had been transported again. She appears in the same way on his famous list of victims which he distributed amongst the jurymen the day before his trial in an attempt to influence them in his favour (it was also published by the A.O.W.J. on May 15, 1725). The D.J. had said that she was committed to Newgate on

2. Although Defoe closes Moll's narrative with the words, "Written in the Year 1683," a time when she was "almost seventy Years of Age," the setting and events conform more closely to the 1722 date of publication. Rather than suggest that Defoe was mistaken in describing procedures aboard prison ships, it would be more to the point to suggest that he was indeed protecting a living "Moll Flanders," for if the historical veracity of the story were taken literally, Moll would have died some years earlier. [*Editor*].

June 16, 1721. If her real identity could be traced, and it could be found that she was in Newgate during the autumn of that year, then the appearance of *Moll Flanders* in January, 1722, seemed to be more than a coincidence. For Nathaniel Mist, editor of the W.J.S.P., had been transferred from King's Bench Prison to Newgate in June and remained there until December. During all this time, Defoe visited the prison regularly to comfort him and see to his wants. Secondly, there was now plenty of published evidence to connect Moll King not only with Defoe, in whose mind she seems to have had a special place, but with Wild. I had learnt that in dealing with Jonathan Wild every irregularity on the documents had a meaning, usually a complicated one. The question "Who was Moll Flanders?" had become "Who was Moll King?", and the answer promised to solve not only an old literary problem but also to uncover some more of the "dark Proceedings" of our "Thief-taker General" during 1721. Travelling between Guildhall and the Middlesex Records Office, I drew up a series of lists of all the women arrested, tried and transported in 1721, 1722 and 1723, using the dates in the newspapers as pointers to show up recurring names.

Out of the several hundred I was able to select three or four possibles, and these eventually were reduced to two—Elizabeth Smith (Moll Flanders was christened Elizabeth) and Mary Godson. The Elizabeth Smiths arrested on the two dates (June, 1721, and September, 1722) turned out to be different women. Mary Godson had been arrested and sentenced to transportation as a *Middlesex* prisoner in July, 1721, and again arrested as a *London* prisoner in September, 1722. She was still in Newgate in March, 1723, as the B.J. had reported, and she was never tried at all. Instead, she was included on a special Order in May and June, 1723, with two others—Mary Chandler and Sarah Wells, alias "Callico Sarah", who is also in Wild's list. These two, together with several others *"double-crossed"* by Wild (the expression possibly derives from his methods of book-keeping), arrived at Annapolis on September 14 on the "Alexander" galley, *Capt. King*. Mary Godson is not on the landing certificate, but right at the top of the list is "Mary King".

Once I had proved that Mary Godson and Moll King were the same, it was possible to trace her history back to 1718, when there is a gap in the records (they have been eaten by rats, I think). In October, 1718, she stole a gold watch and a "clock" from a lady in St. Anne's Church, Soho, and was sentenced to transportation for seven years. Perhaps she was "quick with Child" for she was not transported until February, 1720, under the name "Mary Golstone", and arrived at Annapolis, as "Mary Gilstone" on April 23. "Callico Sarah" was with her this time as well. She was a well-known thief and whore whose importance I shall return to. On May 5 there arrived at Port Oxford a Robert Bird, brother of a thief called Richard Bird, whose name Mary was to adopt when she returned to London. The next documents are her indictments of July, 1721. The first is against Mary Godson alias Bird alias King (I had missed it in my previous search because "King" was buried deep in the Latin) who, with Richard Bird and Humphrey Burton (not taken), robbed the house of one Kinsallaugh in Little Russell Street, Covent Garden. She stole "divers Goods, val. £50" belonging to John Farrell and Martha Kelley. This sounds rather like the place where Moll Flanders was arrested in the novel, "a private Dwelling-house ... inhabited by a Man who sold Goods for a Weaver to the Mercers ...". This was on the July 14. The second indictment says that she was arrested by John Parry (an agent of Wild's) for returning from transportation and being at large in Covent Garden *on and as from 1 April*. She was committed to Newgate on June 15 by Justice Vaughn (Capt. Gwyn Vaughn, of Southampton Street), who, according to a pamphlet, was one of Wild's "tame" J.P.s. This can only mean that between April 1 and June 15 she was employed, under Wild's protection, as a thief. When she was caught, Kinsallaugh was entitled to £40 reward. Wild forestalled this by submitting his own indictment dated April 1, which he had been holding in readiness against such an eventuality, the words of the indictment being purposely vague. Now, it happened that two of his people, Anne Merritt and William Field (later notorious as the betrayer, on Wild's behalf, of Jack Sheppard) were being impeached for robbery by an accomplice, Elizabeth Harris. The indictments, and the names of the informers on the backs, seem to reveal a picture of two parties: Wild's (Merritt, Field, Moll King, Elizabeth Smith, &c.) on one side; Harris, Kathleen Mackaine (later the protector of Jack Sheppard), a family of criminals called Grantham &c., on the other.

Mary Godson alias King was acquitted of the robbery but condemned to death for being a returned "transport". Wild now stood to gain whatever happened. She could assist him and save herself by impeaching one of Harris's friends. If she refused, or her evidence misfired, her death would earn him £40. In the event, Wild successfully defended Field in court and Moll King successfully impeached Richard Grantham, who was transported. This affair throws a chilling light on Wild's methods, but they are shown to be perfectly consistent with what is known about him. Moll King remained in Newgate until January, 1722, during which time Defoe had plenty of opportunities to talk with her at length. That she told nothing of this side of her life to Defoe is not surprising, for she could hardly have been proud of it. Besides, such things were dangerous professional secrets, and we find a similar reticence on the part of others who impeached for Wild and later left dictated biographies (William Hawkins, John Dyer, James Dalton, Roger Johnson *et al.*). It seems likely that Defoe first sought her out when she was under sentence of death, as a suitable subject for a criminal pamphlet to add to Applebee's famous series. After her reprieve, the pamphlet grew into the novel, the first of its kind in English.

Mary Godson was transported to Annapolis on January 29 (two days after the publication of *Moll Flanders*) and arrived on June 16, 1722. She was back in England and Newgate by September 19. For reasons unknown, Jonathan Forward failed to prosecute her (perhaps Wild, or even Defoe had a hand in it) and she was transported yet again, under irregular procedure, in June, 1723. Altogether, she crossed the Atlantic five, or perhaps eight, times, and was never hanged.

Lee suggests that the name "Moll Flanders" came from an advertisement in the *Postboy* throughout December, 1721, and January, 1722, for *The History of Flanders, with Moll's Map*. That is probably true, but I think the idea was first suggested by stories Moll King told Defoe about her friend "Callico Sarah". This was the kind of name Defoe wanted. "Callico" was contraband Indian cloth; "Holland" was Dutch linen (often contraband); "Flanders" was Flemish lace (usually contraband). "Callico" was libellous. "Betty Holland" might have done but it was too close to Susan Holland, whose famous brothel of the 1630s, "Holland's Leaguer", was still remembered in ballads and broadsheets.[3] The advertisement probably gave him the inspired answer.

There was, of course, another Moll King who appeared in Covent Garden in 1721, the wife of Tom King who kept the famous coffee-house shown in Hogarth's "Morning". After a spell in Newgate she died in 1747, leaving some cottages in Hampstead that were still called "Moll King's Row" in the nineteenth century. Although Mary Godson appeared in Covent Garden and changed *her* name to King at the same time as Tom King acquired a wife I am far from sure these two Moll Kings were the same person.

It is also coincidental that a fellow prisoner of Mary Godson's in 1723 was Sally Salisbury, whose publicized affairs with Ministers of State did *not* bring down any Governments. Moralists like Hogarth (in "The Harlot's Progress") and pornographers like Cleland (in *Fanny Hill*) used episodes from her life for avowedly different purposes. Her abortionist was a Mary Davis, who kept a home for

3. The name "Holland" might also be eliminated on the grounds that Anne ("Nan") Holland, a pickpocket, was hanged in 1705. Her biography is included in Smith's *Lives*, which had gone through five editions by 1719 [*Editor*].

unmarried mothers similar to that in *Moll Flanders*. "Mary Davis", curiously, was an alias used by "Callico Sarah", but that again is a coincidence. What is a fact is that Moll King, alias Godson, alias Golston, Guliston, &c., &c., Sarah Wells, alias "Callico Sarah", alias Mary Davis, and Sarah Pridden, alias Sally Salisbury, were finally together in Newgate from January to June, 1723, and Kate Hackabout was in the New Prison, the unwitting sources of so much inspiration to literature and art.

Eighteenth- and Nineteenth-Century Opinions of Defoe and His Writings

Centered asterisks in a selection denote the omission of complete paragraphs; asterisks within paragraphs denote omissions of less than a paragraph. With the exception of William Lee's annotation, all notes to this section are the editor's.

JONATHAN SWIFT

[No Enduring Him]†

One of these authors (the fellow [Defoe][1] that was *pilloried*, I have forgot his name) is indeed so grave, sententious, dogmatical a rogue, that there is no enduring him.

JOHN GAY

[A Wit Who Will Endure But One Skimming]‡

As to our Weekly Papers, the Poor *Review* is quite exhausted, and grown so very Contemptible, that tho' he[1] has provoked all his Brothers of the Quill round, none of them will enter into a Controversy with him. This Fellow, who had excellent Natural Parts, but wanted a small Foundation of Learning, is a lively instance of those Wits, who, as an Ingenious Author says, will endure but one Skimming.

JOSEPH ADDISON

[A False, Shuffling, Prevaricating Rascal]*

When the Count[1] had finished his speech, he desired leave to call in his witnesses, which was granted: when immediately there came to the bar a man with a hat drawn over his eyes in such a manner that it was impossible to see his face. He spoke in the

† From *A Letter . . . Concerning the Sacramental Test* (1708).
1. Lord Orrery (John Boyle, 1707–1762) noted that Swift well knew and remembered Defoe's name, "but the circumstance of the pillory was to be introduced, and the manner of introducing it shews great art in the nicest touches of satire, and carries all the marks of ridicule, indignation, and contempt." The other of "these authors" was John Tutchin, founder of the Whig *Observator*. Both Defoe, as editor of the *Re-view*, and Tutchin published views that were repugnant to Swift.
‡ From *The Present State of Wit* (1711).
1. As the editor of and main contributor to the *Review*, "he" is synonymous with Defoe.
* From *The Late Trial and Conviction of Count Tariff* (1713).
1. In a mock trial Addison satirizes the tariff, or treaty of commerce, which the ministry had agreed to at the peace of Utrecht (1713).

spirit, nay, in the very language, of the Count, repeated his arguments, and confirmed his assertions. Being asked his name, he said the world called him Mercator:[2] but as for his true name, his age, his lineage, his religion, his place of abode, they were particulars, which, for certain reasons, he was obliged to conceal. The court found him such a false, shuffling, prevaricating rascal, that they set him aside as a person unqualified to give his testimony in a court of justice; advising him at the same time, as he tendered his ears,[3] to forbear uttering such notorious falsehoods as he had then published. The witness, however, persisted in his contumacy, telling them he was very sorry to find, that notwithstanding what he had said, they were resolved to be as arrant fools as all their forefathers had been for a hundred years before them.

CHARLES GILDON

[Defoe a Proteus]†

If ever the Story of any private Man's Adventures in the World were worth making publick, and were acceptable when publish'd, the Editor of this Account thinks this will be so.

The Wonders of this Man's [Defoe's] Life exceed all that (he thinks) is to be found Extant; the Life of one Man being scarce capable of greater Variety.

The Story is told with greater Modesty than perhaps some Men may think necessary to the Subject, the Hero of our Dialogue not being very conspicuous for that Virtue, a more than common Assurance carrying him thro' all those various Shapes and Changes which he has pass'd without the least Blush. The Fabulous *Proteus* of the Ancient Mythologist was but a very faint Type of our Hero, whose Changes are much more numerous, and he far more difficult to be constrain'd to his own Shape. If his Works should happen to live to the next Age, there would in all probability be a greater Strife among the several Parties, whose he really was, than among the seven *Graecian* Cities, to which of them *Homer* belong'd: The *Dissenters* first would claim him as theirs, the *Whigs* in general as theirs, the *Tories* as theirs, the *Nonjurors* as theirs, the *Papists* as

2. Defoe wrote the *Mercator; or Commerce Retrieved* (May, 1713–July, 1714) after his *Review* had come to an end. Under the pseudonym "W. Brown" he supported the commercial policies of the ministry. See John Robert Moore, *A Checklist of the Writings of Daniel Defoe* (Bloomington: Indiana University Press, 1960), pp. 232–233.

3. Although Pope undoubtedly knew that

Defoe did not lose his ears, *The Dunciad* states: "Earless on high, stood unabash'd De Foe" (B, Book II, line 147).

† From the Preface to *The Life and Strange Surprizing Adventures of Mr. D . . . . . De F . . . .* (1719). Charles Gildon (1665–1724) was a minor editor, playwright, and translator. In constant need of money, he often wrote polemically in an attempt to attract readers.

theirs, the *Atheists* as theirs, and so on to what Sub-divisions there may be among us; so that it cannot be expected that I should give you in this short Dialogue his Picture at length for the rest of his Life, I may perhaps give a farther Account hereafter.

ANONYMOUS

[Defoe's Readers] †

Down in the kitchen, honest Dick and Doll
Are studying Colonel Jack and Flanders Moll.

ALEXANDER POPE

[On Defoe] ‡

De Foe wrote a vast many things, and none bad, though none excellent. There's something good in all he writ.

SAMUEL JOHNSON

[On Defoe] *

[Samuel Johnson] told us, that he had given Mrs. Montagu a catalogue of all Daniel Defoe's works of imagination; most, if not all of which, as well as of his other works, he now enumerated, allowing a considerable share of merit to a man, who, bred a tradesman,[1] had written so variously and so well.

---

† *The Flying Post; or Weekly Medley* (March 1, 1729). This couplet, often cited by Defoe scholars, suggests that readers of DeFoe's criminal lives were of the lower class. However, Maximillian E. Novak rightly points out that "unless Dick and Doll, like Steele's footman, borrowed a copy from their master or mistress, they were probably reading something they could afford—something rather different from what Defoe wrote." See "Fiction and Society," in *England in the Restoration and Early Eighteenth Century*, H. T. Swedenberg, Jr. (Berkeley and Los Angeles: University of California Press, 1972), p. 62. A variety of chapbook versions of *Moll Flanders*, usually eight to twenty-four pages in length, was available throughout the eighteenth and nineteenth centuries.

Later in the century (1747), in his *Industry and Idleness* series, Hogarth depicted the idle 'prentice asleep at his loom, with a ballad of *Moll Flanders* tacked to the frame above his head. See *Hogarth's Graphic Works*, 2 vols., compiled and with a commentary by Ronald Paulsen (New Haven: Yale University Press, 1965), II, 195.
‡ Quoted in *Observations, Ancedotes, and Characters of Books and Men*, by Joseph Spence (1742). (Pope satirized Defoe as a writer of political pamphlets in *The Dunciad*.)
* From *The Life of Samuel Johnson*, by James Boswell (1778).
1. The first edition called Defoe "a silversmith"; subsequent editions were corrected to read "tradesman."

SAMUEL TAYLOR COLERIDGE

[Defoe Superior to Swift] †

Compare the contemptuous Swift with the contemned De Foe, and how superior will the latter be found! But by what test?—Even by this; that the writer who makes me sympathize with his presentations with the whole of my being, is more estimable than he who calls forth, and appeals but to, a part of my being—my sense of the ludicrous, for instance. De Foe's excellence it is, to make me forget my specific class, character, and circumstances, and to raise me while I read him, into the universal man.

I know no genuine Saxon English superior to Asgill's.[1] I think his and De Foe's irony often finer than Swift's.

CHARLES LAMB

Estimate of Defoe's Secondary Novels‡

*   *   *

While all ages and descriptions of people hang delighted over the "Adventures of Robinson Crusoe," and shall continue to do so we trust while the world lasts, how few comparatively will bear to be told that there exist other fictitious narratives by the same writer— four of them at least of no inferior interest, except what results from a less felicitous choice of situation. Roxana—Singleton—Moll Flanders—Colonel Jack—are all genuine offspring of the same father. They bear the veritable impress of De Foe. An unpractised midwife that would not swear to the nose, lip, forehead, and eye, of every one of them! They are in their way as full of incident, and some of them every bit as romantic; only they want the uninhabited Island and the charm that has bewitched the world of the striking solitary situation.

*   *   *

The narrative manner of De Foe has a naturalness about it beyond that of any other novel or romance writer. His fictions have all the air of true stories. It is impossible to believe, while you are reading them, that a real person is not narrating to you everywhere nothing but what really happened to himself. To this, the extreme *homeliness* of their style mainly contributes. We use the word in its

---

† Coleridge's first comment is from *The Literary Remains* (1830), the second from *Table Talk* (1832).
1. John Asgill (1659–1738), English pamphleteer.

‡ From Walter Wilson, *Memoirs of the Life and Times of Daniel De Foe*, 3 vols. (London, 1830), III, 126–128.

best and heartiest sense—that which comes *home* to the reader. The narrators everywhere are chosen from low life, or have had their origin in it; therefore they tell their own tales (Mr Coleridge has anticipated us in this remark), as persons in their degree are observed to do, with infinite repetition, and an overacted exactness, lest the hearer should not have minded, or have forgotten, some things that had been told before. Hence the emphatic sentences marked in the good old (but deserted) Italic type; and hence, too, the frequent interposition of the reminding old colloquial parenthesis, "I say"—"mind"—and the like, when the storyteller repeats what, to a practised reader, might appear to have been sufficiently insisted upon before: which made an ingenious critic observe, that his works, in this kind, were excellent reading for the kitchen. And, in truth, the heroes and heroines of De Foe can never again hope to be popular with a much higher class of readers, than that of the servant-maid or the sailor.[1] Crusoe keeps its rank only by tough prescription; Singleton, the pirate—Colonel Jack, the thief—Moll Flanders, both thief and harlot—Roxana, harlot and something worse—would be startling ingredients in the bill of fare of modern literary delicacies. But, then, what pirates, what thieves, and what harlots, are *the thief, the harlot,* and *the pirate* of De Foe! We would not hesitate to say, that in no other book of fiction, where the lives of such characters are described, is guilt and delinquency made less seductive, or the suffering made more closely to follow the commission, or the penitence more earnest or more bleeding, or the intervening flashes of religious visitation upon the rude and uninstructed soul more meltingly and fearfully painted. They, in this, come near to the tenderness of Bunyan; while the livelier pictures and incidents in them, as in Hogarth or in Fielding, tend to diminish that fastidiousness to the concerns and pursuits of common life, which an unrestrained passion for the ideal and the sentimental is in danger of producing.

WILLIAM HAZLITT

[Mr. Lamb and Mrs. Flanders]†

Mr. Lamb admires *Moll Flanders*; would he marry Moll Flanders? There ought to be something in common in our regard for the original and the copy.

1. In a letter to his friend Wilson (Dec. 16, 1822), Lamb makes substantially the same remarks but qualifies this estimate of Defoe's popularity, saying: "His novels are capital kitchen-reading, while they are worthy, from their deep interest, to find a shelf in the libraries of the wealthiest and the most learned."

† From "Conversations as Good as Real," in *The Collected Works of William Hazlitt*, edited by A. R. Waller and Arnold Glover (London and New York, 1904), XII, 367.

[Meddling with the Unclean Thing]†

We do not think a person brought up and trammelled all his life in the strictest notions of religion and morality, and looking at the world and all that was ordinarily passing in it, as little better than a contamination, is, *a priori*, the properest person to write novels: it is going out of his way—it is 'meddling with the unclean thing.' Extremes meet, and all extremes are bad. According to our author's overstrained Puritanical notions, there were but two choices, God or the Devil—Sinners and Saints—the Methodist meeting or the Brothel—the school of the press-yard of Newgate, or attendance on the refreshing ministry of some learned and pious dissenting Divine. As the smallest falling off from faith, or grace, or the most trifling peccadillo, was to be reprobated and punished with the utmost severity, no wonder that the worst turn was given to every thing; and that the imagination having once overstepped the formidable line gave a loose to its habitual nervous dread by indulging in the blackest and most frightful pictures of the corruptions incident to human nature. It was as well (in the cant phrase) 'to be in for a sheep as a lamb,' as it cost nothing more—the sin might at least be startling and uncommon; and hence we find in this style of writing nothing but an alternation of religious horrors and raptures (though these are generally rare, as being a less tempting bait) and the grossest scenes of vice and debauchery: we have either saintly, spotless purity, or all is rotten to the core. How else can we account for it that all Defoe's characters (with one or two exceptions for form's sake) are of the worst and lowest description—the refuse of the prisons and the stews—thieves, prostitutes, vagabonds, and pirates —as if he wanted to make himself amends for the restraint under which he had laboured 'all the fore-end of his time' as a moral and religious character, by acting over every excess of grossness and profligacy by proxy! How else can we comprehend that he should really think there was a salutary moral lesson couched under the history of *Moll Flanders*; or that his romance of *Roxana, or the Fortunate Mistress*, who rolls in wealth and pleasure from one end of the book to the other, and is quit for a little death-bed repentance and a few lip-deep professions of the vanity of wordly joys, showed, in a striking point of view, the advantages of virtue, and the disadvantages of vice? It cannot be said, however, that these works have an *immoral* tendency. The author has contrived to neutralise the question; and

† From a review of Walter Wilson's *Memoirs of the Life and Times of Daniel Defoe*, 3 vols. (London, 1830), in *The Collected Works of William Hazlitt*, edited by A. R. Waller and Arnold Glover (London and New York, 1904), X, 379–380.

(as far as in him lay) made vice and virtue equally contemptible or revolting. In going through his pages, we are inclined to vary Mr. Burke's well-known paradox, that 'vice, by losing all its grossness, loses half its evil,' and say that vice, by losing all its refinement, loses all its attraction. We have in them only the pleasure of sinning, and the dread of punishment here or hereafter;—gross sensuality, and whining repentance. The morality is that of the inmates of a house of correction; the piety, that of malefactors in the condemned hole. There is no sentiment, no atmosphere of imagination, no 'purple light' thrown round virtue or vice;—all is either the physical gratification on the one hand, or a selfish calculation of consequences on the other. This is the necessary effect of allowing nothing to the frailty of human nature;—of never strewing the flowers of fancy in the path of pleasure, but always looking that way with a sort of terror as to forbidden ground: nothing is left of the common and mixed enjoyments and pursuits of human life but the coarsest and criminal part; and we have either a sour, cynical, sordid self-denial, or (in the despair of attaining this) a reckless and unqualified abandonment of all decency and character alike:—it is hard to say which is the most repulsive. * * *

We * * * may, nevertheless, add, for the satisfaction of the inquisitive reader, that *Moll Flanders* is utterly vile and detestable: Mrs. Flanders was evidently born in sin. The best parts are the account of her childhood, which is pretty and affecting; the fluctuation of her feelings between remorse and hardened impenitence in Newgate; and the incident of her leading off the horse from the inn-door, though she had no place to put it in after she had stolen it. This was carrying the love of thieving to an *ideal* pitch and making it perfectly disinterested and mechanical. * * *

ANONYMOUS
[Money] †

* * *

Why did not Defoe, with such an unexampled capability as a writer of fiction, occupy himself earnestly in his art? Why did he not expend thought, toil, and long years in elaborating two such works as "Robinson Crusoe," or the commencement of "Colonel Jack," instead of scribbling page after page, without consideration enough to avoid dulness, stories replete with obscenities he must have disapproved, and nonsense that he must have grinned at with

† From "Novels and Novelists—Daniel   XLVIII (July, 1856), 57–71.
De Foe," *Dublin University Magazine,*

contempt even while the pen was in his hand? Forster,[1] in his graphic and fascinating sketch of Defoe and his times, bids us remember, when judging of "Moll Flanders" and "Roxana," the tone of society at the time of their appearance. Without a doubt, measured by the standard of the vicious literature of the Restoration and the two succeeding ages, they do not especially sin against purity of morals. But in this we cannot find a valid apology for Defoe, who, in composing them, put his hand to works that all serious men of his own religious views must have regarded with warm disapproval. Defoe was not by profession amongst the frivolous or godless of his generation; he was loud in his condemnation of the stage, of gambling, and of debauchery; he not only knew that voluptuous excess was criminal, but he raised his voice to shame it out of society,—and yet he exercised his talents in depicting scenes of sensual enjoyment, which no virtuous nature can dwell on without pain, no vicious one without pleasure. What was his motive? Money.

* * * All Defoe's novels, long as they are, are but a string of separate anecdotes related of one person, but having no other connection with each other. In no one of them are there forces at work that necessitate the conclusion of the story at a certain point. One meets with no mystery, no denouement in them. They go on and on, (usually at a brisk pace, with abundance of dramatic positions) till it apparently strikes the author he has written a good bookful, and then he winds up with a page and a half of "so he lived happily all the rest of his days;" intermixed with some awkward moralizing by way of apology for the looseness of the bulk of the work.

* * *

WILLIAM LEE

[Morals] †

When giving an account of the first connection between Defoe and *Applebee's Journal*, I explained the peculiar branch of Mr. Applebee's printing business involving an intercourse with the inmates of Newgate; and fully considered the motives and objects of our author in writing several works for the moral benefit of such convicts as, after being reprieved from the gallows, were about to be transported to the plantations of America for the remainder of

1. John Forster (1812–1876), English historian and biographer, wrote *Daniel De Foe* (London, 1855).
† From *Daniel Defoe: His Life, and Re-*

cently Discovered Writings . . . , 3 vols. (London: Hotten, 1869), I, 355–356, 365.

their lives. The first of such works was published on the 27th of January 1722, and is entitled, "The Fortunes and Misfortunes of the Famous MOLL FLANDERS, &c., who was born in Newgate, and during a Life of continu'd Variety for Threescore years, besides her childhood, was twelve years a whore, five times a wife (whereof once to her own Brother), Twelve years a Thief, Eight years a transported Felon in Virginia, at last grew Rich, lived Honest, and died a Penitent. Written from her own Memorandums." This title was plainly not designed to attract the pure and delicate to proceed farther with the book; but to strike the attention of the unfortunate class for whom it was intended. The very titlepage however suggested a glimmering of hope that they also *might* yet attain Riches, becomes Honest, and die Penitent. That the book was read with great avidity is evident from the fact that three editions were required during the same year, and two the year following.[1] The writer felt the difficulty of his task, and confesses it in the Preface where he says, "the best Use is to be made even of the worst Story, and the Moral 'tis hop'd will keep the Reader serious, even where the Story might incline him to be otherwise." * * * Space forbids my entering upon the narrative; —which, in addition to its moral reflections, abounds with lively interest, arising from unlooked for incidents and coincidents,—is full of rich painting of nature, in the midst whereof the apparently artless story of the vices and follies of the pretended narrator, continually appears more like the gushing of a fountain, than, as it really is, the flowing of a polluted stream.

* * *

Having in "Moll Flanders" portrayed the life of a female Convict, with such moral considerations as in his judgment might help to raise up those who had fallen, so low as to be abandoned by all, except those of their own class; Defoe thought fit to prepare a similar representation of the life of a criminal of the male sex. It is the counterpart of its predecessor; and I cannot doubt that he was actuated by the same good motives as before. He had this additional incitement, that the number of convicts who contrived to return from transportation had greatly increased; and it moved his heart to see these poor wretches, on being identified, taken to Newgate, and from thence to the gallows.[2] There is also reason to believe that he was encouraged to continue his efforts, by the knowledge that "Moll Flanders" had been useful to some of those for whose reading it was specially intended. * * *

1. It is possible that Defoe was indebted for the name of his heroine to the following:—if not, the fortuitous coincidence is at least remarkable. In the *Post-Boy* of the 9th of January 1722, and previously, is an Advertisement of Books sold by John Darby, and among them is,

"The History of Flanders, with Moll's Map."
2. Shortly after *Colonel Jacque* (on the 26th of January, 1723), he published an excellent Essay on this subject in *Applebee's Journal*.

SIR LESLIE STEPHEN

[Defoe's Novels] †

* * * In the preface to 'Roxana,' [Defoe] acts, with equal spirit, the character of an impartial person, giving us the evidence on which he is himself convinced of the truth of the story, as though he would, of all things, refrain from pushing us unfairly for our belief. The writer, he says, took the story from the lady's own mouth: he was, of course, obliged to disguise names and places; but was himself 'particularly acquainted with this lady's first husband, the brewer, and with his father, and also with his bad circumstances, and knows that first part of the story.' The rest we must, of course, take upon the lady's own evidence, but less unwillingly, as the first is thus corroborated. We cannot venture to suggest to so calm a witness that he has invented both the lady and the writer of her history; and, in short, that when he says that A. says that B. says something, it is, after all, merely the anonymous 'he' who is speaking. In giving us his authority for 'Moll Flanders,' he ventures upon the more refined art of throwing a little discredit upon the narrator's veracity. She professes to have abandoned her evil ways, but, as he tells us with a kind of aside, and as it were cautioning us against over-incredulity, 'it seems' (a phrase itself suggesting the impartial looker-on) that in her old age 'she was not so extraordinary a penitent as she was at first; it seems only' (for, after all, you mustn't make *too* much of my insinuations) 'that indeed she always spoke with abhorrence of her former life.' So we are left in a qualified state of confidence, as if we had been talking about one of his patients with the wary director of a reformatory.

* * *

* * * The novel of sentiment or passion or character would be altogether beyond [Defoe's] scope. He will accumulate any number of facts and details; but they must be such as will speak for themselves without the need of an interpreter. For this reason we do not imagine that 'Roxana,' 'Moll Flanders,' 'Colonel Jack,' or 'Captain Singleton' can fairly claim any higher interest than that which belongs to the ordinary police report, given with infinite fulness and vivacity of detail. In each of them there are one or two forcible situations. Roxana pursued by her daughter, Moll Flanders in prison, and Colonel Jack as a young boy of the streets, are powerful fragments, and well adapted for his peculiar method. He goes on heaping up

† From *Hours in a Library*, New Edition, 3 vols. (New York: Putnam; London: Smith, Elder, 1899), I, 5–6, 30–31.

little significant facts, till we are able to realise the situation power-fully, and we may then supply the sentiment for ourselves. But he never seems to know his own strength. He gives us at equal length, and with the utmost plain-speaking, the details of a number of other positions, which are neither interesting nor edifying. He is decent or coarse, just as he is dull or amusing, without knowing the difference. The details about the different connections formed by Roxana and Moll Flanders have no atom of sentiment, and are about as wearisome as the journal of a specially heartless lady of the same character would be at the present day. He has been praised for never gilding objectionable objects, or making vice attractive. To all appearance, he would have been totally unable to set about it. He has only one mode of telling a story, and he follows the thread of his narrative into the back-slums of London, or lodging-houses of doubt-ful character, or respectable places of trade, with the same equanimity, at a good steady jog-trot of narrative. The absence of any passion or sentiment deprives such places of the one possible source of interest; and we must confess that two-thirds of each of these novels are deadly dull; the remainder, though exhibiting specimens of his genuine power, is not far enough from the commonplace to be specially attrac-tive. In short, the merit of De Foe's narrative bears a direct proportion to the intrinsic merit of a plain statement of the facts; and, in the novels already mentioned, as there is nothing very surprising, cer-tainly nothing unique, about the story, his treatment cannot raise it above a very moderate level.

Twentieth-Century
Criticism of Moll Flanders

Editorial commentary in this section is labelled [*Editor*]. All other annotation appears in the original essays. Footnotes to selections have been renumbered in a few cases. The criticism included uses quotations from various editions of the novel, and no attempt has been made to make quoted portions conform with the wording, spelling, and punctuation of this edition. (Asterisks indicate deleted passages.)

VIRGINIA WOOLF

Defoe†

The fear which attacks the recorder of centenaries lest he should
find himself measuring a diminishing spectre and forced to foretell
its approaching dissolution is not only absent in the case of *Robinson Crusoe* but the mere thought of it is ridiculous. It may be true
that *Robinson Crusoe* is two hundred years of age upon the twenty-
fifth of April 1919, but far from raising the familiar speculations
as to whether people now read it and will continue to read it, the
effect of the bicentenary is to make us marvel that *Robinson Crusoe*,
the perennial and immortal, should have been in existence so short a
time as that. The book resembles one of the anonymous produc-
tions of the race itself rather than the effort of a single mind; and
as for celebrating its centenary we should as soon think of celebrating the centenaries of Stonehenge itself. Something of this we
may attribute to the fact that we have all had *Robinson Crusoe*
read aloud to us as children, and were thus much in the same state
of mind towards Defoe and his story that the Greeks were in
towards Homer. It never occurred to us that there was such a
person as Defoe, and to have been told that *Robinson Crusoe* was
the work of a man with a pen in his hand would either have dis-
turbed us unpleasantly or meant nothing at all. The impressions of
childhood are those that last longest and cut deepest. It still seems
that the name of Daniel Defoe has no right to appear upon the
title-page of *Robinson Crusoe*, and if we celebrate the bi-centenary
of the book we are making a slightly unnecessary allusion to the
fact that, like Stonehenge, it is still in existence.

The great fame of the book has done its author some injustice;
for while it has given him a kind of anonymous glory it has obscured the fact that he was a writer of other works which, it is
safe to assert, were not read aloud to us as children. Thus when the
Editor of the *Christian World* in the year 1870 appealed to "the
boys and girls of England" to erect a monument upon the grave of
Defoe, which a stroke of lightning had mutilated, the marble was
inscribed to the memory of the author of *Robinson Crusoe*. No men-

† Written in 1919, this essay is from *The
Common Reader,* First Series (New
York: Harcourt, Brace & World, 1925),
pp. 89–97. Copyright 1925 by Harcourt
Brace Jovanovich, Inc; copyright 1953
by Leonard Woolf. Reprinted by permission of the publisher.

tion was made of *Moll Flanders*. Considering the topics which are dealt with in that book, and in *Roxana, Captain Singleton, Colonel Jack* and the rest, we need not be surprised, though we may be indignant, at the omission. We may agree with Mr. Wright, the biographer of Defoe, that these "are not works for the drawing-room table." But unless we consent to make that useful piece of furniture the final arbiter of taste, we must deplore the fact that their superficial coarseness, or the universal celebrity of *Robinson Crusoe*, has led them to be far less widely famed than they deserve. On any monument worthy of the name of monument the names of *Moll Flanders* and *Roxana*, at least, should be carved as deeply as the name of Defoe. They stand among the few English novels which we can call indisputably great. The occasion of the bi-centenary of their more famous companion may well lead us to consider in what their greatness, which has so much in common with his, may be found to consist.

Defoe was an elderly man when he turned novelist, many years the predecessor of Richardson and Fielding, and one of the first indeed to shape the novel and launch it on its way. But it is unnecessary to labour the fact of his precedence, except that he came to his novel-writing with certain conceptions about the art which he derived partly from being himself one of the first to practise it. The novel had to justify its existence by telling a true story and preaching a sound moral. "This supplying a story by invention is certainly a most scandalous crime," he wrote. "It is a sort of lying that makes a great hole in the heart, in which by degrees a habit of lying enters in." Either in the preface or in the text of each of his works, therefore, he takes pains to insist that he has not used his invention at all but has depended upon facts, and that his purpose has been the highly moral desire to convert the vicious or to warn the innocent. Happily these were principles that tallied very well with his natural disposition and endowments. Facts had been drilled into him by sixty years of varying fortunes before he turned his experience to account in fiction. "I have some time ago summed up the Scenes of my life in this distich," he wrote:

> No man has tasted differing fortunes more,
> And thirteen times I have been rich and poor.

He had spent eighteen months in Newgate and talked with thieves, pirates, highwaymen, and coiners before he wrote the history of Moll Flanders. But to have facts thrust upon you by dint of living and accident is one thing; to swallow them voraciously and retain the imprint of them indelibly, is another. It is not merely that Defoe knew the stress of poverty and had talked with the victims of it, but that the unsheltered life, exposed to circumstances and forced to shift for itself, appealed to him imaginatively as the right matter for his art. In the first pages of each of his great novels he reduces his hero or heroine to such a state of unfriended misery that their existence must be a continued struggle, and their survival at all the result of luck and their own exertions. Moll Flanders was born in Newgate of a criminal mother; Captain Singleton was stolen as a child and sold to the gipsies; Colonel Jack, though "born a gentleman, was put 'prentice to a pickpocket"; Roxana starts under better auspices, but, having married at fifteen, she sees her husband go bankrupt and is left with five children in "a condition the most deplorable that words can express."

Thus each of these boys and girls has the world to begin and the battle to fight for himself. The situation thus created was entirely to DeFoe's liking. From her very birth or with half a year's respite at most, Moll Flanders, the most notable of them, is goaded by "that worst of devils, poverty," forced to earn her living as soon as she can sew, driven from place to place, making no demands upon her creator for the subtle domestic atmosphere which he was unable to supply, but drawing upon him for all he knew of strange people and customs. From the outset the burden of proving her right to exist is laid upon her. She has to depend entirely upon her own wits and judgement, and to deal with each emergency as it arises by a rule-of-thumb morality which she has forged in her own head. The briskness of the story is due partly to the fact that having transgressed the accepted laws at a very early age she has henceforth the freedom of the outcast. The one impossible event is that she should settle down in comfort and security. But from the first the peculiar genius of the author asserts itself, and avoids the obvious danger of the novel of adventure. He makes us understand that Moll Flanders was a woman on her own account and not only material for a succession of adventures. In proof of this she begins, as Roxana also begins, by falling passionately, if unfortunately, in love. That she must rouse herself and marry some one else and look very closely to her settlements and prospects is no slight upon her passion, but to be laid to the charge of her birth; and, like all Defoe's women, she is a person of robust understanding. Since she makes no scruple of telling lies when they serve her purpose, there is something undeniable about her truth when she speaks it. She has no time to waste upon the refinements of personal affection, one tear is dropped, one moment of despair allowed, and then "on with the story." She has a spirit that loves to breast the storm. She delights in the exercise of her own powers. When she discovers that the man she has married in Virginia is her own brother she is violently disgusted; she insists upon leaving him; but as soon as she sets foot in Bristol, "I took the diversion of going to Bath, for as I was still far from being old so my humour, which was always gay, continued so to an extreme." Heartless she is not, nor can any one charge her with levity; but life delights her, and a heroine who lives has us all in tow. Moreover, her ambition has that slight strain of imagination in it which puts it in the category of the noble passions. Shrewd and practical of necessity, she is yet haunted by a desire for romance and for the quality which to her perception makes a man a gentleman. "It was really a true gallant spirit he was of, and it was the more grievous to me. 'Tis something of relief even to be undone by a man of honour rather than by a scoundrel," she writes when she had misled a highwayman as to the extent of her fortune. It is in keeping with this temper that she should be proud of her final partner because he refuses to work when they reach the plantations but prefers hunting, and that she should take pleasure in buying him wigs and silver-hilted swords "to make him appear, as he really was, a very fine gentleman." Her very love of hot weather is in keeping, and the passion with which she kissed the ground that her son had trod on, and her noble tolerance of every kind of fault so long as it is not "complete baseness of spirit, imperious, cruel, and relentless when uppermost, abject and low-spirited when down." For the rest of the world she has nothing but good-will.

Since the list of the qualities and graces of this seasoned old sinner is by no means exhausted we can well understand how it was that Borrow's apple-woman on London Bridge called her "blessed Mary" and valued her book above all the apples on her stall; and that Borrow,[1] taking the book deep into the booth, read till his eyes ached. But we dwell upon such signs of character only by way of proof that the creator of Moll Flanders was not, as he has been accused of being, a mere journalist and literal recorder of facts with no conception of the nature of psychology.[2] It is true that his characters take shape and substance of their own accord, as if in despite of the author and not altogether to his liking. He never lingers or stresses any point of subtlety or pathos, but presses on imperturbably as if they came there without his knowledge. A touch of imagination, such as that when the Prince sits by his son's cradle and Roxana observes how "he loved to look at it when it was alseep," seems to mean much more to us than to him. After the curiously modern dissertation upon the need of communicating matters of importance to a second person lest, like the thief in Newgate, we

1. George Borrow, English eccentric, philologist, traveler, and writer; greatly influenced by Defoe; author of the semi-autobiographical tale *Lavengro* (1851), which contains an incident where the main character encounters an old women selling fruit and holding a copy of *Moll Flanders*, which he tries to buy, but which she will not sell at any price [*Editor*].

2. Mrs. Virginia Woolf *née* Stephen was the novelist daughter of Sir Leslie, part of whose negative assessment of Defoe and *Moll Flanders* appears on pp. 332–333 of this edition [*Editor*].

should talk of it in our sleep, he apologises for his digression. He seems to have taken his characters so deeply into his mind that he lived them without exactly knowing how; and, like all unconscious artists, he leaves more gold in his work than his own generation was able to bring to the surface.

The interpretation that we put on his characters might therefore well have puzzled him. We find for ourselves meanings which he was careful to disguise even from himself. Thus it comes about that we admire Moll Flanders far more than we blame her. Nor can we believe that Defoe had made up his mind as to the precise degree of her guilt, or was unaware that in considering the lives of the abandoned he raised many deep questions and hinted, if he did not state, answers quite at variance with his professions of belief. From the evidence supplied by his essay upon the "Education of Women" we know that he had thought deeply and much in advance of his age upon the capacities of women, which he rated very high, and the injustice done to them, which he rated very harsh.

> I have often thought of it as one of the most barbarous customs in the world, considering us as a civilised and a Christian country, that we deny the advantages of learning to women. We reproach the sex every day with folly and impertinence; which I am confident, had they the advantages of education equal to us, they would be guilty of less than ourselves.

The advocates of women's rights would hardly care, perhaps, to claim Moll Flanders and Roxana among their patron saints; and yet it is clear that Defoe not only intended them to speak some very modern doctrines upon the subject, but placed them in circumstances where their peculiar hardships are displayed in such a way as to elicit our sympathy. Courage, said Moll Flanders, was what women needed, and the power to "stand their ground"; and at once gave practical demonstration of the benefits that would result. Roxana, a lady of the same profession, argues more subtly against the slavery of marriage. She "had started a new thing in the world" the merchant told her; "it was a way of arguing contrary to the general practise." But Defoe is the last writer to be guilty of bald preaching. Roxana keeps our attention because she is blessedly unconscious that she is in any good sense an example to her sex and is thus at liberty to own that part of her argument is "of an elevated strain which was really not in my thoughts at first, at all." The knowledge of her own frailties and the honest questioning of her own motives, which that knowledge begets, have the happy result of keeping her fresh and human when the martyrs and pioneers of so many problem novels have shrunken and shrivelled to the pegs and props of their respective creeds.

But the claim of Defoe upon our admiration does not rest upon the fact that he can be shown to have anticipated some of the views of Meredith, or to have written scenes which (the odd suggestion occurs) might have been turned into plays by Ibsen. Whatever his ideas upon the position of women, they are an incidental result of his chief virtue, which is that he deals with the important and lasting side of things and not with the passing and trivial. He is often dull. He can imitate the matter-of-fact precision of a scientific traveller until we wonder that his pen could trace or his brain conceive what has not even the excuse of truth to soften its dryness. He leaves out the whole of vegetable nature, and a large part of human nature. All this we may admit, though we have to admit defects as grave in many writers whom we call great. But that does not impair the peculiar merit of what remains. Having at the outset limited his scope and confined his ambitions he achieves a truth of insight which is far rarer and more enduring than the truth of fact which he professed to make his aim. Moll Flanders and her friends recommended themselves to him not because they were, as we should say, "picturesque"; nor, as he affirmed, because they were examples of evil living by which the public might profit. It was their natural veracity, bred in them by a life of hardship, that excited his interest. For them there were no excuses; no kindly shelter obscured their motives. Poverty was their task-master. Defoe did not pronounce more than a judgement of the lips upon their failings. But their courage and resource and tenacity delighted him. He found their society full of good talk, and pleasant stories, and faith in each other, and morality of a home-made kind. Their fortunes had that infinite variety which he praised and relished and beheld with wonder in his own life. These men and women, above all, were free to talk openly of the passions and desires which have moved men and women since the beginning of time, and thus even now they keep their vitality undiminished. There is a dignity in everything that is looked at openly. Even the sordid subject of money, which plays so large a part in their histories, becomes not sordid but tragic when it stands not for ease and consequence but for honour, honesty and life itself. You may object that Defoe is humdrum, but never that he is engrossed with petty things.

He belongs, indeed, to the school of the great plain writers, whose work is founded upon a knowledge of what is most persistent, though not most seductive, in human nature. The view of London from Hungerford Bridge, grey, serious, massive, and full of the subdued stir of traffic and business, prosaic if it were not for the masts of the ships and the towers and domes of the city, brings him to mind. The tattered girls with violets in their hands at the street corners, and the old weatherbeaten women patiently displaying

their matches and bootlaces beneath the shelter of arches, seem like
characters from his books. He is of the school of Crabbe, and of
Gissing, and not merely a fellow pupil in the same stern place of
learning, but its founder and master.

E. M. FORSTER

[A Novel of Character]†

* * *

Let us * * * take an easy character and study it for a little. Moll
Flanders will do. She fills the book that bears her name, or rather
stands alone in it, like a tree in a park, so that we can see her from
every aspect and are not bothered by rival growths. Defoe is telling
a story, like Scott, and we shall find stray threads left about in
much the same way, on the chance of the writer wanting to pick
them up afterwards: Moll's early batch of children for instance. But
the parallel between Scott and Defoe cannot be pressed. What interested Defoe was the heroine, and the form of his book proceeds
naturally out of her character. * * * How just are her reflections
when she robs of her gold necklace the little girl returning from the
dancing-class. The deed is done in the little passage leading to St.
Bartholomew's, Smithfield (you can visit the place today—Defoe
haunts London) and her impulse is to kill the child as well. She
does not, the impulse is very feeble, but conscious of the risk the
child has run she becomes most indignant with the parents for
"leaving the poor little lamb to come home by itself, and it would
teach them to take more care of it another time." How heavily and
pretentiously a modern psychologist would labour to express this! It
just runs off Defoe's pen, and so in another passage, where Moll
cheats a man, and then tells him pleasantly afterwards that she has
done so, with the result that she slides still further into his good
graces, and cannot bear to cheat him any more. Whatever she does
gives us a slight shock—not the jolt of disillusionment, but the
thrill that proceeds from a living being. We laugh at her, but without bitterness or superiority. She is neither hypocrite nor fool.

Towards the end of the book she is caught in a draper's shop by
two young ladies from behind the counter: "I would have given
them good words but there was no room for it: two fiery dragons
could not have been more furious than they were"—they call for

† From *Aspects of the Novel* (New
York: Harcourt, Brace, 1927), pp. 56–
63. (This essay was originally part of the
Clark Lectures, delivered under the auspices of Trinity College, Cambridge.)

the police, she is arrested and sentenced to death and then transported to Virginia instead. The clouds of misfortune lift with indecent rapidity. The voyage is a very pleasant one, owing to the kindness of the old woman who had originally taught her to steal. And (better still) her Lancashire husband happens to be transported also. They land at Virginia where, much to her distress, her brother-husband proves to be in residence. She conceals this, he dies, and the Lancashire husband only blames her for concealing it from him: he has no other grievance, for the reason that he and she are still in love. So the book closes prosperously, and firm as at the opening sentence the heroine's voice rings out: "We resolve to spend the remainder of our years in sincere penitence for the wicked lives we have led."

Her penitence is sincere, and only a superficial judge will condemn her as a hypocrite. A nature such as hers cannot for long distinguish between doing wrong and getting caught—for a sentence or two she disentangles them but they insist on blending, and that is why her outlook is so cockneyfied and natural, with "sich is life" for a philosophy and Newgate in the place of Hell. If we were to press her or her creator Defoe and say, "Come, be serious. Do you believe in Infinity?" they would say (in the parlance of their modern descendants), "Of course I believe in Infinity—what do you take me for?"—a confession of faith that slams the door on Infinity more completely than could any denial.

Moll Flanders then shall stand as our example of a novel in which a character is everything and is given freest play. Defoe makes a slight attempt at a plot with the brother-husband as a centre, but he is quite perfunctory, and her legal husband (the one who took her on the jaunt to Oxford) just disappears and is heard of no more. Nothing matters but the heroine; she stands in an open space like a tree, and having said that she seems absolutely real from every point of view, we must ask ourselves whether we should recognize her if we met her in daily life. For that is the point we are still considering: the difference between people in life and people in books. And the odd thing is, that even though we take a character as natural and untheoretical as Moll who would coincide with daily life in every detail, we should not find her there as a whole. Suppose I suddenly altered my voice from a lecturing voice into an ordinary one and said to you, "Look out—I can see Moll in the audience—look out, Mr."—naming one of you by name—"she as near as could be got your watch"—well, you would know at once that I was wrong, that I was sinning not only against probabilities, which does not signify, but against daily life and books and the gulf that divides them. If I said, "Look out, there's someone like Moll in the audience," you might not believe me but you would not be annoyed by my imbecile lack of taste: I should only be sinning against probability. To suggest that Moll is in Cambridge this afternoon or anywhere in England, or has been anywhere in England is idiotic. Why?

This particular question will be easy to answer next week, when we shall deal with more complicated novels, where the character has to fit in with other aspects of fiction. We shall then be able to make the usual reply, which we find in all manuals of literature, and which should always be given in an examination paper, the aesthetic reply, to the effect that a novel is a work of art, with its own laws, which are not those of daily life, and that a character in a novel is real when it lives in accordance with such laws. Amelia or Emma, we shall then say, cannot be at this lecture because they exist only in the books called after them, only in worlds of Fielding or Jane Austen. The barrier of art divides them from us. They are real not because they are like ourselves (though they may be like us) but because they are convincing.

It is a good answer, it will lead on to some sound conclusions. Yet it is not satisfactory for a novel like *Moll Flanders*, where the character is everything and can do what it likes. We want a reply that is less aesthetic and more psychological. Why cannot she be here? What separates her from us? Our answer has already been implied in that quotation from Alain: she cannot be here because she belongs to a world where the secret life is visible, to a world that is not and cannot be ours, to a world where the narrator and the creator are one. And now we can get a definition as to when a character in a book is real: it is real when the novelist knows everything about it. He may not choose to tell us all he knows—many of the facts, even of the kind we call obvious, may be hidden. But he will give us the feeling that though the character has not been explained, it is explicable, and we get from this a reality of a kind we can never get in daily life.

JAMES JOYCE

[Defoe's Female Characters]†

This lady [Mrs. Christian Davies],[1] together with the adventuress Roxana and the unforgettable harlot Moll Flanders, forms the

† From "Daniel Defoe," translated and edited by Joseph Prescott from Italian manuscripts of a lecture delivered by Joyce at the Università Popolare Triestina in 1912 (*Buffalo Studies*, 1964, pp. 3–25.
1. Professor Prescott notes that John Robert Moore states, "We may find under Defoe's name . . . *The Life and Adventures of Mrs. Christian Davies*, written after he died." See Moore, *The Library*, Fifth Series, XI (September, 1956), 157 [*Editor*].

trio of female characters which reduces contemporary criticism to stupefied impotence.

[Molly Bloom on Moll]†

I dont like books with a Molly in them like that one he brought me about the one from Flanders a whore always shoplifting anything she could cloth and stuff and yards of it.

WILLIAM FAULKNER

[Moll Flanders]‡

* * * I remember Moll Flanders and all her teeming and rich fecundity like a market-place where all that had survived up to that time must bide and pass. * * *

ALAN DUGALD McKILLOP

[Genuine Artistic Intent]*

* * *

In *Moll Flanders* (January, 1722, dated 1721), above all the other works, Defoe combines his conception of character as brought out by immediate practical problems, his sense of social and economic reality, his selective and vivid presentation of detail significant for action, his application of a bourgeois success philosophy in a dangerous hinterland beyond the limits of respectability. Moll is a victim of society, showing the workings of economic and social compulsion; an unfortunate adventuress, showing the workings of chance and random circumstance; a cool exponent of self-interest, systematically trying to figure profit and loss in business, love, and crime. Though an outcast from the middle class, she carries many of its standards with her. A foundling at Colchester, she is educated

† From Molly Bloom's "soliloquy" in *Ulysses* (1914). Frank Budgen, friend, correspondent, and critic of Joyce, says: "Joyce was a great admirer of Defoe. He possessed his complete works, and had read every line of them. Of only three other writers, he said, could he make this claim: Flaubert, Ben Jonson, and Ibsen" (*James Joyce and the Making of "Ulysses,"* Bloomington: Indiana University Press, 1960, p. 181.)

‡ When asked what book he would most like to have written, Faulkner mentioned three: *Moby Dick, Moll Flanders,* and A. A. Milne's *When We Were Very Young* (*Chicago Tribune,* July 16, 1927). * From *The Early Masters of English Fiction* (Lawrence: University of Kansas Press, 1956), pp. 28–33. Copyright 1956 by the University of Kansas Press. Reprinted by permission of the author and the publisher.

above her station as a servant girl, and is lured into an illicit affair
with the elder son of the family, and then honestly sought in marriage by the younger son. We begin somewhat on the level of the
domestic conduct-books, with a Pamela-like situation which turns in
the direction of scandalous incident. "He would have me, and I was
not obliged to tell him that I was his brother's whore." "Mrs.
Betty," as she is called, cannot keep for long her aspirations to be a
"little gentlewoman," and though after the death of this first husband she marries a gentleman-tradesman (the very term condemns
him), with his bankruptcy she breaks away from respectability.
Interest in money takes the place of the more intangible manifesta-
tions of pride and vanity. The later discovery that the Virginian
planter she has married is her half-brother mars the narrative with
the coarse incest motive that sometimes intrudes in early popular
fiction. After six years more in England as another man's mistress
she still longs for a "settled life." Her next lover is an Irish adven-
turer, and he and Moll get married under false expectations as to
each other's fortune; but both meet the situation in a good-natured
way, and even with something approaching disinterested attach-
ment, or at least spontaneous sexual attraction. While he is off seeking his fortune—he really turns highwayman—she marries a staid
citizen and until his death seems to be in a safe harbor. A new
period begins when under the tutelage of an old midwife or "governess" she becomes a skilful pickpocket and shoplifter. The nick-
name "Moll Flanders," which she had apparently acquired before
this, now becomes especially appropriate if we can take "Moll" as
almost a generic name for a female criminal. The governess, who
appears and reappears at various points, is one of the most remarkable instances in Defoe of the helper type of character. Moll has
great success in her new calling, and becomes the greatest artist of
her time, but she falls a prey to the infatuation that overtakes
Defoe's protagonists, and will not leave off. Defoe here dwells on
the methods of London thieves, and shows himself versed in the
tricks of the town, pretending that he is putting honest citizens on
guard against such wiles. Though London is not described at
length, the physical presence of the city is intensely realized. Moll is
finally caught, and faces destiny in some remarkable scenes in
Newgate, but her repentance is not so convincing as her anguish at
the thought of being caught, or her pervasive fear of being stranded
without money. She would confirm Samuel Butler's dictum that
money losses are the hardest of all to bear. With her highwayman-
husband she is transported to Virginia, where she reëstablishes herself, and finally returns to lead a settled life in England. Fate, or
the convention of a happy ending, has restored to her the most con-
genial of her numerous husbands.

The action has been summarized to show that much bizarre and sensational incident enters into the record, only to be leveled out by a monotonous evenness of emphasis. Moll reports everything from incest to the contents of a stolen bundle with a deadpan attitude that may remind us of the strict neutrality of naturalism. She compiles data on her husbands as Defoe compiled statistics. This simplification of her attitude is more drastic and less natural than the enforced simplification of Crusoe's attitude on the island. Moll is craftier than Crusoe, and has less mysticism; she indulges in no religious meditations, and feels few secret promptings from guardian spirits, though at least once she seems to be in telepathic communication with her favorite husband. Common decency requires that she should swoon and weep on being reprieved, but her feelings are not elaborated. Yet natural humanity is not completely leveled out. Moll has promptings toward honesty and loyalty, and she can even fall in love in her way, but she feels that she cannot afford to indulge such impulses, though other things being equal she would rather have intelligence and virtue. " 'Tis something of relief even to be undone by a man of honour rather than by a scoundrel." "I would gladly have turned my hand to any honest employment if I could have got it."

> I was now a loose, unguided creature, and had no help, no assistance, no guide for my conduct; I knew what I aimed at, and what I wanted, but knew nothing how to pursue the end by direct means. I wanted to be placed in a settled state of living, and had I happened to meet with a sober, good husband, I should have been as true a wife to him as virtue itself could have formed. If I had been otherwise, the vice came in always at the door of necessity, not at the door of inclination; and I understood too well, by the want of it, what the value of a settled life was, to do anything to forfeit the felicity of it; nay, I should have made the better wife for all the difficulties I had passed through, by a great deal; nor did I in any of the times that I had been a wife give my husbands the least uneasiness on account of my behaviour.

Crusoe is the victim of infatuation and wanderlust; he deliberately leaves the state of security that Moll is struggling to attain. Moll is more completely the prisoner of the immediate situation than Crusoe is even on the island. As a practical woman she has to consider the immediate future, but she does not take long views; she reports her own attitudes and calculations, but she does not look steadily within and struggle with a divided mind. Like the Wife of Bath, she has had five husbands, "withouten oother compaignye in youthe," but she could never sum up her career with such reflections as these:

But, Lord Crist! whan that it remembreth me
Upon my yowthe, and on my jolitee,
It tikleth me aboute myn herte roote.
Unto this day it dooth myn herte boote
That I have had my world as in my tyme.

Throughout her story she uses a stereotyped practical and moralistic style; Defoe's triumph is that he convinces us that it is her personal style. She is so completely occupied with explicit detail bearing on ways and means that she is not disposed to take the aesthetic
attitude required to render fully the immediately experienced present, or the imaginative coloring of recollection and anticipation. It
has recently been suggested that the moral inconsistencies in *Moll
Flanders* and *Roxana* are due to the gap between the state of mind
at the time of action and the state of mind at the time of record:
that is, Moll and Roxana have repented at long last, and incon-
gruously put their repentant attitude into their report of their original misdeeds.[1] The difficulty with this theory is that Defoe is not
much interested in the time-span and the changes wrought by time;
he is never keenly conscious of the double point of view involved
when a character is talking about his own past. But it should be
added that when Defoe is at his best the character at the time of
the wicked action is not so oversimplified as to be unconvincing.
The marvellous episode of the child's necklace may be quoted to
show how Moll's colloquial style, weak compunctions, and ruthless
purposes are fused into imaginative unity:

I went out now by daylight, and wandered about I knew not
whither, and in search of I knew not what, when the devil put a
snare in my way of a dreadful nature indeed, and such a one as I
have never had before or since. Going through Aldersgate Street,
there was a pretty little child had been at a dancing-school, and
was agoing home all alone; and my prompter, like a true devil, set
me upon this innocent creature. I talked to it, and it prattled to
me again, and I took it by the hand, and led it along till I came
to a paved alley that goes into Bartholemew Close, and I led it in
there. The child said, that was not its way home. I said, "Yes, my
dear, it is; I'll show you the way home." The child had a little
necklace on of gold beads, and I had my eye upon that, and in
the dark of the alley I stooped, pretending to mend the child's
clog that was loose, and took off her necklace, and the child never
felt it, and so led the child on again. Here, I say, the devil put
me upon killing the child in the dark alley, that it might not cry,
but the very thought frighted me so that I was ready to drop
down; but I turned the child about and bade it go back again, for
that was not its way home; the child said, so she would; and I
went through into Bartholemew Close, and then turned round to

1. A. A. Mendilow, *Time and the Novel* (1952), pp. 90–92.

another passage that goes into Long Lane, so away into Charter-house Yard, and out into St. John's Street; then crossing into Smithfield, went down Chick Lane, and into Field Lane, to Hol-born Bridge, when, mixing with the crowd of people usually pass-ing there, it was not possible to have been found out; and thus I made my second sally into the world.

The thoughts of this booty put out all the thoughts of the first, and the reffections I had made wore quickly off; poverty hardened my heart, and my own necessities made me regardless of anything. The last affair left no great concern upon me, for as I did the poor child no harm, I only thought I had given the par-ents a just reproof for their negligence, in leaving the poor lamb to come home by itself, and it would teach them to take more care another time.

This string of beads was worth about £12 or £14. I suppose it might have been formerly the mother's, for it was too big for the child's wear, but that, perhaps, the vanity of the mother to have her child look fine at the dancing-school, had made her let the child wear it; and no doubt the child had a maid sent to take care of it, but she, like a careless jade, was taken up perhaps with some fellow that had met her, and so the poor baby wandered till it fell into my hands.

However, I did the child no harm; I did not so much as fright it, for I had a great many tender thoughts about me yet, and did nothing but what, as I may say, mere necessity drove me to.

The hypothetical matter about the parents and the maid is a strik-ing example of the way Moll's mind works, and Defoe's.[2]

Moll's sexual escapades have always given the book a bad name; its immediate success (three editions in 1722, another edition and an abridgment in 1723) was no doubt due in large part to its sup-posed scandalous character. Defoe's full title shows how the book made its market: "The fortunes and misfortunes of the famous Moll Flanders &c. who was born in Newgate, and during a life of con-tinu'd variety for three-score years, besides her childhood, was twelve years a whore, five times a wife (whereof once to her own brother) twelve years a thief, eight years a transported felon in Vir-ginia, at last grew rich, liv'd honest, and died a penitent, written from her own memorandums." Chapbooks put the story within the reach of all, and it was supposed to corrupt the morals of the young. Hogarth's idle apprentice chooses to read *Moll Flanders* (perhaps a broadside ballad version) rather than *The Apprentice's Guide*. As late as 1916 Professor Trent said that the full title was unprintable, and gave no extracts from *Moll Flanders* in his excel-lent book on Defoe. But here there is nothing to compare to the

2. In order to appreciate the effect which Defoe obtains by connecting epi-sode and character, compare exactly the same incident presented as a dream or apparition of the Devil to a distressed man, in *An Essay on the History and Reality of Apparitions* (1727), pp. 207–9.

insistent emphasis on sex in Richardson and Sterne, to say nothing
of the twentieth century. Moll may be *tout entière à sa proie atta-
chée*, but not in the same sense as Venus. Like a good many other
people, she is after all concerned with the social and economic pre-
conditions for sexual union. She is too business-like to be either
demure or lascivious, and she is so consistently on the make that
she imposes strict limits on the range of Defoe's compilation. Here
is Defoe's closest approach to deliberate realism according to a program, and it is this anticipation of the hard-boiled novelist of later
times that gives the story its present high position. The reduction of
the entire record to acquisition and calculation and the spiritual
impoverishment implied in the practical and moral warnings that
echo through the story operate on us with the effect of a marvel-
lously constructed piece of art—no one could be so monolithic by
accident. In the use of casual and apparently unstudied detail which
always bears on the main point, even though given in a repetitious
and colloquial style, Defoe has some advantage over the novelist of
later times who professes to document fully and richly, and also
over the fastidious artist who handles discriminated detail with a
manifest intention to be poignant and precious and symbolic.
Defoe's position is the stronger because he can never go on a walk
with J. Alfred Prufrock. This is not to belittle later fiction with its
collateral influences from poetry and science, but simply to assert
that Defoe's apparent unstudied simplifications yield a result which
justifies our crediting him with genuine artistic intent.

* * *

IAN WATT

Defoe as Novelist: *Moll Flanders*†

* * *

Perhaps the most famous claim made for Defoe as an artist was
made by Coleridge, in a marginal note on the passage in *Robinson
Crusoe* where the hero comes across some gold in the cabin of the
wreck:

> I smil'd to my self at the Sight of this Money, O Drug! Said I
> aloud, what are thou good for, Thou are not worth to me, no not
> the taking off of the Ground, one of those Knives is worth all
> this Heap, I have no Manner of use for thee, e'en remain where

† From *The Rise of the Novel* (Berkeley
and Los Angeles: University of California Press, 1957; London: Chatto &
Windus, 1957), pp. 119–131. Reprinted
by permission of The Regents of the
University of California, Chatto &
Windus, and the author.

thou art, and go to the Bottom as a Creature whose Life is not worth saving. However, upon Second Thoughts, I took it away;* and wrapping all this in a Piece of Canvas . . .

So Defoe, and at the asterisk Coleridge commented:

> Worthy of Shakespeare;—and yet the simple semi-colon after it, the instant passing on without the least pause of reflex consciousness is more exquisite and masterlike than the touch itself. A meaner writer, a Marmontel, would have put an '!' after 'away', and have commenced a new paragraph.[1]

We smile at the phrase 'on second thoughts', with its casual deflation of Crusoe's rhetorical paradox about the worthlessness of gold, and are tempted to see a fine literary decorum in Defoe's avoidance of any further explanation of the compulsive irrationality of economic man. Yet, can we be sure that the irony is not accidental? Is this paradoxical monologue really suited to Crusoe's character or his present situation? Isn't it more typical of Defoe the economic publicist ever on the alert to enforce the useful truth that goods alone constitute real wealth? And if so—isn't the apparent irony merely the result of the extreme insouciance with which Defoe the publicist jerks himself back to his role as novelist, and hastens to tell us what he knows Crusoe, and indeed anyone else, would actually do in the circumstances?

We certainly cannot allow Coleridge's praise to pass as it stands. He used the 1812 edition of the book, which—like most later editions—had put a good deal of order into Defoe's haphazard punctuation: the early editions actually give a comma, not a semi-colon, after 'I took it away'. Further—Coleridge's case for Defoe's literary mastery depends a great deal on Defoe's having first combined the two components of the irony—the uselessness of gold in the circumstances, and the decision to take it nevertheless—into a single unit of meaning, and on his having then refused to give any obvious signal to the reader, such as an exclamation mark. In fact, however, not only is there a comma for Coleridge's semi-colon, but there are lots of others as the sentence rambles on for some fifteen lines, during which Crusoe swims ashore and a storm blows up. This seems to be hiding the effect a little too much: and suggests that the real reason for the semblance of irony here and elsewhere in Defoe may well be the amount of heterogeneous matter which he habitually aggregates into one syntactical unit, together with the extreme casualness by which the transitions between the disparate items are effected.

Coleridge's enthusiasm may in any case serve to remind us of the danger to which, it has been alleged, the wise are especially prone:

---

1. *Miscellaneous Criticism*, ed. Thomas M. Raysor (London, 1936), p. 294.

that of seeing too much. This seems to be what happens in Virginia Woolf's two essays in the *Common Reader*. Do not the texts of *Robinson Crusoe* and *Moll Flanders* provide her with an occasion for being wise, for seeing more than is really there? She writes, for instance, 'a plain earthenware pot stands in the foreground . . . [which] . . . persuades us to see remote islands and the solitudes of the human soul'.[2] In view of the essay 'On Solitude' in the last part of *Robinson Crusoe* it is surely more likely that Defoe's technique was not subtle or conscious enough to be able to evoke the theme of human solitude and to instruct us in elementary pottery at the same time and in the same narrative.

So when Virginia Woolf writes of Defoe subduing 'every other element to his design'[3] I remain sceptical. Is there—either in *Robinson Crusoe* or in *Moll Flanders*—any design whatsoever in the usual sense of the term? Isn't such an interpretation really a kind of indirect critical repayment for the feeling of superiority which Defoe enables us to derive from his humble and unpondered prose, a feeling of superiority which enables us to convert the extreme cases of his narrative *gaucherie* into irony?

Moll Flanders has a few examples of patent and conscious irony. There is, first of all, a good deal of dramatic irony of a simple kind: for example in Virginia, where a woman relates the story of Moll's incestuous marriage, not knowing that she is addressing its chief figure. There are also some examples of much more pointed irony, as in the passage when, as a little girl, Moll Flanders vows that she will become a gentlewoman when she grows up, like one of her leisured but scandalous neighbours:

> 'Poor child,' says my good old nurse, 'you may soon be such a gentlewoman as that, for she is a person of ill fame, and has had two bastards.'
> I did not understand anything of that; but I answered, 'I am sure they call her madam, and she does not go to service nor do housework'; and therefore I insisted that she was a gentlewoman, and I would be such a gentlewoman as that.

It is good dramatic irony to point this prophetic episode with the phrase 'such a gentlewoman as that', where the verbal emphasis also drives home the difference between virtue and class, and the moral dangers of being taken in by external evidences of gentility. We can be certain that the irony is conscious because its tenor is supported by Defoe's other writings, which often show a somewhat rancorous spirit towards the failure of the gentry to provide proper models of conduct: there is a similar tendency, for example, in Moll's later

2. 'Robinson Crusoe', *The Common Reader, Second Series* (London, 1948), p. 58.
3. *Ibid.*

ironical description of the eldest brother as 'a gay gentleman who
. . . had levity enough to do an ill-natured thing, yet had too much
judgment of things to pay too dear for his pleasures'. Here, the
combination of stylistic elegance and demonstrable consonance with
Defoe's own point of view makes us sure that Moll Flanders's reflection after she has been duped by James is also ironical: ' 'Tis something of relief even to be undone by a man of honour, rather than
by a scoundrel'. The verbal hyperbole drives home the contrast
between overt and actual moral norms: 'undone' is a calculated
exaggeration, Moll Flanders being what she is already; and the
ambiguity of 'a man of honour' seems to be used with full consciousness of its subversive effect.

These examples of conscious irony in *Moll Flanders*, however, fall
far short of the larger, structural irony which would suggest that
Defoe viewed either his central character or his purported moral
theme ironically. There is certainly nothing in *Moll Flanders* which
clearly indicates that Defoe sees the story differently from the heroine. There are, it is true, a few cases where such an intention
seems possible: but on examination they are seen to have none of
the hallmarks of the conscious examples of irony given above;
instead, they are much closer to the passage in *Robinson Crusoe*.

A particularly close parallel to Crusoe's bathetic fall from his rhetorical climax occurs after Moll Flanders has revealed the terrible
truth of her birth to her husband and half-brother:

> I saw him turn pale and look wild; and I said, 'Now remember
> your promise, and receive it with presence of mind; for who could
> have said more to prepare you for it than I have done?' However,
> I called a servant, and got him a little glass of rum (which is the
> usual dram of the country), for he was fainting away.

The insistence on credibility—leading to the fussy parenthesis
explaining why rum and not brandy—creates a violent contrast
between the great stress of the emotion and its very humdrum cure.
Life, one might agree, is like that; but any writer who wanted to
insist on the intensity of the emotion would not suggest that a glass
of rum would meet the case. Especially a little one—'little' is a
good example of how a 'realistic' attention to minute but somehow
inappropriate detail can help to create irony.

Formally, we notice, the passage is similar to the gold one; the
transition between the incongruous elements uses the adversative
'however' which insists on the logical connection in the narrator's
mind. If Defoe had merely begun a new paragraph, the irony would
have been much diminished, since it depends on the apparent
insistence that the two juxtaposed items—in each case an emotional
or abstract extreme followed by a more practical consideration—
really belong to the same universe of discourse.

The passage is also typical in content, because the suspicion of irony is aroused by a bathetic transition from sentiment to action which is very common in Defoe's novels, although it is never certain that he intends it ironically. There is the occasion, for instance, when Moll, in her unwonted transport of feeling, kisses the ground her son has trodden on, but desists as soon as it is urged upon her that the ground is 'damp and dangerous'. It is perhaps possible that Defoe was laughing at his heroine's unabashed mixture of sentimentality and common sense; but it is surely more likely that he had to get Moll off her knees before he could get on with the story, and that he did not ponder the means of doing so very carefully.

The lack of insulation between incongruous attitudes seems particularly ironical if we are already predisposed to regard one of them as false. This happens with many of the moralising passages, and Defoe certainly does nothing to obviate our incredulity by the way he introduces them. One glaringly improbable case occurs when an as yet impenitent Moll relates to the governess how she was picked up by a drunken man whom she later robbed, and goes on to improve the occasion by quoting Solomon in the course of a lay sermon against drunkenness. The governess is much moved, Moll tells us:

> ... it so affected her that she was hardly able to forbear tears, to think how such a gentleman ran a daily risk of being undone, every time a glass of wine got into his head.
> But as to the purchase I got, and how entirely I stripped him, she told me it pleased her wonderfully. 'Nay, child,' says she, 'the usage may, for aught I know, do more to reform him than all the sermons that ever he will hear in his life.' And if the remainder of the story be true, so it did.

The two women then combine to anticipate divine retribution, and to milk the poor gentleman of his cash, in order to drive their lesson home. The episode is certainly a travesty of piety and morality; and yet it is very unlikely that Defoe is being ironical; any more than he is later when, by some very human obliquity, Moll Flanders excuses herself from the prison chaplain's appeal that she confess her sins on the grounds of his addiction to the bottle. Both episodes are plausible enough psychologically: the devotees of one vice are often less charitable than the virtuous about the other ones they happen not to favour. The problem, however, is whether Defoe himself overlooked, and expected his readers to overlook, the very damaging nature of the context in which his homilies against alcohol occur. There is every reason to believe that he did: the lesson itself must have been intended seriously, and not ironically; as for its context, we have already seen that there was no way in which Defoe could make good his didactic professions except by making

Moll double as chorus for his own honest beliefs; and there is therefore good reason to believe that the moral imperceptiveness which is so laughably clear to us is in fact a reflection of one of the psychological characteristics of Puritanism which Defoe shared with his heroine.

Svend Ranulf, in his *Moral Indignation and Middle Class Psychology*, has shown, mainly from Commonwealth pamphlets, how the Puritans were much more addicted to outbursts of moral indignation than were the Royalists.[4] One of the strengths of Puritanism, he suggests, lay in its tendency to convert its demand for righteousness into a somewhat uncharitable aggressiveness against the sins of others: and this, of course, carried with it a complementary tendency for the individual to be mercifully blind to his own faults. Moll Flanders frequently exemplifies this tendency. One famous instance is the passage when she consoles herself for having stolen a child's gold necklace with the reflection: 'I only thought I had given the parents a just reproof for their negligence, in leaving the poor lamb to come home by itself, and it would teach them to take more care another time'. There is no doubt about the psychological veracity of the reflection: the conscience is a great casuist. There is, however, some doubt about Defoe's intention: is it meant to be an ironical touch about his heroine's moral duplicities, her tendency to be blind to the beam in her own eye? or did Defoe forget Moll as he raged inwardly at the thought of how careless parents are, and how richly they deserve to be punished?

If Defoe intended the passage to be an ironical portrayal of spiritual self-deception, it becomes necessary to assume that he saw Moll Flanders's character as a whole in this light, for the incident is typical of her general blindness to her own spiritual and mental dishonesty. She always lies about her financial position, for instance, even to those she loves. Thus when the mutual trickery with James is revealed, she conceals a thirty-pound bank-bill 'and that made freer of the rest, in consideration of his circumstances, for I really pitied him heartily'. Then she goes on, 'But to return to this question, I told him I never willingly deceived him and I never would'. Later, after his departure, she says: 'Nothing that ever befell me in my life sank so deep into my heart as this farewell. I reproached him a thousand times in my thoughts for leaving me, for I would have gone with him through the world, if I had begged my bread. I felt in my pocket, and there I found ten guineas, his gold watch, and two little rings. . . .' She cannot even in theory attest the reality of her devotion by expressing her willingness to beg her bread, without immediately proving that it was only a rhetorical hyperbole by reassuring herself that she has enough in her pocket to keep her in

4. Copenhagen, 1938, especially pp. 94, 198.

bread for a lifetime. There is surely no conscious irony here: for Defoe and his heroine generous sentiments are good, and concealed cash reserves are good too, perhaps better; but there is no feeling that they conflict, or that one attitude undermines the other.

Defoe had accused the occasional conformists of 'playing Bo-Peep with God Almighty'.[5] The term admirably describes the politic equivocations about common honesty and moral truth so common in *Moll Flanders*. Defoe there 'plays Bo-Peep' at various levels: from the sentence and the incident to the fundamental ethical structure of the whole book, his moral attitude to his creation is as shallow and devious and easily deflected as his heroine's on the occasion when her married gallant writes to her to terminate the affair, and urges her to change her ways, she writes: 'I was struck with this letter, as with a thousand wounds; the reproaches of my own conscience were such as I cannot express, for I was not blind to my own crime; and I reflected that I might with less offence have continued with my brother, since there was no crime in our marriage on that score, neither of us knowing it.'

No writer who had allowed himself to contemplate either his heroine's conscience, or the actual moral implications of her career, in a spirit of irony, could have written this seriously. Nor could he have written the account of James's moral reformation, in which Moll Flanders tells us how she brought him the riches given by her son, not forgetting 'the horses, hogs, and cows, and other stores for our plantation' and concludes 'from this time forward I believe he was as sincere a penitent and as thoroughly a reformed man as ever God's goodness brought back from a profligate, a highwayman, and a robber'. We, not Defoe, are ironically aware of the juxtaposition of the powers of God and Mammon; we, not Defoe, laugh at the concept of reformation through hogs and cows.

Whatever disagreement there may be about particular instances, it is surely certain that there is no consistently ironical attitude present in *Moll Flanders*. Irony in its extended sense expresses a deep awareness of the contradictions and incongruities that beset man in this vale of tears, an awareness which is manifested in the text's purposeful susceptibility to contradictory interpretations. As soon as we have become aware of the author's ulterior purpose, we can see all the apparent contradictions as indications of the coherent attitude underlying the whole work. Such a way of writing obviously makes severe demands upon the attention of the author and the reader: the implication of every word, the juxtaposition of every episode, the relation of every part to the whole, all must exclude any interpretation except the intended one. It is, as we have seen, very

5. *True Collection* . . . , p. 315.

unlikely that Defoe wrote in this way, or that he had such readers; indeed, all the evidence points the other way.

It may be objected that Defoe wrote at least one avowedly ironical work, *The Shortest Way with Dissenters* (1702). And it is true that there he very successfully imitated the style, the temper and the basic strategy of the exasperated High Churchmen who at last saw an opportunity under Anne for crushing the Dissenters. Actually, however, as is well known, many readers took the pamphlet as a genuine expression of extreme Tory churchmanship; and the reason for this is made clear by a study of the work: as in *Moll Flanders*, Defoe's vicarious identification with the supposed speaker was so complete that it obscured his original intention; his only conscious exercise in irony, in fact, was indeed a masterpiece, but a masterpiece not of irony but of impersonation.

There is not time here to demonstrate this at length, but the contemporary reception of *The Shortest Way* at least shows that it does not constitute irrefutable evidence that irony was a weapon which Defoe could handle effectively. Nor, indeed, is this view held by all those who see *Moll Flanders* as a work of irony. Bonamy Dobrée, for example, in a persuasive commentary finds the novel 'full of delicious irony so long as we keep outside Moll'. But since, as he admits and as has been argued above, it is very difficult to believe that Defoe was objective enough to be able to keep outside his heroine, Dobrée's claim that *Moll Flanders* is 'an astonishing incomparable masterpiece'[6] seems to depend on the view that its irony is unintentional and unconscious.

Our crucial problem, therefore, would seem to be how we can explain the fact that a novel which was not intended ironically should be seen in such a light by so many modern readers. The answer would seem to be a matter not of literary criticism but of social history. We cannot today believe that so intelligent a man as Defoe should have viewed either his heroine's economic attitudes or her pious protestations with anything other than derision. Defoe's other writings, however, do not support this belief, and it may be surmised that the course of history has brought about in us powerful and often unconscious predispositions to regard certain matters ironically which Defoe and his age treated quite seriously.

Among these predispositions, these ironigenic attitudes, two at least are strongly aroused by *Moll Flanders*: the guilt feelings which are now fairly widely attached to economic gain as a motive; and the view that protestations of piety are suspect anyway, especially when combined with a great attention to one's own economic inter-

6. 'Some Aspects of Defoe's Prose',– *Presented to George Sherburn*, ed. Clifford and Landa (Oxford, 1949), p. 176. *Pope and His Contemporaries, Essays*

est. But, as we have seen, Defoe was innocent of either attitude. He was not ashamed to make economic self-interest his major premise about human life; he did not think such a premise conflicted either with social or religious values; and nor did his age. It is likely, there-fore, that one group of apparent ironies in *Moll Flanders* can be explained as products of an unresolved and largely unconscious con-flict in Defoe's own outlook, a conflict which is typical of the late Puritan disengagement of economic matters from religious and moral sanctions.

Most of the other ironies in *Moll Flanders* can be explained on similar lines. One group of apparent ironies, we noted, centred round the deflation of emotional considerations by practical ones: here, surely, we have the rational and sceptical instincts of Defoe unconsciously rebelling against the sentimental scenes and speeches which the genre and its readers required. Another group of possible ironies centres round the amorous adventures of the heroine; we find it difficult to believe that these were told only for purposes of moral edification. Yet the ambivalence here is typical of the secular-ised Puritan. John Dunton, for example, an eccentric Dissenter and an acquaintance of Defoe's, wrote a monthly paper exposing prosti-tution, *The Night Walker: or, Evening Rambles in Search after Lewd Women* (1696–97), in which a virtuous purpose is avowed as strongly and as unconvincingly as it is today by sensational journal-ists engaged in similar appeals to public lubricity. An even closer analogy is supplied by Pepys: he bought a pornographic work and read it in his office on Sundays, commenting 'a mighty lewd book, but not amiss for a sober man to read once over to inform himself in the villainy of the world.'[7]

There are other areas of conflict in Defoe's outlook which explain two further important difficulties in the critical interpretation of *Moll Flanders*. One reason for the feeling that Defoe cannot be serious about Moll's spiritual reformation is that her remorse and penitence are not supported by the action or even by any sense of real psychological change: as in *Robinson Crusoe*, the spiritual dimension is presented as a series of somewhat inexplicable religious breakdowns in the psychic mechanism, breakdowns, however, which do not permanently impair her healthy amorality. But this dissocia-tion of religion from ordinary life was a natural consequence of secularisation, and the same feature of the life of Defoe's time is probably also the cause of the central confusion in Moll Flanders's moral consciousness—her tendency to confuse penitence for her sins with chagrin at the punishment of her crimes. The secularisa-tion of individual morality obviously tended to emphasise the dis-

7. *Diary*, ed. Wheatley (London, 1896), VII, 279.

tinction which Hobbes made when he wrote that 'every crime is a sin, but not every sin a crime';[8] it is surely because Moll Flanders's genuine fears only extend to the probable results of the discovery of her crimes that we feel, to quote Reed Whittemore, that in her moral consciousness 'Hell is almost bound by Newgate's wall'.[9]

Many of the apparent discrepancies in *Moll Flanders*, then, are concerned with areas of individual morality where the last two centuries have taught us to make careful distinctions, but where the early eighteenth century tended to be a good deal less sensitive. It is natural, therefore, that we should be prone to see irony where there is more probably only a confusion—a confusion which our century is much better prepared to discern than was Defoe or his age. It is probably significant in this connection that the most ardent admirers of *Moll Flanders* are unhistorical in their outlook and interests. E. M. Forster, for instance, in *Aspects of the Novel* specifically excludes period considerations from his inquiry; while John Peale Bishop, perhaps accepting but misreading Defoe's concluding assertion 'Written in the year 1683', dates the novel itself in 1668.[1]

There is another historical explanation of a somewhat different kind for the modern tendency to read *Moll Flanders* ironically: the rise of the novel. We place Defoe's novels in a very different context from that of their own time; we take novels much more seriously now, and we judge his by the more exacting literary standards of today. This presumption, combined with Defoe's actual mode of writing, forces us to explain a great deal as ironical. We believe, for example, that a sentence should have unity; if we must invent one for sentences which are really a random accumulation of clauses containing many disparate or incongruous items, we can impose unity only by an ironical subordination of some items to others. Similarly with the larger units of composition, from the paragraph to the total structure: if we assume on *a priori* grounds that a coherent plan must be present, we find one, and thereby produce a complex pattern out of what are actually incongruities.

Life itself, of course, is a suitable enough object for ironical contemplation, and so the tendency to regard *Moll Flanders* as ironic is in a sense a tribute to Defoe's vitality as a writer—it is partly because what he creates seems so real that we feel we must define our attitude to it. But, of course, such an attitude on the reader's part is excluded by genuinely ironical writing more than by any other: every way of looking at the events has been anticipated and either organised into the whole work, or made impossible. There is no evidence of such exclusion in *Moll Flanders*, much less of a com-

8. *Leviathan*, Pt. II, ch. 27.
9. *Heroes and Heroines* (New York, 1946), p. 47.

1. *Collected Essays*, p. 47; the actual date was 1722.

prehensive control operating over every aspect of the work. If they are ironies, they are surely the ironies of social and moral and literary disorder. Perhaps, however, they are better regarded not as the achievements of an ironist, but as accidents produced by the random application of narrative authenticity to conflicts in Defoe's social and moral and religious world, accidents which unwittingly reveal to us the serious discrepancies in his system of values.

That these discrepancies are revealed at all, incidentally, is a tribute to the searching power of formal realism, which permits and indeed encourages the presentation of literary objects and attitudes which had not hitherto jostled each other in the same work but had been segregated in separate ones such as tragedy, comedy, history, picaresque, journalism and homily. Later novelists such as Jane Austen and Flaubert were to incorporate such conflicts and incongruities into the very structure of their works: they created irony, and made novel readers sensitive to its effects. We cannot but approach Defoe's novels through the literary expectations which later masters of the form made possible, and these expectations seem to find some justification as a result of our acute awareness of the conflicting nature of the two main forces in Defoe's philosophy of life—rational economic individualism and concern for spiritual redemption—which together held his divided but not, apparently, uneasy allegiance. Nevertheless, if we are primarily concerned with Defoe's actual intentions, we must conclude that although he reveals the sophistries whereby these dual allegiances are preserved intact, he does not, strictly speaking, portray them; consequently *Moll Flanders* is undoubtedly an ironic object, but it is not a work of irony.

The preceding sections are not intended as a denial of the importance of Defoe as a novelist, but only as a demonstration of a fact that might perhaps have been taken for granted if it had not been challenged or overlooked by many recent critics: the fact that Defoe's novels lack both the consistency in matters of detail of which many lesser writers are capable, and the larger coherences found in the greatest literature. Defoe's forte was the brilliant episode. Once his imagination seized on a situation he could report it with a comprehensive fidelity which was much in advance of any previous fiction, and which, indeed, has never been surpassed. These episodes are irresistible in quotation; and the pre-eminence of *Moll Flanders* is perhaps mainly due to its strong claim to be not so much a great novel as Defoe's richest anthology.

How far we should allow Defoe's gift for the perfect episode to outweigh his patent shortcomings—weaknesses of construction, inattention to detail, lack of moral or formal pattern—is a very difficult critical problem. There is something about Defoe's genius which is as confident and indestructible as the resilient selfhood of his heroine, and which all but persuades us to accept the notorious critical heresy that the single talent well employed can make up for all the others.

The talent, of course, is the supreme one in the novel: Defoe is the master illusionist, and this almost makes him the founder of the new form. Almost, but not quite: the novel could be considered established only when realistic narrative was organised into a plot which, while retaining Defoe's lifelikeness, also had an intrinsic coherence; when the novelist's eye was focussed on character and personal relationships as essential elements in the total structure, and not merely as subordinate instruments for furthering the verisimilitude of the actions described; and when all these were related to a controlling moral intention. It was Richardson who took these further steps, and it is primarily for this reason that he, rather than Defoe, is usually regarded as the founder of the English novel.

* * *

TERENCE MARTIN

The Unity of *Moll Flanders*†

The flat, episodic nature of the narrative in *Moll Flanders* leaves Moll herself as the one immediately discernible principle of unity in the book. Without formal pause, without breaking her story into any mechanical divisions of chapters or sections, Moll relentlessly tells us of her almost seventy years of life in a cumulatively matter-of-fact tone. * *. *

My purpose in examining *Moll Flanders* is to suggest that the episodes themselves (the "very circumstances" with which Defoe is dealing) afford a unity which complements structurally the unity supplied by the novel's heroine. All aspects of the novel's unity, of course, involve Moll herself as principal actor; but in conjunction with the natural psychological progression in the book, there exists, I believe, a formal pattern of circumstance shaped coherently by the episodes which make up Moll's experience.

Let us begin with the second major part of the book, in which Moll Flanders initiates her career as a thief. By leading to her arrest, to her reunion with Jemmy in Newgate, and finally to her return to America, these adventures in theft serve to connect Moll's

† From *Modern Language Quarterly*, XXII (1961), 115–124. Reprinted by permission of the author and *Modern Language Quarterly*.

later life with her earlier; this much is evident even from a bare summary of the plot. But if we examine the details of theft, we find further, I believe, that the second large part of the novel operates as an attempt to win back the relative security of the first part: Moll's desire for economic security manifests itself in a series of adventures which testify to the quality of this desire by falling into a significant episodic pattern.

Moll begins her career of stealing at the conveniently neat age of fifty, after her affair with the elder brother, her marriage to Robin, her marriage to the tradesman, her retreat into the refuge of the Mint, her marriage to her half-brother whom she recognizes to be such during her residence in Virginia, her affair with the man at Bath, her marriage to Jemmy (her Lancashire husband), and her marriage to the banker. The banker's financial ruin and subsequent death turn her into the world "in a condition the reverse of all that had been before it."

Now "eighty-and-forty," she tells us that she is past the time of childbearing. Moreover, to increase her "dismal and disconsolate" state, it is "past the flourishing time . . . when I might expect to be courted for a mistress; that agreeable part had declined some time and the ruins only appeared of what had been." She sees the daily diminishing of her money as a kind of "bleeding to death," a threat to her economic life inducing severe mental distress: "I sat and cried and tormented myself night and day, wringing my hands, and sometimes raving like a distracted woman . . . I had the vapours to such a degree, that my understanding was quite lost in fancies and imaginations."

After living for two years in "this dismal condition," she begins to steal. With the devil prompting her, she first takes a bundle from a maid-servant; among its contents are childbed linen and a small silver mug. Then she steals a necklace from a child. After accidentally getting some pieces of silk thrown down by an escaping thief, she next breaks a window and steals two rings, one diamond and one gold. Shortly afterwards, she steals a watch from a pregnant woman, and, with the devil still urging her onward, she and a temporary confederate-teacher amass twenty-one gold watches.

The significance of the pattern of theft begins to take suggestive shape. Let us admit promptly, and even insist upon, the thick literal texture of Moll's adventures in crime. She steals so many watches because the fashion eminently permits them to be stolen; she steals real objects that come her way, begging, as it were, her attention. But the pattern of theft is there too, because of the very realness of what she steals. At the age of fifty, past the age of childbearing, having buried her last husband (speaking chronologically), Moll requires a new *modus operandi*. Her sex has been her stock-in-trade:

a shrewd bargainer, aware that the market value of a woman depends principally upon herself, she has traded on sex as a commodity
to get on respectably in the world. But age and the death of her husband have left her in a singularly insecure position, in which, conceivably, she might be forced to struggle for survival, rather than for
middle-class respectability.

She begins to steal from impulse, not from any predesigned plan;
her early thefts are uncharacteristic actions, lacking in shrewdness
and conscious design. Indeed, at first Moll has no way to dispose of
what she has stolen; she is threatened with a kind of economic con-
stipation, the grave threat of the capitalist world to itself. The pattern of these impulsive thefts suggests her desire to have back again
the reliable "goods" that have departed—her fertility and the
accompanying sexual attractiveness of younger days. She steals baby
clothes and what might well be wedding rings; she steals from a
pregnant woman; and the necklace (an object to enhance beauty)
she takes from the child is large: "it might have been formerly the
mother's."

This is not to say that Moll is struck with a sudden love of children or with a passion for sexual pleasure. To Alan McKillop's
remark that she is "too business-like to be either demure or lascivious," we might add that Moll has little leisure for sentimentality.[1] We know that she has never wanted children, that despite her
moralistic lecture on maternal duty children are a kind of nuisance
to her because they have no place in her life. But never does she
determine not to have children or to prevent their being born; for
children are a certain sign that she is sexually desirable and that she
has a natural capacity for production. And now Moll, the unintentional producer of many childrren, would have her power back again;
to remain a part of this increasingly competitive society, one must
produce or be capable of producing. Thus Moll steals watches,
quantities of watches, in an effort, as it were, both to steal back
time and to capture the symbolic essence of the business-oriented,
clockwork world around her.

Even the manner of her imperative retreat after the initial theft
of the bundle has about it something impulsive, puzzled, and mysterious. The circumstantial quality of the narrative remains the
same, but the emphasis on subjective and internal detail renders
external reality dubious and uncertain. A sense of indirection, of
being lost in a manifold sense, comes through strongly:

It is impossible to express the horror of my soul all the while I
did it. When I went away I had no heart to run, or scarce to

1. Alan Dugald McKillop, *The Early*   Kansas, 1956), p. 33. [See pp. 346–351,
Masters of English Fiction (Lawrence,   above—*Editor*.]

mend my pace. I crossed the street indeed, and went down the first turning I came to, and I think it was a street that went through into Fenchurch Street. From thence I crossed and turned through so many ways and turnings, that I could never tell which way it was, nor where I went; for I felt not the ground I stepped on, and the farther I was out of danger, the faster I went, till, tired and out of breath, I was forced to sit down on a little bench at a door, and then I began to recover, and found I was got into Thames Street, near Billingsgate. I rested me a little and went on; my blood was all in a fire; my heart beat as if I was in a sudden fright. In short, I was under such a surprise that I still knew not whither I was going, or what to do.[2]

Psychologically valid, Moll's bewildered and trancelike escape is also a seeking, a confused wandering in the pathways of her former life.

Once fully embarked upon her new career, Moll becomes cautious and discriminating in her selection of articles. But she can never get enough: she cannot stop stealing even when she has gained sufficient money to keep her nicely. Where before she was content with economic security in marriage or some stable relationship, she now becomes avaricious. Her stealing thus appears to compensate for what is lost. But it does more than compensate, even as it does less, for it continues to lead her back toward sex and the economic satisfactions of her earlier life. Always one to assume the identity most tactful at the moment, Moll now takes to elaborate disguises. At the behest of her "governess," she dresses like a man and works together with a male confederate, sleeping with him "four or five times" without his knowing her true sex. This is an obviously false kind of return to sexuality, however, and, indeed, when her partner is apprehended for stealing, Moll, closely pursued, evades arrest only by changing into women's clothes and reëstablishing at least that part of her identity. Never again, she vows, will she employ a male disguise.

But before she adopts other disguises, Moll achieves a temporary and thus limited degree of success in her quest to regain her status of younger days. The incident in which she rushes hopefully to a fire only to have a feather bed thrown upon her from an upper window serves as a comic prelude to her affair with the anonymous

2. Compare the account of Moll's second retreat, after leaving the little girl: "I went through into Bartholomew Close, and then turned round to another passage that goes into Long Lane, so away into Charterhouse Yard, and out into St. John Street; then, crossing into Smithfield, went down Chick Lane and into Field Lane to Holborn Bridge, when, mixing with the crowd of people usually passing there, it was not possible to have been found out; and thus I enterprised my second sally into the world." Here is a circuitous route, indeed, but alert, controlled, and with a full consciousness of external reality. So quickly does Moll begin to adapt to the exigencies of her new career.

gentleman whom she meets at Bartholomew Fair. In this first sexual encounter since the death of her banker husband, it is her role of thief that leads her to the bed. She is obviously not interested in sex for its own sake nor bothered by moral scruples: "As for the bed, etc.," she writes, "I was not much concerned about that part." She has, however, brought sex and theft together for the first time, for she robs the gentleman pretty thoroughly in the coach.[3] Reminded of her femininity, her first, and natural, commodity, by the attention she has received, she takes this opportunity to mention that "I did not indeed look so old as I was by ten or twelve years." Though aware of her age, she is "not so past the merry part of life, as to forget how to behave, when a fop so blinded by his appetite should not know an old woman from a young."

The adventure was "indeed unlooked for," as she says; yet in her scramble for security she has stolen her way back to a familiar kind of incident. Although Moll's days for amorous dalliance appear to be at an end, although—significantly—she cannot produce children in this relationship, she sustains an affair with this gentleman for "about a year," her final new conquest. And, very much to the point, she stops stealing for that year and for three months afterwards. "Though he did not keep, as they call it, yet he never failed doing things that were handsome, and sufficient to maintain me without working, and, which was better, without following my old trade." Stealing has led back to sex, only to be displaced by the preferred security of the latter.

The affair has been, however, an "interval," in which she has been forced to adopt the disguise of youth by using "paint" for the first and only time. When it is over, she begins once more to think of theft and "to look abroad into the street again." She takes up "the disguise of a widow's dress ... without any real design in view," and stands resolutely on injured innocence when falsely accused of stealing. But her mode of theft now begins to take on an aspect of caricature. Without knowing why, most uneasy in the disguise, she dresses as a beggar in coarse, despicable rags and—the *voyeur* in addition to the thief—walks about "peering and peeping

3. Though Moll does not conceive of sex as a means to theft, she tells us of a woman whose adeptness at this trade must have qualified her as a sort of culture heroine among female thieves: "I knew a woman that was so dexterous with a fellow, who indeed deserved no better usage, that while he was busy with her another way, conveyed his purse with twenty guineas in it out of his fob-pocket, where he had put it for fear of her, and put another purse with gilded counters in it into the room of it. After he had done, he says to her, 'Now han't you picked my pocket?' She jested with him, and told him she supposed he had not much to lose; he put his hand to his fob, and with his fingers felt that his purse was there, which fully satisfied him, and so she brought off his money. And this was a trade with her; she kept a sham gold watch, that is, a watch of silver gilt, and a purse of counters in her pocket to be ready on all such occasions, and I doubt not practised it with success." To keep such a watch and such a purse for such a purpose would be unthinkable for Moll, counter to her most fundamental attitudes toward wealth.

into every door and window" she comes near. She steals a horse, only to abandon it as useless to her. In a protean burst of inventiveness, she contrives "to appear in new shapes" every time she goes out to steal. She is even invited to join a gang of counterfeiters; but Moll refuses to disguise money, additional evidence of the irrefrangible, not-to-be-hidden reality of money in her world. As if rehearsing for a voyage, she steals an unwieldy portmanteau during a tour of theft that includes Cambridge, Ipswich, and Harwich. It is this journey (and specifically her route of escape after the portmanteau affair) that leads her back to Colchester, back, that is, to the place at which she began her sexual career with the elder brother.

Moll has now retraced the path of her adult life: her career of theft, with its obligation to peer and stalk and hunt, has brought her back to the original place from which she set out to be a gentlewoman. But of course everything has changed; gone are the elder brother and her first husband, Robin, both dead; gone too is her youth. Thus the return, though momentarily pleasant, is of no practical value, for she cannot make another start from Colchester. Rather, she must go back still farther, she must come full circle on her whole life. Moll will not be able to make a new start until she has returned to her birthplace, Newgate.

Stealing, as we know, will bring Moll back to Newgate. After her return to London from Colchester, Moll takes a breath in the narrative; the tone of the story begins to prefigure her impending capture, and she says explicitly that she is drawing toward "a new variety of the scenes of life." Again Defoe proceeds by anticipation: Moll is apprehended in a silversmith's shop, but before she has had time to steal. A matter of perhaps one minute measures the narrowness of her escape. The action here retards the episode of Moll's actual capture, which takes place three days later when, abruptly, she is caught red-handed, stealing not from a shop but from a private house, and sent to Newgate.

The novel's large narrative movement to regain the past and the promise it once held for Moll is now completed, for Moll, sixty years of age, is literally back where she began. Her disguised return to sex as a man has proved false; her actual return to sex, sufficient while it lasted, has proved unproductive; and her return to Colchester has, for practical purposes, proved futile. Thus Moll makes the great return, to the place of her birth, a place of "hellish noise" which she dreads, from which she expects "no redemption but by an infamous death."

Defoe employs a variation on the not uncommon conception of Newgate as a kind of hell; the prison seems to Moll "an emblem of hell itself, and a kind of an entrance into it." The inmates are "a crew of hell-hounds," who welcome her by shouting raucously that the devil has been her champion. Among them, Moll degenerates "into stone"; "I turned first stupid and senseless, then brutish and thoughtless, and at last raving mad as any of them were; and, in short, I became as naturally pleased and easy with the place, as if indeed I had been born there." Now a "mere Newgate-bird," she undergoes a psychic metamorphosis. "So thorough a degeneracy had possessed me," she remarks in curiously studied syntax, the rhetoric of overly formal definition, "that I was no more the same thing that I had been, than if I had never been otherwise than what I was now." The trip home, to the abode of the devil—the only father she appears to have—has disintegrated her personality. She becomes one of the "hell-hounds," part of the total "emblem of hell" that is Newgate.

But only for a short time. When her Lancashire husband, Jemmy, is brought to Newgate, she is "overwhelmed with grief for him." The "for him" is, I think, significant; she reproaches herself "on his account," for once not thinking exclusively and primarily of herself. Reflection now comes easily, followed by abhorrence of her birthplace and what she has become. She undergoes a second metamorphosis, the apparent beginning of a true re-form: "in a word, I was perfectly changed, and become another body." But there is a certain comic audacity in the double metamorphosis; it has allowed Moll to change back into herself. We might say that was no more the something she had become than if she had never been otherwise than what she had been. Importantly, however, her new resumption of identity has a definite meaning for both past and present lives; now Jemmy can know her. From this point onward the novel moves primarily toward revelation, not disguise.

Faced with a sentence of death, Moll repents under the gentle spiritual pressure of the minister. She recapitulates her life history and chooses heaven rather than hell, redemption (which she did not expect out of Newgate) rather than damnation. Her reprieve, however, creates a third alternative which—still true to her youthfully formulated wish of becoming a gentlewoman—she prefers to heaven or hell. Newgate has given her a glimpse of hell from which she has recoiled; if she must choose between eternities, she will choose heaven; but she would rather not choose at all. It is her reprieve and not the contemplation of heaven which allows her to come back, "as it were, into life again" with such a rush of joy that she is rendered speechless, "dumb and silent," finally to burst into a "fit of crying." In keeping with her character and her predominately economic motivation throughout sixty years of life, Moll vastly prefers a secular redemption. She is re-born to a natural, not a supernatural, life. "Really . . . not so solicitous" about heaven now, she must placate the genuinely concerned minister, who would win her to heaven. But Moll, being Moll, is not to be won, by heaven or hell, from herself.

Not until after her re-birth does Moll reveal her identity to Jemmy, speaking of the notorious "Moll Flanders" as if she were another person. At their famous meeting, Jemmy recounts his career in an orgy of stories of theft which show that he, the gentleman, and she, the gentlewoman, have traveled similar roads to the same destination. From the prison, converted from an entrance into hell to an obvious new-gate, they will go to America to be "new people in a new world." On the journey to eternity one travels in the strictest solitude, relying on spiritual treasures alone; "you can't take it with you," as the saying has it. But Moll has chosen practically. She will not only go to the "new world" with a partner, but between them they will have £354 of ill-gotten wealth. And "a worse gotten estate was scarce ever put together to begin the world with."

The structure of the novel calls for Moll's second trip to America, for this is the one aspect of her life which she has not yet doubled back on in any way. Her previous trip, with its discovery of incest, left her with a double identity—that of wife and sister—but concomitantly it introduced her to her mother. The return trip, taken with her "new" husband (as she calls Jemmy), serves to validate and hence corroborate her new, and true, identity: if ill-gotten wealth is her heritage from her father—or at least prompter—the devil, legitimate wealth from a plantation is her mother's bequest. One leads to the other. Theft still functions as a means to reintroduce Moll to her old life, or what has become of it. Though the necessary self-revelation threatens grave social embarrassment which gives her pause, she cannot resist the desire to make herself known, a desire based securely and consistently on her curiosity to know what and how much her mother left her. The human need to establish identity is there, encased neatly in an economic motive.

Although her mother is dead and her brother-husband debilitated, apparently by the very knowledge which has scared but not scarred Moll, she has finally discovered the one part of her old life which can pay dividends. In America she finds change, indeed, but in a context of fertility; secular redemption has met with secular reward; and, logically enough, her son, her "one and only child," sole testimony of her earlier ability to produce, becomes the instrument of that reward. At the age of almost threescore and ten, after eight years in America, Moll will return to England, at last equipped to live as a gentlewoman, having thanked Providence sincerely for her material success.

The unity of *Moll Flanders*, obviously deriving from the heroine, thus involves, I believe, a definable and coherent structural pattern of circumstance, resulting from Moll's different attempts to reach the same goal. Moll would be a gentlewoman: when the sexual means to this goal are no longer effective, she turns impulsively to theft, the pattern of which at first suggests a desire to have back a tested and relatively successful method of living; her avaricious, unreasonable persistence in theft, defining her inability to reconstitute the past as it was, leads her to a secular reformation in Newgate; she employs stolen money to purchase supplies and reach America, the one fertile part of her past life, from which she returns to England financially qualified to be a gentlewoman. Moll has experienced fecundity in incest; the means to being successfully middle-class appear to have been in the family all along.

Contributing to the unity of the novel are the manner in which Moll speaks of theft and the significance of her passion for watches, both of which relate to her middle-class Puritan manner of conceiving reality. Part of the idiom of theft, which Moll quickly appropriates, is to speak of "bargains," the perennial delight of the middle-class woman. Moll goes out to look for "bargains," or perhaps saunters out and chances on one. Watches, her favorite object of theft, signify, as I have suggested, stealing back time. But to the middle-class mind, time is money (the sentimental metaphor "golden hours" probably has a literal, economic origin); the most suitable gift Moll can give to her devoted son is a (stolen) golden watch, the essence of what she has really been trying to steal; and when she tells her husband, Jemmy, that she has lost this watch, she pulls out a deerskin purse full of pistoles given her by her son and announces, "here, my dear . . . is the gold watch." Theft thus becomes in the novel a supplemental way of characterizing Moll's deepest motives.

If Defoe's characterization of Moll is efficiently augmented by the modes and patterns of her conduct, she does not achieve (or even seem to want to achieve) a neat synthesis of the elements of her life. At one time in America, Moll wishes momentarily that she had not brought Jemmy with her, certainly an inauspicious sentiment for the future of the relationship. During the trip to America, she still practices her secret economy of personal prudence by not telling Jemmy about all of her money—a middle-class habit that evolves as it dwindles throughout subsequent history into the wife's private fund in the teapot, a kind of insurance against total dependence, Providence as Small Change. By the end of the novel, Moll has no financial secrets; or, if she has, they are hidden from us as well as from Jemmy. Still, she has curiously preceded Jemmy back to England from America; we leave her as she has so often been, alone. It has taken Moll a Biblical life span to achieve her goal. Were there any implied hollowness in that final achievement, we might still have an ironically moral ending; but Moll, indeed, seems quite content to enter the coupon-clipping utopia of all would-be capitalists; she can now live on her interest.

All this is not to overlook the inaccuracies of detail in *Moll Flanders* or the moot question of a more sophisticated structural unity involving theme, character, and tone. My remarks refer specifically to a pattern in the sequence of events, to a kind of circular unity of circumstance that exists in the novel as a formal, structural counterpart of Moll Flanders' inner existence; in effect, the episodes which I have examined articulate circumstantially Moll's hopes and fears, her devotion to a secular ideal. But working decisively against a more comprehensive kind of unity is the quality of the narrative itself. For it is a narrative of dispersal, insistent only on the reality of what pertains to Moll's individualistic, self-formulated career.

In the very different narrative of *Huckleberry Finn,* for example, Huck describes the world through which he travels in a way that evokes the autonomous novelistic existence of other characters: Jim, the Duke and the Dauphin, Colonel Sherburn, even the men who float twenty-dollar gold pieces down to Huck—these and many others come through in what is startling fullness when we recall Moll's narrative. Of all the characters in *Moll Flanders*, husbands, lovers, relatives, only the governess can approach these as an evoked character, and even she, on analysis, is found to exist in quantitative terms.

Huck has many voices for reporting what is not-Huck; Moll has one voice—her own—for reporting what is not-Moll. In this voice of tabulation, Moll is always in a sense talking about herself, dispersing the reality of those about her into countable units, undercutting the autonomy of everyone but herself. In its way, indeed, this is a feat of narrative, although as historians of the novel we may see that its price is to preclude the achievement of a more highly wrought, more complex kind of novelistic unity. Within the range of determinacy established by the narrative, however, Defoe sets forth in *Moll Flanders* a novel coherent in episode, unified in and by circumstance.

WAYNE C. BOOTH

Troubles with Irony in Earlier Literature†

Confusions of distance did not begin with modern fiction. In all periods and in many different genres we find speakers who win cred-

† From *The Rhetoric of Fiction* (Chicago: The University of Chicago Press, 1961), pp. 316, 318–328. Copyright © 1961 by The University of Chicago. Reprinted by permission of the author and the publisher.

ence when they should be doubted, or who lead critics to dispute the precise degree of their untrustworthiness. In drama (Is the villain always trustworthy in soliloquy?), in satire (Where does Rabelais stand in his work?), in comic fiction (Is Sterne laughing at his narrator in A *Sentimental Journey*?), in the dramatic monologue (What is Browning's precise judgment upon his many vicious and foolish spokesmen?)—in short, wherever explicit judgment has been unavailable, critical troubles, as well as some extraordinary delights, have ensued.

If we are to see what is distinctively troublesome about modern fiction, we should be quite clear about the causes of earlier difficulties with distance.

Lack of adequate warning that irony is at work.—Most successful irony before the modern period gave unmistakable notice, in one form or another, that the speaker could not be trusted. In Lucian's *True History*, for example (about A.D. 170), the narrator introduces himself as a liar like other historians: "When I come across a writer of this sort, I do not much mind his lying; the practice is much too well established for that. . . . I see no reason for resigning my right to that inventive freedom which others enjoy; and, as I have no truth to put on record, having lived a very humdrum life, I fall back on falsehood—but falsehood of a more consistent variety; for I now make the only true statement you are to expect—that I am a liar."[1] While such a warning does not guarantee that the ironies will be easily decipherable, it at least insures that the reader will be working on the right line.

The warning need not be a direct statement, of course. Any grotesque disparity between word and word or word and deed will serve. * * *

Without such unmistakable clues, irony has always given trouble, and there is no a priori reason for assuming that the fault is the reader's. We may be tempted to laugh at the foolish Tories who were taken in by Defoe's impersonated Tory as he argued for extermination in "the Shortest Way with the Dissenters" (1702). But since Defoe gives us a realistic impersonation, without providing the evidences for his unmasking, it is hardly surprising that none of its first readers "did imagine it could be wrote by a Whigg."[2] An intelligent reader, whether high churchman or dissenter, could

1. *Works*, trans. H. W. and F. G. Fowler (Oxford, 1905), II, 137.
2. From a pamphlet published in London in 1703: *The New Association, Part II, With farther Improvements, As Another and Later Scots Presbyterian-Covenant, Besides that mention'd in the Former Part. . . . An Answer to some Objections in the Pretended D. Foe's Explication, in the Reflections upon the Shortest Way . . .* (p. 6). I owe this reference to my colleague, Leigh Gibby. For a discussion of the difference between impersonation and the kind of irony that plays fair with the reader, see Ian Watt, *The Rise of the Novel* (Berkeley, Calif., 1957), p. 126. [See p. 358, above—*Editor.*]

easily read every word without having his suspicions aroused, because Defoe's mock-Tory presents no single argument that might not have been advanced by a real fanatical Tory. A careful student of polemic would of course recognize even on first reading that the arguments are specious; but so are the arguments of much serious polemic. The dialectical route by which Defoe's speaker reaches the conclusion that true charity dictates the extermination of the dissenters is, after all, common in form with much fanatical rhetoric: " 'Tis Cruelty to kill a Snake or a Toad in cold Blood, but the Poyson of their Nature makes it a Charity to our Neighbours, to destroy those Creatures, not for any personal Injury receiv'd, but for prevention; not for the Evil they have done, but the Evil they may do." "*Moses* was a merciful meek Man, and yet with what Fury did he run thro' the Camp, and cut the Throats of Three and thirty thousand of his dear *Israelites*, that were fallen into Idolatry; what was the reason? 'twas Mercy to the rest to make these be Examples, to prevent the Destruction of the whole Army."[3]

To us, knowing the full story of the pamphlet, the signs of Defoe's intentions may seem obvious. How could his contemporaries have failed to recognize the absurdity of this argument? But if we compare Defoe's masterful impersonation with the more fully developed satire of Swift's "A Modest Proposal," we see that the argument for mass cruelty in Defoe is very different from the similarly cruel proposal in Swift. The cruelty advocated by Defoe's Tory, in the name of Mercy, is not unheard of, incredible, absolutely beyond human experience; heretics have been exterminated before, as all his readers knew, and they will be again. Thus the argument, which to any dissenter must have seemed fully as infuriating and outlandish as Swift's argument for child-cannibalism, was not incredible even to the dissenters; on the contrary, it was frightening, and thus for them the irony failed. For the Tories, on the other hand, it must have been both frightening and exhilarating; even for the moderate Tories, it would not, on first reading, seem impossible that an extreme Tory could argue in this manner.

What is even more deceptive is that the appeals to fact, if we can call them that, are not by any means outright lies. He accuses the dissenters of having been cruel, immoderate, and unjust. Most dissenters must have suspected that the charge was at least in part true. Thus the argument, "No *Gentlemen*, the Time of Mercy is past, your *Day of Grace is over*; you shou'd have practis'd Peace, and Moderation, and Charity, if you expected any your selves" (p. 3), is, within its own limits, perfectly sound; and unlike the

"sound" arguments with which Swift begins "A Modest Proposal,"
it does not give way, as the pamphlet progresses, to arguments that
are patently absurd to all reasonable men of both parties.

Finally, there is no statement within the pamphlet of a positive
program which, if read properly, would reveal the true position of
the author. Even after we are alerted to irony, we cannot discover
from the pamphlet alone what Defoe's position is. Compare this
method with Swift's inverted statement of his own beliefs at the
conclusion of "A Modest Proposal": "Therefore let no man talk to
me of other Expedients: *Of taxing our Absentees at five Shillings a
Pound: of using neither Cloaths, nor Houshold Furniture except
what is of our own Growth and Manufacture: of utterly rejecting . . ."*
—the tabulation of Swift's true proposals, as rejected by his
speaker, goes on, in full italics, for half a page. There is nothing of
this sort in Defoe. If any intelligent reader came upon this pamphlet unwarned, with its absolute consistency of tone and sincerity
of purpose showing on every page, he might easily make the
mistake made by Defoe's contemporaries.

Now the curious thing about this comparison with Swift is that
in terms of realistic consistency alone, Defoe's method might seem
the better one. He maintains a dramatic, realistic impersonation
throughout, and he does not engage in any of Swift's winking or
rib-punching. If we judge according to abstract criteria of tone or
distance, Defoe's piece is the better one. It is certainly more significant as a forerunner of modern fiction.[4] But if we are willing, as I
think we must be, to judge realized intentions as revealed in total
structure, Swift's work is superior in its very willingness to sacrifice
consistency to satiric force.[5]

*Extreme complexity, subtlety, or privacy of the norms to be
inferred.*—Even when the reader is properly alerted, he will always
have trouble if the unspoken norms are not fairly simple and generally agreed upon. The debate about where Swift stands in the
fourth book of *Gulliver's Travels* is apparently as much alive today
as it ever was—not because Swift has left any doubt about the presence of irony but because it is very hard to know how much distance there is between Gulliver and Swift and precisely which of

---

4. See Robert C. Rathburn, "The Mak-
ers of the British Novel," in *From Jane
Austen to Joseph Conrad,* ed. Robert C.
Rathburn and Martin Steinmann, Jr.
(Minneapolis, Minn., 1958), pp. 3–22,
esp. p. 5: "Defoe used the device of a
persona so well that his satire had a
doubly ironic effect in that the persons
satirized took him seriously. . . . The
pamphlet brought Defoe to the pillory,
but it also showed his skill in writing
from an assumed point of view."

5. We might also say that our comic delight is less in Defoe, even if we know
that the pamphlet is ironic, because we
have fewer objects of ridicule: (1) no
reader could conceivably be ridiculous
for failing to understand; and (2) the
speaker himself is less absurd than
Swift's. The more realistic his impersonation, the less ridiculously exaggerated he
will be, and the less right we will feel to
laugh at him or at readers deceived by
him.

the traveler's enthusiasms for the Houyhnhnms is excessive. Whatever Swift's satirical point, it is neither sufficiently commonplace
nor sufficiently simple to be easily deciphered. Does he agree with
Gulliver that "these noble Houyhnhnms are endowed by nature
with a general disposition to all virtues" (chap. viii), or is Swift
attacking, behind Gulliver's back, the "absurd creatures" who, in
their cold rationalism, "represent the deistic presumption that mankind has no need of the specifically Christian virtues?"[6] As Professor Sherburn says, it is unlikely "that there will ever be unanimous
agreement as to what Swift is doing in . . . Gulliver's fourth
voyage" (p. 92). Unless there has been some permanent loss of
clues to meanings which were clear to Swift's contemporaries, we
must conclude either that Swift's norms are too complex or that
their relations with Gulliver's opinions are too complicated.

Even if we conclude that the fourth book has been left to some
degree indecipherable, we may, of course, go along with the current
fashion and praise Swift for his ambiguities rather than condemn
him for his inconclusiveness. In either case, we should be quite clear
that the ambiguity we accept will be paid for by a loss of satiric
force. Unless we are quite sure that Swift valued subtleties and
ambiguities more than effectiveness in conveying a simpler message,
it is clearly possible that somebody—whether author or reader—has
gone astray.

Fortunately my main point here does not depend on an assessment of blame: whenever an impersonal author asks us to infer
subtle differences between his narrator's norms and his own, we are
likely to have trouble.

Moll Flanders is a case in point. It would be a clever reader
indeed who could be sure just how much of Moll's behavior is con-
sciously judged and repudiated by Defoe. Ian Watt, one of the
most helpful commentators, finds many passages in which he
cannot decide whether the reader's judgment works against Moll
alone or against Defoe as well. Moll tells her lover, for example,
that she would never willingly deceive him, and adds, "Nothing
that ever befell me in my life sank so deep into my heart as this
farewell. I reproached him a thousand times in my thoughts for
leaving me, for I would have gone with him through the world, if I

6. Irvin Ehrenpreis, *The Personality of
Jonathan Swift* (London, 1958), p. 102.
A substantial bibliography of the controversy over this book can be found in
Kathleen Williams, *Jonathan Swift and
the Age of Compromise* (Lawrence,
Kan., 1958), p. 177 n. See also William
Bragg Ewald, Jr., *The Masks of Jonathan Swift* (Oxford, 1954). George Sherburn and R. S. Crane have given what
seem to me sound arguments for rejecting the strongly ironic reading of the
Houyhnhnms (Sherburn, "Errors concerning the Houyhnhnms," *Modern Philology*, LVI [November, 1958], 92–97;
Crane, "The Houyhnhnms, the Yahoos,
and the History of Ideas," in *Reason
and Imagination: Studies in the History
of Ideas, 1600–1800*, ed. J. A. Mazzeo
[New York, 1962]). But the real point
is that decision is here extremely difficult.

had begged my bread. I felt in my pocket, and there I found ten guineas, his gold watch, and two little rings."[7] Does Defoe intend this final sentence as Moll's unconscious self-betrayal, as I am inclined to think, or is Defoe himself betrayed by it? Watt concludes that, though Defoe *reveals* Moll's sophistries which conceal her dual allegiance here to the lover and to her own economic preservation, "he does not, strictly speaking, portray them," since he is himself their victim; "consequently *Moll Flanders* is undoubtedly an ironic object, but it is not a work of irony" [p. 361]. Everyone finds some examples of intended irony in the novel; everyone finds moments when Defoe seems to be giving himself away. But there is a large tract of Moll's behavior where most of us would be hard put to decide whether the inconsistencies we are amused by were intended by Defoe.

The reader who is untroubled by such problems may argue that his opinion of the book does not depend on whether the artist was on top of its ironies. But for most of us the question is an important one: if we find ourselves laughing at the author along with his characters, our opinion of the book as art must suffer. In any case, whether we read *Moll Flanders* in Watt's manner or join those who see Defoe as a great ironist, it is clear that Moll's point of view has given us difficulties that Defoe could not have intended; the very quality of our interest in the book depends on decisions which even now, more than two hundred years after the event, cannot be made with any assurance.

Vivid psychological realism.—We have already seen, particularly in *Emma,* how strongly a prolonged intimate view of a character works against our capacity for judgment. One of the troubles in *Moll Flanders* is that this effect works to soften our judgment of her worst misdeeds and to confuse us about her minor faults. Trollope reported that even a character as vicious as the protagonist of Thackeray's *Barry Lyndon* (1844) produced this effect on him. The comic villain who tells his own tale is guilty of every conceivable meanness, deliberately harming almost everyone else in the book; he engages in the most outlandish arguments in self-justification, and unlike Moll he dies unrepentant. And yet, as Trollope says, "his story is so written that it is almost impossible not to entertain something of a friendly feeling for him. . . . The reader is so carried away by his frankness and energy as almost to rejoice when he succeeds, and to grieve with him when he is brought to the ground."[8] * * *

7. *The Rise of the Novel*, p. 125. Watt provides a thorough discussion of recent interpretations of Defoe as a conscious ironist. For a more favorable treatment of Defoe's ironies, see Alan D. Mc-Killop, *The Early Masters of English Fiction* (Lawrence, Kan., 1956), chap i. [See pp. 346–351 and 351–362, above —*Editor.*]

8. *Thackeray* (London, 1882), p. 71. First published 1879.

MARTIN PRICE

[Defoe as Comic Artist] †

* * *

Defoe remains a puzzle because he imposes little thematic unity on his materials. Usually the writer who is content to give us the shape of the tale itself has a shapely tale to tell; a tale with its own logic, its awakening of tensions and expectations, its mounting repetition, its elaborate devices for forestalling too direct a resolution, and its satisfying—perhaps ingeniously surprising—way of tying all its threads in one great stroke. Such a tale need not leave those gaps in its narrative that are occasions for us to consider its meaning or theme. In Defoe's narratives the inconsistencies are such that we want to find a significant design, yet they hardly accommodate our wish.

* * *

Moll Flanders is the chronicle of a full life-span, told by a woman in her seventieth year with wonder and acceptance. In one sense, she is the product of a Puritan society turned to worldly zeal. Hers is very much the world of the Peachums, and in it Moll is the supreme tradeswoman, always ready to draw up an account, to enter each experience in her ledger as profit or loss, bustling with incredible force in the market place of marriage, and finally turning to those bolder and franker forms of competitive enterprise, whoredom and theft. To an extent, she is the embodiment of thrift, good management, and industry. But she is also the perverse and savagely acquisitive outlaw, the once-dedicated servant of the Lord turned to the false worship of wealth, power, success.

Her drive is in part the inevitable quest for security, the island of property that will keep one above the waters of an individualistic, cruelly commercial society. Born in Newgate, left with no resources but her needle, she constantly seeks enough wealth or a wealthy enough husband to free her from the threat of poverty and the temptations of crime. But she finds herself fascinated by the quest itself, by the management of marriages, the danger of thievery. When she has more money than she needs, she is still disguising herself for new crimes, disdaining the humble trade of the seamstress. When she finally settles into respectability, it is with a gen-

† From *To the Palace of Wisdom: Studies in Order and Energy from Dryden to Blake* (Garden City: Doubleday, 1964; Carbondale: Southern Illinois University Press, 1970), pp. 264–271, 274–275. Reprinted by permission of the author and Southern Illinois University Press.

tleman, not a merchant; her husband is a rather pretentious, some-what sentimental highwayman, who is not much good as a farmer but is a considerable sportsman. Moll is no simple middle-class mer-cantile figure; nor is she another Macheath. Yet she has elements of both.

There is still another dimension of Moll Flanders. Her constant moral resolutions, her efforts to reform, her doubts and remorse cannot be discounted as hypocrisy or even unrealistic self-deception. Moll is a daughter of Puritan thought, and her piety has all the troublesome ambiguities of the Puritan faith. Her religion and morality are not the rational and calculating hypocrisy of the simple canter—the Shimei of Dryden's *Absalom and Achitophel*, for exam-ple. They are essentially emotional. She has scruples against incest, but they take the form of nausea, physical revulsion. She intends virtuous behavior and is astonished to discover her hardness of heart. Moll's life is a career of self-discovery, of "herself surprised," surprised by herself and with herself. Just as for the earlier Puritan, the coming of grace might be unpredictable, terrifyingly sudden, and very possibly deceptive, so for Moll the ways of her heart are revealed to her by her conduct more than by her consciousness, and even her most earnest repentance arouses her own distrust until it can well up into an uncontrollable joy. Personality is not something created or earned; the self is not the stable essence the Stoic moral-ist might seek. It is something given, whether by God or the devil, always in process, eluding definition and slipping away from rational purpose. Even at her happiest, with the man she has long missed, and in the late autumn of her life, Moll can think of how pleasant life might still be without him. It is a wayward thought, a momen-tary inclination, as real as her devotion and no more real.

What we find in Moll Flanders is not an object lesson in Puritan avarice or in the misuse of divinely given talents. Moll has all the confusion of a life torn between worldliness and devotion, but what remains constant is the energy of life itself, the exuberant innocence that never learns from experience and meets each new event with surprise and force. Moll, like the secularized Puritanism she be-speaks, has the zeal that might found sects as well as amass booty, that might colonize a new world as readily as it robbed an old one. And the form of the old zeal, now turned into a secular world, needing the old faith at least intermittently as the new devotion to the world falters with failure, gives us a pattern of character that is one of the remarkable creations of fiction. Defoe, we are told, seems not to judge his material; Defoe must be a brilliant ironist. Both assertions imply a set of values thinner and more neatly ordered than Defoe can offer. He is aware of the tension between the adven-turous spirit and the old piety; he can see the vitality of both religious zeal and worldly industry; the thrifty efficiency and the reckless outlawry that are both aspects of the middle-class adventure; the wonderful excitement of technology as well as its darker omens. And seeing all of this, he does not seem to see the need to reduce these tensions to a moral judgment. Like Mandeville, who struts much more in the role, he is one of the artists who makes our moral judgments more difficult.

Ultimately, one might call Defoe a comic artist. The structure of *Moll Flanders* itself defies resolution. In giving us the life-span, with its eager thrust from one experience to the next, Defoe robs life of its climactic structure. Does Moll face marriage to the brother of her seducer, a seducer she still loves? It is an impossible tragic dilemma. Yet the marriage takes place, the husband dies, the children are placed; and Moll is left taking stock as she enters the marriage market again. Does she face the dreadful fact of incest? This, too, passes away; she cannot reconcile herself to it, but she can make a settlement and depart in search of a new and illegal marriage. The commonplace inevitably recurs; we have parodies of tragic situations.

Moll herself is not contemptible in her insensitivity. She is magnificently unheroic; and yet there is a modest touch of heroism in her power of recuperation, her capacity for survival with decency. In her curiously meaningless life, there is a wonderful intensity of experience at a level where affection, inclination, impulse (both generous and cruel) generate all the motions that are usually governed, or perhaps simply accompanied, by a world of thought. We have Defoe's own account of this process in his *Serious Reflections of Robinson Crusoe* (iv):

> There is an inconsiderate temper which reigns in our minds, that hurries us down the stream of our affections by a kind of involuntary agency, and makes us do a thousand things, in the doing of which we propose nothing to ourselves but an immediate subjection to our will, that is to say, our passion, even without the concurrence of our understandings, and of which we can give very little account after 'tis done.

This way of reading *Moll Flanders* imposes its own straitening on the untidy fullness of the book. Ian Watt has made a decisive case for the comparative artlessness of Defoe; there are too many wasted emphases, too many simple deficiencies of realization to make the case for deliberate irony tenable. But one can claim for Defoe a sensibility that admits more than it can fully articulate, that is particularly alert to unresolved paradoxes in human behavior. Watt dismisses in passing the parallel of a work like Joyce Cary's *Herself Surprised*. There is point in this dismissal, for Cary has raised to clear thematic emphasis what is left more reticent in Defoe. Yet the relationship is worth exploration. Few writers have been so fascinated as Cary with the ambiguities of the Protestant temper. In a great many characters—among them the statesman, Chester Nimmo, in the political trilogy and the evangelical faith-healer Preedy in the last novel, *The Captive and the Free*—Cary studied the shimmering iridescence with which motives seem, from different angles, dedicated service and the search for grace or the most opportunistic self-seeking. Cary was not interested in "rationalization" but in the peculiar power achieved by the coincidence of religious zeal and imperious egoism. Preedy, for example, seduces a young girl and makes her virtually his slave; but he is convinced that his power to win her love is a sign of grace—that a love so undemanding and undeserved as hers can only be a sign of God's love in turn. Preedy is monstrous in one aspect, terrifying but comprehensible in another; the difference lies in what we recognize to be his object.

Cary's effects are so adroit and so carefully repeated that we have no doubt about calling them ironic. Defoe's are less artful and less completely the point of his tale. Yet his awareness of them seems no less genuine. Defoe's characters have secularized old Puritan modes of thought. Moll Flanders is constantly taking inventory and casting up her accounts as she faces a new stage of her life. Crusoe, too, keeps an account book, and, more like the earlier Puritans, an account book of the soul. The doctrine of regeneration, we are told, caused the Puritans "to become experts in psychological dissection and connoisseurs of moods before it made them moralists. It forced them into solitude and meditation by requiring them continually to cast up their accounts."[1] In the diary, particularly, the Puritan might weigh each night what he had experienced of God's deliverance or of Satan's temptation during the day. "It was of the very essence of Puritan self-discipline that whatsoever thoughts and actions the old Adam within had most desire to keep hidden, the very worst abominations of the heart, one must when one retired to one's private chamber at night draw into the light of conscience. . . . Having thus balanced his spiritual books, he could go to bed with a good conscience, sleep sound and wake with courage."[2]

The "other-worldliness" of Puritan theology was, as Perry Miller puts it, "a recognition of the world, an awareness of a trait in human nature, a witness to the devious ways in which men can pervert the fruits of the earth and the creatures of the world and cause them to minister to their vices. Puritanism found the natural man invariably running into excess or intemperance, and saw in such abuses an affront to God, who had made all things to be used

1. Perry Miller, *The New England Mind*, New York, 1939, p. 53.

2. William Haller, *The Rise of Puritanism*, New York, 1938, pp. 99–100.

according to their natures. Puritanism condemned not natural passions but inordinate passions" (p. 42).

This concern with the uses of things places emphasis not on their sensuous fullness but on their moral function, and the seeming bleakness of Defoe's world of measurables derives in part from this. Characteristically, when Defoe in his *Tour* praises the countryside it is for what man has made of it: "nothing can be more beautiful; here is a plain and pleasant country, a rich fertile soil, cultivated and enclosed to the utmost perfection of husbandry, then bespangled with villages; those villages filled with these houses, and the houses surrounded with gardens, walks, vistas, avenues, representing all the beauties of buildings, and all the pleasures of planting. . . ." So, too, the natural scene of Crusoe's island "appeals not for adoration, but for exploitation" (Ian Watt, p. 70). It is not the things we care about but the motives or energies they bring into play: they may satisfy needs, or call forth technical ingenuity, or present temptations. The physical reality of sensual temptation need not be dwelt upon, for moral obliviousness or self-deception is Defoe's concern (as in the account of Moll's going to bed with the Bath gentleman). If Moll's inventories seem gross, they may also be seen as the balance of freedom against necessity; poverty is the inescapable temptation to crime. And her inventories are, in an oblique sense, still account books of the spirit.

What might once have served the cause of piety becomes a temptation to exploitation. This is the dialectic of which Perry Miller speaks: the natural passion insensibly turns into the inordinate passion. Each of Defoe's central characters at some point passes the boundary between need and acquisitiveness, between the search for subsistence and the love of outlawry. And it is only in the coolness of retrospect that they can see the transgression. Defoe does not play satirically upon their defections; he knows these to be inevitable, terrifying so long as they can be seen with moral clarity, but hard to keep in such clear focus. His characters live in a moral twilight, and this leads to Defoe as a writer of comedy.

We must also keep in mind the essential optimism of the Puritan creed. The Puritans could not, Perry Miller tells us, sustain the tragic sense of life. "They remembered their cosmic optimism in the midst of anguish, and they were too busy waging war against sin, too intoxicated with the exultation of the conflict to find occasional reversals, however costly, any cause for deep discouragement. . . . Far from making for tragedy, the necessity [for battle] produced exhilaration" (p. 37). The battle against sin is not, of course, the only battle in which Defoe's characters are involved, but the struggle in the world demands the same intense concentration and affords the same exhilaration. If there is any central motive in

Defoe's novels, it is the pleasure in technical mastery: the fascination with how things get done, how Crusoe makes an earthenware pot or Moll Flanders dexterously makes off with a watch. The intensity of this concentration gives an almost allegorical cast to the operation, as if Crusoe's craftsmanship had the urgency of the art by which a man shapes his own soul. It is beside the point to complain that these operations are "merely" technical and practical; undoubtedly the man who invented the wheel had beside him a high-minded friend who reproached him with profaning the mystery of the circle by putting it to such menial uses. The delight in mastery and in problem-solving may be a lower and less liberal art than those we commonly admire, but it is a fundamental experience of men and a precious one.

Even more, the energy of spirit that is concentrated in these operations is a source of joy. One might wish that Moll Flanders had founded a garden suburb with the force she gave to robbing a child, and at moments she feels so too; but the strength she brings to the demands of life is at worst a perversion of the spiritual energy the Puritan seeks to keep alive. It is in doing that he finds himself and serves himself, and Moll Flanders reaches the lowest point of her life when she falls into the apathy of despair in Newgate: "I degenerated into stone, I turned first stupid and senseless, then brutish and thoughtless, and at last raving mad as any of them were; in short, I became as naturally pleased and easy with the place as if indeed I had been born there." She loses her sense of remorse:

> a certain strange lethargy of soul possessed me; I had no trouble, no apprehensions, no sorrow about me, the first surprise was gone. . . . my senses, my reason, nay, my conscience, were all asleep. . . .

In contrast is the recovered energy that comes with her repentance:

> I was covered with shame and tears for things past, and yet had at the same time a secret surprising joy at the prospect of being a true penitent . . . and so swift did thought circulate, and so high did the impressions they had made upon me run, that I thought I could freely have gone out that minute to execution, without any uneasiness at all, casting my soul entirely into the arms of infinite mercy as a penitent.

These moments of spiritual despair and joy have their counterparts in her secular life as well. After the death of her honest husband, she is left in poverty:

> I lived two years in this dismal condition, wasting that little I had, weeping continually over my dismal circumstances, and as it

were only bleeding to death, without the least hope or prospect of help. . . .

With the pressure of poverty and the temptation of the Devil, she commits her first theft and runs through a tortured circuit of streets:

> I felt not the ground I stepped on, and the farther I was out of danger, the faster I went. . . . I rested me a little and went on; my blood was all in a fire, my heart beat as if I was in a sudden fright: in short, I was under such a surprise that I knew not whither I was going, or what to do.

This is the energy of fear, but it is a return to life; and before many pages have passed, Moll is speaking with pleasure of her new art.

The benign form of this energy is that of the honest tradesman whom Defoe always celebrates: "full of vigor, full of vitality, always striving and bustling, never idle, never sottish; his head and his heart are employed; he moves with a kind of velocity unknown to other men" (*Complete English Tradesman*, II [1727], i, 106–7). As R. H. Tawney has written, "a creed which transformed the acquisition of wealth from a drudgery or a temptation into a moral duty was the milk of lions" (*Religion and the Rise of Capitalism*, London, 1926, ch. IV, iii). Yet, as Tawney recognizes, the older Puritan view of the evil of inordinate desires still survived. Defoe may call gain "the tradesman's life, the essence of his being" (*CET*, II, i, 79–80), but gain makes it all the harder for a tradesman to be an honest man: "There are more snares, more obstructions in his way, and more allurements to him to turn knave, than in any employment. . . . [For] as getting money by all possible (fair) methods is his proper business, and what he opens his shop for . . . 'tis not the easiest thing in the world to distinguish between fair and foul, when 'tis against himself" (*CET*, II, i, 33–34, 35). This candid recognition of the traps of self-deception leads Defoe to a considerable degree of tolerance. He cites the Golden Rule, "a perfect and unexceptionable rule" which "will hold for an unalterable law as long as there is a tradesman left in the world." But, he goes on, "it may be said, indeed, where is the man that acts thus? Where is the man whose spotless integrity reaches it?" He offers those tradesmen who "if they slip, are the first to reproach themselves with it; repent and re-assume their upright conduct; the general tenor of whose lives is to be honest and to do fair things. And this," he concludes, "is what we may be allowed to call *an honest man*; for as to perfection, we are not looking for it in life" (*CET*, II, i, 42).

* * *

Moll Flanders, like Crusoe, is a creature of mixed and unstable motives. She goes to Bath, she tells us, "indeed in the view of taking what might offer; but I must do myself that justice as to protest I meant nothing but in an honest way, nor had any thoughts about me at first that looked the way which afterwards I suffered them to be guided." It is sincere enough, but the moral twilight is clear, too. She lodges in the house of a woman "who, though she did not keep an ill house, yet had none of the best principles in her self." When she has become the mistress of the gentleman she meets at Bath, she remarks that their living together was "the most undesigned thing in the world"; but in the next paragraph she adds: "It is true that from the first hour I began to converse with him I resolved to let him lie with me." The surprise has come in finding that what she had been prepared to accept through economic necessity, she has encouraged through "inclination."

Earlier in America, when Moll discovers that she is married to her brother and the disclosure drives him to attempt suicide, she casts about:

> In this distress I did not know what to do, as his life was apparently declining, and I might perhaps have married again there, very much to my advantage, had it been my business to have stayed in the country; but my mind was restless too, I hankered after coming to England, and nothing would satisfy me without it.

Here, too, the motives are a wonderful mixture of concern, prudence, and impulse. What is most remarkable about Moll Flanders is her untroubled recognition of her motives, her readiness to set them forth with detachment, at least to the extent that she understands them. She recalls those Puritans who scrutinize their motives as if they were spectators beholding a mighty drama. When Moll robs a poor woman of the few goods that have survived a fire, she records:

> I say, I confess the inhumanity of the action moved me very much, and made me relent exceedingly, and tears stood in my eyes upon that subject. But with all my sense of its being cruel and inhuman, I could never find it in my heart to make any restitution: the reflection wore off, and I quickly forgot the circumstances that attended it.

Fielding was to make something beautifully ironic of this kind of mixture of motives. Defoe uses it differently; candor disarms the moral judgment that irony would require. The stress is more upon the energy of impulse than upon its evil. And the energy is such that it can scarcely be contained by a single motive or be channeled long in a consistent course.

ARNOLD KETTLE

In Defence of *Moll Flanders*†

I

Professor Ian Watt's *The Rise of the Novel* is one of the works of literary criticism of the last decade that have added substantially and rewardingly to our ability to read eighteenth-century literature better. If this paper revolves around some disagreements with Mr Watt that is to be taken as a mark of gratitude rather than an attempt to denigrate. It is because *The Rise of the Novel* has a deservedly wide currency that it is worth examining what seems to be fundamentally wrong in Mr Watt's approach to Defoe.[1]

It is with *Moll Flanders* that I am concerned and I agree with Mr Watt that it is the key work in any estimate of Defoe's significance as a novelist. In *The Rise of the Novel* forty-two pages are spent on *Moll* and constitute the fullest discussion of the book I know. Towards the end of the discussion the conclusions are summarized:

> Defoe's forte was the brilliant episode. Once his imagination seized on a situation he could report it with a comprehensive fidelity which was much in advance of any previous fiction, and which, indeed, has never been surpassed . . .
>
> How far we should allow Defoe's gift for the perfect episode to outweigh his patent shortcomings—weaknesses of construction, inattention to detail, lack of moral or formal pattern—is a very difficult critical problem.[2]

It is a problem, however, about which Mr Watt has left us in little doubt as to where he stands. The passage I have quoted is followed by a couple of pages of generous and perceptive appreciation of Defoe's genius, happily described as 'confident and indestructible'. But these pages cannot eclipse the thirty-five that have preceded them in which scepticism—peppered, it is true, with valuable observations and insights—has reigned. Mr Watt praises Defoe highly

† From *Of Books and Humankind*, ed. John Butt (London: Routledge & Kegan Paul, 1964), pp. 55–67. Reprinted by permission of the author and the publisher.
1. I should add, in fairness, that I am also concerned to correct what I now regard as inadequacies in my own approach to Defoe in my *Introduction to the English Novel*, vol. I (London, 1951). For a realization of these inadequacies I am indebted not only to time, with its gift of second chances, but, in particular, to Mr Watt, to Mr Alick West and to Professor Bonamy Dobrée who was the first person I heard talk of Defoe with the right kind of enthusiasm.
2. *The Rise of the Novel* (London, 1957), p. 130.

for verisimilitude and not for much else. The conclusion is clearly stated:

> His blind and almost purposeless concentration on the actions of his heroes and heroines, and his unconscious and unreflective mingling of their thoughts and his about the inglorious world in which they both exist, made possible the expression of many motives and themes which could not, perhaps, have come into the tradition of the novel without Defoe's shock tactics . . .[3]

Blind, purposeless, unconscious, unreflective: the adjectives are damaging and lead us—for all Mr Watt's scrupulous reservations— in the same direction as Dr Leavis' 'brush-off' footnote in *The Tradition*:

> Characteristic of the confusion I am contending against is the fashion (for which the responsibility seems to go back to Virginia Woolf and Mr E. M. Forster) of talking of *Moll Flanders* as a 'great novel'. Defoe was a remarkable writer, but all that need be said about him as a novelist was said by Leslie Stephen in *Hours in a Library* (First Series). He made no pretension to practising the novelist's art, and matters little as an influence. In fact, the only influence that need be noted is that represented by the use made of him in the nineteen-twenties by the practitioners of the fantastic *conte* (or pseudo-moral fable) with its empty pretence of significance.[4]

It is worth recalling that this footnote—which has, incidentally, along with a couple of others in the same work, had more influence in keeping students of English literature away from the eighteenth-century novel than any other pronouncement—is attached to a sentence which distinguishes as major novelists those who 'not only change the possibilities of the art for practitioners and readers, but . . . are significant in terms of the human awareness they promote: awareness of the possibilities of life'.

It is precisely on such grounds that I would claim that *Moll Flanders* is indeed a great novel.

II

Mr Watt uses, to pinpoint his doubts about Defoe's literary status, the famous passage in *Moll Flanders* in which Moll doesn't steal the watch in the meeting-house.

> The next thing of moment was an attempt at a gentlewoman's gold watch. It happened in a crowd, at a meeting house, where I was in very great danger of being taken. I had full hold of her watch, but giving a great jostle as if somebody had thrust me

3. *Ibid.*, p. 134.
4. *The Great Tradition* (London, 1948), p. 2.

against her, and in the juncture giving the watch a fair pull, I found it would not come, so I let it go that moment, and cried as if I had been killed, that somebody had trod upon my foot, and that there was certainly pickpockets there, for somebody or other had given a pull at my watch; for you are to observe that on these adventures we always went very well dressed, and I had very good clothes on, and a gold watch by my side, as like a lady as other folks.

I had no sooner said so but the other gentlewoman cried out, 'A Pickpocket' too, for somebody, she said, had tried to pull her watch away.

When I touched her watch I was close to her, but when I cried out I stopped as it were short, and the crowd bearing her forward a little, she made a noise too, but it was at some distance from me, so that she did not in the least suspect me; but when she cried out, 'A Pickpocket', somebody cried out, 'Ay, and here has been another; this gentlewoman has been attempted too.'

At that very instant, a little farther in the crowd, and very luckily too, they cried out, 'A Pickpocket', again, and really seized a young fellow in the very act. This, though unhappy for the wretch, was very opportunely for my case, though I had carried it handsomely enough before; but now it was out of doubt, and all the loose part of the crowd ran that way, and the poor boy was delivered up to the rage of the street, which is a cruelty I need not describe, and which, however, they are always glad of, rather than be sent to Newgate, where they lie often a long time and sometimes they are hanged, and the best they can look for, if they are convicted, is to be transported.

Mr Watt's comments on this scene may be summarized as follows. It is very convincing: full marks for verisimilitude and prose. But (*a*) the tone is too laconic, the scene is not planned as a coherent whole; (*b*) the point of view of the narrator is not consistent; (*c*) the relationship of the passage to the rest of the book is suspect; (*d*) the passage suffers from a general fault of the book—repeated falls in tension between episodes. Let us examine these criticisms.

(*a*) Mr Watt complains that

Defoe gets into the middle of the action, with 'I had full hold of her watch', and then suddenly changes from laconic reminiscent summary to a more detailed and immediate presentation, as though only to back up the truth of his initial statement. Nor has the scene been planned as a coherent whole: we are soon interrupted in the middle of the scene by an aside explaining something that might have been explained before, the important fact that Moll Flanders was dressed like a gentlewoman herself: this transition adds to our trust that no ghost-writer has been imposing order on Moll Flanders's somewhat rambling reminiscences, but if we had seen Moll dressed 'as like a lady as other folks' from the beginning, the action would have run more strongly, because uninterruptedly, into the next incident of the scene, the raising of the alarm.[5]

Surely the point Mr Watt objects to is an important part of Defoe's intended effect. Moll isn't a novelist, planning ahead. She lives from moment to moment; she suddenly remembers things she ought to have said before; and she remembers them haphazardly, partly because that is the way people do remember things, but also because she is such an incurable self-deceiver, yet doesn't want to deceive herself or other people. Moll wants to be honest—with herself, with us, even with the woman she steals from—but of course she can't be. And the confusion is expressed in the organization and disorganization of her prose. If Moll's consciousness is a disorganized and impromptu business, so is her life.

(*b*) Defoe goes on to stress the practical moral, which is that the gentlewoman should have 'seized the next body that was behind her', instead of crying out. In so doing, Defoe lives up to the didactic purpose professed in the 'Author's Preface', but at the same time he directs our attention to the important problem of what the point of view of the narrator is supposed to be. We presume that it is a repentant Moll, speaking towards the end of her life: it is therefore surprising that in the next paragraph she should gaily describe her 'governess's' procuring activities as 'pranks'. Then a further confusion about the point of view becomes apparent: we notice that to Moll Flanders other pickpockets, and the criminal fraternity in general, are a 'they', not a 'we.' She speaks as though she were not implicated in the common lot of criminals; or is it, perhaps, Defoe who has unconsciously dropped into the 'they' he himself would naturally use for them? And earlier, when we are told that 'the other gentlewoman' cried out, we wonder why the word 'other'? Is Moll Flanders being ironical about the fact that she too was dressed like a gentlewoman, or has Defoe forgotten that, actually, she is not?[6]

This carries the same point further. Of course, there are inconsistencies here. They are the very life's blood of the book. It is true that Moll speaks as though she were not implicated in the common lot of criminals. She doesn't think of herself as a criminal. When she learns what the other criminals in Newgate think of her she is morally outraged. Occasionally, for a moment, like Joyce Cary's Sara, she catches sight of herself in some mirror and sees herself, surprised. And she *does* think of herself, in the episode under discussion, as a gentlewoman. What Mr Watt sees as Defoe's carelessness I see as his imaginative absorption in his subject, a penetration into the layers of self-deception of which a human being, even a

5. *Op. cit.*, p. 97. 6. *Ibid.*, p. 98.

relatively honest one, is capable. Sir Leslie Stephen's reproach, in the essay Dr Leavis admires so much, that Defoe's novels lack 'all that goes by the name of psychological analysis in modern fiction' makes sense only if one is concerned to blame Defoe for not being Proust. There is no need for formal analysis of Moll's psychological processes in the meeting-house. They are revealed in all their complex, awful, funny, human contradictoriness in the very texture of the scene. This is a triumph of art.

> (c) The connection between the meeting-house scene and the narrative as a whole confirms the impression that Defoe paid little attention to the internal consistence of his story. When she is transported to Virginia Moll Flanders gives her son a gold watch as a memento of their reunion; she relates how she 'desired that he would now and then kiss it for my sake', and then adds sardonically that she did not tell him 'that I stole it from a gentlewoman's side, at a meeting house in London'. Since there is no other episode in *Moll Flanders* dealing with watches, gentlewomen and meeting-houses, we must surely infer that Defoe had a faint recollection of what he had written a hundred pages earlier . . .
> These discontinuities strongly suggest that Defoe did not plan his novel as a coherent whole, but worked piecemeal, very rapidly, and without any subsequent revision.[7]

There is a confusion of critical method here. It may well be (and, as Mr Watt says, external as well as internal evidence suggests it) that Defoe worked piecemeal and that his novels therefore lack a certain planned coherence. But this is a general critical statement about the kind of book we are dealing with, relevant no doubt, but not to be confused with our judgment of artistic success. The passage Mr Watt refers to can be read equally well as a further example of Moll's difficulty of separating the false from the true and of the curious tricks of the extended conscience. She happens to connect watch-stealing with the meeting-house episode because that gave her a shock and imprinted itself deep in her memory; she may even have found it necessary, for her peace of mind, to transform her failure—with its uncomfortable accompaniment of the taking of the boy pickpocket—into a comfortable success. Certainly time has dealt interestingly with the episode. This may not have been Defoe's intention. But certainly the main *point* in the Virginia scene from which Mr Watt quotes is to illuminate the wry twinge of half-conscience, half-triumph that Moll by now feels. She has become complacent in a way which in former days, for all her conscience-blocking, she dared not be. Whether she is referring to the same watch doesn't matter. To suggest that it does would seem to reveal an attitude towards the novel and novel-writing not quite rel-

7. *Ibid.*, pp. 98–9.

evant to the sort of book Defoe offers us. I will return to this point.

(*d*) The question of fall of tension between episodes is a valid point of criticism. That opening sentence, 'The next thing of moment was etc.' does indeed betray a weakness, a technical problem unsolved. There is, it is true, the sense in which Moll does indeed see her life as a kind of inventory of episodes, with nothing much of note between them. There is also the sense in which the book proceeds from one moral warning to the next on the old beggar-book level, and there is no doubt that this aspect of his book tends all the time to conflict with Defoe's major concern—to show us what Moll Flanders is like (in the way that the remnants of the old *Hamlet* revenge-drama tend to conflict with Shakespeare's major concern in his play).

In his analysis of the meeting house scene Mr Watt omits to discuss what is surely its greatest, most moving moment; the taking of the boy pickpocket. The effect here is not at all due to verisimilitude or any of the qualities habitually, and rightly, granted to Defoe; it is almost entirely moral and psychological. The phrase 'and very luckily too, leads us into it. What is lucky for Moll is the lynching of the boy for whom she can afford no more fellow-feeling than a single use of the adjective 'poor' and the dubious consolation that lynching is better than hanging or transportation.

The effect that Defoe achieves here is one that is central to the nature of *Moll Flanders* as a work of art. Moll's reactions to the episode, humanly speaking, are quite inadequate. It is easy, therefore, to underestimate Defoe's art, which can look, at first glance, to be inadequate in the same way. The paragraph is a flat one, a disclaimer, a refusal to see what has happened. But the phrase 'a cruelty I need not describe' is an indication of cowardice not on Defoe's part but Moll's. Of course, she can't bear to dwell on the scene: it is too near the bone. But that last sentence of the paragraph is, objectively considered, all compassion. The phrase 'and sometimes they are hanged', the whole rhythm of the sentence, the toneless forcing out of facet after facet of horror, all these contribute to a marvellous effect. Moll is playing it all down; she can't do anything else, she who has put herself beyond the possibility of looking at such a scene objectively. But Defoe allows *us* to see all round the situation even if Moll can't. And a far more important link between this whole episode and the later reaches of the novel than the link represented by the watch which turns up in Virginia is the connection between this last sentence and the whole Newgate episode of the book. It is only then that we get the full force of the word 'luckily'.

I stress the power of this paragraph because it illustrates very well the nature of the moral organization of *Moll Flanders*, a feature of the book that Mr Watt, and almost everyone else, plays down.

III

The underlying tension which gives *Moll Flanders* its vitality as a work of art can be expressed by a contradiction which is at once simple and complicated. Moll is immoral, shallow, hypocritical, heartless, a bad woman: yet Moll is marvellous. Defoe might almost (though he wouldn't have dreamed of it) have subtitled his book 'A Pure Woman'.

Moll's splendour—her resilience and courage and generosity—is inseparable from her badness. The fair and the foul are not isolable qualities to be abstracted and totted up in a reckoning, balancing one against the other. The relationship is far more interesting. One is reminded, perhaps, of Yeats's Crazy Jane:

> 'Fair and foul are near of kin
> And fair needs foul', I cried.
> 'My friends are gone, but that's a truth
> Nor grave nor bed denied,
> Learned in bodily lowliness
> And in the heart's pride.'

That is too metaphysical for Moll; she wouldn't say that fair needs foul. But the contradiction Yeats is expressing and, in expressing, resolving, is essentially the contradiction Defoe's book expresses. And the phrase 'the heart's pride' is not inappropriate to Moll.

The episode in *Moll Flanders* which tells us most about the underlying pattern of the book is the one very near the beginning in which Moll as a little girl talks of her fear of going into service and her desire to be a gentlewoman. Mr Watt picks out this passage as one of the few examples in the book of an irony that we can be quite sure is fully conscious, and his fastening on the scene tells us that he is a good literary critic. But he lets go much too quickly. This is an absolutely essential episode, as Mr Alick West, in the best analysis of *Moll Flanders* I know, has well pointed out:

> The life the child wants—working for herself in freedom—is the contrasting background to the life the woman gets in a world where a gentlewoman does not live on the threepences or four-pences she earns by her own labour, but on riches of unexplained origin.[8]

This sentence not only shows what *Moll Flanders* is about but illuminates the specific artistic pattern of the book. It leads us straight to what makes Moll at the same time splendid and contemptible. What makes her splendid—a great heroine—is that she wants her independence, to work for herself in freedom. She is a woman who

8. *Mountain in the Sunlight* (London, 1958), p. 90.

is determined to be a human being, not a servant, and the feeling of what it means to be a servant is what generates the impulses which carry her through most of the book, until she too has become a gentlewoman with servants, living on riches whose origin she likes to forget about or to confuse but which Defoe has only too clearly explained.

Unless we see Moll in history we cannot grasp her moral stature as a heroine. Instead, we will bring to her the flat and static sort of moral judgment which she herself (and one side of Defoe himself) brings when she is forced to enter the sphere she calls morality or religion. And here Virginia Woolf's feminist preoccupations offer a more central and artistically relevant approach to the book than any other. The examination of Defoe's social and economic attitudes that Mr Novak[9] has offered us is not, of course, irrelevant; nor are Mr Watt's observations on the significance of the criminal class at this period; but neither emphasis goes to the heart of the matter. Moll becomes a criminal because she is a woman, and it is not at all by a chance in the book's structure that she comes to her second career (that of a thief) by way of her first (that of a wife). Too little is known about the position of women in the eighteenth century, but the general outlines are clear enough and Mr Watt himself in the chapters on Richardson in *The Rise of the Novel* has notably contributed to our appreciation of many of the problems involved. So have recent emphases on the importance of arranged marriages and contemporary feelings about them in Restoration and eighteenth-century literature.[1] Such extra-literary confirmation is not irrelevant to a critical approach to *Moll Flanders* because only on the basis of a just assessment of the facts can we form an opinion as to whether Moll's childish fears about the consequences of not being a gentlewoman are justified—whether in fact they represent an amiable delusion or a naive but genuine moral insight. All the evidence points to the conclusion that Moll is right, that to become a maidservant in that period meant the end of any possibility that could conceivably be subsumed under the words freedom or independence, any possibility therefore of individual human development or flowering. The choice Moll makes is therefore one which, with whatever reservations, deserves our positive sympathy, and the moral tensions about which Defoe's novel is constructed are not trivial or arbitrary.

Not to stress this point is to prejudice artistic judgments. It is only within the social context that we can begin, for instance, to

9. Maximilian E. Novak, *Economics and the Fiction of Daniel Defoe* (California, 1962).
1. Especially C. Hill, 'Clarissa Harlowe and her Times' (*Essays in Criticism*, V (1955), 315–40) and P. F. Vernon, 'Marriage of Convenience and the Moral Code of Restoration Comedy' (*Essays in Criticism*, XII (1962), 370-87).

assess Defoe's treatment (or lack of it) of Moll's role as mother. Mr Watt writes:

> Here the conclusion about her character must surely be that, although there are extenuating circumstances, she is often a heartless mother. It is difficult to see how this can be reconciled either with her kissing the ground that Humphry has trodden, or with the fact that she herself loudly condemns unnatural mothers, but never makes any such accusation against herself even in her deepest moments of penitent self-reprobation.[2]

This puts the cart before the horse. Surely the very point that Defoe has been making us understand is that Moll is *at the same time* unusually honest and extraordinarily dishonest, and that the significance of her situation (whether it be horror or irony) is that she dare not be any more compassionate than she is. What Mr Watt sees as inconsistency I see as profundity. Moll is genuinely sorry that she has been a heartless mother; but that is part of the price she pays *and has to pay* for her independence. The really dreadful aspect of the book lies in Moll's ultimate absorption, via her 'repentance', into the very way of life against which she has so vigorously rebelled.

The Newgate section of the book is an extraordinary achievement and not primarily on the level of verisimilitude. If Newgate is hell to Moll it is above all because it is a place where her habitual habits of self-deception cannot do their job, a real eighteenth-century *huis clos*. Newgate is reality, the eighteenth-century world with the lid off, the world from which Moll set out and to which she comes back, defeated, to emerge as a conformist.

IV

It is worth looking at *Moll Flanders* in its historical context in a rather different sense from the one I have so far emphasized. Moll is perhaps the first major plebeian heroine in English literature. The Doll Tearsheets and Doll Commons of the Elizabethan drama are her literary ancestors, but they are never right at the centre of the plays they appear in, any more than the sensible peasant-bred servants in Molière. Moll is unique. And throughout the eighteenth century she remains so. For Pamela, precisely because she makes the opposite choice to Moll's, is not a heroine. She bears on her shoulders none of the weight of human aspiration which heroism—including the fictional kind—involves. Polly Peachum is nearer to being a heroine; but the Polly of *The Beggar's Opera* needs Lucy Lockit to complete her and together they do—also within the walls

2. *Op. cit.*, p. 110.

of Newgate—throw a great deal of light on the problems and emotions of eighteenth-century plebeian women. Strictly speaking, however, it is impossible to speak of a plebeian heroine after Moll until Jeannie Deans, who is different because she is a peasant, not a townswoman. If one looks further afield the important figure among Moll's successors is another peasant girl, Susannah (Mozart's even more than Beaumarchais'), who is an anti-Pamela and a great advance on the Molière servants.

V

We must see the place of *Moll Flanders* in total history if we are to see it in literary history. The book is not to be judged as though it were an imperfect forerunner of *Pride and Prejudice* or *What Maisie Knew*. Behind almost all the unsatisfactory criticism of Defoe today is a predisposition to judge his books in terms relevant to the novel as it developed in the nineteenth century and to praise in Defoe primarily those aspects of his art which point, so to speak, in that direction. 'Dramatization' (or what Percy Lubbock calls 'scenic' presentation), a conscious manipulation of 'point of view' and a moral preoccupation of the sort one associates with, say, George Eliot: these are assumed to be the elements of maturity in a novelist's development. 'Personal relationships' in the more analytical and isolable sense of the term are seen as the proper, even the ultimate, subject of the novel. And, of course, in an important sense, this is true. Novels will always be about men and women in their living, and therefore personal, relationships.

The trouble with Moll Flanders, however, is that by her very mode of existence she is precluded from having personal relationships of the sort modern critics most value. Mr Watt seems to recognize this when he writes:

> . . . it is certain that, at the end of the long tradition of the European novel, and of the society whose individualism, leisure and unexampled security allowed it to make personal relations the major theme of its literature, Defoe is a welcome and portentous figure. Welcome because he seems long ago to have called the great bluff of the novel—its suggestion that personal relations really are the be-all and end-all of life; portentous because he, and only he, among the great writers of the past, has presented the struggle for survival in the bleak perspectives which recent history has brought back to a commanding position on the human stage.[3]

But he is arguing here that Defoe's positive quality is his concentration on isolated individuals. I think this is a mistaken argument.

3. *Op. cit.*, p. 133.

Moll's life is not an isolated life; she has as many personal relation-ships as anyone else. That she is unable to have full and satisfactory personal relationships is due not to her individualism but to the actual problems she is faced with. Moll is forced to be an individu-alist by her decision to try to be free in the man's world of eight-eenth-century England; but her impulse to be free is due not to individualism but to a desire for better relationships with other people than life as a servant will permit.

The whole nature of Defoe's book—its construction, its texture, its detail, its vitality, its power to move us—is determined by his awareness of the contradiction between Moll's human aspiration and the facts of the human world she lives in. Because so much of the contradiction was, in the year 1722, insoluble and yet had to be resolved, much of the resolution takes the form of ambiguous or ironical statement.

It is interesting to compare Defoe's methods with those of a con-temporary artist facing a comparable problem, the Italian novelist Pier Paolo Pasolini in his impressive film *Accattone*. Accattone, Pasolini's 'hero', is in many respects very like a twentieth-century Moll Flanders. He is a feckless young man who lives as a ponce in Rome, and the film treats his life episodically. There is one scene in particular reminiscent of Defoe's novel. Accattone, needing money to buy a present for his girl, steals a chain from the neck of his young son, telling himself all the time what a swine he is. The moral impact of the film is in one sense much the same as that of *Moll Flanders*: we feel a deep sympathy for Accattone without approving of him, and we are shocked at the human inadequacies of the total situation that is revealed. Yet the similarities are scarcely less striking than the differences, of which perhaps the most impor-tant is that we know precisely where Pasolini stands: there is no moral ambiguity in *his* attitude. Accattone is presented to us clearly, objectively, as a product of contemporary society, and although he is not sentimentalized or excused, the social situation of which he is a part, and at least to some extent a victim, is implicitly condemned.

This is not a matter of chance. Pasolini knows very well that Accattone is unable to resolve his problems; but he also knows that, in the middle of the twentieth century, Accattone's problems are not insoluble. Whereas, to Defoe, at the beginning of the eight-eenth century, Moll's problem is indeed insoluble and this inevita-bly affects the whole nature of his artistic handling of it.

The question 'How far is Defoe's irony intentional?' is not really a fruitful question. For one thing, it is impossible to know the answer for sure; for another, it oversimplifies the nature of artistic consciousness and indeed of all consciousness. Defoe's writing was presumably not *un*intentional, not *un*conscious. He knew what he was doing. But, of course, he will not have been aware of all the implications of what he was doing; no one ever is. It is true that Defoe's own comprehension of some of the most important implications of Moll Flanders' story must seem to us to be incomplete. He underwrites her own ultimate complacency, obviously taking her salvation much too much at its face value. But this limitation is far less important than that 'negative capability' which allowed him to reveal the humanity of Moll. What is important is that he tackled the big, central human problems of his time and went deep, revealing the contradictions as well as the surface qualities, and revealing them in a form which in itself illuminates their nature because it springs from them.

ROBERT ALAN DONOVAN

The Two Heroines of *Moll Flanders*†

* * * In his character as editor Defoe insists in the Preface that the main interest of the novel is in its moral teaching, while simultaneously, in his character as impresario for Moll, he appeals in the long descriptive title to the reader's prurience. Even more important, the novel itself, by making Moll's moral posturing such an obtrusive ingredient of her characterization, can be misleading if the reader takes Moll's moral professions at face value. What I am, in fact, suggesting is that the novel is ironic in that it seems to say one thing and actually says another. The point is not a new one; that *Moll Flanders* is organized by ironies of one kind or another has been argued by * * * others, * * * but the issue of Defoe's intention ought perhaps to be confronted. This is the question which troubles Ian Watt, who, though not disposed to deny the existence of irony in the novel, disputes that it is under Defoe's conscious control.[1] I see no way to prove or disprove the consciousness of the control, but the existence of the control is, I believe, demonstrable in the organization of the novel. At any rate my own object in what follows is to draw attention to what seems to me a consistent principle of organization. In the meantime, perhaps, the

† From *The Shaping Vision: Imagination in the English Novel from Defoe to Dickens* (Ithaca: Cornell University Press, 1966), pp. 34–45. Copyright © 1966 by Cornell University. Used by permission of Cornell University Press and the author.
1. "Whatever disagreement there may be about particular instances, it is surely certain that there is no consistently ironical attitude present in *Moll Flanders*.

Irony in its extended sense expresses a deep awareness of the contradictions and incongruities that beset man in this vale of tears, an awareness which is manifested in the text's purposeful susceptibility to contradictory interpretations. . . . It is, as we have seen, very unlikely that Defoe wrote in this way" (*The Rise of the Novel* [Berkeley and Los Angeles, 1957], p. 126). [See p. 357, above— *Editor*.]

issue of intention need not become too intrusive if we can manage to think of the second, or ironic voice as emanating from Moll herself.

Moll's pretense of a moral preoccupation, equally with her manifest indifference to the psychological and aesthetic aspects of experience, ought to direct our attention to the fact that the subject of the novel is not conceived in any of these ways, and in fact it has been generally recognized that the consciousness which is ordering the experience recorded in the novel is fundamentally concerned with practical matters. Throughout her life Moll remains true to her childhood ambition to be a gentlewoman, which means, apparently, not going into service or doing housework. Her motives are primarily economic, having less to do with social status than with physical and material well-being, and they constitute the mainspring of her character, though as she grows older she conceals this naked acquisitive drive under various disguises, including her puritanical morality. One or two suggestive evidences of what Mark Schorer, echoing a good deal of earlier commentary, calls 'the mercantile mind" ought to be enough.[2] Of the tragedy of Moll's own coming into the world, of her mother's disgrace and transportation, only a single specific detail clings in her memory: her mother's crime was "borrowing three Pieces of fine *Holland,* of a certain Draper in *Cheap-side."* Among the agitations of her conscience after her own first exercise in theft she does not fail to cast up a rigorously exact account of the booty: "There was a Suit of Child-bed Linnen in it, very good and almost new, the Lace very fine; there was a Silver Porringer of a Pint, a small Silver Mug and Six Spoons, with some other Linnen, a good Smock, and Three Silk Handkerchiefs, and in the Mug in a Paper, Eighteen Shillings and Sixpence." And why does she bother to reproduce in toto all three of the midwife's bills when only a single one is applicable? Her inevitable response to experience, of whatever kind, is that of the bookkeeper; the first task is to calculate profit and loss. In this respect at least Moll is very much like Robinson Crusoe; both are centrally concerned with the elementary problem of survival, and beyond that with whatever material amenities a hostile environment can be made to provide. But there is this significant difference between Moll and Crusoe; his principal victory must be won against non-human enemies, but her struggle is with society itself. Crusoe's situation intensifies the practical problems of his life, but it relieves him altogether of the moral and social problems which confront Moll and which she must solve or evade if she is to deal successfully with the larger, more fundamental, and more engrossing problem of economic survival. In *Rob-*

2. Mark Schorer, Introduction to the Modern Library edition of *Moll Flanders*   (New York, 1950), p. xiii.

inson Crusoe the fundamental narrative interest and the basic lineaments of the narrator's consciousness are not overlaid by the distracting complications always present in *Moll Flanders*, which for this reason is a less straightforward, but more interesting, novel.

If the novel's substance, as I have been arguing, is revealed to us through the consciousness of the narrator rather than through the crude cataloguing of incident attempted in the descriptive title of the work, it may be fruitful to turn to the same source for an understanding of the way in which that substance is ordered. One structural principle, of course, is already implicit in the autobiographical format, but the structure so imparted to the novel is very loose and is consistent with a wide variety of artistic or rhetorical purposes. What needs to be established, if possible, is an artistic principle of structure, one that will not only impose unity but make it meaningful. It is clear that the events themselves, considered apart from the way in which they are seen and described, belong to no coherent system. Their order, it is true, is determined in part by the autobiographical plan and by the facts of biology, but there is no inner compulsion that moves us irresistibly from the beginning of Moll's story to the end. Often, indeed, the narrative comes to a halt, as when Moll marries and finds an acceptable mode of life, and it can be made to move forward again only by gratuitously killing off her husband and confronting her all over again with the problem of making her way in the world. In Aristotelian terms, the whole novel consists of "middle," and so no useful purpose can be served by attempting to discover and define a "plot," but it is almost equally unsatisfactory to locate the novel's unifying principle in "character," meaning the Moll who acts and suffers as distinct from the Moll who perceives and narrates. Moll's character, in this sense, undergoes too little change to make its development the sustaining interest of the novel. Furthermore, her character is too simple to permit building the novel around its exposition; we understand Moll as fully as we are going to by the time we are halfway through the book. What remains as a potentially fruitful organizing principle is the relation between Moll as character and Moll as narrator, the curiously devious process by which Moll apprehends and organizes the details of her own experience.

It is not possible, of course, to separate entirely a novel's form from its substance; to say what the novel is about is necessarily also to say a good deal about the way it is put together, for the matter is never conceived without form, and the imaginative act which produces the narrative persona also determines the ways in which it will operate to impose order on the narrative. "Order" is here taken to mean not only sequence but proportion and emphasis, since even a narrative art can be arranged in other than chronological ways.

Nevertheless, though substance implies form, it is still possible, and even fruitful, to talk about form as something different from substance.

I have been examining the details of Moll's story in an effort to determine as precisely as possible the motions of her mind; it is time now to look at the aggregate of these details to see what kind of artistic coherence and unity the novel possesses. For reasons already given I do not think that Moll's purpose (as explained and endorsed by Defoe in the Preface) satisfactorily explains either the selection of detail or its ordering in the novel as a whole. The pattern of temptation, sin, and redemption through suffering, which Defoe as editor tries to force on the narrative, does not really serve to organize it. What does lend coherence to the story is to be sought, I believe, within the fabric of the narration, and specifically within Moll's consciousness as she observes her objective "self" in the role of heroine. Since the novel as a whole is obviously episodic, and the story is continually reaching a full stop, it will be convenient to consider the structure of various episodes, taken singly, before attempting to say anything about the forces of coherence which forge them into a whole.

The first major unit in the novel, bound together by characters, events, and locale, is the Colchester episode, beginning with the death of Moll's foster mother and Moll's subsequent entry into the Colchester household where she occupies a vaguely defined position as protégée and companion and ending with her marriage to Robin, the younger of the two brothers. Now Moll, though professing to care nothing for him, is impelled by the strongest force of her character, her longing for material security and well-being, to desire this marriage, but there are two important obstacles. The first is that she has no fortune, and this lack unites the family against her in spite of the fact that they all admire her. But, as one of the daughters cynically remarks: "If a young Woman has Beauty, Birth, Breeding, Wit, Sense, Manners, Modesty, and all to an Extream; yet if she has not Money, she's no Body, she had as good want them all; nothing but Money now recommends a Woman." She can, of course, marry the young man without his parents' blessing, but since he is the younger son, their prospects necessarily depend on the good will of his parents. The second obstacle is that she has naïvely allowed herself to be drawn into a liaison with the elder brother, without the precaution of agreeing on a fixed settlement. In spite of her professed passion for this brother, Moll would gladly marry his brother and exchange her present precarious situation for a secure and respectable one, and the elder brother, too, would not be averse to such a convenient method of relieving himself without embarrassment from a position that threatens to become both tiresome and awkward. But Moll realizes that she must proceed with caution, for if she accepts this solution with alacrity, then she risks alienating the elder brother by wounding his vanity. She knows, though she is curiously late in acknowledging it to the reader, that she runs the risk "of being drop'd by both of them, and left alone in the World." Moll's master stroke of policy is to declare her undying love for the elder brother and her perfect confidence in his intention to make an honest woman of her. "It took from him," she remarks smugly, "all Possibility of quitting me, but by a down right breach of Honour, and giving up all the Faith of a Gentleman which he had so often engaged by, never to abandon me, but to make me his Wife as soon as he came to his Estate." The result is that Moll has converted one of her most serious disadvantages into an advantage, and henceforward the elder brother will be assiduous, not only to persuade her to consult her own advantage by marrying Robin, but to take her part with the rest of the family in overcoming their objection to the match.

That objection is finally overcome, in part by the elder brother's solicitation, but more importantly by another of Moll's finesses. She simply refuses Robin's offer, and in doing so she attempts (with considerable success) to deceive everyone. To Robin and his parents and sisters it appears that Moll's refusal stems from loyalty to the family and an unwillingness to be the instrument of a schism; to the elder brother it appears that Moll loves him so single-mindedly that she cannot think of making Robin her husband; to the uncritical reader it appears that Moll, being entangled with the elder brother, is unable to break that entanglement so as to permit her to consult her own material and worldly advantage by marrying Robin. To everyone Moll appears in a favorable light because of her unselfishness and her constancy, but the superb irony of all this is that Moll's enjoyment of the good opinion won by her renunciation is not going to cost her the usual price; she is going to have Robin too.

This episode is a remarkably skillful and self-contained little comedy, though its neatness tends to be obscured by the diffuseness and apparent artlessness of Moll's narrative style. But its chief interest and importance in the present discussion is the insight it can be made to yield into the structure Moll imposes on her experience. What is central to her account is not the end achieved but the process of achieving it. Her own little epilogue is suggestive:

> It concerns the Story in Hand very little to enter into the farther Particulars of the Family, or of my self, for the five Years that I liv'd with this Husband, only to observe that I had two Children by him, and that at the end of the five Years he died . . . and . . . left me a Widow with about 1200*l*. in my Pocket.

Obviously the prize, once gained, is of no further interest, and Moll proposes to give us no account at all of the five years of her married life, a period of time which is measured for her characteristically by the bearing of two children and the acquisition of £1,200. What is of paramount interest to her in this whole episode is clearly the means by which the prize is gained, but we must beware of taking her own valuations or interpretive comments too literally. For one thing she is inclined to insist too strongly, as we have seen, on the importance of her own feelings in constituting her dilemma.

Moll's relation to the reader is not an entirely honest one; she is creating a character for us which differs in many respects from the character she presents to other personages in the story, but which is equally far removed from what we may presume to be her real character. In fact, the secret of Moll's worldly success, here and later, is in her ability to assume whatever role is appropriate to her immediate purpose. Here, of course, she differs most radically from Crusoe, who is always himself, since his problem is simply to wrest his subsistence from stubborn Nature. Moll has to get what she wants from other people, a process which involves a duplicity foreign to Crusoe's nature. But Moll's role-playing is more than a technique of her lifelong confidence game; it is, in an important sense, the very center of her being. In the assumption of a specious identity Moll comes as close as she ever can to the disinterested enjoyment of life; her account of the praise lavished on her by the family for her loyalty and abnegation, and of her own "sincerity" in confessing the whole matter to them, breathes her delight in the deception, the special piquancy of which resides in its perfectly ironic quality. Moll knows that she is exactly the opposite of what the family thinks her.

It is not enough, however, to say that Moll enjoys playing a part; she only becomes truly alive when she does. With all her strength and resourcefulness Moll is essentially weak. There is no drive in her character except the vegetable tropism that draws her to comfort and security, and she possesses no inner life at all. A most suggestive passage occurs during her visit to Lancashire, where she falls in with a Roman Catholic family:

> The Truth is, I had not so much Principle of any kind, as to be Nice in Point of Religion; and I presently learn'd to speak favourably of the *Romish Church*; particularly I told them I saw little, but the Prejudice of Education in all the Differences that were among Christians about Religion, and if it had so happen'd that my Father had been a *Roman Catholick*, I doubted not but I should have been as well pleas'd with their Religion as my own.

Moll is clearly what David Riesman would call an "other-directed" person; she has no character or personality of her own, only what she reflects of the society she happens to be in. On Crusoe's desert island she would cease to exist. Her play-acting, therefore, is more than a practical stratagem, more than an amusement, it is the very breath of life, for with no identity of her own Moll must be continually borrowing one.

The attitude at the focus of the first major episode of the novel serves as the center around which all the details are grouped, and this attitude is also, I believe, the center of the novel as a whole. From her childish attempt to assume the role of gentlewoman to her final exit in the character of a penitent, the keen edge of Moll's confrontation of life is pretending to be somebody she is not. Her very name is an assumed identity, for she assures us that Moll Flanders is only a stage name, signifying nothing of her true identity, but only what would now be called her "public image," for Moll's celebrity is considerable. Throughout the later part of her career, in fact, Moll relies heavily on stagecraft. "I had several Shapes to appear in," she acknowledges on one occasion, and she owes her survival after one exploit to the fact that she has disguised herself as a man, and her true sex is unknown to her accomplice.[3] Sometimes, on the other hand, her disguises prove less happy, though the difficulties they involve her in are not practical but psychological. When, for example, she puts on the dress of a beggar woman, she complains that the disguise is "uneasy" and attributes the feeling to her natural abhorrence of "Dirt and Rags," but the reader is inclined rather to suspect that Moll is uneasy as a beggar because she does not have a firm enough sense of her own identity to remain unaffected by the imposture, and of course beggary is Moll's veritable hell.[4]

Most conspicuous of all, however, in the second half of the novel is the affair of the mercer, which occupies such a seemingly disproportionate space in Moll's account of her thieving exploits. Briefly, Moll has dressed as a widow (she thinks of it as a disguise, though she is indeed a widow) and ventured forth "without any real design in view, but only waiting for any thing that might offer." She hears the cry of "Stop Thief!" and presently finds herself dragged into a mercer's shop and accused of theft, for the shop, it appears, has been robbed by a woman in widow's weeds. After receiving a good deal of abuse with only a formal protest, Moll, who is enjoying the

---

3. I doubt whether this ambiguity will lend any support to Watt's contention that "the essence of her character and actions is ... masculine" (p. 113). In view of her lack of tenderness, Moll cannot very well be called *womanly*, but in her practical common sense, in her placing of expedience above principle, and in her unself-conscious vanity she seems to me quintessentially *feminine*.
4. Robert Alter argues that Moll is too unimaginative and literal-minded to be comfortable in any disguise (*Rogue's Progress* [Cambridge, Mass., 1964], p. 42). Disguise certainly may (and in the present instance actually does) threaten Moll's sense of self. What I do not think Alter reckons with is the zest with which Moll nevertheless enters into her impersonations. I shall take up immediately what seems to me the most convincing evidence.

role of injured innocence (her innocence, of course, is only technical, since she has had robbery in her heart) and at the same time is
aware of the practical possibilities of her situation, secures her witnesses for an action against the mercer and his assistant. When the
real thief is brought in, Moll's case is unshakable, and the mercer
eventually has to settle for £150, her attorney's fees, "a Suit of
black Silk cloaths," and "a good Supper into the Bargain." When
Moll arrives to collect this blackmail she carries it off in grand style:

> When I came to receive the Money, I brought my Governess
> with me, dress'd like an old Dutchess, and a Gentleman very well
> dress'd, who we pretended Courted me, but I call'd him Cousin,
> and the Lawyer was only to hint privately to them, that this Gen-
> tleman Courted the Widow.

Since her case is already won, it would appear that this little scene
is to be staged for its own sake. Moll would like to play the piece
out in her character of a respected but maligned widow. Here, as so
prominently elsewhere in the novel, Moll contemplates herself, not
as the innocently covetous thing she is underneath her various disguises, but as the person she appears to be, gaining a few moments
of wider and intenser life by accepting the image of herself that a
temporary circumstance has offered her.

The organizing principle of the novel, the principle that ultimately controls order, proportion, and emphasis, is implicit in this
double function of Moll to serve, so to speak, as both subject and
object. Her consciousness not only reveals the subject to us, it *is* the
subject. The effect is a kind of irony, or double vision, but since the
novel offers us a number of different, perhaps equally pervasive ironies, it will be necessary to make a careful distinction. There is, for
example, the irony implicit in Moll's assumption that the guilt of
her life is her own rather than that of the heartless and venal
society that has produced her. There is also irony of a particularly
devastating kind in Moll's innocent acknowledgment (made overtly
only once, but it underlies her whole moral attitude) that an immoral act is nullified if the perpetrator is ignorant of its moral bearings.
The agent's ignorance, in other words, not only excuses him, it
changes the nature of his act. This amounts to confusing the morality which is an inward condition of mind and spirit with that which
is only reputation. But the fundamental, shaping irony of *Moll
Flanders* is the double vision of the heroine.

Since she herself is unconscious of the irony, it might in fact be
better to revert to a distinction analogous to, but not identical with,
the one already made, between the Moll who acts and suffers and
the Moll who perceives and narrates, so that the duality in her
vision is really a duality in herself. One of her selves, the one whose
impoverished sensibility is displayed to us in the very texture of the

prose, is brutal in its simplicity. She is a kind of vegetable, reaching toward the means of subsistence as a plant reaches toward the light, not by conscious effort, but by some mysterious inherent energy. The other Moll, the unconscious creation of the first, is less the image of what she herself would like to be than of what society would constrain her to be, and her intermittent existence in the various roles she assumes is to be explained not by her conscious or unconscious aspirations, but by her desperate need to escape from the confinement of her nakedly acquisitive self. Her puritanical system of moral valuations, for example, serves in much the same way as her widow's weeds or duchess's costume to confer upon her a moral nature, but one that is quite superficial. Without framing the distinction to herself, Moll realizes that it is better to be a sinner than to be nothing at all. Among the many deceptions that Moll practices, the last and cruelest is of herself, because she has apparently come to take her assumed self for her "real" one. At any rate, she confronts us, finally, in the altogether unearned and unconvincing character of a penitent. What prevents the deception from taking us in, too, is that Moll's undramatic self is there as well, imparting its own unmistakable quality to the narration.

This fundamental irony, produced by the reader's continuous and simultaneous awareness of the two sides of Moll's nature, transforms what would otherwise be a dreary and tedious chronicle of petty deceptions and crimes, unadorned by sensuousness or vividness of description, into a clearly focused and coherent story. Obviously *Moll Flanders* can lay no claim to being tightly constructed, and certainly a great part of its characteristic quality would be destroyed by any effort to contain its substance within the rigidities of a dramatic plot. Nevertheless, the novel does have a more or less clearly defined center in the competing concerns of the two Molls, producing a continuous abrasion that gives to the novel both edge and form. The novel's coherence is a product of its inner form, which has succeeded in energizing and bracing up an otherwise limp and flaccid structure. * * *

MICHAEL SHINAGEL

The Maternal Paradox in *Moll Flanders*: Craft and Character†

The enigma of Moll Flanders' character has occasioned much critical controversy in the past decade, and understandably so. For

† A longer version of this essay originally appeared in the *Cornell Library Journal*, VII (1969), 3–23. The author has especially revised the essay for this edition.

the character of Moll poses complex problems of critical interpretation. Wayne C. Booth has summed up our difficulty in reading *Moll Flanders*: "Whenever an impersonal author asks us to infer subtle differences between his narrator's norms and his own, we are likely to have trouble."[1]

Somehow we must attempt to reconcile the enduring claims of Defoe's novel as a work of art almost universally esteemed by distinguished critics and writers, on the one hand, and the sobering facts posed by the sheer magnitude and variety of Defoe's canon and his habitual haste and carelessness of composition, on the other. Many recent critics of *Moll Flanders* attribute to it a controlled literary craftsmanship that is at odds with most of Defoe's other works, including his novels. In our reading of this novel we must bear in mind that the year 1722 marked one of his most productive quantitatively (over 2,000 printed pages) and his most artistic qualitatively (*Moll Flanders, Due Preparations for the Plague, Religious Courtship, Journal of the Plague Year, Col. Jacque,* among others) —according to William P. Trent, the "greatest *annus mirabilis* in the career of any writer."[2]

If Defoe's creativity reached its height in the year of *Moll Flanders*, it does not necessarily follow that his craftsmanship did also. His narrative technique was always crude.[3] E. M. Forster saw this failing clearly when he compared Defoe's narrative technique to Sir Walter Scott's, remarking of *Moll Flanders* that "we shall find stray threads left about in much the same way, on the chance of the writer wanting to pick them up afterwards: Moll's early batch of children for instance." But unlike Scott, "what interested Defoe was the heroine, and the form of his book proceeds naturally out of her character."[4] Critics of the novel have not analyzed how effectively and consistently Defoe's heroine is enabled to reveal her character through the maternal theme nor how this aspect of Moll's character helps us to understand the interrelation between Defoe's craft and the enigmatic character of his heroine. This essay will attempt such an analysis.

Moll's childbearing record extends over a period of thirty years, from the age of eighteen when she is first seduced by the elder son and marries Robin until the age of forty-eight when her banker husband dies and it is time for her "to leave bearing children." During this span of years she gives birth to no less than twelve children and thereby earns her reputation of "an Earth Mother," as Dorothy

1. *The Rhetoric of Fiction* (Chicago, 1961), p. 321.
2. John Robert Moore, *A Checklist of the Writings of Daniel Defoe* (Bloomington, 1960), pp. 179–184; estimate by Trent quoted in Thomas Wright, *The Life of Daniel Defoe* (London, 1931), p. 313.
3. Arthur Wellesley Secord, *Studies in the Narrative Method of Defoe,* University of Illinois Studies in Language and Literature, IX, 1 (Urbana, 1924), pp. 230–239.
4. *Aspects of the Novel* (New York, 1927), p. 88.

Van Ghent aptly describes her.[5] If her fertility is beyond dispute, her maternity obviously is not; for the fate of many, if not most, of her surviving children in the narrative remains as enigmatic as her character.

Moll's first marriage, to Robin, ends in five years with his death and she thinks it only necessary to record that she had "two children by him" and was left "a widow with 1200*l.*" As an afterthought she notes, "My two children were indeed taken happily off my hands by my husband's father and mother, and that was all they got by Mrs. Betty." Moll's language is indicative of her values; in this case she feels that she has gotten the best of a bad bargain, having successfully fobbed off on her in-laws the care and cost of maintaining two small children while she in turn is "left loose to the world ... young and handsome ... and with a tolerable fortune." Dorothy Van Ghent astutely observes that "schematically, what has been happening here is the conversion of all subjective, emotional, and moral experience—implicit in the fact of Moll's five years of marriage and motherhood—into pocket and bank money, into the materially measurable. It is a shocking formula, shocking in its simplicity and abruptness and entireness."[6]

The formula is applied by Moll to her second marriage, to the gentleman draper, which ends when her huband becomes a bankrupt and flees to France. "Casting things up," Moll finds she can "hardly muster up 500*l.*" Happily, this time she is unencumbered with children. In time she remarries, this time to her half-brother, with whom she goes to live in Virginia. When she discovers that she is living in incest, she already has given birth to "two children, and was big with another." Finally she feels so violently about the relationship and is so fearful of being "with child again" that she asks her husband to allow her to leave for England:

> This provok'd him to the last degree, and he call'd me not only an unkind wife, but an unnatural mother, and ask'd how I could entertain such a thought without horror as that of leaving my two children (for one was dead) without a mother, and never see them more.

Since Moll's husband does not know the true nature of their relationship, he fails to understand fully the cause of her strange behavior. But even though "the whole relation was unnatural in the highest degree," Moll is still the natural mother of the children and her "real desire never to see them, or him either, any more" is, as her husband charges, "unkind" and "unnatural." After eight years she leaves Virginia and her family for England. So complete is her

---

5. *The English Novel: Form and Function* (New York, 1953), p. 43.   6. *Ibid.*, p. 38.

alienation that she shows no concern for the fate of her two surviving children.

In Bath Moll drifts into a liaison with a gentleman who affords her the means "to subsist on very handsomely." Moll is mistress to the gentleman of Bath for six years, "in which time [she] brought him three children, but only the first of them liv'd." When her lover falls seriously ill, she expresses her concern that she "had a son, a fine lovely boy, about five years old, and no provision made for it." Moll's language betrays her true feelings about the boy: the "fine lovely boy" is referred to as a thing ("it") that needs to be provided for. The letter from the gentleman of Bath answers Moll's immediate need: "*I will take due care of the child; leave him where he is, or take him with you, as you please.*" The gentleman at least shows the humanity of referring to the "child" as "him" and, while offering Moll the choice of keeping him, agrees to provide the necessary care. Moll's decision is further revealing of her real feelings about her son:

> . . . it was death to me to part with the child, and yet when I consider'd the danger of being one time or other left with him to keep without being able to support him, I then resolv'd to leave him; but then I concluded to be near him my self too, that I might have the satisfaction of seeing him, without the care of providing for him.

The sincerity of Moll's ostensible anguish over parting with the boy is suspect, just as her entreaty to the gentleman for an additional fifty pounds to put her out of the reach of temptation so that she could "repent as sincerely as he had done" is, by her own admission, "all a cheat." When she proceeds again ritualistically "to cast up [her] accounts," she finds herself aged forty-two and with a "stock" of "above 450*l.*"

Moll next marries James, her Lancashire husband, and soon after they separate she discovers herself "with child." This particular pregnancy puts her "to extreme perplexity" and she grows "very melancholy" because, as she puts it, "I . . . was like now to have a child upon my hands to keep, which was a difficulty I had never had upon me yet, as my story hitherto makes appear." Moll's candid remark about the uniqueness of her imminent motherhood, that she will this time have a child to care for, shows her fully aware of having systematically and successfully avoided the "difficulty" of caring for any of her previous children, of whom at this time five are alive and four reported dead. In time she is "brought to bed" and has "another brave boy." But the child poses a problem to Moll, who cannot avail herself of a good offer of marriage from a banker until she has disposed of him.

This dilemma causes Moll again to moralize on motherhood, its responsibilities and abuses. Her reflections, however, are curiously out of character, and read more like interpolated set pieces by Defoe out of such strenuously religious tracts as *The Family Instructor* or *Religious Courtship*:

> It is manifest to all that understand any thing of children that we are born into the world helpless, and uncapable either to supply our wants, or so much as to make them known; and that without help we must perish. . . . I question not but that these are partly the reasons why affection was plac'd by nature in the hearts of mothers to their children; without which they would never be able to give themselves up, as 'tis necessary they should, to the care and waking pains needful to the support of children.

Coming from Moll, this maternal moralizing is specious and insincere. Up to this point she has manifested very little of that "affection . . . plac'd by nature in the hearts of mothers to their children," whether for the two children discarded with her first husband's parents or the two children abandoned in Virginia or the boy left with her Bath gentleman. Moll, however, does not want to regard herself as a hardened whore and therefore she casuistically justifies her concern for her child: "I was not come up to that pitch of hardness common to the profession, I mean, to be unnatural, and regardless of the safety of my child; and I preserv'd this honest affection so long that I was upon the point of giving up my friend at the bank, who lay so hard at me to come to him, and marry him, that there was hardly any room to deny him." Despite her disclaimer, she is "unnatural" in the end, her "honest affection" being superseded by her selfish desire to marry the banker.

For five years with her banker husband she enjoys "a life of virtue and sobriety," but when he dies she is forty-eight, low in funds, and now at last past childbearing. She mentions that she "had had two children by him and no more," yet the fate of these children is never made clear. Moll describes her happy life with her banker husband in terms which indicate her children lived: "I kept no company, made no visits; minded my family, and obliged my husband. . . ." Moll's "family," however, is forgotten completely in the narrative as she moves abruptly through a two-year transition from widow to thief at the age of fifty.

Artistically we can interpret Moll's failure to mention the fate of her two children as a flaw in Defoe's narrative technique, as simply one of those "stray threads" of which E. M. Forster wrote to describe Defoe's loose way of telling a story. Psychologically and morally, however, the oversight poses no problem to our understanding of Moll's character, for her disregard of her children is a consistent part of her personality and her "history" as she tells it.

So even though Defoe as artist might be nodding at this point in the novel, it doesn't vitiate the portrayal of his heroine. We can accept the view of Robert R. Columbus, who sees Defoe's novel as "a deliberate and conscious attempt to unriddle the soul of Moll Flanders," which he does by imaginatively committing "himself to Moll's own point of view, and her point of view is entirely expressive of his theme."[7] Defoe's identification with Moll, as indeed with most of his heroes and heroines, is clear, but whether the artistry is as deliberate and conscious as Professor Columbus argues remains a moot point. This novel, as indeed all Defoe's other novels, can equally be read as the *unconscious* unriddling of Defoe's own soul.[8] Similarly we can also accept Howard L. Koonce's reading of the novel whereby these narrative flaws are taken as consistent with Defoe's portrayal of an altogether humanly inconsistent and morally muddled Moll narrating her life.[9] Paradoxically, then, the interrelation of craft and character is such that Moll's character and point of view can redeem Defoe's occasional flaws in narrative technique, and critics can promulgate a cogent case for conscious artistry by Defoe at times when he seems most inartistic.

Shortly before Moll is apprehended and committed to Newgate prison, she returns to Colchester, where she grew up and was first seduced and married:

> It was no little pleasure that I saw the town where I had so many pleasant days, and I made enquiries after the good old friends I had once there, but could make little out; they were all dead or remov'd. The young ladies had been all married or gone to London; the old gentleman, and the old lady that had been my early benefactress, all dead; and which troubled me most, the young gentleman, my first lover, and afterwards my brother-in-law, was dead.

Our critical approach to this passage will determine to whom it is more damaging, Defoe's craft or Moll's character. It is a serious oversight for Defoe to have forgotten that Moll's first two children, by Robin, were left in Colchester with her husband's parents, and to fail to pick up such a "stray thread" at this time is indicative of his careless narrative craft. On the other hand, it is utterly devastating to Moll's character and her presentation to us as a mother. For Moll to make inquiries about everyone but her own two children by Robin, the very same children she left with "the old gentleman,

7. "Conscious Artistry in *Moll Flanders*," *SEL*, III (1963), 415.
8. This is the approach taken by Mark Schorer, who interprets *Moll Flanders* as "not the true chronicle of a disreputable female, but the true allegory of an impoverished soul—the author's": "A Study in Defoe: Moral Vision and Structural Form," *Thought*, XXV (1950), 284.
9. "Moll's Muddle: Defoe's Use of Irony in *Moll Flanders*," *ELH*, XXX (1963), 377–394.

and the old lady," betrays her as a mother totally devoid of that "honest affection" she earlier claimed distinguished her from "unnatural" mothers, like hardened whores. No matter how we choose to read this passage it is damaging to Defoe's craft or Moll's character, in my judgment both.[1]

Yet the most revealing and crucial episode in our understanding of the maternal theme in the novel occurs when Moll returns to Virginia aged threescore years and encounters her son Humphry. Many years earlier, when Moll left Virginia, she showed no concern for the fate of her two surviving children by her marriage to her half-brother; she even informed her husband that it was her "real desire never to see them . . . any more" and that they "were not legal children." Now she returns a transported felon and chances to have her brother-husband and son pointed out to her but is fearful of making herself known. Since it would be premature and risky to identify herself at this moment, she prudently lets them "pass by":

> It was a wretch'd thing for a mother thus to see her own son, a handsome comely young gentleman in flourishing circumstances, and durst not make herself known to him, and durst not take any notice of him; let any mother of children that reads this consider it, and but think with what anguish of mind I restrain'd myself; what yearnings of soul I had in me to embrace him, and weep over him; and how I thought all my entrails turn'd within me, that my very bowels mov'd, and I knew not what to do, as I now know not how to express those agonies. When he went from me I stood gazing and trembling, and looking after him as long as I could see him; then sitting down on the grass, just at a place I had mark'd, I made as if I lay down to rest me, but turn'd from her, and lying on my face wept, and kiss'd the ground that he had set his foot on.

Moll's spontaneous overflow of powerful maternal emotion must leave us unconvinced of her sincerity. Moll's maternal feelings are rhetorically contrived and meretricious, coming as they do immediately after she has been informed that Humphry owns the plantation and while she sizes him up ("a handsome comely young man in flourishing circumstances"). Moll's language and stance betray her, for her son's "flourishing circumstances" attract her eye, as does the plantation she stands on and symbolically kisses the ground of, as does the "dwelling house" she sees in the distance. By

---

1. A similar narrative inconsistency occurs when Moll is imprisoned in Newgate and remarks: "in short, I became as naturally pleas'd and easy with the place as if indeed I had been born there." In a gloss to this passage the editor, James Sutherland, observes, "Defoe appears to have forgotten that Moll *was* born in Newgate." While I am inclined to con- cur with Professor Sutherland's explanation, I can also see how critics convert Defoe's omissions into ironies consistent with Moll's muddled first-person narration and point of view. Surely it is a supreme irony for Moll's careless morality to redeem, at virtually every turn, Defoe's careless art!

this late point in her long career, Moll's eyes are too experienced in the sharp appraisal of "handsome," i.e., expensive and desirable, objects not to respond instinctively and passionately to something in which she hopes shortly to share.

Moll's handling of the situation further reveals her calculating efforts to share in the riches now owned by Humphry, the very child she years earlier rejected emotionally and disowned as "not legal." After much deliberation on how best to proceed so as not to "lose the assistance and comfort of the relation, and lose whatever it was my mother left me," she finally resolves upon a stratagem of writing her brother a letter, knowing "that having receiv'd this letter he would immediately give it to his son to read; his eyes being . . . so dim that he cou'd now see to read it":

> I said some very tender kind things in the letter about his son,
> which I told him he knew to be my own child, and that as I was
> guilty of nothing in marrying him any more than he was in
> marrying me, neither of us having then known our being at all
> related to one another, so I hop'd he would allow me the most
> passionate desire of once seeing my own and only child, and of
> showing something of the infirmities of a mother in preserving a
> violent affection for him.

Moll dissembles in expressing "the most passionate desire of once seeing my own and only child," for whom she has preserved "a violent affection." Humphry is far from being her "only child," even her only surviving son; and the "violent affection" Moll speaks of "preserving" for him is a sham, her maternal response being not only sudden but in large part materially inspired. Still, her stratagem succeeds admirably and Humphry dutifully comes to see her "not as a stranger, but as a son to a mother," which convinces her of the complete success of her stratagem concerning the inheritance.

During her stay on Humphry's plantation Moll's behavior is so consistently selfish, calculating, and businesslike that her emotional displays cannot be seen as sincere and natural. Indeed, as soon as she is comfortably settled in the house on the plantation and accorded "all possible respect," she reflects: "thus I was as if I had been in a new world, and began almost to wish that I had not brought my Lancashire husband from England at all." Humphry reads her his grandmother's will, whereby she inherits "a plantation on York River . . . with the stock of servants and cattle upon it," and "tho' [it is] remote from him" he readily offers to serve as her "steward" and manage it so that each year it would yield her "about a 100*l.*, sometimes more." Her response to these "kind offers" is tearful and passionate, and she moralizes rhapsodically on the wonders of Providence.

Emotion, however, as Moll well knows, is cheap, and she transforms the exchange with her son into a proper business transaction, the formula, according to Dorothy Van Ghent, whereby Moll habitually converts "all subjective, emotional, and moral experience":

> . . . at length I began, and expressing my self with wonder at being so happy to have the trust of what I had left put into the hands of my own child, I told him that as to the inheritance of it, I had no child but him in the world, and was now past having any if I should marry, and therefore would desire him to get a writing drawn, which I was ready to execute, by which I would after me give it wholly to him, and to his heirs. . . .

Moll overlooks the existence of her many living children, including the son by her Lancashire husband. Now she sees her affluent security embodied in Humphry, and to her mind she has "no child but him in the world." Again we are faced with the interpretative problem of assuming that either Defoe, in the final rush of finishing off his story, has overlooked this "stray thread" in the narrative or Moll, in her muddled moral way of dealing with her life, has simply forgotten him. Either way, Defoe's craft or Moll's character suffers accordingly.

The workings of Moll's mind require that business transactions, even when performed between mother and son, be balanced neatly, and since Humphry has been generous with her, she feels obliged to reciprocate:

> I made him one present, and it was all I had of value, and that was one of the gold watches, of which I said I had two in my chest, and this I happen'd to have with me, and gave it him at his third visit. I told him, I had nothing of any value to bestow but that, and I desir'd he would now and then kiss it for my sake; I did not indeed tell him that I stole it from a gentlewoman's side, at a meeting house in London; that's by the way.

> He stood a little while hesitating, as if doubtful whether to take it or no; but I press'd it on him, and made him accept it, and it was not much less worth than his leather pouch full of Spanish gold; no, tho' it were to be reckon'd, as if at London, whereas it was worth twice as much there; at length he took it, kiss'd it, told me the watch should be a debt upon him, that he would be paying as long as I liv'd.

The gift of the gold watch in this passage assumes a profound symbolic significance both for Moll and for Humphry. Moll uses the watch as a bond by which she ties her son to the financial contract they have transacted. She presses it on him and asks him to kiss it "now and then" for her sake. The gold watch is a woman's, and by its value (gold) and sexual identification (feminine) stands as a powerful surrogate for Moll herself, of whom it will constantly remind Humphry when she is away. And the watch does indeed become so valued when "at length he took it, kiss'd it, told [her] the watch should be a debt upon him, that he would be paying as long as [she] liv'd." The symbolic contract sealed, there only remains the formal passing of papers to make the transaction legal:

> A few days after, he brought the writings of gift, and the scrivener with him, and I sign'd them very freely, and deliver'd them to him with a hundred kisses; for sure, nothing ever pass'd between a mother and a tender dutiful child, with more affection.

The curious mixture of warm kisses and cold cash is characteristic of the cash nexus in all Moll's actions and motives. The formula for "affection" is the signing of profitable business agreements "between a mother and a tender dutiful child." Her son is so conscious of the debt upon him, symbolically signified by the gold watch, that he informs her she is entitled to the profits from the plantation for "the current year, and so he paid a hundred pound in Spanish pieces of eight," for which she gladly gives him "a receipt."

For all the apparent "affection" Moll feels for her son, what remains of their relationship in the story is largely businesslike. Although ostensibly designed to show Moll in her best light as a mother, the entire relationship with Humphry further condemns her. For his function, by Moll's account, is strictly a utilitarian and economic one: to serve as a means whereby she can swiftly achieve a secure state of affluence.

Moll's maternity affords us a revealing, if unflattering, insight into her enigmatic character, but what does the maternal theme in the novel tell us about Defoe's craft? For all our fascination with Moll, we must remember that she is essentially like Defoe's other fictive heroes and heroines, all of whom adopt the same essential mode of the autobiographical memoir and first-person point of view in narrating their "histories." Moreover, all Defoe's novels show the same errors and inconsistencies in narrative technique and the same resultant muddlement in point of view.[2] In the broad context of Defoe's career as a writer in general, and even in the concentrated period of his novel writing in particular, we should not overestimate his artistry by ignoring the haste and carelessness of composition characteristic of his canon. We can reconcile the greatness of *Moll Flanders* with the imperfect craftsmanship of Defoe as novelist by the paradox of Moll's enigmatic character. Despite the moral muddlement of point of view and the errors and inconsistencies of narrative consciousness, *Moll Flanders* is, as E. M. Forster observed, a

2. Charles Gildon, *Robinson Crusoe Examin'd and Criticis'd,* ed. Paul Dottin (London, 1923); William T. Hastings, "Errors and Inconsistencies in Defoe's *Robinson Crusoe*," *MLN,* XXVII (1912), 161–166.

novel "where the character is everything and can do what it likes."[3] In this way Defoe's occasional lapses in narrative craft are transformed by Moll's character into an unconscious artistry that enhances the psychological and moral delineation of his heroine. Thus we can, like Defoe, have it both ways, acknowledging the imperfections of his craft while esteeming his achievement of creating in *Moll Flanders* a great work *malgré lui*.

MAXIMILLIAN E. NOVAK

Defoe's "Indifferent Monitor": The Complexity of *Moll Flanders*[†]

* * *

Though Defoe's lapses from consistency have often caused his artistic integrity to be called into question, he was a writer deeply concerned with language and the meaning of words—the way an understanding of subtle shifts in meaning distinguishes the good writer from the bad. Let us suppose for the moment that Defoe set out to present a character who passes over certain points of her life with evasive remarks and comes close to lying about others. How would it be possible to handle the language of narrative in such a way that something resembling a true view of the events would be apparent to the reader? Wayne Booth has pointed out the difficulties with proving ironic intent in a novel written in the first person, and Defoe was not above solving this problem in pamphlets employing a persona by ending them with a direct confession of what he called "Irony." But realistic fiction would prevent a device of this kind. What Defoe needed was a method of making meaning transparent without sacrificing the integrity of his point of view.

One way out was through a complex use of language and what Defoe called "Inuendo," by which he meant all indirect methods of communication from irony to meiosis. If we turn to the point in Defoe's novel when Moll has been abandoned by the lover she picked up at Bath, some of the complications involved will be clear. After receiving a note from him cutting off the affair, Moll writes a letter telling him that she would never be able to recover from the blow of parting from him, that she not only approved of his repentance but wished "to Repent as sincerely as he had done." All she needs is fifty pounds to return to Virginia. Moll confesses at once

3. *Aspects of the Novel* (New York, 1927), p. 97.
† From *Eighteenth-Century Studies*, III, 3 (Spring 1970), pp. 351–359, 365. Copyright © 1970 by the Regents of the University of California. Reprinted by permission of The Regents and the author.

that what she said "was indeed all a Cheat," and that "the business was to get this last Fifty Pounds of him," but she does moralize on the situation:

> And here I cannot but reflect upon the unhappy Consequence of too great Freedoms between Persons started as we were, upon the pretence of innocent intentions, Love of Friendship, *and the like*; for the Flesh has generally so great a share in those Friendships, that it is great odds but inclination prevails at last over the most solemn Resolutions; and that Vice breaks in at the breaches of Decency, which really innocent Friendship ought to preserve with the greatest strictness; but I leave the Readers of these things to their own just Reflections, which they will be more able to make effectual than I, who so soon forgot my self, and am therefore but a very indifferent Monitor.

Moll's willingness to confess that any admonitions coming from her about manners and morals might well be regarded sceptically should put the reader on his guard at once. Would we want to hear morality preached by Moll King or Callico Sarah?[1] And after all, Moll has just testified to her dishonesty. Surely at this point simple solutions (i.e., it is Defoe with his somewhat questionable puritan moral standards speaking) will not work.

There are also somewhat disturbing stylistic elements in this passage that might prevent the reader from regarding this as a straightforward confession. Take the phrase, "Love of Friendship, *and the like*." One might almost think that Moll was being witty, that "*and the like*" was intended to imply by ironic understatement all the possible kinds of discourses leading ultimately to seduction. Although Professor Watt has warned us against reading into Defoe what is not there, the fact is that this is an important element in Moll's narrative. She is always qualifying words in order to clarify the distinction between the apparent meaning of a word and the reality behind it. The brother she lived with in incest is "my Brother, *as I now call him*," the first woman who takes care of her is "my Mistress Nurse, as I call'd her," the trunk she steals from a Dutchman is "my Trunk, *as I call'd it*." Whether or not Defoe actually added the italics to these phrases (as he did occasionally in the one manuscript of his that we have), they were obviously intended to suggest the disparity between what something is called and what it is, and to call attention to the narrator's own awareness of this.[2]

1. See Gerald Howson, "Who Was Moll Flanders?" pp. 312–319, above [*Editor*].
2. The tendency of a narrator to suggest moral positions in brief and often oversimplified phrases is part of the tradition of the picaresque from Alemán to Celine. Because I had previously approached Defoe's fiction more from the standpoint of content than technique, like Professor Watt, I sometimes underestimated the very strong influence of picaresque fiction on Defoe's narrative style.

Similar to these kinds of phrases is her simple remark, "I wav'd the Discourse" when her Bank Manager sums up the character of his wife with the remark, "she that will be *a Whore* will be *a Whore*," or her summation of her reaction to the entire tale of this sad cuckold, "Well, I pitied him, and wish'd him well rid of her, and still would have talk'd of my Business." The tone of impatience (the Bank Manager is married and therefore unavailable at this point) is clear enough. Defoe *is* conveying a great deal, then, through tone and language.

In fact Moll is extraordinarily playful in her use of language. When she tries to avoid joining a gang of counterfeiters, she remarks, "tho' I had declin'd it with the greatest assurances of Secresy in the World, they would have gone near to have murther'd me, to make sure Work, and make themselves easy, *as they call it*; what kind of easiness that is, they may best Judge that understand how easy Men are, that can murther People to prevent Danger." And the section in which she enters the home for unwed mothers is full of such implications. After the Governess has assured her that she need not worry about the care of her child if she puts it out to a nurse recommended by the house and that she must behave as "other conscientious Mothers," Moll, who is careful to separate herself from "all those Women who consent to the disposing their Children out of the way, *as it is call'd*," comments on her Governess' language, "I understood what she meant by conscientious Mothers, she would have said conscientious Whores; but she was not willing to disoblige me." Moll tells herself that, at least technically, she was married, but then merely contents herself with distinguishing herself from other prostitutes ("the Profession") by her still tender heart. Even the affectionate use of the term "Mother" for her Governess is suspect. Though she might have a right to that title by her affectionate treatment of Moll, or by being Moll's "Mother Midnight," that is her midwife, the fact is that the name was usually given to the Madam of a brothel. In fact their dialogues resemble nothing so much as those between Mother Cresswell and Dorothea, bawd and neophyte, in *The Whore's Rhetorick* (1683). They too refer to each other as mother and daughter, and Moll's Mother-Governess is not above being a bawd as well as an abortionist and a fence.

Perhaps the way in which Moll describes the suggestion of an abortion and her rejection of it gives the best clues into the complex use of language in Defoe's novel:

> The only thing I found in all her Conversation on these Subjects, that gave me any distaste, was, that one time in Discoursing about my being so far gone with Child, and the time I expected to come, she said something that look'd as if she could help me

off with my Burthen sooner, if I was willing; or in *English*, that she could give me something to make me Miscarry, if I had a desire to put an end to my Troubles that way: but I soon let her see that I abhorr'd the Thoughts of it; and to do her Justice, she put it off so cleverly, that I could not say she really intended it, or whether she only mentioned the practice as a horrible thing: for she couch'd her words so well, and took my meaning so quickly, that she gave her Negative before I could explain myself.

Moll used the same pun a few pages before; if the reader failed to catch it the first time, he might be at least as clever as Moll's Governess and pick it up the second time around. One can assume, then, that, at times, Moll converses in *double-entendres* and expects her listeners and readers to understand them.[3]

Such word play is not uncommon in Defoe's narrative. As I have pointed out elsewhere, Moll points to her misunderstanding of the use of the word "Miss" by the wife of the mayor who comes to visit her when she is a child in Colchester: "The Word Miss was a Language that had hardly been heard of in our School, and I wondered what sad Name it was she call'd me." It is a sad word because it says something about her future quest after gentility and her future life as a prostitute. In much the same way, thinking of the friend who had passed her off as a woman of Fortune, Moll tells of how she decides to take a trip to Bath. "I took the Diversion of going to the *Bath*," she remarks, "for as I was still far from being old, so my Humour, which was always Gay, continu'd so to an Extream; and being now, *as it were*, a Woman of Fortune, tho' I was a Woman without a Fortune, I expected something, or other might happen in my way, that might mend my Circumstances, as had been my Case before." Another instance of this type of word play comes in the section on the counterfeiters. Speaking of her refusal to join the gang, Moll remarks that

> the part they would have had me have embark'd in, was the most dangerous Part; I mean that of the very working the Dye, as they call it, which had I been taken, had been certain Death, and that at a Stake, *I say*, to be burnt to Death at a Stake; so that tho' I was to Appearance but a Beggar; and they promis'd Mountains of Gold and Silver to me, to engage; yet it would not do; it is True, if I had been really a Beggar, or had been desperate as when I began, I might perhaps have clos'd with it for what care they to Die, that can't tell how to Live?

The phrase, "working the Dye," which James Sutherland calls a "grim pun" in his edition of *Moll Flanders*, meant to stamp the coin. A terrible death awaits those who would gamble or stake their

---

3. A more obvious example of this type of dialogue through hints and sugges- tions may be found in the courtship scene with her Brother-Husband.

lives on such an occupation, and in the midst of her punning, Moll is careful to remark that "they" use the term "working the Dye," not she. This is her way of separating herself from such awful people.

It is passages like these that lead the reader to suspect other double meanings. When Moll is made pregnant by her Bath lover, he assumes the name of Sir Walter Cleave, and Moll says that she was made as comfortable as she would have been had she "really been my Lady *Cleave*." In addition to whatever sexual significance might be attached to this word by a wary reader, the fact is that a "cleave" is defined as "a forward or wanton woman" in Francis Grose's *A Classical Dictionary of the Vulgar Tongue*. And significantly enough, in the rather pious chap book versions of Moll Flanders, the name was changed to Clare.

At other times the issue is more doubtful. Is Moll aware of any sexual significance in a phrase like that already quoted in Moll's reflections on her Bath lover, that "Vice breaks in at the breaches of Decency"? If we regard Moll as being, at least in part, a comic figure, we would have to say that Defoe makes her use this phrase with some ambiguity. Is she supposed to understand certain implications in such language? Did Defoe? Having no definite solution, I will follow Moll and waive the discourse. But of Defoe's use of puns and word play as a method to convey subtle meanings playing underneath Moll's narrative there cannot be the slightest doubt.

If some passages raise doubts in the reader's mind, there is good reason for it: Moll, herself, is often undecided or uncertain about the way she should interpret the events of her life, and her language often reflects these doubts. She begins the story of her Bath lover's control over his sexual desires with a remark that reveals her undecided state. He has spent the night in bed with her entirely naked and without offering any advances that might be regarded as completely sexual in nature. Moll comments, "I own it was a noble Principle, but as it was what I never understood before, so it was to me perfectly amazing." Even if one understands by "noble Principle" something that cannot work in practice, we cannot come to such a decision until Moll's final condemnation of the entire relationship several pages later.

Such passages are complex not so much because of the language alone but because Defoe asks us to suspend our judgment on the meaning of certain words and phrases until the events themselves or Moll's last commentary clarifies the situation. Many of Moll's comments on her Governess are rich in this kind of momentary ambiguity. When the woman chosen by the Governess to tutor Moll in the art of thievery has been taken and sentenced to death, the emotions of the Governess have to be ambiguous, since the tutoress has enough information to save her own life by impeaching the Governess. Moll King saved her life several times in this manner. Moll Flanders does not render this mixture of regret for the loss of a friend and apprehension for personal safety in anything resembling straight description:

> It is true, that when she was gone, and had not open'd her Mouth to tell what she knew; my Governess was easy as to that Point, and perhaps glad she was hang'd; for it was in her power to have obtain'd a Pardon at the Expence of her Friends; But on the other Hand, the loss of her, and the Sense of her Kindness in not making her Market of what she knew, mov'd my Governess to Mourn very sincerely her: I comforted her as well as I cou'd, and she in return harden'd me to Merit more compleatly the same Fate.

Moll's bitterness is apparent enough, but the language is sometimes pointed, sometimes neutral in a situation that is inherently ambiguous. The Governess, whose life has been spared at this point and later threatened in the same way by Moll's capture, is sincere in her sorrow, but she does not undergo any change of heart. And Moll may be speaking of one point in the past, but she has her mind set on another point—her future sufferings in Newgate.

* * * it should be noted here that in passages such as these, Moll's narrative may be viewed ironically (by anyone's definition) on the present level of the told narrative, while functioning realistically as a record of the action as it is occurring. Many of the contradictions that appear in the novel are caused by the simple fact that even criminals and fences have to have a morality to live by. Polls among jail inmates revealing strong moral disapproval of crime are commonplace. As we shall see, such moral judgments need not indicate a permanent change of heart.

When Moll commits her "second Sally into the World," she tells of her experience in a manner that is even more demanding of complex understanding. Having led the little girl out of her way, Moll is confronted by the child's protests. She quiets these objections with the sinister remark, "I'll show you the way home." This piece of direct dialogue is given in a narrated scene to underscore its ironic implication—the possibility that to quiet the child while she was stealing the necklace she might have to murder her. After describing her horror at the impulse to murder, Moll tells of her psychological state after this robbery. "The last Affair," she says, "left no great Concern upon me," explaining that after all she did not harm the child and may have helped improve the care that the parents of the child would show in the future. And after estimating the value of the string of beads, Moll begins to extrapolate about the entire incident. The girl was wearing the necklace because the mother was proud; the child was being neglected by the mother, who had put her in the care of a maid; the maid was doubtless negligent and meeting her lover. And while all these palliations for her crime are being offered—and they sound peculiarly like crimes Moll might have been guilty of at other stages of her career—the "pretty little Child" has gradually become the "poor Child," "poor Lamb," and "poor Baby." In blaming everyone else but herself, Moll is revealing that her psychological involvement is far greater than she is willing to admit, and the energy that she exerts to deny her involvement is undercut verbally by the increasing sympathy she tries to arouse for the child.

As for blaming such moralizing on Defoe's simplemindedness, it should be pointed out that a later incident shows a similar unwillingness to accept guilt mingled with a more obvious callousness toward crime. When Moll seduces a Gentleman in a coach, she moralizes on the possibility that the man might have been seduced by a diseased prostitute. Her moralizing, it should be noted, is a blend of past and present reactions:

> As for me, my Business was his Money, and what I could make of him, and after that if I could have found out any way to have done it, I would have sent him safe home to his House, and to his Family, for 'twas ten to one but he had an honest virtuous Wife, and innocent Children, that were anxious for his Safety, and would have been glad to have gotten him Home, and have taken care of him, till he was restor'd to himself; and then with what Shame and Regret would he look back upon himself? how would he reproach himself with associating himself with a Whore? pick'd up in the worst of all Holes, the Cloister, among the Dirt and Filth of the Town? how would he be trembling for fear he had got the Pox, for fear a Dart had struck through his Liver, and hate himself every time he look'd back upon the Madness and Brutality of his Debauch? how would he, if he had any Principles of Honour, as I verily believe he had, I say how would he abhor the Thought of giving any ill Distemper, if he had it, as for ought he knew he might, to his Modest and Virtuous Wife, and thereby sowing the Contagion in the Life-Blood of his Posterity?

What is curious about this is that Moll is substantially creating a fiction as she goes along in much the same manner as she did with the child she robbed. The fiction about the gentleman led astray by the prostitute is highly moral and has little or none of the word play that, as I have shown, is a customary part of Moll's narrative manner. But it is a fiction for all that, a story woven to cheer herself up in the past and present, and the more graphic it is, the more real it is for her.

And then Moll does something that we ought to expect. She betrays herself by telling a somewhat off-color story of how a prostitute once managed to pick the pocket of a customer, even though he was on his guard, by replacing his purse with one filled with tokens during sexual intercourse. Doubtless she tells the sad story of the gentleman who might have picked up a diseased prostitute to her Governess in as moving terms as she tells it to the reader, for she described how that good lady "was hardly able to forbear Tears, to think how such a Gentleman run a daily Risque of being undone, every Time a Glass of Wine got into his Head." But the Governess is entirely pleased by the booty Moll has brought her from the gentleman, and after assuring Moll that the incident might "do more to reform him, than all the Sermons that ever he will hear in his Life," she proceeds to arrange a liaison between Moll and the gentleman. It is impossible to think that Defoe was napping here. Moll and her Governess possess a great deal of morality, but they are criminals nevertheless; and Defoe never lets us forget it. Moll remains throughout the novel an "indifferent Monitor."

* * *

Defoe was a very clever writer, with too little time to be meticulously careful, but with infinitely more craft than an amateur like the Richardson of *Pamela*. It has been a long time since anyone found Shakespeare's clock striking in Athens objectionable, and it is about time that, acknowledging all of Defoe's inconsistencies and errors, we should begin remarking on his brilliance as a writer.

G. A. STARR

[Defoe and Casuistry: *Moll Flanders*] †

Casuistry: That part of Ethics which resolves cases of conscience, applying the general rules of religion and morality to particular instances in which "circumstances alter cases," or in which there appears to be a conflict of duties. Often (and perhaps originally) applied to a quibbling and evasive way of dealing with difficult cases of duty.   OED

Nearly all of Defoe's fictional works cause us to identify imaginatively with characters whose actions we regard as blameworthy. At the same time that they compel sympathy, his heroes and heroines evoke moral judgment, and our two responses are often sharply opposed. Several critics have previously noted the paradox; this monograph seeks to elucidate it by examining the influence of traditional casuistry on the subject matter, narrative technique, and ethi-

† From *Defoe and Casuistry* (Princeton: Princeton University Press, 1971), pp. v–vii, ix–x, 111–120, 134–138, 161–164.   Copyright © 1971 by Princeton University Press, and reprinted by their permission and that of the author.

422 · G. A. Starr

cal outlook of Defoe's writings. The affective problem is posed concisely by Angus Ross, who says of Crusoe, "He knows his disobedience is wicked. So does the reader: but he is drawn on by Defoe to sympathize with Crusoe. . . . the reader is not held at a distance and forced to judge. . . . 'So,' we say, 'if I had been Crusoe, I should have behaved.' "[1] What draws us on to sympathize with Crusoe—and with the more patently "wicked" Moll Flanders and Roxana as well—is in large part Defoe's casuistical emphasis on intention and qualifying circumstances. In terms of overt behavior, we respectable readers are remote from such characters, but there is no such distance between their motives and ours. The difference in our circumstances therefore serves to explain, and to bridge the gap between, our dissimilar outward careers. Moreover, the differences between their situations and ours are shown to be largely accidental: this too keeps us from adopting a complacently superior stance, and from passing rigorous judgment on Defoe's erring heroes and heroines.

This is not to say that Defoe forbids us to judge his characters, or that he asks acquittal for one and all. Both their prosecutor and defender, he tends to seek a verdict of guilty, but also a suspended sentence and even, in some cases, a full pardon. The reader, of course, is both judge and jury, which may be why there is so much of what Ian Watt calls "forensic ratiocination" in Defoe's fiction.[2] Details that appear to be introduced for their psychological, social, or economic import, or for the sake of narrative realism, frequently involve covert appeals for sympathy as well; their function is not only descriptive or analytic, but also rhetorical. Some of them call in question the conventional assumptions and values which ordinarily shape our judgment, and attempt to make us judge more favorably than we otherwise would, given the outward facts of a case. More often, it is the tone rather than the substance of our judgments that they induce us to modify; they insist that reprehensible as a character may be, he merits our compassion, not our contempt. Lionel Trilling has called the traditional English novel "the literary form to which the emotions of understanding and forgiveness were indigenous, as if by definition of the form itself."[3] Recent critics preoccupied with irony have tended to lose sight of such emotions

1. Introduction to *Robinson Crusoe* (Baltimore, 1965), p. 15.
2. *The Rise of the Novel* (London, 1957), p. 85.
3. "Manners, Morals, and the Novel," in *The Liberal Imagination* (Garden City, 1953), p. 215. Trilling's two preceding sentences seem to me equally applicable to Defoe's fiction. The greatness and practical usefulness of the novel, he maintains, "lay in its unremitting work of involving the reader himself in the moral life, inviting him to put his own motives under examination, suggesting that reality is not as his conventional education has led him to see it. It taught us, as no other genre ever did, the extent of human variety and the value of this variety." Tony Tanner has recently made a similar point; the novelist, he says, can effect "a kind of redistribution of our sympathies," which involves "understanding forms of life which hitherto one had rather casually considered as axiomatically alien" ("Realism, Reality, and the Novel," a symposium in *Novel: A Forum on Fiction*, II [1969], 208–209.)

in the experience of reading Defoe: this study tries to reaffirm their importance, and to trace the part that casuistry plays in eliciting them.

* * *

The main effect of casuistry on the action of Defoe's imaginative works is to dissolve it into a series of discrete episodes. Casuistry was not the sole source of fragmentation in Defoe's stories, yet its assumptions about experience probably reinforced episodic tendencies inherent in certain literary genres (such as criminal biography) upon which he drew, as well as in his own improvisatory method of composition. The continuity of each character's struggle breaks down into a sequence of local crises, each somewhat isolated from those that precede and follow it, and I think we can regard such plotting (or nonplotting) as the expression of a casuistical conception of life without implying that it is peculiar to casuistry, or that it is Defoe's only mode of analyzing experience. Watt remarks that between Defoean episodes there is "an inordinate number of cracks," and although Defoe's having "worked piecemeal, very rapidly, and without any subsequent revision" may be chiefly responsible for "discontinuities" in plot, Defoe's casuistical sense of life's intrinsic discontinuities probably contributed to the same effect."[4] Whatever larger thematic coherences his books may have, individual episodes tend to be connected chronologically, not causally, and far from helping to organize them into a sustained narrative, casuistry appears to be one of the factors responsible for their disjointedness. Within the individual episode, however, casuistry often afforded Defoe both his subject matter and a distinctive way of treating it. Many scenes are not only based upon traditional cases of conscience, but organized internally in ways that reflect the casuistical method of posing and resolving moral dilemmas. There is a constant marshalling of motives and sanctions, choices and circumstances, precedents and hypothetical analogues; although this procedure can jeopardize any larger pattern or design a book may have, it can also supply a kind of minimal consistency between episodes, and can give each of them a fullness and complexity lacking in earlier fiction.

* * *

* * * Throughout *Moll Flanders* it is assumed that the respectable reader abhors crime and despises thieves, and that (as one critic has said of Moll herself) he "struggles with no confusion as to what is right and what is wrong," but accepts "a classical moralism which drew a sharp line between goodness and badness."[5] Much of the book seeks to support this "classical moralism," not to subvert it; from the preface onwards, we are invited to abhor Moll's crimes,

---

4. *The Rise of the Novel*, pp. 99, 100.
5. Carl Van Doren, Introduction to *Moll*
Flanders (New York, 1923), pp. xii, xiii.

but urged not to despise the criminal herself. We are asked to distinguish between act and agent—between what Moll does and what she essentially is: without minimizing her culpability, the narrative seeks to deflect our severity from the doer to the deed, and to retain sympathy for the erring heroine.

This kind of appeal to the reader is most overt when she is about to commit her first theft, and plays an important part elsewhere in the book as well. But it is not the only pattern in which sympathy and judgment are related. At times, Moll's story tends to subvert "classical moralism," and casts doubt on the legitimacy of rigid distinctions between "goodness and badness." With this object, considerable emphasis is put on the principle that circumstances alter cases. William Perkins, the Puritan father of English casuistry, had asserted a century earlier that "the circumstances of time, place, person, and manner of doing, doe serve to enlarge or extenuate the sinne committed,"[6] and Defoe frequently reiterates this concept. "Few things in nature are simply unlawful and dishonest," he observes in one work, "but . . . all crime is made so by the addition and concurrence of circumstances"; "Circumstances, Time, and Place alter things very much," he says in another; elsewhere, that "as Sin is Circumstantiated, those Accounts are sinful under one Government, which are not so under another"; and that "what may be simply Lawful, may be unlawful Circumstantially."[7] Moll never explicitly maintains that her extraordinary situation alters the sinful or criminal character of an action, but she often adduces circumstances that serve to palliate if not justify what she has just done or is about to do. In the process, the notion that an act is inherently right or wrong is at least called in question; moral judgment, it is suggested, must take into account the total context of a given act, and the context often works to Moll's advantage.

These are two of Moll's ways of gaining and holding our sympathy: she distinguishes her essential self from her admittedly reprehensible doings, but also lessens the stigma usually attached to specific acts. Other qualities contribute to the same effect, of course. Moll's independence and vitality are captivating;[8] the candor, directness, and very persistence of her speaking voice are disarming;[9] and her siding penitently with the reader against her

6. The Whole Treatise of the Cases of Conscience, Distinguished into Three Bookes (1617), p. 10.
7. The Compleat English Tradesman, I, 241; cf. I, 97–98, "there are very few things in the world that are simply evil, but things are made circumstantially evil when they are not so in themselves"; Little Review (July 4, 1705), pp. 35, 36; A Letter to Mr. How [1701], in A True Collection of the Writings of the Author of the True Born English-man (1703), p.

336.
8. See especially Ian Watt, The Rise of the Novel (1957), p. 132 and passim. A number of Robert Langbaum's remarks about Browning and Tennyson are highly relevant to this aspect of Moll Flanders: see "The Dramatic Monologue: Sympathy versus Judgment," in The Poetry of Experience (New York, 1963), pp. 75–108.
9. On these points see Sheldon Sacks, Fiction and the Shape of Belief (Berkeley and Los Angeles, 1964), pp. 267–270.

former waywardness can also be insinuating. I mention various ways in which Moll gains sympathy, partly to make clear that casuistry is not being proposed as her sole means of keeping our affection, and partly to indicate my grounds for not regarding the book as consistently ironic. Those who find the heroine an object of continual irony imply that we are always coolly judging her, and never emotionally involved in what she says or does. My objection to this is not that we never judge her, but that we are not allowed to do so with any such rigor, or from any such comfortable distance, as we might ordinarily adopt in the face of "all the progression of crime which she ran through in three-score years."[1] Sympathy keeps breaking in, and our ironic detachment—along with Defoe's—is tempered by imaginative identification.

The first important episode in Moll's story is her seduction by the elder brother in the Colchester family, which she does not, at the time, regard as a case of conscience at all. On the contrary, she admits that "I gave myself up to a readiness of being ruined without the least concern." So far is she from weighing her situation morally that she does not even think practically; the brother is more deliberate, but Moll reflects that "he made more circumlocution than, if he had known my thoughts, he had occasion for." Her opinion of the preliminaries to her seduction is that "Nothing was ever so stupid on both sides," and when she says, "I had not one thought of my own safety or of my virtue about me," her point is not that she forfeits both, but that she does so without a thought. By stressing the folly that precedes the act, and by blaming herself for this folly, she seeks to deflect the reader's judgment from a question of fornication to one of stupidity, and to soften his verdict by forestalling it herself. The preface claims that this episode has "many happy turns given it to expose the crime, and . . . the foolish, thoughtless, and abhorred conduct of both the parties." Without denying that Moll's behavior is criminal and abhorrent, Defoe emphasizes that it is foolish and thoughtless, and thus enables her to retain sympathy that she would forfeit if her action had been more calculated.

With the same object, all initiative is ascribed to the man, and much is made of Moll's passivity. As she will do on later occasions, she represents herself as carried along by her circumstances (here, the precarious dependence of her role in the Colchester family); by external inducements well adapted to her situation (here, a great deal of gold); and by the persuasiveness and cunning of others (here, a man full of flattery and stratagems, who knows "as well

1. Preface, pp. 3–4. The debate over irony is surveyed admirably by Ian Watt in "The Recent Critical Fortunes of *Moll Flanders," Eighteenth-Century Studies,* I (1967), 109–126.

how to catch a woman in his net as a partridge when he went a-set-
ting"). Moreover, "Knowing nothing of the wickedness of the
times," Moll is told an "abundance of . . . fine things, which [she],
poor fool, did not understand the drift of"; she acts "as if there was
no such thing as any kind of love but that which tended to matrimony." These touches of the ingenue minimize further the element
of deliberate choice on her part, so that she seems to undergo mischief—to be deluded by the promises and entrapped by the wiles of
her seducer—rather than doing mischief. Along with her passivity
and her naïveté, Moll acknowledges her frailty; yet what appear to
be confessions may tend to raise her, not lower her, in our esteem.
The episode is punctuated by frequent admissions of vanity. But by
mentioning that she had mastered French, the harpsichord, singing,
dancing, and other genteel skills, and that she was "taken for very
handsome, or, if you please, for a great beauty," Moll indicates that
her pride was neither groundless nor self-generated. Other confessions of frailty have a similar effect. She admits at one point that "I
had no room, as well as no power, to have said no"; and, at the
moment of her seduction, that "I could not say a word." She thus
suggests that she was overwhelmed, not induced through inclination
or interest to give her assent, and by presenting herself in this light
—as frail rather than wanton—she further allays our severity. The
foregoing details enforce a distinction between an act and its circumstances; in this case, between a seduction and various factors
that complicate its moral status. These complicating factors tend in
some degree to displace the actual deed as the object of our attention. Moreover, Moll herself is characterized less by what she does
than by an array of motives and pressures that contribute to her
seduction. A summary of her overt actions can only lead to the conclusion reached in the preface that they are criminal and abhorrent.
Yet what Defoe gives us is anything but a summary of overt actions,
and the transfer of emphasis is crucial to our sympathy for the heroine.

  After her seduction, Moll's situation is entangled further by the
younger brother, who seeks to marry her. "I resisted the proposal
with obstinacy," she reports, "I laid before him the inequality of
the match; the treatment I should meet with in the family; the
ingratitude it would be to his good father and mother, who had
taken me into their house upon such generous principles." We
might suppose that Moll's conscience is aroused, and that she has
begun to weigh her conduct in the light of moral principles, but no
such awakening has taken place. "I said everything to dissuade him
from his design that I could imagine," Moll confesses, "except telling him the truth . . . but that I durst not think of mentioning. . . .
I repented heartily my easiness with the eldest brother; not from

any reflection of conscience, but from a view of the happiness I might have enjoyed, and had now made impossible; for though I had no great scruples of conscience . . . to struggle with, yet I could not think of being a whore to one brother and a wife to the other." Moll's celebration of legitimate ideals serves to cloak the truth, her repentance of past "easiness" springs from a sense of lost opportu- nity, and her misgivings over the proposed marriage arise from squeamishness about what she evidently regards as incest. Her reti- cence towards the younger brother, however natural and blameless in itself,[2] leads not only to disguise and concealment, but to a kind of sophistry which exempts itself from the very sanctions it invokes.

What Moll undergoes, then, is not a crisis of conscience. When she says, "I was now in a very great strait, and really knew not what to do," her perplexity is essentially tactical, not ethical. She pro- duces moral arguments for strategic reasons, not because she regards them as relevant to her own decisions, and as we shall find her doing on various other occasions, she endorses doctrines which she does not feel herself bound by. It is easy enough to deplore her pharisaism, and to condemn her failure to take personally the norms of conduct she so persuasively advocates. Nevertheless she herself has acknowledged the existence of moral sanctions, and their hypo- thetical (if not practical) bearing on her behavior. The resulting impression is not one of hypocrisy—it is from her own mouth, after all, that we learn how far short of her lofty protestations her actions fall—but of disarming candor. However deceptive and evasive she may be toward the younger brother, she seems engagingly open and confidential toward *us.*

When Moll seeks her lover's advice about escaping the other

---

2. Cf. Moll's later remark that "I was not obliged to tell him I was his broth- er's whore, though I had no other way to put him off." Jeremy Taylor had ob- served that "*Nemo tenetur infamare se,* is a rule universally admitted among the casuists, 'no man is bound to discover his own shame' " (*Ductor Dubitantium,* ed. Alexander Taylor, in *Whole Works,* ed. Reginald Heber, rev. Charles P. Eden, 10 vols. [1850], X, 113). For a case resembling Moll's, and further dis- cussion of the obligation of self-accusa- tion, see the *Athenian Mercury,* IX, xxviii, 2. A young lady confesses that "*A certain lewd and infamous riffler of my Honour . . . has . . . been a little too busie where he had nothing to do: But I'd since the Good Fortune to enter Mat- rimony with a Person as far above me in Estate as Desert, and . . . manag'd all things so that he knew nothing of the Matter——However, I'm since that ex- treamly troubled for the Cheat I've put upon him, and the Injury I conceive I* have done him. . . . *Your Advice pray in this Condition?"* The Athenian Society replies, "We'll first give you the Opinion of a late Author, and then our own. . . . He tells your Ladyship, 'Your Sin when committed was against Heaven, not your *Honourable Lover.* . . . when he made his *Addresses,* you were not oblig'd to be your own *Accuser,* and . . . 'twas af- terwards no part of yours to unveil the mistake'; and in all this still he is *right,* but here lyes the *Juggle,* Why did you *marry* him, which you ought not in strict *Virtue* and *Honour* to have done. . . . You ought to have been the *Wife* of your first Acquaintance, or else always to have liv'd *unmarry'd,* and are how- ever as Cases are, tho not oblig'd, We think, to accuse your self to any upon *Earth,* yet to do it before *Heaven,* and endeavor to expiate your former long ha- bitual *lewdness* with one, and *cheat* on the other, by a continued hearty *Peni- tency."*

brother's importunate suit, her anxieties are still prudential rather than moral, but they are cast in the form of a traditional case of conscience. The man counsels her to delay giving his brother a firm answer: Moll is startled, and tells him "he knew very well that I had no consent to give; that he had engaged himself to marry me, and that my consent was at the same time engaged to him; that he had all along told me I was his wife, and I looked upon myself as effectually so as if the ceremony had passed." And soon afterwards she declares to him that "I was your wife intentionally, though not in the eyes of the world. . . . it was as effectual a marriage . . . as if we had been publicly wedded by the parson of the parish." Two long-debated problems underlie Moll's reproaches to her seducer: what constitutes a valid marriage, and more specifically, what formal ceremony (if any) is required? Moll echoes attitudes that Defoe had expressed two decades earlier, in the "Advice from the Scandal Club," which in turn are based largely on seventeenth-century casuistical discussions of matrimony.[3] In a *Supplement* to the *Review*, Defoe had pointed out to a querist that "Marriage being nothing but a Promise, the Ceremony is no Addition to the Contract, only a Thing exacted by the Law, to prevent Knaves doing what seems here to be attempted, and therefore the Society insist upon it, when the Promise was made, the Man and Woman were actually Marryed; and he can never go off from it, nor Marry any other Woman."[4] Here Moll uses similar doctrines to affect our attitude towards what she has already done, and what she is about to do. As she pleads with the elder brother, "I am really, and in the

3. See *A.M.*, VIII, iii, 1: the querist reports that "*Having for a long time pretended kindness to a Young Woman, and promis'd her Marriage if ever in a Capacity to maintain her, she thereupon yielded to my unlawful desires. Since this I'm sensible of my Crime . . . but am not yet in a capacity to live with her, tho' she's extremely apprehensive that I'll forsake her, and I under Temptation of doing it.*" He is advised that "His first Duty is, to be sure he's truly sensible of his *Crime*, and troubled for it, and endeavour to make her *Partner* in his *Repentance*, as she has bin in the *Sin*. Then we think 'tis a plain case, that he ought to *marry* her." See *A.M.*, V, ii, 4: "A publick Marriage signifies no more before God than a private Contract . . . only here's the difference, the first gives a satisfaction to the World, and renders the party proper Subjects of the Law as to Estates, &c." Cf. also *A.M.*, XIII, vi, 6, and XI, xxiv, 3. Among the earlier casuists, see Joseph Hall, *Resolutions and Decisions of Divers Practical Cases of Conscience*, in *Works*, ed. Philip Wynter, 10 vols. (Ox-

ford, 1863), VII, 393–395.
4. *Review, Supplement*, I (Nov., 1704), 19–20; in another *Supplement*, the querist is "oblig'd by many Engagements" to a marriage which "forshews nothing but both our Ruins," and inquires whether "I may not leave her, and try my Fortune elsewhere." In reply, Defoe's Scandal Club declares that "his promises to the young Woman cannot be so broken as to marry another, he having engaged (as he says) to marry her; which the Society always allows to be a Marriage, and cannot prevail upon themselves yet to dispense with private Contracts on future Accidents; Promises of Marriage being things not to be trifled with on any Occasion whatsoever" (I [Jan., 1705], 13). Four months earlier, Defoe had observed more cynically that "he that Lyes with a Woman on a promise of Matrimony, is a Knave if he does not perform his promise, and a Fool if he does" (*Review*, I [Sept. 5, 1704], 227; for further discussion of this topic see Spiro Peterson, "The Matrimonial Theme of Defoe's *Roxana*," *PMLA*, LXX [1955], 180–181 and *passim*).

essence of the thing, your wife," she makes it harder than ever for us to be severe toward her. We may not share her view that mutual consent constitutes the essence of marriage, yet we cannot deny her argument a degree of plausibility; we may recall that she was originally willing to accept her lover on any terms (or none at all), yet it now appears that she has somehow been abused. Similarly, to keep us from sympathizing with the duped younger brother at her expense, Moll suggests that she is the victim of a worse betrayal. She reminds her lover of "the long discourses you have had with me, and the many hours' pains you have taken to persuade me to believe myself an honest woman." Such pleas do not alter her lover's determination to palm Moll off on his younger brother, nor do they quite persuade us that she is "an honest woman," yet they induce us to commiserate when we might otherwise condemn.

* * *

Moll's life becomes even more trying on the Virginia plantation than in London. She must act as vigorously and warily as ever, but does not feel called upon to spend so much ingenuity defending her action, because she is convinced of its justice. Again the basic situation grows out of a traditional case of conscience, and again the most interesting question is not where Defoe got his material, but what he makes of it. Moll discovers that her husband is actually her half-brother; what is she to do? The problem had already been considered by Jeremy Taylor and Joseph Hall: both take as their point of departure a Venetian case in which the husband was father as well as brother of his wife, but extend the discussion to all incestuous matches contracted in ignorance.[5] What had been an ethical dilemma for these earlier writers, however, is for Moll chiefly an emotional question. "I was not much touched with the crime of it," she says, "yet the action had something in it shocking to nature, and made my husband, as he thought himself, even nauseous to me." Moll stresses the element of physical revulsion, and although she labels her status "open avowed incest and whoredom," she seems to find the immorality of the match only an incidental aggravation of its enormity. Rather than make Moll grapple with the conventional

5. Taylor, *Ductor Dubitantium,* in *Whole Works,* IX, 149; Hall, *Resolutions and Decisions,* in *Works,* VII, 410–414; cf. *A.M.,* XVI, XX, 1; VI, xxvi, 3. The case seems to have been founded on popular tradition, but occurs as the 30th novel in *The Heptameron* of Margaret of Navarre. In this version, a "council of conscience" advises the guilty mother "never to reveal the secret to her children, who had not sinned, inasmuch as they had known nothing"—a decision endorsed by the English casuists. Horace Walpole heard the story of a lady "who, under uncommon agonies of mind, waited on Archbishop Tillotson, revealed her crime, and besought his counsel in what manner she should act. ... The prelate charged her never to let her son or daughter know what had passed" (George Saintsbury, note to *The Heptameron,* 2 vols. [1903], II, 40). The motif is also used in George Powell's *The Fatal Discovery* (1698): see Eric Rothstein, *Restoration Tragedy: Form and the Process of Change* (Madison, 1967), pp. 146, 156n.

arguments for and against dissolving such a marriage, Defoe subjects her to a conflict in which her keenest impulses are ranged
against the demands of her external situation. Traces of the traditional grounds of debate remain—Moll gives some thought to the
effect of the discovery on her husband and their two children[6]—but
the basic question is whether Moll can regain her peace of mind
without causing "the ruin of the whole family." Defoe's art consists
in first making it appear that she cannot, then enabling her to do so.
Seemingly opposed claims are ultimately reconciled: such a procedure is analogous to the resolution of a case of conscience, but
between a horror of incest on the one hand, and a horror of poverty
and public exposure on the other, Moll's conscience plays at best a
minor part in this episode.

Within a page of embarking from Virginia, the heroine finds herself in Bath. Two decades earlier Defoe's Scandal Club had considered a query that anticipates the scene at Bath—"Whether the
Woman that would permit a Man to set upon her Bed, after she is
in it, and the whole Family before that time being gone to rest,
would not, in all likelihood, admit him in some time into the
same," and thus whether "by the frequent permission of the Man,
the Virtue of the Woman might be seduced." "The Society,"
Defoe responds, "are by no means for allowing indecencies, and
extraordinary freedoms between the Sexes, as what may be in their
consequences Fatal to Vertue; nor do they believe, any one so
secure of their Vertue, as to justifie their Leading it into Temptation; but on the other hand, they cannot suppose every Fredom to
be Vitious. . . . in the present Case, they think the Censure Unjust,
and too severe——But the persons may observe, how neer the brink
of Crime they walk."[7] Thus Defoe had examined this question long
before its incorporation in *Moll Flanders*; both the narrative situation and the ethical problems arising from it are sketched out in the
Review.

6. Moll also observes that "had the story never been told me, all had been well; it had been no crime to have lain with my husband, since as to his being my relation I had known nothing of it" (p. 102). The same point had been made in earlier discussions of the issue. Robert Donovan, however, finds Moll's remark a "most suggestive" indication that "moral distinctions are not real, since they exist only in our awareness of them," and argues that there is "irony of a particularly devastating kind in Moll's innocent acknowledgment . . . that an immoral act is nullified if the perpetrator is ignorant of its moral bearings. The agent's ignorance, in other words, not only excuses him, it changes the nature of the act" (*The Shaping Vision: Imagination in the English Novel from Defoe to Dickens* [Ithaca, 1966], pp. 33, 44). The casuistical assumptions behind Moll's remark may be questionable, but are less extreme than they become in Professor Donovan's formulation. [See above, pp. 396–404—*Editor.*]

7. *Review, Supplement,* I (Nov. 1704), 20–21; cf. the Athenian Society's cynical response to the following query: "*A married Lady meets another Womans Husband, stays frequently with him, some hours at a time, in secret, and permits all the Freedom and Liberty that Man and Wife are capable of, only the last* Favour *excepted, pretending to Conscience and Principles, because she does not go thro' stitch: Pray what do you think she means by Conscience and Principles under such a Practice?*" (*A.M.,* IX, xvii, 4; cf. also XVI, xix, 1).

In the present scene, Defoe greatly aggravates the circumstances of the case. The central question remains the same—whether "extraordinary freedoms" will prove "Fatal to Vertue." But what had been a euphemistic conclusion in the *Review*—"Whether the Woman that would permit a Man to set upon her Bed . . . would not . . . admit him in some time *into the same*"—is here taken literally as a point of departure: the Bath gentleman protests that "if he was naked in bed with [Moll], he would as sacredly preserve [her] virtue as he would defend it if [she] was assaulted by a ravisher." Defoe thus puts the problem in its extremest form,[8] just as he poses other questions about human nature in extreme form by shipwrecking Robinson Crusoe on a desert island. He was to maintain in another context that "it is true, Honour and Virtue may (speaking strictly) be said in some Cases to be preserved, though Decency is not so much, or equally regarded: But let all that plead the possibility of that Distinction *know*, that however possible it may be, it is . . . far from being probable (that where Decency is given up Honour should or can be preserved)."[9] This statement can serve as a gloss on the primary topic of the Bath episode—the hazards, as Moll puts it, of "venturing too near the brink of a command."[1] Its secondary topic is the factor that makes such trials of virtue rash: the power of "inclination" to overturn "moderation," "affection," "noble principle," and reason itself. Thus the Bath episode is concerned with the conditions that lead to misdeeds of all kinds. If there are good grounds for praying not to be led into temptation, there are still better grounds for not willfully seeking it out.

But to isolate such a motif as if it were a "moral" is to make the episode more schematic and tendentious than it actually is. It is true that at the time of writing, Moll reflects upon "the unhappy consequence of too great freedoms between persons stated as we were, upon the pretence of innocent intentions, love of friendship, and the like; for the flesh has generally so great a share in those friendships, that it is great odds but inclination prevails at last over the most solemn resolutions." But her moralizing seldom exhausts the moral issues raised in the course of her story. Detachable from the narrative, her comminatory codas (as Watt calls them) are usually less subtle, let alone equivocal, than the events they so patly "improve." In this episode, various qualifying circumstances prevent us from drawing any simple moral. Those of the gentleman himself

---

8. The Jesuits had pushed this question to the same length; see Nicolas Perrault, *La Morale des Jesuites* (Mons, 1667), p. 20.
9. *Conjugal Lewdness* (1727), p. 4.
1. Bishop Hall reports that "it was wont to be worthy Mr. Perkins's expression to this purpose: 'Let those who must walk close to the brim of a steep precipice look well to their feet, and tread sure; and so they may come off perhaps as safely as those that are farther off; but if a man be to choose his way, let him so cast it as that he may not approach near the brink of danger'" (*Resolutions and Decisions*, in *Works*, VII, 386–387).

are relevant—or at all events Moll is intent on making them seem so. He had a wife, we are told, but "the lady was distempered in the head," and Moll once goes so far as to assert that "he had no wife, that is to say, she was as no wife to him." Whether such a predicament discharges one from marriage vows had been discussed by various casuists. There had been general agreement that it does not, and Defoe never endorses Moll's tacit assumption that it does, yet her bare mention of such circumstances tends to the Bath gentleman's advantage—and indirectly, of course, to her own—since it introduces the kind of complexity that can blunt the rigor of moral judgment without necessarily altering its substance.

* * *

One source of drama in these scenes is a fresh dilemma over revealing or concealing awkward truths. Anxiety generated by a guilty secret had dominated Moll's earlier experience in Virginia, had nearly plunged her into a fatal consumption in Colchester, and had given a somber undertone to her marriage with the banker's clerk. Her conversion, on the other hand, had "unlocked the sluices of [her] passions": confessing her guilt to someone with the story, she had found relief from anxiety. But as John Bunyan, Robinson Crusoe, and others in life and literature had discovered before her, anxiety is not banished once and for all by religious conversion. In prison, Moll had told Jemmy that by accepting transportation to Virginia they would be able to "live as new people in a new world, nobody having anything to say to us, or we to them," and that they would "look back on all our past disasters with infinite satisfaction." Once she reaches Virginia, however, her cares revive: she cannot reveal herself to her former husband and son, because she has come as a transported convict with a new husband, nor can she "so much as think of breaking the secret of [her] former marriage to [her] husband." As in the first Virginia scene, she finds herself trapped between threatening alternatives, and although she now has no incest taboo to struggle with, her dread of exposure proves to be almost as acute and disabling. Once again, her dilemma is more a psychological than a moral one. In the course of reflecting on the compulsion to disburden oneself of secrets, she does say that it works with particular vehemence "in the minds of those who are guilty of any atrocious villainy, such as secret murder"; and it is true that here as elsewhere, Defoe indicates "how necessary and inseperable a Companion, Fear is to Guilt."[2] Nevertheless Moll's comment on her earlier Virginia predicament—that "I had no great concern about it in point of conscience"—applies equally to this new bout of anxiety. What troubles her is not a difficult moral

2. *Colonel Jack*, edited by Samuel Holt Monk (New York: Oxford University Press, 1965), p. 291.

choice in the present, but the danger of shameful revelations about her past.

For Moll, then, this is not really a case of conscience, yet it preserves something of the tone and formal structure of one. "Here was a perplexity," she says at the outset, "that I had not indeed skill to manage myself in, neither knew I what course to take. It lay heavy upon my mind night and day." "Under the certain oppression of this weight upon my mind," she later declares, "I laboured in the case I have been naming." Similar remarks throughout the scene convey the same air of protracted deliberation: Moll's mental state is emphasized, her action correspondingly played down. We may deplore her dissimulation, but her distress invites sympathy. Furthermore, Moll interrupts the account of her own crisis, first to "appeal to all human testimony" in support of her theory that a fundamental "necessity of nature" compels man to divulge secrets; then to ascribe the process to Providence, which uses "natural causes to produce . . . extraordinary effects"; next to give "several remarkable instances of this"; and finally to argue that her remarks have not been "an unnecessary digression." Defoe often establishes the total context of an ethical problem by investing it with greater generality through abstractions, and with further concreteness through analogies. In this respect, too, the present scene is handled in a manner characteristic of a full-fledged case of conscience, even though conscience itself plays little part. Finally and perhaps most importantly, Moll's situation is set forth so as to suggest that the course she will choose is genuinely in doubt. To conceal her story is an almost insupportable "weight upon [her] spirits," but to disclose it to either son or husband will be disastrous. We may surmise skeptically that she will prefer concealment, and she herself hints as much midway in the episode ("let them say what they please of our sex not being able to keep a secret, my life is a plain conviction to me of the contrary"). All the same, Defoe manages to keep the outcome of the episode in suspense by placing Moll in a dilemma that retains the mood and shape, if not the ethical substance, of a traditional case of conscience.

Moll's further dealings with both her son and husband continue to illustrate the kind of double vision which marks Defoe's conception of her throughout the book. A tension between the culpable and the engaging is sustained, in fact, even when the heroine begins to experience the joys of family reunion and capital gain that signalize a Defoean happy ending. The following passage occurs at the end of Moll's first day with her son Humphry. She has already spoken with faint contempt of her husband's ignorance of geography and frontier estate-management, and in lines reminiscent of her scorn for that "land-water thing called a gentleman-tradesman," she has remarked that "he was bred a gentleman, and by consequence was not only unacquainted, but indolent." Here she more openly acknowledges that she finds him a useless encumbrance. Elated by her son's kindness, Moll concludes her account of their meeting, "thus I was as if I had been in a new world, and began secretly now to wish that I had not brought my Lancashire husband from England at all." But as if abashed at her own callousness, she says at once, "However, that wish was not hearty neither, for I loved my Lancashire husband entirely, as indeed I had ever done from the beginning; and he merited from me as much as it was possible for a man to do; but that by the way."

The sequence is curious but characteristic. Are the egotism and treachery of Moll's secret wish nullified by her avowals of constancy? Is the very existence of her wish somehow negated by the assertion that it "was not hearty neither"? When Moll contradicts herself, can her second, more emphatic proposition ever quite cancel the first? It seems to me that her retractions never fully "take back" whatever she has said or done; the process is always additive, so that what appear to be clarifying denials actually tend to make her position more ambiguous. In examining the logically clashing elements of an earlier episode, I suggested that the object was not consistency but comprehensiveness. For all its brevity, the present passage demonstrates the related principle that Moll's arguments regularly end *in*clusively, not *con*clusively. Both generous and selfish, both faithful and disloyal, her attitude towards this charming, good-for-nothing husband is deeply (and understandably) ambivalent; and the scene leaves us feeling no less ambivalent about her. We may recoil momentarily from her heartlessness, but so does she, with disarming humanity: once again, in a manner typical of the entire book, Defoe portrays Moll as both reprehensible and sympathetic.

Daniel Defoe: A Chronology

1660	Born Daniel Foe in London, son of a tallow-chandler.
1662	Act of Uniformity; the Foes become Presbyterians, a group considered to be dissenters from the beliefs of the Church of England.
1665–66	The Great Plague and Great Fire of London.
c. 1671–79	Educated at school of Rev. James Fisher at Dorking in Surrey; later attended Rev. Charles Morton's academy for Dissenters at Newington Green in preparation for the Presbyterian ministry.
c. 1683	At age twenty-three, established as a merchant in London; at various times throughout his career he dealt in hosiery, wine, tobacco, marine insurance, and tiles and brick.
1684	Married Mary Tuffley, who brought with her a sizable dowry of £3,700.
1685–92	Traveled extensively in England and probably in other parts of Europe; published political pamphlets.
1692	Bankrupt for £17,000.
1695	His name first appears with the prefix "De," becoming thereafter "De Foe."
1697	*An Essay upon Projects*, advocating an English Academy, a system of national relief for the poor, education for women.
1697–1701	Supported William III and was active as his agent in England and Scotland.
1701	*The True-Born Englishman*, a satire defending William and his Dutch sympathizers.
1702	*The Shortest Way with the Dissenters*, an ironic attack on High Church intolerance.
1703	Arrested for writing *The Shortest Way*, committed to Newgate, and sentenced to stand in the pillory for one hour on three successive days (July 29–31). Robert

Harley, Tory Minister, helped obtain Defoe's release toward the end of the year; however, during this year of litigation and imprisonment, his brick and tile works failed, bankrupting him again.

1703–30   Served the English government in a variety of capacities; a secret agent for the Tory administration, Defoe worked actively to promote the Union of England and Scotland. After the death of Queen Anne (1714) and the accession of George I, Defoe also served the Whig government, mainly as a journalist.

1704–13   Singlehandedly wrote and edited *The Review*, a newspaper which appeared thrice weekly, treating of topics of public interest.

1713–14   Again arrested for debt and for satirical pamphlets supporting the Hanoverian succession which were adjudged treasonable; released through governmental influence after partial payment of debts and apologies to those offended.

1715   *The Family Instructor*, a conduct manual which went through eight editions by 1720. Popular throughout the century.

1716   *Mercurius Politicus*, a "Tory" journal which Defoe edited on behalf of the Whig Ministry (1716–20).

1719   *Robinson Crusoe, The Farther Adventures of Robinson Crusoe.*

1720   *Memoirs of a Cavalier; Captain Singleton; Applebee's Original Weekly Journal* (1720–26), a periodical.

1722   *Moll Flanders, Religious Courtship, A Journal of the Plague Year, Colonel Jack.*

1724   *Roxana, A Tour Thro' the Whole Island of Great Britain* (1724–26).

1725   *The Complete English Tradesman* (2nd vol. 1727); also a series of criminal "lives."

1726   *The Political History of the Devil.*

1727–30   Defoe continued to write on a variety of subjects which he had found to prove popular over the years and in which he had a special interest, such as projects for social betterment, political tracts, histories, and books of conduct.

1731   Died (April 24) in his lodgings in Ropemaker's Alley, London. Although Defoe's bibliography has not been established beyond doubt, it is clear that in a career devoted as much to business and politics as to literature, he authored some hundred separate works of substance and edited and contributed substantially to more than a half-dozen periodicals.

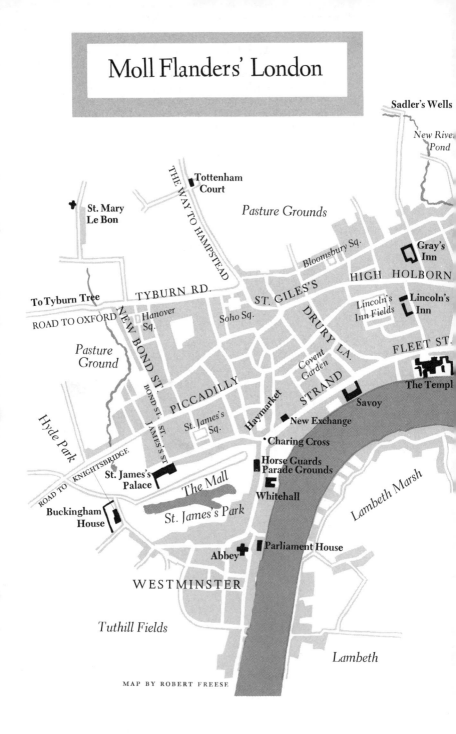

Moll Flanders' London

Sadler's Wells

New River Pond

Tottenham Court

St. Mary Le Bon

THE WAY TO HAMPSTEAD

Pasture Grounds

Bloomsbury Sq.

Gray's Inn

HIGH HOLBORN

To Tyburn Tree

TYBURN RD.

ST. GILES'S

Lincoln's Inn Fields

Lincoln's Inn

ROAD TO OXFORD

NEW BOND ST.

Hanover Sq.

Soho Sq.

DRURY LA.

FLEET ST.

Pasture Ground

BOND ST.

Covent Garden

STRAND

The Temple

PICCADILLY

Savoy

JAMES'S ST.

St. James's Sq.

Haymarket

New Exchange

Hyde Park

St. James's Palace

Charing Cross

ROAD TO KNIGHTSBRIDGE

Horse Guards Parade Grounds

Lambeth Marsh

Buckingham House

The Mall

Whitehall

St. James's Park

Abbey

Parliament House

WESTMINSTER

Tuthill Fields

Lambeth

MAP BY ROBERT FREESE

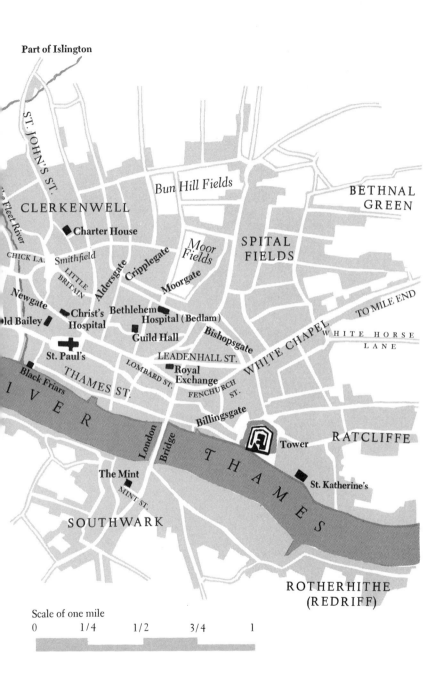

Part of Islington

ST. JOHN'S ST.

Fleet River

CLERKENWELL

Bun Hill Fields

BETHNAL
GREEN

◆ Charter House

CHICK LA.   Smithfield

Moor
Fields

SPITAL
FIELDS

LITTLE
BRITAIN

Aldersgate

Cripplegate

Moorgate

Newgate

Old Bailey

■ Christ's
Hospital

Bethlehem ■
Hospital (Bedlam)

Guild Hall

Bishopsgate

WHITE CHAPEL

TO MILE END

WHITE HORSE
LANE

✚
St. Paul's

LEADENHALL ST.

LOMBARD ST.

Royal
Exchange

FENCHURCH
ST.

THAMES ST.

Black Friars

R   I   V   E   R

Billingsgate

RATCLIFFE

London

Bridge

Tower

T   H   A   M   E   S

The Mint

MINT ST.

■
St. Katherine's

SOUTHWARK

ROTHERHITHE
(REDRIFF)

Scale of one mile

0   1/4   1/2   3/4   1

Bibliography

BIBLIOGRAPHICAL WORKS

Alden, John. *A Catalog of the Defoe Collection in the Boston Public Library.* Boston: Hall, 1966.

Baine, Rodney M. "Chalmers' First Bibliography of Daniel Defoe," *Texas Studies in Language and Literature,* X (1968), 547–568. Includes a shortened text of Chalmers' 1790 bibliography and the correct remark that "if Defoe studies are to progress on any firm foundation, the whole canon must be carefully reexamined for authorship. . . ."

McBurney, William. *A Checklist of English Prose Fiction 1700–1739.* Cambridge, Mass., 1960.

Moore, John Robert. *A Checklist of the Writings of Daniel Defoe.* Bloomington: Indiana University Press, 1960.

Novak, Maximillian E. "Daniel Defoe." In *The New Cambridge Bibliography of English Literature: 1660–1800,* rev. ed. II, edited by George Watson. New York: Cambridge University Press, 1971, pp. 882–918.

See also Chalmers, Dottin, and Lee (below) for additional bibliographical references.

BIOGRAPHICAL WORKS

Chalmers, George. *The Life of Daniel De Foe.* London, 1790 (Garland Facsimile: New York, 1970). Contains a list of Defoe's writings.

Defoe, Daniel. *The Letters of Daniel Defoe.* Edited by George Harris Healy. Oxford: The Clarendon Press, 1955.

Dottin, Paul. *Daniel Defoe et ses romans.* 3 vols. Paris: Les Presses Universitaires de France, 1924. Vol. I is biographical; II is a study of *Robinson Crusoe*; and III contains commentary on Defoe's "secondary" novels, including a bibliographical section on *Moll Flanders,* pp. 645–686. An appendix chronologically lists the works of Defoe, pp. 802–849.

Lee, William. *Daniel Defoe: His Life and Recently Discovered Writings 1716–1729.* 3 vols. London: Hotten, 1869. Vol. I is a life of Defoe; II and III reprint contributions to periodicals which Lee attributed to Defoe. Vol. I also contains a chronological catalog of Defoe's works, pp. xxvii–lv.

Moore, John Robert. *Daniel Defoe: Citizen of the Modern World.* Chicago: The University of Chicago Press, 1958.

Sutherland, James. *Defoe.* London: Methuen, 1937; 2nd ed., 1950.

Trent, W. P. *Daniel Defoe: How to Know Him.* Indianapolis: Bobbs-Merrill, 1916.

SELECTED CRITICAL AND OTHER STUDIES OF DEFOE'S WRITINGS

Where significant commentary in a book-length work focuses on *Moll Flanders,* the page numbers are included in parentheses.

Andersen, Hans H. "The Paradox of Trade and Morality in Defoe," *Modern Philology,* XXXIX (1941), 23–46.

Baine, Rodney M. *Daniel Defoe and the Supernatural.* Athens: University of Georgia Press, 1968.

Bishop, Jonathan. "Knowledge, Action, and Interpretation in Defoe's Novels," *Journal of the History of Ideas,* XIII (1952), 3–16.

Boulton, James T. "Daniel Defoe: His Language and Rhetoric." Introduction to *Daniel Defoe,* edited by James T. Boulton. New York: Schocken, 1965.

Boyce, Benjamin. "The Question of Emotion in Defoe," *Studies in Philology,* 1953, pp. 45–58.

Brown, Homer O. "The Displaced Self in the Novels of Daniel Defoe," *Journal of English Literary History,* XXXVIII (1971), 562–590.

Brown, Lloyd W. "Defoe and the Feminine Mystique," *Transactions of the Samuel Johnson Society of the Northwest,* Vol. 4, 4–18.

Burch, Charles Eaton. "British Criticism of Defoe as Novelist, 1719–1860," *Englische Studien,* LXVII (1932–33), 178–198.

441

————. "Defoe's British Reputation, 1869–1894," *Englische Studien*, LXVIII (1933–34), 410–423.
————. "The Moral Elements in Defoe's Fiction," *London Quarterly and Holborn Review*, April, 1937, pp. 207–213.
Dobrée, Bonamy. "Some Aspects of Defoe's Prose." In *Pope and His Contemporaries*, edited by James L. Clifford and Louis A. Landa. Oxford: The Clarendon Press, 1949. (Pp. 171–184.)
————. "The Writings of Daniel Defoe," *Royal Society of Arts Journal*, CVIII (1960), 729–742.
Fitzgerald, Brian. *Defoe: A Study in Conflict.* Chicago: Regnery, 1954.
Harlan, Virginia. "Defoe's Narrative Style," *Journal of English and Germanic Philology*, XXX (1931), 55–73.
Heidenreich, Helmut, ed. *The Libraries of Daniel Defoe and Phillips Farewell: Olive Payne's Sales Catalogue.* Berlin: 1970.
Hunter, J. Paul. *The Reluctant Pilgrim: Defoe's Emblematic Method and Quest for Form in Robinson Crusoe.* Baltimore: The Johns Hopkins University Press, 1966.
James, E. Anthony. *Daniel Defoe's Many Voices: A Rhetorical Study of Prose Style and Literary Method.* Amsterdam: Editions Rodopi, 1972.
Joyce, James. "Daniel Defoe." Translated from the Italian and edited by Joseph Prescott. *Buffalo Studies*, 1964, pp. 3–25. (Lecture given in 1912 at the Università Popolare Triestina.)
Moore, John Robert. *Defoe in the Pillory and Other Studies.* Bloomington: Indiana University Press, 1939.
Novak, Maximillian E. *Defoe and the Nature of Man.* New York: Oxford University Press, 1963.
————. "Defoe's Theory of Fiction," *Studies in Philology*, LXI (1964), 650–668.
————. "Defoe's Use of Irony." In *The Uses of Irony: Papers on Defoe and Swift Read at a Clark Library Seminar* (April 2, 1966). Berkeley and Los Angeles: University of California Press, 1966.
————. *Economics and the Fiction of Daniel Defoe.* Berkeley and Los Angeles: University of California Press, 1962. (Pp. 83–88, 93–107, 146–149, 152–154.)
Payne, William Lytton. *Mr. Review: Daniel Defoe as Author of "The Review."* New York: King's Crown Press, 1961.
Rogers, Pat, ed. *Defoe: The Critical Heritage.* Boston: Routledge & Kegan Paul, 1972.
Secord, Arthur. *Studies in the Narrative Method of Defoe.* University of Illinois Studies in Language and Literature, IX, No. 1. Urbana: University of Illinois Press, 1924.
Sen, Sri C. *Daniel Defoe: His Mind and Art.* Calcutta: University of Calcutta, 1948. (Pp. 208–213.)
Shinagel, Michael. *Daniel Defoe and Middle-Class Gentility.* Cambridge: Harvard University Press, 1968. (Pp. 142–160.)
Stamm, Rudolf G. "Daniel Defoe: An Artist in the Puritan Tradition," *Philological Quarterly*, XV (1936), 225–246.
Starr, G. A. *Defoe and Casuistry.* Princeton: Princeton University Press, 1971. (Pp. 111–116.)
————. *Defoe and Spiritual Autobiography.* Princeton: Princeton University Press, 1965. (Pp. 126–162.)
Stephen, Sir Leslie. *Hours in a Library.* 3 vols. New York: Putnam's; London: Smith, Elder, 1899. Sir Leslie's comments on Defoe in Vol. I are substantially the same as in his original essay "Defoe's Novels," which appeared in the *Cornhill Magazine*, XVII (1868).
Sutherland, James. *Daniel Defoe: A Critical Study.* Cambridge: Harvard University Press, 1971. (Pp. 175–194.)
————. "The Relation of Defoe's Fiction to His Non-Fictional Writings." In *Imagined Worlds: Essays on Some English Novels and Novelists in Honour of John Butt*, edited by Maynard Mack and Ian Gregor. London: Methuen, 1968.
Swallow, Alan. "Defoe and the Art of Fiction," *Western Humanities Review*, IV (1950), 129–136.
Watson, Francis. *Daniel Defoe.* London: Longman's, 1952.
Watt, Ian. "Serious Reflections on *The Rise of the Novel*," *Novel*, I (1968), 205–218.
————. "Defoe as Novelist." In *The Pelican Guide to English Literature*, Vol. 4, *From Dryden to Johnson*, edited by Boris Ford. Baltimore: Penguin, 1965. (Pp. 203–216.)

CRITICAL STUDIES OF *MOLL FLANDERS*

Where book-length works are not specifically devoted to criticism of *Moll Flanders*, pages discussing the novel are given in parentheses.

Alter, Robert. *Rogue's Progress: Studies in the Picaresque Novel.* Cambridge: Harvard University Press. (Pp. 35–57.)

Bishop, John Peale. "Moll Flanders' Way." In *Collected Essays*, edited by Edmund Wilson. New York: Scribner's, 1948, pp. 46–55. (Originally published in *Story*, 1937.)

Booth, Wayne C. *The Rhetoric of Fiction*. Chicago: University of Chicago Press, 1965. (Pp. 319–323.)

Brooks, Douglas. "*Moll Flanders*: An Interpretation," *Essays in Criticism*, XIX (1969), 46–59.

Chandler, Frank Wadleigh. *The Literature of Roguery*. 2 vols. New York: Houghton Mifflin, 1907. (Pp. 289–293.)

Columbus, Robert R. "Conscious Artistry in *Moll Flanders*," *Studies in English Literature*, III (1963), 415–432.

Dollerup, Cay. "Does the Chronology of *Moll Flanders* Tell Us Something about Defoe's Method of Writing?" *English Studies*, LIII (1972), 234–235.

Donoghue, Denis. "The Values of *Moll Flanders*," *Sewanee Review*, LXXI (1963), 287–303.

Donovan, Robert Alan. *The Shaping Vision: Imagination in the English Novel from Defoe to Dickens*. Ithaca: Cornell University Press, 1966. (Pp. 21–46.)

Edwards, Lee. "Between the Real and the Moral: Problems in the Structure of *Moll Flanders*." *Twentieth-Century Interpretations of Moll Flanders*, edited by Robert C. Elliott. Englewood Cliffs: Prentice-Hall, 1970. (Pp. 95–107.)

Forster, E. M. *Aspects of the Novel*. New York: Harcourt, Brace, 1927. (Pp. 87–99.)

Frye, Bobby Jack. "The Twentieth-Century Criticism of *Robinson Crusoe* and *Moll Flanders*." Ph.D. dissertation. University of Tennessee, 1966. This study contains an extensive bibliography of both *Crusoe* and *Moll*.

Gifford, George E. "Daniel Defoe and Maryland," *Maryland Historical Magazine*, LII (1957), 307–315.

Goldberg, M. A. "*Moll Flanders*: Christian Allegory in a Hobbesian Mode," *The University Review*, XXXIII (1967), 267–278.

Hartog, C. "Aggression, Femininity, and Irony in *Moll Flanders*," *L & P*, 3, XXII, 121–138.

Hatfield, Theodore M. "*Moll Flanders* in Germany," *Journal of English and Germanic Philology*, XXXII (1933), 51–65.

Hibbett, Howard S. "Saikaku and Burlesque Fiction," *Harvard Journal of Asiatic Studies*, XX (1957), 53–73.

Higdon, David L. "Defoe's *Moll Flanders*," *Explicator*, 29, Item 55 (1971).

Howson, Gerald. "Who Was Moll Flanders?" *The Times Literary Supplement*, 3,438 (January 18, 1968), 63–64. Revised and printed as "The Fortunes of Moll Flanders" (Chapter XVI) in *Howson's Thief-Taker General: The Rise and Fall of Jonathan Wild*. London: Hutchinson, 1970. (Pp. 156–170.)

Johnson, C. A. "Two Mistakes in *Moll Flanders*," *Notes and Queries*, CCVII (1962), 455.

Jones, A. G. E. "The Banks of Bath," *Notes and Queries*, CCIII (1958), 277–283.

Karl, Frederick R. "Moll's Many-Colored Coat: Veil and Disguise in the Fiction of Defoe," *Studies in the Novel*, V, No. 1 (Spring, 1973), 86–97.

Kettle, Arnold. "In Defence of Moll Flanders." In *Of Books and Humankind: Essays and Poems Presented to Bonamy Dobrée*, edited by John Butt, pp. 55–67. London: Routledge & Kegan Paul, 1954.

Koonce, Howard L. "Moll's Muddle: Defoe's Use of Irony in *Moll Flanders*," *Journal of English Literary History*, XXX (1963), 377–394.

Krier, William J. "A Courtesy Which Grants Integrity: A Literary Reading of *Moll Flanders*," *Journal of English Literary History*, XXXVIII, 3 (September, 1971), 397–410.

Legouis, Pierre. "Marion Flanders est-elle une victime de la Societe?" *Revue de l'Ensignement des Langues Vivantes*, XLVII (1931), 288–299.

Macey, Samuel L. "The Time Scheme in *Moll Flanders*," *Notes and Queries*, CCXIV (1969), 336–337.

Martin, Terence. "The Unity of *Moll Flanders*," *Modern Language Quarterly*, XXII (1961), 115–124.

McClung, M. G. "A Source for Moll Flander's Husband," *Notes and Queries*, XVIII, 9 (September, 1971), 329–330.

McKenna, Siobhan. *Moll Flanders*. Caedmon Phonodisc, 2s, 12 in., 1p. TC 1090. (Oral interpretation.)

McKillop, Alan Dugald. *The Early Masters of English Fiction: Defoe to Conrad*. Lawrence: University of Kansas Press, 1956. (Pp. 28–33.)

McMaster, Juliet. "The Equation of Love and Money in *Moll Flanders*," *Studies in the Novel*, II (1970), 131–144.

Novak, Maximillian E. "Conscious Irony in *Moll Flanders*: Facts and Problems," *College English*, XXVI (1964), 198–204.

———. "Defoe's 'Indifferent Monitor': The Complexity of *Moll Flanders*," *Eighteenth-Century Studies*, III (1970), 351–365.

———. "Moll Flanders' First Love," *Papers of the Michigan Academy of Science, Arts, and Letters*, XLVI (1961), 635–643.

Oda, Minoru. "Moll's Complacency: Defoe's Use of Comic Structure in *Moll Flanders*," *Studies in English Literature* (English Literary Society of Japan, University of Tokyo), Nos. 187–189 (1972).

Piper, William Bowman. "*Moll Flanders* as a Structure of Topics," *Studies in English Literature*. XCVIII (1969), 489–502.

Price, Martin. *To the Palace of Wisdom: Studies in Order and Energy from Dryden to Blake.* New York: Doubleday, 1964. (Pp. 262–275.)

Rader, Ralph. "*Moll Flanders* and the Concept of Form in the Novel." Paper read at Eighteenth-Century Conference, University of California at Los Angeles, Fall, 1969.

Rodway, A. E. "*Moll Flanders* and *Manon Lescaut*," *Essays in Criticism*, III (1953), 303–320.

Rogal, Samuel J. "The Profit and Loss of *Moll Flanders*," *Studies in the Novel*, V, No. 1 (Spring, 1973), 98–103.

Sacks, Sheldon. *Fiction and the Shape of Belief.* Berkeley and Los Angeles: University of California Press, 1964. (Pp. 267–270.)

Schorer, Mark. "A Study in Defoe: Moral Vision and Structural Form," *Thought*, XXV (1950), 275–287.

Sherbo, Arthur. *Studies in the Eighteenth-Century Novel.* East Lansing: Michigan State University Press, 1969. (Pp. 136–176.)

Shinagel, Michael. "The Maternal Theme in *Moll Flanders*: Craft and Character," *Cornell Library Journal*, VII (1969), 3–23.

Smith, L. W. "Daniel Defoe: Incipient Pornographer," *L & P*, 4, XXII, 165–178 [*Moll Flanders, Roxana*].

Taube, Myron. "Moll Flanders and Fanny Hill: A Comparison," *Ball State University Forum*, IX (1968), 76–80.

Van Ghent, Dorothy. "On *Moll Flanders*." In *The English Novel: Form and Function.* New York: Rinehart, 1953. (Pp. 33–43.)

Walton, James. "The Romance of Gentility." In *Literary Monographs*, Vol. 4, edited by Eric Rothstein. Madison: University of Wisconsin Press, 1971. (Pp. 110–122.)

Watson, Tommy G. "Defoe's Attitude Toward Marriage and the Position of Women as Revealed in *Moll Flanders*," *Southern Quarterly*, III (1964), 1–8.

Watt, Ian. "The Recent Critical Fortunes of *Moll Flanders*," *Eighteenth-Century Studies*, I (1967), 109–126.

———. *The Rise of the Novel: Studies in Defoe, Richardson and Fielding.* Berkeley and Los Angeles: University of California Press, 1957. (Pp. 93–134.)

West, Alick. *The Mountain in the Sunlight: Studies in Conflict and Unity.* London: Lawrence & Wishart, 1958. (Pp. 85–98.)

Whittemore, Reed. "Moll Flanders." In *Heroes and Heroines.* New York: Reynal & Hitchcock, 1946. (A fourteen-line poem.)

Winsor, Kathleen, Louis Kronenberger, and Lyman Bryson. "*Moll Flanders*." In *Invitation to Learning: English and American Novels*, edited by George D. Crothers. New York: Basic Books, 1966. (Pp. 41–44.)

Woolf, Virginia. "Defoe." In *The Common Reader*, First Series. New York: Harcourt, Brace, 1925. (Pp. 89–97.)

NORTON CRITICAL EDITIONS